THE STRANGER PRINCE

The Stranger Prince is Rupert of the Rhine, perhaps the most fascinating knight-errant to have crossed – and nearly turned – the current of English history. The third son of Elizabeth of Bohemia and the luckless Elector Palatine, he lost his chance of a kingdom in his infancy and fought thereafter always in the cause of others – for his elder brother, whom he hated, and for his uncle, Charles I of England.

From this rich career of adventure Miss Irwin has fashioned more than a history of the Civil War, more even than a biography of the reckless fighter called a 'wizard' for his skill in science and the arts; she has portrayed in the round, against the dramatic background of his age, a complex human being who was the model of a fast-dying chivalry, a man whose life was a voyage of discovery and who carried the spirit of adventure in him to the end.

'*Royal Flush*, *The Stranger Prince*, and *The Proud Servant*, books that will never be surpassed' – *Liverpool Daily Post*

D1512656

THE STRANGER PRINCE

MARGARET IRWIN

UNABRIDGED

PAN BOOKS LTD : LONDON

First published 1937 by Chatto and Windus Ltd.
This edition published 1966 by Pan Books Ltd.,
33 Tothill Street, London, S.W.1

ISBN 0 330 20135 2

2nd Printing 1971

Printed in Great Britain by
Richard Clay (The Chaucer Press), Ltd.,
Bungay, Suffolk

CONTENTS

'No sons of mine shall go for knight-errants.'
Letter from Elizabeth of Bohemia

'All life is but a wand'ring to find home.'
Witch of Edmonton (MIDDLETON)

To my Collaborator
J. R. MONSELL

And for our friend
MRS CRANKSHAW

ACKNOWLEDGEMENT

The portrait of Rupert of the Rhine shown on the cover is reproduced by permission of the National Portrait Gallery, London.

WITHOUT WHOM

A BIBLIOGRAPHY has always filled me with awe. How do people know so exactly what they have read? Many of the most illuminating 'sources' of one's work come accidentally in casual, desultory reading, not for any set purpose.

What, for instance, was that crumbling-edged book that I pulled out of an upper shelf in the old library of a country house in County Waterford, in which was a verbatim report of witnesses of the Ulster rising in 1641? There, on the very page I opened, was somebody reporting that he had seen Alasdair Macdonald walking down the streets of Belfast with his arm tied up in a string (not sling), because he had tired his wrist with killing 50 Scots and 40 Englishmen in one day. (Alasdair was the chief abettor of my *Proud Servant*, but it was too late to mention this characteristic touch in that, so I have put it into *The Stranger Prince* instead.) But I saw no more of that book, for the luncheon gong clanged and the afternoon was devoted to live-stock, a cause as lost as that of the Stuarts.

And that collection of King Charles' letters to his wife, printed immediately after Naseby by his enemies as propaganda, which I came on in another house, together with many of the original pamphlets of the Civil Wars. I have quoted extensively from them, but I can't give a list of them, as I could if I had got them out, properly tabulated, in a well-regulated fashion in the British Museum.

If I mention the pleasure which Clarendon's *History of the Great Rebellion* gave me, it looks as though I have read all through the eight volumes, but I haven't; and I had best not admit the odd part the *Fugger News-Letters* played in this book. The *Verney Letters*, the *Annals of the Royal Society*, printed in 1666, the memoirs of Rupert's sister, Sophia, and the diary of that engagingly ingenuous Puritan parson, Ralph Josselyn, kept from about 1630 onwards, are among the original sources that helped me most; also Cromwell's speeches and letters, some of Milton's tracts, and Whitelocke's Diaries. And there are many extraordinarily interesting early local documents collected in *Bristol, Past and Present*, a nineteenth-century work in three large volumes with many old prints. Above all, Warburton's copious letters and pamphlets of the time, printed nearly a century ago, must remain the chief source of any book on Rupert.

But if it be presumption in a novelist to mention sources, it would be ingratitude to ignore them when one comes to the moderns. Eva Scott's and James Cleugh's brilliant biographies of Rupert may well make their many admirers consider a novel on him a further presumption. Clennell Wilkinson's book is particularly interesting on the military side. I acknowledge with delight the help and inspiration I got from them – and also, on the other side, from John Buchan's *Cromwell,* Hugh Ross Williamson's *Hampden,* and Oliver Warner's studies of Monck and Fairfax.

Edmund Gosse's seventeenth-century studies were very helpful, so also that magnificent work of Mallet's on the history of Oxford, and, to skip back more than a century, Strickland's Lives of Elizabeth of Bohemia, and Henrietta Maria.

For 'straight' history, Trevelyan on the Stuart period is as invaluable as delightful; and Green's *Short History* makes the whole century from Thomas to Oliver Cromwell sweep along like some breathless story.

I am most grateful to Mr Alistair Tayler for 'vetting' my proofs, and to Sir Ian Hamilton for doing the same with my account of Marston Moor in manuscript.

And I at last take this opportunity of stating that I would never have written this book at all, or *The Proud Servant,* or *Royal Flush,* if it had not been for the continual creative vision and help of my husband, J. R. Monsell.

October 1936

Book I

MOTHER COUNTRY

CHAPTER ONE

'YOU LET him kiss you! Take you in his arms and kiss you on the mouth! At the very moment when your cousin, your equal, who is so much in love with you, is making proposals for you. And you tell me that you *liked* it.'

'Yes, I liked it,' said her daughter.

Her mother's bright indignant splendour, as of Diana the chaste moon goddess revolted by the grossness of mortal women, dazzled her as always with the sense of her own inferiority. Everyone was right; she and her sisters bore no comparison to their mother, not only in looks and charm, but now she herself in morality also, and, what was worse, in the supreme feminine glory of remaining icily impervious to the emotions she aroused in others.

'Your drawing-master!' breathed the mother. 'I cannot think how he dared —'

'He was probably a little drunk.'

There was certainly the cool note of defiance now in the girl's desperation. After all, what did it matter what one said? It could not, for there was her voice going on speaking, it said – 'You can never have known what it feels like – not to have been kissed.'

She found herself saying it, she finished saying it, she quailed, but she could not stop staring at her mother's lovely and for the moment speechless rage. Her acute observant eyes, trained by a portrait painter, could see through that starry divinity before her to the earthly woman who had been married from the schoolroom to a devoted husband and had borne him thirteen children. But the cold blaze of her mother's angry eyes could outstare any such negligible facts.

Impelled now it seemed by madness, her daughter blurted out one more irrelevancy. 'We are none of us likely to marry. William's proposals will probably be squashed by his grand-mother – and mine. That's all he and I are likely to keep

11

in common – Juliana, our grandmother! And it's not much satisfaction to have a young man in love with you who isn't there.'

To her astonishment her mother answered her, and not at once to dismiss her.

'If the enjoyment of the body is what you understand by being married, let me tell you that it is something that has never been of importance nor interest to me.'

'It had no need to be,' rose to the girl's lips, but her mother's forbearance in answering her had the effect of restoring her sanity. She did not speak it, indeed she had no chance to, for now in a torrent of deep yet ringing sound her mother was speaking.

'What has happened to you all? Are you indeed my children, or are you Negroes that I've conceived in my sleep? You are not of my race and being. You all study and argue and give yourselves airs as artists or philosophers or scientists or God knows what, and yet not one of you has the wit to keep out of mischief, except Eliza, and she is as dull as a sermon, and I've always said that stooping over her books directly after meals would make her nose red – and you saw how it was today after dinner, scarlet as a poppy. Don't you dare to laugh – if you think I am laughing at your sister you are much mistaken. She has some decency, for at least *she's* not yet been caught kissing that shrivelled anatomy who teaches her philosophy, though I dare say she'd do it tomorrow if she thought it would help her abstract speculations – that's what's so hateful about you young people – you've no feeling, no heart, no impulse, and no conscience – and yet you're so conscientious – damnably so – you'd experiment with anything in the cause of your art or science or whatever hocus-pocus you're dabbling in. Lord, how drab it all is, this learning and arguing – my father always said, "Give learning to a hundred women and you spoil ninety-nine". Eliza and Monsieur Descartes, you and Mynheer Honthorst – you are young, you are beautiful, you are *my* daughters, and that is all you can do to amuse yourselves, flirting or arguing, it's all the same, with two middle-aged, middle-class, ugly foreigners who have to think or paint for a living.'

'But, Maman, *I* have to paint for a living. I sold a picture only this week, or we should have had no meat from the butcher.'

'You did not sign it?'

12

'No. Gerard Honthorst did. With his name it fetched a much better price.'

'There you go again, decrying your descent, pretending to be a democrat and a revolutionary, when these slavish shopkeepers here ought to give far more for a picture by one of my children than for one by a mere professional painter. But I am glad you did not sign it. We must try and keep some shreds of dignity, though it's hard enough among all of you. Why must you be untidy because you paint pictures? You don't do your hair with your paint brushes do you, though indeed it has that appearance? And now this squalid little scandal, so careless, so loose-ended – you're all at loose ends, Rupert more than any of you, lounging and loafing about as though there were nowhere in the world to put those long legs of his.'

'He's had them cased tight enough these three years in prison.'

'Then don't remind him of it, and he can start again where he left off. He's only just twenty-two – and prison hasn't changed him.'

'Everyone else thinks it has.'

'Do you stand there only to contradict me? You and Rupert are like a pair of parrots the way you echo each other in flouting authority, and that is how you repay me for spoiling you and thinking you the most amusing of my daughters.'

'*Do* you, Maman?'

'No, no, I do *not* – not now. It is not amusing to kiss the drawing-master, it is sordid and trumpery, and I'm sickened by your aloof considerations on the subject – one can't plunge into mud one minute and be aloof about it the next – but what has happened to the young people, that is what I want to know? They're all as old as sin, and cynical as Diogenes, there's no light nor life left in them, they're "sad as night for very wantonness", and it's a mistake for girls to be so clever, or so tall – I am tall myself but I could never have been mistaken for Rupert in his clothes as you were.'

'His old clothes, Maman. He had outgrown them by several years.'

'It's a mistake all this dressing up – it shocks a great many people, especially our countrymen – they do so enjoy being shocked.'

'Then we do them a service.'

'*We?*'

13

'Yes, Maman. You shock the English visitors too.'

It was irresistible, this kind of word-play. Had she got in past her mother's guard and deflected her from the anger that still flashed in her eyes, however much she might amuse herself with the light and random battery of her words? Her contempt, her perplexity, her impatience with inferior humanity, illumined her face with the light of pure unreason. Her daughter's every word was a venture, made in ignorance as to whether it would cause a fresh outbreak of the storm or a spurt of laughter. Self-interest therefore made her keep a keen watch on her mother's face, though it was almost lost in the artist's pure enjoyment of it.

What a superb advantage her mother's self-forgetful egoism gave her above the common run of anxious watchful critical mortals! She never thought of herself – nor saw anybody else. Even now, in her indignant stare at her daughter, she did not really see her – but only saw what she had vaguely expected her to be, and her disappointment that she had failed to be it. But her mother had no need to understand ordinary mortals – that was not why they worshipped her and followed her fantastic fate – often to their own death or ruin. It was not for her to enter into the lives of others, but to live her own.

'And oh, if I could paint her so!' the daughter's impenitent desire sighed deep within herself even as she perceived that her last shot had miscarried and that wrath, not pleasure, was to be the reward of her rash compliment. Those great liquid eyes, eyes of a wounded stag, of a sad and eager child, hid their scorn for an instant under their white lids as if wearied of the whole base world, then flashed out with renewed fire, while sensitive nostril and proud lovely lip curved sharply like bows drawn to the attack. The imperious head was outlined against the small window-panes; within its circle, though darkened against the light, there shone so royal an ardour of life and indignation that it dulled the wintry Dutch scene outside, the insignificant sun glinting on the canal, the bare trees, the huddled homely figures of The Hague citizens going about their business, to a bleak epitome of commonplace everyday existence.

'There she stands, and ordinary life goes on behind her and it makes no difference,' thought the girl, 'nothing can change or break her, she is there for ever – or would be if I could paint her so!'

So deep was her absorption that she did not even hear the

words that dismissed her, but dismissed she was, she had enough instinct to tell her that, and not to stay one second longer than she knew it.

She left the room, wandered aimlessly down a little passage, banged her head against a low doorway (she could never remember how tall she had grown) and stood staring at a room that seemed full of silent figures, though only three sat there, but each one so intent on a different occupation that the very air held its breath. People were beautiful when they were absorbed. She wished that none would move or speak nor look towards her, that she could stand here invisible, inaudible, till she had drunk in every grave line of their bent shoulders and steady gaze.

Who would notice her first? Not Great Eliza, that was certain. Great Eliza was reading. Her pale profile was sculptured against the torn curtain, exquisite as a cameo; it was doubtful she would even hear that crack of her sister's head against the lintel. And Rupert, if he heard it, would be indifferent, since he was drawing, sprawled half across the table, with that inevitable dog at his feet. Of course it was Etta who sprang from her sewing, blue and crimson silks scattering round her, the raised lid of the big work-box, with its absurd padded picture of Adam and Eve, suddenly shutting down at her commotion.

'Oh, Louey, was that your poor head?'

'I'd be better without it, wouldn't I?'

Eliza's beautiful eyes had lifted from her book and rested on her. She had made no other movement.

'Does that mean – Louise, you did not say anything imprudent?'

'Everything I say or do is imprudent. She looked at me – I wonder I did not go through the floor.'

'Did she make you feel so wicked?' piped up Etta's shocked, childish voice.

'I wish she had. It would have been interesting. No, she made me feel I was a battered spinster who was equally despicable for being one and for wishing not to be one.'

'Before you are nineteen? And I am four years older than you! You can't begin to be a battered spinster before me,' mocked Eliza's solemn tones, weighing each of the four years in the balance.

'My classic seraph, you can spin till you are ninety before you begin to be battered. No Greek statue is ever battered – even

15

with both arms and a nose off. It's I, the miserable Goth, who splash about and make a mess of everything – just like my palette.'

'Do you speak of your taste in wine?'

'Good God, no! Oh this tiresome mother tongue of ours! Let us speak German instead, or shall we use French?'

'Je m'en fiche de toutes ces sales bottes.'

A man's voice had tramped into the flippant sounds, a voice a little too deep even for a man for it still held something of a boy's gruff tones. 'How you women chatter.'

'Have we shocked you, Rupert?'

'No, but I am sick of the sound of your voices.'

He rose and stretched himself, yawning, his huge height and outflung arms seemed to fill the room, his mouth made a gaping O of black weariness and discontent; his sisters gazed at him dismayed.

Eliza expostulated, 'Rupert, dear, can you not get interested in your drawing?'

Louey suggested, 'Would you not like to ride? You must have been cooped up in this room a good hour.'

'I have been cooped up longer than that.'

'That is no reason for your not making use of your freedom now you have it.' Eliza's cool voice came a shade tartly. People were so apt to pity Rupert for having been in prison for three years, it would be the greatest pity if he began to pity himself. After all he had had his drawing, a few books, infinite opportunity for study and invention, and nobody to bother him except to argue about religion. What could one want more?

'One forgets what to do with freedom when one has been deprived of it too long, doesn't one?' said Louise softly to her brother. 'You will get it back in England, where you first found it.'

'I suppose so.' His great eyes were fixed moodily upon her. 'If I go.'

'*If!*'

'Rupert!'

'I thought it was all settled!'

'Cackle, cackle, cackle,' he replied rudely. 'Come, Boy, let's get out of here.'

A big white dog with a shaggy mane like a snow lion sprang out from under the table where Rupert had been drawing, and leaped after him as he strode out of the room, its feet scrabbling and scraping on the tiled floor. The three girls stared at each other's disconcerted faces.

'*She* has been trying to prevent it,' exclaimed Louise, 'I knew it! She hated his going back to England – she says he will only "idle" there. It's always "idle". She would like another nice little war, just to give Rupert occupation.'

'Louise!' Etta was really shocked now, 'you cannot mean that of our mother!'

'Louey never means anything,' said Eliza indulgently, 'but it is true of all our brothers – what else can they be but soldiers? – just as what else can we be but spinsters?'

'You can afford to bring up that again,' Louey laughed ruefully – 'you who refused marriage with a king rather than give up your religion!'

'Give up my freedom of thought rather.'

'Freedom? Freedom!' Up went Louey's voice, down went Louey's voice, sounding the whole scale of incredulous mockery – 'who is free to think anything of themselves? Prejudice, chance, those who brought us up tie us as tight as the Inquisition. And what matters *what* you thought, since a Catholic marriage might have hurt our precious Timon's interests – "My son Carl being more dear to me than *all* my daughters"!'

'Did she say that?' Eliza's voice was cold with anger.

'She wrote it and left it on her table, and Sophie read it and told me.'

'Then you ought to have smacked her instead of repeating it,' said Etta reprovingly.

'I did both. It's no news. Comparisons are as common here as they are odorous. And didn't you know Carl Must Be Considered?'

'I know. I don't care.' It was Eliza again, at her most inflexible. 'My happiness shall not lie in the power of any man, brother or husband.'

'What will you be, then? A nun? Consider Carl, remember.'

'I shall take vows, but not of religion. I mean to devote my whole life to learning and philosophy. One can't do that if one marries, so it's just as well for me that none of us probably will.'

Etta's soft treble, unusually decisive, cut across her eldest sister's argument. 'No. I shall marry.'

The two grown-up girls looked in surprise at the child Henrietta (Etta for short), who had flushed so seriously over her embroidery. Eliza indeed looked at her rather as though she were a mathematical problem.

'How do you know?' asked Louey. 'Your chances are no better than the rest of us.'

'She is the prettiest,' said Eliza reflectively.

'It is not that,' exclaimed Etta, 'I am not half as beautiful as you nor as fascinating as Louey – but it is just that I should not have been born if I had not been going to marry.'

'I believe she is right,' Eliza finally pronounced at the end of her scrutiny; 'all of us others, even little Sophie, are too much interested in other things. But Etta – one can see it is what she is made for.'

' "What are little girls made for?" ' chanted Louey – ' "Sugar and spice and all that's nice" – have you cooked any more comfits today, my sugary plum? You must choose a husband with a sweet tooth or you'll be wasted.'

'Louey, you great tease —'

'No, you'll not be wasted – who'd ever waste the cherub on top of the cake?'

Eliza was not to be deflected by these sisterly cooings. Her speculative brain was puzzled by the contradictions in Louey, the sister nearest herself in age, her most constant companion, whom every year seemed to be making more unlike herself. What did Louey want? What did she mean by the things she said and did? How was it that she never seemed to know? She must know, if only she would think.

Knitting her brows together so that she looked more than ever like a Greek Muse who found the work of inspiring mortals unremunerative, she said:

'William of Brandenburg is deep in love with you. I cannot understand how you could have kissed —'

'No, no, you can't understand, nor will all Monsieur Descartes' philosophy explain it to you. And I can't understand how you could have refused the King of Poland and all his Cossacks for the sake of that tiresome negation you call a religion.'

'All his Cossacks? – a negation? Louey, what do you —'

'Not that you'd have married them all, only reigned and ridden among them. To ride with Cossacks, that would be more worth a mass than Paris ever was to Henry of Navarre. Ah, let us leave these tiresome matrimonial problems. I wish I were going to England. I wish I were going to see our uncle and aunt. They must be a charming little pair.'

18

She screwed up her eyes in the amusing way she had when she was seeing something that was not there, she made a grab at Rupert's pencil and unfinished drawing and began to scrawl up in the corner of the paper, murmuring as she did so – 'That boy can draw! Look at the way he's caught the droop of your head over your book, Eliza – you can see just which bone of the neck that comes from. Oh, and look at the tiny figure of a man trailing a pike – off he jogs to the wars, every millimetre of him alive! I must show that to Gerard.'

Her sisters looked over her shoulder at her own group of little figures sprouting up round two who sat stiffly enthroned, one of them with a pointed beard and eyebrows arching up into a high forehead.

'You have not made our uncle as good-looking as Van Dyck has done,' Eliza commented.

'It is not my business. I am not a Court painter.'

'You can only know what King Charles is like from his picture.'

'No, I know about people from what I hear about them as well as see.'

'Is that why you have made him like a wax figure?' asked Etta – 'a king of a court of dolls?'

'His *people* are not dolls,' said Eliza, 'that is the difficulty. They are rough and unreasonable. I don't want to go to England. I think Rupert was much better where he was – in prison. He was safe there.'

She sprang back in amazement as Louey, uttering a wild yell, crashed the drawing-board to the floor and stamped on it. 'Safe!' she cried. 'Safe! Do you wish we were all born dead?'

CHAPTER TWO

THEIR MOTHER stood where Louise had left her. The eyes that had held her daughter spellbound followed her to the door – a gawky girl, too tall for a girl (her own grandmother had been six foot high, but that was different – Mary Queen of Scots could never have been leggy and lounging). Louise had behaved outrageously, spoken inexplicably, had tried to make her, the most adored woman in Europe, feel old-fashioned and misunderstanding. This cool modern logic had shrivelled all the

19

romance out of girlhood; her daughters were so cold and hard, so unlike women, it was as if they had unsexed themselves – for she had forgotten that her original quarrel with Louey was because she had kissed her drawing-master. She thought only how odd it was she should not understand her own daughter – she who had never ceased to be as youthful, gay and sparkling as when she had left England, a girl of sixteen, who had already been wooed by the King of Spain and the Swedish King Gustavus Adolphus, the greatest soldier of the age.

Ever since that dazzling girlhood, her life had been one long series of disasters and disappointments, but that made no difference, she would allow shadows on her spirits no more than her godmother, the old Queen Elizabeth of England, had allowed shadows to be painted on her portraits.

And the present Queen Elizabeth of Bohemia, now in her twenty-second year of exile from the kingdom where she had reigned one year, sat down in the window that looked out over this neat pretty little town of The Hague – this bourgeois little town where the people were so incredibly slow – sat with the winter sun on her face, closed her eyes against its faint warmth, and saw great suns roll upwards against her shut eyelids, now red, now black. As she watched them, time rolled back against her eyelids, a fiery ball that had never ceased to show her bright colours and then turn them to black – time rolled back within her eyes until she could see nothing but the England where Rupert insisted on going, the England that one day, some day, she herself would surely see again.

*   *   *

She had come to England when her godmother, Queen Elizabeth, died, and her father, King James VI of Scotland, became King James I of England as well. He went south to take possession of his new kingdom, followed some weeks later by his wife and children. Elizabeth was seven then, and the time of year was early summer, and the first people she remembered seeing in this her father's new country had been a company of shepherdesses in shining colours who came out of a green wood and knelt before her mother and herself and told them that the goddess Diana was in that wood and wanted to bid them welcome. So they went into the wood, where they heard music here and there among the trees, and deep in a grove they came upon a group of nymphs in flowing green scarves dancing in a

20

ring, in and out of little flecks of sunlight. Other nymphs stood aside, holding stags in leash whose horns were tipped with gold, and out from the ring came the goddess herself, all white and gold with a crescent moon on her forehead and a bow in her hand, and Elizabeth was told that though she was Diana, she was also her cousin, the Lady Arabella Stuart, who was to be her new governess.

At once Scotland shrank shivering away into a cold uncomfortable place of gaunt grey draughty castles where even her mother, who loved fine clothes, had to wear thick cloth stockings which made her ankles clumsy, and people were always afraid, and her brother Harry had to be shut up in a strong castle away from herself in case the nobles should seize him and try to make him King in opposition to their father. But now here they were at last in the happy settled country of England where their father had always hoped to be, when, if ever, the old Queen should die.

He seemed to have changed back into a child like themselves, so delighted and excited was he when they met him at the end of their long journey; he kissed and hugged them again and again – 'Buss me, my babies, buss your old Dad! We have come into Paradise, we have been wandering in a wilderness, a barren soil, and now we are in the Land of Promise. I have been so fêted, so welcomed, so rejoiced over, it is plain the whole country was groaning under the old Queen and longing for me to come and deliver them. It is a land flowing with milk and honey, the plain country gentlemen here are richer than any lords in Scotland.'

He had just been staying at a very fine place, once a nunnery, at Hinchingbrooke, now a great mansion of warm red brick, whose owner, Sir Oliver Cromwell, knight, was now to be Knight of the Bath also, for the King must knight him over again in thanks for his hospitality – knighting had become a persistent habit with him, he had knighted well over two hundred people on his journey to London and a sirloin of English beef as well, to testify to its superiority to Scotch mutton. Sir Oliver had not only entertained him with such profusion as King James had not seen even in any English country house, but had given him a host of parting presents, hawks, horses, hounds, a magnificent gold cup for himself and a large quantity of gold pieces for his servants – 'and he will not be happy till I go and stay with him again and bring my bairns to play with his little nephew Oliver, but he is too little for your great ruffians, I shall take Baby Charles, who is nearer his age and near as solemn as the wee Cromwell, but, alas, not half as sturdy. But Lord! To think what profit there was in wrecking the monasteries and how Thomas Cromwell feathered his whole family's nest even unto the third and fourth generation – it makes one's mouth water —'

It did, complained Elizabeth as he kissed her again, for she did not mind being slobbered over by her pony but objected to it from a father and a double king who ought to have double his former dignity, but seemed rather to have halved it, as he wept with joy at telling Harry he had just paid over three thousand pounds sterling, not Scots, mind you, 'for a diamond for your hat – it shone so bright I could not resist it, and why should I, we have come into our own at last and my bairns shall have everything their little hearts can desire.'

'Can I have another pony, Dad? Can I have a new fencing sword?'

But Elizabeth grasped the situation quicker than her elder brother. 'Can I have a whole farm of my very own in the country, with all the animals I want on it?'

She could and did; she was given a Fairy Farm stocked with the smallest ponies, cattle and bantam hens to be found in the world, and any traveller who came to England with a new kind of monkey or parroquet or other rare bird or beast was sure to make her a present of it. Never was a child so spoilt in that severe age. Lessons were like a game. You looked at tiny insects and flowers through one kind of glass and they became large; you looked at stars through another and they became near. History was taught with pictures, sorted in packs like cards for the separate countries. And whatever language she was learning at the moment was practised by writing in it to her brother Harry, though the most important part of the letter was the tying it up with floss silk dipped in sealing-wax and so turning it as to form her name.

Harry lived in one palace and she in another, both with odd brief names, Ham and Kew, both surrounded with lovely gardens and both on the river. On summer evenings they glided over the water in boats to pay visits to each other that sometimes lasted for several days, and not even Harry's teasing could spoil her pleasure in them, not even when he told her that the room where she slept at Ham House was haunted by stout King

22

Henry VIII, who liked to see that all was well with his former hunting-lodge.

Well, she did not see King Hal, though she shivered and shook in her big red velvet bed and lay awake half the night expecting to see him; but then she fell asleep, and then she woke, and there, half across the room, stood a tall slight young figure that was terrifyingly familiar. It turned and looked at her and she saw that it was her brother Harry, but even as she screamed to him, knowing that her own Harry could not stand and look so, he was not there!

She fled into the ante-room after that and spent the rest of the night with her maids, lying on a pallet, and Harry was scolded next day for frightening his sister, and the housekeeper declared that Ham House had never been haunted – 'but it is now,' said Elizabeth to herself in answer thirty-five years later – for King Charles had written to her lately that people did not care to sleep in that room at Ham House because they had seen in it the ghost of his elder brother, Prince Henry, who had died at eighteen, just before the marriage took place which he had urged between his sister Elizabeth and the young Elector Palatine from Germany.

That marriage – that delirious dream of excitement, of gaiety, of mad extravagance, of the agony of death – nothing after that, whether of rapture or despair, could equal what Elizabeth had then experienced round about her sixteenth birthday.

Her Danish mother, with the long fair face and the half silly, half quizzical smile in her blue eyes, had wanted her to be Queen of Spain; politics and religion were nothing to her, what she hoped was that her daughter should satisfy her mother's vanity, only partly assuaged by a husband who had become King of England as well as Scotland. A German husband! There had never been such a thing in the royal family before. If Elizabeth married the Elector Palatine, what would her title be? Why, that of any German merchant's wife – 'Goody Palsgrave, Goody Palsgrave,' she hooted at the girl, whose annoyance collapsed in helpless giggles as her mother's teasing burgeoned out into sheer buffoonery, for Queen Anne, rather drunk, as was her habit, with a glazed uncertain eye, would tuck up her skirts over her farthingale and prance about the room like a turkey, in mimicry of the young Elector, who they heard was taking dancing lessons in preparation for his visit to the fashionable Court of England. It all made Elizabeth feel very important, even the teasing did that, since it showed that her mother considered scarcely any marriage important enough for her.

Once before had she been of national importance, when she had been sent to Coventry to escape the wicked designs of those Papists who had deputed Guy Fawkes to blow up the King and the Prince of Wales and the Houses of Parliament all together, and then proclaim herself as Queen Elizabeth II of England.

'What a queen should I have been by this means!' Elizabeth had exclaimed very properly, as her guardian was careful to tell King James, assuring him that his little daughter had declared she would rather have been blown up with him and the Parliament than reign on such conditions. All the same it was gratifying to know that even when she was ten years old people had thought her a right and fitting person to be successor to the proud old Queen whose reign had been one long fairy-tale of glory.

'She was your godmother.'

'She cut off our grandmother's head.'

'She shut up our cousin Arabella Stuart in prison.'

'But she was the greatest monarch England ever had, and the champion of the Protestant faith, and you bear her name and must be as great as she was.'

All these things Harry told her, and Harry thought the match with a German princeling great enough for her, since it would weld the Protestant Powers of Europe together, and Harry must be right, he was so certain about everything, he never hesitated like poor Baby Charles, who stuttered in terrible difficulty to get out the right words, while Harry's words shot out crisp, ringing, confident; he always knew exactly what he wanted, what he thought, and how to say it. 'Two religions will never lie easy in one bed,' he said, and flatly refused to fall in with his father's grandiose scheme to unite Catholic and Protestant Europe by marrying his son to the Spanish Infanta, thus adding the force of his own example to back the advice he gave his sister.

But when the young German Prince arrived – after the greatest difficulty, for the gales that autumn were so furious that they blew him and his eight little ships all back to Holland, and finally her father had to send three of his big ships to bring him to Gravesend, and even then the poor boy had got separated from his baggage and had to make his first appearance at this grand foreign Court in his travelling dress – when he did arrive, and stood there, a very small figure with shy dark eyes that anxiously scanned all his bride's family, it was her little brother Charles, barely twelve years old and usually so backward and retiring, who came forward and did the honours to the new guest, saying and asking all the right things, although he stammered with nervousness.

But her eldest brother Henry, Prince of Wales, who had shown such restless haste to bring about this alliance with the Palatine, stood silent as a statue and as still; and Elizabeth, looking at him in amazement as he neither spoke nor moved to greet his guest, felt an icy chill strike at her heart, as when she had woken in the night to see Harry standing in her room and then disappeared – for there was Harry standing before her, looking at the Palatine, looking at her, and yet he saw neither of them, he was not there at all.

*   *   *

They said he must be ill, but he would not admit it, he rode at the ring next day with the Palatine, and told Elizabeth he liked him very much though he wished he were bigger, 'but there's time yet for him to grow,' said Harry, drawing himself up to his full height, which was considerable, for he had shot up in the last year, outgrown his strength, in fact, and so people reminded each other when four days later he collapsed in the middle of a banquet and fell in a dead faint right across the table. They then began to say how they had noticed he had never been well since the chill he had caught that hot summer evening when he had bathed in the river after playing so hard at tennis, and swum all the way to Richmond.

He was kept in bed, and Elizabeth did not have him with her to help entertain the Palatine at her palace of the Cockpit in Westminster. The playwright Will Shakespeare, who had saved enough of his earnings to go into prosperous retirement in the country (in strong contrast with Ben Jonson and the rest of his fellows who spent all they made a good deal faster than they made it), had been hauled up to town again and ordered to write a pretty play for a musical setting and plenty of ingenious mechanical scenic effects to be acted at the wedding. He gave them a storm at sea and shipwreck on an island, in allusion to Frederick's tempestuous landing, and spirits and savages and drunken sailors and some pretty songs and not much of a story, but nobody cared about that, and transformed King James into a learned magician and the Princess Elizabeth into a lonely maiden who had never seen a man in her life ('the licence of these poets!' exclaimed her mother). It was called *The Tempest* and had so great a success that a much earlier day of his was also revived as it was also about a royal betrothal.

In her years of exile from England, Elizabeth had grown to appreciate Shakespeare more and more and was always quoting him to her children, but at the time she had been amused chiefly by the scenic effects in *The Tempest*, and frankly bored by *Love's Labour's Lost*, and yet there was one line in it that had stuck in her head ever since, for she had never had the heart to look at that particular play again:

'To court wild laughter in the throat of death.'

Wild laughter – that had been the note of her wedding to Frederick, Prince Palatine. How she had laughed at the German sausages she then saw for the first time – for some of Frederick's suite had taken the trouble to bring their favourite food with them – and at the antics of little boys dressed as monkeys on the stage – and at the lovesick glances of the solemn Germans at her pretty maids of honour. And yet she had been tortured with anxiety for Harry, whom she was not allowed to see for fear of infection.

Twice she dressed up as a page-boy and tried to get into his room – once she was near enough to hear him calling in a high strange voice, 'Oh, where is my sweet sister?' But before she could get to him she was recognized and dragged away, and only her fretful old father, of whom she was secretly ashamed because he got drunk and shambled about and spilt his food, only King James, whom everyone knew to be such a coward, was there to sit by his son until he was dead.

*　　*　　*

But the wedding had to go on just the same in spite of the sickness of the Prince of Wales; all that appalling expense could not be wasted (the fireworks alone had cost £9,000), and the Palatine was nearly ruined as it was by the length of his visit and at the end of it the cost of mourning for all his suite, added to the cost of their wedding garments.

'The funeral baked meats
Did coldly furnish forth the marriage tables' —
'Indeed, my lord, it followed hard upon.'

26

What a man that actor must have been! He seemed to have known everything that ever happened.

Not so cold though, the furnishings – those sausages – that sobbing laughter – those crowds packed so tight that the women's farthingales stuck fast in the galleries of Whitehall and a law had to be passed forbidding them – that gorgeous river pageant, an extra show for the Lord Mayor's Day, all ship-wrecked by the tempest of winds and waves that burst upon it even in the placid Thames – those fireworks tearing the night into flame, that cruel fancy of an illuminated hunt when a stag with lighted lamps tied all over its horns was loosed to the pursuit of illuminated hounds, and all the terrified creatures disappeared together in the black river.

The Thames and the Rhine were wedded to music and dancing and the riotous rush of lovely verse, masque followed masque until Sir Francis Bacon was told to take his players away as soon as they arrived, for after two whole nights out of bed for the merry-making the King could not force his eyes to keep open another wink.

And by the end of the festivities Harry was dead; and Eliza-beth was betrothed in black velvet with little white plumes, a fashion so becoming that it was at once the rage for both sexes. She wore it as mourning for her brother, and her stormy and bewildered grief for her lost companion shook her to the depths. It was her young bridegroom's sympathy with that grief far more than his passionate adoration of her that won her to him.

Yet that wild laughter had surged up in her even in the be-trothal ceremony; she had been so convulsed with giggles at the lawyer's bad French accent that she infected the young Palatine and all their company; by the time they got to the religious part of the ceremony the whole building was rocking with laughter, the Archbishop could not proceed with the service and had to cut it short in the middle by giving the blessing.

And it was almost as bad at the actual wedding on St Valen-tine's Day; Elizabeth could not stop laughing and made every-one near her laugh; her mother said it was good for girls to giggle, but many others were shocked and some even took this hysteric girlish laughter for a thing unnatural and an evil omen.

A bad omen also that when at last they left Margate, she and her husband, neither of them yet seventeen, they were driven back into it by an easterly gale after hours of tossing on those seas – but what ill fortune to come, she demanded, could be worse than the agonies of seasickness then endured?

*   *   *

Had winds and waves fought against her family ever since her mother, the daughter of Vikings, had sailed from Denmark to Scotland in a frightful storm raised by two hundred witches who sailed in sieves before Leith harbour to prevent her landing?

For all through that wild autumn and winter and that glittering spring, winds and waves fought against herself. Flying chariots, a marvellous new invention worked with sails like windmills, had been prepared for their amusement at Scheveningen – but just for that once, because it was required of it, the wind wouldn't blow and so the chariots wouldn't fly. And the seas that had done their worst to prevent the Palatine from coming to England and herself from leaving it, the river that wrecked their wedding pageant and had given death to Harry who had promoted that wedding, the sound of their many waters would sometimes throb against her brain, making a very different pageant from that by Mr Campion of the Marriage of the Thames and the Rhine.

The Rhine in that lovely May of 1613 appeared all golden welcome; she was rowed up it day after day in a bright fleet of painted barges, and longed to land among the fruit blossom on its banks and the castles crowning every hill and the little towns as gay as toys. But the towns were not as gay as they looked, plague was thick in them, she was not allowed to land and see their charming sights, she was bored to death with sitting still, she would have given all the compliments comparing her with Cleopatra in her golden barge for one hour of jumping about in the grass with her dogs.

Heidelberg came into the distance at last, as charming as a picture in an old missal, famous throughout Germany for its learning and its art, so everybody told her mechanically as though that were part of its name. Her mother-in-law, the Electress Juliana, anxious, rigid, Puritanical in dress and behaviour, altogether a tiresome old thing, thought Elizabeth, was always impressing on her how proud she must be of her new home in Heidelberg – not a word of how proud Heidelberg must be to have her there, a great king's daughter, who might easily herself have been a great queen – might even have been Queen Elizabeth II of England, had Guy Fawkes had his wicked way. Her mother, Queen Anne, had made Elizabeth promise, rather superfluously, never to forget her own importance. She must always insist on her precedence before everybody else and go in to dinner before her husband and his mother as though she were the reigning queen. This she did, to the amazement of the Germans. But she was so lovely, so young, so gay, it was no wonder her very young little husband wished to indulge her in everything, and no doubt she would soon learn sense under that sensible woman her mother-in-law, the Electress Juliana.

But she did not learn sense, she loathed her mother-in-law, she had to refuse many delightful invitations rather than allow anybody else to go in to dinner before her, and the Electress's discontent with her darling Frederick's English bride made her melancholy horse face daily longer and more sallow.

There were other causes for the mother-in-law's complaint; Elizabeth was so unwomanly, she had not been brought up like the simple German maidens, but more like a boy – and just like any boy, as her devoted Frederick himself had said, she had shown off to him in London by snatching a match from the gunners and firing off one of the big cannon in the Tower. And now she showed no sign of settling down into a composed and dutiful wife; she was never happy except with her dogs and horses, she did not shrink from savage sports but shot a dozen deer with her own hand in a single hunt, and her hunting was so daring that the Palatine was thrown and nearly killed in his frantic efforts to keep up with her horse. To endanger her Frederick's life, the Electress could imagine no greater vice – but no, there was yet a greater, to endanger the life of her child, as Elizabeth did when she insisted on going hunting even when she was with child, but indeed she quite ignored that trifling matter, pretended even that she was not enceinte, and refused gifts for the coming baby up to within three days of his birth.

Children were not her creed, but of her nature; she produced thirteen of them in sixteen years, ceasing only with her husband's death, and nearly all those thirteen were splendid specimens of beauty, vigour and intelligence. But with the arrogance of 'wealthy men who care not how they give', she was not going to take any pride in what her tirelessly magnificent vitality had bestowed on them; she declared that her puppies and baby monkeys were far more amusing, and though her children were allowed to sprawl on to her bed in the morning along with the other young animals, they received no preferential treatment.

Her own country showed its sense of her baby's importance. England went mad with joy over the new little Prince Henry and at once declared him a naturalized Englishman and direct heir to the throne after Prince Charles.

> *'When you are King, diddle diddle,*
> *I shall be Queen,'*

Elizabeth sang to her baby after the Electress had burst into tears of thankfulness over the heir to the Palatinate. These German women were so damp; the men were better; her husband's delightful dry cynical Uncle Maurice, that masterly soldier and statesman who had been so amused by her skill and courage in hunting and her outspoken disgust at the prodigious feasts of pork and eel pies with which he had entertained her, had sent her with his congratulations a present of a diamond necklace for herself and a little crystal ship worth £1,000 for the baby.

A shape carved out of water, the tiny galleon shone before the infant's blinking eyes, and Elizabeth declared that it was the first thing he could see, before even his mother, and when she dangled it before him it was the first thing that his minute crumpled fists clutched out towards.

'In such a hurry to go sailing? That will come later,' they told him.

The baby chuckled; the grave plain little face of his father, not yet eighteen, broke into a slow smile; his mother laughed and clapped her hands and called for her women and cried that she could not bear to stay another hour in bed, she must get up and go hunting, and go she did, so fast that the Landgravine of Hesse-Cassel got a toss and a fractured arm through her determination to follow the fashion whatever pace it set.

'That girl of my nephew's is a public danger,' said Uncle Maurice, and bitter it was to his sister Juliana to hear him say the truth, but in just that particular way, with admiration and amusement and tenderness in every note of his voice. Men liked women to be a public danger, to be a public nuisance too, she added viciously, as the peaceful German State hummed and echoed to all the repercussions caused by Elizabeth. Her extravagance was appalling, the princely allowance sent her by her father was always swallowed up before it arrived, snatched by the greedy sharks that swarmed round her, the very stable-boys running after her and clamouring to her to take their side in some backyard dispute, and take their side she invariably did, while to take out her purse at the same time was an automatic gesture with her. Quarrels and actual fighting between her household and the rest of Heidelberg were loud and furious; a rabble of English, three times the size of her household, had followed her just to try their luck and see if they couldn't get taken on at her Court – and to try one's luck with Elizabeth was to be given or promised whatever you asked for, whether she had it or not.

The Palatine's faithful minister, Schomberg, wrote despairingly to her father: 'Your Majesty must consider that I have a young Prince and Princess, an administrator, a regent, a mother-in-law, sisters, aunts, and every one of these has a train, every one wishes to govern, every one complains I do more for one than for the other. Am I not a miserable man?'

But King James was no comfort, he only added to the confusion, he asked questions incessantly, repetitively, not merely about the expenditure of the huge sums he sent to his daughter, of which he might well expect some account, but as to how many inches his son-in-law had grown in the last year? and how many new dresses his daughter had bought? and were her jewels kept safely or allowed to be squandered away in gifts? and then – oh, horror upon horror! – there followed the fracas of those ruby buttons he had given his dearest bedfellow years ago in dear Scotland, which she had ungratefully and heedlessly given to her daughter, and her daughter had equally heedlessly given to one of her women – but not so heedlessly after all, for it was by way of discharging a little card debt of £300, as at last Elizabeth had to own up to her father, who had to buy the buttons back at his own expense, and somehow managed to blame Schomberg for the whole affair.

But worse to the Electress Juliana than all these scandals was the effect of Elizabeth on the Elector Frederick.

That small shy youth with his cold hands and his sad eyes who used to crouch over the fire and tell stories to the women rather than run out of doors, so that his mother would veil her anxiety with tenderly mocking nicknames – Master Dormouse, little Prince Shiverkin – was changing so fast that his mother never knew what he would do next. Always she had known before, for always he had done what she told him, but now he lived only to do what Elizabeth wished. In a single night he had a carved arch of massive stone raised in her new English garden so that when she walked there next morning she should think enchantment had been at work.

Enchantment indeed was at work, but it was Elizabeth's, not Frederick's. His constitutional melancholy was shot through with spurts of wild gaiety; haste and recklessness were what this slow studious boy now admired above all else. Such unnatural change was a tempting of Providence, thought his mother, and she was right to be afraid, Providence as usual could not resist temptation, and the trial of Frederick's new-found nature was being gradually prepared.

It was a mighty trial, it invoked all the great powers of the world and wrecked the peace of Europe for thirty years, it banded the Protestant States together in plans of a huge war against the Catholic Empire, and placed Frederick at the head of them.

The Catholic Emperor chose this critical moment to die, and his successor, Ferdinand, the elected King of Bohemia, at once began persecuting the most odd among the Protestant sects in his kingdom, who retaliated by throwing his Catholic ministers out of the window. That was in the council chamber at Prague and fortunately there was a dunghill below. A new word, defenestration, was coined in England in honour of the occasion, and its importance deserved it, for this was the beginning of the Thirty Years' War. The Bohemians declared their throne vacant and offered it to their nearest neighbour, the Elector Palatine.

Frederick had been ill with nervous fevers and occasional delirium ever since he had been appointed leader of the Protestant States; now the unnatural division between his old self and his new threatened to split his brain. His mother begged for peace and safety, which was what all his instincts longed for, and instinctive self-knowledge too, for a wise and prudent ruler in peacetime he might well be, but a dashing leader in warfare, never.

And that was just what Elizabeth ought to have for a husband, and Elizabeth ought to have a crown, and go in first to dinner wherever she was, without any question about it. His gratitude longed passionately to requite that lovely generosity of hers which had accepted him without question from the very first and devoted herself to him, though without any sentimental illusions, as her nicknames for him clearly showed. 'My Nigger Duckling' – the Electress was infuriated by that caressing idiocy, just not idiotic enough, for it hit off to perfection the

32

little Elector's rather bandy-legged gait which in haste degenerated into a waddle.

Yet Elizabeth's observant eyes had never transmitted any criticism to her brain. That had simply never noticed that her husband was small, plain and melancholy; she was never bored with him, she had enough brilliance of her own to keep the world always shining round her, she made no demands on it except for mere material things – a kingdom or so, unlimited money to squander – what were such slight tokens in return for the splendour of life and enjoyment she gave it?

Elizabeth could not understand what was troubling Frederick, it must be his mother – 'he is very heavy and extremely melancholy,' she wrote home, 'if I may say the truth, I think there is *some* that trouble him too much.' '*Some*' wanted to make her into a complete German hausfrau, 'which I neither have been bred to, nor is it necessary – neither will I do it'; '*Some*' wanted to diminish her rank 'which I think they do the Prince wrong in putting in his head at this time when he is so melancholy.'

She alternately coaxed and teased him into ambition, demanded why he had married a king's daughter since he dreaded being a king, and offered to deprive herself of her last jewel for armament expenses, such was her appreciation of the hardships of warfare.

His mother wept until her son almost dissolved into tears also, and his Uncle Maurice suddenly demanded if there were any green baize in Heidelberg to make a fool's cap for the boy who could let a crown go a-begging.

Still Frederick wavered between them; he was absent at the coronation of Ferdinand, the new Emperor of Germany, where it was his duty to nominate him; but then a little later he gave him the title of the King of Bohemia; but then, just three weeks later again, he accepted that title himself. He rode all day and all night – he the slow and cautious! – until his horse dropped dead under him, when he came to tell Elizabeth that now at last she would be a queen.

On a dark September day they left Heidelberg in eighteen coaches, left the English garden and the beautiful arch that would bear witness for centuries to the love of

Fredericus V
Elizabetae
Conjugi cariss.

left all the weeping townsfolk, those peaceable placid folk who seemed to have lost their senses, so wildly did they entreat their ruler not to leave them, deaf to all his assurances that he would return to Heidelberg every year – 'but of course he will return,' cried his queen, 'and I shall come and see every summer how my roses are growing.' But they only answered frantically, 'Do not leave us, do not leave us, or we are lost.' But they left them, they left the Electress Juliana in bed, nursing her grief and a brace of Elizabeth's children, and drove to Prague.

'Such a lady going before and marching in the front, who would not adventure life and covet death?' demanded an enthusiastic English reporter, comparing her with 'that Virago of Tilbury, another Queen Elizabeth'.

And now she was at last in good earnest 'another Queen', and no more the Goody Palsgrave that her mother had so jeered at.

But her triumph was robbed of its chief pleasure, for, with her usual perversity, her mother, whose jeers had been the initial germ of this upheaval, had died only just before Frederick and Elizabeth had been elected King and Queen of Bohemia.

* * *

Perhaps it was because she was far advanced in pregnancy with her fourth baby in five years that their entry into their new capital struck Elizabeth as a sort of nightmare. Prague itself in the misty autumnal light, all grey and silver above its wide river, did not look nearly as foreign as those little fairy-tale cities on the banks of the Rhine – indeed her first impression of it, with the false comfort of a mirage to the thirsty traveller in the desert, reminded her with a fierce pang of homesickness of that early home she could just remember, the steep grey city of Edinburgh.

But, as she got nearer, this fantastic resemblance to the northern capital vanished, and she was plunged into an Oriental extravagance that filled her with horror. Women prostrated themselves on either side of her coach, the leaping, yelling figures of men surrounded it, flourishing sickles and flails round their heads, clashing wooden bowls and platters together in a clattering din more deafening than kettledrums; and these, she was told, were not the mad fanatics of some Eastern tribe, but the most prominent Protestant sect in Bohemia, they who had thrown the Imperial ministers out of the window for denying

34

the Communion cup to the laity, and carried their own with them that they might receive the sacrament every day. On hearing this, Elizabeth's bewilderment relapsed into hysterical mirth.

Never was her wild laughter more dangerous than now. The dark faces of that savage band of fanatics gazed disconcerted at this woman, the 'Pearl of England', beautiful as an angel, fair as ivory and gold under her canopy of violet velvet, who shook and contorted her face with laughter as though possessed by a devil. Frantically Elizabeth tried to control herself, stared to right and left of her at the avenue of statues that went all the way along the bridge over which they were passing, statues of heroes and old Bohemian warriors, but above all of saints.

Their icy stillness behind all the twisted faces of those shrieking men had at first glimpse given her a shock, as though she had seen two rows of corpses greeting her arrival into her new capital. Her terror affronted her, she would not admit she had been startled, but rushed instead into anger.

What were all those saints doing in a Protestant city, whose faith she and her husband had sworn to uphold? They should all be thrown into the river before she would cross the bridge again.

What was the fair foreign queen saying, now that she stared with angry eyes upon their guardian statues? The question went from mouth to mouth among the crowd; after some days the answer, losing nothing in the translation, ran like fire among dry stubble.

But Elizabeth could know nothing of that as she gazed up at the grim grotesque fortress of the Edissa, a thing so old that no man could tell in what dark heathen ages it had been built there at the foot of the White Mountain. Though she shivered at the sight of it, nothing would induce her to go and sleep in the comparatively modern comfort of the Queen's Palace that had been prepared for her. Since Frederick had got to stay in this frightful dungeon, she would stay too.

The fanatics continued to clash their wooden bowls even when they waited on her at table – an honour she had to accord them though they made deplorable waiters, spilling the dishes over her dress when startled by her little dogs and pet monkeys. As lunatic as they, were the women of the country, who were deeply shocked by her low-cut dresses in the English style, and yet bathed naked in the river themselves along with the men. They brought her absurd presents of sacks of cakes and loaves of bread made in great rings, which the English pages stuck on their hats and danced about in before the Queen, who laughed too helplessly to make any attempt to scold them. That caused great offence; it had always been the custom for the Bohemian countrywomen to bring such presents for the christening of a royal baby, and here was their new foreign queen flouting them.

The baby was her fourth child, born late in December in the dark tower of the Strathoff, and christened Rupert. The countrywomen declared loudly once they were outside the palace that the splendid great baby who crowed so lustily in his cot should be their next king instead of the little Prince Henry, born an alien, whom Frederick had announced as his successor – although it was just this error that had helped to dethrone his Catholic predecessor, Ferdinand, now sitting in Imperial state in Vienna and listening sardonically to the reports of the magnificent christening given to Rupert, in spite of its homely peasant accessories.

'A Winter King and Queen made of snow,' he said, 'and when the snow melts, they'll go.'

And melt they did, the first thaw showing when Frederick gave the order to knock down those statues on the bridge. Good King Wenceslaus fell first, and the sainted Queen Elizabeth. The whole of Prague rose to the rescue, Frederick had to recall the order, King Wenceslaus and Queen Elizabeth stood again in their ancient places to show that stone is stronger than snow or feeble human flesh.

Frederick's new country would not support him when the Imperial Catholic forces invaded it, and a brief campaign showed him this. He returned from it, however, with premature hopes that the invaders were retiring for the winter months; his army were confident there was no immediate danger, and he had been absent from Elizabeth so long he had to see her again. Ambassadors had arrived from England to discuss the situation, and a banquet was given in their honour.

Through the music and the polite speeches came the sound of thunder, steady and persistent – it was not thunder but the booming of big guns, and it came from the direction of the White Mountain. The embarrassed guests had only just realized this when a page came and whispered to the King, and straight on top of him a haggard bloodstained figure rushed into the hall, told him that his army was defeated and the enemy would be in the city within a couple of hours. There was nothing for it but flight, and that so instant that no sooner had the horses been rushed out of the stables, thrust between the shafts of their coaches and had their harness flung over them, than they were off.

No one dared wait to collect their possessions lest they should find themselves left behind; people rushed in all directions, screaming 'The Cossacks are upon us!' They dropped shapeless bundles as they collided against each other and forgot to pick them up, dogs barked furiously, horses neighed in shrill terror, and all the time that dreadful steady thunder came nearer and nearer. Frederick and his guards held the defences as long as possible while the coaches of his queen rumbled once again over the unlucky bridge, where two rows of dead faces mocked their flight.

'All, all is lost!' sobbed the women in the coaches, and remembered that first this and then that of the Crown jewels had been left behind.

'It's more to the point that all my night-clothes have been forgotten,' their queen told them in exasperation.

It was just over a year since she had first come to Prague, and once again she was on the eve of a confinement. Her mind was more taken up with the coming baby than anything else, for the terrific bumping and jolting of the coach at this rate might precipitate its birth at any moment – 'and then what shall I christen it?' she thought, in the effort of a mind in desperation to fasten itself on any trivial point.

Her women, straining from the coach windows, cried now that they could see the Cossacks in hot pursuit, now that they had checked it to plunder some baggage wagon. They enlivened each other by recalling the unimaginable cruelties of the Cossacks to their captured victims.

Their queen answered, 'If it is a boy I will call him Maurice. Pray Heaven he'll be one half as good a soldier as the uncle.'

To be a soldier, that was the one thing that counted these days.

'Now I know what I am,' her husband had sighed just now as he lifted her into her coach. Whatever that was, it was not a soldier. No soldier would go on a campaign as if it were a University course with eight boxes of books like her poor little Nigger Duckling. ('But why *eight*, Nigger? You cannot possibly read them all.'

'But I cannot possibly tell which I shall want to read.')

Yes, a soldier, that was what Maurice must be, and his name

would please the old man, his great-uncle. Names were beginning to run out in the rapid increase of her family; there was Henry, named after her dead brother – thank Heaven he had been sent away from Prague some time ago when the city began to get dangerous – and there was Charles Louis, named after her second brother and one of Frederick's relations, but always called Carl to distinguish him, and the little girl Elizabeth, named after herself, both of whom had been left behind, again thank Heaven, with her mother-in-law; and there was Rupert, named after the famous Rupert the Red, who built Heidelberg three centuries ago – would Rupert be a soldier too? He should be a grand fighter, to judge by his tempers.

Where was Rupert by the way? With his nurse of course, she must have seen to him; but as she made her feverish inquiries, she could get no decided answer, nobody could remember seeing the baby, and when she cried to the coachman to stop the horses his only answer was to whip them on. She called to the cavaliers who rode beside her carriage, and some of them galloped back to the rear of the train to see if they could get any news of him. Back they came at last and one of them was carrying him.

Rupert had been flung into the back of the last wagon as it clattered out of the palace courtyard. Some servant must have seen the baby lying there forgotten and picked him up just in time to throw him in among the boxes, where he would soon have been knocked about to death if it had not been for those healthy lungs the Bohemian women had so admired. His ferocious yells were heard even above all the clatter and jingle and shouting, and he had been picked out of the lumber and put into one of the more advanced coaches. Now here he was on his mother's lap, still yelling, and staring at her with a scarlet indignant face.

'Rupert the Red!' she exclaimed, and burst into fits of laughter.

The angry baby roared louder than ever.

'The poor forsaken lamb!'

'And was he quite forgotten?'

'In another minute he would have been dead.'

The murmurs of the women were hardly audible, but sympathy is felt more than heard, and Elizabeth knew quite well that for once the sympathy of her immediate followers was against her and with her son. She could not endure it, she who was beloved by everybody who knew her. Resentment welled up in her against this brat who so furiously resented her laughing at him, and had worse reason for resentment in her having forgotten him – she knew that, but she would not think of it, she would put it at once behind her, bury it so deep that soon it too would be forgotten.

And forgotten it was.

But now, more than twenty years later, sitting in her armchair in the winter sunlight of that brisk little bourgeois town that had been her refuge ever since, sitting there dozing over old memories and present troubles and the difficulties of growing daughters and the greater difficulties of faster growing sons, something still lurked in the recesses of her memory, waiting to pounce out on her.

For in all the twenty years that had followed that escape from Prague, years of endless fruitless failure to get back to their lost kingdom or even to Heidelberg, now a tortured wreck from the wars of Catholics and Protestants – her palace a haunted shell, her English gardens trampled down, and only the carved stone arch remaining in them to testify to Frederick's love that had ruined his country for her sake – in all those twenty years of defeat, of debt, of dragging poverty and humiliation, of the agony of her loved ones' death – her eldest son Henry drowned before he was fifteen, her husband dying broken-hearted, hearing through his delirium his drowning boy's cries to him for help – through all those desperate, hopeful, disappointed years, it always seemed in each fresh grief as though there were some special point of bitterness that had for the moment eluded her, some added sharpness of self-reproach for her, who never reproached herself any more than she reproached others – something that she could not at the moment recall, but which, if she were to probe deeper, she who never probed, she would find to be in some way connected with that difficult lad, her odd, angry, perverse and vaguely unsatisfactory son, Rupert.

CHAPTER THREE

RUPERT WOULD have said he could remember nothing of his escape from Prague at the age of one. But the jolting, jostling and shouting, the shrill neighing and trampling, the helter-skelter scurry of men and horses running for their lives, made its indelible though forgotten impression on him, so that to the end of his life it had the effect of quickening his blood as to some early familiar tune. What music, drink or love did for most men, danger did for Rupert. The mere physical shock of that escape, which would have made a weaker infant into a nervous wreck for life, only heightened his innate appetite for action and danger.

His baptism of fire had been early, yet other elements had been potent in his infancy as strange and as fierce. For the first year of his life he had been a prince in state as well as name, the son of a reigning king and queen, born as were none of his brothers into the barbaric magnificence of the Bohemian Court at Prague. He had been born in the grim old fortress of the Strathoff, under a coverlid of velvet lined with sables, and rocked in an ivory cradle which was studded with gold and precious stones, the gift of his father's female subjects, whose round slant-eyed impassive faces, framed in massive embroideries like the faces of jewelled idols, had thronged persistently round their infant prince, admiring his scarlet countenance and royal roaring.

His baptism had been an international affair, held with tremendous pomp, and though he naturally could remember none of it consciously, yet he had been told of it so often that it had become a favourite fairy-tale, with himself mysteriously somewhere in the middle of it. The Russian Embassy had come to the christening in fifty coaches, and on each coach were chests covered with red leather, containing presents, chiefly furs, and at the banquet they drank so much brandy and heavy Hungarian wine that most of them had to be carried home. And the Muscovite Embassy looking like gipsies (for they economically wore their ordinary clothes because it was raining), brought for their christening gift a coach drawn by six white bears, another by six black, and another by six stags; and the white bears danced to the company – 'which is why you're such a bear now,' Carl expounded. And his principal godfather had been that scoundrelly adventurer the King of Hungary, Bethlem Gabor, believed to be a heathen, that is to say Mahomedan, who for a last exotic touch cajoled Rupert's father at the christening into his unholy alliance with the infidel Turks.

The savage music of the Tartar hordes had drummed and throbbed in his infant ears; his eyes had blinked at innumerable jewels, at the uncouth prancing of wild beasts, at the bright weapons of warriors with the sallow high-cheek-boned faces of the tribes of Tamerlane.

And this semi-Oriental splendour, forgotten as it was, endured in continual reminders. His brothers and sisters would never let him forget that eccentric baptism; they declared that Bethlem – or Bedlam – had left a mark on him for life by sponsoring him in the names of the Pagan fiends, Mahomet and Termagant, so that no wonder the fury of his temper soon earned him his second christening as Rupert the Devil. And nurses and servants impressed his gorgeous infancy upon him, just to point the contrast to the puzzled child with not half as much pocket-money as the children of the Dutch merchants, who yet were not considered grand enough to play with him. 'Ah, to think of that cradle that rocked Your Highness,' they exclaimed, rocking their heads, and told Rupert of the fierce barons who had dandled him in their steel-clad arms, delighted with the first royal prince to be born in Prague for a hundred years, and declared him their future Grand Duke of Lithuania and King of Bohemia, though his father did not wish the two elder sons to be set aside for him.

A vision of that one year of uncertain splendour, doomed to vanish in the flight from the White Mountain before he could even retain it as a memory, early helped to give his eyes that wistful and bewildered look which strangers found so touching, though his mother and brothers would have told them to see Rupert in one of his rages before they chose their adjectives.

Perhaps his pride bore also some unconscious inheritance from that first year, for certainly it was far greater in him than in any of his brothers. Henry's temper was too sweet for pride, and Carl, though proud of his birth, soon recognized that his chances of getting on in the world would depend on what he could persuade other people to do for him. But Rupert could never be brought to conciliate anybody to his own advantage; if he disliked or despised anyone he showed it instantly; and from his early childhood it was so natural to him to command that he reduced his younger brothers and playmates to a slavish obedience such as his elder brothers could never exact.

Yet he (and Maurice too) was always on much more easy terms with those far beneath him in rank than Carl approved of – indeed his natural taste for low company was one of the many faults listed by most of his elders against him. Perhaps even that

41

too bore some lingering influence from his cradle, when all the peasant women who chose came into the palace and crowded round him with their homely presents of bread and cakes and went away so much better pleased with his lustily crowing welcome than with anyone else in that scornful alien Court.

Whatever that first year had left with him of fierce and barbaric glory and pride and headlong danger, was unconscious; and for Rupert consciousness meant vision, for the part of him that was the most acute and aware was always his eyes. From the moment that he was old enough to focus them, they took in exactly how people moved inside their clothes when they did things, and communicated it to his brain, not in words but in a rapid outline that could later be put down on paper. He saw how his sisters curtseyed to him and his brothers at mealtimes, suddenly transformed from lively little animals into a stiff pattern; he saw how his father sat so much more still than any of the rest of them, while his eyes would roll round, the white patches showing at the side of the dark brown circles, set in hollow melancholy caves of furrowed skin, as they followed his mother's every movement, whether violently despairing, or exaggeratedly comic; and he saw just how the great Duke of Buckingham's splendid legs came striding into the room when he visited the Palatine with proposals of help from his friend and master, King Charles of England, and of marriage between his own little daughter, Lady Mary Villiers, and Rupert's eldest brother Henry.

Legs the Duke remained, silken, strong, superbly shaped, and a voice like a deep jubilant bell ringing out from somewhere above them, and only a rare glimpse of a pointed beard thrust out in laughter above shiningly clad shoulders. For Rupert, like most shy children, looked no higher than his own level when with grown-up people, and so at six years old was only dimly aware of the Duke of Buckingham from his waist upward. But he knew that as those legs strode through the house or spread themselves at their ease like brilliant maypoles from the shabby seats of the armchairs, glorious things would come dropping down from the heights above them in a casual inconsequent way as if they had been dropped by a god – delicious sweets, and gold coins 'to buy yourself a new pony', and a fat round watch in white and green enamel for himself, and a brooch of diamonds for Eliza, and a little jewelled Italian dagger for Henry.

He also became aware of the effect that this magnificent stranger had upon Henry.

Seen later in the halo light of his early death, Henry was so much the perfect elder brother as to seem hardly credible, and yet there were his letters in the careful childish handwriting, treasured in dried rosemary and lad's-love in his mother's cabinet, to prove that he was every bit as gentle and sweet-tempered as they remembered him. 'I have a bow and arrow with a beautiful quiver tipped with silver, which I would fain send you, but I fear it may fall into the enemy's hands,' he wrote to his younger brothers.

Carl of course remarked that he could afford to be equally generous in the same conditions – Carl could find the thoughts for such remarks even before he could find the words for them. 'Timon the Cynic,' his sister Elizabeth nicknamed him from her reading, which was as precocious as Carl's cynicism. It was Henry who reported that the baby Rupert's first spoken words in his father's German were 'Praise the Lord'; it was Carl who declared that Rupert's first word in his mother tongue was 'God-damn'.

'I have two horses alive that can go up my stairs, a black horse and a chestnut horse,' wrote Henry, this time with no intention of making a present to his very small brothers, not yet promoted above hobby horses.

Those 'two horses alive' proved the most unendurable to read in later years, far more even than the grave and tender evidences of Henry's devotion to his brothers and sisters, bidding them pray every night that they should be restored to happiness. His father adored him above all his other children, but poor Frederick's chance of being adored himself could stand no competition with his dazzling spouse. Henry's almost protective affection went out to his father – his idolatry was reserved for his mother. 'I shall marry my mother,' he announced at an early age, and when it was explained that this was impossible, he then declared that he would marry nobody.

No age would have been early enough for Carl to display a similar innocence; the wistful radiance that surrounded Henry seemed to have marked him from the beginning with foreknowledge of death. The little crystal ship worth £1,000 that Great-Uncle Maurice had given him for a christening present was always his favourite toy; when he grew too old to play with it like a baby, he stuck it in his window for the light to shine through it, and wrote with a diamond on the pane beneath it

'Mediis tranquillus in undis.'

On windy nights the roar of those waves on the long low shores of Holland could be heard within the little panelled room snug as a cabin where the boy slept, and his crystal ship glimmered in the window, a minute ghost of the future.

Great-Uncle Maurice died, and now the ghosts from the future took the splendid and tantalizing form of ships laden with gold and silver from Mexico, looted from the Spanish galleons. For the Stadtholder had taken shares in a Dutch company to raise a fleet for the excellent purpose of intercepting and looting the Spanish fleet on its way to the Spanish Nether-lands. The old soldier who had delighted in Elizabeth's English freedom and boldness and had backed her against his pious sister and timid nephew, had done his best in his last years to take the place of her father, that canny Scot who was depicted in all the Continental caricatures as carrying a cradle behind his daughter and showing his empty pockets and scabbard while he stumbled down a staircase labelled 'Peace'. Any help King James gave was surreptitious, he did not even allow public prayers for his daughter and the desperate condition of Pro-testantism abroad. But he signed his letters to her 'Your old Dad.' – 'An odd sort of Dad,' growled Great-Uncle Maurice, 'who won't fight for his children nor pray for them!'

It was left for him to do what he could for 'little Frederick's girl', and when he died he bequeathed his shares in the Dutch shipping company to his favourite.

So that 'What shall we do when our ships come in?' became the children's most popular game.

But now into their schoolroom and their childish games came the legs of the Duke of Buckingham, and the great world with them, and suddenly everything was different, for one of their tight little company had become a man and a proposed bride-groom, and there was this magnificent man of the world talking to Henry with the most delightful easy assumption of equality. He brought a miniature of the bride-to-be, a very little girl, younger than Rupert, with a rather sly almond eye; bored but determined, she held out a tiny scarlet and silver apron full of flowers towards the outstretched arms of a baby brother. But they all fell in love, not with the absent Mary Villiers, but with

44

the present father-in-law, and his dazzling promises of what they would all do when they came to England.

England had always been a paradise of the past from their mother's stories of her Fairy Farm, her kind tutor with his marvellous microscope and telescope, her river palaces where she swam and hunted and danced and watched masques and plays with her now long-dead brother Harry. Now her brother Charles had just come to the throne and his friend Buckingham was by far the most important person in the kingdom – 'more important than Charles it seems,' said Charles' sister, drily at first, but she could not really disapprove, Buckingham's affection for Charles was so warm, and his belief in the glorious new reign that they two were going to build up together was so happy and confident.

Buckingham went away, and now a new game was added to the repertoire – that of their all going to England to stay with their Uncle Charles for Henry's wedding, sailing up the Thames in a river pageant and hunting at Windsor. To go to England – that would be home indeed, their mother's home, in a way the Palatinate could never be.

Henry now had a new correspondent and signed himself 'your most affectionate friend' to his future father-in-law for two years after Buckingham had left them, until the terrible news came that Buckingham had been stabbed by a mad assassin just as he was going on board ship. So there and so shortly was the end of England's ruler and King Charles' friend and Henry's.

Would the marriage be carried out just the same? Nobody quite knew – so many glorious hopes seemed bound to end in darkness, it was scarcely worth while to consider whether the Villiers marriage, with Buckingham dead, was still one of them.

But then incredibly something did happen that had been hoped for, their ships that had been given up for lost did come home, and after three years of silence there was the news of the Dutch fleet bringing the captured Spanish galleons into the Zuyder Zee with £870,000 worth of plunder.

Now all the family ran wild with excitement, they rushed about the house beating drums and trays and ringing bells and killing innumerable Spaniards. A steady stream of growing children were coming along to be conscripted as armies or enemies; Rupert, aged nine, was now commanding five youngers – Maurice, who would never change his position as his devoted ally, and Louise, or Louey, who was generally his opposing

45

rival, and Edward, or 'Wilful Ned' as they nicknamed him in disapproval, for even at four years old Master Ned would take his marching orders from nobody but himself, and when challenged as to whether the treasure he carried of a rattle and a nutcracker were for the Dutch or Spanish fleet, would only reply from fat, blown cheeks, 'For me.' The tiny pink and white Henrietta, Etta, or else the Cherub, never minded if she were an Inca, a conquistador, or a pirate, and the baby Philip could just crawl along as the baggage vans in the wake of the armies.

Rupert, increasingly proud of his studies in military science, was never tired of practising them on his devoted victims. Just now he stood halfway in the family between these undoubted children and the three elders, at this time so much older than he. Elizabeth was so much more learned and grown-up in manner that they all called her Great Eliza after the old dead Queen of England, who had been godmother to their mother. And Carl was so much shrewder that he seemed the eldest of all, and Henry, lucky, glorious Henry, nearly fifteen, had just left his studies at Leyden to start on his first military campaign, and had persuaded his father to take him with him to Amsterdam to claim Great-Uncle Maurice's share of the plunder from Spain.

Amsterdam had run as mad with joy as the household of royal children, or rather it had run mad drunk. In that first raw foggy, frosty week of January, the Zuyder Zee was as crammed with boatloads of holidaymakers, all singing, laughing, roaring and rollicking, as if it were carnival time on the canals of Venice. Frederick and his son crossed it with scores of other passengers on the common packet-boat – disappointingly to Henry, who had thought that now they were to be really rich and able to live like the princes they were. But his father preached economy and prudence to him, his favourite virtues, now to prove fatal. For the small overcrowded packet-boat was run down in the foggy dusk by a heavy Dutch boat loaded with beer. The packet sank, and the beer-boat began to sail off from the disaster, but the skipper of the packet swam after it, yelling that the King of Bohemia was drowning. Frederick was picked out of the icy water, but his son was not among those who were saved with him, and he thought he could hear his voice crying, 'Father! save me, Father!'

Frantically he commanded the beer-boat's skipper to put down the rowing boats and find his son. A face like a round red cheese grinned drunkenly back at him 'Ya, ya, we will do

anything you want.' Nothing was done, the sailors were too
sodden to trust themselves in small boats among that helter-
skelter of sea craft that had thrown every rule of the waterway
into the waves. The wretched man tried to fling himself again
into those black freezing depths, but the skipper was not so
drunk as to let a king drown once they had rescued him – 'Na,
na, that would only make trouble.' The night closed down on
Frederick, blacker than his worst melancholy could ever have
imagined, and in the frozen mist of dawn they found Henry's
body still clinging to the mast of the sunken packet, the ice
congealed on his face, which yet looked peaceful and childish.

'Mediis tranquillus in undis' – the prophecy was fulfilled, and
the crystal boat had come into its haven.

*   *   *

They thought his mother would die when the news was
broken to her, ill as she was at that moment after the birth of
yet another child. Now at last the seas, that had striven to
prevent her mother's wedding and her own, had done their
worst by her family; the sound of many waters throbbed in her
brain so that she could not hear the voices of her friends as they
strove to recall her to consciousness. But in a few weeks she had
recovered her health and that amazing vitality that simply
would not let her body remain sad, however tragic her fate. 'I
am still of my wild humour to be merry, in spite of fortune,' she
had once written, and that 'wild laughter' would always echo
round her, though another Prince Henry, more dear even than
her brother, had died more young and tragically.

Economy and prudence had failed Frederick utterly; they
called down a miserably sordid aftermath of the tragedy of
Henry's death in the shocked reproaches of public and particularly English opinion, for as King Charles I had as yet no children, Prince Henry was his heir – and that the heir apparent to
the English throne should be run down in a common packet-
boat was a scandal scarcely to be believed.

The treasure so dearly paid for melted away almost as soon as
it was brought home. Soon the family was in poverty deeper
than it had ever yet known, so that it was sometimes in straits to
get enough to eat. Queen Elizabeth's passion for hunting proved
quite useful in supplying venison, and now Carl and Rupert
were allowed to accompany her, to their intense pride. Rupert's
most famous exploit in the hunting-field took the ignominious

form of wriggling so far down a fox's earth in order to rescue a favourite hound which had followed the fox that he in his turn got jammed. Both the Prince and his tutor were missing; the hunt, after a long search, discovered a pair of legs sticking out of the ground, and dragged out backwards first the tutor, whose hands were clutching Rupert's legs, and then a crimson, choking boy with earth all over his hair and face, and his hand clutching the hind legs of a whimpering hound, whose teeth were fastened in a bedraggled fox. So famous did this become that drawings of the scene were printed and passed into various countries, and Carl was gently sarcastic on his younger brother's methods of getting notoriety.

It was impossible to get accustomed to 'old Timon' in Henry's place as eldest brother and heir to the Palatinate; Rupert certainly did not try much, and it was chiefly owing to his furious quarrels with Carl that he acquired so early his own nickname of Rupert the Devil – and that Maurice, as a secondary result, earned his of the Twin, for Rupert and he became quite inseparable now that Rupert had no elder brother that he cared to make his companion. Carl was more friendly with their elder sister for his acid wit appealed to her scholarly mind, but rather oddly it appealed far more to their mother's.

Elizabeth had always really been fondest of Carl even while her devoted Henry was alive. Devotion after all was the daily breath in her nostrils, but there was something in her second son that baffled and piqued her; his sleek charm made him her complement, where the headlong tempestuous Rupert was her counterpart. Not that his mother would ever have recognized Rupert as her counterpart. Carl was so neat, precise and elegant, never at a loss what to say; he made his brother, only two years his junior and already his equal in height, seem in comparison a backward hobbledehoy, shy and tongue-tied, with great brooding eyes looking out through his tumbled hair that was always untidy and too long where it flopped across his forehead.

Yet strangers were aware of his fiery vitality, as urgent as his mother's, but suppressed in her presence. There were reasons too deeply buried ever to be recognized, why she could never be quite fair to Rupert. She was convinced that his stubborn refusal to study the classics was due only to his incorrigible idleness. But Rupert's determination carried weight with his tutors – a rare achievement. He pointed out that modern languages would be of far more use to him in his future life as a soldier of

48

fortune (for everyone seemed certain that would be his career) and from that moment he refused to touch Greek or Hebrew, and only as much Latin as would enable him to understand any necessary parley in it. He was practically tri-lingual in English, French and German as soon as he could speak, other languages followed, also geometry, because it was useful in fortification, and out of that art grew another that could not be claimed as useful, but Rupert found he simply could not draw a fortification or a map or a plan of battle without a host of little men running across the paper, all alive and active in the business they were on.

Fencing and vaulting and exercises on the great horse and at the pike and musket were as much a part of play to him as riding, so that he was rather astonished at the solemn praises they called forth from his masters. They remarked that at only eight years old he 'handled his arms with the readiness and address of an experienced soldier', and their reports to his mother of his later prowess in all military studies were so glowing that she simply could not understand it, she had never noticed any sign of genius in Rupert, always so sullen and silent – his sister Elizabeth now was an absolute little paragon of learning, but what use was that in a girl? but anyway she was sure his brother Carl was a deal more clever, just as his brother Maurice was certainly far more amenable – and they even made a fuss about those little figures he put all over his paper, but all children liked drawing little figures – there was Louey now, more than three years younger than Rupert, and you could not keep her away from chalk and paper. And then she remembered with an absent air that a certain schoolmaster had told her that the stupidest boys who showed no aptitude for their lessons often proved quite good at military science.

'Was Gustavus Adolphus a stupid boy, Madam?' asked Rupert, scowling under his heavy fringe of straight hair. Of course she was annoyed, nothing could have been more tactless at the moment, unless it were deliberate impudence, just when the greatest soldier of the day was actually bringing his Swedish armies to the help of the Palatine and the Protestant cause.

An endless succession of romantic knights-errant from England – and other countries too – had been dazzled into fighting for their 'Queen of Hearts', as they were now all calling Elizabeth. They fitted out expeditionary forces at their own expense, wore her colours, and bound badges on their arms proclaiming their intention to fight 'For God and For Her', and did their best to turn the bloodiest and beastliest war that modern times had yet seen into something resembling a chivalric crusade.

It was part of Elizabeth's careless charm that she was so little impressed by her slaves. 'I am never destitute of a fool to laugh at,' she declared – 'when one goes, another comes!'

The Swedish King Gustavus Adolphus had made very ardent offers for Elizabeth's hand when she had been a girl, and they had been firmly rejected by her father, for the position had been widely different then – Elizabeth, the only daughter of one of the greatest kings in Europe, and Gustavus, who had been brought up like a poor student, the heir to a very uncertain and divided throne. Even after he came to it he had to fight for six years to make it secure against the Catholic claimants.

But there he was now, the most powerful soldier king in the world, coming to the rescue of the distressed princess he had failed to win in youth, and there could be no more romantic situation, if it were not for the fact that he had never set eyes on her, and that the real motive behind his campaign was that Catholic France under Richelieu had, with remarkable religious tolerance, hired the Protestant champion to fight against Catholic Germany and Spain. 'It takes a Cardinal to do that sort of thing really well,' said Carl.

After a few victories Gustavus invited Frederick to join him; and his active wife was at once hopeful that a little campaigning might cheer him up and benefit his health, which had been failing ever since Henry's death. She had just given birth to her thirteenth child in time to christen him Gustavus in compliment to the great commander. ('Pray Heaven I am not now starting on a second dozen!' she remarked cheerfully.)

It was a good thing to have a reason for a name – they had all drawn lots for that of the twelfth child out of a hat, and nobody had owned up to the contribution of Sophia, that daring innovation to the English part of their cosmopolitan ears. But as that was the one to be drawn, her mother, strict gambler, insisted on abiding by it.

Frederick said goodbye to Baby Sophie with especial tenderness, for she was a lively brat that had often teased him out of his melancholy. He left The Hague with a certain amount of relief, for 'a great city is always detestable', he was wont to complain, 'but of all *canaille* save me from the *canaille* of The Hague!'

He called at Leyden on his way to say goodbye to Carl and

Rupert and see how they were getting on at the University there. They were getting on very well indeed and grown considerably taller than their father, and distinguished themselves in his presence both in examinations and in a grand college tournament where they bore off most of the prizes between them, and Rupert in particular attracted the attention of all the ladies for being so young, so daring, so angelically beautiful. But he was too young to take any notice of that – too young to accompany his father to the wars as he begged. 'Shall *we* ever fight by the side of Gustavus?' sighed Rupert as he watched him go, the image of his father's pathetically frog-like countenance still in his mind, the round eyes so anxious, yet so anxious even now to be hopeful.

The reports of him were all very cheering once he had reached Gustavus (which was not for many weeks owing to the usual amount of books and heavy coaches which had to be pulled out of the winter bogs on the roads by large, white, incredibly slow oxen), but, when he did, Gustavus put him on his right hand and called him 'my brother' as often as he spoke to him, and embraced him so often that the minute Frederick was almost suffocated, and bragged to him of his victories, and then suddenly rose at the end of dinner to address a full-length sermon to the company just to show that he could do it as well then as when he preached to his troops from the saddle, and hauled him off to a carnival where he disguised himself as a waiter and the bewildered Frederick as a Jesuit friar.

But in spite of all this boisterous camaraderie Frederick was not allowed to levy troops from his own subjects lest it should interfere with Gustavus' own recruiting, and was soon writing to his wife with all his old dejection that he could not imagine why the King of Sweden had asked him to come – he had much better have stayed at The Hague. Perhaps he had – perhaps in either case his days were numbered and he was glad of it – anyway he caught a fever on the campaign and died of it just a fortnight after Gustavus was killed in battle.

He was in his thirty-sixth year, a worn-out man who had no will to live. The last voice he heard was that of his dead son Henry calling him, but his last words and prayers were for his wife Elizabeth.

*   *   *

The news of Frederick's death came to his family when Carl and Rupert were home on their holidays from Leyden. It shook

Rupert, not yet thirteen, into a storm of passionate grief and pity – blindly, incoherently, he felt that love of his mother had ruined and finally killed his father – and yet that love had been the only joy and glory of his father's life. The pitiful puzzle of human things had early become almost more than he could bear.

'But is the battle lost that you are crying?' asked little Philip, staring in astonishment at his grand elder brother sobbing like a baby, for even at five years old Philip knew that military disaster mattered most. But four of his brothers, being older, knew how much had been lost. Who could help them now? Once their uncle's friend had come striding down from the skies with his pockets full of presents, to help their parents and take Henry as his son-in-law. Now Henry was dead and Buckingham was dead, but there was still his friend and their uncle, King Charles of England, the one safe and contented country left in Europe. So these four sat down to write to him – ('We will make it a round robin,' said Rupert, who did not want to sign his name just under Carl's) – 'to commit ourselves and the protection of our rights into your gracious arms' and to remind him that without his protection 'God knoweth what may become of Your Majesty's nephews

Carl

Rupert   Maurice

Edward.'

The four boys' heads, the eldest barely fifteen, the youngest just eight, clustered together over the letter. 'Is there anything we could add to make it stronger?' asked Carl, 'such as for instance that money is very hard to come by?'

'Or,' suggested the practical Ned, 'that the house is overrun with rats and mice?'

'And creditors,' added Maurice.

'It would make a good Litany,' giggled Ned – 'from rats, mice, creditors and all other vermin, Good Uncle Charles deliver us!'

The others looked doubtfully at their frivolous younger brother.

'I said it was a mistake to bring you into this,' said Maurice, the next of age and therefore the most severe on youth.

'I have as good a right to be in it as any of you,' protested Wilful Ned, 'and for that matter so has Philip.'

'And why not Gustavus?' demanded Carl's sarcastically drawling tones. 'I expect he can make his mark in the cradle.'

But Maurice was already smacking Ned's head, and Carl having again asserted that the letter wanted working up, Rupert suddenly burst out in a roar that Carl was a whining merchant who wanted to ask for cash down, that not a word should be added and he would have it sent this instant to prevent it.

Their uncle, reading their dignified and pathetic appeal, would have been astonished if he could have seen the furious fight that attended its writing, from which Carl emerged with a black eye and Rupert with a bloody nose and Maurice with some scratches and Ned, less hurt than any, howling with rage.

'Who can be making that horrible commotion?' demanded their bereaved mother, and then when she heard who was there, 'Oh, Rupert – naturally!'

She had been prostrated by the news of her husband's death – speechless, unable even to weep, she had lain for days like someone that had been physically crushed.

Her sanguine temperament had expected him to step into the dead Gustavus' shoes in the last fortnight and lead his composite armies with even greater success than that superb general had done. There was no logical procession to her in Frederick's life and death – at one moment he seemed to her on the point of conquest and recovery of all his lands, reunion to all he loved, and a fairy-tale happy-ever-after conclusion – at the next, a loving but mysterious God had struck him down in death, and their cause once again into failure. Her despair was proportionately the more violent and unreasoning, her recovery the quicker.

Yet she wrote sincerely five months later when she said, 'though I make a good show in company yet I can never have any more contentment in this world', for she had been as fond of her poor little Nigger Duckling as he had been dazzled and blinded by 'his Star' as he called her with his last breath, mercifully never quite seeing into what slough of despond her bright blaze had led him.

And for her part she never thought how much happier and more glorious and suited to her lordly temper would have been her marriage to the conqueror Gustavus Adolphus – perhaps she knew instinctively that it would not have been – and wisdom deeper than her conscious thoughts told her what combustion might have flared to their undoing at the conjunction of two such uproarious spirits.

Certain it was that no man could have given her more superb children in health and beauty and wits and high spirits than her poor little weakling husband had done; while all that Gustavus left to carry on his new-won power was one queer small sickly girl, Christina, who was already beginning to show perverse instincts and, what was almost more shocking in the daughter of the Protestant champion, a strong inclination towards the Roman Catholic Church. There was some idea of marrying her to Carl as a corrective to both these tendencies and a brilliant advantage to him, but it came to nothing – everything came to nothing, his mother declared in a most unwonted fit of despairing petulance. Her adored elder son was not even the soi-disant King of Bohemia – that hollow title that had cost them and half Europe so much tragedy was now only attached to her; and Carl's, as Elector Palatine, seemed as impossible to regain as that had been.

For the first time she was showing some faint signs of growing older, worn out not only by her great sorrow but by so many small worries. One of the smallest was her last baby, Gustavus, the only one of all her children (except two which had died in infancy) to lack her splendid constitution. The tiny, always ailing baby seemed a sign that her apparently inexhaustible youth and vigour had at last failed.

And on the other hand the superabundant high spirits of that family were causing her a great deal of annoyance, for no tutors seemed able to restrain the older boys, and the girls were growing as bad, or at least Louise was – they never thought what anyone might think, they were always dressing up in some absurd disguise and conducting impromptu plays or careering about the streets of The Hague or arranging some mad and horribly noisy form of hunt or paper-chase, or worse, some outrageous practical joke on the prosy Dutch citizens who really bore it all very well, for like many sturdy democrats they were secretly greatly flattered to have all these young princes and princesses, penniless though they were, but such beautiful children – regular pictures, as could be seen whenever they would sit long enough to let themselves be painted – to have these royal young rascals making free with them and their houses and all their solid respectable comfort.

But it was quite another matter when a company of English

Puritans came over to offer their 'godly condolences' to the queen whom they had always regarded as the martyred saint of the Protestant cause. Their visit happened to coincide with the Carnival and the young princes' mad 'mask of Yagers', and the godly English retired horribly shocked by their mumming and merrymaking, their 'songs, dances, hallooings and other jovialities', having found no moment at which they could appropriately offer condolences. It caused some scandal, and Elizabeth might scold and swear at her family, 'but', said Carl, 'they were far more scandalized by you, Maman, when you bore down upon them in the hunt in your cavalier hat and coat and they saw that instead of a stout widow and mother of thirteen you looked like an elegant young man'.

Which cleverly diverted Elizabeth's wrath on to the Puritans – a detestable conceited sect that persisted in regarding her as their patron saint ('Not now, Maman!' interposed Carl), when she had never liked them any more than her father, who could not abide them, and now here they were giving her brother Charles all the trouble they could – she only hoped that new Oxford Chancellor of his, Bishop Laud, would be able to keep them under, for the man seemed an honest fellow and determined, though too fantastically a pacifist for her taste.

Which meant that Laud had written in answer to her appeals for help (for she wrote to the most influential men in every kingdom as well as to their monarchs) that he could not wish to recover her rights 'by effusion of Christian blood' until all other means had been tried – to which she replied that 'wars alone made good peaces' and that she hoped her dear brother King Charles would have luck in them. 'I know your profession forbids you to like this scribbling of mine,' she added with that comradely candour that had made such different types of men adore her – 'You will think I have too warring a mind for my sex; but the necessity of my fortune has made it.'

King Charles had written the most sensitive and tender letter begging his 'dearest and only sister' to make her home with him for his sake if not for hers – but she would not, she must devote herself to her children, she declared – and perhaps, even before she thought of them, the image of her brother's bustling little French Papist wife stood in her mind – how could she go as a suppliant and beggar to another woman's home?

But certainly above everything these great boys of hers must first be attended to, she could not have them sprawling about

The Hague, running wild and ruining their opportunities now that they had no father to guide and restrain them (never did she see her Nigger Duckling when she argued thus, but some demi-god whom she yet believed to be Frederick so devoutly that it never occurred to her a miracle had taken place).

Well, there was always the army, the perpetual struggle of the Protestant States of Holland against the Spanish Netherlands which was connected with the more recent efforts to recover the Palatinate; and Great-Uncle Maurice's brother, Great-Uncle Henry, now offered to take her two elder boys with him on the next campaign.

Rupert, not yet thirteen, seemed a little young for this, but it was he who had really prompted the offer. As great a favourite with Henry as his mother had been with Maurice, he had sat and cracked nuts between his fingers over his great-uncle's golden Rhenish wine and listened to his uncle's complaints of his escapades beginning – 'Now look here, my boy, this really won't do –'

'What a youngster like you doesn't yet understand –'

'What you need, my lad, is some sound discipline of the sort I had at your age –'

'Isn't a soldier's training the best discipline?' asked the boy.

'Ah,' sighed Great-Uncle Henry, leaning back with his hands across his pork-fed stomach, 'you'd find life a very different thing in the army.'

'That's what I want,' said Rupert, gazing up at last from under the heavy square-cut fringe of golden-brown hair. The sudden fire in his sombre eyes almost startled his Dutch uncle out of his post-prandial complacence.

'Good God,' he exclaimed, 'and what, may I ask, do you hope to get out of it?'

'I don't know,' said Rupert. It was obvious he had never asked himself such a question.

'Drink some more of this good Rhenish to begin with,' suggested his uncle, 'it's time you began to learn to carry your liquor.'

'No, thank you, Uncle.'

'Why? Your mother? Are those the English notions now? Not what I remember of them in your grandfather's day,' he added, chuckling heavily – 'How that old fellow could drink, and his wife too! I've seen the whole Court reeling drunk. But your mother needn't think I would teach you the same.'

'No, sir, it isn't my mother. It's only that I' – the boy turned crimson as he blurted out, 'I want to be a soldier. I don't want to do anything to get in the way of that. And I ought to begin at once. Take me with you, sir.'

'That's all very well,' snorted Uncle Henry, blowing through his cheeks, 'but you're not yet thirteen. What will your mother say?'

What she said was – 'He cannot too soon be a soldier in these active times.'

That was after she had consented to Carl's going with the army, so, after all, Rupert – well, it did not so much matter.

And she helped the boy write a letter in ten languages asking for a commission, which his great-uncle had imposed as a condition, thinking that would stop him – but not a bit of it, for Rupert reeled it off in English, French, German, Dutch, Spanish, Italian, Swedish and dog Latin, and then his mother came to his aid with Danish, which she remembered from her mother, and broad Scots from her father – 'and that's the most necessary of the lot, with all the Scots soldiers of fortune you meet abroad.'

So Great-Uncle Henry was beaten, and Rupert went to the wars. But when his mother heard how petted and fêted he was by all the soldiers, no less than by 'that damnable old fool Henry', she began to fear for the effect of camp life on his character and to try to recall him, especially after a tournament in which old Henry commemorated a victory at The Hague, where Rupert carried off the palm with such strength of arms and grace of carriage that the ladies behaved in the most idiotic fashion over him.

Back he was hauled to the maternal side, more sullenly angry and injured than she had ever known him, and so unbearable did he make himself, refusing any study that was not of arms, that his mother could do nothing but again let him have his way – which this time was to enlist as a private soldier in the Stadtholder's Life Guards, for he had determined to work his way up through the ranks so as to know all the conditions of a soldier's life.

As a private he endured the hardship of two sieges and the revolting sack of a town, but as a private no less than as a prince he was protected by his adoring comrades in arms, who were not going to let the little rascal come to harm in spite of the reckless daring which positively shocked the old soldiers.

'Thinks the General slow, does he?'

'Always for charging the enemy, is he?'

'The God-damn young fool – well, he'll learn sense in time and be a proper soldier,' so they consoled themselves, laughing in admiration of the boy, who returned from his second campaign more spoilt than ever.

'If *this* is army discipline!' breathed his mother in despair.

Something quite different would have to be done about him.

* * *

Carl had gone to England. His kind Uncle Charles had been asking him to visit them for some time, and was now fêting him as if he were the powerful prince of a rival State instead of a very poor young relation. His brothers and sisters heard with derisive envy how he had been given a household of his own, horses, servants, a chaplain.

'For "chaplain" read "tutor"!' interpolated Louey, and she was to some extent right, for Mr John Wilkins was an Oxford scholar who had been chosen for his higher mathematics – 'what *are* higher mathematics?'

'Higher than Carl's,' Rupert told her.

' "River picnics, city banquets, hunting parties, masques, plays, fireworks in the gardens all night" – oh, England must be Paradise! Why can't we all go?'

And Carl was winning golden opinions there in spite of his mother's coy doubts of her favourite at the beginning – 'I fear damnably how he will do with your ladies, for he is a very ill courtier – desire them not to laugh too much at him.'

Laugh at her Carl, so smooth and polished in spite of his youth – what fools they would be if they did! Her letters were of course merely the inverted pride of the correct Oriental – 'My poverty-stricken house – my base and miserable offspring.'

But now came a truer occasion for humility – her brother, the most elegant and accomplished monarch in Europe, whom she had not seen since she was a glorious bride, was inviting Rupert to join his elder brother – Rupert the Devil, with all the coarse ugly oaths of the camp in his babyish mouth, and his furious tempers, and his bewildered inattention to ladies however young and pretty.

Now in sober truth it was 'my base and miserable offspring' – for which very reason she could not write of him with such gay and careless disparagement as of Carl. 'For blood's sake I hope he will be welcome,' she began doubtfully, and then something of the same old joke that he would 'not be thought a very *beau garçon* which you slander his brother with', and then, anxiously, an entreaty to give him good counsel, 'for he is still a little giddy though not so much as he has been. Pray tell him when he does ill, for he is good-natured enough, but does not always think of what he should do.'

She dared not say more for fear of putting them all too much against the troublesome violent headstrong lad. They would know what he was like all too soon, she added to herself with a sigh.

Did they? She began to wonder. She began to doubt. She began to be bewildered, incredulous, amazed.

Carl had been popular enough as soon as he arrived at the English Court, he was so 'handsome, modest and very bashful' – he was 'so sweet, so obliging, so discreet, *so sensible of his own affairs and so young as was never seen*' concluded another and more ambiguous report, which continued no less ambiguously – 'he gains upon His Majesty's affection by assiduity and diligent attendance'.

But now came Rupert, quite incapable of assiduous and diligent attendance – much more rough than sweet, often disobliging and very indiscreet – but younger than Carl in years and younger by centuries in spirit, and so unaware of his own affairs that never to the end of his life did it occur to him that they might be used to his own advantage instead of to another's.

And Rupert won – won all hearts and amused, interested attention. His elder brother had been all very well, a nice well-behaved lad enough, but apart from his rather neat little dry comments one always knew what he would say, and that was whatever would please the most important person present.

But this other young fellow, ah, that was different – something odd there and unexpected, a spark of the genuine fire of genius, one could not tell how or where it would flare up, but it was there beyond question – 'spirit and action – observation and judgment – certainly he will be *a great man* for whatsoever he wills, he wills vehemently, so that to what he bends, he will in it be excellent' – so ran the report to his mother, and then in slight bathos but none the less approval, 'His Majesty takes great pleasure in his unrestfulness, for he is never idle; in his sports serious, in his conversation retired, but sharp and witty when occasion provokes him.'

' "In his sports serious" – oh, well, I suppose that explains it,' decided his mother over the baffling problem of Rupert's superior popularity to Carl's. She could remember her England well enough for that. And it gave an extra edge to her complaints, for she was sure he was spending 'his time but idly in England' – 'he will never mend there' – ('And when was he broken?' asked Louey pertly of her sisters) – *she* knew what England was like and how the young men went so mad over sport that they could think of nothing else (she might have added the women too, if she had remembered her own unceasing passion for sport, but she was not given to introspection) – and either it made them damnably conceited or else it caused their death, as with her own poor dear brother Harry – those fierce games of tennis, that long swim – but for them he might have been alive now, and *he* would never have let himself be married to a French Papist ('Two religions will never lie easy in one bed') as poor helpless Baby Charles had done.

For Charles had not at first intended to marry the Princess Henrietta Maria – he had only seen her at the French King's wedding to Anne of Austria as he and Buckingham passed through Paris on their way to their ridiculous unlucky wooing of the Spanish Infanta – and Elizabeth was quite sure that the little French princess, child as she was, had then inveigled Charles into his later marriage to her. And in Charles' wife lay the secret of Elizabeth's growing nervousness over Rupert's visit.

Henrietta Maria, or Queen Mary as she was more simply called in England, was a born proselytizer, and many rising young men at her Court had turned Catholic in compliment to her gay Parisian charm combined with religious fervour. If Rupert were to follow the fashion it would seriously prejudice his brother's cause as the Protestant Elector.

Carl could see that quite as clearly as his mother, and did a good deal to goad on her fears in his letters, telling her that Rupert was 'always with the Queen, her ladies, and her Papists'. Carl himself had been a great deal more with the Queen and her ladies before Rupert had come and put his nose out of joint, but the wise young man was naturally not going to mention that cause of annoyance to his mother.

CHAPTER FOUR

CARL WAS careful to remember his dignity, for he was haunted by the fear that since he was dispossessed and penniless others might not remember it. He was conscientiously concerned for his harum-scarum family for their own sakes as well as his own, and what worried him most was to find people in London gossiping about them.

What, he demanded of his mother, was this disgraceful story of Lady Laveston giving Louey a box on the ear in front of about twenty people in the Prince of Orange's garden, and never even asking her pardon for it? Louey was thirteen now and should be treated with the full respect due to a princess, even if she had been indulging in her usual impudence. Those 'imaginary portraits' of hers – wicked caricatures for the most part – they would only get her into trouble.

Carl was convinced that all his family would get into trouble; that was why it was so important that he, the eldest, should keep out of it, should do the right things and make friends with the right people, lest the grave men who had supported his mother as the heroine of the Protestant cause for a generation might now be alienated by his wayward brothers and sisters. Rupert particularly needed watching, but there were reasons why Carl had no wish to be too much in his company.

It was naturally galling to find himself playing second fiddle at Court to the younger brother who had hitherto been despised for his rough manners. He swore he would not compete, but go where he was appreciated, and this urged him on with his accustomed diligence to cultivate the most important Puritan and political leaders.

An instinct for the winning side of the future had begun to develop itself in this prematurely disappointed young man. He did not believe that everything was really going so well in this charming country. Puritan feeling was being steadily fanned to more and more strongly outspoken resentment against their Roman Catholic Queen and her priests in petticoats and her unscrupulous Parisian ladies, all meddling and intriguing in honest, manly Protestant England.

Carl found he could do a little intriguing himself in an honest manly fashion. He declared he owed too much to his kind uncle and aunt to dream of criticizing them, but he thought it scandalous that they were not better served – the sly Papists round the Queen were getting all the reins of government into their hands, and the King was so simple and open-hearted he never saw how he was being led by the nose; for of course it was his wife who got her own way in everything, and Carl would be very much astonished if she did not contrive to bring up all her children as Roman Catholics at heart. His intimate knowledge of his uncle's family circle naturally gave weight to all he said, and his lost sense of importance was soothed and nourished – not merely by the present attention he was winning.

For if the tide of Puritan feeling *should* turn the country against King Charles' children and demand another and more undoubted Protestant heir to the throne, then he himself as Charles' eldest nephew stood next in the succession. His new friends told him what lamentation had been raised in all staunch Protestant households when the little prince Charles had been born six years ago to the Queen of England, and so barred the succession from the Protestant Palatines. 'God had already provided for the nation in the hopeful issue of the Queen of Bohemia,' so they had said quite openly (it was really an amazing country!) and had refused to ring the bells in some of the churches for the birth of the Prince of Wales.

The son of 'our English Elizabeth', that was what all true Englishmen had wanted for their next king, not the son of 'the Popish brat of France', and so they let Carl know, with many demonstrations of their sympathy, and hopes that public feeling might even yet bring about that desired event, in spite of the sturdy little boy whose black eyes watched his cousin Rupert so adoringly, but not his cousin Carl.

This prospect, however remote, was the more dazzling to Carl because he had begun at last to give up all hope of his own country of the Palatinate – a wretched land by now in any case, tortured by years of war and famine.

It did not for a moment occur to him that he might be helping to bring that same condition on this country of his uncle, who had after all done him no serious injury in preferring Rupert's company to his – he did not think in terms of war, for there was no reason why it should come to that, the people here in England were a peaceable level-headed folk who knew what was good for them and their trade and never carried things as far as they did on the Continent.

And, after all, if he did not look out for himself it had begun to grow plain to him that nobody else would.

So he paid discreet visits to the house of Mr Pym, the Puritan leader, after dark, and walked there (for the sake of the exercise, he said) unattended, like any ordinary citizen, and dressed like one (but then his tastes were sober, as he had already assured his Puritan friends); and there he met the very wealthy Mr Hampden, who had suddenly become the most talked of person in England because he had preferred to stand his trial rather than pay his taxes, purely as a matter of constitutional principle.

Mr Hampden had brought with him a country cousin who was talking violently in a harsh, uncontrolled voice when Carl entered, fulminating against the foppish novelties Archbishop Laud was introducing into the Church; all bishops, he swore, were anti-Christian mushrooms. Some of his companions looked nervously at the new arrival, and one said that the innovations were really of slight account.

'Nothing is of slight account,' persisted the speaker, 'if it tends towards Rome. Laud is bringing back flat Popery.'

He was a big ugly man who stared rather rudely at Carl, so the young prince fancied, as he affably made friends with these commoners, showing them how different he was from the rest of his family, how he had hoped to make his uncle understand something of his and these gentlemen's point of view through his young brother, who was, alas, so much more of a favourite with the King and Queen than himself. He lamented that Rupert had been brought up as the darling of the brutal and licentious soldiery and could understand no really advanced or enlightened view.

Really, the stare of Mr Hampden's cousin was quite uncomfortable – an uncouth, slovenly-looking person. He managed to ask his host privately who he was, and learned that he was a Mr Cromwell from Huntingdonshire who did not like foreigners.

The presence of the young Palatine was in fact rather a nuisance to his company, who were willing enough to consider him as a possible substitute for his uncle's family on the English throne if sufficiently well trained by them, but could not naturally discuss their plans and complaints half as freely when he was there. But Carl had a vein of stolid German insensitiveness which kept him sitting on very placidly, lamenting that his young brother could not understand a constitutional principle, while his unwilling hosts regretted that he thought himself capable of doing so.

He had a shock when at last he went, for there, coming in through the doorway, was the Queen's great friend, Lucy Countess of Carlisle, in a black cloak with the hood slipping back from her thin, clever face, and her white arm raised against the doorpost with a black ribbon fluttering from it, for she had always worn a black ribbon on her arm, ever since an obscure Devonshire parson called Mr Herrick had praised it in a neat little milliner's verse.

The King's nephew and the Queen's friend stared at each other, almost equally annoyed to be discovered by the other in that company. But the woman of the world was the quickest to smile and make a casual reference to Mr Pym's delightful evenings where one met everybody of interest irrespective of the difference of opinion. She proved her point by chatting familiarly of the last letters she had received from the Lord Lieutenant of Ireland, Tom Wentworth, and how she had been urging the King to reward his services in that detestable country by making him Earl of Strafford. He was as strong a 'King's man' as Mr Pym was a leader of the discontented Puritan party, and Lucy Carlise prided herself on her intimate friendship with both – on her liaison with both, said scandal, but not those who knew her. Her beauty had been great, but was now fading or rather sharpening into a refinement of feature and critical expression that made more appeal to the mind than the body – and indeed she had always done so. Her last love affair had been with the all-conquering Buckingham nearly ten years ago, but he had quickly left her arid charms for the richer beauties of Anne of Austria, and Lucy's jealousy was supposed to have been the prime motive in that troublesome and mysterious affair of the diamond studs that the French Queen had given Buckingham. She discovered from that moment that intrigue and secret power held an attraction far more satisfying than passion to her irritable and sexless vanity.

Rupert had hated her at sight and called her an ingrowing toenail, though unable to explain why.

For the first time since he had come to England, Carl shared his brother's opinion. He longed to warn his uncle against the brittle mocking creature that stood in the doorway and sparkled on about 'Tom' and 'Growler' (her nickname for Pym), while she looked him through and through. The only difficulty was that she might also warn King Charles against himself.

*　　*　　*

After an evening with Pym and Hampden and his country cousin, Carl, slightly conscious of the incongruity of his visiting list, went to call next day on Archbishop Laud, and there to his astonishment he found Rupert helping the old gentleman to piece together the fragments of stained glass scattered on his table. The glorious old windows in the chapel at Lambeth had all been smashed up in Henry VIII's time in the popular passion for the Reformation—'De*formation*,' muttered Archbishop Laud, his plump white fingers quivering over the heavy jewel-like fragments. With infinite patience he was determined to fit them together himself, to restore them to their old position, while the glazier, deeply shocked but not daring to protest, had been set to work to mend together the pieces of the broken crucifix.

Laud had fined people heavily for thrusting their walking-sticks through church windows, and insisted on their receiving the Communion on their knees instead of sitting or standing about anyhow with their hats on their heads to show they were as good as God. The Communion table in his chapel was no longer a bare board in the middle of the church but was in its old position against the east wall, and behind it a piece of elaborate embroidery that painted in exquisite minute stitches the scene of the Last Supper, recovered with some difficulty from the parson's wife, who had cut it up for a petticoat.

Carl pulled down his lip as he looked at it; that long upper lip, slightly pursed at the corners, was always apt to give him a bitter look, enhanced by the narrow line of moustache that had just, to his intense satisfaction, begun to show itself, running downwards from the scornful nostrils to the corners of his mouth and looking at a distance like two sharp elderly lines. He knew from the glazier's face what the common people thought of such 'Romish' shows, and it was more worth while to take note of that class in England than on the Continent; besides, it wasn't only the common people – he had a message for the Archbishop which showed what way public opinion was going among the best educated – but he had no chance yet to give it while that young ass Rupert went on taking up all his attention with this childish puzzle – as if the glazier couldn't do it better than either of them!

'Look, sir,' Rupert was saying, 'that bit of blue fits in there – I said that would be the sky.'

'Bless your sharp eyes, so it is, and I was looking for Saint Peter's head. Well then where does the head go?'

'He's stooping, it comes in down here. That bit of yellow must be the beginning of his halo.'

'Aha, and here's the rest of it. Why did Your Highness tell the King you would not take Holy Orders? I shall tell him you are admirably fitted for them. Now here are two fingers, raised to bless. I shall put that piece there and look for the arm afterwards.'

At last Carl broke in.

'Your Grace, I was dining with Bishop Juxon today and he asked if you were going to pay attention to those libellous verses you showed him.'

The Archbishop's eyebrows shot up into his hair so sharply that his horn-rimmed spectacles slipped down his nose; his rosy indignant face looked ridiculously like that of a small boy who is just about to swallow a dose of medicine.

'The verses? But Juxon himself advised that nothing should be done – too vague he said.'

'So he said. He was telling me about it because he knew I should be interested.'

'Why?' interposed Rupert, his eyes and hands going on with the puzzle while an impatient foot kicked against the table over which he leaned.

'Anything to do with the English Church naturally interests me.'

'Don't see why it should.'

'No, for you've never had the smallest concern for religion.'

'Nor have you. But you've got to play the Protestant champion or where are you? Nobody in England is going out to fight just for a German Elector.' And he jogged roughly against his elder brother, pushing him out of the way while he thrust out his arm for a minute piece of emerald glass.

'Sirs, sirs!' exclaimed Laud in panic, fumbling among the folds of his cassock – 'I have the verses here – perhaps you would like to hear them?'

That would keep the young savage from flying unprovoked at his brother's throat for another ten minutes at least.

'As Your Grace pleases,' said Carl, with icy dignity. It was what he had aimed at in bringing up the subject, as he made it his business to find out what undercurrents of discontent there were in this supposedly well-satisfied country. The Archbishop adjusted his spectacles, unfolded the paper and began to read, while Rupert went on fitting bits of glass together, humming a little low tune as if he were not listening. Carl made up for his brother's bad manners by frowning and nodding his head attentively at every other line. The poem, named 'Lycidas', was supposed to be about a young man who had been drowned, a Cambridge Fellow, son of the Secretary for Ireland, Laud said, and wrecked on his passage to that country, but so far the poet was showing discontent only with his own trade and asking if it were not better

> 'To sport with Amaryllis in the shade
> Or with the tangles of Neæra's hair?'

'This is damned dull,' interrupted Rupert, 'where's the libel?'
Laud was not to be checked. Without skipping, he read to the end, only pausing to explain which lines were an undoubted attack on bishops under the guise of false shepherds, and that

> 'The hungry sheep look up and are not fed
> But swoln with wind'

referred to their congregations —
'And the wind to their sermons!' chimed in Rupert, pleased with his ingenuity 'but he shouldn't call bishops —

> 'Blind mouths that scarce themselves know how to hold
> A sheephook —

How can a mouth be blind *or* hold a sheephook?'
Laud, who had suggested a bishopric as a suitable profession for Rupert, began to think he had made a mistake.
The two boys went out into the crowd of Lambeth poor who were always clustered thick round the gates waiting for the Archbishop to come out and give them the alms he never refused. They rushed forward at sight of the Princes, but not so hopefully, for they knew that these gilded youths, the King's nephews, had no pocket-money but what their uncle gave them, and that their nickname throughout England was the Pauper Palatines. Carl heard someone whisper it behind him with a snigger at the small coin he had handed with so magnificent a

gesture to cover his uneasiness at the amount. He was exasperated into a thrust at Laud.

'That old fellow is making the Church of England more and more like that of Rome.'

'Then he's making the best of both Churches.'

To Rupert the Church of England had been one of the most delightful novelties in it. The gaunt Calvinistic services abroad had been the only form of Protestantism he had known; nor could one enjoy the beauty of the Catholic Church without treachery to one's family and country. England, with her genius for compromise, seemed to have discovered the golden mean.

But Carl, with his glancing flick of sarcasm, replied, 'It won't do. How are people to know this is Protestantism if it's not ugly?'

Encouraged by Rupert's grin (there were times when old Timon really was not so bad) he continued on his favourite, rather priggish note of warning. 'The sermon last Sunday! Laud talks as though Divine Right means that everything the King says or does must be right. It's caused a lot of unpleasant comment, I can tell you.'

But Rupert had not even heard the sermon, it had bored him profoundly, and he had spent the time surreptitiously drawing a caricature of the Archbishop in the flyleaf of his prayer-book. The tightly buttoned little mouth opening into a round O of incredulous disgust that the world should contain all kinds of men and opinions, the fretful eyebrows peaking halfway up the forehead, the glazed, rather bovine stare of the assertive eye challenging his congregation, all made as trenchant a criticism of Laud as any that Carl had heard. But it was made unconsciously and therefore without acrimony. Rupert could not understand why Carl and others should get all worked up over a little man whose job it was to stand up in the pulpit and talk for an hour on end without anyone answering back.

Words never hurt anyone – or he had never thought so until he came to England. It must be because in England they had nothing else to hurt them that they considered them such deadly weapons. In other countries war, plague and famine stalked side by side through a burnt-out wilderness where the blackened skeletons that remained alive ate grass for food and had no strength to bury the dead. Civilization had slipped, Europe was falling back into savagery. The English, secure in their island, were free of it; but also they did not realize it.

They were not as free as they might be, said Carl. No Parliament had sat for eleven years.

'Why should they sit? Last time they did, they all burst into tears.'

'One must move with the times. The country expects more Parliaments now.'

'The country's got on very well without 'em. A lot of talk only makes trouble.'

'It's bad to have people grumbling in private.'

'It's worse in public. And *I* don't know what they can find to grumble at, however good the English may be at it.'

'There is a very grave discontent underneath.'

'Let it stay there then. They're better fed, housed, clothed, and fairer treated than any land in Europe. Isn't that good enough for them?'

'Not for noble minds. Their discontent is not of the body, it's of the spirit.' Carl spoke portentously, feeling how much older he was than his young fool of a brother.

'Christ's blood, what do they want? They ought to be in Heaven. If I were my uncle I'd send a few of them there. *I'd* give 'em something to be nobly discontented about – a few months in the trenches to start with!'

There was no doubt that Carl had been strictly fair when he had talked about the effect of the brutal and licentious soldiery on Rupert.

CHAPTER FIVE

FOR ALL the life that he could remember, Rupert had been a pauper with high-sounding titles but often with a coat too short at the wrists, and more accustomed to find creditors than courtiers at his parents' house, a smallish house and in no way resembling a palace. He had been as poor a student at Leyden as many of the technically 'poor students' there, who were admitted at reduced terms. He had served as a private.

And then, from the scrambling anxious poverty-stricken little house at The Hague where the titles sounded so sham, vaguely expecting something like his Great-Uncle Henry's comfortable bourgeois state as Stadtholder, he came to England and the most civilized Court in Europe.

His mother had always considered him rougher, ruder and more troublesome than his elder brothers; and he came to an uncle and aunt more gracious and courtly than any people he had ever met, who instantly preferred him to his mother's favourite. It was of no use for Elizabeth in the repeated alarms caused by Carl's reports to send again and again for Rupert to come home; his uncle and aunt flatly refused to send him. They delighted in the company of this shy boy who expected nothing better for himself than the life of a soldier fighting for his brother's inheritance.

'Why, he is born to rule himself!' his angry aunt exclaimed with flashing eyes. 'He would manage three kingdoms better than his brother could a single miserable little electorate. What can we do for him?'

Laud's suggestion of a bishopric and Sir Thomas Roe's of a wealthy marriage were both equally to his distaste. He could not imagine why anything should be done for him except to give him employment for his trade. He had a reasonably high opinion of himself as a soldier but was quite unaware of his other gifts, was astonished they liked his drawings – 'Oh, but you should see Louey's – they are far better, and she is much younger – Gerard Honthorst thinks the world of her.' He was passionately interested in pictures, spent hours walking up and down the galleries at Hampton Court towering over his tiny, very erect uncle, while King Charles showed him his collection, the first on such a scale ever to have been made by an English monarch.

'But for you, sir,' his nephew announced with a touch of Germanic solemnity, 'your people would never have known what Mantegna was like, or Breughel – they must look on you as their greatest royal benefactor.'

'It does not seem yet to have oc-oc-occurred to them,' replied his uncle drily.

They were happiest of all when they were hunting, a sport King Charles cared for as passionately as his sister Elizabeth. Rupert, mounted on the superb Irish hunter his uncle had given him, felt that he had never ridden like this before. The English woods, the village greens where the thatched cottages looked like friendly mice and children ran to cheer the royal huntsmen and throw them flowers, the wide green lawns of private gardens sloping to the river side, were all new to him. The German peasants he had seen were still serfs who wore wooden shoes and

70

ate grass herbs and roots, lucky if they were not in districts devastated by the wars. But these rosy brawny peasants were free men, fed on quantities of bullock's beef and mutton, hares, rabbits and all kinds of game; they continually had time to play on their village green, the cry 'All fellows to football,' fetching them even from their work in the fields to kick at the blown swine's bladder that made their ball.

His eyes looked round him everywhere with delight, and King Charles, seeing the boy so happy beside him, could again feel himself also a gay young man. He enjoyed telling Rupert of his single adventure, that mad journey through France and Spain when he had set out to woo the Spanish Infanta as Mr Thomas Smith, a servant, carrying the portmanteau of the irrepressible Buckingham, who travelled as Mr Brown. For the first time in his backward youth he had then realized the fascination of women, in the half Oriental seclusion of Spain, mysterious behind mantillas and barred windows; he had thrilled to the discovery that he was a young prince on an adventure, personable, brave, and – 'why should I not match even Buckingham in daring, carry the fort by storm, and climb the garden wall to woo a princess?'

It had shocked everyone inexpressibly – in fact, ever since, the whole Continent had known for a certainty that all the English were incurably mad.

'So it was —

> *"Adieu and farewell to you,*
> *Ladies of Spain,"* '

sang King Charles on his big white horse, throwing back his fine head so that the small point of his beard thrust out against the blue sky, where the larks were carolling shrilly against his snatch of song,

> ' *"For we've received orders*
> *To sail for old England,*
> *And we hope in a short time*
> *To see you again."* '

'But you never did see them again, Uncle?' said Rupert, secretly marvelling that his uncle should ever have climbed a wall or shocked a lady.

'No, Rupert, we never did. It was the little French princess, as quick and dainty as a kitten, that we'd seen dancing and miming at her rehearsal in Paris on our way out – that was the one we saw again. "He needn't have gone so far as Spain for a wife," she said, when she heard of our visit incognito – so she tells me now – and her mother was furious that she had not been let into the secret and so seen to it that her daughter had worn a prettier dress.'

But fate had not been baulked by that – the grave Spanish lady was left to walk undisturbed in her garden, and the Princess Henrietta Maria came to England to be King Charles' queen — 'and not as old then as you are now, Rupert, think of that, and she your good aunt!'

They came in from riding to where 'his good aunt' was inspecting with cries of delight a new consignment of rare plants from Paris for her especial garden, the pond garden at Hampton Court. Her small daughter Mary was helping her unpack them, and Charles should hold this precious root if he were very careful, for it would have the loveliest flower in the world.

'What is it called?' asked Rupert.

'Some Latin rigmarole. These gardeners are so pedantic. But we will give it a name.'

'Call it *"ma mie"*,' said Charles.

The little Princess Mary asked gravely what that meant.

Her father, stroking her sleek curls and gazing over her head at his wife, replied, 'It is the short for *"mon amie"* – and for Marie.'

His wife blew him a kiss. Rupert stood looking at his uncle and aunt, both so charming, so good-looking and so small, as though they belonged to a miniature and more refined race than the gross full-size mortal, both so free from the squalid poverty and ugly gnawing anxiety that had seemed till now the essential condition of all grown people, even of his mother.

She had just been making a specially determined effort to recall him, which he had repulsed with even greater determination. He blurted out – 'Is it because this is an island where no one – not even —' (no, he could not say 'not even my mother') 'can get at one —' and stopped, having made nothing clear but that England was to be preferred to all other places in the world.

His uncle's slow smile showed that he understood. His little aunt sprang up impulsively and kissed him on both cheeks. These people were his friends. As he tasted the knowledge in delight and awe, he heard his uncle say, 'Would you not like to have an island of your own, somewhere beyond seas?'

It was said so smoothly that Rupert scarcely noticed. But the question was repeated, the island was named – the magical name of Madagascar – the third largest island in the world, and so remote that he might be able to conquer India from its base. And this was not a mere idle game of pretence – King Charles had been thinking it over seriously and discussing it with practical people. He was convinced that England's genius lay in colonization – that the little fringe of trading villages that had sprung up on the coasts of America were only the beginning of what she might do in that great continent and indeed all over the further parts of the world.

The sea, within easy distance of The Hague, had always given a tantalizing tang to the air in Rupert's nostrils. He had sometimes gone sailing with the fishers, and was apt to hang reprehensibly about the little doorways of low taverns where the Dutch sailors would reel out with their enormous breeches tucked into their boots, shouting their hoarse shanties. He had watched and waited as a child for their uncle's ships to come home with the plunder of the Spanish galleons from the River Plate; the people he liked best to meet in England were sailors who could tell him of the sea-dogs of the old Queen's day; having gambled away their fortune in a night, they would set out to voyage round the world and return laden with emeralds and pearls. So mighty, so pure was the sea, that it had even washed out religious differences; for the Catholic gentry had brought their ships up to fight by the side of Drake's and Howard's in the Armada.

Now God had ordained a fairy-tale to come true for his own especial benefit; the King of England was going to build a fleet for the colonization of an island in the furthest parts of the world; an Order in Council was passed for twelve ships of war and twenty-four merchantmen to be fitted out at once, and to be followed later by twelve more. And Rupert was to be leader of the expedition, ruler of the new colony, and 'Universal Admiral'. He might become Emperor of India.

He now spent most of his time in the London dockyards; he pored over shipbuilding plans and the study of navigation, chemistry, mineralogy, and the reports of the island's soil and produce.

His friends were all hot on the plan. Mr Endymion Porter, a middle-aged wealthy diplomatist and connoisseur, comfortably settled in the exquisite structure of art, music and congenial society that he had gradually built round himself, actually

73

intended to fling it away and follow this boy of sixteen into the wilds. So did the popular young dramatist, Will Davenant, whom everybody believed to be the son of old Shakespeare, but a deal more of a courtier and less of a poet. He at once composed a long poem called 'Madagascar' in praise of England's new soldier-and-sailor prince. Ballads about this new sea-adventure were hawked and sung in the street, not much worse – nor better – than the courtly Davenant's; it even almost reconciled some of the less truculent spirits to the payment of the ship-money tax towards the upkeep of the navy – but not the sounder heads, for after all enthusiasm was one thing but money was another. Everywhere was heard that new and ringing word, Madagascar – it sounded in Rupert's ears like a trumpet call which no power on earth should prevent his following – and it had the effect of a red rag on a bull when it was repeated to his mother.

'Rupert's romance of Madagascar!' (spat out like that between a hiss and a snort it certainly sounded a mistake!) Had her brother gone mad like Don Quixote that he 'promised his trusty squire to make him King of an island'? She wrote to all her friends in England, entreating them to put such 'windmills' out of the boy's head, she wrote to Rupert that it was 'neither feasible, safe nor honourable for him', and that there was 'work enough to be had for him in Europe'.

He did not answer her.

Her great friend, 'Honest Harry' Vane, told her it was 'a fine thing'; her greater friend, 'Honest Tom' Roe told her it was 'a most desperate, dangerous, unwholesome, fruitless action'; a London merchant gave his blunt opinion that it was 'a gallant design, but one on which he would be loth to venture *his* younger son'.

And Elizabeth, more frantic than ever, both wrote and swore to Heaven that 'no sons of hers should go for knight-errants'.

If ever the Fates smile ironically, they must have smiled then.

Rupert said nothing, not even when his mother's Dutch agent came to England on a special mission to point out the distress he was giving to his grandmother, mother and sisters. Having answered not one word, he returned to the latest map of the expedition, and appeared to be measuring how many hundreds of miles lay between his distressed grandmother, mother and sisters, and the island of Madagascar.

*   *   *

If the future were dazzling the present was intoxicating, and women as well as men combined to make it so, though Rupert made no effort to rival his brother as a *beau garçon*. The superficial experience he had had as a young boy with the camp-women who had tried to pet and chaff him on his last campaign only made him the more diffident with the beautiful and brilliant creatures at his aunt's Court. These were beings of another world, they sailed about inside skirts like inverted tulips; they smiled up at him with enchanting but alarming friendliness; they quoted long romances and declared that no one had lived who had not also read them, so that Rupert had no prospect of ever living at all; they talked French so badly and with such an air of it being the only way to talk it that he found himself conscientiously mispronouncing words in imitation until his aunt caught him at it and laughed at him for carrying Court fashion so far.

These kind beauties were eager enough to wake up the shy handsome lad whose war experience was that of a man, his fast-growing strength and stature that of a youth who did not yet realize how it would out-top others – his movements restless, abrupt, now bounding with superfluous energy, now sinking into slack inertia with the suddenness of a young animal that flings itself all in one instant from furious activity into a deep pool of sleep – while his sulky mouth, his great dreaming eyes, the soft curves of his cheek and chin, were still those of a boy, almost a child.

'Ce grand bébé là, je le trouve adorable —'

'C'est bien vu, ma chérie. Mais est-ce qu'il trouve —' (Lord help her, why had she tried to keep it up – what *was* 'the same thing' in French? Why, the same thing of course!) 'trouve la même chose en ta cas?'

'Tiens!'

That was not fair. Anybody could say 'tiens', and it had the merit of meaning anything one chose it to mean. This was what they had to pay for having a Parisienne perched as vividly as a humming-bird on the English throne.

She was not one half as beautiful as many of her ladies, she was brown, sallow even, for all that her dear friend Lucy, the Countess of Carlisle, had shown her how to paint as cleverly as herself ('When I was a stupid little *jeune fille* she gave me my first hare's foot – is there any greater proof of friendship?' Queen Marie would demand, quite forgetting the proof she

herself had given, in visiting Lucy when she had the small-pox).
She had thin arms a little too long, and her teeth undoubtedly
stuck out, but she had the magic power of making all these
things appear as attributes of her superior 'chic', so that the
larger fairer women round her, with their fresh rosy skins and
sumptuous shoulders, felt that they were a lot of clumsy
cabbages.

Rupert shared that opinion. When he watched the Queen's
glancing, laughing, shining black eyes, her one beauty, it never
struck him that she had no other – except indeed her hands, and
even more her feet, which turned into will o' the wisps when she
danced and into little mice when on cold evenings she snuggled
them confidentially into her tiny red velvet fur-lined boots. Her
hands too claimed their expensive tributes, dozens of pairs of
scented chamois gloves embroidered in different colours sent
over by her Paris tailor, rings of emeralds and ruby and diamond given with kisses on the thin brown fingers by King
Charles.

His love for her was of a deep, slow-growing root. When he
had married her she had been an obstinate child of fifteen, hot-
tempered and sometimes bad-mannered, offending her English
hosts in country houses by noisy talk and laughter with her
French servants while Protestant prayers were being held, but
making up for it by some flashes of tact from the future woman
of the world – when her blunt new subjects asked her if she
disliked Protestants she replied airily, 'Why should I? My
father was one.' But though she never forgot she was the
daughter of Henry of Navarre, she never learnt the suppleness
of the man who had thought Paris worth a mass; she would not
be crowned with her husband nor even walk in the coronation
procession to that Protestant ceremony.

Worst of all in her husband's disapproving eyes, utterly bewildered as he was at having this termagant to tame, she was
furiously jealous of his friend the Duke of Buckingham, who
was so much more impossibly handsome and flamboyant and
outrageous than any English gentleman should be, even if he
did begin by being Irish. It was hopeless for a schoolgirl to
compete with this man, who had scandalized Spain and infuriated France, made war in order to woo a queen, and told the
most severely dignified monarch in Europe to carry his portmanteau for him. But Buckingham, always generous, gave her
her opportunity by getting killed.

In a burst of relief that her wish had been granted, and of remorse that she should have wished it, the little Queen flung herself on to the apparently impossible task of consoling the stunned lifeless creature that was now her husband. Her vitality and warm impulse towards living and loving, the simplicity of purpose in a practical Frenchwoman which showed her that she would never be happy in a foreign country until her husband loved her, the admiration she had felt from the first for his dignity and his delicate beauty and the unconscious courage that had enabled him to grow from his stunted childhood into a man who could walk as well as other men, talk, though slowly and stammeringly, nearly as well, and ride a great deal better – all these together, no longer baffled by any rival, achieved their purpose. Charles now was guided by her and felt for her the same unquestioning adoration, but mingled with a tenderness he had never known before, that he had given to his elder brother Harry and to the friend that had taken Harry's place.

Those had been a boy's emotions – now she had made a man of him. A man and a child also she had made – for her fierce protective maternity showed him what he had missed in his mother, the silly starved woman in dresses stiff as armour with jewels, who had stifled her disgust of her husband in shrill laughter, in noisy games, in such pranks as getting drunk or blacking her face and neck and arms in order to dance in a masque as a Negress. That Court where his father had rolled about too drunk to stand without help – flopping abjectly over the necks of beautiful young men who endured his kisses in contemptuous acknowledgement of their mutual needs – theirs for money, titles, position, and his for what he conceived to be friendship ('Christ had his John and I must have my George,' so he explained his passion for George Villiers) – a Court whose manners were the more revolting for the veneer of learned pedantry that James contrived to smear over it in his determination to show that a man might be a pig but was at least a learned pig – that Court of his parents, Charles had managed to outgrow as he had outgrown his own childish weakness.

So decent and sober had life become at Charles' Court that the reckless young adventurers who turned up there hoping to try their luck, as good-looking young men had done in the last reign, had left in disgust for the greater freedom of the German wars, where a man had the chance of loot and rape to counterbalance the hardship and danger – they were at any rate preferable to watching the King watching the Queen and the Queen watching her babies.

These were at the time of Rupert's visit a steadily increasing family, a baby in arms, a busy trotting prattling little boy, James, a wise little girl, Mary, and the eldest, Charles, a fine upstanding boy of six who had greeted his tall cousin with a steady stare from round black eyes that looked as solemn as an owl's, but generally managed to see anything odd or comic in a stranger's appearance, so his mother told Rupert disconcertingly. He had been so ugly and dark a baby, 'but *black*, as black as a little nigger!' that she had been ashamed to own him, but so big and strong always and looked so grave and important, she was sure he knew a great deal more than she did – in fact she had always been exceedingly proud of him, and was now more so than ever since she could show actual written examples of his precocity and sly fun.

'He will be a charming letter-writer when he is older.'

'If he is not too lazy,' said his father.

There were so many directions in which she could fulfil herself that sometimes she felt dizzy with happiness. Even her extravagance was only another charm in her husband's eyes, her frequent bankruptcy another source of amusement in her own; she cried she must win a thousand pounds from Charles that evening at the cards – but they must not stay up gambling late tonight, for tomorrow would be the first of May and they must all be up before dawn to take her nephew a-maying – 'to think this is the first time Rupert will fetch in may in England – but not his last by many a May Day!'

'Am I not to fetch in may too, my aunt?' Carl asked with pointed politeness.

'Why yes, dear Carl, as many bundles of it as you can carry! I only singled out Rupert because it will be his first, while you must have seen many May Days in England.'

'I have not been here so long as that.'

'No? It seems like it – we know you so well.'

The soothing addition came just a fraction of a second late – a snigger from young Walter Montagu, son of the Earl of Manchester, had been plainly audible. The crimson Carl silently vowed he would not go a-maying but find better work for to-morrow's morning. With the steeled assurance of a proud nature that has taught himself to swallow rebuffs, he walked over to young Montagu, who looked startled at his approach, expecting trouble over that unlucky giggle. But Carl as usual was on business.

'I heard you telling someone just now, Mr Montagu, of a country neighbour of your father's, a Mr Cromwell.'

'Why, yes, Your Highness, I was saying he was a rude fellow who had been giving trouble on the Fen Drainage Committee in Cambridgeshire. He attacked my father on it more than once, did his best to pick a quarrel with him, but that's impossible, my father being the most good-natured man in England —' (young Montagu heard himself rattling on in an eager attempt to show that he too meant to be good-natured, and pulled himself up) 'Has Your Highness heard of him?'

'Scarcely, except that he's a cousin of this Mr Hampden who's been giving us so much trouble. And you said that your father, my lord of Manchester, would be relieved once his noisy neighbour had set sail tomorrow for America. Do you think his cousin Hampden intends to emigrate too?'

'I have no notion.'

'Wat Mot,' as his friends called him, a light-hearted young man who had written a heavy masque for the Queen to act in, and been in return converted to her religion, was bored by the Germanic passion for acquiring information. But impervious to his boredom, it plodded on.

'Do you know what ship he sails in?'

'Lord no! Your Highness had best ask my father – he might, as he knew of the sailing.' He turned back to his companion as Carl threaded his way through the card tables to find the Earl of Manchester.

'What is he trying to ferret out?'

'Something to his advantage. I've never seen a man so busy for it – or with so little result.'

'Hush, here's a song. A fellow can never start talking but he gets music turned on him like a cold douche.'

Will Davenant was singing an aubade of his to remind them all to rise early tomorrow:

> 'The lark now leaves his wat'ry nest
> And climbing shakes his dewy wings.
> He takes this window for the East,
> And to implore your light he sings —
> Awake, awake! the morn will never rise
> Till she can dress her beauty at your eyes.'

With his foot raised on a stool to balance his lute against his knee, he leaned forward as he sang, gazing adoringly into the eyes of the Queen. They sparkled with a hundred things unsaid as she listened to the compliment; Rupert watched them in a fury of envy that he too could not write verses and sing them to her.

He told his servant that night to pour a jug of water over his head if he did not wake the instant he was called next morning. But he did not need it; he sprang out of bed in a shivering ghostly grey light, washed and dressed in a violent hurry and dashed down the stairs out into the courtyard to find himself the first. Soon came the others, yawning and shivering and laughing, at last came the Queen – but not the King – 'Your industrious brother has some news for him, Rupert, and is as pleased as a dog with a bone. Charles thinks he should stay to attend to it – there is always something.'

They rode out into a grey mist, chill at present, but harbinger of a hot spring day; the river was a streak of silver, the Houses of Parliament were milky clouds carved into towers, seen for an instant and then vanishing.

> '*The glories of our blood and state*
> *Are shadows, not substantial things.*'

Rupert, determined to be a poet if only at second hand, quoted the verse he had heard in a play at Court, pressing his horse nearer the Queen's.

'But heaven!' she cried, 'do you call those Houses our glories? They do nothing but sob and squabble in there, whenever there *is* anyone there – but thank the saints they've been empty some years now.'

They rode on through fields that glimmered with white and gold flowers as thick as the stars in the Milky Way, the cobwebs on the wet grass all shaking with diamonds. The damp delicious smell of the dew stung their nostrils; the air tingled with the shrill sounds of birdsong and clattering hoofs and the high whinnying neigh of horses snuffling in the new morning.

On a flat-topped grass-covered mound, spangled with dandelions, some lambs were capering in a ring, leaping and bounding over each other in a rhythm that seemed as if it must answer to music unheard by grosser human ears. He drew rein an instant to watch them, and at that they at once stopped, all turning their silly daisy faces towards him, then went bucketing away over the field.

'And they turn into sheep!' he exclaimed, pointing at the heavy lumps of wool that were grazing near by.

'And girls turn into women!' answered his aunt ironically, 'and I am getting rheumatic.'

He did not believe her.

The sun was beginning to shine on the dim trees, although they could not yet see it. An orchard of fruit trees caught its first rays, pear-blossom snowy white, apple-blossom showing its first pink buds, were frothing and foaming up through the mist like clouds of the sunrise.

Wherever he rode in these fields and woods round Westminster, Rupert was not on earth but in a seventh heaven of delight. The gay voices round him said no words that he distinguished, he heard them as he heard the blackbirds and thrushes, the larks and the cuckoo, all calling and trilling and laughing their happiness, his happiness, together. More voices, of those unseen like the birds, now swelled the chorus. A song sung in parts in rough harmony, male and female, came ringing clearer and clearer as past them through the trees there trooped a procession of country boys and girls, brown, barefoot many of them, but in holiday clothes – scarlet waistcoats and blue and red aprons, and ribbons tying up the girls' loose hair – all bearing great branches of whitethorn, and some, little osier baskets full of primroses and violets.

'Look, look!' cried the Queen, 'they are bringing in May before us. How they put us to shame! Rupert, hold my horse. I must get down on the instant' – and down she got and ran to a bush that was a fountain of white blossom, snatched at a branch, cried out that it pricked her but that she must have it, those boys and girls had crowned their May king and queen already.

'And I will crown you,' said Rupert.

He had thrown her horse's reins to a servant, he was beside her, tearing boughs from the bush so fiercely that he was scattering a shower of tiny snowflake petals all over her green hat and riding dress, tearing his hands too, but he never noticed that until she cried out that there was blood on them. 'Will you crown me with bloody hands?'

'I wish I could,' he said, 'with the blood of all your enemies.'

'Young savage! But I have no enemies.'

'And never shall – none to hurt you – if I am here. Oh, Madam, promise me that wherever I am, at the uttermost ends of the sea, if ever you and my uncle have need of me, you will send for me.'

Madagascar at that moment was a childish fancy; what happiness could he find there comparable to that of fighting for these two, so precious to him, so much smaller than him?

'Dear Rupert – your mother was right. A knight-errant – rise, Sir Quixote!'

He had kneeled to pick up her glove, and she touched his shoulder with the whitethorn; for an instant in all this shining countryside there was no one but he and the little creature whose dark eyes were now smiling at him, brilliant with tears. He said to himself, 'This is I, Rupert, and I am in England on May Day, and I am her knight, and his, and I will keep the vow I heard the boys say at Eton, "my friends and my friends' son never to forsake."'

He knew in that moment the pride of manhood such as even his first battle had not given him, for then he had fought only for his own hand, but now he would know the joy and responsibility of fighting for those he loved.

The Queen, with a branch of whitethorn sticking out of her hat like an absurd feather ('my father's famous white plume of Navarre,' she cried), led them all on to Chelsea village to see the pretty church by the river and Sir Thomas More's house and garden beside it, 'and you black Protestants shall lay a wreath before his tablet in the church – the first martyr you made here and the noblest – and all so that that fat rogue Thomas Cromwell might get another wife for his fatter master, King Hal! All the mischief in the world is done by fat men – mark that, Harry Jermyn, and stop drinking sack.'

They drank bowls of milk and cream at Chelsea, and ate new spongy buns warm from the oven and crisp with sugar, they strolled along the river bank and the village street and pointed out the maypole on the village green, hung with garlands of wild daffodils. All the houses had burst into leaf and blossom; green branches, branches of whitethorn and wild white cherry were twisted all up the doorposts and over the porches, the whole street was dancing green and white in the little breeze that had now sprung up and driven the mist away in big white clouds that gleamed in the sun.

Back they rode, past rings of dancing figures and the wheedling music of bagpipes and flutes, through the village of Kensington and the fields of Hyde Park, up the long hill towards the windmill on its height, and the Piccadillo bowling green, down to the river and Whitehall.

The Queen ran into the palace with branches of whitethorn bundled in her arms. 'Oh, Charles, you should have come with us – were you coming to meet us? See, I crown you King of May,' and she stuck a branch of blossom in his hat, for he was hatted and booted, ready to start out.

But – 'Take it off, sir, take it off!' cried Lucy Carlisle, and snatched the whitethorn from the Queen's arms.

'Why, Lucy, are you mad?'

'It is unlucky to bring may or whitethorn *into* the house – it was so in the old heathen days that they chose their victim, bringing in garlands for the young man who was to be King of Summer for a day, and sacrificed at the end of it.'

'Learned Lucy!'

> *'Learned Lucy Locket*
> *Has John Selden in her pocket!'*

cried Suckling on a pirouette, checked instantly for respect.

'His toes are as malicious as his verse,' laughed the Queen, enchanted to catch out her clever friend. 'Come, Lucy, confess!'

'Yes, I'll own I learned it from Mr Selden, and he, I suppose, learned it from some old book – what odds does it make? Any milkmaid knows – though not the reason – that you must not bring may into the house.'

'Shoo! Then out they go. I'll not make the King a victim.'

'You've al-al-already made him that,' he said, smiling at her. His smooth face showed no line of worry, but Rupert suddenly wondered if Carl's news had disturbed him and asked what it had been. Mr Hampden had been giving trouble again. The King had had to issue a mandate to prevent his leaving the country.

'Because he lost his case he wants to emigrate to America in his pique, and a cousin of his too, another wealthy landowner. We can't have all the richest men leaving the country like this. They tell me 3,000 people emigrated in the last year alone. And it's not what it used to be, just the scum of the country going, poor work-people and artisans with a bee in their bonnets like that first boat-load in the *Mayflower*. Any country would be glad to be rid of them. But now it's quite a different class, people of wealth and position. That's very sound, in moderation, but Hampden and this man Cromwell – they will only stir up trouble there.'

'Cromwell? You were speaking of someone of that name this morning,' Rupert said to his aunt.

'Yes, my ignoramus, of old Thomas Cromwell, who pulled down the monasteries in Henry VIII's time and chopped off heads like so many thistles – but that was a hundred years ago and nothing to do with us now. What shall we do with the rest of our May Day holiday?'

Rupert wanted to go and see the ship start for America. The Queen clapped her hands at the notion. The King, alas, again could not come, but she made Carl come instead, for her conscience smote her for having been unkind to him last night. His chaplain was with him, so he came too, and a distinguished French poet who had just arrived with a complimentary poem was also pressed into the party, and off they went to speed down the river on the turning tide in a light barge rowed by ten oarsmen to see the magnificent new ship that the Pett brothers had just built. She was the largest England had ever had – 169 feet 9 inches in length, and with a depth of hold of 19 feet 4 inches. Well might she be called the Sovereign of the Seas.

There she lay at anchor down in the Pool of London with royals and topgallants on all masts, the gilded carving glittering on her stern, the officers shouting commands and the sailors running up and down her rigging like mice. Rupert caught in his breath as he watched them unfurl the sails and saw that great spread of canvas flap bellying out before the breeze. It was good to think of Madagascar after all. New lands, new life – even a new kind of ship to sail under the sea – what was this new invention that Carl's chaplain, the Reverend Mr Wilkins, was speaking of to him in his eager amiable voice? A diving bell that might be directed and navigated as if on the surface of the waters, and with windows so as to observe the nature of the deep-sea fishes – 'I am confident that it would be possible to achieve some such submarine vessel,' he was saying.

The Reverend Mr John Wilkins had proved an unexpected friend of Rupert's, but then he was not at all like most young parsons, especially those who were now making themselves popular at Court by wearing fine vestments and bowing to the altar 'with one eye on the Queen and the other on the Pope', as Carl had expressed it. Mathematics, mechanical geometry, music and experiments in every branch of science were the major passions of his generous and acquisitive mind; compared with them it was only a mild though steady flame of his that burned for Robina Cromwell, the youngest and prettiest of a large family of sisters in Cambridgeshire, whose only brother, Oliver, did not much approve of him. He was publishing a work on the 'Discovery of a World in the Moon', proving that it might well be habitable, and even suggesting the possibility of a voyage to it by means of volitation.

'You mean by a rocket?' Rupert had always been passionately interested in the construction of weapons and firearms; their use for other purpose than destruction struck him as a whole world of discovery in itself.

Carl, who had been computing with his companions the probable statistics of village maidenheads lost before 7 am every May Day, now listened amusedly to their talk of submarine boats and rockets to the moon, while the lazy ripples from the tide lapped against their barge. He thought his chaplain an odd fish to combine so much science with religion – 'they're bound to clash sooner or later,' he observed rather astutely, 'and then where will you parsons be?'

'With our minds opened by God to receive every branch of His knowledge – so I hope and pray!' exclaimed John Wilkins.

'You are optimistic,' drawled Carl.

The two young Princes looked at the son of the Oxford goldsmith; he had more reason for hope in future mankind than the dispossessed sons of generations of kings.

But all his confidence suddenly died away, he looked perplexed, unhappy, and at the same moment Rupert saw Carl's head turn and follow Mr Wilkins' stare at the shore.

'Surely that is Mr Hampden,' he said.

'And my brother-in-law-to-be with him!' said John Wilkins.

Two men on the shore in grey cloaks and riding boots and plain broad-brimmed hats, who had been watching the ship with many others, were now looking down into the brightly painted little barge with its freight of blue velvet cushions and gorgeous young people.

'That is very awkward. I hope they will not think we have come to laugh at their discomfiture,' said Carl.

'Oliver is sure to think it,' said Wilkins.

'Who is Oliver?' asked the Queen, her attention caught by the sudden interest in the shore from this corner of the barge.

'My future brother-in-law, Mr Cromwell, Your Majesty, the big fellow who is standing there beside Mr Hampden.'

'Oh, the two gentlemen you have just prevented from sailing in this ship, Carl— How soon are you to be married, Mr Wilkins? Will you be sorry not to lose your brother-in-law?'

'My wife will be, Madam, for she tells me her brother had set his heart on America.'

'Every schoolboy does that. It's what America was discovered for – that everyone may feel it would be all quite different if only they could start life over again out there.'

'Wat Mot' was purring in appreciation. 'Yes, Madam, and say how real, now noble life will be out there, when all they mean is that they won't have to put on a clean collar so often.'

'Oh, hush, they'll hear you,' said the Queen, but the laughter rippling over her face was as clear as his tones had been over the water. It was also clear, even at this little distance, that Mr Cromwell's collar was not clean.

'Mr Wilkins, would you not like to get out and speak to your prospective brother-in-law, or is he in too bad a temper? It's the fat men who make mischief, we decided this morning. See what you can do to prevent it.'

With a faint reluctant grimace Mr Wilkins rose to obey orders. He knew that Robina's earnest and vigorous brother thought him a dilettante, a Court lapdog, worst of all a likely candidate for a bishopric, and Oliver did not approve of bishops – quite apart from that, his temper had every reason to be unbearable this morning, and the mocking scrutiny of his discomfiture by these brilliant young people of the Court would not have improved it.

'You wish we were in your submarine boat now,' Rupert whispered to the chaplain as he clambered past him, then flung back his head in excitement, for a wave of song had come rolling out from the ship, a shanty sung by the sailors as they hoisted anchor. The great white-and-golden creature trembled, braced herself, heeled slightly, then floated majestically out towards the sea.

She would sail thousands of miles, she would crest the globe of the world and go over on the other side, she would come to the land that had been discovered to the west of the setting sun to give new hope to the tired old world. It was bad luck on those two men standing on the shore, Mr Hampden looking stoically resigned, Mr Cromwell heavy with discontent, as they watched the ship sail out with the tide that was to have taken them to America.

The Queen was reading out the poem that Monsieur de Saint Amant had written in praise of her and 'ce pays bienheureux'. 'It is charming,' she cried, 'that all foreigners find England so happy. So do my nephews – do you not, Rupert?'

He was still looking at those two sombre figures, and answered absent-mindedly, 'I wish they had not been left behind.'

CHAPTER SIX

A T T H E house of Mr Endymion Porter, the most cultivated man in Europe, Rupert met all the famous and fashionable people in London, just the society in fact that one would have supposed his mother most desired for him, to correct the rough training of camp life and give the polish she had complained he lacked.

But Carl's enquiring finger sought out its danger spot. '*Mrs* Porter,' he wrote home, 'is a professed Roman Catholic.'

In spite of that, Rupert continued to see all he could of Mr Porter and his friends and to make friends himself, for the first time in his life, not just with the schoolboys and soldiers who happened to be doing the same job of work as himself, but with all sorts of unexpected people, from his uncle himself to the Reverend Mr Wilkins. He got to know such men of the world as that amusing fellow, Harry Jermyn, always to be seen about the Queen, and that extraordinary fat versatile creature, Sir Kenelm Digby, hardly human in his cleverness, who never stopped talking; and foreign artists whom he had met before at his mother's house, but now met on quite different terms, all grown men together – Paul Rubens, who had painted the ceiling of the banqueting hall at Whitehall and insisted that no masques should be acted there, lest the smoke of many lights should damage the colours, Van Dyck, who had already painted Rupert's portrait as a child in Holland and now wanted to do another. He had been induced by Mr Porter to pay a visit to King Charles' Court and was so happy there that he vowed he would never go back to his own country. There was the dignified old architect, Mr Inigo Jones, with eyes as piercing as in youth, and a grey beard that could not disguise the fine jutting line of his jaw. He was anxious to rebuild everything in England in the 'Italian Palladian style', and already his stage scenery had revolutionized the drama ('killed it dead,' growled old Ben Jonson). There was the musician, Mr Lawes, who sang the airs he had set to little songs tossed out by the courtiers, careless and defiant as a gambler's fling of the dice upon the table —

> *'If she think not well of me*
> *What care I how fair she be?'*

'Capping verses' was a favourite game at Court; one after the other of the ring of young people clustered round the King and Queen, brilliant in wits as well as in scarlet silk, in wine-dark velvets, in tossing feathers, in cloth of gold and silver sewn with jewels, would throw a fresh line into the common pool of verse, rhyming to the one before, or the one before that.

> *'I loved a lass a fair one*
> *As fair as e'er was seen*
> *She was indeed a rare one*
> *Another Sheba Queen*
> *But fool, as then I was*
> *I thought she loved me too*
> *But now alas she's left me*
> *Falero, lero, loo!'*

It was to some such inspiration of a round game played with delightful intimate companions, of a page's thrumming lute, inconsequent laughter, and the bright acclaiming eyes of a little Parisian lady who was the Queen of England, that such songs were tossed out into the scented air.

> *'She would me "honey" call,*
> *She'd – Oh, she'd kiss me too!*
> *But now alas she's left me,*
> *Falero, lero, loo!'*

Never were there such people as the English for music. King Charles played the viola as well as a professional, nearly everybody could play at least one instrument, and as for singing, they sang whenever they met, in parts; they rose from table to rush to the harpsichord; they sang while they were waiting to be shaved, a lute being provided in every good barber's shop for the customer who had to wait his turn; they had boys to sing to them while they ate or played cards or dice or bowls or other gambling games – and they played furiously high, sometimes losing thousands of pounds in the course of one tender love song.

No money, no love, that was the sad result of such sweetly accompanied action; Sir John Suckling's young sisters came crying on to the bowling green at Piccadillo, begging him not to gamble away their marriage portions, but that did not move him, nothing could sober the fiery beacon of his debauched nose, although his wild scared eye, squinting over his cups, seemed frequently to be signalling a warning of danger to it.

'But I'd forgive him everything, for the sake of that one song in that dull play of his, *Aglaura* —

'"Why so pale and wan, fond lover?"'

Songs again, and now one pretty song was worth a whole dull play according to Mr Porter – but old Ben Jonson would not agree; he wheezed and snorted, and the greasy pink coverlid heaved like a mountain in earthquake as his enormous belly shook from the eruptions of his splenetic criticisms and huge hollow laughs that had once held the gaiety of the best company that ever man had known, but now echoed in a poor room empty of all but a conscientious patron and a nervous young prince who had been dragged unwillingly to see an old dying man.

Rupert would never have gone if it had not been for his mother saying – 'And whomsoever else you see or don't see in England, you *must* see Ben Jonson, and remember that he wrote me those charming verses,

"Queen and huntress chaste and fair — "'

Everybody seemed to have written his mother verses. He had stayed with the old Provost of Eton, Sir Henry Wotton, who had written 'You meaner beauties of the night' in her honour (Mr Porter said it was one of the best poems in the English language), and had fished with him and Mr Izaac Walton in the pleasant reaches of the Thames – a slow sport in very elderly company for young Rupert, who preferred a hard game of tennis or a gallop with the hounds.

But that had been a minor infliction to this torture of being taken to visit a decayed dropsical old creature who could not be many months, weeks even, from his death, who had risen from being a bricklayer and a common soldier of fortune to poet laureate at the Courts of King James and King Charles and yet now was dying disappointed. They had not been able to employ him in the Court masques of late years, his quarrels with Inigo Jones had been too violent, his furious jealousy, as author, of the scenic artist had led to one disgraceful scene after another. Once Inigo Jones' name was put before his on the programme – that finished it. Ben had once killed a man in a private quarrel, but he was too old and fat by now to move quick enough, and that saved them both. But Ben lost his place at Court.

He was given odd sums of money by the King and Mr Porter, but it wasn't odd sums he wanted, it was security for his old age, he complained (not recognizing that with his age very little more security could be needed), and the one thing that went on coming in regularly was his allowance of sherry sack from the King which the rascally doctor tried to prevent his drinking, for gout and the dropsy were finishing him off, there was no doubt of that.

But remembering that he was Ben, *the* Ben, and must show that the old dog still had his teeth, he hastened to tell them that the theatre had been killed stone dead by these filthy modern mechanical inventions – 'all paint and carpentry, and the author such a fool that he puts his own money into it and spends a fortune, several thousands, on costumes and scenery – and where's the play? In *print*, Lord help it! since nobody's had a chance to notice it in the theatre – a miserable bull-calf's pizzle of print in the middle of a bare field of margin, a skeleton child embedded in the great bed of Ware that can hold seventeen of my size – *there's* my Suckling's suckling!'

And with a roar of rage that was by now almost happy, he flung poor Sir John's *Aglaura* right across the room at Rupert's feet. Rupert sat looking down at it, for it was easier than to look at the old man roaring and sighing in bed with his rocky face aflame with gout and fury.

Now he was tearing to pieces a masque by Mr Milton, all speeches, allegory, no plot – 'they can't tell a story nowadays, that's what the matter with 'em, they can't tell a story. Old Will Shakespeare was right with that catchpenny line of his in the play where everybody's mad – mad prince, girl mad, father senile, nobody talks sense but the ghost – but what he said in it was – "The play's the thing." They've all forgotten that – they've run mad over what they call novelty, and forgotten that the one new thing that matters is new plays. They ran mad over *them* once – everyone so hot to see a first night that they all, lords and stinkards alike, paid double prices for their places. The play was the thing then, he was right, and you may laugh at me for a vain old fool but there'll never be better plays written than mine and Will's – and why? Because they were wanted – and now people don't want 'em any more, they only want new inventions to make the scene twirl round and round or up and down!'

In the pause in the hurricane Mr Porter agreed that plays weren't what they had been; he thought the genius of the age had moved to song-writing, the verses of the young men today had a casual audacious charm as if the rhyme and rhythm had just sprung out of their spoken speech.

'The Puritans will soon put a stop to that if they get into power,' came in ominous growl from the bed.

'Yes, and they've put a stop to one or two of your plays before now, Ben.'

'They'll put a stop to *all* plays if they get the chance. Here's this pestilent fellow Prynne writing that every honest actor should be whipped and branded.'

'Well, he's only got his own ears cropped by it.'

'He's got a deal too much sympathy by it. There's a bad spirit abroad. It'll be down with plays and dancing and songs too before they've done. You're right about the new songs, Mr Porter, a deal of 'em are very easy and pretty, though that's not so new, it's been done before, you know.' His swollen lips began to shape words that fell like thistledown on the stuffy air of the small room.

> '*Beauties, have you seen this toy*
> *Called Love – a little boy,*
> *Almost naked, wanton, blind,*
> *Cruel then and now as kind?*
> *If he be among you, say!*
> *He is Venus' runaway.*'

The miracle had happened. Behind that bloated face and tun of belly and gusty bellows of a voice, there sang a fancy of exquisite delicacy. Rupert listened to it amazed, then remembered – 'But this is the man who wrote —'

He looked him full in the face now as he said – 'My mother, sir, told me to ask you – do you remember the poem you wrote her on her wedding? She told me to tell you it was the first

thing that made her feel herself a woman, that you, the greatest
of our poets, should call her a goddess.'

> *'Thou that mak'st a day of night,*
> *Goddess excellently bright!'*

murmured Mr Porter reminiscently.

'She does that whenever she can,' said Rupert with an impudent grin, but it froze on his face as he saw to his horror that
tears were pouring down the furrows and hillocks of that vast
face in the bed.

'Do I remember it?' cried Ben, 'do I remember your mother
when her every step was a dance, and joy so strong within her
that it shone out of her eyes and her hair, and the very feet of
her laughed? Do I remember old Will coming up to town again
to yark up a wedding play for her, that fairy-tale *The Tempest*,
the last play he ever wrote – and a damned bad play too – but
there he was in town again, going to rehearsals – trusting to
them for all corrections, the rascal – and meeting me at The
Mermaid for sack and supper after them, all as in the old days!
He's dead, Will was right there too, he's dead, and I hang on –
an old dog that has lost his favour. They don't kill off the old
dog, that would hurt their tender feelings, they only take other
favourites in his place, these clever new puppies, and cosset 'em
in front of his eyes and scold him if he growls at them – "back
to the kitchens you stinking old cur, that's the place for
you." '

'I can do nothing,' thought Rupert. He was humiliated that
his mother, who had been so proud to be praised by Ben, could
do nothing for Ben. Princes should not be without power or
money or even any place to call their own. It was worse than
ridiculous, it was shameful. He had a few pounds of pocket-
money from his uncle but he could not insult Ben by giving him
that. In his restless misery he had got up before he knew what
he was doing, now he had to do something to justify it, he went
over to the bed and held out his hand and then found himself
utterly tongue-tied. That mountain in the bed had forgotten
him, forgotten the laughing lovely princess that had become
Rupert's mother, he had begun to mumble now to himself,
something about that rascal Inigo Jones who had plotted and
worked against him from the start – 'they used to call a villain
an Iago – but an Inigo, that's what it should be, for the blackest
villain out of Hell is an Inigo.'

Mr Porter was exceedingly apologetic when at last they got outside.

'Poor old Ben, I'd no idea he was so far gone or I'd never have taken you. But he gave you a faint taste of his old quality at the beginning, didn't he?'

'Oh, yes,' said Rupert savagely, 'the old dog could still do some of his tricks.'

Mr Porter thought he was resentful on his own account – and no wonder.

They heard a few weeks later that Ben was dead at last. He was buried in Westminster Abbey and King Charles planned a splendid monument for him.

CHAPTER SEVEN

RUPERT WAS invited by Mr Endymion Porter to his place of Aston-sub-Edge in Gloucestershire to see the Olympic Games on Cotswold. It was Whitsun, and the Games had been held there in Whitsun week ever since Captain Dover took charge of them thirty years ago, so his host told Rupert as they rode down the rough country lanes in the fine spring rain that leaves the shape of the clouds still clear in the blue sky.

Mr Porter was a delightful companion for a journey; he had been everywhere, done everything; he had been a page to the famous Spanish general, Olivares, and read *Don Quixote* to him to keep him entertained while Velasquez painted his portrait; he had gone to Spain again as interpreter to demand Spanish aid to recover the Palatinate for Rupert's parents, in the days when old King James had dreamed of a peaceful Europe, united by British wisdom – he had liked the term British, as it included the Scots, but other people had laughed at it as they did at his peace policy and his hope of the Spanish alliance and of Catholics and Protestants settling down amicably together. Rupert thought that in this country even that was possible; Mr Porter, not quite so optimistic, agreed that in Madagascar at any rate everyone should be free to worship as they liked.

There beyond seas would be the freedom men had failed to win at home – so they planned, hoping, as the reward of their enterprise, for a Golden Age rather than gold – forgetting that so had the pioneers hoped who had founded a brave New

England, but had limited those hopes to their own creed only.

Some quality of eternal youth had made the portly middle-aged patron of poets and artists almost as hot on this new adventure as the boy beside him; but he naturally saw it with a larger vision, he talked of its effect on the King's dominions, how every day they were being strengthened by new and fruitful plantations. Trade was flourishing; the credit of the English merchants was higher than that of any other nation in the foreign bourses, and the forty additional ships built with the new Ship Money had enabled the English fleets to regain the command of the seas and secure a world trade for their ports. Lightly, easily, he built up for Rupert the ideal of empire that he would follow in his island, and almost in the same breath told him how in Seville a man would kill a bull for sport after baiting him with his scarlet cloak – 'but don't talk of that to Captain Dover.'

'Why not?'

'You'll see tomorrow.'

Tomorrow he was half wakened by a strain of music and voices like the sound of flutes or birds, so clear, unearthly, they must be the voices of the cherubim descending from the clouds.

> *'My soul, there is a country*
> *Far beyond the stars,*
> *Where stands a wingéd sentry*
> *All skilful in the wars.'*

Was it of heaven they were singing, or of Madagascar? Madagascar also was far beyond the stars – no, beyond the seas – 'so this must be heaven,' he said aloud, struggling to lift his head from the clouds – or was it the big white pillows? His host, in a dressing-gown of Chinese embroideries, was laughing down at him.

'Aston-sub-Edge has had its noblest compliment,' he said.

The cherubim were still singing in parts, very sweetly and tunefully, though the pronunciation of the words was rough and unfamiliar. Young choir boys from the village and the musicians of the choir with their violas and pandoras had come to stand outside the guest's door and wake him with sacred music, as was the custom in this country in even the humblest villages. Mr Porter paid them their small fee and sent them clattering downstairs to get some breakfast in the kitchens; he apologized for the rough Doric of their accent, 'I fear you can have hardly distinguished the words. But to my mind Sir Philip Sidney knew how to write a hymn better than any of these modern punsters who try to be so clever with their God.

> *'The closest closet of my thought*
> *Lies clear revealéd to Thine eyes,'* —

do you call that a hymn?'

'No, sir, but the sun's shining – could I get a bathe before breakfast?'

After breakfast they rode through Chipping Campden, a village of unpretentious palaces whose spacious rooms and courtyards and long walled gardens opened out unexpectedly from behind their modest front doors. In one of these they found Captain Dover, a plump gay figure who sported a yellow favour in his hunting-cap. His bright eye, accustomed to observe and command, rolled over them as he urged with passionate insistence that his guests should breakfast all over again before going on with him to the Games. When at last this attack had been beaten off, they all went on about half a mile above the village to Dover's Hill, which had got its name from the gallant captain, as well it might when it could be seen what an army he had summoned and organized year after year on those heights. Dover's Hill, a long low plateau, steeply overhung the Vale of Evesham, a wide plain obligingly mapped out for a race-course by Nature in conjunction with Captain Dover.

An enormous gaily-dressed noisy crowd swarmed over the plateau and down into the plain, and through it strolled the competitors, leashed greyhounds, led by their owners, country lads on their sturdy ponies and farm horses, swaggering in front of their sweethearts, who had helped plait up their steeds' tails and manes with ribbons, and hung garlands of flowers round their necks till they looked as gay as the Morris dancers that were practising their steps in rings to the high drone of the bagpipe players, seated on the ground. Rupert pointed out a pony whose ears were dangling with cowslip balls, and Mr Porter told Captain Dover that Europa would have deserted her bull for his horses. Captain Dover told Rupert that horse-racing and greyhound-coursing were the two best sports in the world, urging his views on his princely young visitor with a proselytizing vigour.

'Not better than hunting?' queried Rupert.

'Hunting – pah – hounding a wretched animal to death – I beg Your Highness' pardon – hunting is necessary no doubt – foxes and such vermin must be destroyed – venison is good to eat though only with so many wine sauces that you can't taste the meat and that shows what it is, nothing but thin wood and stinking – but with racing you have all the skill and gallantry and none of the cruelty.'

Rupert looked in amazement at this robust and tender-hearted squire. Nowhere even among the most timid and sensitive ladies had he heard the opinion that hunting was cruel. What would his mother say, who frequently shot sixteen buck with her own cross-bow in a single hunt? Yet this man was the most passionate sportsman he had met, giving his whole time and wealth to the organization of these games for the entire countryside. The English were a contradictory race. Captain Dover was amusingly contradictory even in his anti-cruelty, for – 'How do you get your greyhounds to course without a hare?' asked Rupert.

'I don't,' replied the captain, 'but the aim is to win the prize rather than to kill the hare. It's the principle that matters.'

'I seem to have heard that before in England,' said Rupert, 'but as long as it isn't a constitutional principle I don't mind.'

'His Highness thinks us an unduly political and contentious people,' explained Mr Porter, grinning in his recognition of a thrust at Carl. Captain Dover broke into tempestuous assent. Disputing, complaining, finding the difference between all men rather than their agreement, that was the curse of Englishmen today. It was all the fault of the Puritans. They had made people feel it was wrong to enjoy anything except the destruction of enjoyment in others.

'Fault-finding, back-biting, are these not vices?' he cried to the clear blue skies, where the white clouds were coursing as swiftly as the 'silver-footed greyhounds' in the vale below.

The cause of his animosity soon thrust out. The Puritans had attacked, were continually attacking his Games. They had discovered 'wicked horrid sin' in every branch of them, from the youths climbing up the greased pole, scrambling along in sack races or, blindfolded, chasing a man with a bell round his neck and his hands tied behind his back, to the girls who dared raise their immodest voices in part singing, or dance a country dance, in which none of the opposite sex were included, to the music of the bagpipes.

'These Protestants,' he snorted, 'they are like the lady in the play, they do protest too much. The King himself cannot tell them to go out on Sunday after service and play games and enjoy themselves, without giving them mortal offence. They don't *want* to enjoy themselves, they want to be miserable, to make everybody else miserable —' his round red cheeks had suddenly a bluish hue, the light had gone out of his eye, he looked round him and said in a whisper, 'They'll spoil it all yet.'

It did not look as though they would. Thousands of happy shouting boys and girls were testifying to their power to maintain their pleasures against the encroaching fog of gloom whose chill breath Captain Dover seemed to have felt even now upon his neck. They danced and sang and ran and rode and wrestled and climbed and jumped and fought with cudgels and quarter staves and single sticks, with judges everywhere to keep order and award prizes – a good five hundred they would amount to by the end of the day, Mr Porter told Rupert, and all given by the jovial Captain.

Military rank he had none except that bestowed by the admiring obedience of his volunteers. He was an attorney who had never practised for gain, since he had discovered the law divided more men than it brought together, and to bring people together, as in their thousands on this sparkling Whitsunday, was his only ambition. His modest fortune he used for that, his legal learning to help his neighbours make up their differences, without reward to himself. The finest place he had got for himself was his absurd toy, 'Dover's Castle', a movable wooden fortress built on a pivot, so that he could swing round and view any corner of his games from it; it was furnished with a couple of real guns which he could fire off to start each contest, enormously impressing the crowds.

Above the little portcullis of this 'castle' he appeared at the end of the day to give prizes, in a costume which made Rupert gasp. It was gorgeous but shabby and quite thirty years out of date – a slashed satin doublet and a hat with bedraggled plumes, and a stiff ruff sticking out like a plate all round his cheerful pink face.

'What the devil is he wearing?'

'Your grandfather's old clothes,' replied Mr Porter with his

97

inscrutable smile, as though the follies and humours of mankind had long ceased to perplex him. 'He asked me to get him a suit of them when he first applied for my patronage of his games. That was just after King James had come to the throne, and I was Gentleman of the Bedchamber, so it should have been easy, but the old King never liked to part with anything he had worn – he was like the old Queen in that, who had three thousand dresses when she died. But I told him what good work Captain Dover was doing to advertise His Majesty's Book of Sports – reading it aloud to his household at family prayers – and that helped me to the oldest royal doublet and most out-of-date ruff. He's worn them on these occasions ever since and nobody notices there's anything odd in them. Good God, what is he saying? He's calling Your Highness!'

'Winner at the quintain and presumptive winner at backsword play if not prevented, His Highness Prince Rupert of the Rhine, Prince Palatine, the Prince of Paladins,' Captain Dover was shouting.

Rupert had insisted on trying his luck at the homely version of the quintain that had been set up here, with a bag of meal to swing round and catch the unwary tilter behind, spattering him with flour if he failed to strike the dummy figure in the right place. He had ridden at the quintain often at his schools of arms, and too easily avoided the disgrace of a whitened behind to be pleased with the roars of applause that had greeted his victory.

So he thought it more fun to try a newer sport, and had managed to give the slip to Porter and engage in a bout of backsword play, where the aim was to draw blood on your opponent's head with a short stick in your right hand while guarding your own head with your left elbow; your left hand was forced to keep down by holding the end of a handkerchief tied round the knee. Fencing and sword play was of no help in this strange technique, you stood as close to your opponent as if you were fighting with your fists, and it was something so new to Rupert that the moment he saw it he could not rest till he had learned it. He had already flung off his coat and hat like the other competitors and without giving his name demanded to enter.

But he had not joined in it three minutes before the crowd round them were shouting – 'Blood! Blood! Your game's up, young gentleman! Your head's broke!' He could not believe it.

'I'm not touched,' he cried and tried to fight on, but they pulled him off, and even as he protested he felt a splash of rain in his eyes, no, by God, it was blood trickling down from a cut in his forehead, so they were right after all and he had been beaten at once, more shame to him, and here was Mr Porter pushing through the crowd with a face like thunder and hauling him off before anyone should discover that it was a prince of the blood royal who had so demeaned it.

And here, after all Mr Porter's pains, was Captain Dover cheerfully publishing it.

'And why not?' he declared as Mr. Porter expostulated, but Rupert came forward to get his yellow Cotswold favour for the quintain prize and stick it in his hat – 'They'll all like him the better for it – and where's the lad that broke his head? Here he is now, Prince, and I'll wager you'd have broken his as soon as you'd got the hang of it.'

Rupert turned to see his once cheerfully grinning opponent now gazing at him in blank dismay. He did not know how bad the scar on his forehead might look, it was all very awkward and tactless of Captain Dover to give him away in his determination to advertise everything and everybody; there did not seem anything to be said, but at least there was always something to be done in England and that was to shake hands, so he did it and remarked, 'Do you think they'll have dinner soon?' But his sturdy opponent could not recover his speech till well after that event. To have blooded the King's nephew – to have broke his head on Cotswold! Well, it would be something to talk about ever after.

Captain Dover thought so too. He sat beside his royal guest in a long tent at a rough table made of boards set up on trestles; they ate Cotswold lamb and beef and great gouts of clotted cream on their apple pies (but why not apfelstrudel? and nobody in this country realized what an excellent mixture was black rye bread and butter with young radishes) and drank Cotswold ale and cider, and the sunlight shone through the tent in a rich haze made up of the steams of hot meat and trampled grass and the breaths of many men eating and drinking and talking and laughing in unity.

He was getting on now, an old man, Captain Dover told him, and every year was perfecting his life's work to a more glorious consummation. This was the finest Whitsun of them all – and he had thought last Whitsun was. Last Whitsun had set the seal of the Muses on his physical labours, all the best poets in England had contributed together to do them honour – Ben Jonson and Drayton, both dead now, but luckily, said his callous host, not till Ben had at last grumpily assented to his persistent petitions – 'And old Heywood, who can't last much longer himself – Ah, you don't get poets like them nowadays.'

So he told this young prince they called Rupert of the Rhine, who wasn't drinking nearly as much ale as you'd think for a lad of his size and spirit, 'They're all too much the gentlemen now, going to college and Court and what not instead of picking up their verses in the street and the tavern as they used to do. I might ha' got Will Shakespeare to contribute too if I'd only thought of it in time, for I used to see him sometimes at Stratford when I walked over on market days from Bourton-on-the-Heath, and he mentioned my greyhound-coursing in one of his plays, so I'm told, though I never had the patience to read through 'em all and see which – but there, he's been dead too long, and now some of the others are too, and it will be my turn soon I don't doubt, but as long as the Games go on, what does it matter if I've shot my bolt? Here's the little book and I'd be honoured if your young Highness would accept of it – perhaps you might even add a couplet or so yourself to my own copy?'

Rupert drew a caricature instead, of himself having his head broken at backsword play, which made the Captain shout and shake with laughter. They went out from the stuffy glowing tent into a pale evening where the jostling crowds had mysteriously become part of the mist-grey plain and the translucent sky, and even the calling voices sounded fine-drawn and remote. Faces shone as red as polished apples in the after-glow of sunset. Groups of girls were dancing in their print petticoats and aprons, giggling wildly as their swains applauded. The grass was all trampled and dusty; painted carts drawn by donkeys went jolting over it, barefoot children ran in and out among them, bobbing up from under their very wheels, yelling to each other, clustering round the bright booths where toys and ribbons were sold, and the mysterious tents where you had to pay your penny first before you could see the marvels of the Irish giant or the fattest woman in the world or the mermaid caught on the Cornish coast in the equinoctial gales.

'Cross my palm with silver, pretty gentleman, and I'll tell you all the world holds in waiting for you.'

100

'All the world, I hope,' Rupert answered, and put a crown piece in the dirty seamed hand before him. A pair of dark eyes glittered up at him from between two great gold rings.

'What country do you come from?' he asked.

'I am a Bohemian, my noble young lord.'

'And so am I,' Rupert all but answered.

The English scene shimmered round them while the gipsy bent a head as gaudy as a parroquet over the hand of the foreign Prince. She babbled of far countries (for all young gentlemen liked the notion of travel), lovely ladies dying for love of him, when he wanted only one word – Madagascar.

'Do you see – an island – anywhere?' he faltered, ashamed to be so childish.

At which hint of course the gipsy was willing to see an archipelago. His life it seemed was thronging with islands; tufted with palm trees like cockatoos, they rose out of the sea and spread their coral reefs for him.

'That would make an awkward landing,' Rupert interrupted. 'Is there no one special island among them?'

Yes there was one, but not among these exotic growths. There was an island that would mean more to him than any other place in the world.

Would he then be the ruler of that island?

He would be asked to rule, he was told, and would refuse.

It all sounded disappointing and unlikely, fortune-tellers were all frauds, and he was annoyed when Mr Porter caught him at the silly game.

He said goodbye to Captain Dover and rode back to Aston-sub-Edge and went to his room with the mullioned windows and the uneven wood floor, and sat on the edge of a very wide bed hung all round with tapestries of Diana making love to Endymion, which his host had relegated to the spare-room because he was so sick of the classical allusions to his own name, and peered sleepily by the light of two tall candlesticks into the little book in compliment to 'the great Inventor and Champion of the English Olympicks, Pythycks, Nemicks, and Isthmicks', Captain Dover.

Dipping carelessly here and there, it struck him that the poems were as much prayer as praise, prayer that the old merry life of England which these poets, some now dead, some old, could remember in such free profusion, might yet continue. Like a new Saint George of Merry England, Captain Dover was making his gallant stand to keep it alive against those who

> *'teach that dancing is a Jezebel,*
> *And barley-break the ready way to hell;*
> *The morrice, idols; Whitsun ales can be*
> *But profane relics of a jubilee;*
> *These in a zeal to express how much they do*
> *The organ hate, have silenced bagpipes too,*
> *And harmless maypoles all are railed upon*
> *As if they were the towers of Babylon.'*

*   *   *

'A broken head?' enquired Carl, raising his eyebrows in delicate disgust at his young brother, who was prompt to give him what he wanted.

'Village sports. Low company. Warn Mamma.'

CHAPTER EIGHT

CARL WAS not left out in his uncle's schemes of colonization. King Charles offered him the West Indies, on the same plan as Madagascar, and he had begun to wonder seriously if he had not best accept it and give up that endless struggle for the Palatinate. It certainly looked as though the Protestant Powers had lost ground for good in Germany. Even in the last century the heroic William the Silent of Holland had so despaired of the contest against Catholic Spain that he had been on the point of throwing it all up and emigrating to America. And Carl had far less reason than he to hang on to a patrimony he had never even entered. All Europe was looking on the New World as the path of escape and hope; now even Carl, most practical and disillusioned of young men, was turning his face towards that glow from the west.

If Carl should abandon his own cause and 'go for a knight-errant', no one could object to Rupert doing the same. Rupert watched his brother's West Indian plans begin to develop in incredulous joy; would God really make the fates move as he longed? It seemed too good to be true, and he was right, it was; for just as Carl had lost all hope in his cause, the tide began to turn, and the Cardinal Richelieu, that incongruous supporter of

Protestants, promised to join with King Charles in the aid of his nephew.

The Cardinal believed in the balance of power; no nation, except of course France, must be too victorious or too prosperous. For that reason he was even now helping to stir up rebellion among the Scottish Presbyterians by promising to finance their armies against King Charles, and thus destroy the irritating peace and comfort of England; but this King Charles did not yet know, and was eager to join with him in the scheme for his nephew. He at once promised Carl a fleet and ten thousand pounds; the older English nobles opened a subscription list; the younger hurried to enlist.

England's response was touchingly ardent and generous, it looked on the struggle as a crusade both for the Protestant cause and for wronged beauty in the person of Queen Elizabeth. Carl was astonished and even made rather uncomfortable to find how much disinterested emotion did after all exist. Old men would tell him how they remembered seeing his mother ride to hounds or dance at Court or finally sail down the Thames away from England – 'ah, my young lord, you don't see women like that nowadays' – and how proud they were to pledge their rent-rolls to her support and send their sons to fight for her.

The one person to hold back in all this enthusiasm, and show no desire to rush to the front, was Rupert. Would he forget that his vocation was that of a soldier to serve his brother? Rupert's friends thought it time he did forget it, but Carl naturally did not share their opinion. Now that there was a prospect of a campaign backed by English help and French money he had become as enthusiastic at the thought of action as his cooler temper would permit.

The plan he had himself so lately entertained of a colony in the West Indies was now only a silly dream – and Rupert surely would not stick to *his* silly dream and go wandering off to the other side of the world, leaving his brother to fight alone for his inheritance? Carl put it to him as persuasively as he knew how, but could only write of the result to his mother – 'When I ask him what he means to do, I find him very shy to tell me his opinion.' Which was no wonder, since it would at once be told to their mother.

It was difficult for Rupert to know his own opinion. To serve his father's lost cause – that had been his duty and his desire since early childhood – and he supposed it would have to be the same now it was Carl's. It was the cause of his mother, too, and of all of them, naturally, but somehow now it was particularly Carl's, it made a difference.

There was Carl nagging or coaxing away, his mother scolding, his aunt shrilly indignant against her scolding; and through it all his uncle moved gracious and imperturbably serene, showing him the newest designs in shipbuilding, inspecting all the vessels already built with his usual thoroughness, going into every office and even down into the holds, and examining and counting the ordnance; he went on discussing the climate and the flora and fauna of that far country, making plans for when he would visit Rupert there in his palace as Governor of Madagascar. He never saw that it was all crumbling, dissolving round them both, that those ships would never sail for Rupert, that he would never govern that island, that it was just another dream, like the treasure-ships from the Spanish Indies, that would end in nothing.

For how could he turn his back on his father's country to go to the other side of the world when half the young men even in this country were clamouring to go out and help fight for it?

But he could not bear to tell Carl that yet. They were all so damnably eager and anxious. Let them wait. They were so cocksure the scheme of Madagascar was all nonsense – *he* could have shown them the contrary!

In this uncomfortable silence he and Carl went with the King and Queen on a State visit to Oxford, saw Archbishop Laud in his element there as Chancellor, and were given honorary degrees – specially invented for this purpose – and presents. Rupert's was a Caesar's Commentaries in English, and Carl's, Hooker's *Ecclesiastical Polity*, which hit off their respective tastes very nicely, and so did the Queen's, of a pair of embroidered gloves, but the gift to the King of a Bible printed in Edinburgh, even though worth £80, was perhaps a little tactless after all the trouble those Scottish theologians had given him at his Scottish coronation a few years ago.

Some of the younger men at Oxford had just been debating the thorny questions raised by the Scottish liturgy – Laud was furious with them, he had thought that at least the scholars of Oxford would behave like gentlemen and not like Scottish savages, whatever the rest of the world was coming to.

Rupert scarcely listened to their episcopal host's pedantic arguments on the Scottish questions. He left Carl to make intelligent enquiries at the right moment, while he himself sat crumbling the little loaves before him that had been moulded and decorated in the semblance of bishops and doctors, and watched the deep sunlight slanting across the old silver plate on the long table of St John's. Even the colleges in England were palaces, thought the Leyden 'poor scholar'. The extravagant glories of scenic effects in the play that was acted before them afterwards in Christ Church Hall, written by the Proctor, surpassed anything he had ever imagined possible. Inigo Jones had prepared them, free from old Ben's snorts of contemptuous fury. There was a storm at sea with waves rolling and churches and houses moving up and down, and glimpses of landscape with rocks and trees – also a chair that glided perhaps unnecessarily but very marvellously on to the stage without any assistance. The courtiers yawned and talked through the play, pronouncing it the worst they had ever seen, except at Cambridge – these dons were no good at plays – but Rupert sat entranced – was it perhaps because it was called *The Floating Island?*

And next night there were more exotic scenes of Persian temples and a sun that really shone, and distant forests and villages with men that actually seemed to move about in them. Was it all done to mock his hopes of that island, somewhere beyond seas, that just now had been so nearly his, but was floating like a wind-blown cloud farther and farther away from him, never now to be reached and won?

They were shown over all the best colleges and the Bodleian, and the King sat in the window and examined the old manuscripts and insisted on going up into the gallery to see the coins, with a patient interest that his nephews could not emulate, and his Queen contrived to avoid altogether, by taking so long over her dressing that they had to go on to their sight-seeing without her. But she made up for it by her enthusiasm for everything she did see – and might she borrow all the stage machinery and properties for her own Queen's Players at Hampton Court, if she promised never to allow them to be prostituted upon any mercenary stage? She had acted often in masques herself and talked stagecraft in a most professional way to the delighted undergraduates.

The whole visit went off beautifully, for no one seemed to notice how cold and thin were the welcoming cheers of the populace in the streets – after all, when did Town here ever count against Gown? Chancellor Laud, more genial and less exacting than they had ever known him, now he was in his beloved Oxford, congratulated himself on everything as he bade his royal guests farewell – the weather had been perfect – he had firmly insisted on the undergraduates wearing cap and gown, cutting their hair and pulling up their stockings (their slovenliness revolted the neat little Chancellor, who had been the son of a draper) – and, most remarkable of all, out of all the silver plate used during the visit only two spoons had disappeared.

'I suppose they will say I took the one and you the other,' remarked Carl in his acidly thoughtful manner to his brother as they drove away in the royal coach.

'They may call us the Beggar Princes,' replied Rupert, 'they haven't started calling us the Robber Princes yet.'

'They will, Rupert, they will.'

*   *   *

'The dream of Madagascar, I think, is vanished,' wrote 'Honest Tom' consolingly to his royal mistress.

It had been touch and go after all at the end. For marriage with the monstrously rich and very good-looking daughter of the great French Huguenot, the Duc de Rohan, had been dangled in front of Rupert as a bait to keep him in Europe, and had had the directly contrary effect of making him decide to fly immediately to Madagascar. He would not lose his liberty, he said, for all the money in the world.

Carl objected that her money would buy him his liberty – 'besides, you might fall in love with her.'

'Then I should be still the more obliged to her and the less free.'

'This island nonsense has gone to your head. Are you going to play at Don Quixote all your life?'

Carl had condescended to back the alliance, pronouncing it to his mother as 'no absurd proposition', for though Mademoiselle de Rohan was not royal, she was 'great, both in means and birth, and of the Religion', thus putting these qualities in the proper order. But he saw he had for once been a fool and driven his pigheaded young brother on to 'this island nonsense' more firmly than ever.

Just as he was despairing, his mother conceived a masterstroke of strategy. She let Rupert know that she was sending Maurice to serve in the army of the Prince of Orange so as 'to learn that profession by which I believe he must live'. If only

Rupert would join his brother he would 'spend this summer better in an army than idly in England'. There was the hint of a taunt in the suggestion – was Rupert going to let his younger brother win his military honours before him? It is true the Dutch army was not fighting directly for the Palatine, whose expeditionary force was not yet ready – but then neither was the expedition for Madagascar – and was Rupert to dawdle on in the luxury of the English Court while his younger 'Twin' underwent for the first time all the hardship and danger of a campaign?

He did not think of it as hardship and danger, though he somehow did not like the notion of Maurice being in his first battle without him there to look after him, for he knew what to do quicker than Maurice, besides he was a year older and had already had experience; but he thought chiefly what magnificent sport he and Maurice would have, fighting together, far better than anything he had had before; for then he could never get anyone to join him, they had all been so busily engaged in looking after his safety and had only laughed admiringly at his complaints of the army's slowness and his anxiety to be 'always charging the enemy'.

But Maurice was his ideal second-in-command, he knew that from all the times they had hunted and played together – Maurice always obeyed instantly, unquestioningly, so that the two of them were like a single driving force with Rupert as its motive power.

So Maurice finally tipped up the scale against Madagascar, and Rupert went hunting for the last time with his uncle, King Charles, on the very morning that he was to sail for Holland – a stormy late summer morning with the white clouds chasing each other across the blue sky and the wind roaring and swishing in the tree-tops overhead. Apples had begun to redden in the Kentish orchards, and their red walls, built when stout Harry was King, glowed themselves like ripe fruit. The river, spangled with white waves, gleamed through the forest trees as it broadened even farther and farther out to meet the sea, and the ships slipped down fast before the wind, white sails, red sails, seen like gigantic birds before the forest shut them out. It was hard by here at Gravesend that the Princes were to embark. Rupert had been in England eighteen months – and a whole lifetime of enjoyment.

He rode so recklessly that his uncle, a daring enough rider

himself, warned him jokingly not to break his neck. His nephew's flushed face looked round at him, his eyes unnaturally brilliant with the tears he would not shed.

'I wish that I could,' he replied, 'and so leave my bones in England.'

CHAPTER NINE

WELL, AS he remarked a few hours later, they left quite a lot of themselves in the Channel. It was an appalling crossing. Rupert was sick enough to wish he had never come to England at all rather than endure this on his return. He arrived at The Hague in a very bad temper and at once quarrelled with his mother. She had just failed to induce Carl to pay a few of her most pressing debts out of the enormous sum he had raised in England, largely by virtue of her name, and had been told by him that 'everything ought to be sacrificed to the head of the family'. In a bitter and disappointed mood she unwisely asked Rupert a great many questions about his aunt – of course she had tried to convert him to Papistry? – how far had she succeeded? – had Rupert remembered what he owed to his brother, and his whole family?

'*Yes,*' replied Rupert in an angry shout.

'How dare you answer me like that, sir?'

'How would you have me answer you, Madam? Shall I tell you I would have been converted to my aunt's religion if I had only stayed another fortnight?'

'Is that true?'

'I am not a liar.'

'You are an insolent passionate boy. Get out of my sight.'

He was quick to obey, fuming. Here he was being treated like a child again, when he was full seventeen and a half now and had been offered command as Universal Admiral.

With a furious swish of silken skirts (oh, how old!) the Queen rushed to her writing-table to reproach her sister-in-law, who took up the cudgels with equal spirit and replied that if only she had known the state of Rupert's feelings she would not have let him go when he did. The quill pens fluttered and scratched, the two queens wreaked their passions on the paper that would outlast them by centuries, and Rupert fled from the family row to the safety of the Dutch campaign.

Carl had gone off to arrange his co-operation with the Swedish army, and their mother was left in quiet again to write in her old careless fashion of 'the death of hares, and which horse ran best, which, though I say it that should not say it, was mine'.

Rupert found Maurice with the Dutch army besieging Breda, which was held by the Spaniards. The brothers' delight at meeting again was too great for either to say anything much for some time – they could only sit and stare and grin and ask 'How goes it?'

Maurice, his junior by a year, had grown almost as tall and strong as himself, shooting up into another young giant and quite out-topping his eldest brother, as they had written to Carl while he was still in England, so that in disgust Carl had sent home his measurements 'without my shoes' to disprove the slander. But they had not disproved it, and Maurice was very proud of this, and of being a soldier, and of making friends with two young English volunteers in the Dutch army, the Lords George Goring and Harry Wilmot, who swaggered about in superb clothes with an incomparable air of insolence. They had a terrible reputation with women and were generally drunk.

'But they are fine soldiers too, Rupert.'

'They can't be fine soldiers when they're drunk.'

'They say it inflames their wits.'

'Damned lie – it damps them and makes 'em soggy.'

'Oh, well, be pleasant to them, for they are very good fellows and they think the world of you from all they've heard of you here in the army, and long to meet you.'

But Rupert preferred some of the other English commanders – Sir Jacob Astley, an odd downright old fellow with a keen sense of humour, which he needed, being one of the many great friends of Rupert's mother. She had enjoined 'Honest little Jacob' to 'skip over quickly like the little ape you are', and keep an eye on her two boys. He had the sense not to tell them this.

Rupert also liked Goring's lieutenant, the squat, sallow George Monck – 'now there's a soldier,' he said at once, and was not deterred by the young exquisites' opinion of 'little Monck' as a bear, next door to a Puritan, and a damned Mahomedan water-drinker.

Rupert soon put Maurice to the test as his second-in-command. One thick raining misty night there was a lull in the fighting all along the lines, the besiegers felt it safe to sleep, and

Rupert had gone with Maurice to their tent but would not lie down; he prowled restlessly about. 'What the devil is the matter with you?' complained Maurice, who was dropping with sleep, 'they'd never think of attacking on a night like this.'

'That's just what they know we're saying.'

The next time Maurice opened his eyes, Rupert was not there.

Maurice was out through the tent in a flash, snatching up his sword as he went, hurrying towards the beleaguered town. Soon a tall black silhouette shaped itself in the darkness, and he caught up his brother. 'Come on,' whispered Rupert, 'I've been listening. There are sounds within the walls.'

'Won't you give the alarm?'

'Might be a false one. Let's make sure first.'

They went softly through the squelching mud, past the few men on duty, right through the trenches and up to the great glacis that sloped up towards the walls of the town. Here Maurice thought they would stop, but Rupert began to creep up the glacis itself, and Maurice crept after him. They reached the top, crouching down so as not to be seen by those within the town. There they lay flat, straining their eyes and ears through the mist, feeling the rain on their faces. They were a part of the night itself and of its alarms, they were together, and they moved as one. At first they heard nothing, then Rupert clutched at Maurice's arm, for a dog yelped within the town – had someone trodden on it? Now they heard the muttering of men below within the walls and the clink of arms. They backed noiselessly down the glacis and ran at top speed to give warning that an attack was being prepared.

Their fellow-officers had thought a raw thick pestilential night like this just the occasion for a cheering debauch. The Princes plunged out of the wet darkness, the silence, the throbbing suspense, into the glare and noise, the smell of drink and smoke, the sudden stuffy heat of the marquee. There they all were, drunk as lords, said the Dutch of their aristocratic English volunteers – drunk as Dutchmen, said the volunteers. Rupert's eye caught the flourish of a long white pipe, the gleam of light on a tankard, the pool of white and red cards on the dark table, the hot faces that raised themselves stupidly, some swaying upwards, at sight of the two dripping wet dishevelled boys.

'The Princes, God damme,' shouted Goring, sprawling across the table – 'and weren't they tucked up in their cots hours ago?'

'You damned sot – they're planning a sortie.'

'A damned sottise! We've heard nothing.'

'How could you hear anything – dead drunk?'

'You were hearing your dreams, Your Highness – snorr-k! – snorr-k!'

'We've been up the glacis and looked down into the town. I tell you they're planning an attack.'

They took his word for it then and rushed to give orders, not quite as coherently as might be, but still effectually enough to have a stout resisting force all ready to thrust back the Spaniards when they stole out for their surprise attack.

The old Prince Henry was as much horrified as delighted when he heard of his great-nephews' exploit. A pretty thing it would have been if he had had to write home to their mother that both the Princes had been killed in such a lonely and dangerous piece of scout-work. Determined not to allow any more unnecessary risks, he ordered Rupert to attend him personally, at the moment when he was sending a message to Monck to lead a particularly dangerous attack on a strong hornwork which guarded the defences of the town. But Rupert, forestalling the Prince's aide-de-camp, dashed off himself to Monck with the order to advance, and was next seen in the forefront of the storming party, scaling the redoubt. There was some desperate hand-to-hand fighting; it was Sir Jacob Astley and his musketeers who finally carried the fort, and by then it was found what heavy losses the attacking party had suffered. Goring and Wilmot were both badly wounded, but Rupert, who had rushed into the front line, was untouched. He lay resting on the rampart with a few English officers, when, from a heap of dead men whose clothes had already been torn from them by the marauding soldiers, there suddenly rose a naked figure with a neat round paunch and spindle legs who made them a jaunty little bow, asking politely, 'Messieurs, est-il point de quartier ici?'

'Jack Falstaff, by God!' shouted Rupert through their laughter, 'how long has he been shamming dead?'

'Jack Falstaff' he remained for good, returning with them as a comic trophy, and the story of his discovery was Rupert's only response to his great-uncle's complaints of his 'rank insubordination – flat mutiny'.

Breda surrendered soon after that, the campaign was over, the Princes were once again looking round for new employment.

Not Maurice, however. His career was taken out of his hands by his mother, who suddenly decided that he had had enough soldiering and must have his education finished at a French University so that she should not have to blush for his manners as well as for Rupert's. Maurice was furious at being 'sent back to school', together with his younger brothers Edward and Philip too, after the honours he had won in this last campaign. The honours were the chief reason for Elizabeth's decision, since she could not bear to risk all three of her sons together when two of them had already shown how reckless they could be.

So off poor Maurice had to go to books and lectures again in Paris, while Carl and Rupert levied troops with the English subscription money and rode on white horses at a victory tournament given at The Hague to commemorate the conquest of Breda, and carried off so many prizes, which were conveniently though unromantically of hard cash, that they issued a printed challenge to all fresh comers. There were balls too and hunting parties; the brothers were fêted everywhere and treated like heroes, for the thought that they might not return alive from their desperate venture gave an added charm to the beautiful young men, and *so* young – Rupert only eighteen, but with three campaigns already behind him. The Hague went carnival-mad over the possible victims, who felt themselves already victorious in this festal air, and were so full of high spirits and conceit that their mother could not tolerate their rudeness and indifference to her commands. They had got utterly out of hand, there was no dealing with them, she declared; and after three furious quarrels in two days – baffled, indignant, and wildly envious of the young adventurers who had inherited her rampageous vigour – she left the parties she so loved and fled to the peace of her country house at Rhenen, some time before Carl and Rupert rode out to win back their country.

CHAPTER TEN

A FEW WEEKS of triumph and rejoicing at the wrong end of the campaign, and Rupert was riding out to rescue his country for, and with, his brother. It was a pity it was 'with' as well as 'for', for Carl, though an amiable enough companion just lately at The Hague, where they had both been rollicking on an up-roarious holiday, was nothing like Maurice as a comrade in arms. Where Maurice had instinctively known and responded to his thought, Carl argued with it and talked round it 'like a woman', Rupert objected, to show how unsoldierly he con-sidered his brother. Carl talked round that too, not unnaturally – 'What you mean is, I don't always obey you like your slavish Twin. I'm in command of this expedition, not you—and you'd best learn to take orders as well as give them, or you'll make enemies. Goring says you were damned insolent to him – he calls you the Princely Pup.'

'I don't care a rush for a sink-pot like Goring.'

'He's as brave as you. And he's lame for life from that wound at Breda – very gracefully he limps too, especially with the ladies,' added Carl, in one of the malicious twists that he so enjoyed giving the conversation that he could not resist them even when they worked against his argument.

Their burst of laughter recovered Rupert's good humour. It was no good being angry because old Timon was not Maurice. And he himself was in splendid fettle, so gay that it was hard to keep from singing aloud as when he had ridden down the Eng-lish lanes, warm with the smell of bracken in the sun. Now he was riding at the head of his own cavalry regiment, a full-fledged colonel with his first command, over the flat Han-overian plains that lay near the Lower Palatinate, and his powerful white horse, that whinnied with pleasure whenever the bugle sounded, was as proud as he in his white-plumed helmet and doublet of scarlet plush, and scarlet-and-silver sword-sash wound outside his gleaming breastplate.

It did not occur to him that four thousand men was a very small force with which to conquer the Emperor's armies, or if it did, the odds only gave the greater spice to the adventure. They were out to take a chance, and take it he did with a schoolboy daring and impudence when they passed near the strongly garrisoned town of Rheine, turning his advanced guard out of the way in order to 'affront' it. Out poured the cavalry from the city, a force twice the size of Rupert's. Old soldiers from the Swedish and German wars behind him were muttering that they'd best turn and be out of this as fast as they could. Rupert knew nothing of that, and if he did, would have cared less. Now was the moment he had always longed to taste, his first cavalry charge, his first chance to prove himself as leader. He drew his sword and rose in his stirrups, shouting the command to charge. His horse's shrill neigh and plunge forward responded as if they were one flesh. The men and horses round him caught the fever; his shout, his waving sword, his mad rush forward fired their blood with his own fierce joy; they hurled themselves on against that advancing host, confident that they had only to reach them to rout them; they rode through them, cutting them down, sweeping them back into the town – and it was with difficulty that Rupert restrained himself and his men from following them into it.

And if anyone asked' as the regiment re-formed itself and continued its line of march, what was the use of that? the answer was that every man and horse in Rupert's regiment now felt that a mere odds of two to one was of no account to them. There was another encouragement to morale; when Rupert's mount had for a moment been stationary in the struggling jam, he had been fired at by one of the enemy who took deliberate aim with a carbine within a range of ten yards – and the carbine had missed fire. This story was added to those of him at Breda – 'always in the trenches – doing scout-work at night on his own – first up the scaling ladders in that desperate attack on the redoubt when all the fine officers behind him were wounded – and never a scratch from first to last'. So Rupert began to win his reputation of a charmed life.

They reached Lemgo, a town rich in provisions and poorly defended, and were settling down to besiege it when they heard that the Austrian armies were marching towards them in numbers far greater than their own. General King, a Scottish veteran, commander-in-chief of the Palatine forces, advised them to fall back in the direction of Vlotho. They were in a defile among the hills when the Austrian horsemen crashed down on to the Palatine cavalry and broke both its first regiment and its second, driving them back on to the swords of their own troopers, who in their turn scattered and fled in a horrible headlong rout, swelling the torrent of the enemy as it now swept down upon the third regiment.

That was led by Rupert and formed chiefly of English volunteers. 'For England and Elizabeth!' he shouted as they faced that wild spate of sabres and horses; the two Fairfax brothers took up the war-cry, and little Lord Craven, who was here for no other reason than that he longed to give every day of his life, every penny of his wealth and every drop of his blood in unrequited service of Elizabeth, could smile even in this moment at the boy's unerring instinct in action.

Rupert's regiment charged at the charging Austrians, the two waves of cavalry crashed together, the horses rearing upward on its crest, for a moment they hung in suspense, swaying this way and that, then it could be seen that Rupert had turned the tide, his men were overwhelming the Austrians, pushing them back. He sent back a colonel for the fourth cavalry regiment, still untouched behind them, to come to his support. But no support came. The Austrians, pursued by Rupert's men, had reached their reserves, and now, reinforced, were wheeling round to charge again. Another body of the enemy came over the hillside down on his flank; his men were now outnumbered by more than ten to one – and where was that fourth regiment? And where was General King?

General King, that tried professional in charge of the expedition, had in very cool blood sent away his baggage and was fast packing off as many troops as he could after it. He bustled Carl into his coach and six and drove him off the field, thus avoiding the enemy's fire but nearly meeting death by water instead, for the river Weser was in flood, the coach and horses were swept away, so were Carl's cash-box and the Garter that had been so magnificently bestowed on him in England; Carl himself was only saved from drowning by snatching on to the branch of a willow tree that overhung the swirling, roaring waters.

By now Rupert was alone in the confusion – riding madly here and there through the host of his enemies to find any of his own men left, escaping death it seemed at first by a miracle, but soon he saw by an accident, for he was wearing a white cockade, which happened that day to be the badge the Austrians were wearing to distinguish their own side. At last he saw the blue-and-white banner of the Palatine and a handful of men defending it desperately, hopelessly. He flung away the incognito that had saved him, by setting spurs to his now sobbing horse and charging to their help, only a minute or two before they had all fallen or surrendered. He was left alone with his horse shot from under him, but fought till he was borne down by the sheer weight of numbers, the hands of a dozen Austrians clutching at him.

'Do not kill him,' shouted their officer, certain that they had caught someone of importance in this furious foe, almost a giant in height, a commander if not a king in bearing.

'Who are you?' he demanded, striking up Rupert's vizor while five or six of his men seized his arms, tearing his sword from him.

A boy's hot and angry face glared back at the officer and shouted hoarsely, 'A colonel.'

'Christ, it's a very young one!' exclaimed his captor.

Rupert hoped to keep his identity hidden and perhaps escape; but it was no good, the reputation of his height and his courage had preceded him, everyone began to be certain it was the Prince, and soon he was identified. He offered as a bribe all the money he had on him (as usual it was very little) with promises of more; a day or two later a woman tried to help him to escape; it was all useless; his guards were doubled, he was being hurried deeper and deeper into Germany, right across Germany into Austria, and every day made it the more certain he was the prisoner of the Emperor Ferdinand.

The campaign was over almost before it had begun. Little Lord Craven (who had headed the subscription list for it in England with £10,000, and accompanied it chiefly to keep an eye on Elizabeth's two boys) had also been taken prisoner, and he offered twice his ransom if he were allowed to stay with Rupert in imprisonment wherever it were. That was refused. The English subscription money had been exhausted and most of the English lives thrown away through the treachery or tepidity (almost equally treacherous) of the Scots mercenary who had been hired to teach the lesson of warfare to these young fools of gentlemen amateurs.

CHAPTER ELEVEN

ONCE AGAIN the Emperor Ferdinand sat in Vienna and made caustic comments on the news of that troublesome family, the Palatines. So the young cub was caught at last, and the one that was the most dangerous of all that litter. Rupert had always been a danger spot in the way of his Catholic empire, ever since that fantastically gorgeous christening in Prague when even his name, Rupert, had been a defiance, since it had been given in memory of his Imperial ancestor. He was the only one of his family to be born in the purple, when his parents were for their one brief year a reigning king and queen, on the throne they had

116

so hardily snatched from Ferdinand. His birth late in December, just nineteen years ago, had been a menace to the Emperor as his christening had been an open challenge.

'Winter King and Queen of snow,' he had said then in grim mockery of all that regal pomp in the capital that should have been his, 'and when the snow melts, they'll go.' They had gone, gone before the snows of the next winter; but the baby that had roared so imperially in his jewelled cradle and had fought his way out of death in a baggage wagon by the sheer force of his lungs, had with every growing year made himself more evident. He had fought for Protestant Germany since he was thirteen and won a European reputation for courage, determination and skill in arms, acquiring before he was out of his teens a half-legendary character. It was always Prince Rupert this and Prince Rupert that. There were prints of him all over Europe (before even his first campaign) – a crude picture of a boy being pulled out of the earth with his pet hound and a fox; there were stories of his popularity in England with the King, with artists and men of letters, and more spectacularly with the common country people whose sports he had shared; there were glowing descriptions of the tournaments in Holland at which he bore off all the prizes, and foolish young women told their friends that they were dying for love of him.

All of which was oddly irritating to the Emperor Ferdinand, a cold sober young-old man whose one passion was ambition, who knew how to bide his time, the last person likely to envy the flamboyant publicity so heedlessly won by his opponent. But Ferdinand knew that that half-legendary character puts a magic weapon into the hand of a popular leader. People in every country felt more intimately concerned in the fate of this penniless, landless boy than in that of the all-conquering Emperor – and more than ever now that the Gazette had printed that he was last seen completely surrounded by the hosts of his enemies, refusing quarter to the end and fighting 'like a lion'. The report of his death had caused the deepest mourning and lamentation in England, where many public games were cancelled and people wept as for the death of a son.

Then came the news that he was not dead but a prisoner somewhere in the heart of Austria.

'I'd make the first report true before the second has time to get round,' growled the old Duke of Bavaria, an unpleasant and unhealthy old man who had yet managed to live till he was over eighty, to marry the Emperor's young sister and to acquire an heir, though few people believed that to be the work of his diseased body. Still, as a good father (or foster father), the old Duke was determined to hang on to whatever he had grabbed of the Palatine possessions; he had declared himself Elector years ago in Frederick's place, with the unsavoury title of Arch-Sewer as well. 'What the sword has won, the sword shall keep,' he put it grandiloquently, and his young wife was as fierce in greed as himself, desperately anxious lest her imperial brother should forget that 'we are no longer in the days of chivalry'.

Ferdinand was the last person to forget it, though he refused to show his modern and advanced point of view by dropping Rupert down an oubliette. But he had caught the young cub and would not let him go till his teeth were drawn. No ransom, such as Lord Craven and other English friends at once offered, should buy his freedom; this boy was too dangerous to be at large as an enemy, but he should be released if he showed himself willing to be friends.

And for three years the Emperor exhausted himself in trying to make terms with his helpless prisoner.

Would he consent to change his religion and become a Catholic?

The suggestion, the prisoner told the Emperor, was 'an affront rather than a favour'.

Would he ask the Emperor's pardon for taking up arms in Germany against the Imperial power?

He 'disdained to ask pardon for doing his duty against the enemy of his house'.

Would he accept command under the Emperor to fight against the French and Swedes?

He would not, for the Swedes had been the most faithful champions of his father's cause.

He was told he might be permitted to see the Emperor.

He replied, 'Tell him, the Emperor *shall see me*.'

Jesuit priests were sent to convert him, and he would not receive them. When they were forced on him and argued most eloquently, he would not answer them.

Sometimes he was treated harshly, guarded night and day by twelve musketeers, and only allowed to walk about the battlements. Sometimes he was given freedom to practise exercises in the gymnasium or on the great horse, to perfect his marksmanship with the pistol and the new screwed gun or rifle, to ride and play tennis with his polite gaoler, the Count von Kuffstein, and dine with him and his pretty daughter, even to walk and talk with the daughter alone, except for the supervision of a discreetly distant guard – a hopeful idea of the Count's to win his heart to the Church by the fairest means at his disposal.

But fair means or foul made no odds at all; Rupert only grew the more defiant, the Emperor the more perplexed, the old Duke of Bavaria the more furious, and the prisoner's fame the more romantic.

There he was shut up in the lonely old fortress of Linz on the shores of the Danube, and his gaoler's only child, a flower-like young girl, deep in love with him; yet nothing could win him from his loyalty to his brother's cause – and to another woman, said the most hopeful romantics, chief among them Mademoiselle de Rohan herself, who enraged her family by refusing all the good offers she received for the sake of this hero she had never seen and who might never come out of prison.

Suzanne von Kuffstein had no reason to feel jealous of the French heiress, for Rupert never even remembered that she had been offered to him. The Austrian girl had been told by her own father to get the young man to talk to her, and so win him over gradually to the true Church. It was a sacred trust. She would gain a soul for the Church and she would heal the sore and disappointed heart of the prisoner.

She was sixteen, and the tall angry young man who defied her father, her Emperor, her Church, and all the powers of her world, was only just nineteen. There was a sombre, half savage beauty about this magnificent young animal, caged, but never to be tamed. Unless she could do what the Emperor, the Jesuits and her father himself had failed to do?

They walked on the battlements or on the terraces of the garden and looked at the fast flowing river beneath them, and Suzanne said it was always called the blue Danube and Rupert said no, it was green, as green as ice, and she at last induced him to show her the things he was always scribbling on bits of paper and would hide as she came up, and they were just what she had suspected, drawings done on the backs of letters or any scrap of paper – of the sentry changing guard, of a cannon cut sideways to show how it worked, of a group of eager female heads bending towards each other on long full throats, shaded by floating curls – and asked with a little catch in her voice if it were true that the English ladies were much more lovely than those of any other nation, and he replied, staring at her, 'No, but they were more lively,' and she then wished he had said 'Yes'. And the more they talked, the less they talked of religion.

But she did tell him that her father had been converted when he took service with the Catholic Emperor; she did remind him that Henry of Navarre had been converted when he had become the greatest king France had ever had; the implication being that it could be no shame for a young prince to be converted to win his freedom – and perhaps her love. But she could not bear to press it.

So dark and strange a look would shut down on his handsome face that she shrank from it, wondering if it were so that Lucifer had looked when he had defied God and His angels. Was it indeed pride alone that kept him so rigidly determined against any gesture of compliance? It could not be his faith, for he showed small affection for the Calvinist preachers, and the only time when he mentioned religion with any sympathy was when he spoke of the brave old hymns, the glowing windows and the short services that Archbishop Laud was bringing back to the Church of England.

'But he is bringing them back from the Church of Rome,' she demurred.

'That's what the Puritan fellows say. They can't believe it's Protestantism unless it's ugly.'

He heard his last words echo in Carl's voice, and fell silent, gnawing his thumb. She looked at him in dismay. Something had made him angry again. But he was always angry. A contained fury of boredom, brooding, restless and yet static, gleamed under the lids of his half-shut eyes as in the yellow slits of a lion's eyes drowsing in captivity. Why was he so obdurate? Was it all for his brother's sake?

Once she summoned up courage to ask him, and wished she hadn't.

The eyes opened wide enough then, they blazed upon her, he laughed, and she wanted to say, 'Oh, don't!' but could not speak again, and now words were coming from him, no longer repressed, slow, each one under guard, but rushing from him headlong like that rapid ice-green water below (never again would she see it as blue).

'For my brother? For Carl? Yes, I did it for him! I was to

120

have been Universal Admiral of an English fleet and gone to Madagascar, and I gave it up to fight for Carl. I was a fool. Carl has shown his sense, so has General King, that canny Scot. It's I who am the young fool they say, who don't yet know my job as a soldier! But I won my part of the battle. If I'd been supported I might have won it all. It was their damned caution lost the day.'

He saw that she was crying; and when he asked her why, she sobbed out, 'For you.'

Women could be kindly and pitiful then, they could mind injustice. Suzanne indeed minded so much that he wished she would not. Her sweetness, though not stupid, exasperated him even while he admired and was grateful for it. She gave him nothing to contend with, and that was what he had learned to expect from a woman. And her sympathy stirred his resentment yet deeper, for it was what another should feel more than she.

He said, 'If a miserable hireling fails me or —' (no, he could not say 'or my own brother') 'what's that to do with me?'

And if his mother failed him, what was that to do with him? He had not made her, but she him. He would not let her break and tear his heart.

So he thought with fierce, false passivity, while she was busy writing to her friends – 'I confess in my passion I did rather wish him killed than in his enemies' hands. – I pray God I have not more cause to wish it before he be gotten out.'

It was the old fear – would Rupert be seduced from the religion and therefore the cause of his house? Would he forget – or simply not care – that his apostasy would work to the prejudice of the Prince Elector?

Rupert sent her his assurance that neither good usage nor ill should ever make him change his religion or his party. But his mother was the one person who could never feel sure of him, though with pitiful and not altogether truthful unction she told her friend Sir Thomas Roe, 'Honest Tom', that 'he will never disobey me at any time though to others he was stubborn and wilful. I hope he will continue so,' she added, quite destroying the effect of this confidence. And then, really very oddly, 'I am comforted that my sons have lost no honour in the action and that him I love best is safe.'

It seemed as though all the old bright clarity of vision had gone, since Rupert's fighting, which the neutral and impersonal Gazette had reported to have been 'like a lion', could so drop in value to his mother's 'have lost no honour' – faint praise shared somewhat dubiously with 'him I love best', who had fled without fighting at all.

Carl himself made a rather wry face over it. 'Lost no honour,' had he, in that desperate wetting? Well, he had rather have lost it than his horses and his cash-box! The 'old soldier' contempt for heroics, which General King and other tough mercenaries of the German wars had shown, helped his 'Timon' attitude and fortified him against the indignation and sneers of his sisters and younger brothers. Maurice was wild with grief and rage and began to agitate to be taken into the Swedish army where he might find some chance to rescue his brother, for there were Swedish garrisons not far from where Rupert was at Linz.

This was not till later, not till the weeks had slipped into months and the months into one year, two years, and there was Rupert still at Linz, growing from a boy into a man so fast that now he measured six foot four on his bare feet, and all his clothes were too short for him and even his bed had to be altered since he could not lie straight in it. But nothing else showed the passage of time; years, months, weeks, it was all one, they slipped past him on the flowing river below in one long hour of desolate leisure, while he stared at the unchanging scene on its banks, all his furious energies quenched and stilled, his senses and emotions tantalized by the shy adoring Suzanne, and nothing that he could do to prove the rising heroic manhood in him but to deny, to reject, to refuse.

After his first stunned rage he made occupations for himself with cool common sense; went on with his military and mathematical studies, took all the exercise he could get, planned out different methods for improving firearms, made himself an exquisitely observant artist, practised etching as well as drawing, and experimented with a new form of that art.

It was suggested to him by the dark pattern of rust on a sentry's half-cleaned musket, giving a rich depth of background that he longed to transfer to the medium of engraving. He could not achieve it – but he would some day. In the meantime he did bring to perfection an instrument for measuring perspective in pictures which the great master Dürer had begun to invent but never completed.

Lord Arundel, the English ambassador at Vienna, sent him a sprawling white woolly puppy of a breed so excellent that the Grand Turk had asked his ambassador to send him one of them. Rupert trained his pup to various tricks; he also tamed a more difficult subject in a young hare, caught near the castle, so that it followed him like a dog and did whatever he told it; nor did 'Boy', his other pet, ever dare snap his jaws at it.

So this detached, practical Rupert whom no one, not even himself, had yet known, went about his new business of keeping himself sane and interested, and yet all he did was in such strange suspension of the greater part of his faculties that he seemed to be moving, talking, eating and drinking in his sleep.

'The dream of Madagascar I think is vanished,' Elizabeth's Honest Tom had written, and vanished it was, clean out of Rupert's vision, for he found he did not dare to dwell on it.

No other dream took its place of what he would do; to dream thus was to long yet more fiercely for his release, to be tempted perhaps to compromise with his enemies in order to gain it. Best not look forward then. What indeed was there to look forward to? Even if he escaped, would it be only to service again of Carl, who had betrayed him by his failure to support him?

Yet he must not betray Carl by making terms with his enemies. It was the one thing he could look forward to with certainty, the one solid rock in the mirage of this unreal because unchanging present, the one thing that made him know he was still a man.

He might consent to forget it, to make his peace with the intractable present, to shatter that invisible wall that divided him from everybody else, since they were free and he was not, if Suzanne could succeed in becoming the chief thing in his life, as she now so nearly was. She stood beside him in the summer garden while the bees hummed in the grey scented shrubs that had such sentimental names in English, 'lad's-love' and 'rue', as he told her, and her blue eyes brimmed over in that disconcerting way of hers as she replied, 'Perhaps they think the one is worth the other,' and then ducked her fair head suddenly down over her basket and lifted a big dock leaf to show him the tiny wild strawberries she had been picking in the pine woods. 'Take some too,' she said, and picked up a handful of them to eat, holding them out to him. They sparkled scarlet in the sunshine, staining her plump white fingers with little beads of juice like blood. He took her wrist and bent his head and ate them out of her hand and then kissed it, each finger in turn – 'Ach, God!' she said in a soft whispering cry, '— the sentry! – what are you doing?'

'Eating your strawberries,' he answered, lifting his head and laughing at her and then growing grave as his eyes slid from the line of her throat and small swelling bosom to her hips; they narrowed as she had seen them do in anger, they were hard and wary and something was alight in them like a flame; and because she was very young and really innocent she thought he was angry with her, perhaps because she was the daughter of his gaoler. She could not live if he were angry with her, it was too cruel, too unfair, when she so longed to make him free and happy, she would give her life for him if she could, but he would never believe that, he seemed to think all women unkind and unjust.

The silence grew in the rich sunlight; the tinkle of cowbells in the distance, the ripple and gurgle of the river below, the hot incense from the pine forests were all part of it. She did not want to break it but she must tell him not to look at her like that, not to be angry – 'How I wish I could help you!' she said.

'How I wish you could!' he answered, and still he looked at her, but her unawareness of his feelings, her distress for him, made him ashamed; he must not look at her with lust in his heart when all she thought of was for him, even hoping to help him escape, planning wild romantic schemes of disguise, a boat down the river and herself somewhere in the picture as his faithful page, as she did not like to suggest marriage to him – 'I know you do not want to be tied to a wife – and if you did, there is that French lady waiting for you who is a great heiress and of far nobler blood than I, and you might like her when you see her.'

'Nothing would make me marry an heiress and be chained with gold to her bed.'

'You think of all marriage as chains, don't you? Would mine chain you?'

'Faster than most, Suzanne,' and it was true, for he would be very grateful to her and he did not want to be grateful and kind and tender, he wanted to conquer and subdue and show a woman that he did not care, she should not hurt him – show *what* woman? He did not know.

For he was still under an enchantment and did not know it. There was a song his mother had sometimes sung, remembering it from her Scottish nurses, perhaps even from her first seven years in Scotland.

> *'There came a wind out o' the north,*
> *A sharp wind and a snell,*
> *A dead sleep it came o'er me*
> *And frae my horse I fell,*
> *And the Queen o' Fairies she took me*
> *In yon green hill to dwell.'*

He had begun to escape her power; the sophisticated English Court ladies, the rougher but much more easy and accommodating attractions of the women near the camp at Breda, his eager admirers in those last few gay weeks at The Hague, had all helped to awaken his mind and senses and prepare him to fall in love.

But now he was no longer awake. A dead sleep of sudden stunning inactivity had fallen on this growing giant in the first flush of his manhood. Even sentimental kind little Suzanne was only part of this present sleep from which he knew he must one day awake. And behind her tender prettiness which made him think of apple-blossom and fawns and fresh young growing things, behind the soothing certainty of her adoration of him, her timid questing smile that so unconsciously betrayed all she longed for from him – was the love that had baffled and perplexed and tormented him all his life, since long before he could remember – a love that teased and delighted him, amused and thwarted him, kept him angry and excited and never appeased, for never could he win the recognition that he had a right to expect from that love.

Why was it his mother could never trust him as she trusted Carl? – not even now, when he was in the absolute power of his enemies and proving by one arrogant gesture after another that they could never make him desert her cause? His defiance of the Emperor was aimed not at him but at his mother, betraying him sometimes into heroics that he would never have uttered but that he hoped they would be repeated to her – so that then at last she might believe that 'he would rather breathe his last in prison than go out through the gates of apostasy'.

Small chance had Suzanne's gentle bait for apostasy against

that Queen of Hearts. Among all those hearts the Queen owned and valued so lightly, she scarcely ever noticed how secure was her hold on that of her third son. Nor did he know the effect on him of his mother's deep enchantment. He knew only that it was more gay and pleasant to be with her in her good moods than even with his adorable little French aunt – that more even than to hunt with his uncle in England he wished now to hunt again with her in the woods round Rhenen, where they would leave all the other huntsmen far behind and they alone gallop together through the green branches as if to the end of the world.

She was so amusing when she talked – so magnificent when she was angry – so exciting when she laughed – and she was always laughing, however sad she might be, for there was always some glinting star of courage in her that whatever happened could not let her be sad.

'I am still of my wild humour to be merry,' she had written when tragedy and, worse, the nagging sordid miseries of debt and poverty had crowded in on them and would have utterly cowed any fainter spirit. But with as proud and gay a heart as in her regal splendour of Bohemia, so she still held court, when her chief courtiers were her favourite dogs and her pet monkeys chattering in their little scarlet coats.

Children, monkeys, dogs, all sprawling over her bed together, that was one of Rupert's early recollections of her – and then there were weeks when they did not see her at all, while she went off to some other house, and then suddenly would appear with a crowd of grand English visitors to whom she would show off all her fine children, 'as though we were a stud of horses', Carl had said bitterly – little reason as he had for it, he the one she had always loved best even when he was still only the second son, and so she had frankly admitted to everyone.

Frankness, gaiety, courage, those golden qualities dazzled everyone about her till they could no more see herself when they looked at her than they could see the sun.

And now in the dark hour of his imprisonment Rupert's eyes were still so dazzled that they could not see Suzanne whole-heartedly as she saw him.

The dream of Madagascar had vanished – this dream still held him. His anger told him his mother loved Carl and not him, whatever he might do or Carl fail to do. His dream told him that one day she would love him and not Carl.

126

So his mother's ingratitude held him spell-bound; while Suzanne, deprived of that unreasoning and resentful fascination, won only Rupert's gratitude, his tenderness, his romantic and chivalrous devotion.

CHAPTER TWELVE

THERE CAME news that broke his sleep at last. His captors were murmuring that the Swedes were giving trouble again, they were uncomfortably near Linz, and Prince Maurice was with them. Now that wild fancy of a boat slipping down the Danube in the dark became a hope; Maurice was daily coming nearer to him, planning his escape, Maurice who knew his mind in action almost as soon as he knew it himself; between them they would contrive something. Rupert's spirits soared; it was the moment when he gave the Emperor the most hearty snub he had yet bestowed on him, saying that he disdained to ask pardon for doing his duty. The Emperor in reply cut off his freedom to ride and walk with von Kuffstein, confining him to the actual walls of his prison, and commanded that an extra guard of a dozen musketeers should attend him night and day. Though this severity was aimed at bringing him to his senses, Rupert knew that it was done at this moment because there was a real fear of his rescue, and this confirmation of his hopes made it possible to bear those twelve bovine wooden faces always round him. But there could be no hope, in their presence, of rescue through any subtle strategy. The Swedes might be able to muster in sufficient force to attack the town and castle, that was the only chance.

He slept now with his ears open as on active service, his senses straining out into the silence beyond the heavy breathing, the clumping movements of his guards making the lumbering noises of cattle in a pen. Surely some other sense beyond the accustomed five would tell him when the Twin was near, breathing with him that aching agony of desire for his freedom. That night on the glacis at Breda, Maurice had followed and found him then in the thick darkness, sharing his thought and intention – as he had done before, he would do again. Please God they would fight together in many a campaign yet – 'God, set me free – God, let me fight again with him beside me – let us

127

go on together – cut out victory if you like – women, money, anything you like – only let us go on together.'

A guard snored as he stood, another jolted him awake, there they all were round him, shutting him into the midst of their pen, breathing his air, thinking their slow laborious thoughts – could God hear him through them all?

*   *   *

Maurice had come near, quite near him. Then Maurice was further off. Maurice had gone away. There was no longer any chance of escape. That other sense told him this, for his guards would say nothing; they stared at him and shook their heads when he spoke to them, pretending not to understand him – when he could speak the different German dialects as well as the ten modern languages displayed in his now famous letter to Great-Uncle Henry. They did not relax the guard, but that gave him no hope now; they would probably keep it on for a precautionary measure after this scare, keep it on for as long as he was here – and how long would that be – how long, O Lord, how long?

Time lapsed again; there were no longer days and weeks slipping away down that ever moving river – only one indistinguishable interminable hour. Until something happened that broke it up, made him think 'tomorrow' and then 'yesterday', though at first only with a recurring rush of fury and disappointment, filling his veins with life again, but a life that stung.

He saw the countryside from his battlements filled with the Imperial troops; there was the blare of trumpets, the Imperial flag waved from the castle tower, a very great personage had come to stay. It was the Archduke Leopold, the young half-brother of the Emperor, who had been sent with an army to disperse the Swedish troops from near Linz. That done, he came to stay a night or two at the castle, and asked to see the prisoner.

· Rupert received the brother of his arch-enemy with rather less than the aloof courtesy that had become his best behaviour in prison. So this fellow had come to take a look at him, had he, and take word back to his brother how the prisoner was bearing his disappointment?

'I have to congratulate Your Highness,' he said in a bitter drawling voice that he did not know he ever used till now, when it came curling out like a snake from his half-closed lips, 'as far as I can gather from the presence of your armies in this countryside, you have been successful in your manœuvres against the Swedes.'

He was looking down on a slight young man who could not be more than two or three years older than himself, and looked younger by reason of his fair hair and skin and the grave candour of his blue eyes. Yet it was not a boy's face that looked up at Rupert, it was too much aware for that, too understanding, a face that showed knowledge of suffering, and reluctance that any other should know it. Looking at him, Rupert remembered that the Archduke had been nicknamed the Angel, though whether for his fair beauty or his pious disposition he had not heard.

Leopold on his side, seeing the curled-back, wolfish smile, the contemptuous eyelids of the prisoner, had good reason to remember that his nickname was Rupert le Diable. He felt a cold selfish qualm that told him to get out of this uncomfortable situation as quick as he could, there was no need for him to stay to be insulted. He waited till that passed, deliberately recalling the mood in which he had planned to come and see this fierce stranger, then said rather hesitatingly, 'I am sorry if my visit offends you. I do not wish that. I have long wanted to meet you.'

Rupert bowed. There was silence again, heavy as lead. Once again Leopold drew up all his resources and pushed that silence aside.

'They say this is no longer an age of faith, that men and nations care now only for power or self interest. If that is so, the world, for all its discoveries, is dwindling into a smaller and a meaner place. But you have enlarged it. You have shown you care for your religion enough to sacrifice all else that you care for. The world has good reason to thank you.'

Rupert stared at the young man. Was there some trick in this, subtler than any the Jesuits had used? How was this pious Catholic going to try and convert him if he began by thanking him for not being converted?

But Leopold did not try. In the clear light of his simple good faith, Rupert began to be ashamed of his own suspicions, and even of the stubborn pride that had lain at the root of his refusal to change his religion. Not faith but politics, that was what it had chiefly stood for. So pulled about had it been by argument and controversy that he had grown sick of the very word, disbelieving of any reality behind it. In Leopold he was astonished and even a little envious to find a freshness of faith that did not seek, did not even wish to interfere with his own.

He nearly blurted out: 'You are wrong. I am acting a part. I have no faith, I wish I had.' But to what would he lay himself open by such a damning admission? This quiet youth with the steady eyes seemed fit to be trusted, but no one should be trusted, nothing should be said that might be used against him and the cause of Protestant Europe. So he said nothing.

Yet inevitably, unwillingly as it was on Rupert's side, the two made instant friends. Each understood what the other said and believed it; their sincerity was equal, though Rupert's was defiant, and Leopold's the simpler since he had no need of defiance. Leopold made friends too with Boy, a good preliminary though done instinctively, without design.

'He'll be a powerful dog when he's grown,' he said, pulling gently at the soft puppyish ears.

'His dam pulled down eight buck in a morning's hunt – so Arundel told me when he sent me Boy.'

'Von Kuffstein told me you had another pet – a young hare you tamed yourself.'

'I did, but I let it loose.'

'Did Boy go for it?'

'No, I'd trained him not to. But a hare should be free.'

He had said it simply, but Leopold's gaze made him flush – did his visitor think he was making a coy parable of his own condition? Then let him say it straight out – 'I feared,' he said proudly, 'lest it should find captivity as irksome as I do.'

'So you turned it loose in time,' said Leopold. 'Later would have been too late for it to live with its own kind again.'

He too might have been accused of speaking in parables, for he was noting the savage sensitiveness that must have grown in prison on this lad, whose magnificent careless strength should have made him easy-tempered. But it might well spoil that temper for life to be mewed up here during his most vital and urgent years.

Leopold did what he could at once. The guard was removed and Rupert was allowed more liberty than he had yet enjoyed. He could pay visits of two or three days on parole to the neighbouring nobles, who were all eager to entertain him with hunting parties and banquets. The despairing prisoner suddenly found himself a fêted guest; everybody knew that the Emperor's brother had made friends with him and was anxious to do the same; he was the fashion; young men talked anxiously to him of the English hunters and race-horses, hoping they had said the right thing, and copied the straight fringe across his forehead until he cut it off.

When even the new lighter saddles were called 'after Rupert le Diable', so that trade herself had set her sanction on him, the Emperor began to see that his own case was hopeless. Half his family were on Rupert's side, and the half that he cared for; his young brother Leopold was always at him now, urging him to free his prisoner, and his wife backed up Leopold. Only his sister, whom he despised, and her husband, the Duke of Bavaria, whom he disliked, urged him to remember the true Church and to arrange a hunting accident that should finally dispose of the prisoner.

The Duchess of Bavaria urged it on her knees, clasping those of her brother, while she sobbed in anguish over the Palatine property that might be snatched from her defenceless infant if this devil prince should be released to win back his own again. Whereupon the Empress grew furiously jealous – were her sister-in-law's pleadings to prove more powerful than her own? Family quarrels seemed doomed to rage round Rupert; while he enjoyed himself, with eager young Austrian nobles and their pretty, gentle women courting his favour (not quite as pretty and gentle as Suzanne, he just had time to remember), the Imperial Court was wracked with feud and party on his account; wife and sister-in-law, brother and brother-in-law all ready to fly at each other's throats.

It was the weight of England that finally turned the scales. King Charles had been negotiating urgently on his nephew's behalf, and 'Honest Tom' Roe had been sent to Vienna for the purpose; but pleas, ransoms, none of these things had so much effect as a private message whispered into the Imperial ear by the English ambassador at Vienna after long consultation with Roe. King Charles, he said, would certainly have employment for Prince Rupert that would keep him out of mischief on the Continent for a good while yet, if not for ever. Those Irish troubles were all breaking out again.

'What Irish troubles?' asked Ferdinand, and was hastily told 'the same ones', for Lord Arundel could not start explaining the Irish question now.

He pointed out instead that the Prince looked on England as his true home, and must be disgusted with the way the Prince Elector had failed him on their campaign. He would be more eager now to strike a dozen blows for England than one for the Palatinate. Only let him go free and he would cease to be a bone of contention, a storm centre that might at any moment blow up into a real danger. Coercion would make him an enemy for life, said Honest Tom (who knew his subject, having tried and failed to manage Rupert in England), but gratitude was certain to make him friendly.

Ferdinand gave in. After three years of frustrated attempts to make his own terms, he was constrained by the sheer force of his prisoner's character and its effect on public opinion to let him go free on his own conditions, not his captors'. One last gesture of authority he attempted. Rupert must promise not to take up arms against the Empire again. Rupert, having received a strong hint from Roe that King Charles would be glad of his services, consented to give a verbal promise. Ferdinand, fighting a losing battle, protested that it ought to be down in writing.

'If it's to be a lawyer's business,' sneered the prisoner, 'let them look closely to the wording of it!' No one quite knew what to make of that, but Ferdinand dropped the suggestion hurriedly.

There was one last point. No prisoner of the Empire was legally free until he had kissed the Emperor's hand. Rupert made a face over that too. It would mean going under guard to Vienna, formality, fuss, an implied act of homage. Honest Tom had begun to feel he would never breathe freely till his charge was out of Austria; he consulted with von Kuffstein, who was as anxious as Roe for that event, since his foolish daughter would evidently not consider any useful match while this handsome young Prince was in the country. Between them they concocted a pretty little plot; Rupert was given parole to join a hunting party which was taking place on his route to Vienna, a hunting party arranged, it was known, for the Emperor Ferdinand.

The horns were heard in the forest. Rupert galloped ahead alone through the trees of late autumn, their branches now etched in bold bare lines against the white sky, now blurred with a flurry of rustling brown and gold that flew out in scattered flecks all round him, swirled up from under his horse's hoofs, bringing the wet reek of rotting leaf mould into his nostrils, streeled down the wind and away. Once he had kissed the Emperor's hand he would be as free as they to follow the wind or his own will.

He heard shouts, urgent, alarmed, a frantic baying, the shrill neigh of a terrified horse. He stuck spurs into his mount and galloped out into an open glade where a ring of huntsmen were confronting a wild boar which had turned at bay, its back against a broad oak. It was an enormous and savage beast and must have escaped more than one hunt; its wicked watchful little red eye, the long white scar down its bristling back, the murderous rushes it made at its persecutors, all showed a well-practised ferocity. Blood dripped from its long curled tusks, and two of the hounds were limping away, yelping painfully; just as Rupert came on to the scene, the brute made another rush and sent a third hurtling through the air; a man sat on the grass at a little distance, staunching the blood that was flowing from a wound in his leg.

None of them now dared make the next move; the picture painted against the gold woods of the crouched men in green, the uneasy hounds, the squat hideous shape of the boar, that potential thunderbolt, held for an instant the alert stillness, the flat bright colours of a hunting scene by Breughel.

There was a sudden stir as Rupert leaped from his horse, snatched one of the short flat-headed boar spears from a huntsman, and drove it deep into the boar's heart. It was the most approved method of dispatching a boar and raised a shout of applause; the Emperor rode up from the edge of the glade to congratulate the bold and lucky stranger, and leaned from the saddle (but not very far, for the young boar-slayer was remarkably tall) to give him his hand. The young man kissed it, falling on one knee and holding the Emperor's hand in a grip like steel as he pressed his lips to it, so that Ferdinand felt a shock of amazement, there was something so fiercely intentional in the action. A pair of glowing dark eyes were looking up at him over his hand, eager, amused, a little anxious – they seemed to tell him, 'What a host of things we could both say!'

Why had he not known it from the beginning? The height, the handsome arrogant head, the slaying of the boar in this fearless and easy fashion, they all bore out what Leopold and everyone else had told him of his prisoner. The young rascal had got out of the tiresome formality of kissing his hand in Vienna by doing it here in this unceremonious fashion; once

133

again he had taken his own way with his captors – and had added another story to his name.

'Prince Rupert,' said Ferdinand, snatching at that small crumb of advantage that he would not admit his surprise, 'today your luck is equal to your pluck – and you'll admit it's not easy for it to be so always.'

They rode on to Vienna together, Rupert now a freed man, no longer under a guard, but a guest in the Emperor's suite; and that cold, busy, rather weary man took a real though watchful and sometimes ironic pleasure in the company of the young man he had not been able to subdue.

As in the fantastic whirligig of a dream, Rupert's life, which had dragged on such slow and leaden steps for these three years, now rushed into a crowded helter-skelter of balls and hunts and long, dizzying drunken feasts, at all of which he was the fêted and honoured guest. It was bewildering, it was also a little boring. 'What shall we do with him if he will not drink?' asked his hurt hosts when he abruptly left in the middle of their orgies, but found that to please him they had only to arrange hunting parties instead.

These were good, but the noise and the roaring good-fellowship stunned him after his long silence; in the thick of all the glittering gaieties Vienna spread for him he sometimes felt as though that invisible wall were once more enclosing him, shutting him off from these companions who were so excited to see him, stretched out their hands so eagerly to him, but could not reach him.

And they tried hard, for still they hoped to win him for the Empire; the women made love to him, assuring themselves that it could be no sin if by so doing they won a convert to their Church; the Emperor himself made a last, almost desperate attempt to gain him as an ally by making him an unconditional offer of command in his service against the French Armies. There could surely be no objection this time; Rupert would not have to change his religion, he was to be left entirely free; and the French had just given him every reason to attack them, since Richelieu had suddenly abandoned his rather feeble support of Rupert's family and clapped the head of it, Carl, into prison as he was passing through Paris.

This argument, however, did not move Rupert at all. It wouldn't do his brother any harm to kick *his* heels in prison for a bit, he told Leopold, and anyway Carl would be certain to wriggle out of it soon, as he did out of most things. Rupert himself was anxious to go home and then to England, and cheerfully declined Ferdinand's last and most magnanimous offer. At last Ferdinand lost his temper, but he could do nothing else and quickly realized it – 'the young devil's got the better of me all along,' he growled to Leopold – 'if his brother's anything like him, I pity Richelieu.'

He said goodbye with as good a grace as he could, warning Rupert not to go anywhere near the domains of the Duke of Bavaria on his way home, 'for if he catches you he'll wring your neck out of pure paternal feeling for his son and heir'.

'The Arch-Sewer is bound to protect his issue,' replied Rupert in a far from pleasant joke on the bad old man's well-known malady; but it gave no offence to the Arch-Sewer's brother-in-law, who roared with laughter and confided in return the surprise he had felt at the aforesaid son and heir, 'for I had always supposed my sister to be virtuous!'

Really it was a thousand pities this boy would not stay with them; a touch of the Devil would do no harm with his own Angel, for fond as the Emperor was of his half-brother, Leopold, he sometimes found his air a trifle rarefied to breathe. But Rupert only stayed as long as politeness demanded and then hurried off, avoiding the country of the wicked ogre of Bavaria, but passing through Prague, the home of that first year of his life which he could not remember.

He stood on an old bridge and saw stone statues staring at him with the passive immutability that had overcome his parents' attacks: he walked through the fantastic bazaars among women whose almond eyes slanted up at him from a rich frame of crusted embroidery. These were the women, some of them perhaps the very same, who had come and rocked him in his jewelled cradle and declared that he should be their future prince, 'King of Bohemia, Grand Duke of Lithuania.' He walked among them now, a stranger.

It was mid-December and he would be twenty-two next week. As on the day of his birth, and the day when he last left the city, the snow was sprinkling small and white against the grey skies and the grey frowning arches, over the rugged stone towers and delicate green domes of this city that stood halfway between east and west. Over it all towered the White Mountain where his father's armies had been defeated; and here he now stood on the cobble-stones of the courtyard where he had been forgotten, then thrown into the last coach to follow his mother.

Nothing came back. He was looking at a strange city as for the first time. Yet it had made the first year of his life and therefore all succeeding years.

Once more he turned his back on it and went to find his mother.

CHAPTER THIRTEEN

ONE NIGHT, within a week of Christmas, Mr Boswell, the English ambassador in Holland, had been paying a call on the exiled Queen of Bohemia, and finding her, as did everyone else, the best company in Europe, had kept on putting off his departure until at last he fled precipitately just as the Queen and her daughters sat down to their very simple supper. Eight o'clock – it was a gross breach of etiquette even in such an old friend to have stayed till the very meal, and then refuse her invitation to it since he knew well there would not be enough to go round.

But how delightful it had been, the peculiarly English jokes and laughter, the easy-going good-humour, the sense of camaraderie, of smiling intimacy in a foreign land. The Queen had somehow managed to make incomparably funny the account of her sons' escapades, which through one mischance or prank after another had caused them all to be imprisoned at the same time. That consummate rascal Richelieu had contrived what was virtually a kidnapping of the three younger boys while at school in Paris, together with Carl, who had visited them on his way through. Their distraught mother, 'Niobe all tears', had rushed to Great-Uncle Henry, with the result that Carl had been retrieved by the English ambassador in Paris and enjoyed himself there enormously and very extravagantly (at his Uncle Charles' expense) and then gone on to spend another pleasant Christmas in England. Maurice had been allowed to return, and was paying different visits on the way; but poor Ned and Philip, the schoolboys, had been kept as hostages until their mother's consummate guile could lure them from the Cardinal with the usual safe excuse of their being required for Great-Uncle Henry's army, 'which I can assure you, Mr Boswell, they shall not enter till their beards touch their toes'.

136

The bright grave eyes of her daughters watched her as she chattered. In her shabby dark silk dress, its heavy folds gleaming here and there with the pearls of her grandmother, Mary Queen of Scots, lately retrieved by an admirer from pawn, she looked out at the world and not at anyone in particular, her splendid forehead crowned with her still dark hair, her mobile lips flashing into smiles, her shining eyes astonished, amused and somehow aloof.

They never noticed those watching eyes of her daughters, as much amused as hers, but so much more aware. Some chance reference to a merry party at last swung them into her ken. 'Oh, but that was when these girls here acted "Medea", and this great tomboy Louey – look how tall she has grown! – took the part of Jason and wore an old suit of Rupert's that he had worn as a boy – and do you know, she was so like poor Rupert that had you seen her then you would have called her by his name!'

'Poor Rupert' – the sighing of his name buried him more deeply in prison than he ever yet had been, so deeply that it might have been the grave, for there it is that 'poor' is fastened down like a tombstone on to one's head for ever. Mr Boswell looked uneasily at his company. He did not know exactly how matters stood. There were always so many rumours of Rupert's immediate release, only to be contradicted within a few weeks. The hush of that 'poor Rupert' had quenched all the merriment. Mr Boswell knew he must ask for news, and at the same moment that he ought to and now wished to go.

He took his leave with exclamations at the lateness of the hour, hurried down the smooth polished staircase, out into the courtyard where the stars were twinkling frostily over the skeleton trees that overhung the tall brick walls. But the courtyard that had lain so still and bare under those stars when he had entered was now filled with clatter and bustle and the heavy black shape of a coach whose horses were just pulling up, snorting and trampling, the steam of their sweat rising in a hot cloud through the iced air.

A young man sprang out of the coach, took three strides across the courtyard and hurried up the steps.

Mr Boswell stepped aside to let him pass, then as the light from the portico fell on the stranger's face he gave a cry, for the young man, so much taller, leaner, sterner than he remembered him, with weary, dust-grimed face and an almost desperate resolution in his stride, was the lad with rounded cheeks and big childish eyes whom he remembered as Prince Rupert.

If Rupert saw him he did not stop, he went on into the house, into the room where his mother and sisters sat at supper, in a little pool of candlelight treed round by dark shadows. Their startled faces lifted against the light, their eyes widened in question at the sound of his stride; he saw them so for one instant as he stood in the doorway, then came their fluttering uprush from the table like a flock of doves, cooing and clamouring their amazement at sight of him.

The pool of candlelight lay quiet and empty now of human movement; it had all crowded into the shadows round the impassive figure that still stared stupidly, still felt himself swinging in the saddle, then in the coach, still could not believe that here he was home again.

Their questions and exclamations broke against his stunned senses; his mother leaned against his breast, her burning eyes asking a thousand things of him, his sisters' eager faces swayed behind her – how many were there of them – three? No, four! Then that was Sophie, the baby, that pretty tall child – and Louey, now a grown-up young woman, was the tallest of all, her eyes, gay and welcoming, holding his above the heads of her mother and sisters.

'I had forgotten there were so many of you,' he said. His bewildered words fell like marching footsteps into the broken rhythm of their unheeded talk.

A moment's silence followed them, then a rush of laughter.

'The barbarian! He's forgotten us!'

'He admits it to our faces!'

'Oh, Rupert the Rough and Rude!'

'So many women,' he added in explanation. 'Where are all the brothers?'

'That makes it no better.'

'He has only come home for Maurice!'

'You must answer our questions first.'

'We've heard nothing of you – nothing.'

'We'd never even heard you were free.'

And all the questioners opened fire again, but in the middle his mother seized him by the arm and pushed him into a chair in that circle of light at the table and gave him a glass of wine and put food before him and said, 'Fill your mouth with that, and talk later. Girls, be silent if you can' (she had talked more than any of them), 'and if you *must* speak – no questions! Where did that dog come from?'

A joyful and indignant barking had swallowed up all the lesser human sounds as a big white dog bounded into the room and up to Rupert's side. He seemed the only thing that Rupert could answer for – or to.

'I left him shut into the coach – hullo, old fellow, so you're annoyed about it are you? Take a bit of meat to stop your chat. How did you get out? Yes, I was coming back to you – you needn't have worried. His name is Boy. Arundel gave him to me, and the Angel has promised me a mate for him later.'

'Who the devil is the Angel?' asked his mother.

'Oh – the Archduke Leopold —' said Rupert, and promptly fell into silence, in despair of ever bridging the gulf of these last three years. He could never tell them all that had happened – all that hadn't happened. He sat within the circle of light, eating and drinking, the blood gradually finding its way back into his numbed toes and fingers, while the cold and the dark and the headlong speed of his journey were slowly forced outside, shut out beyond the walls of this familiar room.

It was true then. He was at home again with his mother and sisters. Their faces shone round him; their lips moved and smiled against the darkness, while their lovely eyes never left his face. Eliza's pale cameo carved in still lines beneath the braids of her dark hair, Louey's gallant head with its oddly inconsequent features, Etta the Cherub, too transparently fair to be quite human, Sophie, pert as a bright bird – above all his mother, whose face could never be described – they were all there again round him; and it was not a dream. His breath choked in his throat, he found to his horror that it was all he could do not to let go at last of the grip he had kept on himself these three years – to fling restraint from him, and the manhood he had won in so cruel a school of denial – to drop his head on his arms and burst into tears among them all.

CHAPTER FOURTEEN

NONE OF the brothers was at home. The sisters talked a great deal. The frost was too hard for hunting. The familiar streets seemed to lead nowhere in particular. He could study or draw or do exercises in the gymnasium, but so he could in captivity.

It was odd, now one could do what one wanted, how difficult it was to know what one wanted to do.

Except to go to England – he knew he wanted that, but difficulties were always being put in his way. He sat thinking of the Kentish woods and orchards, the little mouse-like villages where he had last hunted with his uncle, while he drew figures that had nothing to do with that. There were others in the room as quiet as he, and Boy under his chair, but then Louey came in, full of some quarrel with their mother, something about Gerard Honthorst – their mother would call him the drawing-master – and the silence split up as so often at her entry, and the air was full of the odd chirping cooing sound of girls' voices. It suddenly made him feel more caged even than in prison; he pushed back his chair with a jerk, yawned and stretched himself, said something irritably surly in one or two languages, and marched out of the room.

But once outside he was no clearer as to where he wanted to go next, so he stood staring, waiting, then thought, 'Why not get it over?' and turned towards his mother's room; then remembered that she had just been having a quarrel with Louey and would not be in the best of moods; then shrugged angrily and told himself he would not be made to consider her moods as though he were a courtier suing for her favour; and strode on, first through a door into a little ante-room, and then through a low doorless archway and then another, all the rooms leading into each other, and empty, the windows bright with pale sunshine, and a frosted hush upon them, so that he unconsciously slackened his step, treading more softly, and even Boy, that white shadow at his heels, scraped less harshly on the patterned stone floors as he wént slower.

In the last room sat his mother in a tall chair facing the windows. She did not turn her head; she sat so still that it gave him a slight shock, for his mind had held the impression of her in fiery animation, and now here she was more still than he had ever seen her. Her eyes were closed, the lashes lay in two dark half-moons upon her worn cheeks. He had never seen before that they were worn, that there were lines at the sides of her eyes and between her nose and mouth. She sat defenceless before him, unable to dazzle and bewilder him.

He had never seen her helpless, or tired, or that she could one day be old; now he saw, and an unbearable tenderness crept for the first time into his thoughts of her, making him angry for her as well as against her, angry at what the world had done to this glorious creature.

It was not fair to stand and pity her when she could not know. He moved so as to wake her, and saw her eyelids raise themselves slowly without a flutter and her eyes look calmly up on him.

She was not surprised to see him before her, for she had been thinking of him just now – what was it she had been thinking – or dreaming? Yes, she must have been dreaming, for it all seemed to have been happening all over again just now as she sat here in the window and saw the wintry sun roll upwards against her shut eyelids, now red, now black – and with it time had rolled back as far as she could remember, back even to the old cold days in Scotland, and all the wanderings since then that had finally left her stranded here in this little Dutch town, left her sitting quiet here for one-and-twenty years, ever since that headlong flight from Prague when Rupert, roaring and resentful, had been left forgotten in the courtyard.

And before consciousness had utterly dispelled her dream, she knew for one instant what was that special point of bitterness that had always for the moment eluded her, that added sharpness of self-reproach for her who never reproached herself any more than she reproached others – that something which, if she were to probe deeper, she who never probed, she would find to be in some way connected with that difficult lad, her odd, angry, perverse and vaguely unsatisfactory son, Rupert.

She opened her eyes and saw Rupert standing before her. Heavens, how tall he was! His shadow fell over her, in some way ominous and overpowering. The knowledge that she had had of him and herself, in that instant of her dream, vanished as always in her waking thoughts; all that was left of it was an instinct to assert herself at once, lest he should get the upper hand.

So she looked at him calm and full without blinking and said, 'It is the sun, I was not asleep.'

Now if it had been Carl, how delicately he would have mocked her!

But Rupert said nothing.

'Not quite asleep,' she continued, as in vain hope of attracting that piquant attack, 'only enough to remember all the things that happened before you were born. I suppose it seems very surprising to you that anything could have happened before you were born.'

141

'No more than that they should happen after I am dead.'

'Oh, *that*,' she said impatiently, for *that* introduced religion, which always bored her as a subject for speculation, and indeed all these young people nowadays talked a great deal too much of religion and death and the future life – and what was the result? Only that they were none of them certain of their faith, as she was. 'But since you have brought it up,' she said, 'we may as well talk of it, for that is my chief objection to your going to England.'

He looked bewildered, for he still thought they were talking about before-birth or after-death, he did not see as Carl would have done at once that her mind had skipped two or three steps and was well in a new subject.

'Your aunt Henrietta Maria,' she began, then drew a deep breath, for there was always so much to be left unsaid when she spoke of her sister-in-law. She had to content herself with adding only, 'You know well enough what she is like.'

'Better than you do, Madam.'

'What, are you being rude?'

'No. But I have stayed a year and a half with her, and you have never seen her.'

'I doubt it,' said the Queen, skipping back two steps now instead of forward. Rupert, she was distressingly sure, would never know what his aunt was like. 'But even her most partial nephew must admit that she is proselytizing mad. But for the life of me I don't know what to do with you. What does one do with one's boys nowadays? You cannot kick your heels here for ever.'

'I have been home three weeks.'

'You will be just as idle in England as you are here, unless there is a chance of your being sent to Ireland to help put down the Papist risings. Carl writes something about it from London. Where is his letter? Jacky, have you stolen it, you bad boy, you little rascal?'

The monkey chattered back at her tender tones. She discovered the letter thrust as a marker into a new book of French plays and turned it over and over.

' "January 2nd" – um, um – now where is it about Ireland? More horrible details of the massacres in the Irish rising last autumn – that's no matter – more risings, that's what's important – oh, yes, here it is about sending you or Maurice. Carl says King Charles approves of it, but that "the Parliament will employ none there but those they may be sure of. I shall speak with some of them about it, either for Rupert or Maurice. This last might, I think, with honour, have a regiment under Leslie, but to be under any other odd or senseless officer, as some are proposed, I shall not advise it." There – you call him selfish, but you see how he looks after his younger brothers' interests. What are you scowling at? Are you jealous at his putting Maurice first? But he was with the Swedish army all last year, so his experience of warfare is much more recent than yours.'

Still Rupert did not answer, although his lips moved slightly as though he were memorizing some words. But when she began to speak again, he interrupted —

'Whatever you say, I shall go to England.'

'And why, pray?'

'My uncle may need me.'

'Again, why, in heaven's name?'

' "The King approves, but the Parliament does not," so that settles it, apparently. "The Parliament will employ none but those they may be sure of." "Sure of" for their own purposes, I suppose.'

' "Enter First Murderer, a Parliament man." Don't be so foolish, Rupert. If you could only remember all the things before you were born as well as I do, you'd know how Parliament is always giving trouble. They clamoured for a Protestant crusade in my father's time to help our cause, and then would not vote sixpence towards it, the damned hypocrites. The English Parliament are notorious – why, the Spanish Ambassador said they were the best thing that could have happened in the interests of Spain and the Pope. They drove my poor father nearly out of his mind.'

'I don't care what they did to your poor father. I'm going to prevent their doing it to my uncle.'

'You are unbearable – the most rude, wilful, obstinate, pigheaded young beast imaginable.'

'Why should Carl go to England and not I? He was there first before, and you did not want me to go then. It's always Carl first. *I* am not to get in Carl's way, *I* am not to change my religion because it might interfere with Carl's chances. Well, I didn't change it in prison.'

'Of course you would not give up your brother's cause to win your freedom,' she broke in, lightly dismissing the sacrifice of those three years of his youth.

'No, I did not give up Carl's cause —' he thought, but did not add, 'when I went on fighting till I was taken, while Carl got away.' He gulped and said instead, 'I would sign no bond when they released me. I gave my word and that was enough for my enemies. It's not enough for you.'

'Don't be absurd and heroic. I trust your intentions but not your youth. Your enemy's force is easier to withstand than your aunt's persuasions.'

'That's all changed. I might have been persuaded when I was a boy – not now. No one is ever going to meddle again with my religion – it's my own affair, if I have any – and if I haven't, no one shall meddle with the lack of it – not my aunt, no, nor mother.'

'Good God, what a passion you are in! Have all my children taken leave of their senses? First Louey and her damned filthy pig-faced drawing-master, and now you – there's not one of you shows any decency or restraint except Carl, and so you all hate him because he knows how to behave.'

'Knows how to behave, does he? Knows how to get into a coach and drive away, knows how to curry favour with the Parliament and work with them against our uncle, knows how to look after himself first and last and leave everybody else in the lurch – as he'll leave you too in time, and even then I suppose you'll go on loving and trusting him and thinking him the best of us all.'

'How dare you say such things of Carl!'

'I say, curse Carl!'

'You can curse your brother!'

'I can curse my mother if you like.'

'You monster, you Nero – out of my sight before I curse you too.'

He turned on her, his lips livid. That unwonted tenderness for her, as he had watched her asleep just now, rose and tore him. She had cheated him of that moment, and betrayed it. What worse could she do to him than that? He knew he was a better man than Carl with his pretty ways and little sharp sayings that suddenly pricked out among them, showing a disbelieving soul, wary, acute, and unfathomably selfish. But that was all she wanted for a son.

'You've cursed me always,' he told her, 'you've never believed in me. You will one day. One day you'll see what Carl is like.'

'Go, go, *go* —'

144

He went.

She sank back in her chair, trembling. The sudden silence shut down on her. She could think of nothing that she ought to do or say, though her own child had defied her, cursed her, shattered her by the cataclysm of fury that even now seemed to be hurtling all round her. No one had ever had the power to shake her thus. His boyish rages had bewildered her, but now he was a man he terrified her. And she had never been frightened by any man before. That dark flush that mounted to his forehead, that blind look in his eyes – and yet they had been looking at her so very intently just before, as though they saw something she could not see, something that made him very sorry for her, though in the next instant that very same vision was causing in him a cruel exultation.

What was it he saw? Could he be right? Could Carl be selfish, even treacherous, – *could* he desert her?

She pressed her fingers over her eyes, shutting them tight.

'No, no, *no*,' she cried, and heard the rhyming echo of her call to Rupert to leave her – it had been more an entreaty than a command, and this too was an entreaty – to Carl. But she found she could not think of Carl, for Rupert loomed over her, dominating her, oppressing her. How dared he treat her so? He was jealous of Carl, of course, he had always been jealous of him, a detestable quality, she would not let herself be cowed by it, for that was all it was that had frightened her.

She shook herself, got up, walked up and down, told herself that Rupert certainly could not stay here since she could not control him – had never been able to control him. He must indeed be possessed of a devil, as his brothers and sisters had guessed when they gave him his nickname. Those rages of his, even in the cradle – none of the others had shown anything like them. He was the same Rupert now, though grown so tall and lean. Yes, he was much leaner since his imprisonment, and even more restless.

'Your dog Boy is less of a puppy than you,' she exclaimed impulsively, as though he were still there. And pacing now in more regular and martial tread up and down the room, she began to hear what she would say to him before he went to England so as to wipe this unhappy insane quarrel from both their minds. She would tell him to enjoy himself with his uncle and eat plenty and put more flesh on his lanky bones and not trouble with the stupid English politics, for England was the only happy, peaceful and prosperous country in Europe, her only trouble was that she was too happy and so waxed fat and kicked now and then.

He would be in time to see the snowdrops coming out at Kew, and the hedges bursting into bud round old King Harry's Privy Garden at Hampton Court, none of which she had seen since she had lived there as a child.

'I think *I* am jealous, and that is why I did not want you to go,' she told the young man who still seemed to be towering against the chequered pattern of the leaded window-panes, making the whole room look lower, a bright little box unfit to contain anything so large and young and powerful. Was she jealous too of that youth and power, setting out for England as to a new adventure, while she thought of it as an elderly woman, weary for home?

She only hoped it would not be too much of an adventure – those Irish troubles, what use could any man be in them? and when he was, he only lost his head for it like poor Tom Strafford. 'So don't go to Ireland, go to England,' she told the absent Rupert, 'and thank your uncle nicely for all he did to get you out of prison,' and she would send a letter by him about Louey and William of Brandenburg, for something must be done about all these great girls growing up round her, and Louey had been right in one thing – her grandmother and William's, that insufferable old Dowager Electress Juliana, only made all the difficulties she could between the young people, just as she had tried to do between herself and Frederick when she had been her mother-in-law. It was a great pity that the money Charles had already sent over for Louey's dowry had had to be used for Carl – it might even give him a bad impression of his nephew, though of course he must know that sons, especially eldest sons, must come first.

Rupert could tell her how Carl looked – no, she had better not ask him that – and see some English plays – Ben's or old Shakespeare's – and a picture flashed into her mind of a little man with a bald forehead and globular light eyes like gooseberries, running about from behind the scenes when they did *Love's Labour's Lost* for her wedding —

All her thoughts stopped, suddenly brooding on the strange title. How was it she had never noticed its significance for her poor Frederick, broken in his struggle to win a crown for her? And for all those men who had broken themselves in her cause for no other reason than their love for their 'Queen of Hearts'. Was it one hundred thousand men they said had died by now in her quarrel? She clenched her hands and told herself a little breathlessly, 'A stiff, pretty play, it had a few good lines in it, though I have not looked at it since.' There was one —

> *'To court wild laughter in the throat of death.'*

Ah no, to remember that was to remember Harry dying and calling for his sweet sister, while she had laughed so insanely through her wedding that had been Harry's loving labour – was that, too, lost?

Not with all these splendid sons to justify it. They would win back her kingdom and theirs in time, they would ride out to protect those they loved, as Rupert, silly romantic lad, imagined he was doing now.

Was her love's labour to be lost with him, the boy who had given her greater pangs than any other, both in his birth and ever after? She would not have it so, she would not care about her dignity as queen and mother, or how it had been outraged; she would go to him and reach up her hands to his shoulders and say everything that she had just been saying to him in her mind.

Now she ran out of the room, called to the servants, to her daughters, to go and find Rupert for her. They stared at her, those great girls, round-eyed and disconcerted.

'Rupert has gone,' they told her, 'he told his servant to pack a portmanteau and follow him to Scheveningen to catch the English boat. But Rupert himself rode off with Boy just half an hour ago.'

Book II

DEBATABLE LAND

PART I

CHAPTER ONE

RUPERT STOOD on deck. He and Boy alone were motionless among the scurrying of the crew and the bewildered passengers who called for their baggage, cried messages to their friends on shore and screamed for the captain that they might impart this or that direction to him. Boy's leonine white mane rose stiff in anger at the undignified helter-skelter. His puppyhood had passed in hermit-like seclusion, unperturbed except by the necessity to curb his natural instincts in the presence of Rupert's young hare which he had tamed to follow him 'like a dog', as he said, quite ignoring Boy's disgust at the comparison. There came, however, a blessed day when his master turned his rival loose, and from that day Boy reigned alone in his continual companionship.

But for the last few weeks there had been a bewildering change in that companionship; he had been hustled from place to place, surrounded by crowds of people and sometimes other people's dogs, more impertinently gregarious than he had ever learned to be; he had gone long journeys in coaches and been made sick by their jolting more times than anyone could count, and yet was unreasonably scolded every time – and now here he was being jolted up and down again, but in a still more horribly subversive fashion. The planks on which he stood beside his master, bracing his legs to grip them, went up into the air and down into the sea; great birds wheeled and squalled round him and rode upon the waters in an unnatural and derisive fashion; but though all creation combined together to mock him, he could not summon up enough of his shivering spirit to answer his defiance by so much as one feeble bark. He opened his jaws and was sick instead.

'You're in a hurry, Boy,' said his master, 'what will you do when we're in the open sea?'

Certainly it was rough enough already. A February crossing

to England was likely to be that. But the wind was in the right direction, that was the main thing, they were moving fast out of the crowded tossing harbour. Jostling, jostling, shouting, for some reason that he could not remember, Rupert's blood was always quickened by them. Noise, scurry and confusion – that perpetual accompaniment to his life except for the drugged dream of the last three heavy years – these were now affecting him unconsciously, making him feel he was on the march again, while all the time his eyes, like sentinels, remained acute, aware. They took in every detail of the staggering steps of the passengers, of the sure easy roll of the crew, and now on one side of the great sail, now on the other, every rocking peak and angle of the reddish coloured town on the low grey shores that he was fast leaving.

Those low lands of Holland had been home to him and his family ever since he could remember. But as he turned at last from it and faced out towards the grey mist of rain that shrouded the western horizon, he felt that after nearly five years he was now at last turning towards his home, and that was England.

A lovely and gracious land, where no one had quarrelled with him that he could remember, it was hard to believe in so peaceful a place. He tried to fix in his mind the serene face of his uncle, the laughing face of his little aunt, and the glad welcome that he knew would be his.

But he found he could see nothing but his mother's face fallen from all its fiery life into its tragic mask of sleep. He wished now he had not torn up the letter unopened that she had sent after him by so fast a messenger that he had arrived just before his baggage. It had been stupid of her to demand his instant return once he had started – she might know him better than that by now. Her letter had probably only contained her message all over again, in more violent words than her messenger had dared to give him – but all the same he wished now he had not torn it up unopened in front of her messenger – that had been a needless insult and he could not forget it for he found himself repeating it over and over – 'I wish I had not' – Yet why should he trouble, since his mother would probably forget even to ask the messenger if he had read her letter?

He turned on his heel and marched up and down the deck. He was pleased to find he had got his sea legs – the last time he had made this crossing he had been horribly sick – but no more

so than Carl, it gave him satisfaction to remember. He stopped
to watch the sailors at work on the yard-arm and found he had
not forgotten the technical details that he had learnt so eagerly
in the English dockyards when they were building the ships for
his expedition to Madagascar. That island had vanished, but
here he was sailing to another as dear and familiar to his
dreams. He remembered the game of 'capping verses' that he
had loved to play on dark rainy evenings with the King and a
few of his friends – sitting in a circle on gilded chairs, each had
contributed a line in turn; great men had strolled in and out
of the game, lending themselves for a moment to that golden
leisure, and famous musicians played in a further room. There
was a boy who sang songs dating back to the old Queen's reign –
a charming one Rupert suddenly remembered now.

> *'Cupid and my Campaspe played*
> *At cards for kisses; Cupid paid —'*

The lovely notes came tripping into his mind after all these
years, he whistled them as he walked up and down, thinking of
that gracious and splendid Court that at last he was to see
again.

* * *

A rift of stormy silver light pierced the clouds on the horizon,
it gleamed on white walls that rose sheer and unearthly out of
the dark sea; after three days of straightforward sailing he was
seeing once again the cliffs of Dover. But here suddenly the wind
dropped, then changed to a southerly quarter while the ship
tacked and veered and tacked again, taking nearly all day to get
to port. For some time Dover was tantalizingly near, he could
see an unexpected bustle going on in her harbour, which was
filled with ships, and an unusual number of horsemen were
riding up and down between it and the gaunt old castle on the
cliff. One ship in the harbour was flying the Royal Standard.
The sailors could tell him nothing, for the boat had touched at
various Dutch ports on her voyage and had not been in England
for several weeks.

When he landed he learned the reason of the bustle; the King
and Queen were staying at Dover Castle, seeing off their little
daughter Mary to Holland. She had been formally married to
the young Dutch Prince William this last autumn, as Rupert
had heard in prison, and now, though still no more than twelve
years old, she was to be shipped off to her husband – her mother

having decided at the last moment to go with her in consideration of her tender age. It all sounded very natural, yet Rupert felt puzzled and dismayed as he climbed the hill to the castle. Why should the little princess be sent off so much earlier than was the original plan at the wedding? She had been the favourite of her father, who delighted in her babyishly practical remarks. *He* could not have wished her to go, and yet here he was consenting to her departure when she was still far too young to be a wife in earnest, consenting too to the voyage for his queen, whom he had vowed never to allow on the sea again, since she had all but died of the rough weather when she had last ventured.

The people at the castle were astounded to see him, it even struck him that they were alarmed. They looked significantly at each other when he demanded to be taken straight to the King without any formality.

His Majesty then expected him?

'Ever since he got me out of prison,' Rupert retorted bluntly.

The looks became charged with still more meaning, irritating him profoundly. People should not be allowed to think without speaking. In spite of their efforts to stop him or at least forestall him, he insisted on marching down the stone passage to the room where the King was sitting with the Queen. Now there would be no more mystery – only the clear light of their welcome.

He came hurrying in on top of the servant that announced him – he was here, at home again, what need was there of ceremony? He heard the scrape back of a chair on the stone floor, the swirling rush of a woman's skirts – now his aunt would try to fling her arms round his shoulders to kiss him and he must remember how tiny she was and stoop very low. His uncle too was not much bigger – he smiled as he bent his head under the low stone doorway at the image of those gracious miniature figures whose faces were now to shine on him again.

He stood, feeling oddly isolated, in a dark tapestried room. Yes, they were there, they had risen at his entrance, but his aunt had not rushed towards him, she was clinging to her husband, and their two pale faces stared at him aghast.

Rupert's alarm rushed headlong into anger, and with his temper went his manners.

'What the devil?' he began – and then, 'Am I not welcome here?' and suddenly he remembered that Carl had been in

England now for several weeks, perhaps had 'gained upon His Majesty's affection by assiduity and diligent attendance' until he had ousted Rupert from his uncle's friendship. If that were so, he was not going to try and compete with his brother's subtle persistency.

He was not wanted at home, he was not wanted here, very well, he would find somewhere else to go. He had already turned towards the door when they called him back, called him their dear, dear nephew, told him he did not understand, they would explain everything later, but he must not think they did not want him, they would be gladder to see him than anyone on earth, if only – but never mind that, never mind anything but that he was here with them again, and for this one evening anyway they would all enjoy being together.

There it came again, that questioning shock, interrupting the reassuring flow of their voices, his aunt's chirruping French accent, his uncle's stammering speech, coming with more difficulty than Rupert had ever known it. 'For this one evening?' What was happening then in England? They were seeing off the Queen and Princess Mary to Holland, he had learnt that – but why could he not then go back with the King to London?

'I do not know,' said the King's slow speech, 'when I shall go back to London.'

He had not stammered then; the words had fallen with a dreadful finality; Rupert found them repeating themselves in his mind – 'Back to London – when I shall go – I do not know —'

He must hear everything at once, he could not wait. But he had to wait. There were messengers from London, and the King remained with them for hours. The Queen had to attend to her daughter's clothes, the trousseau had all been prepared in such a scramble, they had had to leave London in such a hurry, and now some of the most important dresses did not really fit. This disaster was upsetting her more volubly than graver matters.

'What sort of impression, Heaven help us, shall we make at the Court of Orange?' she demanded shrilly, and then found consolation in the thought that she would now at last see 'your dear mother and my sister-in-law, the hope and joy of every good Protestant soul in England – and if anyone is capable of putting hope and joy into a Protestant soul, she must indeed be the wonder of the world!' added the little Queen with so much bitterness that Rupert was not sorry to be dismissed.

Whatever bitterness he might feel against his mother, nobody else was entitled to that privilege.

So he borrowed a horse and went a long ride with Boy over the frosted downs that glimmered pale and grey beneath the misty copper ball of the sun. Sometimes he saw an English village huddled down in a hollow; once he rode through one, and people came out of their cottage doors to stare at the very tall young man with his big white dog who came clopping down the quiet street. It struck Rupert as too quiet to be natural; he pulled in his horse at the corner of the street and asked the reason of it from a little knot of village youths who were standing there, stamping their feet and blowing on their fingers while they sniggered over some dirty story.

'It's Sunday,' they answered, their blue-cold faces gaping up at him.

'But it's after church hours. Why is there no football? Where's the village maypole?'

Sunday afternoons in country villages, with all the boys and girls in their best clothes keeping themselves warm and merry with games or dancing, had been one of his pleasantest memories of England; it was impossible to believe that that too had changed.

But – 'It's Sunday,' was all the answer he got again.

'Confound your mutton faces, what's that got to do with it? Isn't the King's Book of Sports read from the pulpit in all churches, telling you all that if you go to church you can play at your sports after?'

'That is the King's command,' replied a man who had just joined the little group, who shuffled apart at his approach, nudging each other. Here was Parson himself, let Parson answer the big stranger. 'I have to read the King's command from the pulpit, but I read God's command after it, and tell the people to choose between them. "Keep the Sabbath day holy — "'

'Is that what your friends are doing here? I did not notice it,' cut in Rupert, scattering them by the sudden urging forward of his horse. In another minute he would have cut that insolent blackguard across the face with his whip. Telling the people to choose between their king or God! He was preaching rank disaffection and dared admit it openly. He must warn his uncle.

He did so, late that evening after dinner, when at last the King could make leisure for a long private talk with him. But he found he had no need to warn the King. Charles' wan smile cut across his story of the mischievous parson with only a hint of mockery.

'If that were all the mischief!' he sighed longingly, and then fell into silence.

Where could he begin to answer to the young man's eager questions? Where had it all begun? Back in that trouble with Scotland, four years ago, when that country's national pride had flared up so furiously at the attempt to bring her Church into union with England's? He had had to call a Parliament to vote for subsidies against the invading Scots, and Parliament had proved more friendly to the invaders than to their king. In fact they had subsidized them to keep the threat of that army up on the Border, while Parliament, guarded as securely by those distant pikes as though they were behind each member's chair, sat on at Westminster to do what they wished. They had at once imprisoned Archbishop Laud and murdered Strafford, Charles' strongest and most faithful servant, after a trial that was a mockery of the law.

Rupert had heard vaguely of these things while in prison, had thought it very strange that little Laud, whom he remembered as such a friend of his uncle's, should be in the Tower – still odder that Strafford should have been beheaded after his fine work in Ireland – but one never knew what lay behind such matters, especially when they had anything to do with Ireland, which was known abroad as the grave of English reputations. Now, to his amazement, he learned that his uncle had nothing to do with either of these matters – 'but they could not behead him without your signing the death warrant,' he blurted out.

That pale pointed face before him changed dreadfully. Rupert wished he had not spoken.

'You are young,' said his uncle presently. 'Is there anyone yet that you love more than yourself, whose little finger is dearer to you than your whole body? No, do not answer —' (though Rupert had no intention of doing so) 'until you can tell me too if you have ever heard a mob howl for blood, the blood of that loved one. It was so they howled through the London streets for Strafford's death or the Queen's, all night long beneath the windows of Whitehall, so that none of us dared go to bed that night, but stayed out on the stairs, marking out positions at the corners where a few men might make a stand for perhaps half an hour against the multitude.'

'What a beast thing is fear!' thought Rupert, watching the

154

reflection of that ghastly night on his uncle's face, knowing that it had been put there by fear for his beloved wife. What woman was ever worth the life of a friend? They took your love and used it for their own purposes, and never noticed that they had it. So he thought, brooding on Elizabeth, Carl and himself, while he listened to his uncle's hesitating voice speaking of Strafford.

'His success in Ireland made him enemies here. Pym swore years ago that he would never leave Strafford till his head was off his shoulders. In London the best weapon for an enemy is to work up public opinion. It's easily done. They had only to tell the prentices that Strafford was a tyrant and that all prices would be halved and all wages doubled from the moment of his death. The printing press helped. They published all the counts against him and not one of his answers.'

'God preserve us from the scribblers and speakers!' burst out Rupert – 'we'll live to regret the day the Press was invented.'

'Pym has announced publicly that all Papists should be treated like madmen, imprisoned and scourged. The Queen they have always hated, both as Frenchwoman and Papist' – so the sad, stumbling voice went on – 'They knew that she was trying to get the Army to save Strafford – from that instant it was a question of his life or hers. Now – who knows – it may be mine. Bloodshed does not appease blood lust – it whets it. The crowd complain that nothing is the better for Strafford's death – they may well ask whose death will make it so. They have burned churches and murdered officers who were even vaguely suspected of Papacy, but all that Pym says is, "God forbid the House of Commons should proceed in any way to dishearten the people to obtain their just desires."'

'Who is this fellow Pym? I believe Carl spoke of him, but I don't remember.'

The shadow of a smile crossed the King's face. 'The leader of the House of Commons. All his speeches at Strafford's trial were in praise of law – but he had to make a new law to get his death – and organize the mob to get it carried through. In the name of law they have destroyed law.'

With bowed head and in scarcely audible tones, he added, 'Whatever they want, it makes no odds now. I owe a life.'

Ought he to speak out his forebodings thus? It was tempting to tell things to Rupert, he was so tall and strong – young as he was, he seemed firm, decided – almost it was as though he were once again telling things to Buckingham, or, far back in his boyhood, to his 'sweet, sweet brother', to whom 'I will give anything that I have, both my horse and my books and my crossbow.'

'It would all have been so different if Harry had lived,' he said.

Rupert stared. 'He would have been King.'

'And I would have been Archbishop. So he told me, to tease, and I used to cry and say I would not be. And now they call me King.'

'You *are* King, sir, and will prove it to this rabble.'

Rupert was annoyed to hear himself speak so. Was this the powerful monarch of a great and peaceful country that he had thus to reassure? His expectation of England had been shattered with a vengeance. The gracious First Court of Europe was now a terrified suspicious scramble. He had heard fragments here and there from different courtiers through the day and tried now to piece them in with the astonishing things that dropped one after the other from his uncle's fine yet strangely immobile lips.

In the past that immobility had been part of his serenity, but now it wore an unnatural air as though it had been painted on his face like a mask. He appeared almost indifferent when he spoke of what had happened since Strafford's death last summer – that perhaps was natural, since nothing could ever again hurt him as had done his own betrayal of his friend. So broken had he been by it that he had let pass unchallenged a bill for the perpetuation of the present Parliament that had shown so plain a desire for his ruin. 'I signed it without thinking,' he admitted now to Rupert.

Rupert shifted uncomfortably in his chair, listening to the sea wind as it moaned round the old castle and away over the downs. What help could ever come from outside if one did not act and strike oneself? One would be no more than a leaf blown drifting on the wind. His uncle's fatalism seemed to accept every blow instead of returning it. What had happened to his courage?

He did not yet see that it lay in the grave with Strafford.

Charles had in fact tried to act decisively only last month when he had descended on the House of Commons with the intention of arresting the five most dangerous members in it. But they had had warning of it, and fled.

'Warning? How?'

'Through Lucy Carlisle, I believe myself. My wife told her – and she is Pym's friend – some say his mistress.'

'And she is alive?'

'Oh, yes, she is still with the Queen. There is no proof against her, and if there were, it may not have been deliberate.'

'These women! And they get off scot free.'

'Chivalry, Rupert! You haven't much, I fear.'

'God's blood, no!'

'They blame me now for the attempt, not the failure. Yet no one blamed the old Queen when she clapped the five most troublesome members of her Parliament into prison – kept some of them there for life too.'

'No, they wouldn't blame *her*. Chivalry, Uncle Charles!'

From the moment of Charles' attempt, and failure, London was too unsafe for him or any of his family, and here they were at Dover on this device of sending his little daughter prematurely to Holland with her mother, who had secretly packed the Crown jewels in her trunks to sell abroad and so raise money for armaments. It was money that had been the real difficulty first and last. The Court was not one quarter as extravagant as it had been in the old King's time, or even the old Queen's; but every year money was less in value – some said it was all this influx of new gold from the Indies that raised all the prices every year higher and higher.

Certainly the country would have to see in time that it must share in the expense of its government by paying regular taxes towards the upkeep of its services – but that was just what the Parliament men would not see. They were all calling themselves leaders of liberty, although their most notable acts now they were left in undisturbed power in London were to fine and imprison citizens who dared proffer petitions asking that the City government should not be too violently altered.

A tradesman called Sandeford had just been fined, pilloried, whipped at the cart's tail from Cheapside to Westminster and finally condemned to hard labour for life because he said the Parliament leaders were traitors – a punishment that did not show any striking advance in clemency since the Star Chamber had condemned Prynne to have his ears clipped for his persistent published libels on the Queen – and London had howled in fury at such a sentence!

Rupert sat frowning, caring nothing for such comparisons.

These dogs were not to be argued with, but shot. Why had nobody done it? Where – on a sudden afterthought – was Carl?

In London, which was apparently safe enough for *him*. 'But he has been most helpful as a go-between, for he is friends with many of the Parliament and does all he can to help the peace between them and us.'

Rupert's frown deepened.

It only cleared slightly, most unworthily, when Charles let him know, with faint apologies, how absurdly Carl had added to his difficulties at Mary's wedding, to which he had come uninvited, by asserting his claim to precedence over the little Prince of Orange, who at thirteen could behave far less childishly than Carl. 'I cannot imagine what happened to your brother. He shut himself up in his room and refused to come down, partly because of the precedence – and also because he said he had been affianced to Mary since her babyhood – though you know that nothing had ever been definitely settled about that.'

It was almost reassuring to know that 'old Timon' could behave so idiotically as well as so badly. There could not after all be anything very sinister in a young man who sulked so openly. But he had been a continual nuisance and expense to his uncle, Rupert could see that, and he much doubted whether Carl was doing anything to earn his keep now among the mischief-makers in London. He remembered words that Carl had dropped from time to time on their former visit about the popularity of their mother in England and the passionate desire in that country to be ruled by the Protestant son of a Protestant mother; they had been dropped five years ago, and now Carl was older, more astute in spite of his childish evidences of the family temper, and probably more scheming – and everything that had happened since in England was making a richer hunting-ground for those schemes.

A few months before Strafford's death Charles had found a writing scratched with a diamond on one of the windows in Whitehall – it cursed the Queen and the Prince of Wales and prayed for the succession of the Palatine Prince Carl to the throne of England. The King had smashed the glass with his own hands – 'but it makes no odds, since that is what they feel,' he said, anxiously watching Rupert's face and wondering if he ought not to have told him, since there was little enough love lost already between those brothers.

158

Rupert started up, banging his fist on the table, so that Boy leaped from under his chair and stalked disgustedly over to a corner, where he turned round three or four times in protest before he curled up again.

'Send Carl packing from London,' commanded Rupert. 'And let me go there instead.'

He had broached the one subject that his uncle had not yet dared to touch on. Now he answered his nephew almost timidly.

'My boy, you can't stay here now. You must go back.'

'You don't trust me to help you?'

'I daren't.'

'Has Carl been making difficulties?'

'Perhaps – in a way. It may have been he who let it be known in London that I had got you out of prison because I hoped for your help here.'

'Why should it not be known?'

'You are a foreigner.'

'*I!*'

'Yes, Rupert. Your mother is still the idol of the English, but your father was a German – you have fought in the German wars – you have won a terrible reputation for strength and valour in them. It is strange – I do not know how it is, but they dread your name in London more than any other since poor Tom Strafford's.'

Rupert did not care to think how it was.

'Why should they fear me? England is my home. I have never hurt anyone here. And what have I done abroad except fight till I was taken prisoner?'

'You'd had three campaigns before that one, Rupert. You'd already worked your way up from the ranks.'

'I've never heard it as a reproach before.'

'No – but —' (Charles was disconcerted at that sudden stiffening, doubted whether the last five years had made his nephew's temper any less difficult) – 'the German wars have such a name for barbarity – and you were at the frightful siege of Tirlemont when most boys are at school.'

'I saw little enough of it and took no part in it – *they* saw to that, with all their talk of my tender years.'

'That is just it. They say here that you have been steeped in blood since you were thirteen.'

'They did not say it when I was here before, and my bloody

159

career had started then. *They* say! Who are they? And who cares what they say?'

'Rupert, I care, I *must* care, at all costs I must avoid war in this country. It is not Germany, it is England, it has been at peace in itself for a century and a half – and warfare since then has grown infinitely more terrible. Civil war in this country now would destroy the old merry England for ever.'

'That is already destroyed.'

He did not know why he said that. A group of idle insolent sullen youths at the corner of a village street, why should they have had the power to make him feel that the England he had once known had changed for ever?

CHAPTER TWO

'YOU MUST go back.'

His uncle's command must be obeyed. He still hoped for peace, though Rupert saw it was hopeless, said so, asked what was the use of trying to keep up this pretty fiction of rights and wrongs and 'Who began first?'

'Let us begin first by all means – if we don't get in the first blow, they will, and so get the advantage.'

But his uncle talked of sacred trusts, and Rupert began to see that he was looked on as the stormy petrel, harbinger of disaster, and so with unusual meekness, while longing to stay on and fight, had to content himself with a sworn promise from his uncle that he should send for him the moment he thought that fighting was going to begin. So he left within three days, together with his aunt and little cousin, and went back to Holland.

King Charles rode out along the cliffs to see them go; the ship sailed out to sea, and all the time they looked back, he was still there. Rupert found Mary crying quietly and steadily as though there was nothing else to do but cry.

'You will come back and see him again,' he told her.

'That is a lie,' she answered with the finality of twelve years old, 'I shan't ever see him again.'

'Or England?' he asked, shocked into taking her seriously.

'Oh, England – I dare say!' the patriot princess shrugged. 'Anyone can see *England* again!'

They were met on their landing in Holland by Elizabeth and her two eldest daughters, and the affectionate greetings between Elizabeth and Henrietta Maria left everybody depleted of compliments ever after.

They all drove in one large coach to the Court of Orange, and Elizabeth never looked at Rupert nor he at her, but she and everyone else went on talking, talking, and his aunt made great fun of the crop-haired prentice lads who had been the stormy centre of all the trouble in London, continually rioting against the courtiers – she had nicknamed them 'the Roundheads' as against 'her gallant Cavaliers'. Why '*her* Cavaliers?' thought Rupert, unreasonably irritated, as he looked at Louey, who looked at her aunt, and the little vivacious Frenchwoman looked back at her tall niece; and long before they got out of the coach it was an assured thing that Henrietta Maria would take her side against her obtuse mother and her wickedly unfeeling old grandmother, and above all her utterly unsatisfactory, unconsolatory religion.

As for Louey's engagement to the absent William of Brandenburg —

'But, my poor child, of course I understand – it is a martyrdom you have suffered – lovely, ardent, still in your teens, and to have had all that boy's passion for you wasted when you were not old enough to have any more satisfaction from it than the pleased vanity of a child.'

Somehow this frank outpouring of sympathy made Louey feel rather hot in a way that her mother's equally frank abuse had never done. But it was delightful to have the little Queen of England so much interested in her – here was this full-grown woman, a wife, a mother, a great queen and the daughter of the greatest king France had ever had, treating her on the most delightful terms of intimacy as though they were equals in age and experience. They shared confidences, little foolish secrets, minor plots. Religion between them became as exciting and dangerous as a flirtation; Louey confided her hatred of the dreary Calvinistic services and the long sermons, which their mother made fun of as much as anyone – 'and yet we all have to stick to them for the rule of the game, lest it should hinder Carl's chance to get back to the Palatinate. Religion should not have to do with politics.'

'Religion has nothing to do with politics!' cried Queen

Henrietta, with passionate sincerity that quite overlooked the mischief that her religious methods had made in England.

She persuaded Louey to attend a private mass in her chapel, and of course the lynx-eyed brat, her younger sister Sophie, saw her coming out of it with her eyes red from emotional weeping.

Her mother countered her aunt's attack by devoting herself to her new little niece Mary, who at once became her 'best niece'. She inquired rather persistently after Queen Henrietta's 'poor mother', Marie de Medici, a truly terrible old lady who had come on to The Hague after being turned out of first France and then England, having done all the mischief she could without ever being fully aware of it.

A passionate but clumsy intriguer, wildly extravagant, and cluttered with servants as quarrelsome, egotistic and unpractical as herself, the Dowager Queen had helped the English people's discontent to boiling point, so that Parliament had actually raised £10,000 to get her to go away – to which King Charles thankfully added the same amount from his own purse. As for her daughter, the Queen of England, she had walked about her room wringing her hands and saying 'There is an end to my freedom', when she heard that her mother was coming to pay them a visit.

But when she was driven out with yells and booings and handfuls of mud and even stones by those hearty lads, the London prentices, who had unmistakable methods of expressing their dislike for foreigners and Papists, then her daughter not unnaturally felt both indignation and remorse, and did not care to be reminded of such feelings by her sister-in-law's spurious sympathy. For all her correct formulas Queen Elizabeth made it quite plain that she shared the feelings of the London street boys, and would not have objected to heaving half a brick herself at her brother's mother-in-law.

The only person who ever said a good word for her was Etta, the Cherub, and that was because Marie de Medici had given her a recipe for lemon cakes. They were very good cakes – everybody had to agree to that.

Everybody at The Hague seemed to have grown ten degrees more feminine since Queen Henrietta had arrived. Rupert found his mother and sisters unbearable and let them know it; nor did he like his aunt much better at the moment, though he had admired her pluck and now her business-like qualities in disposing of the Crown jewels and buying ammunition. But he was glad that she was not ready to go back with him when at last he got his summons from his uncle, the following summer.

'This is a man's business – you leave it to us and come back when it is all over,' he told her kindly as he kissed her goodbye, and she uttered a sharp yell of exasperation.

She had not found the just grown-up Rupert nearly as pleasant as the great boy of sixteen who had sat at her feet and watched her with shy adoring eyes while she sang him little French songs in her clear treble voice, songs that always had the same sort of tune, and refrains of 'Giroflé! Girofla!' 'Oh gai oh gai!' 'Ohé! Ohé!' like the trilling and chirruping of birds. He never asked her to sing to him now, and when she did at Louey's beseeching, she would sometimes catch those brooding eyes of his fixed upon her with no shy adoration, but a strange, aloof almost resentful expression.

For he could not help looking at her and weighing her as the price of his uncle's honour and loyalty to his friend – and found her far too light for it. Did she know what she had cost King Charles? Did she think herself worth it – think anyone in the world worth it? 'God keep me from ever loving a woman!' prayed the boy passionately.

And his aunt, not unnaturally annoyed at the unreasoning new sullenness in this young oaf, and disappointed in her attempts to win admissions from her sister-in-law as to Rupert's failure to improve with age ('What a pity that Rupert —!' 'Can you not make Rupert —?' 'Why cannot Rupert —?'), sat down and wrote to her husband, warning him on no account to trust too much to his nephew, for 'He should have someone to advise him, for believe me he is still very young and self-willed. I have had experience of him, and he is not to be trusted to take a single step out of his own head.'

But Charles was so weak; she wished she were returning with Rupert to counteract his influence. A new sense of life was quickening her pulses. Up till now, absorbed in her adoring husband, her many babies, her private conversions, her passion for acting and dancing and her reform of the Englishwomen's hideous dress into the most graceful fashions of the age, she had had no wish to take a part in public life. But now, since the English people insisted on driving her into it, they should see that not for nothing was she the daughter of Henry of Navarre!

That astute monarch might well have shuddered had he known his effect on his daughter's resolution!

Nor was her nephew easy at this change in her, and not merely on his own account. He had heard her urgent, one might almost say her hammering, instructions to her husband as she bade him farewell.

'My dear heart!' Charles had said to her again and again, and sighed so deeply that it seemed indeed that he was bidding farewell, not to a separate being, but to the heart out of his body.

But to him she had said, 'Do not look back. There is no more room for repentance. You must dare. Do not delay longer now in consultations. It is action must do the work at this hour – *action*, ACTION, ACTION!'

Well, at least she could not begin to meddle yet, for here he was going back to his uncle without her. But he wished she would not write so many letters.

He had got quite ill with the boredom and uncertainty of waiting for his uncle's summons all through that dull cold spring. Maurice had come home and was determined to accompany him to England, but even Maurice roused his temper. He wanted to go over that time when he was in the Swedish army, and the plans he had made to rescue Rupert – 'What's the use now, since they never came off?' Rupert growled ungraciously. Linz was a hundred years ago – but England lay just ahead.

His mother, for all she refused to take sides with his aunt against him, remained as aloof as she had been all through his return visit. He thought she had never forgiven his affront to her; and she would not have forgiven it if she had remembered it, but in reverse to the usual procedure, Elizabeth was much more apt to forget than to forgive.

She now had a much deeper cause for resentment against Rupert than any mere personal insult. He was going back to fight for her country, so much more hers than his, and she could not go too without everyone thinking her a nuisance of a woman – and yet how well she could lead and influence her own countrymen she knew, from her long experience with them abroad, when every year her effect on them was more instant and magical than even in the old days of her lovely girlhood. A power far stronger than mere youthful beauty now bound them to her. She had become a legend and an institution, the Mecca of every young Englishman's pilgrimage abroad. – 'And did you

164

see the Queen of Bohemia?' was certain to be among the first three questions asked of any returned traveller, and if he had not done so then it was of small use for him to tell that he had been rowed in a gondola or had hunted with the King of France.

'I am on show here like any Fat Woman or Dancing Bear,' Elizabeth mocked herself, but with pleasure, for it was something to provide the most famous and popular Court in Europe when your curtains were only held together by the darns in them, and your velvet chairs were so shiny with the nap all worn off that it was best to pretend they were leather. But she knew well enough that hers was not the freak popularity of an anomaly or raree-show – the Beggar Queen or the Proud Pauper. That was not what sent thousands of Englishmen to fight under her Standard whenever it was raised, and made them find in her again and again a second Queen Elizabeth, potentially as great as she who had inspired her people to shatter the Armadas of Spain.

Whatever she was doing now – riding or walking or trying to make polite conversation with that dreadful little woman her sister-in-law, who was as plain as she was supposed to be pretty, and even had sticking-out teeth, though that was the libel her countrymen invariably fastened on the Englishwomen – whatever she sought to fix her attention on – even on the fact that she was in her late forties – she could only see herself as in the daydreams of a schoolgirl, dressed in men's clothes and riding at the head of her troops, as her grandmother, Queen Mary of Scotland, had done, staying hours in the saddle through the wild wind and rain of her northern country.

'What is it you are repeating to yourself, dear sister?' asked Queen Henrietta, looking up from her embroidery at the tall Englishwoman pacing up and down with that amazing springing step like the step of a young deer.

> *'Oh my soul of heavenly birth*
> *Do thou scorn this basest earth,'*

replied Elizabeth. 'I wrote it when I was eleven and very pious.'

'Tiens! Can you really remember your childish fancies?'

Remember them? Why should she not? Nor did they seem like childish fancies, but her present thoughts. Did one really change so much since one was grown up? It was a shock to think she might have done so in others' eyes if not her own –

but no, there were too many proofs against it. The tribute the arrogant old rascal Ben Jonson had paid her –

> 'That most princely maid whose form might call
> The world of war, to make it hazard all
> His valour for her beauty.' –

That had been when she was fifteen, and it was the sort of thing men had gone on saying of her ever since, because it had gone on being true ever since, however much a tiresome little Frenchwoman might sit and hum over her finicky sewing as if to belittle it. She had the gift of leadership, magnetic and decisive, to her fingertips – and Harry had had that too – but Baby Charles, could he ever outgrow his baffled babyhood so far as to win to it?

She thought of the pale persistent little boy who had shown an almost inhuman courage in the efforts with which he had outgrown his early delicacy. Why, he could neither walk nor talk at four years old, and by the time he was twelve he had made himself a splendid horseman! But he still was not higher than five foot one, he still stammered, and like most tall strong elder sisters she was convinced that whatever he did would go wrong. That very resolution of his, it seemed to her to have a fatal quality, it was so entirely independent of what others might think and feel. Those who knew him might love him devotedly, despairingly, but those who did not might feel him as chill and alien as a being from another world. A word that she had forgotten for forty years leaped unbidden to her mind —

'He is fey,' she said to herself, and straightway she was back in Dunfermline, a shivering child of five years old, sitting cramped and quiet in her corner under the wide chimney so that the maids should not see her as they whispered together of the bonny young Earl of Gowrie and his brother, the Master of Ruthven, not yet nineteen, whose heads her father, King James, had ordered to be stuck up on the Tolbooth in Edinburgh only a week or two before Baby Charles was born.

'What good can come of *that*?' they asked each other – and even as they whispered and shuddered, frightening each other for the pleasure of it as they pulled up their wide farthingaled skirts, exposing their thick cloth stockings to the comfortable blaze – and as Elizabeth crouched hidden behind the pile of logs, hearing the voices and seeing only the fat female calves and the stars that seemed to rock in the wind at the top of the wide chimney – there came a scream so horrible that none dared cry out or move, but sat frozen until it came again, and nearer, and now in the room – and there was the baby Prince's nurse, fled from his cradle, having seen what no human being should have seen. A black pall, soaked in blood, had fallen from nowhere over the cradle – so she said when at last they could get her to speak through her raving hysterics.

They rushed to the cradle and found little Charles sleeping as peacefully as a waxen image, his blankets and silken coverlid all as they should be – though it was strange, even unnatural, that he had never waked at that blood-curdling shriek torn out of the nurse as she ran from the room.

And now it seemed utterly unnatural to Elizabeth that this thing that had so terrified her in her infancy should have lain forgotten, together with nearly everything else that had happened in those first years of her life in the grim castles of Scotland.

> *'The King sits in Dunfermline town,*
> *Drinking the blude-red wine —'*

That was another thing she had forgotten, once the King, her father, had come south to England.

'It's not an easy thing to be King of Scotland *and* England,' she thought – and now that she had once remembered that horrible portent of Charles' infancy her head became so full of it that she had to tell it, and so she did, to Eliza, whose cool philosophy might perhaps dispel her uneasiness – and if it did *not*, then what the plague was the good of philosophy? Alas, she found it no good at all.

Eliza told Rupert.

'Why have you told me?' he demanded.

'I thought you would be interested.'

'Women – are they human?'

'I never thought you would take it so seriously – an instance of superstition in a barbarous land like Scotland. What struck me most was the Gowrie and Ruthven executions. Why was that? It was a conspiracy against King James, wasn't it? I once saw an old print of it, done in Geneva, so it must have made a wide stir.'

'But then you don't know my uncle,' he muttered in extenuation.

If she did, her coldness would be inexcusable.

Did a man really carry his fate from the cradle? The Calvinist doctrine said so, and that was the only religion that he and his family might have.

'Then God is a monster!' he broke out.

'Rupert, are you mad?'

He was really intolerable, always running down women, and now even God! Well, there was one good thing about the war in England if it really came to that – it would give him employment, and Maurice too.

Even Louey was glad when he went. 'Men are dreadful unless they are doing something,' she said.

His mother only seemed to realize his departure at the last moment, when she ran after him to give him a small female monkey with two smartly cut velvet jackets, one green and one red. (She had had no new dresses herself for years.)

Only one person was happy because of Rupert, and that was Maurice. At last one of Rupert's dreams was to be realized. Maurice was sailing with him to England, and they were going to fight together for their uncle.

CHAPTER THREE

'THESE ENGLISHMEN are amateurs,' said Maurice.

Rupert scowled doubtfully at his brother. His instinct was to clout him over the head for speaking of 'these Englishmen' as though he were a foreigner, and yet he had better reason for Maurice's opinion than Maurice had. He had been woken up at Nottingham on the night of his arrival by what he had at first taken for the Archangel Michael. On rubbing his eyes he perceived his visitor to be an elegant gentleman with an almost ridiculously beautiful face set in an aureole of fair curls, who asked him, in a waft of heliotrope scent and the fashionable drawling stammer that was supposed quite erroneously to copy the King's, whether he had any ghost of a notion as to what God-damned object from hell a p-petard might happen to be?

The furious barking of Boy was at first all the answer given. Only the snobbery innate in even the noblest dogs restrained him from fastening his teeth in those exquisite satin breeches.

Rupert had just had such a horrible crossing that he had been in real danger from his violent and perpetual sickness, but had

had to struggle on deck to order out the guns to beat off a Parliament ship that threatened to search his boat. The Parliament ship signalled two others to the chase, but his ship managed to make Tynemouth late in the evening; he and Maurice landed in boats from outside the harbour, and set off straightaway to ride through the night to Nottingham without pausing for any rest. Three hours' pause, however, they had to make, for by a freak of English weather there was a hard frost that August night, and Rupert's horse fell, throwing him on to his shoulder and putting it out of joint. A bone-setter was found who put it back for him out in the road; Rupert at once rode on, and at last reached Nottingham and bed, only to be woken up within a couple of hours by what on second thoughts was a 'God-damned object from hell'.

'A petard,' it proceeded languidly. 'His Majesty sends to me from Coventry for a petard. It's a word I never heard except in the p-play where somebody gets hoist with his own petard, God knows why.'

'God damn your eyes,' retorted Rupert, stumbling out of bed – 'are you supposed to be a soldier?'

'I am George, Lord Digby, the Governor of Nottingham,' replied his visitor frigidly and without any trace this time of a stammer.

The answer to this awe-inspiring intelligence was a cracking yawn while the naked giant stretched himself till he seemed as if he would go through both walls and ceiling.

'Have you no officers on your staff?' he grunted at the end of his yawn.

'Naturally, Your Highness. But they none of them can recognize a petard when they see one. They are gentlemen, not base mechanics nor professional soldiers.'

A gleam of impish humour impelled his thrust, but Rupert ignored it. 'Take me to the arsenal,' he commanded as he pulled on his breeches, stamped himself into his boots and flung a voluminous scarlet cloak round his shoulders.

'Will not Your Highness take cold without your doublet?'

'No,' was the curt answer.

There was no petard to be found in the arsenal.

'There!' exclaimed Lord Digby, 'I knew there was some good reason for not recognizing it.'

Rupert looked at him as if to discover some good reason for his existence, but failed.

'Isn't there anybody here who's not a gentleman?' he asked, then swung round as a man came in, stooping his head under the low doorway – 'You, sir, are *you* not a gentleman by any chance?'

The man, who had bowed to Digby, looked comically from him to the Prince. He was a pleasant square-set fellow, trim without being elegant, and his shrewd yet candid eyes and wide grin promised intelligence as well as good humour.

'I see my answer should be in the negative,' he replied, 'but may I ask the reason of the inquiry, sir – and the inquirer?'

Rupert was suddenly aware that his naked chest and arms must look surprising.

'I am Rupert of the Rhine,' he told him quickly so as to forestall the elaborate introduction that was obviously forming on Digby's pursed lips. 'I am looking for a petard, and Lord Digby tells me there's no officer of his so ungentlemanly as to know one when he sees it. I hoped you might be a common soldier like myself.'

'Save me from His Highness' sarcasm, Will,' implored Digby. He twirled up his fair moustaches, exposing a red full mouth rather too small for his face. 'Will' answered gravely.

'I am Captain Will Legge, but I can assure Your Royal Highness that my commission is prior to this war, which by the way is going to be declared tomorrow. There's no petard here, but we might make one out of two apothecaries' mortars.'

'God's blood, that's a good notion. You must be a very common fellow.'

Rupert's new comrade grinned at him in a deprecating manner.

'Plenty of private gentlemen will try and make themselves soldiers now,' he said. 'Your Highness will have to deal leniently with us.'

Rupert felt a trifle ashamed.

'If only they aren't so damned proud of being fools,' he muttered – 'look, where are the mortars? Let's see to it.'

He and Will Legge set the artificers to work to construct the petard and send it off.

Digby, who had left them, now suddenly appeared again, looking more than ever like a rather dissolute archangel as he held his hand aloft in a superb gesture and declared he had ordered a petard that should hoist them more comfortably than any apothecaries' stuff. He led them back through his own apartments. Some squat-bellied black bottles had been placed at the end of a table, three slender-stemmed wine-glasses, three long curved clay pipes, and a jar of tobacco. Candles had been lit on the table and spacious leather chairs drawn up round it. Rupert, having done his job, was already half asleep again and had no wish to sit up and drink, but at Digby's invitation Captain Legge gave him a glance that was an unmistakable appeal.

Well, he owed the fellow something for that notion about the mortars, and he liked him, so he would stay a few moments since he wished it and seemed to be a friend of this fantastic fribble. The fribble was pouring red wine into the glasses, saying they were the only vessels for it – good wine tasted like ink when drunk out of pewter or leather, even silver was wrong, because metallic – besides, the beauty of the liquor was half its enjoyment, he declared, holding his glass against the light.

Puffs of blue smoke going up (mingling pleasantly with the faintly warm smell and taste of claret), the faces of his companions, the one so round and feminine, the other so square and masculine, the long red jaws of Boy opening in yawns that expressed his master's boredom for him, these outlines of the little scene sketched themselves before Rupert's heavy eyes while he sat wondering how quickly he could break through the flow of Digby's flamboyant talk. It was airily ironic, it blazed into magnificent indignation, it glanced over the odd events that had led the country into this incredible position, admitted frankly that he had sympathized with the Parliament at first himself ('because I shall be certain to hear of it from others if not from him', thought Rupert cynically), and so indeed had his good friend, Ned Hyde —

'Who's Ned Hyde?'

'The soundest legal brain in the country.'

(A damned lawyer then, and a rebel at heart.)

But it was always the way in any reform, the moderates got swept aside, the hotheads rushed on —

'Then let 'em find a stout row of pike-heads to rush on,' said Rupert, perversely playing up to the simple soldier rôle, since Digby was trying to impress him over politics; but Digby had already sheered half off from them to tell him how that inimitable fat rascal, his cousin, Sir Kenelm Digby, had been hauled before the Parliament as a traitor for his help to the King, and had quelled them all by the sheer gift of the gab, for he had talked without pausing for breath for two hours on end, and would doubtless have still been talking at them but that in pure self-defence they had had to release him – 'as Your Highness observes, it runs in the family,' he added, swinging round that startlingly brilliant blue eye at Rupert.

He was an actor playing for applause, willing to be a buffoon if he could so win it, or if the touch of buffoonery would excuse that unfortunate piece of ignorance of the weapons of war. All his eloquence was aimed at Rupert; Will Legge was evidently the old friend whom there was no need or perhaps no hope of impressing.

Captain Legge puffed stolidly at his pipe, leaning back in his chair, listening to the one of his companions and watching the other with an amusement which betrayed itself only in the twinkling corners of his eyes. Yet he, too, obviously wished Digby's impression to be favourable; once or twice he spoke to correct some extravagant statement, but in a tone of humorous affection, and he cordially backed up the amateur when he sought to express his admiration of Rupert's military exploits.

All England, Digby told Rupert, yes, even these damned 'Roundheads', had thrilled with pride as for their own prince when they heard how he had fought at Breda and at Vlotho. His admiration was whole-hearted, passionate, spoken even more in his bold appraising eyes that scanned the long lean lines of the young man's figure as it lounged forward, one bare elbow propped upon the table, the dark eyes wary against his; yet through it all there ran a vein of egoism. Rupert in his boyhood had been a prodigy – so in his own way, it was implied, had Digby. Assert himself he must, but he wished to do so by Rupert's side, not against him.

But Rupert would not ask questions, would not be interested, would not acknowledge the charm of this beautiful creature whose first false step of affectation had instantly antagonized him. As soon as he could he made his escape, and Captain Legge took him back to his room, helped pull off his boots, saw him roll himself up again in his blankets and promised he should not be disturbed again.

The boy's face on the pillow was asleep even as the Captain repeated his command; a boy's face it was now in repose, with the frowning lines suddenly smoothed out, the lips pouting a little instead of compressed, and the eyelashes lying thick and heavy on his cheeks in two dark half-moons. Will Legge looked at him with a sudden love, sharpened by anxiety. This lad had served in the toughest war of the age as volunteer, private, and commander, and so had more practical knowledge and experience, yes, and genius too from what he had heard, than any leader on the King's side – nor, was it obvious, would he mince matters in showing that he knew it.

But how would they take it, all these fine gentlemen who had lived so softly and given account to no one, to be schooled by this arrogant youngster? Lord Digby was eldest son of the Earl of Bristol, a tender and intimate friend of the Queen, accustomed to worship; and his genius for intrigue could generally get him whatever he did not win by these qualities. But the young foreign prince had contemptuously brushed aside all his importance and fascination and made a hare of him at the outset in front of an insignificant officer. It was characteristic of Will to give himself that description which no one else would have done, not even a man so much obsessed with his own significance as George, Lord Digby.

But Rupert's sleep was entirely untroubled by any thoughts of Digby; all he remembered on waking was that there was someone he hoped he would see a good deal of, and that was Captain Will Legge.

*　　*　　*

King Charles arrived at Nottingham the next day and greeted Rupert, who had ridden out to meet him, very sadly. He seemed stunned that 'it should have come to this', though Rupert had thought it had come to this six months ago when he had paid that flying visit that was then held to be premature. He wished they had not lost that half year – in this time he could have built up a magnificent body of cavalry, which he must now do in as few weeks as possible. Naturally he said nothing of that to his uncle, who was far too melancholy already and in danger of infecting all his followers. They assured him that Parliament could not really intend a civil war, that they knew their leaders only meant this flourish of arms as a demonstration in order to bring him to terms.

But he told Rupert privately that he thought it was 'the hand of a cloud that would presently overspread the whole kingdom in disorder and darkness'. They were riding into Nottingham in a tearing northerly wind; they had to clutch their cloaks and hats as they fought against it, ducking their heads until their horses' tossed and flying manes blew in their faces and made Rupert sneeze violently, in answer to which his new black

Barbary horse, the instant present of his uncle, replied with a long indignant neigh. The narrow streets of Nottingham were a whirlpool of dust and straws, the old castle frowned down upon them as their horses struggled up against the wind towards it, for here they were to hold their councils and raise the King's Standard.

'This is more than half a gale,' said Rupert, thinking of the rough seas he had lately left. But his uncle's thoughts were of the future.

'A dark and dangerous storm,' he murmured. 'Shall I ever return to the port whence I set out?'

Rupert just caught the words, blown past him like a sigh, together with a rag and a rustling onion skin.

'By God, but you shall be in London again and at peace within the year!' he swore, shaking back his shoulders and promptly losing his hat, which danced deliriously down a side alley with three little street boys whooping and hallooing after it. He had had to shake his uncle's gloom off himself as Boy shook himself after a swim. Plans raced through his head, he was stretching his mind and limbs with the old vigour that had grown so unaccustomed to him for the last three and a half years. But now he was free again and had the grandest work ahead of him that any man could have – to fight for the uncle who had befriended him, and set him on his throne again.

Then he remembered Carl. Where was he?

Carl had gone north to York to meet his uncle after Rupert had sailed for Holland last February, and had been with him most of the time since. But now he was seizing the occasion to get a permit from Parliament to cross to Holland before hostilities actually started, and had gone to London for that purpose. 'He would not wait to see you, though I told you you would probably have arrived by now.'

Rupert showed no surprise, though his face was very black.

'But here I have yet another gallant nephew instead of him,' said King Charles in affectionate greeting to the newcomer, Maurice.

*   *   *

The two Palatine Princes, standing close together, gazed in some wonder on the small assembly in the dismantled hall of the old Castle, chill with years of emptiness.

'Are these *all* the loyal lords?' Maurice asked his brother in an audible whisper, and was told to shut his mouth.

But it was what everyone present was feeling. Thousands of men had trooped into and round Nottingham, but it was only apparently to see what was going on. They were not going to commit themselves till they saw what their neighbours were going to do. War was a serious matter and no one had the ghost of a notion as to how to begin it. The stormy weather added to the damp on all men's spirits; some of the showy Cavaliers, who had ridden up with a flourish to be the first to offer their services, had got drenched through and were eager to change into other clothes, however old. Even Sir Edmund Verney, the King's gallant Standard-bearer, told his clever legal friend, Mr Hyde, that he 'did not like the quarrel'. But he added that he had eaten the King's bread and served him near thirty years and would not now do so base a thing as to forsake him.

This mood of depressed resignation to loyalty seemed the best that men could muster. And for the worst, there were many to whisper that the scanty drums and trumpets made so thin a ceremony that it would have been better to have had none; that only one regiment of foot had turned up; that the trained bands mustered for the King's bodyguard were so few that there was great danger of his being taken prisoner any night while he slept; that no arms nor ammunition had yet come from York – and indeed was there ever going to be any King's army at all?

The yeomen, the backbone of England, were holding aloof, thinking of their farms. The soldiers of fortune were wondering whether they hadn't better back the Parliament. Rupert had found that a few untrained and practically unarmed troopers on poor horses, with about a quarter of the number of helmets and cuirasses required for them, constituted the royal English cavalry he was to command. But all he had said to Maurice was, 'We'll soon change that.'

The King seemed chiefly concerned with the incorrect wording of the Proclamation that was to be read when the Royal Standard was set up, and sat correcting it in minute neat marginal notes. At least no one could ever say that this had been of his doing. The die was cast; the gates of Hull had been closed against him, and the Parliament had made the first overt act of war. Now there could be nothing for it but to raise his Standard and summon all loyal Englishmen to join it.

Yet some there still hesitated; Mr Hyde was advising the King to wait even now.

'For yet further insults?' demanded Rupert, frowning at the

man, a stout youngish lawyer, and not troubling to lower his voice. Boy, close at his heels, echoed his master's voice in a defiant bark. If the company had been dogs instead of English gentlemen and nobles, there would have been no doubt that their hackles had stiffened. They had not reached growling point, but they moved and spoke low together with the precise deliberation of dogs stepping stiffly round a stranger. Maurice moved a little nearer still to his brother.

A fair man of great dignity who had been watching them with thoughtful, sympathetic eyes, now came over to them. He had already been introduced to the Princes, he was James Stuart, Duke of Richmond, but they had had as yet no talk together.

'I had the misfortune to be abroad when you were last in England,' he told Rupert, and stayed chatting for a few minutes with the two brothers with a grave friendly courtesy, reminding them of his cousinship, since he too was a Stuart, and making them feel more at home in this strange country. When they were all three at ease together, he said quietly, 'Ned Hyde has been hoping for peace negotiations with the Parliament. He has a very sound head.'

'It looks thick enough,' said Rupert, staring at the massive square forehead, the fat cheeks and rather protuberant bright eyes of Mr Hyde.

Maurice gave a loud laugh which annoyed Rupert, for he knew that what he had said was not witty though it was rude. He did not wish to be thought a boor by this quiet cousin of his with the kind eyes and sensitive mouth.

'I spoke so to him,' he said, 'because he seemed to be of the Peace-at-any-Price party, and all this delay is torturing the King – his mind is torn enough as it is. For God's sake let him get it over and raise his Standard.'

Richmond nodded in agreement and forbore to smile at '*all* this delay' (which in the Prince's experience had amounted to three days, but to many months for the rest of the King's friends).

He introduced the Palatines to Mr Hyde. Rupert spoke to him pleasantly enough, having grasped by now that some very various people seemed to think his opinion worth considering. But Maurice, having taken his cue from his brother's gibe and going as usual a little beyond it, was very haughty and off-hand, and Mr Hyde, who had a good conceit of himself, was quick to resent it, glaring up with his round eyes like an angry little owl at the two brothers.

Certainly they were rather overpowering; Maurice was an inch shorter than Rupert, but even so, six foot three in stockings was a height beyond that of anyone else there; and though only an exact year younger than his brother, he appeared more – a fair, shock-headed youth with thick light eyelashes that drooped in sulky shyness.

The introduction to Mr Hyde would have gone very badly but for the tact of Richmond, who at once abandoned the present situation to tell Rupert that Hyde had been a great friend of Ben Jonson in his last days, and that the old poet had spoken even as he lay dying of the visit the young Prince had paid him a week or two before – 'Ah, they've all got to come and see Ben,' he had mumbled. – 'Not much of a compliment to Your Highness,' smiled Richmond, 'but that you gave him his last satisfaction.'

'Oh, yes, we'd all got to go and see Ben,' said Hyde, 'and hard it was to keep it up too when he held half the night too short a time for talk to spread itself comfortably. There he'd sit propped up in his chair at The Old Devil Tavern – he never would go to The Mermaid after his crony Will Shakespeare left the town – and expecting one to pay him court there night after night. And I was leading a busy life as a young man of the Middle Temple – making friends, going everywhere, having to prepare a thesis every single night for my uncle, the Chief Justice, who held it an excellent way to get me on in law —'

Ned Hyde seemed to think he was quite as interesting as Ben Jonson. Rupert reminded him that he was not, by asking abruptly, 'Did he get his fine monument in Westminster Abbey?'

'It was never carried out, Your Highness,' said Hyde, stiffly again now. 'The general disturbances of late have left many things unfinished.' And he turned away, but Richmond said, 'Somebody paid a stone-cutter one and sixpence to carve the words, "O rare Ben Jonson", on his tomb. A brief epitaph, but I don't know where you'd go for a better.' Rupert nodded.

Maurice looked at his brother in astonishment to hear such talk at a time like this, all about a dead poet he'd never heard him mention. He could not feel at home in England like Rupert; he had not spent eighteen months of his boyhood there, being spoilt and petted to the top of his bent. Nor had he his brother's quick wits and his genius for languages, so that he talked slowly and with more of a foreign accent; he was extremely shy with these grand English nobles, and Richmond's quiet refinement, for all his kindness, made him feel like an awkward German bumpkin. He had got on well enough with Goring and Wilmot at Breda, but there was nothing hearty about this superb new cousin, nothing of the dashing cavalry officer, the type of young man to be attracted by the Palatine brothers, when not jealous of them. Yet Rupert seemed instantly at home with Richmond. A glimmering sense visited Maurice that Rupert-in-England was something beyond and even different from the Rupert that he knew, and it increased his feeling of isolation.

The Standard was raised on the Castle Hill that wet stormy evening, more like November than August, and six men had to hold it up, while a herald read the Proclamation but could not read the King's corrections, so that the most frequent announcement was a loud aside of 'What's this?' to his nearest neighbour. But in any case it did not much matter, for the words were blown away indistinguishably.

And the wind blew down the Standard in the night; it was found next morning lying like a blood-red pool upon the ground.

CHAPTER FOUR

GEORGE LORD DIGBY suffered from having begun his career too early. He had been an exceptionally beautiful and brilliant child, and everything had happened to throw these gifts into prominence against a dark background of family disaster. His father, Lord Bristol, had been the handsomest man at King James' Court until young George Villiers, soon the Duke of Buckingham, appeared as the King's cup-bearer, a Ganymede to Jove, and put the more aristocratic nose of Bristol out of joint. It was useless to put that nose in the air; Buckingham remained in favour just as firmly when the old King died and the new King Charles I came to the throne. The whole Court had to adapt its ways to those of this extravagant yet simple-minded favourite; and young Digby's earliest memories of his father were of his contemptuous remarks on the upstart who was turning the First Court of Europe into a children's romp – country dances the only ones now at Court, and 'little children running up and down the King's lodgings like little rabbit-starters about their burrows'.

Young Digby noticed one of these 'rabbit-starters', a little girl with dark almond-shaped eyes who went past him on the stairs at Whitehall two or three times in a scarlet and silver apron with a basket of flowers on her arm, and told him with an insufferable air that Mynheer Honthorst was painting her portrait for the young Prince Palatine.

But family disaster went deeper than mere disfavour. Bristol's quarrel with Buckingham blazed out over the failure of that unlucky plan of Charles' Spanish marriage (Bristol was Ambassador to Spain at the time) and this led finally to his being sent to the Tower. Then it was that young Digby stepped into public life, and at the age of twelve pleaded his father's cause before the House of Commons. Everybody who heard him prophesied an extraordinary career for the young orator; his eloquence and still more his self-possession were amazing, and yet his grace and dignity never lost the touching quality of a young boy's.

But what impressed his audience more than anything, though this was not perhaps admitted so freely, was his radiant beauty, of a quality half childish, half feminine, and wholly angelic. In that dark old stuffy hall, dedicated to the deep purposes of stern men, who were, however, to show themselves in that session extremely hysterical, young Digby got such an opportunity as he could never get again to make the world fall in love with him. He perceived it and was intoxicated by it; his power over all these captious, argumentative politicians, whom the King himself could not manage, transported him on wings of self-confidence, he soared above the common earth, his fair hair flying, his eyes a blazing blue, he was glorious, he was irresistible —

He was doing lessons again next week.

Everything went on just the same after all. The years went by, Buckingham was assassinated and Lord Bristol came out of the Tower (a garrulous, indignant old gentleman who would never let his son speak), and still Digby got no chance to spread his wings as in that dazzling trial flight. A born aristocrat, he sought neither place nor wealth, he wanted only to be acknowledged as above all men – he was not yet sure in what respect.

He could talk brilliantly about anything in the world; he involved himself in love-affairs for the pleasure, it was said, of getting out of them again; his friendships were more durable, and it was noteworthy that he valued those with men such as Hyde and Will Legge which could give him the sense of stability he lacked. He wrote poetry and plays, and his natural grudge against the Court led him to follow the fashion among the advanced young writers of treating Caesar's murder as an act of vengeance for outraged liberty. But however daring his plays, he realized that they were not good.

A horrible doubt sometimes assailed him that perhaps he had shot his bolt at twelve years old, and would never again do anything quite as remarkable. The troubles with Parliament should give opportunity to his genius, but he could not make up his mind as to how he wanted to use it. He disliked tyranny, so he helped Parliament attack Strafford; but he hated injustice, so he attacked Parliament's Attainder Bill against Strafford. He urged the King to 'do something extraordinary' and arrest the five most troublesome members of Parliament, and then whispered in the House of Lords that the King must have been very mischievously advised to attempt it, and that he would make it his business to find out who had so advised him.

Yet his starts and swerves, like those of a too high-bred horse, from one side to the other, were due not to any conscious treachery but to that persistent question, 'Is this going to be *my* chance to do something extraordinary?' Any little slips he might make in the process of discovery could not really matter since anyone of such brilliant parts could easily set them right. He made friends with the King and Queen by frankly admitting his early and quite legitimate sense of grievance against the Court, and won their confidence as well as their dazzled admiration by the skill with which he helped to get the Queen safely away from London and abroad.

Something of the 'enfant terrible' had lingered on in the grown man from his precocious boyhood; he loved to shock staid fellows like Hyde and yet win them to him again whenever he wanted; to demonstrate that whatever he did must not be judged by ordinary standards, since he was a law unto himself.

Now into his world had come Prince Rupert, two or three years younger than he, who had made himself as remarkable at thirteen as Digby had done at twelve, but had gone on doing it ever since. He had had exceptional luck, of course; it is not everybody who can be a disinherited prince, a cavalry leader and a prisoner whose gaoler's daughter is in love with him, all before he is out of his teens. Digby, despite this handicap, was quite ready to be magnanimous; he had felt a generous glow of enthusiasm more than once over the splendid young pauper's defiance of the established powers of Europe, and now imagined a picturesque alliance between them, a Young Party that would set at odds all the stuffy councillors about the King, and the King's own anxious endeavours to be constitutional when the constitution was being wrecked round him.

His imagination was the more warmly fired by Rupert's looks; this wild young giant who strode half-naked among the weapons in the arsenal like some Viking god of old, was the fitting counterpart to himself, not so regularly beautiful, of course (Digby had never met anyone, male or female, who was that), but dark and fierce and sudden like a flame. He was the one man he had ever seen that he might acknowledge as his leader – as long as Rupert in his turn acknowledged all Digby's astonishing qualities.

But Rupert had not acknowledged them, did not appear to see them, had shown himself in fact quite bored with Digby. It was no good forming a Young Party by himself if the youngest would not join him; however banal it was to be in the majority, Digby felt himself forced to join that instead; to agree with the safest and stuffiest of the old fogies he had longed to flout, that nothing could be more unfortunate than the arrival of this headstrong youth at such a moment of national crisis. A penniless half-foreign adventurer with nothing behind him but a reputation for courage and resource won before he was nineteen and so probably over-emphasized, he was plunging into matters of which he knew nothing and setting all the King's wisest councillors at naught. A very natural jealousy joined hands with distrust and caution against the raw young stranger; and the versatile Digby helped to knit them together.

Now he was slapping Harry Wilmot on the back and telling him he'd always guessed that he and Goring should have got the credit for that brilliant counter-attack at Breda, which had somehow been given to the Princes because they'd liked to crawl about in the trenches and play at being common soldiers, damme! Here was Rupert being made Knight of the Garter and Commander of the Cavalry for no other reason than that he was the King's nephew.

And now he was pulling a long face with Mr Hyde or his grave little friend Lord Falkland, who had just been made Secretary of State, over the danger of loosing this thunderbolt in England. What did the Prince understand of politics?

And what, asked Rupert in his turn, did these politicians understand of war?

He was disgusted to find the councils of war continually resolving themselves into political discussions. He had thought they were fighting the Parliament, 'but wherever you get a lot of Englishmen together, there'll be a parliament', he complained to Maurice. It amused him to have Boy beside him in the Council and pull his ears so that he should add his yap to the discussion, but it did not amuse the councillors. And they were terrified as well as scandalized by his cool assumption of authority.

'Have you heard the latest of His High Illustrious Arrogancy?' demanded Digby, and the title stuck. He had actually demanded that he and his cavalry should be exempt from the general command of old Lord Lindsey, the Commander-in-Chief. That meant that he would be free to do just what he chose, for nobody was appeased by his saving clause that he should take his orders only from the King himself. For Rupert to take orders from his uncle, was to give them.

Charles, in fact, was almost drugged by his bewilderment. No sooner had he raised his Standard than Lord George Goring sent word that he would not be able to hold Portsmouth any longer against the Parliament forces unless he were relieved. There was no hope of relieving him, and Charles had only dared raise the Standard at that moment because he had thought Portsmouth secure – as indeed it should have been. But Goring surrendered it on excellent conditions for himself, with leave to depart for The Hague, for no reason one could see except a pleasant holiday there.

'Goring may have been drunk – or bribed – or merely bored,' Rupert suggested, and Charles, pained as he was by Goring's defection, was still further pained by his nephew's harshness.

'You fought by his side at Breda – I had hoped you would be friends.'

The Parliament held London and therefore all the financial resources of its money-lenders and merchants, and had already put twenty thousand men in the field, chiefly from the trained bands of London prentices under the Earl of Essex, son of that unlucky Earl who had been beheaded by the old Queen, and long since disappointed in the Court on his own account, since his wife had run away with one of old King James' handsome young friends.

Another and more terrible grudge from the last reign had cost King Charles the Navy, for the sailors had never forgotten that his father had sacrificed Raleigh as a vain sop to Spain. And the Navy would be able to keep the English trading centres open to the Parliament and cut them off from the King.

So there was Charles, without army, navy, trade or money, or his capital, surrounded by advisers who either swaggered gloriously like Wilmot or Digby about wiping off in a week or two these insolent base-born 'Roundheads' (the Queen's nickname for the cropped-haired prentice lads was being applied to their whole party) – or else were so cautious and constitutional, like Mr Edward Hyde, that it seemed the war would be ended before they had finished discussing the legal rights of its beginning.

The magnificent certainty of Rupert was like a strong wind blowing away the fog of these conditional clauses on the one hand and vain boastings on the other. Charles showed from the first that he relied utterly on this young man of twenty-two, who was so like what Harry might have been had he lived, so unlike what he himself could ever have been.

Hyde might doubt and question and complain that the Prince did not care what was said of him or what he said to others. Digby might say it was disgraceful that the pauper son of a deposed foreign king, who showed his preference for low company, should lord it over the highest nobles in the land. Councillors and courtiers alike might remark that his favourite comment in the council chamber was 'Pish!' or 'Pooh!' when it was not something equally disconcerting and more blasphemous. Yet however many of them combined together to grumble at this unmannerly young cub who had been set over them, they were forced to recognize that the King was heart and soul behind him, and that it was the first axiom of the royal command that 'Prince Rupert's pleasure was not to be contradicted'.

So Rupert and Maurice stood shoulder to shoulder, contemptuously ignoring all other points of view than this – how best and most quickly to end the war.

The King had hardly raised his Standard before he tried to make terms with Parliament, sending Lord Falkland, the most passionate wooer of peace in his camp, to treat with them, but as they insisted that every penny the war had cost must be paid for out of the confiscated estates of the King's friends, even Falkland could not wish the King to betray all those who had stood by him.

'There is no hope then,' the King said despondently, and Maurice asked his brother if their uncle were a coward, and got as badly cuffed for his stupidity as in the old days.

Now Rupert must raise troops from the scattered country districts who were hoping to remain neutral, and lick these raw recruits into something like the shape of regiments. Even the trained bands which the old Queen Elizabeth had established in every county against invasion had only trained one day in every month, and then only in the summer – and only the Londoners had learned to shoot.

With the common soldiers, down to the lowest in the ranks, the brothers could get on instantly. There was no complaint of 'the Palatine pride' among the men. They found these royal lads simple enough to understand them, even when they did not understand all their words; they were proper upstanding lads, they were, who had been through the mill of a soldier's life themselves down to the lowest ranks and knew everything there was to know about it. They were tough youngsters, mark you, you couldn't play any tricks with them, they made you work like the devil, but they worked every bit as hard themselves. As for the elder, you couldn't see his horse's heels for the dust – he was in every part of the country at once – Nottingham, Warwickshire, Worcester, Leicestershire and Cheshire, and yet all the time steadily building up an army and doing it in a few weeks too.

That was the sort of young fellow to have at the head of things, not a dreary slow-coach like old Essex, who was the most popular leader on the other side because he was always seen smoking a pipe, which made people trust him as a comfortable homely body, but that did not make him a soldier. Still less did his manner of setting out on his campaign with a grievance against his Parliamentary masters, and a coffin, winding-sheet and hatchment all ready – an odd way to encourage his followers – 'though, damme, his death *would* be the best encouragement they could get!' said Rupert, telling the tale to his men while they swabbed down their horses and had to hold on to them for laughter – and asked themselves what could such a commander do, even with 20,000 men and all the wealth of

London behind him, to men who had Prince Rupert at their head?

The news had got round that he had sent a personal challenge to Essex – 'My lord,' he had written, 'I hear you are in command of an army' (there was a fine beginning!); and informed him that he also commanded an army, but that it would save a deal of trouble if they two should meet and fight it out together. And very sound too. There'd be a damned sight fewer wars if only all commanders knew they'd have to do the fighting themselves. But of course the Great Cuckold wasn't going to risk *his* skin – not he!

And it wasn't just the pluck and quickness and impudence of the boy. He saw to it that their bellies were filled and that they'd something between them and the wet ground at night; he managed to get the best horses for them and equip both them and their mounts somehow – saddles, spurs, iron to make armour, cloth to make coats, even feathers for their hats, so that they quickly became known as Rupert's Gay Riders instead of just a lousy rabble – ah, he knew what a commander's job was, and no wonder his ranks were swelling every day, now double, now treble their original number.

And as for the notions he had in training them you'd never heard the like. For the volunteers and mercenaries who had served in the German wars were full of the cavalry reforms of Gustavus Adolphus, how he had extended their front by reducing their lines to four deep instead of six (the old Dutch formation), and increased their speed by instructing them to reserve their fire until they were near enough to see the whites of their enemies' eyes.

But for Rupert, who had already reduced Gustavus' four lines to three, the most modern tactics were not modern enough.

'The side that wins this war,' he told Maurice, 'is the side that gets in first with the best cavalry.'

'Then we must be that side, for the country gentry are coming in to the King's Standard, and they are better horsemen than the townsmen.'

'There are country gentry on the other side too, plenty of 'em. There's a fellow in Essex's army who's just raised a troop of sixty horse at his own expense and practically taken command of Cambridge. That's why the £20,000 worth of college plate we were expecting has never got through to us. He's only a raw

185

volunteer – a Captain Cromwell. He took three of the heads of colleges prisoner while they were in chapel and packed them off to London.'

'There's a soldier for you!' sneered Maurice, 'to attack some old dons in chapel – that shows a lot of spirit!'

'It shows sense – which our fellows don't. That man knows how to move quickly. Well, we've got to move quicker. They talk of ten and twenty-year-old reforms as new – I want something newer.'

'Newer than Gustavus?' exclaimed the Twin's shocked tones.

'And older.' He sat frowning, a lock of hair falling into his eyes as in the old days at school in Leyden when he had been plotting some escapade. Maurice knew better than to interrupt him at such moments. He was making his plans in pictures, not in words, seeing before his half-shut eyes all that he had heard of those furious charges of the Cossack tribes that had driven him as a baby from Prague.

He had determined to revive as much as possible the shock tactics of the mediæval cavalry, when the stallion himself, armed with spikes on his forehead and knees, screaming and tearing the foe with his teeth, was as much a weapon and a fighter as his rider. That had been dropped since the terrifying invention of gunpowder, and even Gustavus' idea of cavalry was only that of mounted infantry who should get as near as possible to their foe before they fired.

'But why fire at all?' demanded Rupert, 'why break the charge just when you've worked it up? I'll have no volley till the enemy is in retreat – if then! Let the sword, and – more – the horse, do the work.'

If Maurice, fresh from the latest Continental schools of arms, was startled, the conservative English commanders were horrified. To ride straight into the ranks of your enemy, allowing them all the advantage of firearms and not use them yourself, it was merely treating honest Englishmen as gun fodder, and none of the commanders would hear of it.

'You will hear well enough in battle when I give the command,' said Rupert, and they perceived that 'Prince Rupert could not want of his will.'

His methods were soon put to the test. He and his officers were surprised in a field near Powick Bridge, a little way from Worcester. He had left some of his force in the town to strengthen a convoy of sconce pots and silver plate which the

186

dons of Oxford were sending to the King: and hearing that
there were some enemy cavalry hovering somewhere south of the
town, he had gone to look for them, but could not find any
trace of them. The weather had turned from a wintry August to
a grilling September; they had taken off their armour and coats,
laid aside their weapons and were some of them asleep.

Rupert was watching the stream below glinting here and there
through the trees in the slanting light of the evening sun behind
him. In the lazy warmth, a strange inertia fell on him, relic of
the long days at Linz when he had nothing to do but watch the
river go by. He thought, not of his frantic activities these last
few weeks, not of his quest today, but of bathes he had had in
English rivers – the smell of bedstraw hot in the sun as now,
then the plunge into cool earthy water under overhanging
branches, into shadow deep as a cave – a kingfisher flashing blue
past him in the sunlight beyond the shade – a trout that he had
caught in his hand – a moorhen's nest with eight speckled eggs,
and the leaves of yellow flags pulled and interwoven by the hen
into a hiding-place over it.

Suddenly he saw through the trees the glint of steel above
that of water, – two abreast, for the bridge was narrow, along
the little lane that led from it, came horsemen who rapidly
deployed from behind the trees into the meadow below, more
and more, a heavy weight of cavalry. He sprang up with a shout
of 'the Roundheads!' and vaulted on to the nearest horse. The
cry was taken up, the scattered Cavaliers clambered on to the
first saddles they could find, and their startled men behind them
saw the gay-coloured officers hurling in a body down the slope,
shouting 'For the King!' and headed by those two young limbs
of Satan who were waving their rapiers and galloping straight
into the thick of the enemy.

Their men thundered after them, and the Parliament troop,
nearly a thousand strong, heavily armed as they were, resound-
ing tinnily and apparently imperviously to the Royalists' blows,
yet broke utterly under the shock of a force half their number.
They were driven back across the bridge and along the Upton
road, losing their commander, about sixty men, and five or six
colours; they fled headlong for more than nine miles without
even looking back to see if they were still pursued. Some swam
across the Severn, losing many of their helmets and swords in
the river. On the opposite shore they met a hundred of Essex's
picked bodyguard who, aghast in their turn at seeing their

comrades weaponless and their heads 'unpotted', were swept along with them in their panic.

Rupert lost only five troopers, but every single officer except himself was wounded, and Maurice badly, in the head. His horses, not so good as his enemy's, had to abandon the chase after taking many of their horses and some Scottish officers as prisoners, a useful point, since it proved that the Parliament were employing 'foreigners' though they were outraged at the idea of Irish soldiery for the King.

Digby and other courtly detractors pointed out what Rupert knew well enough, that the Prince should have been court-martialled for letting his little troop be caught napping like that. But his instant reaction to danger being to attack instead of to defend, he had turned what should have been disaster into victory. His horsemen, without armour, pistols or directions, had, by the sheer instinct to follow their leader, put a well-prepared and heavily armoured force of twice their size to abject flight.

The happy confidence of the Parliament that in sending out their large and well-furnished army to seize the King and disperse his little rabble of followers, they would be finishing the war at the first blow, was now shattered. 'It is such a blot,' wrote one of the Parliamentarian captains, 'as nothing but some desperate exploit will wipe out' – and the saying was rumoured abroad.

'Let 'em find their Rupert first,' laughed Rupert's men, '*then* they may look for their exploit!' There was no holding them now in their pride of their leader.

'My Prince Paladin,' the King called him.

All the younger nobles and officers clamoured to serve under him, even to a half-brother of Digby's, to Digby's disgust. Rupert got more letters of admiration than he could deal with, entreating him – 'to command my attendance and I will break through all difficulties to come to you'.

' 'Tis not advance of title I covet but your commission.'

'I must confess I have neither desire nor affection to wait upon any other general.'

To swear by his name became a favourite army oath – 'Rupert take you!' was equivalent to 'the devil take you!' and spread through the countryside so that his old childish nickname, 'the Devil', was now revived everywhere, and in terror-stricken earnest. Everything about him helped his spectacular and mysterious reputation – his height, his abrupt and taciturn manner, his scarlet cavalry cloak, his big black Barbary horse, 'the Corsair', his fierce white dog, commonly supposed to be a poodle because of the thick mane of hair on his shoulders, although he was so big and strong that he pulled down as many as half a dozen buck for his master in one morning when he went hunting.

How was it one heard of the Prince as having been in different places at great distances from each other at almost the same moment? How was it he alone among his officers was not wounded at Powick Bridge, though he charged in ahead of everybody among the enemy with neither helmet nor breastplate, and only a sword in his hand? How was it his brother, who had been reported dead from a head wound that would certainly have killed most men, was next heard of as 'abroad and merry'?

Even his marksmanship was unnatural. He had put a bullet from a horseman's pistol through the tail of a weathercock on a church steeple sixty yards off, and when his uncle declared it must be just a lucky chance, he did it again with his second shot. Clearly his connection with gunpowder must have been established in another and lower world.

Rupert the Devil had his familiar spirit, the dog who sat in the King's own chair at council and to whom the roaring young blades paid almost as much court as to the Prince, drinking his health on their knees and promoting him to 'Sergeant Major General Boy', and 'the Four-legged Cavalier'. Boy had been taught by his young master to 'die for the King', but to 'hold up his Malignant Leg at Pym'. He helped make a showy target for Parliamentary press propaganda in London. Pamphlets poured out against Rupert, with crudely printed little black pictures of him on horseback with a sword in one hand and a pistol in the other, and Boy prancing in front of him; he was described variously as 'a loose wild gentleman', the Mad Prince, the Wizard Prince, and Prince Robber.

It was useful propaganda for Rupert's own side, for it made his name so widely feared that the Parliament troops would not hold any place where he was likely to march; and recruits went on pouring into the King's army, whose spirits were enormously raised since that grey gusty evening when the King's Standard had been laid low in the mud.

And this new hope and cheer were all due to one young man. But he was still young enough to be hurt by the injustice of his enemies – and sometimes as it seemed to him the injustice of his friends.

He had arbitrarily levied a loan of £500 from the city of Leicester (he had tried to make it £2,000) in a letter which carried its sting in its tail, for Rupert was not proof against the feminine practice of postscripts, though in this case his PS was masculine enough, being a hint that unless he got the money, 'I shall tomorrow appear before your town in such a posture with horse, foot and cannon as shall make you know it is more safe to obey than to resist His Majesty's command.'

The King had had to apologize to the Mayor and disclaim his nephew's high-handed action. Rupert could see no sense in it. Parliament, alarmed by the reports of Powick Bridge and the King's continual fresh recruits, had begun to raise forced levies and confiscations ('*They* take men and money by force and yet you won't let me lift a beggarly £500!'); they had refused to make peace unless the Royalists and 'other malignant persons' (*i.e.* Rupert and Maurice) were made to pay for every penny the war had cost. Why should the Royalists alone carry on the war by voluntary contributions only? It was damned unfair on the loyal contributors.

But his hard common sense was too logical to appeal to his English comrades. 'That money business at Leicester' was quoted by Digby as only another proof (together with his taste for low company and for knowing his job with professional thoroughness) that the Prince was not quite a gentleman.

Rupert was mystified by the complaints against him. His troops had got to live on the country, hadn't they? He always gave a receipt signed with his own name for future settlement. Nor did he understand the journalistic mind sufficiently to see that the English variation of his name as Prince Robert was quite enough in itself to account for his being referred to in print as Prince Robber. (What was it Carl had answered in the coach at Oxford over those two lost spoons? 'They haven't started calling us the Robber Princes yet' – 'They will, Rupert, they will.')

Then there was his reputation for cruelty.

Ladies left alone in their country-houses, with their husbands at the war, interrupted the even tenor of their letters on the marriages of Doll and Mag and Bet, and the proper way to make broom beer and Daffy's Elixir, with a little start and a sigh, as the quill pen fluttered desperately on – 'My fear is most of Prince Rupert, for they say he has little mercy when he comes.'

Yet Mrs Purefoy and her daughters could give a very different testimony.

He arrived at Caldecot House with a troop of five hundred on a fine Sunday morning early in September, and summoned it to surrender, for it was a garrison held in the name of Mr Purefoy, a Member of Parliament, who was away on active service against the King. The summons was refused and Rupert gave the order to attack.

Church bells were ringing in the distance; a soft misty sunshine was spread over the scene like the bloom on a plum; the place had ripened through nearly two centuries of peace. The house, originally a Norman castle but with added modern wings of red brick, raised its battlemented head over heavy trees and roofs of outhouses, golden with lichen moss, sure testimony to the long quiet years that had added each ring of bark and each mellow brick outside the fortified walls. Generations had gone by since these had last stood for defence in war.

Over the courtyard arch was painted an inscription, partly overgrown and nearly rubbed out by wind and weather, but Rupert could just make out the words, 'For God and the King'. He had seen the same on the walls of other country-houses whose inhabitants had last gone to war when they followed their King to France or Scotland, fighting beneath his banner at Agincourt or Flodden Field. It was strange to see it on the walls of a house held for the Parliament against the King.

His men forced the gate of the outer court, but as they did so the defenders behind the stone walls picked off three of his officers and several men. The assailants, firing blindly with their horse-pistols at an unseen enemy, were exposed to a thin but incessant musket fire within close range. It did deadly work. The attack was called off, renewed, and lasted several hours; the men began to grumble and beg that they should leave it; it was a hopeless and far too costly job – look at the numbers they had lost already.

But Rupert only sucked his finger and held it up to tell the way of the wind, which had been rising steadily all the afternoon. As he had thought, it was blowing straight from the farmyard to the house; he ordered one or two of the barns to be fired, and under cover of the clouds of smoke he was able to push his advance right up to the doors.

They were flung open from within; the house was surrendered; a little elderly lady in a grey silk dress, the Sunday
dress of nearly all elderly ladies throughout the country, came
forward and went down on her knees before the Prince with a
certain stiff deliberation, due in part to reluctance but more to
rheumatism.

'Your Highness,' she said, 'I surrender my husband's house
into your hands. I beg you to spare the lives of my garrison.'

'Have any been lost?'

'None, sir.'

'Then you owe us about a score.'

'We have not the half of that number with which to pay
you.'

'What, you have not had ten men to hold this house?'

'Not five. My son-in-law, Mr Abbot, and three serving-men
are all the male garrison. But we have twelve muskets, and my
two daughters and two of the three maidservants kept them all
reloaded as fast as they were fired.'

'Did the third maid shoot?'

'She was too frightened to touch a firearm even to load it, but
she was useful in melting down the pewter plates and saucepans
for bullets.'

Rupert gave the enemy general an amazed and wary glance.
'Four men only? I'll swear there were five muskets at the same
time in play.'

In his astonishment he had forgotten to tell her to rise, but
now at his outstretched hand, she did so, stiffly, while a faint
pink stole up over her round cheek-bones. 'I used to shoot buck
with my crossbow,' she said, 'and as I had a good eye, I thought
for some time past I might as well keep it in with a musket
also.'

'Will you take a command in my troop?' said Rupert, 'I'd
rather have you than most officers I have met in any war.'

And he repeated his offer to Mr Abbot in all seriousness, once
he had got his men clear of the courtyard – without loot or
further damage – no easy job, for they complained that they had
had all their work and the death of several of their number for
nothing.

Mr Abbot's offer from the Prince was declined, to his
chagrin. He could not understand how people like these could
take up arms against their King and on behalf of grudging
hypocritical curs like the Parliament.

Mrs Purefoy, who modestly began every argument with 'My husband says', said that it was not because they admired this particular Parliament, in fact they had not at all agreed with some of its decisions, but that if the King beat the Parliament he would certainly destroy its power for good and all and reduce it to nonentity.

'I've never heard any Englishman admire a Parliament in being,' said Rupert, 'and yet you must fight for a mythical one that might one day exist. It must be because it gives a hope to each one of you to be sitting there one day yourself and talking politics.'

'Not to me, Your Highness,' said Mrs Purefoy.

He looked at her keen profile, her alert and combative eye. She must have been between fifty and sixty but was as wiry and intelligent as a terrier.

'Yes, to you too, Mrs Purefoy. If Englishwomen go on talking politics as well as you've just talked them to me, you'll not be satisfied till you too are sitting in Parliament.'

'Your Highness could not have expressed more perfectly your contempt for politics,' she replied.

He flushed, for he had thought he was being rather gallant, and he had evidently only been boorish. But his admiration for her prevented his resenting her rebuke. She had resisted his attack on the house for several hours and killed some of his men, so she had a right to say what she liked, damn her!

'Yes, it's true I despise politics,' he said, 'and I'm told I do not sufficiently admire women.' He took her hand and stood looking down at the plain little figure. 'Well, here's one I admire'; he stooped down and kissed her hand, then bowed to the rest of the company and walked out of the hall to rejoin his followers. He looked back at the door for one instant on the warmth and brightness of family life that was already resuming its sway after the accident of its brief siege. The maidservants had been ordered to set the place to rights and were making up the fire and removing the furniture from the shuttered windows; young Mrs Abbot, exhausted, had sunk on to a chair and was surreptitiously clinging to her husband's hand, while her sister brought her water.

It was their mother who saw the Prince to the door, entirely unaffected by the late contest, except that a wisp of grey hair had escaped from her cap and lay as yet undetected across her forehead.

'Poor boy, some woman has been unkind to him,' she said as she came back into the hall, then caught sight of herself in the little mirror her husband had brought from Venice, and scolded her daughters for not telling her that her hair was untidy.

CHAPTER FIVE

RICHARD SHUCKBURGH, Esq. of Warwickshire, out with his pack of hounds for his Saturday's hunting in the misty mid-October sunshine, met a great gathering of gentlemen riding towards him, who stopped him and asked if he had seen any troops in this part of the country.

'Troops?' he repeated, amazed as he became aware that more and more men were riding up over the brow of the hill, 'why, what are you?'

'The King's army,' they told him, and there in their midst was a grave gentleman on a superb horse, and from the respect they were all paying him he knew this must be the King himself. Off went his hat, and he bowed so low he nearly fell off his horse – but he still did not know what it was all about.

They told him there was a war on between the King and the Parliament and they were expecting the first big battle now at almost any minute – in fact he and his pack of hounds had probably been hunting plumb between the two armies.

Well, it was the first Mr Shuckburgh had heard of any war; he'd heard tell from time to time that folk were making trouble in London, but they were always making trouble there. He was a peaceable man himself and cared nothing for politics, and he had not been obliged to go to market these two months past, so he had been a bit out of things, but now as sure as his name was Dick Shuckburgh he would go straight home and put his hounds back into the kennels and collect his tenants together and what billhooks and hayforks they could lay their hands on, and come after the King's army as fast as they could follow, and pray Heaven they'd join it before the big battle began.

'Bring your hounds too,' called out a young gentleman on a big black horse who looked rather like the King (and bore himself just like one) but drawn out from a delicate miniature figure to a mighty size and strength – 'we might get some hunting after the battle.' There was a shout of laughter near him, and

194

'Trust Prince Robber to think of that!' called out some of the fine gentlemen – and 'Your Highness has added Prince Poacher to your other names already, we know that!'

But it seemed quite reasonable to Mr Shuckburgh that he should bring his hounds on the campaign, and he promised to do so. 'Come True, come Trusty, come Tripe, come Trixie,' they heard his voice and his huntsman's hallooing over the common, while his hounds' tails flickered and glanced away like running water in the pale sunlight.

Next day came the warning of a very different hunting. Digby had reconnoitred with four hundred horse and reported that the country was completely clear of the enemy. But Rupert's quarter-master went into Wormleighton to arrange quarters for the troops and crashed into Essex's quarter-master who had come on the same errand, promptly took a dozen prisoners, and learned from them that the bulk of Essex's army was at Kineton, only four miles off. So back they came just as the King's army had settled down for the night, expecting to get their first real rest the next day, with the news that Essex's army was close at their heels, and unless they wished to look as though they were running away, they must turn and fight them.

No rest next day then nor even that night, and no chance to forage for food though many of the men had had nothing but a little bread for the last forty-eight hours, and some not that. And now, just as they had turned in, they were beaten up out of their quarters and told they had got to take up their positions in the nipping early frost of an October night and wait for the dawn.

There would have been far less grumbling and shivering if they had been going to make a surprise attack at dawn with their gay rider Rupert the Devil at their head, and a good chance to wipe out the entire Parliament army at one blow. Rupert knew that, and urged it passionately.

He had good reason for his confidence. In just one month he had managed to convert 800 raw, badly mounted, unpaid, un-trained, and all but unarmed men into a well-knit, well-drilled force of 3,800 horse.

And Essex had no notion he had come up so near to them or he'd not have been in such a hurry, for he hadn't got all his enormous army together now – 'there are two of his regiments still behind, under old What's-his-name who wouldn't pay his tax.'

'John Hampden,' they corrected coldly, but Rupert didn't wait to hear the name, he was continuing a quarrel with Lord Falkland, who had quite rightly objected to the Prince's refusal to take instructions from him though he was the King's secretary.

'In neglecting me,' said the little man stoutly, 'you neglect the King,' and his sad anxious eyes turned valiantly upwards like those of a small water spaniel at a very big mastiff.

'I'll neglect God and the Devil both,' Rupert burst out, 'until we get this plan of attack settled in the right way.'

'The right way meaning Your Highness' way?' sneered Digby.

'Yes,' said Rupert.

Old Lord Lindsey had resigned in a huff his command as General-in-Chief, since Rupert and the cavalry had been excepted from it, and had gone back to his own regiment. The general command had been given to Patrick Ruthven, equally old and practised in both Swedish and Scottish wars, but generally drunk and always deaf. He heard not a word of the discussion that was now raging round him, but nodded very wisely to completely opposite advice. Finally it was decided that it was impossible to make a night march in order to risk a surprise attack when the troops were so tired and hungry. Besides, they were now holding a very good stance on high ground above the Vale of Red Horse, and it would be idiotic to throw away such an advantage.

Rupert's position when in private with the King had been virtually that of Commander-in-Chief, and certainly with full command over the King himself, whose letter he now had in his pocket dated '4 o'clock this Sunday morning.

'Nephew, I have given order as you have desired; so I doubt not all the foot and cannon will be at Edgehill betimes this morning, where you will also find

'Your loving Uncle and faithful friend, Charles R.'

That was the sort of letter an uncle ought to write!

But now in open council there was opportunity for every one of the commanders who had quarrelled with Rupert to challenge his position, and moreover he found that his uncle's support, on which it depended, was veering from one point of the compass to the other. Again and again he was reminded that he was a foreigner who did not know the country or the character of his men, above all that he was years younger than anybody

196

present. Raging, he was forced to agree to the general plan and wait for dawn on the slope of Edgehill.

When it came it revealed what he had suspected overnight, that the slope was too steep to admit of the cavalry charging down it, and that though nothing could be better as a position for defence, it was useless for attack. They would have to throw it away and descend into the plain before they could begin. And though Rupert had got all his cavalry massed, they had still to bring up the rest of the army, and it was not until well past noon that the descent could begin, with all Essex's army spread out below, not more than a mile off. The advantageous position that everyone was insisting on last night would have to be thrown away before the battle began.

Rupert was in a black rage, but at least he had got his way over the formation of the cavalry, which was drawn up only three deep, and not in the old six-line formation of the Dutch that Lindsey had insisted on, until at last he had thrown up his command. And Rupert's further innovation of charging without firing, which had caused such opposition, must of necessity be carried out since they were so short of ammunition. But he was perfectly confident of the ultimate result and so were the other cavalry leaders; they had seen how the Roundheads ran for it at Powick Bridge; they were nothing but base tailors and tradesmen who could not stand up to a man of spirit, damme, so Lord Wilmot swore, who had the left wing of cavalry while Rupert had the right, and had fortified himself with so much spirit from the brandy bottle that his young commander hoped sardonically he would know the enemy when he saw them.

Old Sir Jacob Astley, major-general of the infantry, whom Rupert had met at Breda (the 'honest little ape' of his mother's letters), was not so confident as 'all these gay young lads'. He ordered his regiment to stand to attention for a prayer, 'as if he were a damned Roundhead,' complained Wilmot, but the prayer was far briefer than theirs.

'Lord, I shall be very busy this day. I may forget Thee, but do not Thou forget me. March on, boys.'

On either side the cannon thundered across the sunlit haze of the plain to declare that the battle had now begun. Banners of every colour were waving over the different regiments; blue, orange, scarlet, green and yellow flaunted the fact that here were Englishmen about to take each other's lives.

197

The King looked long through his telescope at the army spread out before him. At last he laid it down. 'I never saw the rebels in a body before,' he said.

The higher ground for the King's army was so far from being an advantage that for the most part their cannon balls went clean over the enemy's heads and dug themselves deep in the fields behind. It was three o'clock by now and so late for an autumn day's fighting that many were advising postponing it till the next day.

'Those who say so are speaking from full bellies,' cried Rupert, who knew that the common soldiery would get no food till they had won it at the point of the sword. Another night's starved waiting was more than flesh and blood could stand and he would not even hear it considered. He rode down the ranks from one wing of the cavalry to the other, reminding them that as soon as he gave the word of command they were to charge as close together as possible with their swords in their hands, and receive the enemy's fire without waiting to fire a shot in return. 'Charge them then in God's name and the King's! Drive them from the field, and the day is ours.'

It was what he had urged in council. The Royalist foot would then advance and clear up the work. He knew that with their inferior numbers and inexperience the simplest and boldest methods were the best. And the men, like their horses, were champing with impatience, hunger and cold.

A regiment raised by Parliament for service in Ireland, who had deeply resented being used against the King, seized this spectacular moment for changing sides; rode out from the Parliament ranks, fired their pistols into the ground and wheeled their horses round to join in the attack against their former side; its leader shouted to Rupert as he galloped up that his name was Sir Faithful Fortescue.

'Faithful you have been, after your fashion,' Rupert answered, 'but for God's sake tell your men to tear off their confounded orange scarves, or ours will be stabbing them in the mêlée.'

Then he gave the order. 'Use your swords alone. Charge!'

Orange scarves were the prevailing mark of the Parliament army, and as they saw their own orange scarves riding back on them, horror and dismay were added to the dread they already had of Prince Rupert's cavalry.

Now all that they had dreaded was upon them; they saw that

cavalry come wheeling round from their right front, swinging inwards towards them, they felt the earth shaking under the thudding of their horses' hoofs, louder and louder – but now surely they would stop and fire their carbines as cavalry should, before advancing again in the recognized manner at a good round trot. But no – these devils came charging on at a hand-gallop, faster and faster, gaining impetus all the way, roaring and cursing and brandishing their bright steel till they crashed right in among their foes, driving the first rank in upon the second till the whole line broke in utter confusion with men and horses going down right and left, and the remainder wheeling round and galloping back to Kineton hell-for-leather, scattering their own regiments of foot and sweeping their own reserves along with them and part of their infantry, on past Kineton, some of them even on to London.

Rupert had tried to rally his men and return to the battlefield long before then, but it was of the very nature of that deadly charge, inculcated by him through weeks of hard training, that once launched it was difficult to recall.

Its exultant impetus had carried the whole of the Royalist cavalry forward in one surging wave, sweeping with it the troop of gentlemen rankers under Sir John Byron, who should have kept close round the King, but had been fuming at their nick-name of the King's Show Troop and determined to show their pluck equal to Rupert's Royal Horse Guards. On they all hammered, hacking down their enemies as they galloped for more than two miles, driving them through Kineton and on into the open country beyond until they were brought up by John Hampden and his two regiments as they came up belatedly to join the battle.

This was the instant of their proof and their victory, they were certain that the whole Parliament army was routed, they were mad with excitement, ravenous with hunger, and in Kineton they found Essex's baggage wagons crammed with provisions and plunder.

By the time Rupert had beaten them off and got them back to the Vale of Red Horse, the frosty blue dusk made it hard to see what was going on. Whatever it was, these scattered groups of infantry, and here and there Parliamentary horse, fighting together in a thick cluster, could not mean the complete crumpling of the Roundheads' battle front that he had expected to find. All the different-coloured coats of the regiments made it almost impossible to distinguish friends from foes – a few regiments were standing firm and unbroken, but for the most part men were mixed up in inextricable confusion, and many had been cut down or taken prisoner by those whom they had taken for their own side. The King's bodyguard under Byron were nowhere to be seen, and the main body of infantry round the King had been suddenly attacked by the very bodies of cavalry which Wilmot was supposed to have accounted for.

For Wilmot also had charged on the left on to Kineton, Digby blindly following with his reserves, but had gone so wide that he seemed to have driven through thin air for the most part, missing the Roundhead cavalry reserves altogether. He had remarked airily after his charge that the ground was as hummocky as a camel's back and easy for men to hide in, but even Falkland, who had chosen to fight with him rather than Rupert, could not believe that it was hummocky enough to conceal about six hundred men on horseback.

These six hundred or so of Roundhead cavalry had in their turn charged through the Royalist ranks, cut the traces of the King's cannon, and rounded on the line from the rear. The King himself, with Richmond close beside him, had been in considerable danger, fighting gallantly with his own hand and encouraging the men round him who at one point were urging him to fly. The Royal Standard-bearer, Sir Edmund Verney, had been killed and the Standard taken, though they had had to cut off his hand with it.

It was a bewildering finish to what had appeared to be a triumphant victory. Rupert did his best to muster his men together for another charge, but they were exhausted, their horses were blown and sweating, their tails quivering. Only Wilmot's force, having had no real fighting, were still fairly fresh and in their ranks. He was urged to make another charge, but could not see what all the fuss was about, now the battle was practically over.

'The day is ours,' he said, mopping his forehead with a handkerchief far too beautiful for its usage, 'let us live to enjoy the fruits of it.' And the word went round.

But was the day theirs? Not a man in either army could really feel confident of it.

It was growing too dark to go on fighting. Somebody called Mr John Smith had ridden through the enemy's ranks, wearing an orange scarf torn from the dead foe, trotted up to Essex's secretary, who was holding the Royal Standard, told him that he was only a civilian and a penman, and must hand it over at once, and then coolly took it back to his own side. He was knighted for his exploit on the battlefield, and so was Mr Richard Shuckburgh who had fought doggedly all day, although in utter perplexity as to what was happening – in which he did not much differ from his commanders.

The King's two sons, Charles, the Prince of Wales, and James, the Duke of York, aged twelve and nine, had been left on top of the hill in charge of Dr William Harvey, who was so much interested in a new theory of his concerning the circulation of the blood that he continued to work it out on paper instead of watching the course of the battle. So that he and the two Princes would have been taken prisoner by a stray force of Essex's, had not Mr Hyde noticed that their position was becoming dangerous, and got them away in time.

Old Lord Lindsey stood no longer in Rupert's way. Mortally wounded, he had been taken prisoner and treated with great consideration by the Parliament commanders, who sent to ask what they could do for him. In reply he raised himself on his elbow and reproached them bitterly for their disloyalty in stirring up rebellion against their King. Cold-hearted knaves who could eat the King's bread and then turn against him, on the one side, and on the other, hot-blooded young fools who must needs try and bring their new-fangled notions into warfare – what would the country come to between them?

He had only a few hours of that bitter autumn night to consider the question before he died.

*   *   *

'Good night, Mr Hyde,' said a husky, gentle, yet rather discordant voice.

'Good night, my lord – Falkland is it not? This mist thickens the dark.'

'It's crept into all our minds.'

'Well, the night at least is certain – that common friend to weary and dismayed armies. It's parted them, even if no certain victory has.'

'My new commander thinks his victory certain. Listen to that.'

A drunken chorus reeled out of the makeshift tent contrived for Wilmot and his friends.

'The Prince is not there?' said Hyde.

'No, he'll not drink. And he hates Wilmot as much now as Digby.'

'He hates too many, and does not care how plainly he shows it. No man can afford to despise the affections of men too stoically – if he does, he will find himself unfortunate.'

'You are generally right, Ned. Yet I doubt if you have said – or will ever say – the last word to be said about Prince Rupert.'

The chubby, confident lawyer wheeled round on the minute form beside him in the darkness. (Lord Falkland was no taller than the King.)

'I'll say that the man is a strange creature,' admitted Hyde with the deference he paid only to his sensitive friend. 'But I thought you too had quarrelled with him.'

'I have, and am the less likely to know him truly. Can the truth ever come out in a quarrel?'

'It must in this great quarrel of the country. No one could have been more eager for reform than either you or I, we have worked for it all our lives. But you've said it yourself, that your great reverence for Parliaments in the abstract has been destroyed by the utter disingenuousness this Parliament has shown. They have set out to destroy law, with the word "law" always in their mouths.'

'And they will keep it there. Do any of us, party or individual, ever admit the true cause of our quarrel? We complain of the Prince, that he is a wild and arrogant, probably a bloodthirsty youth. But do we ever say that he is a superb young animal, and that I am too short and you will soon be too fat?'

'I see no occasion to say it,' observed Hyde coldly.

'Precisely. Nor will this Parliament ever see occasion to admit that they forced the horror of civil war on this country in order to abuse the privileges they were afraid the King might abuse.'

Falkland was well launched now and almost happy. As they paced the crisp frost-laden grass together, they might have imagined themselves once again on the lawns of his beautiful country house in Oxfordshire where Ned Hyde had been encouraged to bring down reading parties of clever young legal and literary friends. It had been a modern symposium of the most advanced and humane thinkers of the day. To reason, to speak freely, to discover the truth, it was so the world would now be governed; even the disturbances at Westminster were but the growing-pains of an ever-increasing liberty of thought, and were greatly alleviated, at a distance, by the comfort of speculative discussion.

But the darkness could not shelter their illusion; all round them they could hear the groans of the wounded and dying. This was no longer the modern world; civilization had slipped and fallen once again; England was following the rest of Europe back into barbarism.

*   *   *

Rupert's tense excitement would not let him sleep. He sat by a crackling fire of branches with Boy crouched between his knees for warmth. The sharp tang of the frosty autumn night, of mud and of apple orchards in the mist, stole in like the icy breath of a ghost across the warm smell of burning wood.

A fiery exultation tingled in his blood as though he were still clamped on to his saddle with the Corsair stretching out in full gallop under him, and the enemy flying before him and his men sweeping along all round him, all as he had planned and had trained them to do – oh, they were grand fellows, these English, they would make the finest cavalry in the world, he had always known it and now he was proving it, he was doing it – there was nothing he could not do with them, they had swept everything before them, they could sweep on to London now that the road to it had been laid open, and he could finish the war at a blow and put his uncle on his throne again and then go off to look for other adventures, for the world was wide and he was young and he had all his life before him to do what he liked with it.

A terrific sense of new life surged through his veins; the long imprisonment that had cramped every form of initiative lay far behind him, he had crawled out of it like some newborn insect emerging damp and untried from its chrysalis, and now with one rattle of his sabre wings he had darted with dragonfly brilliance into the swift power that his enemies had described as 'a perpetual motion', a wildfire that 'flew with great fury'. He had in a few weeks proved himself leader in this war, and he was fighting it, not for that swine Carl, but for his beloved uncle.

But through the fierce glow that burned within him there stole from the surrounding night a thin cold breath that whispered to him things he did not want to hear. It was no good shirking it – what was it he must think of? He had won all his part of the battle, but the others had not won theirs. Curse Wilmot! – but it was no good laying the blame on others. He had gone a bit mad himself, hurtling on and on in pursuit of the enemy, and when he started to pull up his rascals and get them back, he had had the devil's own job to haul them off the baggage carts, and no wonder, for they had done their work magnificently and here was their reward.

But what a mess when they returned! How had it happened, and why? There had been no co-ordination, and the reason was simple – lack of a Commander-in-Chief. He had seen to it that there was no one from whom he himself had to take orders. But he could not impose his orders on other branches of the army. He and his regiments must do their work unaided and if possible unhindered by the rest. And they must do it quickly. For that clumsy unenterprising army they had attacked today had at least been an army, acting from a centre, with its cavalry in co-ordination with its infantry.

There had been a good brain behind that attack of the Roundhead cavalry reserves – a cool brain – since it could operate after the best part of its own side had been smashed. Whose was it? Not Essex's!

Yes, there was good material there, once they had found a man who could make use of it. At any moment that might happen, and old Essex, with his pipe and his stammer (no affected copy of the King's but his own sad inheritance of fear and distrust), might have to give way to some new commander in whom the war had discovered military genius.

At present he knew there was no one who could touch himself. But he must use his hour while he had it.

*   *   *

Less than two miles away Mr Hampden walked up and down the plain with his cousin, Captain Cromwell of Essex's horse.

'That was a bad business,' said Mr Hampden.

His companion's assenting comment was not blasphemous but quite unprintable. He was a thick-set middle-aged man with the appearance of a country gentleman who prides himself on being a simple farmer.

'Essex ought to fight again tomorrow,' said Mr Hampden.

Captain Cromwell's answer was again unprintable, this time because it was a snort. But the snort became a chuckle and presently he said, 'Did you see him at the end of today – snatching a pike from one of his men and swearing to die in the ranks since the battle and the whole cause were lost? *He* a commander! Let him stick to being a lord! And Lord Wharton was one of our stout fellows who hid from their charge in a saw-pit – did you know that?'

Mr Hampden showed a wish to change the subject at the first mention of lords. 'By the way,' he observed thoughtfully, 'the battle *was* lost, wasn't it?'

'It's not lost till we say so. If our men have no guts, we must give 'em 'em,' he added in a growl that was lost in his boots.

Hampden demurred. 'Your own little lot and the rest of those cavalry reserves had the guts to drive in on top of the King's own guards and all but take him prisoner.'

'*After* their charge had gone by. D'you know how they missed us? Because we snatched off our orange scarves and shouted "For the King!"'

'So that was it! Well, our men will have to learn how to face a cavalry charge some time.'

'They must learn to do more than that. They must learn to make one. To attack – always attack – I see now why that is the only way to win a battle. *Their* cavalry never paused to fire until our miserable horse was in full flight – they scarcely waited to use their swords – their horses, ridden at that speed, were their best weapon. I shall remember that.'

'You'll never get ploughboys and tapsters and serving-men to show the spirit of those young fellows today. Even their troopers are mostly gentlemen's sons, younger sons, persons of quality.'

'Then,' said his cousin, 'we must get men of a spirit that will go on as far as gentlemen will go.'

'How far is that?' asked Mr Hampden with a sigh. 'This war may go farther than any of us can see.'

'That may well be,' replied the other, 'for you never go so far as when you don't know where you are going.'

'Oliver,' said his cousin, 'I never know when you are speaking with heaven-born wisdom, or merely being hazy.'

*   *   *

'James, are you asleep?'

'I *was*.'

'Liar! That whisper couldn't have waked you. I wish I knew where Cousin Rupert is.'

'Charles, what have you got in your head?'

'Well, you know how he and Cousin Maurice stole out at

night at the siege of Breda and discovered the enemy's plans. Why shouldn't *we* do that?'

'Perhaps they haven't got any plans.'

'Well, they'll have to start making some. Cousin Rupert's beaten their heads off.'

'They weren't beaten in the middle. Mr Hyde said so.'

'He's only a lawyer and he always thinks he knows everything.'

'He got us away from the enemy. Dr Harvey's an ass with that old blood. Does it really move, Charles?'

'Certainly it does. It flows bad up one leg and good down the other. I think science is interesting. Cousin Rupert knows a deal of it. He says gunpowder can be made ten times more powerful. I wish he would do it at once and end the war.'

'I like the war. It's better than doing lessons with the girls at St James's.'

'I don't like these beasts trying to turn my father off his throne – and me.'

'And me then.'

'No. I'll be King but not you. You're only my younger brother.'

But James was asleep again and in another instant Charles was too.

*   *   *

The moon slid down into the mist. In his coach, surrounded by his guards, the King stared out at the night, 'that common friend to weary and dismayed armies,' which now lay in a black pall over the whole plain.

CHAPTER SIX

'THE ROAD to London is open. Let me push on at once with the cavalry and three thousand of the infantry, and I will seize Westminster and the rebel part of the Parliament and occupy Whitehall Palace until Your Majesty comes up with the remainder of the army. Tomorrow night you shall sleep in your own chamber at Whitehall.'

It was 'early morning courage', the most difficult of all. Rupert's voice still had the ring of victory in it; his eyes, though smarting with lack of sleep, were bright and confident; the tireless strength of the young giant was exasperating to those weary and discouraged men who stood on the cold hillside in the raw morning light after the battle. Many of them had had no sleep at all that night, some had wounds with the blood dried and congealed on them. They were stiff and aching with cold, their eyes smarting, their mouths dry and foul; they longed for a feather-bed and peace to thaw out and forget the last twenty-four hours.

There was nothing good to look back on that they could see; it had been a horribly bloody business; out of the thirty thousand men in the two armies, nearly six thousand must now lie dead upon the field – so the clergymen were saying who had been busy all night trying to administer to the dying – and of those nearly all have been cut down by hand. Artillery and musket fire had been feeble in rivalry to the desperate courage of these men, determined to prove themselves on the battlefield, many of them before the very eyes of their King. More than sixty corpses of the Royal Guards alone had been found heaped on the spot where Sir Edmund Verney had had the Royal Standard hacked from his dying clutch. Yet what had this frantic valour achieved? The losses seemed almost equally heavy on both sides, and both armies were pretty much where they had been before the battle began. It was true that Essex had been foiled in his objective, which was to prevent the King from obtaining the London road. It lay open to the Royalists' line of march, and now that young firebrand Rupert was urging them to press forward on it at once.

But nobody could feel the vigour or the hope for such an undertaking; how could they get the men together, all scattered as they were, half-frozen, half-starved, crawling miserably behind that stricken field in search of their own officers and troops? One after the other the officers in that improvised council of war pointed out how impossible it would be to rally their men and put enough spirit into them for such an enterprise.

Yet Rupert's own spirit seemed enough of itself to create an army out of these broken units; he had already got his own men together, and as he spoke again, it seemed he would be able to inspire even this chill and dispirited group. He urged them that now was the moment to strike home, now while Essex was still staggering from the blow they had given him, and before London had time to complete its defences. London had been their objective from the first, and their advantage that it was so definite. The Parliament could only aim at capturing the King's person, but the King's aim was to get back into his capital, and never was there so good a chance of doing it as now.

'Give me twenty-four hours,' he cried again, 'and the King is back in his palace tomorrow!'

Could he fire these sheep? They had not been sheep yesterday, they had fought like lions then – but he knew what it was like the morning after a fight, he and Maurice had had a job with their own men this morning, but that was done. Now, if only he could stir the leaders, the war would be over tomorrow. It was their mutton heads he feared; they would think and doubt and 'see all sides', a fatal practice – what in God's name were they seeing out of their blear eyes now?

The younger ones were stiffening themselves a bit; Wilmot, for all that he had had a thick night on top of a hard day, was stretching his arms and legs, stamping the life back into his feet and murmuring that there was some stuff in this notion; and Digby looked for a moment as though a fire had been lit behind his blue eyes.

There were a few of the cautious, deprecating question-statements that Rupert found infuriating in warfare; was it wise to move until they had ascertained the exact position of Essex's forces and the extent of their own losses? These would soon be overcome; it was not these moderates, bent on showing off their military knowledge, that made him anxious. It was the men who were not soldiers at all – the King's civilian counsellors – the King himself. He was staring at the King, wondering what he was thinking, trying with almost agonizing effort to make him think as he did, when a mighty voice broke into the ring of the council.

'By God,' said an old man with a face like a Viking's and a head like a snow-white lion's, 'if the Prince is allowed to take London, he'll as like as not set fire to it!'

It was the old Earl of Bristol, Lord Digby's father, who had relinquished his grudge against the Court the moment war was declared, and marched to join the King.

There was a murmur of assent, swelling to an outcry. There was not a man there who had not some part of his family or property or at least friends in London; they were not going to risk them in the power of a half-foreign youth who might run mad with the lust of battle. They had seen or heard how Rupert had fought yesterday – was such Berserk fury to be turned loose on their own capital?

Ned Hyde took up the case. He had already formed a considerable one against the Princes in private, his chief charge being that they 'neglected any consideration of the country', and also, though he did not add it, of himself. Falkland had touched jokingly on a tender spot when he spoke last night of his friend's grievance. These young men with their angelic faces but devilish tempers, their tall elegant figures (so different from Hyde's short and tubby form) but abrupt and often rough manners, treated him, who was in his own opinion the only completely wise and far-seeing counsellor about the King, with the contempt of the insolent young soldier for civilian brains and sentiment.

This charge he could not make in public; but he could concentrate on one more deadly – that these strangers were riding rough-shod over his beloved English earth. Were they to be allowed to wreak their will on London itself? Sooner let the Parliament win a hundred battles! At least *they* were Englishmen through and through, brought up in England.

And of England he spoke, of the horror of a country divided against itself, of a war 'without an enemy' in which Englishmen dreaded to hear their foes cry for quarter in the English tongue. His bright conceited eye softened to an unimagined tenderness as he mentioned his own little village of Dinton, its church and thatched walls and barns like fortresses, which had remained unchanged for three hundred years and would so remain he hoped for three hundred more. That was the England he longed to restore before it was irrevocably poisoned by hates that would last long after the cause of them was forgotten.

Rupert heard him aghast. What on earth had all this fine sentiment to do with their next move? Were men really attending to this? – was his uncle?

'Christ's blood,' he broke out, 'do none of you *want* to win the war?'

'We do not!' cried Digby. 'That's the plain answer to it – which Your Highness, being a stranger, cannot understand.'

Why had he said that? Digby himself was astonished to hear his own words. A longing to put himself against this arrogant young man, that had been his motive, conquering his first impulse to ride with him – for what a glorious entry they might have made into London together! But it would not have been

209

together – Rupert would have been well ahead, taking all the glory, while Digby was far back with the reserves. And Rupert had slighted him.

So now when he spoke, before he had intended, in his eagerness to get in a thrust at the foreigner who thought he could lord it over Englishmen, he found himself committed against the march to London. Now he would have to give good reasons for his surprising statement, but that never worried any of his family – they were so good at finding reasons that they would often argue passionately first from one side of a case and then from the other, for pure love of their own ingenuity.

But in the second's pause he made to give effect to his riposte, another and very different voice had taken up the discussion. In no eager confidence such as Rupert's, but with sad earnestness, Richmond had come in on his side. Everyone there knew that his gallant young brother George Lord d'Aubigny had been hacked down in Rupert's charge. All the deep tenderness of his nature had gone out to him and his gay pretty little bride Kate, now after a few weeks a widow. He had as much reason to loathe the war as any man there – perhaps he would say so, appeal to their sympathies; and if so, they would all go out to him, for everyone admired and respected Richmond; the trouble was that he gave them so little chance to show it, his peculiar mixture of diffidence and pride keeping them all aloof from him.

But that still obtained. It was not in Richmond to show his wounds. There was no tremor in his voice as he asked them to see to it that this war should not drag on needlessly, a mere to and fro of wasted deaths and bitterness, for lack of the decision necessary to end it at one clear stroke.

'But what is the use?' his heart was telling him, 'they don't care to hear what a cold dull fish like you has to say.' They would have listened to d'Aubigny – that boy whose gay spirit had been equal to the young Prince's and now was quenched, while his body lay rotting on the Red Horse Vale.

While Richmond was speaking, Digby remembered that he could not risk another quarrel with his father since he was heavily in debt to him. So after a few seconds' calculation he had decided that his most effective rôle at the moment would be the head of the moderates. His half patronizing friendship for Hyde had given him knowledge of his views, and he determined to exploit them now with a force of statement that the lawyer would hardly dare put into them. His eloquence was more dangerous to Rupert than Hyde's, for he had fire and beauty equal to his opponent's. Trust to that to put out the effect (if any) of Richmond's grave reasoning!

In a ringing voice he proclaimed, 'Victory is to be feared as much as defeat. A too violent victory, won by the downright soldierism of the Prince and his troopers, will only embitter England against the King for ever. There is no hope nor confidence in any mere military victory. Only the temper of the English people as a whole can give His Majesty the victory he desires.'

'Then what in God's name is the sense of taking up arms?'

But even Rupert's hard young logic was un-English, and he saw this in their eyes. His wrath was choking him. He had won the best part of the battle for his uncle, and all his reward was to be told he was a stranger who wished to lay his sacrilegious foreign hands on things holy. *He* set fire to London! *He* sack the city! How dared they say it?

'I think there is none here that would call me a coward,' he heard his voice begin on its low, snarling note of anger – what had he been going to say? He must pull himself up, he must not ruin everything. He went on instead – 'But I would hold it the greatest honour of my life to bring His Majesty back into his capital without the shedding of one drop of blood.'

Did they believe him? Did his uncle believe him? He could think of nothing more to make them do so. He began a word or two but felt it useless. He said almost piteously, 'Although I cannot talk, I can fight.'

They all knew it. That was the trouble. And still the King had not spoken, and his face was like a mask; it was drained of blood, drained of all feeling, the eyes hollow and dark.

'Sir,' said Rupert, looking full at him, 'will you not enter your capital?'

A long shivering sigh passed over that slight form; Charles, who had not slept, was finding it increasingly difficult to think. He had been up before it was light and had ridden over part of the battlefield to see the dawn come creeping up over the bodies of his subjects, dead and dying, friend or foe, it made no difference. The names of men he knew well who had fallen in the fight kept on repeating themselves in his mind – chief among them George d'Aubigny – and his friend Sir Edmund Verney, and all the gallant gentlemen with him who had been slaughtered defending that insensate Standard, won back by a schoolboy's trick. War was as futile as it was bloody and horrible. What satisfaction could it be to enter London as the conqueror of his own people? In hesitant, unhappy speech he began, 'I am afraid —' then stopped, though he did not see the amazement on all their faces, then went on – of the temptation of an absolute conquest. I never prayed more for victory over others than for victory over myself.'

Was his uncle a half-wit – a coward – a saint? Whatever he was, he had flatly declined to be a victorious general. Rupert broke away from that little group of men before he should disgrace himself.

That then was over.

He at once swung his attention away from it and on to the news that Essex's army had begun to retreat – got leave to go after them, and dashed off with a few troops to Kineton where he smashed up their rearguard, captured eight cannon and seventy colours, wagon-loads of arms and ammunition and all Essex's private baggage, plate and papers. Among these last he found letters from his own secretary, Mr Blake, a cheerful little man with a bright beady eye, who had all this time been in the Parliament's pay to the tune of £50 a week, and was demanding a rise on it; he'd rise higher still when he hung for this!

And so in immediate action Rupert tried to forget that he had not been allowed to march on London and set the Thames on fire.

CHAPTER SEVEN

'Farewell my Lord Wharton, with hey!
Farewell my Lord Wharton, with ho!
He swore that all his lies were true,
And it concerned him so to do,
For he was in the saw-pit too,
With a hey, trolly, lolly, ho!'

THE SONG came reeling into the room in a voice rich with delight in its own invention, the words obviously improvised, with pauses here and there, to the well-known tune of a marching song. 'Get the boys to march to that,' shouted Lord Goring, appearing in the doorway as he finished his song, and flourishing his hat in an absurd bow in answer to the applause of the little knot of officers gathered together in Wilmot's quarters in one of the houses at Banbury.

'Goring! By all that's rascally!'

'You old ruffian! You back!'

'Well, Goring – home from the wars?'

That was Wilmot's flick of irony, acting merely as a stimulus to the returned prodigal.

'Home from the whores – and sharp shooting to be had among 'em too – I'm a worn-out warrior – virtue has gone out of me.'

Wilmot was still regarding him with an amused but wary eye. 'Making up for lost time, aren't you, to be singing songs already about Edgehill! How soon will you say you were there yourself, hey George?'

'By God, that's a good notion!

"For he was in the saw-pit too,"

- hey Harry? Or will you not allow me that much honour to be hiding in a saw-pit with my Lord Wharton of the Parliament?'

'Wharton said "it pleased God then to begin to show Himself" – was that when you came into the saw-pit?'

Goring swung round, snatched the mug out of Wilmot's hand and drank it off.

'My greed is greater than thine,' he observed as he handed it back empty. 'Let us, my friends, never forget the immortal words of Sir Philip Sidney when he wouldn't stand the other fellow a drink.'

His eyes were twinkling with laughter, his moustaches twirled upwards with a mocking swagger, even his limp appeared a mere humorous affectation. Red sleeves slashed with white satin and frothing with lace, great hat cocked at a tilt and brandishing a plume like a banner, ribbons and love-locks flying, sword-sash gleaming with silver, all the superb absurdity of fashion in its extreme was flaunted by him so triumphantly that it seemed the natural and perfect wear for a soldier and a gentleman.

Once the company had recovered from the first start of pleasure which was Goring's inevitable first effect, they began to remember that hadn't there been something mighty strange, not to say fishy in his late conduct? What of that business of Portsmouth? They began to ask him in tones that tried to be sneering but somehow, whatever they felt about it, would turn into a mere friendly jocularity.

'What happened at Portsmouth?'

'Yes, tell us – did you get converted at Portsmouth and hand it over at the end of a sermon?'

'Or did they give you cash down for it, and how much?'

Goring's eye roved round his company, taking them all into his confidence.

'Portsmouth!' he ejaculated, rounding his full lips so that the word shot from them like a cork out of a bottle, 'all this about a hole like Portsmouth! Why did I give it up? Why, how could I bear to keep it? Everybody in Portsmouth is either in church or in bed – and not with the best people. It's a place only fit for Puritans, and so I told 'em – and so I shall tell the King.'

'God damme, what *will* you tell the King?'

'You can leave it to me,' – and well they knew they could. It was no good trying to hold him to it. He glided with the grace of the perfect skater on thin ice to the more congenial topic of Paris, for he had come home by there and seen poor Suckling just before that fiery nose had lit him to hell at last – 'Didn't you know he was dead? Killed himself, they say, for fear of poverty, though as it was by putting his foot on a razor blade in his boot, it's more likely he did it when drunk. Well, he's put his foot in it for the last time.'

Suckling had raised troops of horse with Goring for the Scottish War three years ago, and spent £12,000 out of his own pocket on scarlet coats and feathers and white doublets for them. His coach had been captured by that grim little Scot, General Leslie, full of money and gorgeous clothes, and Parliament nearly captured himself for the Tower, but he had escaped to France – only to die thus miserably.

Not a man in the company but had known Suckling, and most of them had been known as his Roaring Boys, had sung his rollicking songs with him, smoked and diced and played bowls with him, and learnt from him the daring view that Will Shakespeare had been a better poet than Ben Jonson. Now they looked uncomfortably on each other and even felt a lurking suspicion of Goring which his betrayal of Portsmouth had not aroused. Had he done anything for poor old Suckling? Not he! Perhaps he had stood him a drink!

And Goring, seeing, guessing their thought, went one further as usual. ' "Why so pale and wan, fond lover?" ' he quoted from Suckling's own song, flinging an arm round Wilmot's shoulders. 'It won't do him any more good than you. Look at this I had in Paris. You know I was at The Hague first.'

'God damn your fat effrontery! Must you start showing your love-letters all round your company like a conceited schoolboy?'

'Ah, Harry, wait. It's such a love-letter as should be framed and set up in the King's picture galleries – it's for that I show it – pure disinterested love of art! That a princess should do it for me is a mere nothing – princesses are cheaper than prostitutes.'

Rupert, coming in with an order for Wilmot, found a group of officers clustered round Goring, bent double over something he was showing them, and acting in illustration of it. 'You see, there are the Brethren, and the Elector's preaching to 'em – see what that balloon is, coming out of his mouth? – "And fifthly my brethren I say unto you, as Cain said unto the Lord, Am I my brother's keeper, however mad he be?"'

Goring was speaking in a snuffling high-pitched whine, the chapel-voice of most of the Puritan preachers, and his congregation answered with hollow groans and 'Amen' and 'Yea verily', bursting out into guffaws and sharp yells of laughter. They scattered at sight of the Prince, with sly, self-conscious looks, but Goring boldly faced him, holding out a letter on a very broad sheet of paper where the writing kept breaking into little pictures, comic, but beautifully drawn.

'I congratulate Your Highness on so brilliant an artist for a sister – and my unworthy self for being given such an illustration of her genius,' he said with exaggerated respect.

Rupert could not prevent that rush of blood to his face, turning it crimson. He had known at his first glance at the madcap figures dancing over the paper that this was Louey's work. The English Puritans at The Hague in their high steeple hats and Carl addressing them were unmistakable, not only in themselves but in the wickedly mocking eye that had penetrated and fastened them, quivering with absurd life, upon the paper.

He saw no more than that, for Goring was quick to whisk the letter away – 'in order that I may guess it to be indiscreet!' thought Rupert; but he had held it there long enough for Rupert to see how long it was and how full of drawings – 'and she's done all this for that swine Goring to brag about to his friends and say what he likes of her' – even sharing their family jokes and animosities with him, for that scene of Carl excusing himself for his mad brother must refer to Carl and himself. Yet

215

he could not show his anger, for to do that was to give Goring the greater rein for scandal. He could hear the voices clacking – 'A quarrel over the Princess Louise – her brother took exception to a letter she had written to Lord Goring,' and the amused echo, 'Oh, *Goring!*' as though that explained everything.

All he could do was to outface Goring till those lascivious knowing eyes had to drop at last before the scornful stare from under the Prince's eyelids, and then say quietly in answer to his greeting, 'And I congratulate Your Lordship in your turn on your courage in returning to England to stand your court-martial.'

He then gave his order to Wilmot as curtly as if he were speaking to a corporal, turned on his heel and swung out of the room, to hear the laughter and mimicry begin again as soon as he had closed the door.

He could not kick his heels in this damned city another moment. What the devil were they doing, tinkering at the defences of Banbury when they ought to be on their line of march to London, even if he had been stopped himself from going on ahead?

He sent for Maurice and told him to take over for the moment; he himself might be away for a day or two. He dressed with some care in his soberest suit of clothes, swung a grey cloak round his shoulders, and looking like an ordinary country gentleman, he rode off by himself, unattended by even his servant, Tom Draycott, on a solitary reconnaissance.

He had done this already two or three times and gained some information and a good deal of fun by it, jogging off by himself through the English countryside that he used to enjoy while hunting. He liked talking with the country people, and apart from any actual intelligence he might pick up, it was useful to find out their opinions, though he had collected many far from flattering to himself.

An old woman near Worcester, in whose cottage he had bought a meal of collops and eggs and very small beer, had abused 'the Dragon Prince' heartily to his face, declaring that the country had been the worse ever since he had come into it – 'It was he brought the war – never tell me he didn't, for the proof is, it started the moment he set foot in England. That's what comes of bringing a stranger prince into the country. He might have kept himself where he was born!'

And Rupert had as heartily agreed with her while he ate her

collops in her tiny smoke-filled kitchen and thought of Prague and what might have happened had he been able to 'keep himself there' to be the King of Bohemia and Grand Duke of Lithuania.

But this time he could not believe he would have either fun or adventure; a drizzling rain stung his face, there was no shape nor colour in the late October scene, only a dreary greyness, and all the time he was thinking savagely of Louey's letter. He could even sympathize now with Carl's annoyance at her making herself conspicuous – there had been some row about it last time he was in England, and Louey a mere child – what was it? Some English lady boxing her ears, and he had thought old Timon a fool to fuss – but this was quite different.

That picture of Carl puzzled him, or rather the mock speech that he had heard Goring declaiming as he came into the room: 'Am I my brother's keeper, however mad he be?' Were the Parliament complaining to Carl on Rupert's account? 'She might have written to tell *me* instead of that toss-pot, Goring.'

He grew increasingly bitter as he realized that never in his life had Louey done an illustrated letter for him, until at last the corollary forced itself on his unwilling attention that never in his life had he written to Louey. Goring doubtless had done so from Paris, and doubtless Louey had laughed over his letter as much as those fellows had laughed over hers. His jealousy was working him up into a most unwonted fit of homesickness. His mother had never written to him since he had come to England – nor again had he to her, but that also was different, he was here on a man's job and far too busy – besides, he was fighting for her country and she might have the decency to feel some gratitude – but she had no decency, none of the family had, he'd swear she'd been just as much amused with Goring as Louey had been – all women were. And men too, he finished gloomily, thinking of that hilarious group that he had interrupted.

In a fury of irritation (to add to everything else, the drizzle had become a downpour) he stopped at a wayside inn for a drink and shelter. A fire of turf sods on the flat hearth-stone gave a smoky glow to the dark little room where some yokels were huddled together, their coats of rough homespun steaming from the rain and smelling like wet sheep. At sight of 'gentry' they at once made way for him to come near the fire, and a fellow at the further end of the wooden settle began to get up as

Rupert sat down, half lifting a battered slouch hat, but seated himself again at his gesture. Rupert sat drinking his ale and talking to the man about the bad weather. He discovered that his trade was to sell cabbage nets, an article of which Rupert had never heard before. Idly, with the interest that any new technical subject, however small or out of the way, always aroused in him, he asked him questions on the purpose, price and nature of cabbage nets, while a plan began to shape itself in his mind.

A few weeks ago he had actually sold apples to the Roundhead troops on Dunsmore Heath; it had been a mad risk, and his friends would not believe on his return that he could have disguised his height and bearing as those of an English peasant, but he had done it successfully, having bribed a countryman to change places with him and driven his apple cart right in among the army. The cart had been the best part of the disguise, for he had sat huddled forward in it under his ragged cloak, and nobody could have guessed the almost hunch-backed peasant to be six foot four in his stockings. And now here was this fellow saying he was going to ride into Warwick and sell his cabbage nets to the Roundhead army. (Rupert noted with amusement that the Queen's nickname for her enemies had reached the peasantry and even presumably the sympathizers.)

'Why don't you take them to the Cavalier army at Banbury?' he asked. 'I hear they give good prices.'

'Ah, but you never know where you are with those rascals.' The man was looking very knowing. 'They're a mad lot they are, always roistering and kicking up their heels in their satins and feathers.'

'Do you know where you are with the Roundheads?'

'Lord yes, they're a sober lot, even when they're drunk. *They* don't dice and bet and swear and skylark.'

'You're wrong, my man. I've got a friend in the army now at Warwick and he made me a bet of £5 that I'd never do an honest day's work. I'd give a crown to anyone here who'd help me to touch him for it.'

He looked round his company as he spoke, and they shifted their feet and glanced sideways at each other, all obviously racking their brains to think how to earn such easy money. The man beside him on the settle began to chew the cud of some great thought, to rock himself gently until at last it bubbled up as he leaned right forward and tapped Rupert on the knee. 'Why, sir, what you could do is to buy my cabbage nets and sell 'em in Warwick instead o' me!'

Rupert stared at him as if slowly taking it in, then slapped him on the back, told him what a good fellow he was, what a grand notion he'd had, stood drinks all round, gave him his crown on the spot and set about changing clothes as far as it was possible. The man's slouch hat and ragged coat, which had belonged originally to a very fat man and hung in flapping folds all round him, were almost enough disguise in themselves; and the man with the longest feet in the company sold him his rough shoes and cloth gaiters to wrap round his legs instead of his boots, which were too good for a cabbage net seller.

Off he jogged to Warwick on a wretched old horse, remembering to hunch himself up on the saddle with his coat pulled over his knees so as not to show his height – and that was the last that the net seller saw of him that day.

He began to get restive for his horse; the gentleman had paid a good price for the cabbage nets but not for the horse, and though his own horse, an infinitely superior animal, was in the stable, the inn-keeper refused to consider it the net seller's perquisite. But their argument was interrupted by the return of the gentleman, who had sold all his cabbage nets, was delighted to have 'played that touch' on his friend, and proved more generous than ever as he resumed his own clothes. The net seller held his stirrups for him, chuckling: 'Shall I tell 'em in Warwick that it was a gentleman sold 'em my cabbage nets?'

'Tell 'em it was the Devil himself!' Rupert laughed back as he swung into the saddle.

The man's jaw dropped, he stared after the tall figure galloping down the road with his cloak flying out on the wind.

'The Devil? The *Prince*!'

*   *   *

Rupert rode back to Banbury, hot with the news he had learned from the Roundhead soldiers in Warwick – pleasant fellows some of them had been too, and none so different from his own troopers. They got cashiered if they called their comrades Roundheads, so strong apparently had been the temptation.

He found the King's army had moved on to Oxford, the King was already settled at Christ Church College, and there was a council meeting in progress. He plunged into the midst of it, and the first thing he saw was Goring twirling up his moustaches as he talked low with Digby. It was a bad check. Goring was not going to be court-martialled then, he was going to be trusted and admitted again into all the secret councils. He had known it all along. Why had he ever hoped anything else? For an instant he glared at him before he even remembered to salute the King, who asked him coldly whether he had enjoyed the leave he had taken.

'I took it, Your Majesty, among the rebels' army at Warwick. I went in among them in disguise to discover their news. All London's in arms since the news of Edgehill. They are digging trenches in Finsbury Fields and the village of Pancras, and redoubts in Hyde Park. All the trained bands have been called out under Colonel Skippon, a good soldier from the German wars – the Parliament are raising men and money as fast as they can by conscription and loans. Every day strengthens their position. More than that – Essex's main army is now ahead of us on the road to London.'

'The P-P-Parliament,' said the King, 'have reported Edgehill as a victory for their side.'

'Lord Wharton has publicly admitted that both wings of their army were destroyed – in any case, London is scared out of its wits and we must get there before they fortify it any further.'

His peremptory tone raised a good many eyebrows. London apparently was not the subject for debate at the moment, but Edgehill. An inquiry had been set on foot as to why the enemy had not been more effectually beaten.

'Well, I gave a good account of their horse,' said Rupert.

'*And* of their carts!' called out Goring, and was echoed by bursts of angry laughter. It was plain how the inquiry had been answered – by blaming Rupert for the delay of the plunder of Kineton. And Goring was even now carrying Louey's letter in his pocket – this traitor, who had already wormed himself back into the King's confidence, this loose-lipped swaggerer who thought he could fight the better for a tongue like a bit of old rabbit fur – no, Rupert could not hurl back insults like a fishwife – only his sword could answer Goring. He had already drawn it without knowing, as he turned on him with the one word, 'Draw!' He saw Goring fall back amazed, and the Duke of Richmond and Will Legge spring out from among all those men and fling themselves upon him, snatching at his sword hand, crying out to him in horror, Will calling, 'Sir! You are in the King's presence!' and Richmond, deep and stern, 'You insult His Majesty!'

His sense swam back into his dizzied brain; slowly he turned and faced the King.

'Sir, I did not intend disrespect. But your counsellors are unjust to me.'

'In their accusations of violence, nephew, you have shown how little they are unjust.'

It was the sternest speech the King had made him, and he signed to Richmond to lead him away from the royal presence. The Duke hauled him off, more angry himself than Rupert had ever seen him.

They plunged down a corridor into a little dark room looking on to the quadrangle. Rupert threw himself into a chair, rubbing his head which he had banged in the doorway. Richmond stood looking down on him.

'You are here to defend His Majesty's honour. Is this the way you show others how to respect it?'

'I forgot the King,' said Rupert ingenuously.

'And trusted him to forget that the penalty for drawing a sword in his presence is the loss of your right hand?'

It was an unlucky reminder, for it savoured of a threat and at once set Rupert on fire again.

'Let him take it, if he's such a fool! He'll not find another to strike as hard blows for him.'

'He knows that. Give others the chance to know it too, instead of letting them think you a swashbuckler who fights only for his own hand.'

'Let them think? *Let* them think! What do I care what they think? But they – all of them – even the King – have they nothing but lukewarm milk in their veins?'

He broke off as he encountered Richmond's gaze, which wore an inscrutable expression. What could his grave cousin be thinking? He was very angry with him, he knew that, and Rupert wished he were not, for he admired and respected Richmond more than anyone he knew in England.

Would he always turn the people he cared for against him? His uncle had spoken in such icy reproof to him just now; his mother hated him, and no wonder, for he had cursed her in one of their quarrels. He began to bite his finger and kick his leg over the arm of his chair; presently he flung himself out of it and strode up and down. 'I don't know what's the matter with me,' he said, 'something comes on me from outside and shakes me to bits and then I see what's happened – what I've said or done in my rage. Perhaps they're right and I'm really mad. Perhaps that is what you are thinking. I wish I had fallen in that charge instead of d'Aubigny. I saw him cut down. He died gallantly.'

It was the first time he had dared speak of Richmond's young brother, knowing how fond he had been of him. D'Aubigny had only just been married too. He wished passionately that he himself was not giving Richmond so much trouble.

Richmond said nothing about d'Aubigny. He answered, 'I don't think you are mad. But anyone of your headlong vigour must have been tortured in that long imprisonment.'

'It's done me no harm. I fly about fast enough now.'

Richmond had seen that, had realized what furious release of energy was now being hurled out upon England, and how nervous it must make cautious people. Prison had taught no patience to Rupert; he had been tied and bound, all his strength put into resistance; now he could tolerate nothing and no one that got in his way. He was an irreconcilable; and his uncle, though as gentle as the nephew was fierce, was also one. Richmond feared for them both, but more for Rupert, for he saw that Charles could hurt Rupert as Rupert could never hurt Charles.

The young man that was flinging himself about the room in his angry bewilderment did not guess at his cousin's brooding anxiety for him; had he done so, it would have lowered his opinion of him to that of a fantastic – he only allowed his uncle to be fantastic, and that grudgingly. There would have been some truth in the charge; Richmond, sensitive almost to morbidity, too fastidious to like many, was very slow to give his friendship, for he knew it, once given, to be an integral part of him that could only be torn from him with agony. Pride also forbade him to give anything of himself easily and unwanted, a pride far deeper than that of his birth and position, the pride of 'a great and haughty spirit', as Mr Hyde had dubbed it, with that final and satisfied air in labelling the qualities of his acquaintance which often made them resent it worse than harsher criticism.

It had been a surprise to many when this reserved, rather melancholy man took the Princes into his friendly care, risking the snubs that Rupert had already shown he could give so

222

casually to the English nobles. It must be, people thought, because the King had asked him to befriend them, for Richmond, punctiliously loyal in all things, was ready to submit even his friendships to the King's approval. And no doubt it had been partly out of courteous hospitality to his kinsmen and the King's that his friendship had begun with these two half-foreign youths, secretly shy in spite of their glad defiance of others' opinions. But with Rupert it had quickly developed into something far deeper than this kindly impulse, while there remained an almost womanly tenderness and desire to protect his young cousin at the root of Richmond's feeling for him.

Rupert, as he had seen from the first, could have no shred of power in this his mother's country except such as he could build up for himself in the freedom given by the royal favour. Once that were withdrawn, he would be nothing but an alien adventurer.

To his severely controlled mind Rupert's furious disrespect to the King had been almost criminal. Yet it could not diminish his affection, and it had even aroused his envy. He longed for something of that hot fervour in himself.

'When you are in love,' he said strangely, 'you will give great happiness.'

Rupert thought he had already been in love – several times, though he did not wait to distinguish which had been the most important occasion. 'But you,' he said, 'haven't you been in love?'

Very quietly Richmond answered, 'I have never been anything else.'

'You have loved so many?'

'Only one. My wife.'

At once Rupert felt he had been indecent and did not wish to recall or inquire whom it was that Richmond had married.

CHAPTER EIGHT

I T W A S the Parliament cavalry leader, Colonel Ramsey, who brought the first news of Edgehill to London; he and his troopers came charging down the streets, shouting that Essex's army had been cut to pieces and that Rupert's men were hard on their heels, galloping towards London and 'hacking, hewing and pistolling everyone they met'. This report was presently contradicted, but whichever way you spoke of the battle it had certainly given the chance to the Devil Prince to march down and storm and sack London at the head of his hideously merry men.

That was something that brought war home to a man. It couldn't be allowed, even if it meant letting all the prentice lads off from their work for a month or so and carrying on the shop or the business with only the wife and an old man or two to help.

The war couldn't last for more than that, they all knew it – worthy Mr Richard Baxter himself had said he would not give it a month. Parliament held all the money, and a pretty penny it was costing them – £30,000 a week, and all of it coming out of the pockets of honest plain men who'd never wanted a war – all they'd wanted was to be let alone and not be bothered with priests prancing about the high altar as they would call it, and having the impudence to tell the lads they could play games on Sunday, when it was much better for them not to be encouraged to play games at all, since it only took their minds off their business and made them eager to be off early from work to get to football or even such low rascally pleasures as play-acting. *That* had been put down with a firm hand, thank the Lord – as soon as Parliament had established itself in London and could make laws unhindered by the King, it had made it an offence to act stage plays, and condemned actors to be whipped and branded.

This campaigning would take off more time from trade than plays or games, but then it was worth it for it was in a righteous cause, and when they had won the war they would make those loose ruffianly swearing fine gallants about the Court pay for every penny of it out of their estates. That would teach them to jeer at honest God-fearing citizens.

Meanwhile Parliament settled their terrors comfortably for them concerning the result of the battle of Edgehill, which the insolent Royalists were calling a great strategic victory. They passed a resolution in Parliament 'that their army had the victory', so there was the question settled by Parliamentary vote, and nobody could doubt it after that.

So Parliament appointed a day of solemn thanksgiving to God for laying open to their enemies the road to their capital, and gave £5,000 to the Earl of Essex (and they surely would not have paid him all that for a defeat), and the citizens, somewhat reassured, sent their lads off from the shop to dig trenches in Finsbury and Lincoln's Inn Fields, and raise barricades in the chief streets and chains across the narrow ones to keep out the enemy. The gallants jeered worse than ever, the few that were left at large in town, and a new song was sung in the taverns called 'Cuckolds come dig' – an insulting reference to the traditional family misfortune of city merchants.

It infuriated them worse even than the propaganda of Rupert's atrocities and endeared them all the more to their Commander-in-Chief, Lord Essex, whose humiliating divorce case in the last reign had caused every shop in London to buzz and whisper the latest scandalous reports of the horrible home life at King James' Court. The old King's insolent favourite had made the poor earl a cuckold – it was only fair that now he should get his own back by fighting the old King's son.

Colonel Skippon, from the German wars, in charge of the defences, was cheered with great affection as he rode down the lines of his new recruits, exhorting them to 'Pray hard, boys! Fight hard!'

John Milton, pessimistically putting more faith in the pen than in the sword, pinned a sonnet to the door of his pretty garden house in Aldersgate Street, one of the quietest houses in London, entreating the invader to

> *'Lift not thy spear against the Muses' bower.'*

All the city wives were doing war-work: they carried earth in basketfuls to help build the ramparts, they packed great hampers of provisions, huge meat pies and loaves of bread and flagons of ale or rough wine, and piled them up on the forage carts for the brave boys who were marching out to defend the Parliament. The King was a noodle who collected pictures, his wife was a Popish brat from France, his nephew a bloodthirsty foreigner, and the bishops were spies and tyrants in petticoats – but Parliament was a body of honest Englishmen like themselves. So they hung their windows with orange flags and ribbons, that being the badge of the party since Essex's colours were deep yellow, and waved their handkerchiefs and cried good luck, and the boys waved back and marched down the west road from London and stopped pretty often to sit by the roadside for refreshments, and so went on to Turnham Green in force to check the King's advance on his capital.

For an advance had at last been agreed upon, as long as it was done in proper order instead of one of the Prince's wild dashes, and Rupert had been allowed to make an impossible attempt on Windsor Castle from the grounds of Eton College, where his men entrenched themselves with four rather elderly guns and tried to attack from there. But it could not be done; they could fight men, said his horsemen, but not stone walls.

He went on with his cavalry to Kingston, cut his way through the trained bands who were all drawn up there ready for him, and took Maidenhead.

'Horrible news from Colnbrook' was the next headline to startle London. The Prince had taken that too and had 'deeply vowed that he will come to London, swearing he cares not a pin for all the Roundheads nor their infant works and saying he will lay their city and inhabitants on the ground'. That was a bit of news to turn men pallid!

Two London merchants were captured under suspicion of being spies and taken to him at Egham to be questioned. They found a very tall young man lying on his bed with all his clothes on, not having had time to undress. A big white dog leaped from his feet and barked as his master raised himself on his elbow and stared with heavy sleep-laden eyes at Mr Tebbit, chandler, and Mr Elworthy, huckster, both of Cheapside.

A sense of urgency filled the air; the young man who had shot up so quickly, spoke so little and watched them so keenly, was a creature of more fiery and desperate purpose than could ever inform their lives. Both were certain that he had his clothes on because he had taken a vow never to undress or change his linen until he had set King Charles back in his palace of Whitehall.

The Prince seemed as much interested in their clothes, for he had picked up one of the hats they had laid respectfully on the table, and all the time he questioned them and listened to their answers and watched their faces he was tossing and turning over a bunch of ribbons in it.

'Are these your favours?' he asked in his deep voice that held a foreign intonation rather than accent – 'I'll swear there are none of the King's favours here.'

Mr Elworthy blushed crimson.

'They are the favours of my mistress, Your Highness,' he said.

The Prince smiled and handed back the hat without saying a word.

The sergeant who had led them to his room tapped Mr Elworthy on the shoulder, who looked mystified at him and then at the Prince and gathered that the audience was over, for Rupert had stretched himself on his bed and was already asleep.

The next day, as they were led past under guard, they saw that strange young man again, walking on Hounslow Heath beside a tiny, very erect figure with a pointed beard whom they had once seen riding in state to be crowned King at Westminster, dressed all in white like a bridegroom, and he was a bridegroom then – but the old wives had shaken their heads and said they did not like it, for white was also the colour of the grave.

The Prince wore the same handsome scarlet coat that he had had on the night before, but now as he talked with the King he took it off without any more ceremony than if he had been talking with an equal, and handed it to a servant and put on a rough grey coat, pushing his long arms into the sleeves with violent energy, and buckled on his sword belt, and then to their amazement he scratched his head in front of His Majesty and pulled at his dark curling hair, all with the same restless angry abstraction, as though he were thinking not at all of what he was doing nor of whom he was talking to, but was desperately considering something of far deeper importance, something, moreover, that disturbed him passionately.

As well it might, for the King was withholding his consent from Rupert's plan of an attack upon Brentford because he was again considering negotiations with Parliament. Yet Essex was advancing upon him, and if he did not take Brentford he would be completely surrounded.

But – 'I do not wish to lose the hearts of the Londoners,' said Charles.

'Sir, they are already lost to you. They are flocking to Essex's standard, marching out in thousands against you. They cry "For the King and Parliament!" because they are such hypocrites they can even now pretend they do not fight against you but against us, your wicked advisers.'

The King turned on him such a long and heavy look that his nephew felt a strange chill, as though his uncle had touched him with a cold finger.

'Yes, Rupert,' he said at last, 'they do not love you.'

'Do you wish I had not come to fight for you?' was on Rupert's lips – but why ask it? His uncle could only disclaim

227

and protest his gratitude, and Rupert had no wish for gratitude; he wanted to finish well what he had begun, and he wanted to get his uncle's consent to take Brentford.

He got it, he took the town and guns and ammunition, after hard fighting; Charles lost what was left of the hearts of his Londoners, and was accused of breaking faith in not letting himself be surrounded; and after all it was too late, as that whole march on London was too late once Rupert's initial chance of dashing on it had been discarded, for by then Essex's army, now twice the size of Charles', barred the way at Turnham Green, and Rupert was forced to retire from Brentford.

The retreat under fire was a triumph of discipline and quiet order, an answer to those who had said all along that Rupert was no general but a mere mad young daredevil. But now the fire of his headlong charges had to give pride of place to the cool courage with which he stood his mount in the river beside the bridge for hours, his tall figure and black horse a conspicuous target for the enemy bullets which splashed all round him, while he cheered his men to keep their ranks in good order as they retired and to fire steadily upon the advancing enemy. It gave him a reputation almost miraculous, not only for courage but for a charmed life. The Prince cared nothing for danger, it was plain, because he had secret knowledge that no human power could kill him – and where could he get that knowledge from except from his master Satan?

*   *   *

The town of Oxford had made up for its coldness at that visit when Rupert was given his honorary degree, and had greeted the King with tremendous enthusiasm. It was now the King's capital, Christ Church his palace, his Court flowing out into the colleges, his camp into the low-lying meadows; his great guns were parked in Magdalen Grove, and Rupert's headquarters at Abingdon.

Rupert's fiery concentration helped turn the city into a sternly practical centre of warfare with the same unbelievable speed and efficiency as that which had recruited and built up and drilled and licked into shape his magnificent cavalry in the space of a few weeks. That had been gay work, with all these gallant fellows coming in faster and faster in their eagerness to serve under him, and shaping so splendidly under his creative will that the raw civilians, who did not know enough even to ask for 'quarter' instead of 'mercy', would not in a few days have dreamed of asking for either.

Now that furious building up of material had to be consolidated and dug into its citadel. Rupert had learnt the value of a spade as well as a sword in the school of Gustavus. He had trenches dug across St Giles' and at the back of Wadham, and all undergraduates had to take a day off a week to help dig them; they formed a regiment too and paraded in Christ Church meadows; and a mathematical don at Queen's made plans for fortifications. Brasenose Tower and the Law and Logic Schools were turned into stores for corn and victuals, New College walls were fortressed, and Magdalen Tower was the chief point of observation. The old college plate that Laud had treasured so carefully down to its last spoon was melted down for the Royal Mint at New Inn Hall. Magdalen and All Souls brought in most – Corpus so little that they were suspected of hiding it.

In that soft air, among those grey buildings dedicated for centuries to the quiet pursuit of learning, Charles was in his true kingdom; he should have been a don, even as Laud, his tragic little Archbishop, now in the Tower under the advancing shadow of the Parliament's determination on his death, should have remained always and only a don.

When Charles read Spenser or Tasso or listened to the singing of the Magdalen choir-boys, he lost all sense of his present troubles. Meeting Rupert on the lawns in Christ Church gardens, he stopped his nephew, who was hurrying through them, to tell him that he had now no doubt at all – then waited an instant to master his stammer, while Rupert from his uncle's serious tone started half a dozen guesses as to what urgent matter had at last freed his mind from doubts. No, continued Charles, whatever Spenser had written about his grandmother Queen Mary as Duessa, he was undoubtedly his favourite poet. The even flow of his verse was like that of a broad river, and he began to quote a line while Rupert, staring at that even flow of the Cherwell below them, glinting silver in the winter sunshine as it showed here and there through the grey drooping forms of the willows, wondered how quickly he could break away to the gun emplacement at Magdalen.

'Sleepe after toyle, port after stormie seas,
Ease after warre, death after life, does greatly please.'

The words echoed in his impatient ears even when he had seized his chance to stride away. He should be glad that his uncle had regained so much of his old imperturbable serenity. Gone was the haunted creature that he had had to leave at Dover this year, gone also the sad uncertain man who had seemed to dread his victory over his people almost as much as defeat. In his place had come again the exquisite connoisseur Rupert had first known and loved, who had made him feel that the enjoyment of music and poetry and pictures was as important as the actual business of living. But now it could not be – now they had got to attend solely to the business – and then let the King enjoy his own again!

Maurice came to him one morning at Abingdon with a perplexed face and a letter in his hand from his uncle.

'Does he often write like this?' he demanded, laying it in front of his brother.

Rupert found all his English relatives' letters rather difficult. Even James of Richmond, his greatest friend, wrote him long letters full of goodwill and really helpful advice, when extracted from their confusing context. But he was apt to curse his involutions and repetitions as he did his uncle's. In this letter Charles was being classical and a little arch.

'What the devil does he mean?' he exclaimed as he began –
' "Nephew Maurice, though Mars be most in vogue yet Hymen may sometimes be remembered." '

'It's that girl of yours,' Maurice complained, 'the French one. She's gone on refusing good matches ever since they suggested you to her, and now her family won't wait any longer.'

'I know. My uncle spoke to me about it. But I'm not in any way engaged to Mademoiselle de Rohan. I've never seen her, and I never wanted her, and I said so when I was here six years ago and I say so now. Why should he write to *you*?'

'He thinks I might do instead. He asks if I will "take my brother handsomely off".'

' "Take me handsomely off!" Very handsome, as it's to the tune of £80,000 a year.'

'He thinks it a pity to let it go out of the family.'

'Well, why don't you, Maurice?'

But the Twin refused as flatly as his elder had done. To be saddled with a wife, however rich, beautiful and faithful (to all other offers, even during the three years Rupert was in prison, she had only replied – 'as I have been inclined so I am still'), seemed an intolerable burden to these unbiddable paupers. The only result was that Rupert continued to chaff Maurice mercilessly about it, all the more as Maurice's steadiness and coolness in withdrawing their forces from any attack in which Rupert had too hotly engaged had begun to earn him the nickname of 'the good come-off'. The brothers were an excellent supplement to each other, but what everybody realized, except Rupert, was that Maurice was only the shadow to his brother's flame.

*   *   *

Proposals of matrimony were not the brothers' worst grievance against pen and ink. Libels on Rupert were now pouring out thicker and thicker from the London printing press. 'Call Prince Rupert to the Bar.' They ranged from serious charges of the slaughter of civilians, including women and children, at Kineton, brought by Lord Wharton (who had extricated himself from the saw-pit after Edgehill but not from the rotten reputation he had got there), to rude joking dialogues between Boy and some 'true English dog' of the Parliament who told that 'bawling shag-haired Cavalier dog' that he would have no outlandish cur domineering in his country. The pamphlets on the pet that his mother had given him at his departure for England were much ruder – they described this 'Malignant she-monkey, a Great Delinquent' as 'a kind of old, little, wrinkled, old-faced, petulant, wanton and malignant gentlewoman, the little whore of Babylon in a green coat', and its relations with various officers, with an obscenity that wavered between the conflicting aims of humour and high moral indignation.

Rupert himself, 'the Bloody Prince', 'the Debauched Cavalier and his unbridled Roarers' (for the tradition of Suckling's Roaring Boys must be carried on), were all sons of Belial living in 'a wilderness of Tobacco' with 'Legions of Whores'; they swore as well as smoked, and openly declared they would rather be in hell with their comrades than in heaven with the Roundheads, such a statement proving them to be 'worse than the heathenish Turk or Cannibals'.

These puerile charges worried Rupert no more than the persistent accusations of witchcraft which included Boy as his 'familiar', a demon in the guise of a white dog who whispered instructions from his master Satan – and that was why he always accompanied the Prince, even in the King's council chamber.

231

But Wharton's speech against him at the Guildhall and later in print was a more substantial affair and had serious consequences, not only to Rupert and the King's cause.

His evil reputation was getting his family into difficulties. It was Parliament who paid his mother her revenue, and Parliament, terrified by her son's victories and indignant at his mother's attitude towards them, was now refusing to pay it. Carl, of course, had been writing to express his affection and respect for Parliament and his complete dissociation from Rupert ever since the war began. It had been the sole reason for his departure from England, so he quite unnecessarily pointed out, that he had feared lest his continued presence might be the cause of any embarrassment to Parliament. Now he pointed out with equal superfluity how impossible it was for him – or his mother – 'to bridle my brother's youth and fieriness.'

But even Elizabeth's pride had to stoop to try and placate the Speaker when letters from her to Rupert were intercepted and caused a storm of censure. She became very womanly, as she only did under great stress, protested that she really could not remember what may have happened 'to slip from her pen in the private relation between mother and son', but whatever it was, she had never intended it should give the Parliament the least distaste (as indeed she had never intended the Parliament should see it). Her apology was fruitless in the matter of hard cash. Parliament stopped her pension.

But it gave a passionate hope and gratitude to Rupert. Whatever had been written in those letters that he would never now see, it must have shown more praise and sympathy than he had ever had from her pen. He burned with pleasure that she should have written so to him – and with indignation that she should be made to suffer for it. He must do what he could to repair it, even at the cost of his dignity (had she not been forced to forego hers too in her appeal to the Parliament?) – even at the still heavier cost of taking up pen and paper.

So he wrote his only answer to the libels, though it was against his instinct and his principle to do so, as he showed scornfully enough in his opening; 'it will seem strange, no doubt, to see me in print, my known disposition being so contrary to this scribbling age.'

That he favoured 'Popery' scarcely required any answer, but he forced himself to remind these fools that 'the world knows how deeply I have smarted and what perils I have undergone for the Protestant cause, what stately large promises were offered me, would I consent. And what a wretched, close imprisonment was threatened me if I refused to change my religion, when I was captive to the Emperor of Germany!'

'But they *know* all that!' he exclaimed, throwing down the quill in disgust and looking up at Will Legge, who was puffing at a long pipe, lounging against the window, his blunt nose silhouetted against the small panes. 'Come out of that "wilderness of tobacco" – I'll not be answered by a grunt and a puff.'

Will removed his pipe for an instant. 'Never mind what they know. Write it.'

'It makes no odds to them.'

'No. But you'll have said it.'

Rupert abandoned the sketch he had begun of Will's nose, a fascinating shape rather like a duck's bill with the same look of humorous wisdom. 'The Seven Deadly Sins are written on your nose,' he observed as he wrote on: 'I would to God all Englishmen were at union among themselves.' His greatest victory would be to see His Majesty enter London in peace; 'whereby that ancient and famous City would manifestly perceive how desperately it has been abused by most strange, false and bottomless untruths.'

There was a new charge, more preposterous than any yet conceived. It had begun with a caricature of Rupert tying up a child to a stake for Boy to devour; now one of the most popular branches of propaganda was the accusation of cannibalism. A refined taste in cannibalism, it should be said, for the Cavaliers were supposed to eat only children, not adults – and that not from necessity so much as from a perverse and wanton taste, a new exotic fashion in wickedness, set by the Stranger Prince.

At first no one had believed these accusations could be taken seriously; but they grew more and more circumstantial and venomous; they gave a great opportunity to appeal to the 'women of England' to save their precious infants from the power of the Prince. 'Rupert take you' had become more than an oath, it was now a curse and a terror. Women told their children, especially the plump ones, not to play in the street lest the Dragon Prince should ride by and snatch them up on the point of his sword to be roasted and eaten at supper and the bones thrown to his dog.

'They must be very stupid,' said Rupert, staring at some of these warnings. 'What d'you say, Boy? Does Boy eat Boy?'

233

Boy was busy trying to eat a flea.

'On the contrary,' replied Will, 'they are very clever.' He had knocked out his pipe against the stone window-frame and was scratching at a grease mark on his buff leather coat. There was something very solid and reassuring in his absorbed attention to this small matter. Rupert pushed away the reports of his cannibalism.

'I shall not answer them. When charges get too absurd there is nothing one can say.'

'There is nothing one can say in any case. The people believe what they want to believe. All this is shot at you because you are the best-known person in England, the best loved by your own side and the best hated by the other.'

'All the hating doesn't come from the other side.'

'You have to pay for getting your own way.'

'But these idiot lies —'

'In war there must be an ogre. The fact that you are half foreign and inordinately high has cast you for the rôle.'

Was it only that?

Was he just the bogey man of children's tales?

A memory from his own childhood stole into his disturbed thoughts – of himself and Maurice sitting up in bed, clasping their knees, while 'each particular hair' on their heads seemed to start and rise, and Carl in his precise and unchildish tones told them what was happening at this moment in Germany. Their parents' palace at Heidelberg, where their father had set up a beautiful arch for their mother in her 'English garden', was now a haunted shell; nobody lived there, and yet lights were seen in all its windows at night, and one of the Emperor's generals had feared to advance on it because it must be so well garrisoned.

It was strange to think that ghosts should now be in their home, which Carl and Eliza could both just remember. It was not so strange as what Carl had said next.

'The people eat grass and die of hunger by the roadside. And in the houses queer new joints of meat have begun to appear at table – *long* joints.'

'Why are they long, Timon?'

'Arms and legs are long. The people are eating human flesh.'

Was that then where it came from? Was he supposed to have learned cannibalism in the German wars, and had Carl, with that mocking flick of his peaked eyebrows that seemed to make light of all he said and beg you not to take it seriously, yet managed with his foreign rumours to plant a seed very helpful to Parliament propaganda?

Into his hand as it hung limp at his side Boy had thrust a long cold damp nose and presently began to lick it. His master was unhappy among all these crackling unsatisfying bits of paper. Why would he not leave them and come outside? He thumped his tail hopefully on the floor as Will lounged over to the table and leaned over the Prince's shoulder, but no, it was only to pick up another bit of paper and flap it down again on the table.

'Have you noticed this one?' said Will, and his broad finger pointed to three questions in one of the pamphlets:

'Why camest thou hither? Thou hadst a dukedom already, and would thou have a kingdom too? Is it that thou aimest at?'

'I have a dukedom, have I? Grand Duke of Lithuania, Prince of a haunted ruin at Heidelberg, none of which I've ever seen! So now I come here to snatch at my uncle's crown, is that what they think?'

'It don't matter what they think. But don't give *our* fellows excuse to say it.'

'What fellows?'

'Fellows with a sense of their own importance, like Digby – don't ride too rough-shod over 'em. It's worth noticing – and now don't think of it again. Have you written it all now?'

'Roughly. Will this do?' He tipped back his chair, tapping his quill against the table. Boy sat up in anticipation, again scenting a speedy departure out of doors, then flopped down again with a deep sigh as Rupert went on – 'I read you the beginning. Here's my answer to their charges – "I take that man to be no soldier or gentleman that will strike (much less kill) a woman or child, if it be in his power to do the contrary; and I openly dare the most quicksighted of that lying faction to name the time, the person or the house where any child or woman lost so much as a hair from her head by me or any of our soldiers. And this I would have asked Lord Wharton at Kineton – *if His Lordship had stayed so long as to be asked the question!*" '

'That's a sharp counter-charge – into the saw-pit, hey?'

'Here's my real counter-charge. – "Whom have *we* ever punished for speaking against us? As the rebels most Jewishly whipped to death a citizen of London —"'

235

'I thought Jews got whipped to death themselves rather than whipped others.'

'Confound it, isn't that what I said? Well, let it go. Listen. "What house have *we* ransacked, as they did the Earl of Northampton's? What churches have *we* defaced as they did at Canterbury, Oxford, Worcester, and many other places? Whose pockets have *we* picked even to the value of threepence, under pretence of searching for letters, as they lately did in Gloucestershire?" '

'Put in this last week too at Windsor and Uxbridge – but go on.'

'Can't read this – something about "let God and posterity judge".'

'Humph. Posterity will judge that whichever side wins was right.'

'Well, I'll leave it. Is this good? – "My uncle is only guilty of this, that he is too good to be their King." '

'It's pressing it home good and hard, your usual method in a charge.'

'And I say he's "the best defender of the Protestant religion in Europe", and "what a gracious supporter he has been to my mother and to my brother the Prince Elector" – that's as much as I can do by way of a whack at Carl, to remind him how rottenly he's paid it back – so that "in common gratitude I do my utmost in defence of His Majesty". And here's my ending – "He that has any design against the Protestant religion, the laws of England or hopes to enrich himself by pillaging the City of London, let him be accursed".'

'*That* won't exonerate you from "belching out cursed oaths!" '

'Curse you, Will, let me finish – "And so, whether peace or war, the Lord prosper the work of their hands who stand for God and King Charles!   RUPERT".'

He sprang up, scraping back his chair and stretching his arms above his head until he rapped his knuckles against the low ceiling, and gave a piercing whistle, 'Come, Boy.'

RUPERT'S RESOLVE to take London had never swerved. At first he had hoped to take it in a single-handed dash with his cavalry; when that had become impossible, through the loss of the initiative he had won at Edgehill, he had hoped for a concerted march on it with the King's army. But Essex and the city had been given too much time to collect reinforcements, and the Royalists had had to turn back at Turnham Green.

Now a vaster plan took shape in his mind. The King was secure at Oxford, with all Wales at his back, and could communicate with the large armies that had risen at his call both down in Cornwall and up in the north under Lord Newcastle, a gallant Royalist of enormous wealth and power in his own wide lands, where, moreover, he stood as a barrier between the Parliament and that dubious Scottish army that still hung like a threatening storm cloud on the Border, ready to burst on one side or the other at the bribe of a Presbyterian Church of England and several years' pay.

Let Newcastle then march south to the Thames below London, and the Cornishmen march up to the opposite bank, and the King's army tackle Essex from Oxford on the west, and London would be surrounded. It was a fine tight plan, but, said the doubters in the academic groves, the young man who proposed it was thinking in terms of regular armies and did not know the reluctance of the English peasant to fight away from his home, or his tendency, once he had cleared the enemy away from it, to go back and work in his own fields.

Nor did he know my Lord of Newcastle.

'And what is wrong with Newcastle?' demanded Falkland, 'a man of great courage and devoted loyalty.'

'I hear he has the misfortune to have something of the poet in him,' replied Hyde drily. 'He has made Will Davenant his second-in-command for no other reason than his verses.' He expatiated on Newcastle's ignorant and unprofessional attitude towards war, until it struck Falkland that perhaps his friend was rather too ready to find fault with everybody, since he now distrusted Newcastle for lack of the very quality he so much resented in the Princes.

The three-fold plan began from the west. Rupert rode out from Oxford again, establishing outposts for the King at

Abingdon and Wallingford, at Banbury and Reading, until the ring of forts, moving ever farther out, reached to within thirty miles of London. He marched day and night to take Cirencester, and during this march meteors tore the black wintry night, 'a strange fire falling from heaven', which his enemies seized on as a portent of this modern Lucifer.

Having taken it, he swept on to Gloucester, to be told by the governor that he 'held it for King and Parliament and would not surrender it to any foreign prince'. The pretence of the King's enemies in declaring they were fighting for the King made Rupert fume even more than the 'foreign prince' – 'and thank God that I am foreign, for where but in England would you find such God-damned imbecile hypocrisy?'

But the town was too strong for him, as he could measure with a glance for all his 'rashness', and he was off again, this time to Malmesbury for one night, then to Chipping Sodbury for another, then to Durdham Down above Bristol (his diary at this time was a traveller's itinerary). Bristol was the second town to London in importance, the key city to the west, which he hoped to take the night he arrived. Colonel Fiennes had been made the governor of it by the Parliament, but there was a plot among the Royalists in the city, over two thousand in number, who were desperately sick of being insulted, imprisoned and plundered as 'Popish malignants' because they wished to preserve their churches from being desecrated, and the altars, organs and stained-glass windows in them from being destroyed.

Two leading merchants, Mr Yeomans and Mr Boucher, were to muster men and arms in their respective houses on this cold night in early March to secure the Frome gate, and as soon as it was taken, to ring out the bells of St John's church for the sailors to join the revolt, the bells of St Nicholas for the butchers, and the bells of St Michael's for Prince Rupert himself, as signal that he was then to march down and take the city.

So he appointed a party at the Gallows on St Michael's Hill, just outside the lines, and the rest of his army over at Westbury, Horfield and Durdham Downs. It was a frosty spring evening, the pale sunset had glimmered into twilight and the stars were crackling overhead as bright as musket flares over the dim grey spaces of the downs as he rode from one part of his army to another to make sure that all was in readiness to leap to the signal when the church bells should come pealing up for him from that misty old city sunk in the marsh of the river bed below.

He had thought of everything; the Bristol Royalists were to wear white tapes on their breasts and at the back of their hats so as to distinguish them, the watchword was to be 'Charles', and his soldiers had been ordered to make a peaceable entry with no bloodshed. He had mentioned the plan to no one in Oxford in his determination to keep it secret; if it succeeded it would be the most triumphant bit of organization and exact timing that could be conceived, a clear proof to all those sneering civilians round the King that he was not a mere reckless young fool, a 'dashing cavalry leader' (God, how sick he was of the words!), but one who could think in advance with as cool a judgement as any of them.

The night stepped on, minute after minute under those sparkling skies; the night was silent; no bells rang out to startle the ice-still air; the dark smudge of the city lay quiet below. At four in the morning, rolled in his cloak, he lay down on a horse-cloth on the ground up in his main camp on Durdham Downs. He closed his eyes, and dreamed that he and his cavalry were escorting King Charles into Bristol, which was now to be his capital instead of London, and therefore he must be crowned again. 'But there must be no bloodshed,' the King told him – 'they call you "that bloody cavalier". My nephew must not be bloody' – and all this while Rupert was putting the crown on his head, when suddenly, as he looked down at his hands, he saw that the crown between them was a bloody circle. People were crying out at the sight, there were shouts and tramping steps and confused frightened sounds all round him. He sprang to his feet, demanding what had happened.

Men were running into the camp, gasping breathless reports of an attack – the enemy, horse and dragoons, had fallen on them out of the night as they had sat round their camp-fire on St Michael's Hill, and they had legged it back to their main body, for they did not know how many might be coming on out of the darkness, nor how quickly they might be surrounded.

Rupert looked at his watch. It was just after half-past four. He sent out scouts. At dawn he said they should display their force before the city and see if there were still any chance of entering it. But it looked as if the plot must have been betrayed, or how did Fiennes know of his outpost on St Michael's Hill?

At seven o'clock he took his army to the edge of the downs, but three cannon shots from Brandon Hill was the only message he got from the city.

He gave the word for the army to wheel about, and was on the point of ordering a march back to Chipping Sodbury, when an extraordinary figure came running towards them like an animated scarecrow. Black mud was caked all over him like a solid suit of armour, he was trying to rub it off his face but his hair was stiff with it. The soldiers roared with laughter at him, all the louder when he shook his black fist in their faces, shouting at them, 'I am Mr Taylor, merchant and alderman of Bristol, you rascals, and one time captain of her trained bands. Take me instantly to your Prince. I can tell him of the plot.' He was taken quick enough then.

At sight of the young man on horseback leaning a little forward in his stirrups to hear what he had to say, the 'blackamoor', as the soldiers were calling him, broke out excitedly, 'God bless his most gracious King Charles! If it had not been for that detestable traitor Clement Walker, he would have sat in Bristol arrayed in the purple robe of authority, his serene brows adorned with the golden crown of dominion!'

'What has Clement Walker to do with it?' demanded Rupert.

'He – or Dobbins, who knew of our meeting at The Rose tavern – or damned talking females – they have betrayed us —' his voice ended weakly, he swayed suddenly forward.

'Bring him brandy – and food,' Rupert ordered, and sprang from his saddle, declaring that he would breakfast with Mr Taylor. Some bread and cold meat were brought them on the instant and two leather cups rimmed with silver and a squat round black bottle with a thin neck in the middle of it, full of brandy, from which Mr Taylor drank copiously, rubbing his hands as he set it down.

'Ah, I needed that,' he said in a far more natural voice than when he had uttered his aspirations for King Charles, and he went on talking rapidly while he stuffed his mouth with bread and beef. 'I was with Yeomans at his house in Wine Street last night – my own house being in the next street, Broad Street, with a large garden at the back and a stable in Tower Lane,' he added quite unnecessarily. 'Well, I was with Yeomans at ten o'clock when he got warning that our plot had been discovered to that arch fiend Colonel Fiennes. I volunteered to go down and warn Boucher in Christmas Street and tell him to dismiss his men. Yeomans said, 'Go at once or you may be too late.' He was very sad, I am certain he knew that those would be the last words I should ever hear from him – and now I shall never see him again nor Boucher either – they will be hanged and go down into silence.'

He broke down, the tears making little sooty channels on his cheeks. Rupert poured more brandy into his mug and held it out to him.

'Don't think, man – drink. They'll never hang prisoners of war. Loyalty to the King is not treason.'

Mr Taylor, with his lips glued to the cup, shook both it and his head sorrowfully from side to side. 'Then it will be,' he said as he set it down and wiped his hand across his eyes, making a great smear over his face; 'you, sir, are young, you know Englishmen separately as decent honest fellows, you don't know that clubbed together in a committee or a court of law or Parliament, and talking about principles, they can deceive themselves into bloody cruel unnatural actions and yet think themselves righteous.' He seized another piece of bread and meat. 'I am not a young man,' he said with his mouth full, 'fifty-six I shall be next June, but it would not have been safe for Clement Walker to have crossed my path as I went last night to Boucher's. They were all there as arranged, close on sixty of 'em. I told my news; we had scarcely begun to discuss what to do when we heard them banging on the outer door and shouting to us to put out lights for them. We *did* put out lights, but not as they commanded, we extinguished every lamp and candle in the place, and then in that horrid confused darkness with the soldiers shouting and battering on the door, then —'

He paused to drink again.

'What then?' asked Rupert eagerly.

Mr Taylor looked at him over the cup with round solemn eyes, their whites showing up like a Negro's in his grimy face. He said impressively, 'Every noble feeling and patriotic sentiment fled before the instinct of self-preservation.'

'I don't doubt you. But how did you preserve yourself?'

'The window was the only chance, to jump from it into the river-bed just below – luckily it was low tide, though the mud banks are near as dangerous to drown in as the water —'

'Ah, the mud! That explains —'

'My appearance? I must apologize to Your Highness —'

'No, no, man, go on. You jumped into the mud —'

'Not for some time. The window was jammed with men trying to get out. I have said there were quite sixty of us – there was only one window large enough – and the enemy were breaking in the door. But there would have been time, had we set about it in orderly fashion one by one we could all have escaped – as it was, time was wasted in struggling, and many were taken in the end.'

'But not you.'

'No. I – well, I fought my way to the window. I heard them drop, drop into the shining bed of the river like that – flop, flop —' he brought his open hand down flat on his knee – 'I could hear them floundering, choking in the mud. I could see nothing but the ruddy glares of light from the cabins of phantom ships in the distance, reflected in the sluggish water —'

('This man should be a Rembrandt – but get on with it for God's sake!')

'So you dropped —?'

'Commending my soul to God's Providence,' said Mr Taylor in stately fashion, 'I dropped from the window and fell with my face in the mud.'

'How did you get out of it?'

'The plumber, Edward Dacre, 11 St Michael's Hill, whom I shall always remember in my daily prayers, and recommend him too as a good and skilful workman who does his utmost to give satisfaction at moderate charges —'

'It's no good recommending him to me. My chances of requiring a plumber in Bristol seem devilish thin. Did he pull you out then? How did you get here?'

'Our situation was critical. The enemy had got into the house, they were firing repeatedly from the window, but without any effect except to awaken all the dogs in the street and start them barking. And the mud crawled all over us, closer and closer —'

Mr Taylor was too much of an artist to resist re-tasting his late horrible experience, but suddenly thrust it from him with a convulsive shudder. 'We got on to a plank,' he said, 'and slipped down the river in the darkness to the fishermen's huts at Hotwells. There Dacre stayed to rest, but I climbed up here to find Your Highness. My friends are in torments and chains, darkness and misery. I do not know why I have escaped.'

He looked round him, bewildered, on the grey March morning. The wind blew fresh in sudden gusts, the trees tossed against the sky; the river, now at high tide, wound silver grey through its deep gorge below them, covering with fresh sea water that loathsome slime that had so nearly filled his mouth for ever.

CHAPTER TEN

MR TAYLOR rode back to Oxford with Rupert, who promised that he should be given a commission in the auxiliary forces now being raised in that neighbourhood – he had been one of the Captains of the Bristol trained bands for fourteen years and only resigned three years ago when he became alderman and then mayor – and Rupert had formed a good opinion of him as a potential soldier. He liked his candour, his violence, his keen unconscious vision. He liked his pride in his city, and learned from him all that he could of it and its sea trade and its communications with Ireland and foreign parts.

It was from Bristol that Buckingham's army was to have set out to fight in France, 'and a bad time we had with them – as unruly a mob of ruffians as ever you saw, until one day comes the news that the Duke had been stabbed – and pouff! all at once they were lambs – 1,500 soldiers stranded at Bristol, walking the streets like ghosts and not knowing what to do. They were sent to Ireland at last – poor devils!'

'Why were they?'

'People are always sent to Ireland when they don't know what to do with 'em. You can see the caves now down by the docks at home where they used to chain up the folk to be sold as slaves in Ireland – their own flesh and blood too – younger brothers and sisters, anyone they didn't want. But that was long ago, mind you. Bristol shows other slaves now. Many's the blackamoor I've seen down at the port.'

He spoke of travel with the pride and excitement of the stay-at-home trader; Bristol merchants had been familiar with Greenland through their North Sea fisheries ever since John Cabot, the Venetian merchant and Bristol citizen, had with his English crew discovered the icy wastes of Labrador, and his son Sebastian had pushed on still farther north to Hudson Bay and south to Maryland. Taylor himself had bought a share in three ships, the *Great St David's*, the *Faithful Lady* and the

Bonaventure; he had thrilled to the proposed adventure of Madagascar six years ago, and had determined that his excitement should not be merely vicarious, for he would have put money into it too.

'Tell Your Highness what,' he said confidentially, 'I might lend £100 towards these auxiliary troops you speak of – at six per cent,' he added thoughtfully.

He was a big powerful man with a peaked beard and eyes that twinkled with interest in everything he saw or heard or said. Rupert found it almost as interesting as Mr Taylor that the merchant had married a daughter of Alderman Henry Yate, soap manufacturer, that he had been apprenticed as a lad to his trade the very year that King James came to the English throne ('*Queen* James we all called him, as we'd called the old Queen, King Elizabeth – but bless my soul I'm forgetting, he was Your Highness' own grandfather!') and that he had been church-warden of St John's in '28 and '34 and got Bishop Skinner to threaten to interdict a fair in that parish if the congregation would not set in order a pair of decayed organs in that church. 'But now all the organs are interdicted, the clergy turned out of their living to starve, while croaking cuckoos are thrust into their places to defile and destroy what they can of their church to prove the purity of their faith. And my friends will die horribly.'

His head sank on his chest, he could talk no more, not even of his city nor himself.

His gloom was justified. All the prisoners taken in Bristol on that frosty night in March were chained by neck and feet in the dungeons of Bristol Castle, allowed neither fire nor lights nor any visits from friend or wife or child; the leaders, including the absent plumber, who had had too much wit to return to 11 St Michael's Hill, were solemnly tried and condemned to be hanged for 'treason to the nation'. The King's threats and entreaties went for nothing.

Then the city itself intervened. They had been told the Parliament stood for the liberties of Englishmen – was this liberty, that they should see their most respected merchants ('Yes, and Mr Yeomans had been their sheriff too, only two years ago, as I was in '26, and as good and just a sheriff as ever they'd had – bar one!' Mr Taylor told Rupert) swinging before their front doors, and all because they thought the King had a right to enter his own city of Bristol? But even Mr Aldworth, the present mayor, and his aldermen had no more power than the King!

Fiennes indeed, disturbed by the outcry from the town, hesitated to carry out the sentence until he had again asked the Houses at Westminster for his orders. But they had already told him to 'proceed with all celerity and severity'; the feeling of the town made no difference, except that Fiennes had to keep the city gates shut and all the streets lined with troops to prevent any attempt at rescue. The executioners did their best to impress the Parliament by their 'severity'; Yeomans and Boucher, so weak from their hideous imprisonment that they fainted as they were brought out, were not allowed to be attended on the scaffold by their own clergy, but by the enemy's chaplains; and even those last thwarted devotions were disturbed by Captain Langrish, who taunted and jeered at the prisoners all through their prayers. Captain Clifton gave the final touch of 'severity' when he hacked with his sword at the hand that Yeomans' brother-in-law put out to stay the wild swing to and fro of the body as it was jerked off the ladder.

'And those contemptuous cruelties, done in deliberation and cold blood, are respectable, because supported by a mock trial and orders from Parliament,' so Mr Taylor burst out in his rage and tears to Rupert.

'It's no good talking to a bloody foreigner, Taylor,' said Rupert ironically.

The executions at Bristol shocked the nation. They were the first lives to be deliberately taken by either side outside the heat of action, and many devoted adherents to the Parliament thought it a pity to have started that particular precedent.

Its effect on Rupert was to make him more scornful than ever of his enemies' complaints of him, and of his friends' anxious warnings. 'Remember the Bristol merchants,' he would say when told that Englishmen would not stand this or that – 'it strikes me that Englishmen will stand anything, as long as they can pretend that it's legal. I have neither the time nor the inclination for these formalities.'

When about this time his troops stormed Birmingham and took the town on their first assault, the Parliament declared that 'the Cavaliers rode through the streets like so many furies or bedlams. They shot at any door or window where they could espy any looking out.' As usual Rupert did not trouble to see to it that any Royalist answers were issued. But as many of his men were shot down as they rode through the streets there was good reason to fire on citizens who looked out of windows. Rupert had ordered one or two houses to be fired to help his entrance into the town; later it was found that other streets were in flames, and he at once warned the city authorities and did his best to help them stop the fire which was spreading rapidly in a high wind among the wooden houses.

'Do they take me for a fool?' he demanded when he was shown the accusing pamphlet with its sarcastic title, 'Prince Rupert's Burning Love to England discovered in Birmingham's Flames' – 'what military objective could I have had in burning the city?' It was the main difference between him and both his allies and enemies, that he thought of Birmingham in terms of 'military objectives' rather than as a town 'as famed for hearty wilful affected disloyalty to the King as any place in England.'

He pushed on to Lichfield, but it was too hard a nut to crack by storming, for the Cathedral Close was strongly fortified, and the answer to his summons was a derisive jangle of bells from the Cathedral tower. So he set to work to dig trenches as near as he dared round the Close; they became rivers of mud in the bad weather, but he went on working in them himself to encourage his officers, an example of such force that even so magnificent a courtier as Digby followed it, working in mud up to his waist in the moat until he got shot in the leg. Will Legge was also wounded. Lichfield was proving too costly. Rupert cast about for newer methods. Remembering those on the Continent, he collected a platoon of miners from the Staffordshire colleries near by, got them to tunnel under the walls of the Close and to spring the first mine ever used in warfare in England, to make a breach in the walls.

But the Roundheads fought on undismayed by the novelty; they took some prisoners and hanged one of them in derision in front of the walls, inviting the Cavaliers to take pot-shots at their comrade.

'God damn me,' swore Rupert, 'I'll not give one man quarter after this!'

And he read what he could of a letter from his uncle entreating him in a charming rambling sermon to remember his courtesy and humanity to the people he fought against and act towards them always as a father, while he watched his big guns being brought up to play on the breach. By next day he had forced a surrender, and despite his former threats, gave all the honours of war and compliments to the enemy officers on their gallantry as they marched out. In the Cathedral he found the tombs broken open and bones scattered and the altar used as a butcher's shambles. A calf dressed in linen was bleating by the font, left there after a mock baptism. He was glad he had paid his compliments before he saw all this.

All through the tough and tedious siege he had been pestered by frantic appeals which besought him to be in half a dozen different places at once. Now he found there was no help for it; in spite of the King's repeated urging of him to continue marching north, he must retrace his steps and relieve Reading, which was being besieged by Essex, so that at last even the King's secretary had to write that if Prince Rupert did not come, Reading would be lost. But when he came it was too late, for Reading had already surrendered. Its defeated Governor was court-martialled, and the King proved implacable against him, not on his own account but because the Governor had consented in the articles of surrender to give up the Roundhead deserters to be dealt with by their own side. Rupert got him off by enlisting his young cousin Prince Charles to beg his life from the over-scrupulous King; – 'Your father is too much of a gentleman for this rough business,' he told the boy, who was at once on fire to show that he was as rough a soldier as Rupert.

And now the northward march could not be continued, for since Reading had fallen, Essex barred the way. Rupert had to make his headquarters again at Oxford and content himself with night marches and surprise attacks, often close to London. Any Cavalier who rode clattering into a village demanding levies or provisions in the name of Prince Rupert was sure to get them, for you never knew but what the terrible prince himself might come riding up after him on his black Barbary horse, singing as he rode. War was a game to him and his brother, a game they had played since childhood, complained the towns-folk. A horse taken was a horse taken, even if worthy Major Medhope of the Parliament swore that he only requisitioned 'Popishly inclined' horses – but all the same many earnest citizens felt they could better put up with it when their peace was disturbed by sad stern men in the name of conscience, rather than by these 'gay riders'.

Rupert's forays from Oxford had earned him still another nickname, the Terror of the West.

On a June morning a certain Colonel Hurry, a long lean loose-knit Scot whose years of service abroad had put a high shine on his ruddy weather-beaten face, rode up to Rupert's headquarters at Abingdon with important news. On being asked for his credentials, he replied that he had this moment come over from the Roundheads.

'A deserter?'

'A soldier of fortune, Your Highness – and may I bring it to you! Twenty thousand pounds in gold are not to be sneezed at.'

He explained that this sum of army pay for Essex's men was on its way from London to Thame, that Essex's outposts were half asleep as usual, and that if Rupert could get through their lines and catch the convoy he would be making a grand scoop for the King. Hurry knew the country backwards and would lead them with his maps.

So Rupert's bugles blared out his orders for 'Boot and Saddle', and in the double quick time his men took to get ready he had a chat with Hurry, who amused him by telling him of the very similar difficulties the commanders were having on the other side – Essex now simply could not be got to tackle Oxford seriously, he was as much afraid of extreme measures against the King as the King was of them against his people. 'Hampden prods at the old cuckold to invest Oxford, but no, he says there are floods in Port Meadow, and his men haven't got their pay.'

'So Hampden's the fire-eater, is he?'

'Not really, Your Highness – but he's got his cousin behind him, Colonel Cromwell – there are the makings of a soldier in him,' added the professional, with a tug at his scrubby moustache.

'Colonel now, is he? His men are getting as good – or as bad – a reputation for horse-thieving as my own.'

Hurry grinned. 'You know what he says? Tells his men to trust in God – but to keep their powder dry!'

By the afternoon Rupert was jingling over Magdalen Bridge and out of Oxford with seventeen hundred men and some officers as eager as himself – Will Legge and Dan O'Neill, that jolly Irishman, and Harry Percy, the brother of Lucy Carlisle, and Colonel Lunsford, who was getting as alarming a reputation as Rupert for witchcraft, and all because he had two brothers, also Colonels, so that he was constantly being heard of in three places at once. They rode through the outlying posts of

248

Essex's army as it was getting dark, and dashed through Tetsworth, fired at from all sides, but keeping to Rupert's express orders and not replying by a single shot. On they went all through the light short midsummer night, with the scent of honeysuckle and meadowsweet coming clear and fresh through the smell of sweat and leather, and now and then the shrill pipe of a startled bird piercing the steady clank, clank of moving horses and the low murmur of men's voices.

As the dawn began to come up white over the edges of the Chiltern hills, they cleared two villages, and in the second one, Legge leading the forlorn hope, captured one hundred and twenty sleepy Roundhead soldiers, utterly surprised at enemy troops so far behind their lines. Legge also took their standard, showing some buff and bossed Bibles on a black ground, and best of all, several scores of horses.

Rupert pushed on up over the hills, but the sun had risen on a white, empty road – 'Gone to earth!' he exclaimed, looking round in vain for the convoy – 'they may be in any of these woods.' The noise of the fighting in the villages must have given the alarm, and they could not wait to search the woods since they could see from the heights that the Roundhead army was now awake and on the move. He was miles behind their front line and Oxford a long way off. He must pull off his forces, and this he did very coolly, drawing his converging enemies after him until he reached Chalgrove Field. Here he ordered the infantry to press forward towards Oxford and secure the bridge over the Tame at Chislehampton. He then lined the road on either side with his dragoons, while he halted with his cavalry in a cornfield, to lure the enemy on into the trap.

As he was making these arrangements, the enemy dragoons opened fire on him from behind a hedge and he saw one of his men in front of him crash over on his saddle while another clutched at his sword arm.

'By God,' he swore, 'this insolency is not to be endured!' He swung his horse's head round, put it at the hedge and plumped into the middle of the amazed Roundheads. About sixteen of his men followed him, and the enemy fled back to their cavalry supports. Rupert collected a few more horsemen and then charged. The Roundheads stood their ground for a bit, but the rest of the cavalry under Dan O'Neill and Harry Percy swung in on their right flank. There was brisk hand-to-hand fighting for a few minutes, the Roundheads showing far more mettle than at Powick Bridge, but soon they were scattering in every direction. Rupert managed to rally his troopers this time from pursuit, left some dragoons to guard the bridge, and gave his men the night's rest they needed on the other side of the river.

He got them all back into Oxford in triumph by noon next morning after a ride of fifty miles through their enemy's country, having soundly beaten them in two small actions and one pitched battle in less than forty-eight hours with a loss of exactly twelve men.

They were all full of glee in their exploit, increased daily as the news trickled in that over sixty of the Roundheads had fallen and that somebody had seen Mr John Hampden riding off from Chalgrove Field swaying over his saddle bow from a mortal wound. He had heard the firing and leaped from his bed to join the fight and now lay dying in a cottage at Thame.

Rupert thought the death of this Roundhead leader, 'the fellow who started all the trouble when I was over here before', a feather in his cap; but his uncle, so far from being grateful, was really distressed and was sending his own surgeon, Dr William Harvey, to attend him, when they heard that he was dead – 'of his own acid temper', said George Goring, who had picked up the odd medical detail that Hampden's wounds could not heal because his blood was 'acrimonious', as was shown by the scurf he often had on his face.

CHAPTER ELEVEN

QUEEN HENRIETTA MARIA had returned to the North of England early that spring. She had been abroad nearly a year and had accomplished her business with the Dutch merchants, bartering the Crown jewels for armaments, with all the determined ferocity of a Frenchwoman who is bargaining for those she loves. People who had thought of her only as a drawing-room darling, a Parisienne whose weightiest concern had been to reform the clumsy dress of Englishwomen and wheedle silly young men into Catholicism, had been amazed at what she had accomplished.

They were the more astonished at her heroism. The Dutch Admiral Tromp had escorted her ships home, and a storm had arisen so frightful that for more than two weeks they were tossed backwards and forwards between England and Holland. Two of the ships went down and the sailors despaired. It was the Queen who kept all their hearts up by declaring that 'Queens never drown', though she was so horribly sick that she had good reason to wish they did. When at last they could make a landing, the Parliament ships trained their guns on the house on the Yorkshire coast where the Queen and her ladies had taken shelter, the house was set on fire, they were driven out in their nightdresses in the middle of that bitter night in early March, and one poor woman went mad from the continued terror and exposure. But the Queen was not to be cowed for an instant; she even ran back into the burning house to rescue her little dog.

A new life and force had taken possession of her, and it made some of the King's friends as uneasy as it did his enemies. There was an enquiry at Westminster as to the propriety of opening fire on a woman and a queen. Pym settled the sex question by ignoring it. For the 'queen' part of it, the Queen was a simple subject like anybody else; having refused to take part in her husband's coronation ceremony because of its Protestant nature she must now accept the consequences. And he proceeded to impeach her for high treason for bringing arms into England. The Queen laughed.

It was the King who was appalled. 'She is in danger only for my sake,' he said, and then – 'how content were I to be tossed, weather-beaten and ship-wrecked, if she were in safe harbour!'

'The danger of his love for the Queen,' Hyde pronounced in his sententious fashion, 'is that it is more compounded of conscience and gratitude than of desire. And the danger of the Queen is not so much that she has influence over him, as any woman may have over her husband, but that she is determined everyone shall see it.'

He had just been made Chancellor of the Exchequer and knighted, and knew that the Queen would like him no better for it. Nor did the Prince, who was always finding Sir Edward too busy to attend to his wishes. But in the matter of the Queen they were in accord.

Rupert had observed that after a letter arrived from his wife King Charles was not nearly so apt to obey him with that immediate confidence that he expected of his uncle. He did not feel as deeply complimented as the King intended he should

251

when, directly after Chalgrove Field, he gave his nephew a deed of chivalry to perform in going to meet the Queen so as to guard her from Essex's army and escort her in safety to himself at Oxford. Goring had been despatched the previous winter to help Lord Newcastle clear the North, and in spite of his former record he had done excellent work at the head of the cavalry and now got the country safe enough for the Queen to start on her journey south.

So Rupert set out to guard his aunt, with memories, not of a May Day morning in the woods near Westminster when he had burned to serve her and she had dubbed him her own true knight with a branch of whitethorn, but of her with his sisters and mother at The Hague, of maddening feminine allusions to he knew not what, and little intrigues in which she was always taking somebody's part against somebody – generally against himself. But then he had been a sullen boy, so cramped and dulled by his imprisonment that it had been difficult to distinguish friend from foe. Now he was a man who had come into his own in every way, no longer stunted before he could be tried, but fulfilled to the utmost of his powers. So why should he fear woman any more than man?

The women of England had certainly given him no cause to do so. They had offered themselves to his embraces with a persistency that would have been embarrassing if Rupert had allowed himself to be embarrassed by what was to him mainly a matter of time. He must get what sleep he could, and that was always too little; therefore how could he love? So he answered his admirers, with a simplicity that shocked them. Sometimes with even greater simplicity he handed them over to Maurice, who was quite content to 'take his brother handsomely off' as long as matrimony was not involved. To win the attention of his more aloof and elusive brother, even for a week or a night, became a target for as fierce competition as that among his soldiers in battle. Sometimes the two were mingled, for many women armed themselves and rode to fight under the Prince's banner.

Now, though he would have to encounter his aunt again, in compensation there was Essex too, whose army was also marching with very different motives to meet the Queen. At one point Essex dared approach him too near, and Rupert got the news while he was in the middle of shaving, dashed out with the soap still on his face, flung himself into the saddle, rode out at the head of a hastily mustered troop, routed the enemy, and returned to his razor.

'That was quick work,' said Will Legge.

'Not very. The shaving water has got cold.'

Essex learned his lesson and did not get up so early again. Rupert's men now rode out singing,

> 'Farewell my lord of Essex with hey,
> Farewell my lord of Essex with ho,
>   He sleeps till eleven,
>   Leaves the Cause till six or seven,
> But 'tis no matter – their hope's in heaven
>   With a hey trolly lolly ho!'

But there was not much chance for Essex's army to sleep till eleven, for the Prince's army harried them so perpetually that they had everlastingly to be on duty and declared themselves weary of their lives.

The King's secretary wrote long letters, and the King himself long postscripts to them, full of anxious instructions lest the Queen should come by Stratford-on-Avon and 'the Earl of Essex may force her to fight before it be possible that His Majesty can come up to her'. But in spite of all their fears Rupert outmanoeuvred Essex and came as arranged to meet the Queen at Stratford.

She was already there when he arrived, with a large force of foot, horse and artillery, and was already finishing supper in a charming old-fashioned house, the biggest in the village, belonging to a Mrs Nash.

'Here I am, your She-generalissima!' she cried, as she stood on tiptoe with her hands on his shoulders to kiss her nephew on both cheeks. He had never seen her look so well; she was rosy and sunburnt from riding with her troops and picnicking in view of them all, and in all weathers, rain, frost or bitter wind.

Energy and excitement shot out from her like sparks from a cat's fur; she was twice the woman she had been, indeed it did not seem safe there should be so much of any woman in so small a compass – it seemed possible that like a charged mine she might 'go off'.

Rupert had found no opening for any speech whether of welcome, congratulation, or condolence, for with that inimitable air of hers that transformed this pleasant middle-class room into a Court drawing-room, yet kept all its informality, she was bringing him up to a simpering lady and telling him, 'Now you must meet your hostess, a most illustrious lady, for she is the grandmother of your mother's favourite poet, and Mary here must cap your quotations from him, for all your English poets are alike to me, all their verse sounds like water hissing on hot iron – and you need not scold me for being rude since Mrs Nash agrees with me! She says her grandfather had a regular income paid him on condition he wrote two plays a year. No *true* poet would have done that.'

Mrs Nash's grandfather turned out to have been Will Shakespeare, and the regular income had been large enough to buy this house, the 'New Place', and leave it to his descendants. Mrs Nash was fashionably deprecating about her famous grandparent, whom she believed to have gone up to town sometimes to make merry with his old companions, Drayton and Ben Jonson, and to have drunk so much with them on the last occasion that he died of it.

'The English always say their ancestors were a poor lot, and drank,' remarked Rupert, glancing at the books which had belonged to the dead poet. Mrs Nash blushed hotly at the snub. His aunt excused him with a peal of laughter.

Their skirts swished and whispered; the low, beamed room was full of the July evening sunshine, mellow and somehow miraculous, making the whole of this scene like something in a play – a play of Shakespeare's perhaps, he did not know which – and presently he found that what he was really doing was watching 'Mary here', her long eyes laughing both at him and Mrs Nash, and a little lizard in her hat made of emeralds, winking green sparks at him out of the dusk beside the low window. For she stood beside the window against the light, and only her hands showed clear in the glow, and they were long and still like lilies, while the Queen's fluttered about.

He only just noticed in time that his aunt was telling him about that terrible crossing from Holland and her poor ladies, what they had suffered! And she, too, of course, but it had been almost worth it for the amusement, for 'only imagine, dearest nephew, they were so certain their last hour was upon them that they confessed everything – oh, but *everything*! quite regardless that I was there to hear them – and afterwards you can imagine their repentance – of their confessions, not their sins!'

He asked about the ships that had fired on her house – what had Tromp been about not to drive them off?

'And cause an international incident? No, he said there was a fog and I dare say there was – that fog of war we hear so much about!'

'It was clear enough for you to miss Mitte, Madam, and run back into the flames to find her,' said 'Mary'. She had spoken at last, and in just the voice he had known she would have, deep and gay, a voice rather like his mother's when she was happy, out hunting. He must find out who she was. His aunt had assumed that they knew each other, so that she had curtseyed and he had bowed without introduction. But he had to ask how his aunt had run back into danger, and he had to admire and pat the cause of it, an ugly little mongrel bitch, 'poor darling Mitte', who was now frantically trying to make friends with Boy. The big white dog wore his most patient air of the martyred gentleman, gazing at his master with wounded eyes over her fluffy yapping head as if to ask how long he must endure these underbred effusions.

'Our Cavalier dogs,' exclaimed the Queen, 'what high adventures they share with us! Your "Boy" is a great public figure.'

'He's not a popular one with half the nation – nor will Mitte be with the other half after running you into such danger.'

He turned to 'Mary' for confirmation, hoping to hear that voice again. But she was patting and stroking the dogs and would not even look up. Yet every curve and lissom line of her was aware of him; he was sure with a most unwonted certainty that she was wanting to look round at him, and only did not because she wanted still more to tease.

His aunt recalled his roving eye. He had to hear how one of those tiresome Scots nobles, the Earl of Montrose, had come and worried her with their tangled Scottish politics when she was still worn out with fright and cold and seasickness. She had met the Marquis of Hamilton just after, 'another Scot you know, Rupert, but so different', and he had reassured her completely by telling her what a vain foolish person Montrose was.

But supper was not finished (nor begun for Rupert), and the golden light was deepening and reddening down the long Spanish table, making little pools of fire beneath the glasses, and shutting out in deep shadow the books that Shakespeare had read.

He was sitting now at his aunt's right hand, and 'Mary' was beside him, her fingers playing with the stem of her glass, and her face in the glow of the sunset when she turned to speak to him. He thought she would never do so, and he did not know how to make her, until Harry Jermyn, the Queen's Commander-in-Chief, fair, fat and florid in black satin and soft white boots, came in and sat on the Queen's other side, and at once there was a great deal of talk between them, though at first the Queen included Mary too, this time calling her 'Butterfly'.

He seized his chance to detach her from the general talk.

'Why do they call you that?' he asked.

'Your Highness doesn't think I'm like one?'

'No, for your hands stay still.'

She glanced round on him, her eyes full of laughter. 'I thought Your Highness never noticed what women were like.'

'Who's told you that?'

'My husband has told me a great deal about you.'

Damn it! He obviously ought to know who she was. His social memory was poor, but surely he could never have met this pretty creature and forgotten her. And yet there certainly was something familiar about her face – was it those long eyes? Where *had* he seen her? Discretion was the better part of valour; he went on eating his roast chicken and peas. Those two plays a year had provided old Will's descendants with an excellent cook.

'You don't care to know what he says of you?' she pursued devilishly.

Should he confess he had no notion who she was?

He turned and looked at her, and forgot what she had said and what he had been going to say, forgot everything but that her eyes were the most tantalizing, provocative things he had ever seen; it must be they that had given her the name of Butterfly, for the lights and colours dancing in them under those soft eyelashes were like clusters of butterflies fluttering in the sunlight. The setting sun shone full on them now; there were yellow lights in them, there were orange lights, and a circle of very dark blue – no, grey – no, brown – went all round them. He had never seen such eyes, but – '*Where* have I seen you before?' he exclaimed.

' "Did not I dance with you in Brabant once?" ' she answered lightly.

'Do you often talk in blank verse? Oh, I see, you are quoting. A play, isn't it? That's suitable here.'

'*Love's Labour's Lost* – I hope that is not suitable here!'

He just caught the last words uttered on a quick breath, half laugh, half whisper, before the Queen swept up their conversation. 'Yes, his plays, Rupert; it is true, isn't it, that you and your brothers had to learn William Shakespeare's plays at Leyden?'

She had been talking with Mrs Nash, and Rupert had to tell her how highly Shakespeare was thought of in the German university; his mother too held the Continental opinion and was always quoting him; no doubt in time England would follow suit, especially since Suckling had set the example.

'Ah, poor Suckling!' sighed the Queen, but her grief had a metallic ring in it, a perfunctory Last Post, sounded that she might rally her troops round her yet again and prevent her nephew and Mary from galloping off the field.

It gave him a delightful thrill that he could give no other name to her. But he could not get back to her now that his aunt was on the alert, watchful, determined they should all talk together. Why could women never leave anything alone? Mary did not talk nearly as freely to his aunt, he could see that – her words slid out prettily then but insipidly, all showing what good little girls they were, like débutantes making their Court curtseys. He would like to tell her that to tease her – that would rouse the devil in her again! But he did not see how he was ever going to tell her anything. Were they all going to talk general conversation for the rest of the evening?

Thank God, no! That good fellow Harry Jermyn had just tipped him the faintest flick of a wink as he lifted his glass to him in a toast to somebody's memory, Shakespeare's or Suckling's, Rupert hadn't noticed which, and was now talking so earnestly with the Queen that he leaned farther and farther over the table to her, till his broad shoulders quite obliterated her diminutive person by the window from the two who sat farther down the table in ever deeper growing shadow.

'And now,' said Rupert, 'who are you and where have I seen you?'

'That is hardly gallant, unless you have never seen me.'

There was no good little girl now in her tones, though they had gone so low he could scarcely hear them.

'I am not a gallant.'

'So *she* evidently thinks. You had best pay her more court after supper.'

'Why, what use is a nephew for a gallant?'

257

Mary shook with silent laughter. 'Oh, sir, forgive me, but this is the direct "Rupert touch" that everybody is speaking of! "What use" – then is gallantry only for an end?'

'Your honesty should acknowledge it. Your poets do. No, not Shakespeare this time – I am tired of him – but that old fellow Donne – doesn't he say that the lover who would ignore the one right end of loving is like a man who would go to sea for no other purpose than for to be sick?'

His gaze beat hers down, though she tried manfully to meet it, to keep the blood from flooding into her face. Well, she deserved it for taunting him with 'the Rupert touch'. Let her have it then! And hers was a grand spirit, she was rallying to the attack again – but he would get in first. 'Do you still want me to pay court to my aunt?'

'No.' She had not shown much fight after all – but now she came on again with wicked eyes – 'I have too much respect for your uncle.'

'Your innuendoes are atrocious, Madam.'

'And so are your statements, sir.'

He gave a burst of laughter, and now her startled lips shaped themselves into a round 'Oh, hush!' but he was damned if he'd hush. Why should they mind about the Queen? People were free enough to enjoy themselves, God knew, in her Court – and since this Butterfly would not tell him who she was, then he was all the more free to enjoy her. She had made him realize that everybody was speaking of him, that he was successful in war – and why should he not be in love? His diffidence in that respect should certainly have been beaten down by this time.

Yet now that he was suddenly, overwhelmingly, delightedly in love, his mother's assertions that he was too rough to please the ladies would come back into his mind. They had been made so early and so long before they could be refuted that he had never dreamed of their contradiction. Now he had a double contest before him, to prove his mother wrong, and to win this brilliant Court butterfly.

And as they rested on her, dark and heavy, his eyes betrayed this latter purpose as clearly as if he had spoken it aloud. She looked at him in an excitement that answered his own; but slowly she began to change, and into her face, which had been alive with pleasure and mischief, there now crept a light dismay.

'What has happened?' he asked, 'what are you thinking of?'

'My husband.'

A stale cheap trick, to make him jealous. He was angry and showed it. 'What has he to do with us – here – now?'

That was true – her transparent face showed it, as her thoughts sailed swiftly across it on the high wind of his emotion. They were together here and now on this July evening, with the warm light fading outside the window and the hum of bees and scent of roses coming in through it; they were as remote from the busy company round them, from the usual background of their lives, as if they existed only in one of those plays that that bald-headed old gentleman had written twice a year in this long low room.

'Did not I dance with you at Brabant once?'

The silence between them lasted perhaps half a minute and then she was saying in a rather breathless voice —

'But I think you had better know who I am.'

'You would not tell me before – why should you now? I will tell you who you are – a butterfly that nobody has ever captured.'

'Oh, but they have!'

'They?'

'Caught me in a tree and packed me in a hamper and sent me to the King!'

What strange fooling! Was she hysterical? But he only asked gravely, 'And what did the King say?'

'He said it was a pity butterflies should wear black, and he made me leave off mourning. I was in mourning for my first husband, for I was a widow before I was eleven. And I nearly was your brother's widow,' she finished with a gasp, and leaned back in her chair, for now at last she had said it, and whatever happened now he could not blame her.

But, Oh! what would he say? why did he not say it? what was he thinking, this man who had won so terrible a reputation as a soldier, yet had greeted his aunt like a tongue-tied schoolboy, and then had launched out so surprisingly at herself – a magnificent creature, every movement like that of a young tiger in its contained fury of energy – would she ever be able to get him out of her head?

He said very low, *'Who* are you?'

'I was Mary Villiers.'

Once again the splendid legs of George Villiers, Duke of Buckingham, strode across Rupert's remembered vision.

Buckingham had been murdered, Henry drowned – and here was Mary, whom none of them had ever thought of.

'No,' he said, 'we never thought of you,' for he must speak to stave it off, that other thing that was forcing its way up into his mind, that other splendid figure, not Buckingham, but a noble young bridegroom in the chapel at Lambeth Palace, and the King, wearing his George and Garter, leading up the aisle a little figure so gorgeous he could scarcely see her.

It had been only one of the many grand functions he had had to attend when he was on that visit to his uncle six years ago; it had taken place just before he left England; he had met neither bride nor bridegroom, and had got away from the wedding to the river as soon as he could, but he had thought for a moment – 'she should have been Henry's wife', and then forgotten her, and now here she was again – and the thing he did not wish to see was coming nearer and nearer, coming between them.

'You were Mary Villiers,' he said, 'so then you are now —'
'The wife of your friend Richmond,' she answered.

CHAPTER TWELVE

AT SIX years old Mary Villiers had been betrothed to the eldest son of the Prince Palatine, who was the heir-presumptive to the throne of England. Her portrait was painted in the big family group that the Dutchman Gerard Honthorst did of her father and mother and herself and her baby brother George when the painter was on a visit to England. He told her charming stories of the young Prince Henry, all of which Mary secretly disbelieved, for she knew they wanted her to like him, and equally well she knew that little boys were not like that. There was young Charles Herbert now, a horrid little boy with pimples always breaking out in a different place on his face, who pulled her hair and told tales against her when she scratched him in return.

She wore a scarlet and silver dress and a silver lace cap and apron for her picture, all of which she liked, but she had to hold out the apron full of flowers to her baby brother, and of that she grew very tired. Her arms got stiff and ached, and Baby George was not really there, she was only holding them out to an empty chair; – none of the family were there, they were all painted separately in turn, which just showed you what liars painters were, for at the end there they all were sitting together as though they never were apart, and Baby George was holding out ecstatic hands to the flowers she would never have dreamed of handing to him; and her mother was sitting fair and placid beside her father in a way she had small chance to do in real life; and her father sat there all smooth and soapy with a large glassy eye looking out of the canvas, as pink and white and sweet as a great doll – and nothing could be more utterly unlike him.

'Mary, Mary quite contrary,' her father called her, but she would not say she liked the picture, and she would not give Mynheer Honthorst a kiss and thank him for making her so pretty. She was a great deal prettier than that when she danced about, and all the praise and petting she got had already begun to make her aware of it. She could run wild wherever she liked in the King's palace; staid old courtiers complained that the place had been turned into a rabbit-warren of children, as she scampered up and down the corridors, thankful to be released from her sittings and to stretch her legs and lungs again in freedom. A miniature was done of her from the picture to be sent to Prince Henry; and her father read out the boy's letters that assured his prospective father-in-law 'how much I am your most affectionate friend'.

Buckingham pulled his Mary's hair (but in a charming caressing way, very different from Lord Herbert's furtive tugs) and told her with his usual gay imprudence that she might well one day be Queen of England, 'but don't be as contrary as the last Queen Mary', – for the song was all about her, she had turned England Catholic again, and the 'silver bells and cockle shells' had been the bells in High Mass and the cockle shells in the hats of the palmers, and the 'pretty maids all in a row' had been the nuns. But that was all over now, the palmers and the nuns mostly in prison, so that the common jail-birds complained that to go to prison nowadays was as bad as going into a monastery or nunnery. Mary would be the Protestant Queen of the young Protestant German Prince who all good Englishmen were longing to see on the throne of England.

Buckingham's exuberant and happy mind was brimming with vast plans for Europe, all to be negotiated by himself. He urged on a war to restore the Palatinate to Prince Henry's father; he organized another to help the Huguenots in France, which he would lead himself, and so perhaps contrive another opportunity to make love to that fair Queen of France that was always known as Anne of Austria. Nothing could daunt him. He wriggled through all the persistent attacks of the English Parliament until he boasted he was 'Parliament proof'; and he even baffled that jealous snake, Lucy Carlisle, when she had stolen from him at a dance a diamond stud given by Queen Anne, and tried to send it to Richelieu in proof of the French Queen's infidelity. But Buckingham, as Controller of the English Ports, had all the ports closed while another stud was made and sent secretly to Anne to produce in refutation of the charge.

'That was the end of poor Lucy,' he was apt to say, 'she took to intellect after that – ugly fellows like Black Tom Wentworth and Pym.'

Such a fate seemed to him worse than any vengeance, but indeed he never bore malice, he was too happy, too confident – a man who could escape both politicians and women must well be invulnerable. But he was murdered as he set off to France; and then they heard that Prince Henry was drowned; and then the Queen Henrietta Maria had a baby boy, so in any case Henry would not have been King of England; and then Mary was married, in form only of course, to young Lord Herbert; and then Herbert died too (thank Heaven!); and it seemed as though she had worn nothing but black ever since she had had that picture painted of her in scarlet and silver.

Until one day she climbed a tree, in hopes of tearing her clothes to rags, and was nearly shot by a short-sighted courtier. He had some trouble in getting her down from her perch – 'And what shall I do with you now I've caught you?' he asked.

'Pack me up in a hamper and send me to the King!' she exclaimed. She had been set to read North's translation of Plutarch in her lessons; the story of the young Cleopatra, sent to Caesar in a bundle of rugs, had been an alleviation, was now an inspiration.

How the King's grave face lit up when he saw her jump out of the hamper! He kissed her and told her she was the image of her madcap father, and that there was never a day in his life that he did not long to hear his laugh again.

'And so do I,' said Mary, 'for everything has been dismal since he died, and I am still wearing black.'

But that was the last day she wore it.

The King insisted that she and her two younger brothers should now be brought up with his children, and as his children – there should be no difference between them. Little George Villiers, now the second Duke of Buckingham, was growing into a great rascal, with all the vitality of his father and even more of the mischief. He was three years older than Charles the Prince of Wales and always getting him into trouble.

As for Mary – 'that girl is bound to make trouble wherever she goes', said the Queen, and refused to give her a place in the Queen's bedchamber when she was only thirteen, because, as she frankly told her husband, she was so pretty that she would set everyone by the ears. So King Charles told Mary in consolation that she should have the greatest and the handsomest young nobleman in the kingdom for a husband as soon as he came back from his travels. And that was his own cousin, James Stuart, the Duke of Richmond, now making the grand tour of Europe.

In the meantime, as for some strange reason the Queen did not seem to care much for poor Mary, she was sent to one of the new boarding-schools for girls that King Charles had started under the governance of refugee French Huguenot ladies. He believed in women's education, and was determined to restore it to the high level of the last century – 'My grandmother, Mary Queen of Scots, was the most charming woman of her age, and no one thought her the less so because she could talk Latin and write Greek.'

Women's education was one of the many innovations the Puritans objected to; women's place was the home, except when it was at church. But Mary's French and English governesses did not advance her education very much. They taught her to cover boxes with shells, to twist tiny toy stags and birds out of wire and cotton, to make perfume sachets out of walnuts, and to write shorthand. There was a craze for shorthand – all the girls took notes of the sermons in it, to the fury of their fathers when they caught them pulling out their little books and scribbling in church with that affectedly intense air.

Mary did not make notes of the sermon, but she wrote them to her guardian, King Charles, to tell him that she had learned no Greek and Latin at school, and how much she wished to return to Court. She was always hearing of different masques being acted there in honour of the two young Palatine Princes who were on a visit to their uncle, and surely, of all people, she should have met them, since she was to have married their brother.

But the Queen was determined that Mary should not return to Court 'until she has a husband to look after her', and it was only when the Palatines were just leaving England that the Duke of Richmond returned to it, to be appointed Privy Councillor at the age of twenty-one and given one of the richest matches in the kingdom. The grave, sensitive young man, who was both too haughty and too diffident to take any relationship lightly, was married before he knew her to this girl, just fifteen. 'Lucky dog!' 'Lucky devil!' said his friends at his wedding to that lovely child.

They did not know James Richmond. Mary was the most exquisite thing he had ever seen, a glancing, dancing creature all light and laughter. So easily hurt himself, he was as much afraid of hurting her as if she had indeed been a butterfly in his hands. His passionate love for her was a responsibility so great as to be almost agony. Such a sentiment would have been quite incomprehensible to her father; indeed it was as though Mary now for the first time knew what it was to have a father. She had been accustomed to admiration since she was born, but this tender, reverent care of her was something new and enchanting; she revelled in it, traded on it, laughed at it, rebelled against it, and then was suddenly sorry and coaxing and asking for it all over again. She gave her husband the most perfect happiness and misery he had known; he knew that she had not yet learned to love anybody as much as he loved her, that perhaps she would never learn it, and if she did, who could tell whether it would be himself or another that would teach it to her?

She could not naturally see what troubled him (and he was wise enough to hide it from her all he could), for she adored him and told him so, he was so courteous and dignified, a great gentleman, as even her dazzling father had never quite been – and as for her first detestable little boy husband – well, it had been very fortunate for her that he had died before the marriage was consummated, she knew that now – and what a different woman she would have been if she had not been married to her dear James.

Sometimes she almost wished she could have been a different woman. How different? With whom? There were so many to answer the question that it became tedious; she could not imagine herself in love with the numberless men who fell in love with her.

When the King raised his Standard at Nottingham there were many who thought that the war might only last a few weeks, and Richmond persuaded his wife to visit her mother's relatives in France to be safely out of the way. But when it showed every sign of continuing, she joined the Queen and her ladies in Holland and crossed to the Yorkshire coast with them. She had had a very amusing time as well as a good deal of hardship and terrors; she had been looking forward longingly to hearing James' low tender tones to her, to telling him everything (well, practically everything), to feeling blissfully safe in his arms once again.

But now she had met the Prince – and there was no safety there!

It was the most cursed luck that she had met him before she had met James again, that he had not known her, that her insatiable love of mischief must at once fasten on that trivial fact (for why should he have known her when he could only have had a glimpse of her at her wedding when she was almost a child?) and led him on till he had all but declared his sudden passion for her, before she had at last insisted on declaring herself.

Would Richmond see anything? He always saw a great deal more than he said. But, being in love with Richmond, she was able to enjoy her fears – as indeed she enjoyed most things – this heavenly high summer weather at the moment, and the ride through the smiling Warwickshire country, so little changed by the course of the war that judges could still be met ambling from town to town on circuit. She leaned out of the little casement window when she went to bed in Will Shakespeare's house, and breathed the sweet sharp smell of dew on the new-cut hay, and saw the moon caught like a white flower in the branches of a tree, and all the leaves cut in a black still pattern against the glimmering sky, and a bat go swooping and looping through the pale air, now a jerk, now a shudder, its black wings spinning the shadows together; and she thought that whatever might come of it, it was a delightful thing to be not yet twenty-one, to be the prettiest of all the Queen's ladies, and to be certain that the most famous young Prince of the day was in love with her.

RUPERT DID not lean out of his window that evening at Stratford to look at the moon, or wonder which was Mary's window, or do any of the recognized actions of a young man in love. He had flung himself on a bed that was too short for him by at least two inches, stuffed his hand into his mouth, and tried to stifle his rage by wreaking it on himself until the physical pain should deaden the mental. Why should this cursed luck have hit on him? He knew now that he had never been in love in his life, not even with the lovely little Suzanne; now that at last it had come to him after all these years (his age, twenty-three and a half, did not occur to him as hers had done to Mary) it must needs be with the wife of his greatest friend.

She had taken good care to keep it from him too, had known what restraining effect that would have, had not wanted that restraint. His fury now was all against her, but with a grain of bitter pleasure somewhere in it, for all this showed she was nothing but a whore, she had probably cuckolded her husband scores of times – what else should she have done, a woman like her, all these months away from him, nearly a year, in France and Holland?

Why then should he have any scruples? Because he was Richmond's friend, what did he owe him? Richmond had been very kind to lecture him for his good no doubt, to write him tedious letters – God's blood, what a fool to send a wife like that away from him, whatever the danger! He deserved to be cuckolded. 'I would have kept her. I'd have killed anyone who looked at her, I'd have killed her if —' His impotent anger shook him with dry, empty sobs, he would have liked the whole world in his hands to tear it to pieces.

This evening he had known a boy's and a poet's gay rapture; it had been torn from him; and Mary, instead of an unknown enchantment, was his enemy. 'Have your will of her, you will be quit of her then,' said this new implacable voice within him. There came an echo to it in that often-uttered belief, that 'Prince Rupert could not want of his will'.

He sat up, staring into the darkness. She was in this house, she must be within thirty yards or so of him, it seemed he had only to stretch out his hand to seize her and pull her down beside him.

He opened the door and called softly to the servant who lay there on a bench in the passage.

'Send Tom Draycott to me.'

Draycott would find out where she was, nothing ever baffled him. He pulled the curtains back from his windows and began to dress himself. The moon had swung clear of the tree and was staring into the room hollow and bright. Its light lay in a white pool on the floor, the shadows were cut sharp and black all round it, his suit of wine-coloured velvet lying over the massive chair was black, only the great scarlet cloak still burned darkly red.

The mere fact of moving and doing something pulled his mind into some sort of working order, though all it could do was to run here and there, destroying his world in advance for him, to make his work the easier. It was a lascivious, sneaking world, rotten at the core. Harry Jermyn, that 'good fellow' whom he had always liked, was probably even now lying with the Queen, as half the army believed. The war excused everything. He had been sentimental about Richmond, who felt that he in some part took the place of his young brother, d'Aubigny, killed at Rupert's side in that first charge of his at Edgehill – but what odds did that make? Kate d'Aubigny made a pretty little war-widow, and how much was she a widow? Not often, he'd swear. It was all in d'Aubigny's sacred memory, was it, that she mixed herself up with plots that had to be carried in her curls, and wrote long letters to himself with the reproachful postscript, 'I hope you have received my other letters?'

He had never doubted her before, nor believed the scandals about the Queen, and he had been proud to think that he was more to Richmond than any other friend – but all this he now tore to shreds in sardonic exultation so that neither affection nor conscience should get in his way.

Tom Draycott came in with a lighted taper in his hand and apology in his tone. 'I stayed on in the stables, sir, talking to the King's groom who has just come with letters. He says the King will come as far as Edgehill tomorrow to meet the Queen, bringing his army and all the Court, and then go back and make a state entry together into Oxford.'

He had stuck the taper into a stand where it flickered a little, the yellow light driving the white light from the window. Colours came back into the room, chief among them Tom Draycott's shiny red face, his mouth opening and shutting

under its bristling moustache, saying these things so brightly –
'at Edgehill tomorrow' – 'all the Court.'

Then Richmond would be there with the King; tomorrow
night his wife would lie in his arms after nearly a year. And he
would have been cuckolded by his friend the night before.

Draycott was looking at him in question. 'You've dressed
again, sir?'

'Yes. Get a horse saddled for me. Not the Corsair. He's done
enough work today. I'll take the chestnut mare. And keep Boy
here.'

Boy, already miserable and uneasy at this utterly different
being in the room in place of his master, now looked anxiously
from one to the other at the sound of his name.

Rupert swung out of the house, galloped out of the sleeping
village, through his troops bivouacked round about it.

The sentries were startled by that curt familiar voice flinging
the answer to their challenge like a stone through the night. –
'Rupert rides,' ran the whisper through the horse lines, and on
what mad errand? There were many who believed that Rupert
could ride on the wind if he chose, like the wicked squire of
Tumpleton no farther off than the next county, who still rode
through the air on windy nights and had kicked off the top of
the church steeple with his horse's hoofs.

Rupert was clear now of that vast hive of men which never
ceased to hum faintly; he had left the smell of horses and
trampling clanking noises behind him. He had no notion where
he was, in what direction he was going. He saw a windmill
standing stark and black on top of a low hill; he heard the long
hoot of a hunting owl; then he saw and heard nothing more.
His brain seemed to spin round and round in his head, loud and
senseless, saying the same thing over and over. He must want of
his will. He must not go back tonight. He must ride on till he
had tired himself out, on and on through that grey country
under the gaping moon, a crazed, driven thing, knowing only
that he must not go back.

Tomorrow Richmond would meet his wife – after that, let
him look to himself. He stuck spurs into the chestnut mare, she
was flagging but he drove her on, senselessly, purposelessly,
cruelly. God, if he could snatch Mary up into his saddle and
ride to hell with her!

Trees and hillocks round him were growing more distinct.
The edge of the sky was silver grey in front of him. That

must be the dawn. He was riding due east, straight towards the enemy's country, for the Parliament held the eastern counties.

That was Hampden's country, the fellow he had killed last month at Chalgrove Field, and his cousin Cromwell's, who was doing useful work in the Eastern Counties' Association, so Hurry had told him. The ordinary everyday things of his life and work were creeping back into his brain with that prosaic grey light of a dull morning. He turned the mare's head and rode back.

When at last he found Stratford the sun was well up; the heavy dawn had been preliminary to a blazing July day, that hive of men and horses all round the village was humming in full blast, clustering round the smoky fires. He took a bathe in the river, went back to his room, flung himself on the bed and plunged into sleep.

CHAPTER FOURTEEN

MARY RICHMOND did not find it delightful next day to know that the Prince was in love with her. It would have been better not to have made so certain of it and so soon, for now even her father's daughter had to realize that she could not eat her cake and have it. The Prince was in the blackest of moods, and much as she would have enjoyed coaxing him out of it, he gave her no chance to do so.

'Oh, well,' she sighed philosophically, 'there will be plenty of time in Oxford!'

Rupert had breakfasted so late that he actually had it with Harry Jermyn. That jovial person rolled an amused enquiring eye over the young man's haggard countenance. What fools these youngsters were! Luckily he had known the Prince well enough from boyhood to tell him so.

'*You've* no reason to lie awake at nights,' he said, 'unless it's to good purpose. If ever our Butterfly lights on anyone, I'll bet a thousand pounds it will be you.'

'If ever —?' repeated Rupert stupidly.

'Yes, you may look incredulous. It's what we've all felt, and done our best to disprove, but to no purpose. There's never been any real scandal about her all the time she's been abroad even.

The minx can't be serious – or so I'd have said till last night. But that was quite another matter.'

'She didn't seem very serious.' (God's blood, no – how she had laughed and made him laugh!) He looked down the long room which seemed so bare and dull this morning.

'Did not I dance with you in Brabant once?'

'Serious is a stupid word,' said Jermyn, 'but you can take it from me, who have been to and fro upon the earth to some small extent – a rolling stone may gather no moss but it picks up a reasonable amount of maidenheads and doesn't need telescopes to see the signs of surrender – and I should say you've got no reason to despair.'

His pink and white face was full of gross good nature before he obliterated it in a tankard of beer – 'Own brother to Pandarus,' thought Rupert sourly, but what reason had he to feel squeamish? and Harry Jermyn had always been a good friend to him. All he said was, 'three thousand foot, thirty companies of horse and dragoons, six pieces of cannon and two mortars, that's what I make the sum total of the Queen's army. Can you get them on the march in two hours?'

*   *   *

Edgehill was a very different place now from what it had been in the frosty days of last autumn when there had been held a very different tryst. The mid-July heat lay in a blue haze over the low rounded hills, the valleys were pools of shadow, the sheep like a cirrus of small cloud clustered together under the clumps of heavy trees. There was excellent grazing for them, the grass grew as green and lush as in a churchyard.

The King rode out at the head of his army to meet his Queen; he took her in his arms and kissed her again and again. She clung to him and told him she had not been able to sleep for thinking of this meeting after so many months, and then broke away to check her tears, and laughed instead and told him she would not speak to him alone – no, but never, never, never – until he had done justice by dear kind Harry Jermyn who had done everything for her and her army since she had arrived in England, and now he promptly must be made a peer.

Gazing on her like a man in a trance, the King said, 'Whatever you will, dear love, dear heart.'

Some moments later he turned to Rupert, who was standing

by his horse looking gravely on, and said, 'Nephew, you have brought me safely the thing I love best in the world.'

'Essex didn't give much trouble,' said Rupert awkwardly.

But everyone knew that was because Rupert had so watchfully kept his army between Essex's and the Queen's. It was he who had brought about this meeting, but expected nothing in reward, not even his uncle's thanks.

'A knight-errant – that is a strange thing for you to be in this modern age,' Mary Richmond said, as she came up to him with her husband.

He had seen how she greeted Richmond; it had been to turn away from that that he had watched the King and Queen. Now he had to see again the deep happiness that had flowed into her face, making it a thing more shining and lovely than he had yet known.

At Richmond he dared not look. It struck him as it had struck Mary that Richmond would see a great deal more than he would ever say.

He must speak – this silence was shouting at them – but he could not think what she had said – something foolish about himself and knights-errant —

'It was what my mother swore we should none of us be.'

'And so you all are? No, not all – not your brother Carl, Lord help us! But is that how things work in your family?'

'They don't work. We are always at sixes and sevens.'

If Richmond did not help him now, he was done. But why should he help? He was probably amusing himself by watching his friend's discomfiture. He had got his wife again, he was secure, 'a stranger shall not meddle with his joy'.

Rupert looked helplessly round him for an excuse to get away, but now Richmond was speaking – what was he saying? He must try and listen. Mercifully he was not thanking him as the King had done for making it safe for his wife to come to him! He was speaking of Maurice, congratulating Rupert on him, as though he knew all about something Rupert had not yet heard of.

And before Rupert could ask him, the King and Queen had joined them, and the King was echoing Richmond – 'Yes, Rupert, you must well be proud of him – his first great success without you.' He turned to his wife: 'Rupert gave you my message, I had no time to write of it to you too, and thought it more important to advertise him. Am I forgiven?'

'Not till I know the charge!' cried the Queen. 'What is all this, Rupert? *Did* I have any message from you?'

She did not, she knew it as well as he, she was only asking so as to make him confess. And for the life of him he could not think what message he should have given, until suddenly it broke on him – those letters that Draycott had told him came last night – he had not had them till this morning, when he had thrust them into his pocket until he should finish ordering and dispersing the troops – he had been late enough over that, God knows! He pulled out the papers in his pocket. There on top of them, damning him at the first glance, was a letter with the royal seal unbroken, 'to my dearest nephew'.

The Queen's shrill laugh sounded a paean of indignation. 'And now perhaps your dearest nephew will open his letter and tell me what it is I should have heard several hours ago! Another time, Charles, it might be wiser for you to write to your wife and give *her* your messages to pass on – they are more likely to reach their destination!'

Richmond's quiet voice came like balm after her speech – 'The Prince has had to arrange the line of march all this morning, Madam.'

Rupert shot him a grateful glance. Their eyes met, and Rupert forgot the business of the letter as he thought, 'The man's my friend. I can't ever change that.'

And he resigned himself stoically to his aunt's innuendoes that he was too careless and haphazard to be trusted with any serious business. Most fortunately this was not serious (but if it had been —!). It was a simple matter of good news.

Maurice had joined Lord Hertford and his Cornish army against Sir William Waller, a Parliament general (far too elegant with his long curls to have earned the term Roundhead) who had been so successful down in the West that the cockney prentices had nicknamed him 'William the Conqueror'. Sir William and his troops had been quartered at Bath very comfortably and with ample provisions, but the Royalists, who had to keep the field, had lured him out on to Lansdown for a fight which went so hardly for themselves that out of the two thousand cavalry under Maurice and his second-in-command, only six hundred answered the roll-call at sunset. The conquering William fell back upon Bath till the next day when, rather nervously and tentatively, he pursued the Royalists as they retired after their losses to Devizes, where they raised barricades in the streets and dug trenches for defence as fast as they could.

Maurice and Hertford moved even faster; they rode thirty miles across country to Oxford, left their Cornish cavalry at the first Royalist post they came to, and galloped on in person to the city for reinforcements. Fifteen hundred horse under Wilmot and some ammunition was all that could be spared, but they were Rupert's horsemen, raised and trained by him. They had to push back without the Cornish cavalry, who were too exhausted for a return forced march, but there was not a moment to lose, nobody knew how long their friends could hold out in Devizes, and as it happened (though this they did not know of course till later) Waller had already written announcing their capture to the Parliament, and promising to give a full list of his prisoners the next day.

As Maurice and Hertford, with the Oxford cavalry under Wilmot, came over Roundway Down, Waller hauled off his men from besieging Devizes and moved out to attack them. He sent Haslerigg's Lobsters out first against them, cavalry regiments in full armour with long-tailed helmets to guard the back of the neck, which made them look as though they were wearing lobsters on their heads. But Byron, whose unwarranted dash with the King's Show Troop at Edgehill had caused such confusion, now fully justified his daring; he made a bold counter-charge, routed the Lobsters and drove them in among their own foot.

Maurice's charge completed the havoc. There was an appalling panic, the Roundheads stampeded, riding each other down; 400 dead were left on the field, 900 taken prisoner, the premature Conqueror gathered the remnants together and fled to Gloucester; and the victorious Royalist horse trotted back towards Oxford under Maurice, Hertford and Wilmot, leaving what was left of their Cornish army to occupy Bath.

The King and Queen met the conquerors at Woodstock, Maurice flushed with victory, and all the praise he was getting – from the Queen particularly, for he had not only won a victory but he had not neglected his letters and messages to her.

'Your first great victory without your brother, Maurice! You are no longer a mere "Twin", you are a man on your own legs – a host in yourself!'

But Maurice, though glowing with new happy confidence, refused to have his head turned. He staunchly declared that his victory was really Rupert's – 'but it's true, sir, indeed it is,' he insisted as his uncle and aunt laughed at him for his modesty – 'it was Rupert's horse that won the battle. Even Wilmot has to say so, since he led 'em. Our western cavalry never had the same drive – the Cornish foot were grand fellows but left their horse lagging every time – we never got our chance to smash Waller till we got Rupert's cavalry.'

'Dear Maurice, that is very pretty of you,' said his aunt as though she were speaking to a child, 'I'd tell you not to be a goose, but that the modest soldier is always a pleasant rôle, and I can see it's having a good effect on my Magpie here' – (For why should Rupert have his 'belle amie' and not Maurice, who deserved one at least quite as much? His aunt was the last person to allow such injustice.) So she turned to pretty Mrs Kirke beside her, and asked, 'What do you say, Mag? Ought he not to be rewarded?'

'For what, Madam?' answered Mag Kirke. 'His was the oddest speech I ever heard! I thought no soldier ever praised an ally, and no man a brother.'

Maurice stared at her wide smiling mouth, her crisp curls bubbling up all over her impudent bird-like head, her sophisticated dress slashed and cut with the blue that matched her eyes.

'Why, madam, I expect they don't when they're with you – they've something better to praise.'

The Queen went scarlet with suppressed laughter and hastily engaged the King in what was apparently a very earnest and private conversation, leaving Maurice to follow up his opening volley on Mag Kirke with the defensive measures of shy answers to her admiring questions. In ten minutes he was headlong in love with her; by next day, after the dinner at which he entertained the King and Queen and Court, Mrs Kirke was telling her great friend Mary Richmond that she was enchanted with his boyish roughness – 'so strong, he lifted me straight into my saddle – I just shot up into the air – remarkable elevation!'

'That sounds Popish. Do you speak of the Host?'

'No, but of *our* host. I'm no Catholic for all my devotion to our dear Queen. How she watches you and t'other Prince by the way!'

'T'other indeed! It's Rupert who is *the* Prince. Yours is a mere heavy dragoon!'

'Well, I'd not exchange Maurice for him. He looks very grand riding at the head of all the cavalry, but a most formidable young man.'

'He was not so formidable two days ago,' sighed Mary.

'It's your work then? I thought as much. Can't you be kind and promise fair, even if you don't fulfil? For an experienced campaigner you must have manoeuvred badly.'

'Damnably.'

'So? Why, my Butterfly, your heart must be engaged!'

'Not unless it can be halved. And at least it has not turned German. Would I ever say "So"? Would my Prince ever say it? Your Maurice is only a so-so Prince!'

The laughter of the Queen's ladies mingled with the reports of good news as they rode into Oxford in a triumphal procession. Bells pealed, flags and scarves flew everywhere, crowds cheered frantically, some of them running for miles beside the King and Queen; children scattered flowers; streets and windows were thronged with eager happy faces; scholars in scarlet hoods held up the procession to read their poems of thanksgiving and praise. The most charming of these was by the young Proctor of Christ Church who had written that tedious bad play, *The Royal Slave,* on the last royal visit, but everybody was agreed that he made up for it now with his verses to the Queen on all that she had gone through on her return to England.

> '*Courage was cast about her like a dress*
> *Of solemn comeliness;*
> *A gathered mind and an untroubled face*
> *Did give her dangers grace.*'

Comely she certainly was in her pride and happiness, but there was not much sign of solemnity, nor much reason for it now that everybody was certain the war was practically over. The fighting had lasted barely a year, and the King's armies, which had begun in such miserable scattered scarcity, were now everywhere victorious. The great Lord Essex and all his men had not been able to prevent the Queen coming all the way down from Yorkshire to join the King with the armaments she had so pluckily won for her husband's cause.

But not this, nor Roundway Down, were the chief reasons for cheer. The Parliament was crumpling from within, they heard it on all sides. The latest reports from deserters told of quarrels raging among the chief commanders. Waller blamed Essex for his defeat – had he not been sleeping and feeding his great body so well at Thame, he might have come to his help. Essex was indignant as usual, but not very articulately so.

Parliament men were openly pleading for peace in the House of Commons – 'the cup of trembling that had passed round the other nations had at last come to Englishmen' – but must they drink it to the dregs? 'Blood is a crying sin: it pollutes the land. Why should we defile our land any longer?'

London was seething with peace demonstrations – cartoons of Essex sprawling in his chair, with his pipe in one hand and a glass of wine in the other, had been chalked all over the walls; women had stormed the Palace yard and yelled for peace and for Pym's death – 'The dog Pym!' – 'Traitor Pym!' – just as Pym had once encouraged them to yell for Strafford's death. 'God forbid,' he had then declared, that 'he should prevent the free expression of their just desires.' But now that their 'just desires' were dangerous to himself, he called out the cavalry and artillery to ride down the servants that had once proved useful to him. 'Women killed at Westminster' – that was no good for their propaganda, chuckled the Cavaliers at Oxford. Public opinion would force even Pym to make a reasonable peace; this summer was certain to see the end of the war.

And in the meantime the courtiers and Queen's ladies thought it a charming picnic to lodge in the poky dark little college rooms at Oxford. Their horses' hoofs clattered under the arches and came out into the sunlight that filled the courtyards, where undergraduates stood staring at this bright invasion. Everyone felt elevated and a little strange, it was so odd to see this ancient monastic city transformed into a Court. The Queen's rooms were at Merton, and soon her ladies spread themselves like flowers over its grey-walled gardens.

A private way had been arranged between her rooms and the King's at Christ Church; it went through Merton Hall and the grounds of Corpus and led right into the King's own apartments; it was all a part of the new air of amusing mystery and intrigue now breathed in the learned city. Gossip would grow here in a hotbed, as Mary discovered from Mag when the Court walked from dining in state with the King at Christ Church to the special service for public rejoicing over the victory of Roundway Down. They went across the lawns, where the evening sunlight lay in a deep pool, a stream of colours and plumes and glancing movement pouring into the dark chapel, and

Mary turned her head to catch Mag's whisper, and whispered back,

'What, are they talking already? That rascal Harry Jermyn, I suppose. What do they say?'

' "They'll make a fine pair." '

'Do they ever say this – "He is a friend of Richmond"?'

'They add, "He'll get over that." '

'And what of me?'

'You'll be forgiven, a Duke's daughter and a Duke's wife.'

'Ah, yes, my strawberry leaves shall cover a multitude of sins!'

'Hush, stop laughing, here we are in church.'

'You are mighty serious, but I know you. Don't sit next me or you will make me giggle all through the service. Now – is my hat right? Do you like the lizard?'

They composed their faces to those of serious angels as they went into chapel – angels they seemed at least to the two young Princes seated in state beside their uncle. They had mentioned neither of the two ladies to each other. Rupert introduced Maurice to the Duchess of Richmond afterwards. She reminded him of her betrothal to Henry, which had happened when Maurice was too young to remember it.

'So you should have been my brothers,' she said, and later, as she turned away with Rupert, 'I am glad that you are not.'

It was said very low, as if she had meant it only for herself, it was said with a kind of soft heartlessness as light as the flutter of a butterfly's wing. But all the warm busy air round them, humming with chatter and bustle in the evening sunlight, seemed to stand silent as she said it. He looked down at her face; it was hidden from him under the tilt of her hat. Only the little green lizard in its crown winked and sparkled back at him. All his wits seemed to be leaving him, he had to tug at them, to tell himself – 'This is not happening – it cannot happen.'

At last he found he could speak, and he must speak.

'It makes no odds,' he said. (How could it, when Richmond had said, 'Only one. My wife'?)

Now he had done it. She would be offended and leave him, and all this senseless buzzing round him would be the only thing to listen to.

But she looked up and smiled. She was not offended. They were still walking together. It was the company who had gone; no, it was they who had gone into the little farther garden at

Merton, they were walking up and down, up and down on its lawn, speaking hardly at all, for if he spoke he would woo her, he would break this enchantment, and for the moment he was at peace, living this moment with her as if it had been, would be, for ever; walking up and down on this silent lawn while the white roses hung above them on the walls, and their shadows grew faint and faded away, until they themselves were no more at a distance than two grey shadows walking in a college garden where the sun had set.

CHAPTER FIFTEEN

IN AN old room in the heart of 'the lady-barracks' at Merton, the mongrel Mitte flounced out of the basket that held her new litter of puppies, and trotted about, gazing up in entreaty at the greedy female humans that were sipping wine and nibbling biscuits and examining the bowls of rare new flowers picked from St John's gardens for the Queen, who was herself a great gardener. They held out morsels to Mitte, asked after her babies, laughed at the airs she had given herself ever since she had become a war heroine, with the Queen risking her life to save her. Just look how languidly she waved her long plumed tail in imitation of their fans! And once she could coax no more titbits out of them she stood critically surveying the company with her globular brown eyes, seeing that her mistress was not here, and that nobody else was worth her attention.

Mitte was assuring herself that all was as it should be. She was back in the familiar surroundings of silk laps and sweet biscuits and caressing voices, and no loud noises of guns and shrieks of fire, no sudden snatching up and being carried helter-skelter through the cold night. The world had been made safe for her and her puppies, she turned with a deep sigh of content and flopped back into her basket.

Outside the sunlight blazed down upon the sultry stone walls, the steady clang of hammer and pick sounded from the gardens near by where a bastion was being built.

In here the light was dimmed by the leaded panes of old greenish glass, it was cool and airless, and the silken figures swimming across in their wide skirts from one to the other had a veiled look as if seen through water like mermaids in a cave.

Except Mag Kirke, where she sat with her lute beside her and a piece of wire and cotton in her hands, for she had pushed open the small window behind her, and the sunlight made a fiery halo round her fair head and bared, golden, neck, while her rose-coloured skirts swept down round into glowing shadow.

'You will be as sunburnt as a milkmaid,' they warned her.

'What if I am! We're not still in Queen Bess's day, all trying to look like white parchment.'

'Lord help us, what a memory the girl has!' cried Kate d'Aubigny. 'When were *you* at the old Queen's Court?'

'Dear fool, I can sometimes talk with old ladies. Would you never have the manners to do so?'

'Not I, I find it too sad. How can a woman go on living after thirty?'

'You'll put off that age limit long before you reach twenty-five.'

'The Queen says no woman keeps her looks after twenty-two,' and Kate added in a whisper, leaning forward, 'because she lost them then herself!'

She spoke restlessly, darting her pretty, eager head from side to side as though she were trying to soar out of her smart black and white dress. She might talk and laugh and flirt, and dress in elegant new variations of mourning, and engage herself in such dangerous war-work as carrying papers into London in her curls – but it all made no difference, she could never stop thinking of her young husband, killed as he rode, killed just after he had married her – 'or at least a summer, just this one summer in Oxford!'

But she never said it. She was quicker to laugh and move than anyone, she swung round now before anyone else had noticed, to exclaim at her sister-in-law, Mary Richmond, who had just flung open the door and stood there in a cap and gown borrowed from an undergraduate, the most becoming dress in the world they all declared, and why, demanded Mary, should their sex be deprived of it?

Weren't their brains as good as the men's? Clever, courageous Kate had proved they were, Mary would prove they were – she mounted on a stool to lecture them. – 'My sisters, it is unquestioned that men's praises of female virtue are apt to be excessive. Why should the men have all the vices – all the advantages I mean – why should not women wear caps and gowns and smoke and dine in Common-rooms where the wine is better than at Whitehall? I put it to our learned friend, Lucy, Lady Carlisle, here present, that she shall be our first Principal – and then I am sure the battle-cry of our philosophic armies will be "Let us get back to First Principles!" '

She jumped off her stool, snatched off her cap and gown and swept a curtsey to Lady Carlisle, who was smiling thinly at this fooling. 'Something has put you in a very merry humour,' she observed.

'And now *she's* put you in your place,' murmured Mag, thrumming on her lute to cover her remark, as Mary sat down beside her. The two friends chattered on the window seat. Mary was out of everything, must hear a whole year's scandal.

The sunlight ran rippling from her dark hair down the long curve of her neck and sparkled all over the tiny seed pearls sewn on the back of her dress, as the two friends swayed backwards and forwards in their laughter over odd fragments of gossip.

Their gaiety had in it a frightened fugitive quality. Outside their gossip of loves and scandals, death was waiting to snatch the cause of them; the fine young men they spoke of might be hacked to pieces before they saw them again. The shadow fell across even their glancing talk.

'And young Campion?'

'Oh, didn't you hear? He was killed at the Lichfield siege.'

And abruptly Mag pushed away the toy stag she had been making for the baby Prince Harry of Gloucester, the youngest of the Queen's children, and asked Mary to play the lute for her and she would sing a song to it to keep herself from yawning, for she was more than half asleep this morning. They tried over a song of poor Suckling's, the tune pricking through the hum of female voices:

> '*Out upon it, I have loved*
> *Three whole days together;*
> *And am like to love three more,*
> *If it prove fair weather.*'

Fair weather it had proved and was proving – hot sun and exquisite twilights and sapphire nights under the July moon when courtiers and ladies danced in the quadrangles and couples walked in the cloisters slower and slower as they whispered low. Three whole days there had been of this courtly pleasure since the King and Queen and the Princes Rupert and Maurice had ridden together into Oxford.

A shrill sound tore across the tripping tune. A trumpet blared across the blue sky behind them. As rain follows thunder and lightning, there followed the patter and rattle of footsteps through the cobbled streets, of voices calling, and now louder and louder the tramp of armed men, the clatter of horses, and short shouted words of command.

Prince Rupert's trumpet had sounded yet again for 'Boot and Saddle'.

Down fell the lute and the song into silence. Out flew Mitte from her basket in a shrill succession of metallic tiny barks, in furious protest against this new disturbance. Up rushed the company in a swirl and a swish and a twitter – 'The Prince! It's Prince Rupert's trumpet!'

Mag caught Mary's hand, pulled her out through the door, across the gardens, under the stone archway, down the little side street towards the High.

'Did you know of this?' panted Mary.

'Not one word. I'll swear Maurice did not know himself. O Lord, we shall miss it all – come, quick, quick!'

They reached the broad highway, they stood in the crowd like any common citizens' wives waving their handkerchiefs to see the soldiers go by, sharing the cries and comments all round them.

'They're in full force. This must be for something big.'

'They're going out by the West Gate.'

'They're going to attack Bristol, I'll be bound. They'll conquer all the West first and then march on London.'

'The war will be over long before *that*!'

'Oh, the brave boys! I love to see them. They're coming, they're coming!'

'That's Lord Hertford, that is.'

'Oh, lift me up, Father! Where are the Princes?'

'You'll not need lifting to see the Princes on horseback. They're head and shoulders higher than the others.'

'That's him – on the black horse – *that's* the Prince! Hurrah! Hurrah!'

The line of the crowd swept forward like a breaking wave on the cheer, till those in front drove it back——

'Mind there now! Don't drive us under the horses!'

The great banner of Prince Rupert, five feet long, black and gold, rippled and poured out against the burning blue ahead.

Drums were beating. The trumpet sounded again, ahead of

them now, out by the West Gate. Mary Richmond caught at her friend's hand, with a laugh that had the sound of a sob in it.

'Three days!' she cried. 'He has stayed in Oxford

"three whole days together!"

And that is all – before he marches out again!'

'By God, mistress,' said a hearty red-faced butcher beside her, 'you don't know the Prince if you think that so short a time!'

'No, you don't know the Prince, do you, Moll, and that's your sorrow,' whispered Mrs Kirke – 'and he's taken my brave Maurice too, hang him!'

'Oh, confound your Maurice! There's none to be compared to my Prince!'

'Congratulations, sweetheart! I did not know you had secured him for yours.'

'Miaow!'

Laughing hysterically, the two friends backed out of the crowd. What was there to do? Go back and finish that song of Suckling's, a silly fellow who had not even the pluck to go on living? There was no one now to whom they wished to sing it.

Oxford was empty, the King and Queen were mere cyphers, all the gay and bold spirits of the place had left with the Princes, riding out through the West Gate to march on Bristol.

*   *   *

Once again they were riding together to battle. There was compensation in that, even for Maurice, who was more luckily situated than Rupert. Mr Kirke, whoever and wherever he was, was nothing to him, and it seemed not very much to Mrs Kirke. Maurice would certainly have liked to linger in Oxford a bit longer – 'Three days wasn't much after those forced marches and a stiff fight.' He broke off, ashamed of his grumbling. 'The fact is,' he said apologetically, 'I'm in love.'

'And so am I,' said Rupert.

Maurice began to ask a question but bit it off as he looked at his brother's face. Rupert presently went on to say that Hertford seemed a good soldier, hadn't Maurice found him so?

Maurice had, but demurred that he was a Catholic.

'What the devil does that matter? Let him be a Mahomedan for all I care.'

'Oh, you – naturally you wouldn't. Weren't you baptized by

one, you old heathen Termagant! But it gives the Roundheads a chance to call us "the King's Popish army".'

'They'd take it anyway.'

Maurice's more serious objection then appeared.

'His Lordship says I take too much on myself – and he a lousy civilian! And yet he's made General of all the Western forces, and I win his battles for him as his mere Lieutenant-General. It's time I were a full general.'

'It is. I'll see to it with the King.'

'Now the Queeen's come, it's she you'll have to reckon with when you want anything. They are all saying so.'

'I wish to God she'd stayed away.'

'I thought you were her favourite.'

'Years ago – and that was in peacetime. Women ought to keep out of war.'

'Except when one's on leave,' said Maurice, smiling reminiscently.

*   *   *

They stood in the churchyard on Clifton Hill, a little knot of officers come to take observations, having left Rupert's men encamped on Durdham Down and Hertford's and Maurice's beyond the Avon. Across the deep gorge where the river crawled sluggishly at low tide like a thin silver snake between wide banks of shining slime, were the hot deep woods in their heavy July foliage, and the great cleft of blue shadow that Mr Taylor told Rupert was called Nightingale Valley – 'the woods are shouting with them on moonlight nights in spring – you were too early for them in March'.

'You ought to have put off your plot for them,' said Rupert. He stared down at the city below, its grey old walls glowing in the sun. 'Looks as soft as a plum,' he murmured, thinking for the flicker of a half-shut eyelid against the dazzle how he would like to draw that faint, Dürer-like scene.

'Looks a damn hard nut to crack, *I* should say,' corrected Will Legge (now Colonel), but the results of Rupert's dreaming gaze were practical enough.

'You, Maurice, and my Lord Hertford' – (Hertford stiffened to a ramrod – their names should have been put in the reverse order) – 'can take the Cornishmen down on the other side of the river and attack from the south of the city. There'll have to be a concerted attack from six different points that I can see. They've strengthened these forts since March, thrown out

283

breastworks between them all along their line. What's that fort opposite, Taylor? Only two hundred yards off, but they don't seem to have spotted us, the slack dogs.'

'It's Sunday, sir,' excused Taylor. 'That's Brandon Hill, the crown of the city defences.'

'There's only one weak spot that I can see —'

Boom – whizz – plonk! The deep summer hush was broken by a cannon ball fired from Brandon Hill fort into the churchyard, spinning round and round, raising a shower of earth and felling a couple of tombstones. Boy, well accustomed to cannon fire, but not to such sudden interruptions to a quiet gentlemanly talk, leaped up against his master, barking his indignant inquiry.

'I thought you said it was Sunday,' said Rupert in disapproval as he patted Boy's head reassuringly; 'irreligious dogs, aren't they, my Boy? Did the draught give you a cold, Maurice?'

'Swallowed a crumb of earth,' said Maurice, who was coughing violently.

'It was certainly very near us,' said Lord Hertford anxiously. 'Having made our observations —'

'One moment, Hertford. Do you see what I mean, Will? That higher ground outside the line on Kingsdown – he's put no fort there, only a small sconce on the hill. If I plant a strong —'

Boom – whizz – plonk! A piece of the churchyard wall went scampering down the hill, the stones bounding like footballs.

'Yes, yes, sir,' broke in Hertford, 'but they're taking dead aim at us, it's madness to be so foolhardy.'

'Foolhardy – *I* foolhardy!' Rupert seemed deeply insulted by the suggestion. To get a clearer view he mounted a square tombstone, oblivious of the fact that more than three foot of him thus made a target for the gunners of Brandon Hill fort, turned his back on Hertford, who meditated a dash through the vestry door into the church, and continued to point out to Maurice and Will Legge and Taylor, whose knowledge of the city was useful, the advantage of a strong battery in the spot which Fiennes had neglected. 'Then we can attack the line there with fire pikes and grenadoes and run up some scaling ladders under cover of its fire.'

'Yes, sir, but —' Taylor ducked as a third ball came crashing over and carried away the lychgate, '– but if you please we're under no cover *here*, and if they pick off all the senior officers before the fight begins, there'll be no fight.'

'You're right, they seem to have got our range.' Rupert stepped down from the wall. 'That church is the place to hold once we get into the city —'

'St Mary Redcliff's, bless her!' Mr Taylor, forgetting his admonitions, was bobbing up on the tombstone just as the Prince got down. 'She's part of the city wall and the strongest part of it. Once we hold her we'll soon avenge old Yeomans! Wait till I meet Clement Walker —'

'Don't wait, Taylor! Here comes another!'

And the party decamped.

CHAPTER SIXTEEN

NEXT MORNING, Monday, the two Royalist armies on either side of the river had orders to deploy in full battaglia, marching with a very wide front to make the most of themselves, to the edge of Durdham Down on the one side and along the river shore on the other, so that the forts should see them as large as life or as far as possible a little larger. Then Rupert sent his trumpeter on behalf of himself and Hertford to Colonel Fiennes to summon the town to surrender. Fiennes wrote back that 'being entrusted to keep the town for King and Parliament, he could not as yet relinquish that trust until he were brought to more extremity'.

'He shall have his extremity,' said Rupert grimly. He was anxious to forget his frustration in action; there at least he would not be denied, and these insolent rebels who dared take the King's name in vain should know that here at any rate Prince Rupert 'could not want of his will'. It would be a sharp and costly action but he swore to himself that it would be short.

Colonel Fiennes was not much of a soldier, but he held a strong position, and the bulk of the city was so determinedly for the Parliament that the citizens made far better fighters than his soldiers. Between six and eight thousand of them could be called up at a moment's notice. The women too had hastily formed a labour battalion to stop up the gates with earth and woolsacks, and offered to work in the fortifications and go with their children 'into the mouth of the cannon to dead and keep off the shot from the soldiers if *they* were afeared!'

This was discovered by Mr Taylor and reported to the Prince

with the oddest mixture of pride and rage – 'You can't beat our brave Bristol wenches, damn their Puritan souls – but that's their thrift, that's all it is. You may find the young ones for the Cavaliers but their mothers are all for "pure religion"; it's good for trade, keeps the boys out of mischief, Church costs nothing but the playhouse does.'

He was in a state of dancing excitement at the hope of his city being now taken for the King after the tragic failure of his attempt in March.

As night came on and firing opened between Lord Grandison's quarters and the defenders in Prior's Hill fort, he declared it to be 'a beautiful piece of danger to see so many fires incessantly in the dark', and complimented Rupert on his military masquerades. He was busy with reports from here, there and everywhere, for his lifelong knowledge of the city gave him an uncanny cognizance of what was happening in it. He declared he saw an enemy cannoneer who was 'vapouring in his shirt on top of the fort' for the cool night air killed for his foolhardiness, as disapprovingly as if he himself had never jumped up on the tomb in Clifton churchyard. These 'leaden courtesies' (Mr Taylor's name again – Rupert said he should write all the despatches) did not achieve much else, however; by Tuesday morning most of the batteries were in position, and various skirmishes went on, while Rupert left his headquarters at Captain Hill's house at Redland and crossed the Avon for a council of war with Hertford and Maurice.

It was decided that there should be a general attack by both armies at dawn next day, the signal shot to be fired from the two demi-cannons at Lord Grandison's post; the password to be 'Oxford' and their men to know each other by all wearing green bows and leaving off their collars.

Rupert returned to his headquarters by the evening, where his field officers had been summoned to receive his orders. A messenger also was waiting for him with letters from Oxford, but he did not attend to him until he had given all his directions and seen to it that they were sent also to the officers of the foot. Then, though pretty weary and furiously hungry, he opened them before he would eat or drink – he had learned his lesson about letters at Stratford. There was another from the King – he had already had one on the march, and this was on the same errand. Sir William Waller had slipped out of Bristol before the Princes approached and gone on to London to collect reinforcements for Essex, 'wherefore I desire you to hasten those brigades of horse, and as many regiments more as you may spare, for I believe numbers of horse are not much useful for a siege. This is all for the present.'

'All,' was it? As if he could spare a man or horse at this moment!

Still more maddening was a letter from Harry Percy at Oxford telling him how hurt the Queen was that he had not written to her since he had left, although he had found time to write to others. 'I hope your successes in arms will not make you forget your civility to ladies,' wrote her dear friend. God, what a sentence to read while storming a town!

There were kind messages, too, of hope for his success from the Duchess of Richmond, who did not write herself but took the occasion to show how open was her friendship with the Prince (and how proud she was of it, though this did not occur to him).

How should he answer them, and through that pert-nosed fellow Percy, who was always gossiping with his sister Lucy Carlisle? He would not answer them, that was all, and damn his civility to ladies!

He thrust the letters away from him and sat down to a rapidly cooling chop and mug of ale. Then he would snatch some hours of sleep lying dressed on his bed, before the dawn attack.

But would he? A pair of almond-shaped eyes looked up at him from under the tilted brim of a hat, then turned away. 'You might have been my brother. I am glad that you are not.' What then might he be instead? It was plain, wasn't it? What a fool he had been to ride away! But she loved Richmond; he had seen her face when she met him, there was no getting away from that. And he must think of tomorrow and tomorrow and tomorrow.

Did all his colonels understand that the first thing was to make it practicable for the cavalry to get through ('numbers of horse are not much useful for a siege', aren't they!)? 'Grandison and Bellasis understood – Wentworth seems a bit thick-headed – the Cornishmen are as hot as pepper and Maurice will look after them,' – so he kept saying to himself over and over, round and round, to drive out the sound of a low voice, vibrant with laughter, that fluttered inconsequently through his mind.

Bristol must be taken tomorrow – but now it was already

tomorrow – he must get up before the attack began. But what was all this noise? He leaped from his bed to the window at the crackle of musketry. 'God, they've begun fighting on the other side of the river!' He hurled himself from his room and ordered the signal to be fired for the general assault.

*   *   *

Six separate attacks were made at dawn, and five of them failed. They started indeed before dawn, before the signal and before all of them were ready; and that was the fault of the Cornishmen across the river on the south side, who were so eager to be first into the city that they set off in the dark before three o'clock in the morning on a scaling party, before they had got the necessary ladders and faggots for filling up the ditch. The sound of firing warned their fellows that the fight had begun and so hurried up the whole assault by about two hours. Maurice dashed up to the line as soon as he heard what had happened, to find the Cornishmen's attack had failed, and drew them off in perfect order from a desperately close fight where stones were used as well as bullets. He galloped from regiment to regiment, cheering the soldiers, helping the officers to keep their companies by their colours, and earning once again his reputation of the 'good come off'. This he did largely by using the magic of his brother's name; Rupert, he declared, had just entered the city from the other side of the river.

Rupert had not, but he soon did.

'I knew you'd back me up by making it true,' Maurice told him later, grinning.

'Then your luck was better than your lie, for at the time you said it there seemed no earthly chance of getting in.'

It was the sixth attack that won, an attack that had been intended only as a feint to distract the enemy, but it showed up a weak spot in the breast-works between the two forts at Brandon Hill and the Windmill. Rupert's men stormed it, hurling hand grenades till the defenders fell back, then scrambled over the breast-works as best they could on each other's backs and shoulders, sweating with anxiety, and began to tear down the earthwork furiously with their halberts and partisans, best of all scrabbling with their hands. The instant a sufficient breach was made, one of the colonels rode along the inside of the line with a fire pike, routing out the few remaining defenders who now ran, shrieking 'Wildfire!'

All this time Rupert's men were pouring through the rapidly widening gap, but before they could rank themselves in order they were charged by a troop of Roundhead horse. All the storming party could do in the time was to discharge their muskets, swing them round in their hands and use them as clubs. But a few more fire pikes came up, and they did the business; the defenders' horses could not face the leaping flames and the troop turned and fled, revealing the fat round shoulders of their officer in the rear who now desperately tried to force his way through his flying men.

'Why, it's Langrish, curse him!' yelled Taylor, who had insisted on accompanying the storming party. Beside himself on recognizing his private enemy who had tormented Yeomans' last hour on earth, he spurred after him, to get a discharge of powder in his face from the Captain's pistol – but in recompense he killed him dead.

Now behind Taylor and the dragoons with him there came a charge of fresh Roundhead horse, which drove them all the faster down the narrow lane towards the city, after Langrish's flying company. At the end of this lane was a strong post called Essex-work, heavily held, so that Taylor and the dragoons were galloping straight into a trap. But the men in the fort, seeing their own cavalry in rout before a hotly pursuing Royalist force, did not wait to see that the force was itself being hotly pursued; they fled for dear life, leaving the post empty.

But Taylor and the storming party were still in a desperate position until their reinforcements could come up; they had forced their way into the suburbs but had no space to deploy their troop, and there was every chance of their being caught in a deadly ambush in the dark lanes between high walls if they tried to advance. In a racking torture of uncertainty they waited in Essex-work, under continuous fire from the surrounding houses.

They had small hope that any would come to their aid, since they heard from fresh men coming up that the attack was being beaten back all along the line. Young Lord Grandison had been killed, and his infantry were utterly disheartened with the death of their leader on top of their heavy losses. Owing to the premature start of their assault, their scaling ladders had not been forthcoming any more than the Cornishmen's; Colonel Harry Lunsford found one of the enemy's ladders leaning against a haystack, brought it up yapping with pride like a dog that has found a stick, and climbed nearly to the top of the palisade, but it was too short, and he had to come down, untouched by the enemy's fire – a miracle, said his more pious colleagues, showing God had work for him – but the work lasted less than eight hours. That attack too had failed, and the attackers were beating a retreat.

The assault on their right had fared no better, and the men were turning. It was at that moment that Will Legge came galloping up with news of the dragoons' entry (with Mr Alderman Taylor) between the Brandon Hill fort and the Windmill.

Rupert, who seemed to be everywhere at once along the line, rallied the flying infantry in person and led them back to the attack with the good news, as coolly as if they had just taken the wrong turning. He was galloping back again to bring up the cavalry, when his horse ('thank God, not the Corsair!') was shot under him, but he walked on without hurrying until he got another. His commanders swore afterwards that it was only owing to his presence that the attack was not given up through sheer despair – no other man could have turned it.

Will Legge, with Colonel Lunsford at the head of his horse, galloped through the breach to the help of Taylor and the dragoons; and horse and foot together now went crashing down the steep lanes into College Green to seize the Cathedral, down the interminable stairs of Christmas Steps, down Steep Street, down into the deep hole that is the heart of Bristol city.

Here was the worst fighting of all. The pent-up mass of the invaders, jammed and jostling together through those narrow lanes, presented an incessant certain target for the townsfolk, who kept up a deadly fire from the windows only a few feet above their foes. Lunsford was shot through the heart on the steps; but he was only one among hundreds, with an appallingly high proportion of valuable officers, picked out by the observant marksmen above.

Sweltering in the stuffy heat of those narrow airless streets in the hollow, with the sun beating down upon them, and their comrades being picked off like flies from their horses by the cool aim of the snipers in the shade and comparative safety above, was a hell worse than any battle in the open. The infantry stormed and took some of the houses, and now the house-to-house firing became like a bout of scolding out of windows.

The blind, close, nagging fight dragged on into the grilling afternoon, when gradually it slackened, and the men began to ask each other what was happening; the sound of a drum throbbed in the distance, and the word, 'A parley!' 'A parley!' shuttled from mouth to mouth. The men lowered their smoking muskets.

Presently they heard Rupert's trumpet-call blare out in answer to the enemy's drum, giving the order to cease fire. The noisy city grew strangely quiet. Then in the hush, two officers went by towards the Castle under a flag of truce. Soon the rumour became a certainty. Fiennes had asked for a parley. Fiennes had surrendered the city. Bristol was won for the King, taken by storm on the third day of its investment.

Then it was that Mr Taylor turned to find Mr Clement Walker.

There were many old scores to be wiped off by the Royalists in the city, who had had a very bad time from their neighbours since the plot, and who knew by now which of their neighbours had helped betray that plot. They were eager to point out the houses of 'the most pestilent rebels' to the victorious soldiery, egging them on to plunder, though little they needed that.

With them too were deserters from the Parliament garrison, among them a deeply injured private who sat in a tavern among a half-sympathetic, half-jeering crowd of his recent enemies, hiccuping out his grievance against his late commander. '*I* saw that weak spot in the line between Brandon Hill and the Windmill, pointed it out, I did, and said "Plant a gun there," I said, "and you'll sweep the whole valley." And all old Fiennes said to me was, what d'you think he says? "Shut your saucy mouth," he says. When he gets his court-martial for this day's work he'll wish he'd listened to me – but all you good fellows ought to thank me with another drink that he didn't.'

The conclusion was not very clear; some were still sober enough to point out that he was devilish lucky they didn't run him through for what he'd just told them. Was there nothing more he could tell? What of the houses in Steep Street and on those bloody steps? They'd give him another drink soon enough if he'd point out the house whose owner shot down their Colonel, jolly old Harry Lunsford. They dragged him to see the place, Lunsford's Stairs, they were calling it, and it was called so ever after.

Pillaging was stopped from time to time by the officers, but it kept breaking out in different parts of the city all through the night. Rupert had hoped to show that his troops could storm this city without pillaging, but he had to content himself that at least there was no wholesale destruction. He had refused early this morning to fire the ships they had seized in the river to help the storming party near the quays, because he would do nothing that might do permanent injury to the city – at least they should have no grounds to sneer again at his 'burning love to England'.

And he arranged with Fiennes that he should have a strong escort of Royalist troops to protect his garrison when he marched out of Bristol with the honours of war at nine next morning. That pompous person, however, whose fulsome drooping moustache spoke a world of contempt for other people's suggestions, and who had preferred to lose the city rather than listen to a saucy common private, marched his troops out unexpectedly at seven o'clock, without waiting for their guard. They had therefore no protection from the mob – Royalist soldiers who had been man-handled under safe-conduct by Roundhead troops at Reading, stragglers and sharks who followed in the wake of an army, released prisoners, injured townsmen, and street ruffians of no persuasion whatever – who set upon them at the gates of the city to harry and plunder.

Rupert heard the tumult, shouted to Maurice, and without waiting for any guard the two of them leaped into the saddle and came hurtling down upon that disordered, dangerous crowd, so that they began to stampede from the Princes alone before the troops had arrived to keep order. The old soldiers in the crowd complained bitterly; they had only been getting a bit of their own back for what the Roundhead rank and file had done to them at Reading when none of the Roundhead officers had bothered to interfere.

Even Fiennes was impressed by so much zeal, and went out of his way to put it on record that 'the Prince was so passionately offended' at the bad behaviour of the crowd 'that many of them felt how sharp his sword was. So far from triumphing and rejoicing at these disorders, the Princes did ride among the plunderers with their swords, hacking and slashing them.'

But 'hacking and slashing' – that was the picture left in the mind, it did not much matter for what reason or against whom – against Englishmen all, that was the one clear fact, and the hacker and slasher a stranger Prince.

*　　*　　*

'Bristol taking, Exeter shaking, Gloucester quaking!'

Now it was Rupert's turn to have the bells ringing in Oxford and thanksgiving services held in the chapels. People were beside themselves with joy; they repeated what the soldiers in the attack had said, that no other commander could have done it but the Prince; the King sent public messages to him of praise and thanks; it was felt everywhere that this young man of twenty-three had as good as won the war.

It was the greatest and clearest gain for the King since the war had begun nearly a year ago, and it seemed as though the whole Roundhead front were crumpling simultaneously under the blow. Their strongholds at Berkeley Castle and Dorchester at once surrendered, and Portland, Weymouth and Melcombe Regis the very next day; the Roundheads fled from the islands of Purbeck and Portland, leaving in all 1,500 arms, 120 barrels of powder and 60 pieces of ordnance in the Royalists' hands.

The Parliament general, Sir Thomas Fairfax, had been defeated at Alderton Moor and was now shut up uselessly at Hull. Massey, the Governor of Gloucester, was throwing out feelers towards surrender, saying that he would not mind doing so to Colonel Will Legge, who had once been his superior officer. Three of the most important and influential Parliament lords went over to the King. The Earl of Essex himself, their Commander-in-Chief, wrote to the Parliament advising them to make peace as soon as they could.

Recruits poured in from Bristol, and the city subscribed to show their love and affection to His Majesty; '£10,000 worth of love and affection is worth having!' said Rupert with his sardonic laugh. The ships in the Kingsroad harbour had declared themselves for the King on the morning of the attack on the city; a Royalist fleet could now be rigged out there, and the ships known as 'the King's whelps' had already begun the work. So now the King would be master, not only of all the West of England between Shrewsbury and the Lizard's Point with free access from the Welsh recruiting centres, but also of all the traffic of that inland sea of the Severn, of the shipping of the Welsh and English coast and of Ireland.

Amongst the paeans of rejoicing caused by all these glorious events, nobody had time to notice an insignificant engagement at Gainsborough on the other side of England, where Colonel Cromwell defeated a Royalist force. Some Cavaliers from

Newark soon won Gainsborough back, so there was no reason to notice it, except that it had been the only success at this time won by the other side, and it was won by a body of cavalry only half the size of the Royalists. Whoever else was demoralized by the Royalist supremacy, it was not Colonel Cromwell, and he had no reason by now to complain of the cavalry of his own side.

But nobody thought of that down in the western seaport city, now devotedly loyal and eagerly welcoming the state visit of the King and his two sons and ministers, all to be lodged at the houses of different aldermen, all imploring His Majesty to make his headquarters now in Bristol.

> *'Bristol is my home,*
> *In Bristol city I met my doom,'*

sang the sailors as they rolled up from the quayside under Rupert's windows.

CHAPTER SEVENTEEN

THE REAL reason for the King's triumphant visit to Bristol was no compliment to Rupert. He had come to hold an inquiry into complaints against his nephew. Lord Hertford had made charges against him of 'arrogance and ambition'. Rupert had decided the terms of Bristol's surrender without waiting to consult his fellow-commander. And Rupert had taken for granted that the King would give the Governorship of Bristol to him, instead of to someone appointed by Hertford.

'As every soldier in my ranks took it for granted!' Rupert burst out to Richmond, one of the many ministers to come down with the King, who had told him of the impending charge. 'Damn his eyes, of course I took it for granted. I took the town, didn't I? The Governorship is nothing but a form. Do you think I'll cool my heels here for long?'

What Richmond thought, and did not say, was that Rupert's private enemies must be feeling themselves very secure to make this public attack on him, and straight on top of his greatest triumph. They would not have dared do it a month or so ago. What then had made the difference? Was it the arrival of the Queen?

Since she had come, she and Digby had worked hand in glove together. And there was now open hostility between him and Rupert; at the siege of Lichfield he had resigned his commission and preferred to serve henceforth as a volunteer, rather than under the Prince. Richmond suspected that it was largely owing to him that there was this public inquiry into the conduct of 'His Most High and Mighty Illustrious Arrogancy'.

But Rupert's enemies got small satisfaction from it; the King confirmed him as Governor of Bristol, and agreed to his request that Maurice should be given independent command and not under Hertford. Then Rupert, prompted by the wise Richmond, asked that Hertford's nominee, Sir Ralph Hopton, should be made Lieutenant-Governor, and privately promised to give him an entirely free hand – 'You'll not find me wanting to interfere with civil government, I can tell you.'

He had already interfered, as it happened, by a rough and ready attempt to deal with the unemployment question in Gloucestershire, having ordered all the clothiers in the county to keep their people at work for a month; although, as the employers now complained bitterly to the King, the war had deprived them of most of their chances of selling their cloth and they had masses of it lying useless on their hands. The war was ruining trade in the West, the most hopeful chance for it would be if the King would make his headquarters here in Bristol instead of Oxford. There was a good deal to be said for this, and Rupert and Hyde found themselves unexpectedly in agreement in saying it.

Rupert was still prejudiced against Hyde, largely because he excused his own loyalty with tedious definitions such as 'the necessity for a personal embodiment of the law'.

('And what does that mean?' Maurice had asked ingenuously. 'A King!' Rupert had answered in a snort of contempt.)

If the temperaments of those two men had been as sympathetic as their views they might between them have put the King back on his throne then and there. For Rupert as well as Hyde was of the opinion that now was a time when the King might safely and honourably treat with his enemies. And he went out of his way to be friendly to the three lords who had just forsaken the Parliament and brought them himself to the King to be reconciled – hoping to encourage more such desertions.

But the Queen was irreconcilable. She had prevented Charles

from receiving the penitents up till now, and was furious with Rupert for making him do so against her wishes. These rats who deserted their sinking ship – were they to be treated the same as loyal gentlemen? And by the same token, now that the King was winning, let him beat his enemies to their knees until they squealed for mercy, before one began to talk of peace. That peace talk too was Rupert's doing, was it?

It was. But everything that she did not agree with was certainly Rupert's doing – even the siege of Gloucester, which the King had undertaken instead of pressing on to London. And here, had she but consented to know it, Rupert was in agreement with her.

He hated sieges and thought this one an unnecessary waste of time. He was not allowed to repeat his success at Bristol and take it by assault, for the loss at Bristol had been too heavy, the King told him.

'If any of them had ever been in a real war!' he exclaimed despairingly to Will Legge. Then they might see with how comparatively few losses he had brought off most of his triumphs. Could not Will, or Richmond, explain to the King how far more necessary speed was at this juncture than anything else? He appealed to them because he had an uncomfortable inkling that he himself was losing hold on the King. The taking of Bristol ought to have strengthened it, but no, his advice was set aside and the siege of Gloucester dragged on; and all Rupert could do was to refuse to command it – a negative sullen gesture that only fed his bitterness and the King's annoyance.

Nor could he really keep out of it. He had set himself to build up and reorganize his cavalry, and brought it up to 6,000 strong – yet for all that he was continually slipping over to Gloucester, hoping each time to arrive at the moment of the final assault, and then staying on in the trenches, encouraging and helping the men in what he felt to be a futile business, and running continual risk of being shot. But Gloucester, though weaker than Bristol, held out, and in the end the King had to raise the siege and retire before Essex who had by now lumbered up to its relief.

After three days at Gloucester, Essex made one of his few sudden movements in the war and surprised Cirencester, which Rupert had seized with such an adroit swoop this spring. Rupert was furious that the result of his work should have been lost, and nothing done to prevent it.

He had sent back intelligence of Essex's movements to the King, but he got no orders. He mustered his cavalry on Broadway Down and waited there all day. But no word came. At last as the early September dusk shut down in a thin rain over the rounded Cotswold hills, he set off himself, with only two men, and rode across the enemy's line of march, seeking for the King's headquarters.

Presently he came to a snug farmhouse sheltering under tall elms in the soft darkness. There was a light in its windows, and he went up to make inquiries, but saw as he came near a scene that held him still and amazed, staring at something that seemed to have been there from the beginning of time, and that he would see ever after. For there inside the square frame of the window was a bright still picture of a low-timbered room in candlelight, and a little table at which two men sat with grave and intent faces, playing cards, while a third leaned against one of the chairs, looking on, with a glass of wine in his hand.

And the man with the beefy red face, looking on, was the deaf old Ruthven who had been made Lord Brentford and nominal Commander-in-Chief a year ago, and one of the two men who played was Harry Percy, his sharp nose silhouetted against the whitewashed wall, and the other was the King.

'I knew it,' said Rupert aloud.

But if any had asked him what he meant, he could not have told what it was that in that instant he found he had always known about King Charles.

The few seconds that held him there to a vision far beyond their compass were dashed from him with a curse – he strode into the room, seized Brentford by the shoulders and thrust him out of the way, and crashed his fist down on to the table, so that some of the cards bounced off it.

'Here have my men been in the saddle all this day long,' he cried, 'waiting for Your Majesty's army up on the downs.'

'A serious matter,' sneered Percy, 'that His Majesty should keep the Prince waiting!'

Old Brentford, distinguishing no words as usual, gazed anxiously at his glass to see how much of it had been spilt and hastily finished the remainder, muttering in his thick northern voice, 'Impertinent pup! Impertinent pup!'

The King said nothing, but stared with freezing dignity at his nephew. Once that would have made Rupert wretched, but now he had looked through a window and seen what his uncle's opinion was worth.

Nothing mattered now but that Essex should be prevented from joining forces with Waller and making a combined attack on the King. Every hour of this wasted day they had been marching towards each other – 'while we fool here doing nothing to prevent them. Let me get ahead and engage them before they meet. We can still do it if we ride all night.'

Charles looked at Brentford: Brentford looked at Percy. All three wished to justify themselves by showing that Rupert was mistaken, that it was his usual reckless folly that insisted on rushing after the enemy instead of letting well alone. But as usual Charles waited for others to speak first. So old Brentford protested that it was very hazardous to risk the cavalry unsupported, that there was no such hurry, they had found comfortable quarters for the men, and no good ever came of night marches.

Rupert's blood was up, he forced his uncle to take his commands, while Percy watched the King ironically, seeing how little he liked his nephew's imperiousness even though he had to submit to it.

*   *   *

Rupert went off as suddenly as he had come, and led his men that same evening in chase of Essex. All that night and next day they marched until they reached Faringdon, when Rupert called a halt for his exhausted men and sent on Hurry (now a proud Sir John, increasingly apt to insist that his name was really the Norman Urré) to try and find out where Essex was. He brought back word that the Roundhead army was straggling over Aldbourne Chase, 'as loose-knit as a flock of sheep', and obviously making for Newbury. Rupert rapidly got his men on the move again – all grumbles at their broken rest checked the moment they heard that at last their quarry was at hand.

Fast and silent as hunters they rode through the old forest where the autumn sunshine lay deep and still on the mossy rides. Rupert in front of them caught the first glimpse of the enemy through the trees, and saw that as usual the cavalry was riding ahead. In the trusting manner habitual in this war, they had sent out no scouts, and had left their foot trailing after them some way behind. He unleashed his squadrons on them before they had an instant to form or to grasp what was happening, and disorganized them utterly. They put up a brave fight and managed to get in touch with the main army in spite of Rupert's flank and rear charges to prevent them, but they had to retreat with heavy losses to Hungerford.

Harry Jermyn and Digby were both wounded in the action, though slightly, and a beautiful French marquis (who had insisted on serving as a volunteer) mortally, and by a common pikeman. This indignity seemed to hurt him worse than his death-wound – 'Vous voyez ici,' he said reproachfully, 'un grand Marquis mourant.'

Rupert had done what he wanted. Charles was able to come up in safety and occupy Newbury instead of Essex.

Now it was Rupert's turn to advise passive measures. He had placed the King between Essex and London, and there was no sense in turning back to fight Essex again, when the Roundhead army was still strong and longing for a chance to retrieve their position since they were cut off from supplies and shelter. They were short of provisions and very near mutiny after this last defeat – let the Royalists wait snug and secure in Newbury, and let the next few days do the work for them.

But with the King had come the Queen. And with the Queen had come her own army, raised by her bargaining and her heroic energy on the Continent, and her own Court from its separate palace at Merton, and she was determined that Rupert's advice should not be put above hers. Her pent-up jealousy of him was ready to burst into the open, for it had by now convinced her that he was trying to undermine her influence, flout her authority, and make her contemptible with the King.

And chief among 'her' courtiers had come George Goring, raging at having missed 'that jolly Chase at Aldbourne' where, as he said, he had often chivied the does but had never had a chance at the bucks. He had drowned his disappointment in his accustomed fashion, but even in his cups he could exercise an extraordinary fascination. With the gaiety of a schoolboy rather than a toper he urged on a battle, appealing to the King 'to give me a chance now, sir, and yourself, and all of us, to show what we can do before the very eyes of your Queen – the very bright eyes of your Queen!'

If Rupert had taken that cue he might yet have got his own way. But he loooked through the Queen without seeing her bright eyes, or anything in her but an exasperating obstruction, and he only said coldly that Essex's army was now reinforced by six companies of fully trained London prentices under the Colonel Skippon.

'Little Cockneys whose shops have been closed while they are allowed out by their masters!' exclaimed Digby, a world of aristocratic contempt in his tones. With his arm tied up in a sling, and his blue eyes ablaze in his interestingly pale face, he urged that now was the moment to smash the enemy utterly while they were still staggering from their knock.

Only Harry Jermyn among 'the Queen's courtiers' took Rupert's side, prompted partly by genuine liking for him and respect for his opinion, and partly by jealousy of Digby, who was getting altogether too important with the Queen.

'Yes, by all means let everybody else fight. You and I, Digby, the wounded heroes, are safely out of it!'

'This is serious, my Lord Jermyn,' said the She-Generalissima. 'Charles, if you do not fight, *my* army will. I have brought my own men from abroad and I mean to use them.'

The King flushed at her tone. He had been brooding bitterly over the unmannerly rebuke Rupert had given him two nights ago, had longed to prove himself before the eyes of his nephew as well as his Queen. Gloucester had been a humiliating disappointment; he had let Cirencester slip through his fingers; he burned to show himself a man of action.

'Very good,' he said, 'we will fight.'

'Very good!' cried Rupert. 'Good to fling away our advantage? Here we are in a strong position, keeping Essex away from London and his supplies. Let him attack us if he's such a fool – but why should *we* be fools?'

The Queen's eyes were glinting with yellow sparks. She looked indeed a little mad. 'How prettily and respectfully your nephew gives you his orders,' she purred. 'Rupert must be Right – that is the one rule in this war. Very well then, you can choose between us – if you listen to him, I will draw off my men tomorrow and never fight with or for you again. My God, if my father were only here!'

Even Goring was startled into sobriety. That white plume in Henry of Navarre's hat – it had gone to his daughter's head! He yearned to whisper this to Jermyn, but the silence was so intense he got no chance.

Rupert had not known it was possible to want so strongly to kill a woman. He had seen his mother angry often enough, an enraged lioness, but this little French cat clawing at him was out of his ken. He dared not look at her, nor, after the first glance, at the King. Charles had been told to choose between his wife and nephew; that would settle it. He would choose his wife. Tomorrow they would go out of Newbury and fight Essex's army.

*   *   *

By the morrow George Goring was singing and fighting drunk, and told everybody that this was the moment to win the war once and for all while they were all merry, damn 'em and ram 'em and sink 'em in hell!

'– And are *you* merry?' asked Rupert in surprise at Lord Falkland's usually melancholy little face, which now wore a smile.

'Yes,' he said, 'for I shall be out of it all by tonight.' The rather hoarse voice had a sweetness of expression that Rupert had never heard in it. He stared at the insignificant figure that now wore a strange dignity, and wished for an instant that he had not somehow always been at loggerheads with Falkland – there were so many others he would rather be at loggerheads with – such as that roaring madman, Goring, now riding down his ranks, incapable of giving any clear command as he shouted to his men.

Falkland was right, he was out of it all by night.

The lives of hundreds of men and of many of their finest leaders, that they had refused to risk in an assault on Gloucester, were now squandered in an attack that had no more object than that of meeting an enemy who had already been defeated.

But now that enemy was drawn up on high ground in a position of great advantage, and the Royalists could only charge uphill against them. Again and again Rupert's splendid cavalry, which he had brought to such perfection that autumn, thundered up under the hail of bullets against the City regiments. Those little Cockneys that Digby despised stood firm to their pikes through charge after charge. They had good artillery behind them, while the King's was utterly feeble; otherwise they were unsupported, and had the demoralizing spectacle of their own cavalry flying all round them at the first onset of the Cavaliers.

Their training in the London parks had been their only experience of warfare. Yet they held that solid fortress of pikes, and from it their musketeers kept up their incessant and deadly fire, while Rupert's horse hurled themselves again and again on to their very points. Not till night fell did the Cockneys leave the field, cracking deprecating jokes in their cheery nasal voices, observing that they had not been such a lousy crew as old Skippon had sworn they were. They had made it safe for their army to retire towards Reading, once night had stopped their slaughter.

For only night had stopped it, allowing the King's forces to creep back without too much disgrace into the town they need never have left, there to sleep or die.

For Rupert there was no such rest. Indefatigably (inhumanly, thought his weary troopers) he set about collecting what horses and what men were still capable of carrying on, and led off a body of cavalry silently in the middle of the night, riding over the battlefield and startling the ghoulish robbers of corpses who had settled like a flock of vultures on their spoil under the glimpses of the moon. By riding all night he got in front of Essex's army and surprised them early the next morning in the midst of a defile along a road between high hedges. Then his trumpet rang out for the first time on that march.

'Rupert's trumpet' – 'Rupert's horse' – the word rushed down the wearied columns, who had only just left the safety of the open country, and threw them into a sick frenzy of terror. Whoever lay dead among the King's men, *that* man could never be killed. He had shown himself a target again and again, in the trenches like any common soldier or walking about at a casual pace when his horse was killed, but himself nothing could touch. Sir Philip Stapleton had stood within a few yards of him in the battle of the day before, had taken careful aim and fired in his face. But the bullet had glanced off his helmet – the bullet had yet to be found in hell that could kill the Wizard Prince.

And now when his side was defeated with heavy loss, driven back to its quarters after an all-day battle, and the Parliament men could at last say that this was a certain victory – here he had shot ahead of them all, and fallen on them out of the sky to snatch their triumph from them.

His cavalry came crashing in on them through the hedges; huddled, frantic, they could scarcely draw their swords without wounding each other, they had no space to fight in nor to see what was happening, their struggle was a nightmare, blind and helpless.

But Rupert could not keep it up; his cavalry were utterly worn out and there was no fresh force to support them. He had to fall back, leaving his enemies in utter confusion in the narrow road to collect their dead and drag themselves on to Reading, while he at last staggered back through a noisy town into a room where the sun shone blindingly, tumbled on to a bed with his cloak and boots still on him, and slept through the confusion of tramping, shouting and bugling outside the window, as only a man of twenty-three can sleep who has fought two fights and been close on thirty hours in the saddle.

CHAPTER EIGHTEEN

THEY WERE back in Oxford and everyone was laying the blame for Newbury on everyone else. Rupert badly missed his 'Twin' – 'the Shadow' most people now called him; and like a shadow Maurice had gone into eclipse in the West, for, having taken Dartmouth and Exeter, he fell a victim to a miserable low slow fever which was playing havoc with the western troops that autumn. No one knew how to account for this, the 'New Disease', though Dr Harvey said it should be called influenza because of its 'dangerous and fraudulent influence'. Maurice was so ill with it that his mother at The Hague gave up going to any parties because she expected to hear of his death by every post. The King and Queen did hear of it in Oxford, and the Queen, having got her own way and some reason to regret it, felt an impulse of her old tenderness towards Rupert as she braced herself to tell him of his sorrow.

'How will he *bear* it?' she cried to her husband; 'poor boy, in Maurice he always had someone to believe that all he did was perfect, and now —'

Her tongue failed her, only her little busy hands could express how lost Rupert would be without that unfailing adoration.

But Rupert, when they told him, quite declined to be lost.

'Maurice is not dead,' he said, and nothing would shake him from it. If Maurice were dead he would know it, apart from any report. He would not have been able to ride along the river side and fly the pair of hawks Lord Ormonde had given him at the herons that flew over Long Meadow, and never once have known that Maurice was dead. So he obstinately refused to believe the news, which took all the wind out of the sails of his

303

aunt's sympathy and left her flat in exasperation. It was intolerable the way Rupert *always* thought he knew best.

But he was right; Maurice was not dead, though the doctors had thought him past all hope – and then suddenly they found that he was not after all dying, but sleeping naturally for the first time for weeks, and from that moment he began to mend.

'And what moment was that?' Rupert asked curiously when at last, late in November, a very pale and feeble Maurice was strong enough to travel back to Oxford. They compared the landmarks of various dates and found it must have been on the very afternoon that the report of his death reached Rupert and was so resolutely rejected by him. To both of them this had a queer significance, as though Rupert had actually kept him alive by believing it so passionately. Neither said it, for they knew each other too well to need to do so. But from this time on Rupert felt a new responsibility, as though Maurice, the Twin and Shadow of himself, had a less stalwart hold on life than he, and kept that hold largely through his brother.

'I must not let Maurice die,' was the sudden shape this fancy took in his mind.

Pretty Mag Kirke did her best to cheer and cosset Maurice, but his life belonged to Rupert, not to her – and that was the shape it took in Maurice's mind.

'And your affair?' he asked, 'how is that going?'

'What do you mean?'

'The Duchess, of course.'

'There's nothing there. What makes you think there is?'

'One hears people talking,' said Maurice uncomfortably, and at once shied away.

That made them both shy when, the next minute, Richmond came in with his wife to inquire after the invalid, with a bottle of rare old port commandeered from the Christ Church cellars, which Mary had insisted on carrying to Maurice under her cloak as though she were playing Lady Bountiful in her husband's village. But the brothers showed no amusement, and she, piqued by their lack of cordiality, asked if their visit had interrupted some more important matter.

Maurice at once expostulated in the unconvincing manner of people who are being polite – oh, no, not in the least – they had not been talking of anything of importance – but his brother crashed in on top of him, annoyed at being driven into a corner.

'You are wrong. We were talking of gossip,' he said; 'that is of more importance here than anything else in the world. Who cares now about the war between King and Parliament? It is the rivalry between the Queen's Court at Merton and the King's at Christ Church that counts.'

'Oh Heaven!' cried Mary, 'you cannot know what it is like from within! We call Harry Jermyn the post-boy now, he is everlastingly trotting out on some fresh errand to intrigue for this, that or t'other post for one of the Queen's courtiers before one of the King's can get it. Poor Falkland was scarcely dead at Newbury before she laid hands on the Secretaryship of State, and said "That's mine! For Digby!"'

'I heard Lord Falkland put on a clean shirt that morning at Newbury because he knew he would be found dead,' said Maurice simply.

'Because he knew Digby would step into it! Dead men's leavings must be suitable for his High Digby Daintiness! There's one good thing – Wilmot is madly jealous of him, since he used to be far more of the Queen's pet before Digby appeared, so between them they may eat each other up.' She stopped short with a sidelong look at Richmond out of her furred cloak that made her look like a wicked squirrel. 'How I *hate* gossip, don't I, James?' she laughed.

'Yes, you do,' he replied unexpectedly, 'when it is growing as dangerous as now. It will lose the war if we let it.'

'*We?*'

'*If* we lose the war, it will have been by not marching on London after Bristol,' said Rupert. 'Gustavus would have got there in a week.'

'And Rupert in two days,' said Mary softly.

'After Edgehill,' he replied with the literal-mindedness of the good soldier, 'not from Bristol. The King now admits it was "a capital error not to march on his capital".'

'Is that a joke?' asked Maurice.

'A bad one,' said Mary.

'A sad one,' said Richmond.

He had hoped to find Rupert eased out and in a lenient mood after his relief from anxiety for Maurice. Richmond's intimacy with the King, whom few men knew intimately, made him more aware than any of the effect of the Queen's quarrels and intrigues. Charles was being allowed less and less peace, until his nerves were tired and fretted beyond endurance. Sometimes he stole away to the Bodleian with Jeremy Taylor or Archbishop

Usher, but these godly and learned men, though his friends, could not make up for the peculiar sympathy and humanity of little Falkland, with whom he used to walk hour after hour in Christ Church meadows.

But now the showy Digby stood in Falkland's shoes, and Charles' chief counsellor was his wife.

'If you cannot make friends with the Queen,' he said to Rupert, 'there will be little hope for the King.'

'If she hates me, she must do so, and there's an end of it,' he answered.

'She did not always hate you,' said Mary. 'Lord, how tired I got of hearing your praises when I was at last allowed to come out of school!'

'It suited her to be kind to me then – it plagued my mother – and I was not old enough to get in her way.'

'Do you think so harshly of all women?'

'No, not all.' He felt himself flushing, but she came quick to the rescue, though with something he did not care to hear.

'You have a grudge against them anyway, a deep and early one, and it's hardened your heart – all for one woman's sake.'

Maurice stared bewildered at her talk. 'He had his gaoler's daughter in love with him for three years,' he said; 'I'm damned if I know what grudge that should give him.'

'Cousin Maurice, you are getting much better!' said Mary, 'as for your brother, there's only one way he can make friends with the Queen, as for any handsome young man – and that is by being or pretending to be in love with her – and that, James, you know as well as I do.'

'I know that she is a brave woman who has been excited and embittered by her misfortunes. You can remember, Rupert, how different she was before all this fell upon her.'

'Well, I for one,' cried Mary, 'can never remember the time when she was not the most jealous creature alive – even of poor me, a child, when they sent me in that absurd hamper to the King.'

'At your own suggestion,' Richmond put in, smiling.

She flung herself upon him – 'James, I could murder you! – Let us go back before our matrimonial squabbles tire out the invalid.'

They walked back to Richmond's rooms across the lawn, while his wife congratulated Rupert on Maurice's looks, and at the little dark arched doorway of the college asked him to come in with them, turning, with Richmond beside her, both smiling their welcome, with the stairway winding up into the darkness behind them.

He hesitated, and at that moment a messenger came hurrying across the quadrangle after them and handed him a packet. 'I was taking it to Your Highness' rooms,' he said, 'from the Lord Secretary of State.'

'Bring it with you and read it,' said Richmond.

They went into his rooms. Rupert broke open the seal of his package, saw the black print of a pamphlet, and gave a glance at the accompanying letter from Digby, all apologies for troubling him with so mean and lying a matter, but one that it were best that he should know of before his enemies used it against him; these newsrags were for the most part vulgar libels, but the observation and subtlety of this particular one made it the more dangerous.

'I'll not read it,' said Rupert. 'What does Digby mean, to send me such stuff? I get 'em every morning.'

Mary took it up and read out, " 'A Looking Glass wherein His Majesty may see his Nephew's love," – no, I should not read it – they may have only got hold of some dispute between you and the King and magnified it a hundredfold.'

But all the same she went on reading it to herself, while Rupert turned aside with Richmond to the window and said, 'They couldn't very well magnify the last. He accused me outright of "a damnable lie".'

'And what did you accuse him of?' retorted Richmond. 'I was there, remember.'

'I am what I am,' replied the Prince haughtily.

'Nor would you have it otherwise. You would alter others if you could, but not yourself.'

Rupert's great eyes were fixed upon him, Richmond thought in reproach, but presently the young man said very low, 'Sometimes I wish it, but don't know how. You love God. Will you pray for me?'

'I have done so ever since I first saw you at Nottingham,' said Richmond.

Rupert turned and stared out at the gust of wintry rain that was now spattering the small window-panes, humbled by this 'intent affection', as the elder man had himself once called it.

Mary suddenly cried out behind them, her voice sharp with distress and anger. 'Oh, but this you must listen to! – it is the most monstrous, sickening lie. – They say this of you – "This whole war is managed by his skill, labour and industry." '

'I am sorry you think that such a lie – I grant it's an over-statement.' (How pretty she was in a rage!)

'No, but listen, sir. Your enemies don't praise you out of love. It goes on, "If the King command one thing and he another, the Prince must be preferred before the King. Having won the hearts of so many soldiers of fortune – he is already their chief-tain and their Prince, and"' – she lowered the pamphlet for a moment and her voice dropped to a whisper as she finished – ' *"and like enough to be their King!"* '

'Go on.'

' "Many of our debauched and low-fortuned young nobility and gentry suiting so naturally with this new conqueror, will make no bones to shoulder out the old King." '

Rupert stood like a block.

'Why should Digby have sent this to me?' he asked at length.

'Because,' Mary broke out, her eyes blazing – 'because Digby, Wilmot, Percy, all of them are saying openly that it makes little odds now whether the Prince or the Parliament win – the King anyway will be ousted!'

Her heavy cloak had slipped from her like a cloud, her dress shone out from it, the soft curves of her shoulders rose under their rippling sleeves; every movement that she made was a focus of light in the dim room.

Rupert scarcely heard her words, only her tone, not meant to charm, but full of generous indignation for him. At this mo-ment, when she was least conscious of being a woman, her loyal friendship took him by surprise; he looked at her, and the things that he thought he had buried surged over him.

Richmond had been horrified by the accusation, and by Mary's news that it was being made in their own camp as well as in their enemies'. He expected to see an answering horror on Rupert's face, and saw that he was not thinking of it; he was looking at Mary.

What he saw in his friend's face made him feel grey and old.

'Shall I now look at her?' he thought, 'and try to see what she is feeling? Shall I stay here to feed my suspicions, watch and listen and weigh their words?'

No, he would not be that ignoble thing, a jealous husband. He went to the door.

'Where are you going?' cried Mary.

'To question Digby,' he replied.

The door shut behind him.

Mary flung up her arms as though they were indeed wings, but caught and bound. 'Oh,' she cried, 'how I wish he were cross and unreasonable and beat me, and then I should be free.'

'For what?' asked Rupert, and saw the answer as he said it, and strode across the room to her. But she too had been startled by what she had said, and picked up her lute even as she spoke, saying coolly, 'We've talked enough in all conscience. What shall I sing to Your Highness instead?'

So she was being feminine again! He was going to ignore the check, to force that defensive weapon of the lute from her hands, but her face had changed again, it had turned to him in sudden frightened entreaty. He had never seen her like this, helpless, bewildered, and could not refuse that mute appeal to his generosity. 'Sing, then,' he said gruffly, and then, smiling, 'sing —' and he sang the first two lines under his breath —

> 'If she be not fair for me,
> What care I how fair she be?'
> 'But, sir, consider, is that fair to me?'

So she sang back, and then before he could take up this challenge also, broke into the impudent little modern song. The rain pattered its soft drumming accompaniment against the window pane. He looked at it and thought of Richmond's face silhouetted against it, as he had seen it when they had talked at the window just now. So short a time ago he would have said that no woman in the world was worth a friend like that. Why must he be torn between these two? A blind rage swelled up in his veins. He did not even notice when she stopped singing.

'What are you looking at so intently?' she asked, and went to the window. 'Oh, I see, it's my lord of Montrose. He does not mind the rain, does he, but these Scots never do. I think him very good-looking, but you should hear what the Queen has to say about him!'

Rupert at once felt more friendly to Montrose than he had yet done. But this room was stifling him. Either he must take Mary in his arms or he must go. He went.

CHAPTER NINETEEN

THE YOUNG Earl of Montrose was in Oxford on the same errand as when he had met the Queen after her landing on the Yorkshire coast last spring. She had thought his advice that of a scare-monger, a hot-head; he was not allowed, therefore, to have any better success when he troubled the King with it through this summer and autumn. He warned Charles that the Scots army on the Border, never yet disbanded, was even now in treaty with the Parliament. But the Scots had been treating with both sides ever since the beginning of the war, and Lord Hamilton, who must know best, said they would go on bargaining to the end and never really move.

So nobody would listen to the quiet dignified young Scot, who went about Oxford like a man out of his element in this glib chattering Court, where gossip and personalities counted for more than war news and politics. Rupert, who might well have been friends with him, had heard that Montrose had helped start all the trouble in those Bishops' wars some years ago, when Scotland had been so jealous of her national liberty, and had thus thrown a lighted torch into the piled pyre of England's disaffection. He had been friendly with the deserter lords from the Parliament, who were mere cyphers to him, but could not forgive this keen-faced young Scot with the compelling eyes, just because his instinct was to think very differently of him.

Pym died that winter of cancer, and the Court congratulated themselves that with him and Hampden dead, and Essex being steadily discredited, and Waller too (he and his army had not made the faintest attempt to come to Essex's help at Newbury), there was now no outstanding leader left on the other side, and no factor that could possibly help their enemies to win the war.

And then they heard the Scots were moving, even as Montrose had warned. Hamilton was either false or unbelievably stupid. The bolt fell on the King as if out of a clear sky, instead of from the threatening clouds that had been piling up against him in the North all this time. He was stunned by it at first, then he asked for Montrose.

'I will go and find him,' said Rupert, and swung out of the council chamber with Maurice, who had pulled his arm once or twice before to get him away.

'What the devil's the matter?' Rupert asked irritably once they were outside the door. 'You might have known I'd want to find Montrose myself.'

'I didn't, for I thought you didn't like him.'

'Well, I do now. Understand that. Why were you pulling at me then?'

'Your collar's dirty. They were looking at it. Come and change.'

'To hell with my collar! I'll go without.'

He tore it off, and trampled it underfoot in his haste as he strode on, until Maurice's miserable face made him realize what a guy he must look. Maurice was proud of his brother's restrained elegance, which had led the younger men of the Court right away from the more showy and fussy styles of the conscious leaders of fashion such as Digby and Goring, a victory as galling to them as any of the Prince's, though Rupert did not know of it. That he should wear a dirty collar, or none, was in Maurice's eyes a base surrender to his rivals.

But he would not waste any time – 'I'll wear this,' he said, and knotted his lace handkerchief round his neck, while the groom brought up the Corsair. They rode to Montrose's rooms in the High, but he was not there; they went everywhere they could think of in search of him, and finally as the raw wintry dusk shut down on Oxford in a veil of river mist, they met him on Magdalen Bridge as he rode back from Headington.

Rupert reined in his horse and said, 'My lord, there is news for you.'

'Good or bad, Your Highness?'

'Both. The Scottish earl, Argyll, has sent General Leslie with eighteen thousand foot and two thousand horse on the march against us.'

'In God's name, then, what is the good news after that?'

Rupert wanted to say – 'Because you are proved right at last – and I was a fool not to back you with every ounce of my strength from the beginning.'

But looking into the other's grave and piercing eyes, as the misty light from the lamp on the bridge flickered up and down, he felt that this man would never want justification or apology – such things were superfluities to him.

He said instead what he knew would be reassuring: 'The King, my uncle, is angry with Hamilton at last; he will be impeached.'

He bent and patted the Corsair's neck, for in that instant he no longer wanted to meet the other's eyes, something had just said to him, 'This man can master himself as well as others – he should be able to help the King better than I.'

It was with difficulty that he spoke again, and sullenly – 'The King asked for you.'

And he wheeled the Corsair round as he spoke and was starting him away at a canter, when he heard Montrose's voice calling after him to come with him to the King.

So they all three went together, and Rupert listened to Montrose's plan to raise an army that should first secure the King's power in Scotland and then come south to fight for him in England. He asked for no more help than a small body of troops from Ireland to be landed on the west coast of Scotland, and a party of horse to enable him to cut his way up through the Lowlands to join them. He would have to fight his way through Leslie's armies, which until this moment had lain inactive, but now were garrisoning all the fortresses along the Border line in what might well prove an impregnable barrier.

But he made no reference to that, nor to the fact that this was what he had wanted to do all along, and so get in first before his enemies; all he said was, 'Your Majesty's affairs will at any rate be in no worse case than they are at present, even if I should not succeed.'

'Let me go with him,' burst out Rupert, 'and a thousand of my horse.'

God, what it would be to fight by the side of this man! They would then have one really decisive clear-cut campaign. Between them they would conquer Scotland in a few months and roll success down into England.

'Maurice can stay here in my place,' he added defiantly, for none of these fellows appreciated what a splendid soldier Maurice was, and even as he told himself that, his heart sank, for he knew that Maurice was splendid chiefly as his second-in-command – and yes, it was just as he knew it would be – Montrose was refusing his help. Neither of the Princes, he said, could be spared from England now, and he could collect most of his horse from the Marquis of Newcastle as he went north. He refused, too, the title of Lieutenant-Governor of Scotland – let him earn it first – or rather, let Prince Maurice wear it, and he be his deputy, the King's Lieutenant in Scotland.

'*I!*' exclaimed Maurice. He had flushed up to his fair hair, and tried not to smile too widely in his pleasure, for surely it must be a mistake and the Scot had meant 'Prince Rupert'. But Rupert too was smiling and looking at Montrose, and King Charles was nodding in pleased assent, so it was all settled.

The night wore on in work, while below the little college windows a courtier stepped discreetly to his assignation, and some noisy undergraduates went singing drunkenly home from a supper party. The King went to bed in the small hours of next morning, a very different man, happy and confident, from the aghast creature that Rupert had left sitting in that chair when he went out to look for Montrose.

Lord Ormonde was there now instead of him, that good-looking Norman Irishman, tall as were all the Butlers, and pleasant as ever, though he thought it a desperate enterprise. He had been sent for to discuss the question of supplies from Ireland, where he had lately been appointed Lord Lieutenant.

'Dan O'Neill asked me to tell you how passionately he had always wished for your appointment,' Maurice told him.

'Ah, well, I dare say he may wish it, and I dare say again he may unwish it,' replied Ormonde in his easy-going tones, Irish only in intonation, as Montrose's were Scottish.

Rupert was pleased to discover Ormonde had no great opinion of his fellow-countryman. Dan O'Neill had annoyed him by sly compliments about the Duchess of Richmond. That was another thing that would have made it so much easier to share this venture of Montrose, desperate as it was, than stay here fighting he knew not what enemies in the dark.

If they turned Richmond against him too? But they should not – never.

He was pulled away from his disturbing thought by hearing Ormonde say – 'Antrim could spare some of his forces. There is that red-headed giant, Alasdair Macdonald, whose father, Colkitto, has been shut up in prison by the Campbells – he and his men would welcome fighting for their own again in Scotland.'

'Did he not rise in the '41?' asked Montrose.

'He did indeed, for I met him walking about the streets of Belfast with his arm tied up in a string, complaining that he had made his wrist ache by killing fifty English and forty Scots in one day. I wouldn't swear it's true, but he's a mighty fighter.'

His Majesty's newly appointed Lieutenant-Governor of Scotland fell forward in a sudden heap on the table, sound asleep, and Boy, who had been sitting in the King's chair since he had gone to bed, sprang down with an indignant bark.

'He's been ill,' explained Rupert, and hounded his brother off to bed.

But soon he too fell asleep; and when he woke the room was empty in broad daylight, and he was lying on the fur rug near the fire, where Ormonde and Montrose must have pulled him for comfort, and Boy was lying across his chest to keep him warm. He staggered up, thrusting his knuckles into his eyes that were smarting with tears as well as sleep, for he had been dreaming – 'dreaming that you were someone else,' he told Boy – 'and it's the first time I've ever wished it!'

The mild morning air blew fresh on his face as he walked out into the quadrangle. Undergraduates were hurrying out of chapel with their black gowns flung anyhow across their shoulders. A courtier in hat and cloak made a gay patch of colour as he came through the archway; Rupert noticed there was something odd about his dress, and in the same instant his hand flew to his own throat. Yes, that was it, the young man had knotted his lace handkerchief about his neck instead of a collar, even as Rupert himself had done. The correct young man must have observed him yesterday evening, and taken his carelessly improvised neckgear for the latest and most princely fashion.

And so in the last few hours, while they had debated the Scottish invasion and Montrose's wild throw against it, cravats had been born.

CHAPTER TWENTY

RUPERT, WITH envy in his heart, saw Montrose ride north to conquer a hostile country united against the King under Argyll's rule.

But only a month later in early spring it was decided that he himself must go north. The central position of the war had swung right round from the South-West to the North-East (although Maurice had had to go down to Dorset again to besiege Lyme Regis); and this was what Newcastle had been hoping, for he had long been certain that he would be the determining factor that would decide the victory for the King. So he told his friends, while he wrote extravagant compliments to Rupert. But now Rupert would have to go and help him, though he was the last man Newcastle had wished near him to dim his glory.

'If it had been Montrose now,' thought Rupert as he rode up through England, measuring the chances of making some great decisive blow that would smash this new threat of the Scots Covenanters and the steadily consolidating power of the Parliament armies both together. Their new man, Cromwell, now Lieutenant-General of their horse, was making a very different thing of their cavalry.

Rupert had had a troublesome time these last few weeks; making continual demands for men, money and ammunition, which his uncle told him were as impossible to grant as if he had asked for the flesh off his bones. He had been given titles instead, created Duke of Cumberland and Earl of Holdernesse so that he could sit in the Royalist Parliament at Oxford – also President of Wales and the Marches. Digby managed to make a deal of trouble over this last honour, by far the most important; he insisted that it should be given to Ormonde instead, and when that was settled by the impossibility of Ormonde being in Wales and Ireland at the same time, he did his best to make Ormonde feel aggrieved with Rupert over the Prince's preferment to himself.

But Ormonde calmly refused to be aggrieved, and Rupert himself was the most indifferent of any. Richmond and Will Legge and Arthur Trevor, his devoted, exasperated and amused secretary, entreated him to give what time he could spare from his public to his private interests; his answer was that he had none to spare.

He had scarcely been in Oxford the last few weeks, but darting far out through the surrounding country. On one raid with a very small force he captured an entire regiment of Fairfax's, on another he lost more than 400 men through the sudden violence of wintry weather, on another he narrowly escaped a plot of Essex's, who had written to London the day before that he would have the Prince in the city the next day, alive or dead. He marched by night as often as by day; 'In the morning in Leicestershire, in the afternoon in Lancashire, and at suppertime at Shrewsbury. Without question he has a flying army!' declared the news reports.

'Rupert is coming,' began the terrified dispatches of his enemies, demanding help, and were sometimes finished, 'Since I began this, Rupert *has* come!'

There was consternation even in the pride of his own side, for every garrison under his charge knew that at any moment of the day or night he might without any warning swoop down and subject it to his eagle scrutiny; and every private country gentleman who hoped to keep comfortably out of the war knew he might suddenly be confronted with a tall stern young man on a black horse who would give him three stiff alternatives and three minutes to decide them in; 'Sir, you have a house which may be used by the enemy, so must be used for the King. You can defend it yourself with your own men if you will – or else have it defended by a garrison of mine – or else . . .'

'Or else, Your Highness?' in a faintly hopeful tremor.

'Or else blow it up.'

No, he could spare no time to combat the delays and doubts that Digby threw in the way of every scheme that might advance him. The Presidency of Wales was of real military value since it would give him the right to raise taxes and recruits and appoint commissioners – but the North was waiting for him.

The Scots Covenanters were gradually spreading out into England; Newcastle was terrified of being surrounded by them from the North and the Parliament armies coming up from the South; the town of Newark was all but starved out by the besiegers; and the Countess of Derby, who was desperately defending Lathom House, had only one hope, in Rupert, with whom she had played at soldiers as a child in Holland.

And as if he were likely to forget the truculent chubby little French girl who had refused to let him carry off all the honours of their battles in the garden at The Hague, her English husband had implored his help for her, telling him – 'I hourly receive little letters from her who haply a few days hence may never write me more.'

Yet Newark must be rescued first – but for all the backing he could get at Oxford it might not have concerned them there if all the North were lost together. Rupert had left that good fellow Arthur Trevor to ferret out what support he could to send after him, and set off with only a very small force, snatched here and there from among the garrisons in his charge.

The enemy were quicker than his friends to follow him; a note from Trevor warned him that 900 dragoons and a regiment of horse were pursuing him, 'which I hope they will all be damned.' And if Trevor could not raise the help he was demanding from the King with a persistency that earned him the nickname of the Terrier, attacking His Majesty every morning (for he was not the man to be turned aside by one denial, nor by fifty), then 'I will raise my siege, burn my hut, and march away to Your Highness'.

But not even that solitary reinforcement did Rupert receive. No matter; he had sworn to march north, and march he did.

The besiegers of Newark heard 'an incredible rumour' of the approach of his minute force, and laughed at it. Even Rupert would hardly come near them when they could meet him with 2,500 horse and 5,000 foot. But long before it was light he and his men charged down upon them, causing utter confusion in that first bewildered shock in the cold darkness before dawn. And before they could recover from it the northern gates of Newark opened and the besieged garrison sallied out to join their force with the Prince's. 'Let the old drum on the north side be beaten early on the morrow morning,' had been the only message Rupert had dared send to the garrison, lest it should fall into the hands of the enemy; but the governor had guessed that by 'the old drum' he had meant the Scots veteran, Meldrum, in command of the Roundhead besiegers, and had been ready for the attack since midnight. The besiegers, caught between two fires, fought desperately all day before they surrendered.

Three of them together made a frantic attempt to kill Rupert, one of them reaching out of his saddle and seizing him from behind by the collar, while the other two rushed upon him in front. But one fell from his saddle with a bullet through his head, just as Rupert managed to run another through with his sword even as he was hauled back by the collar grip, and then as he was choking, it loosened, something flapped heavily against him, and Dan O'Neill severed the hand that clutched him.

'That was the tight fist that was twisting your collar,' he said later with a broad grin. 'Your honour's luck is too good to be lucky – haven't you got such a thing as a scratch about you at all?'

A spent shot was found in his mailed gauntlet. 'Worse and worse,' groaned O'Neill. 'I believe all the devilish stories about you now, sir – why, it's not even grazed the skin!'

Rupert's little army marched in triumph into Newark, where the starving townsfolk went nearly mad with joy to see them, their gaunt faces stretched in hoarse, feebly frantic cheers.

As wild almost was the chorus of praise and congratulation

from outside the relieved city. His prestige was stronger now than it had been since the war began. People said that the very sound of his name made his enemies fall before him. A Lichfield lawyer embarrassed him by insisting on serving dinner to him on his knee. Street ballads were hawked and sung in all the Royalist cities, telling as they had done after Powick Bridge and Chalgrove Field, how

> *'The crop-ears marched without much fear,*
> *Not knowing Rupert rode so near.'*

The Court poet, Sir William Davenant, who was so proud of his reputation as Shakespeare's son, did his best to refute it in his poem.

> *'The women kiss his charger and the little children sing,*
> *"Prince Rupert's brought us bread to eat, from God and*
> *from the King."'*

The prose congratulations were even more lyrical. 'Letters, letters, letters – how can I read 'em all? Stay, that's Richmond's – leave me that and burn the rest.'

Will Legge, his acting secretary for the moment, looked at him quizzically. 'There's one from the King.'

'Does he promise more men?'

'Not as far as I've read. But – "I assure you that this, as all your victories —" '

'Write back – "I assure you that this, as all your letters, is of no interest unless you promise men." '

He was struggling with the long, confused and tortuous sentences that Richmond so oddly used to convey his very simple and direct feeling for him. He told Rupert of the 'jubilee all men are in at your last great victory' – 'Yes, but it's not really important in itself, only as the first step to the North – can't they see that at Oxford?' the Prince exclaimed.

Will sniffed deprecatingly. His young friend was too apt to despise the opinions of others, even when in his own favour. 'The King says here it "is no less than the saving of all the North".'

'God damn me, what a lie! Here's even Newcastle showing more sense – a flood of compliments, but if he's cut off in York, "that great game of your uncle's will be endangered if not lost".'

And his spare hand tugged distractedly at his long curls,

318

rumpling them up over his fingers, while the other turned and tossed Newcastle's letter, tied up so elegantly with floss silk and scented wax, and his eyes saw only Newcastle's next sentence – 'Could Your Highness march this way, it would, I hope, put a final end to all our troubles.'

He knew even better, because more dispassionately than Newcastle, who was troubled about his own precarious position, that this was true, that it was indeed the only hope of putting 'a final end to all our troubles'.

But how could he march north with far fewer men even than he had marched with to save Newark? for the bulk of them would have to go back to defend the garrisons from which he had taken them, and now he had not enough even to man the fresh outposts he had captured.

He had now to interrupt his northern campaign to go back to Wales and get recruits from there and Ireland, and it was owing to Digby's opposition to his Presidency that this had been delayed till now.

The recruiting, too, was interrupted: the King demanded his presence at Oxford for no very adequate reason (once again the work of Digby), and for twenty-four hours Rupert planned furious refusals – wasted labour, for next day another messenger arrived, the King had changed his mind (or, rather, followed someone else's) and Rupert need not return after all.

Rupert dreaded the sight of a letter as he had never dreaded an enemy. The King, he wrote, must either follow his counsel or Digby's, and if he would choose Digby's, then 'Rupert must leave off all'. Since he was not there in person to dominate the King, his advice was never followed, and that in spite of the fact that the Queen was no longer with him, for she was with child and set off to bear it in Exeter, which she thought safe, in spite of all Rupert could tell them to the contrary. But his chief fear was that it gave such evidence of fear. And the King wanted to send Prince Charles to Bristol – but in that he was thwarted by the boy himself, one of the staunchest of Rupert's allies, for he flatly refused to go where his cousin Rupert did not wish. 'He left me my lesson before he went away,' said young Charles, showing a most unwonted obedience.

Rupert hoped presently to have the boy with himself. The excitement and uncertainty of this half camp, half Court life at Oxford was having a bad effect on young Charles. He liked being with the soldiers, which Rupert had thought sound, remembering his own boyhood's passionate interest in the talk of old campaigners round the camp-fires in the German wars. Some of the best lessons in soldiering he had had then, seeing it, as it should always be seen, from the point of view of the common ranker.

But young Charles' interest was very different. Not of night marches and surprise attacks and the wet dead life in the trenches was the talk to which he listened, but to stories of women told by swaggering ruffians who held it a point of loyalty to be as un-Puritanical as possible, inconsistently regardless of the fact that no Puritan's private life could be more blameless than their King's.

Mary Richmond's brother, the young Duke of Buckingham, who had been brought up with Prince Charles ever since his father's murder, was a still headier influence. Three years older, he was beginning to enjoy women on his own account, and still more to brag of them to 'little Charles'; he had his father's beauty and careless magnificence; most important of all, he was an inspired mimic and could show the grain of pomposity or weakness or roughness in everyone, so that as he acted them, Hyde became a fussy windbag, and Maurice a mere boor, and Rupert a mere savage, and there was no one in the world worth admiration. But young Charles had not yet learned that lesson with regard to 'my cousin Rupert' as he proudly called him.

Not till the end of April was Rupert's new army ready; mainly of little quick-eyed, quick-talking Welshmen, and 'Irishes' whom he felt instinctively to be the best potential fighters he had ever yet commanded – 'I am mightily in love with my Irish soldiers,' he wrote gratefully to Ormonde, and no one had ever seen him so sick with rage and disgust as when the news came of a boat of Irish reinforcements captured by a Parliament ship, who took all English on board as prisoners but tied the Irish back to back and flung them into the sea. Most of these were English soldiers who had been garrisoned in Ireland.

Just as they were ready to march northwards once again, there came another letter from the King, commanding him and all his new army to come to him instead to Oxford.

For some moments the Prince stared moodily at the messenger, and the man, shifting uneasily on his feet, never knew how near he had been at that moment to death. For with him and the letter destroyed, how was the King to tell that they had not merely fallen into the hands of the enemy? But it would only delay the matter; he might be recalled later and at a still worse moment.

He sent the man back instead, with such urgent, even frantic reasoning against the change of all his plans that the King allowed himself to be persuaded; he would ask no more of his nephew than a regiment of his horse, two thousand of his foot, and his certain promise to join him in Oxford by the beginning of June.

But this was to change all his plans as much as the other. How could he set Newcastle free from York and help him conquer the advancing Scots with such a diminished army? But nothing he wrote could make his uncle understand; he himself was absent, Digby present, that was the whole crux of the matter. Seeing this as he read Charles' bland, imperious epistle, he saw there was only one thing to be done – he must once more interrupt his march north and go himself to make his uncle understand.

Not waiting to collect more than about a dozen of his horse as escort, he rode at a mad pace to Oxford, blind to the risk he ran, to everything but the appalling urgency of this present moment in the late spring of 1644, when he rode through the dark, rode through the dawn, never noticing the big lambs that bounced coquettishly away from his little company of dusty, galloping riders striving to keep up with the ferocious rider at their head.

At last Oxford lay in the plain below him, a dim and unsubstantial city whose beauty could only at this moment increase his anger. Was there a curse on this soft, sleepy place, so that nobody there could take in hard facts and act on them but at once they melted in the river mist? Always he was being called back for the discussions he so hated, in this grey old city that lay smugly secure in the learning that was its real concern, and where the turmoils of this present moment, urgent and keen as the cold east wind whistling in his ears, would leave scarcely a mark.

In times to come, undergraduates would come and go as they had always done, and which of them would remember the gun emplacements at Magdalen, or the royal council chamber at Christ Church, or the Queen's gardens at Merton where he had walked with Mary?

CHAPTER TWENTY-ONE

I T W A S Mary he saw first. He came on her in Magdalen Walk by the river, where he had been told the King would walk after morning chapel, and so hurried to catch him there the instant he should come out. And there he saw two girls sauntering and laughing under the pale green willows that overhung the river. It was the Duchess of Richmond and her friend Mrs Kirke, but they looked more like two milkmaids in their fresh, light-coloured gowns, carrying in their hands their broad-brimmed hats filled with wild flowers, white and gold, while a blackbird in the branches above them shouted for joy.

They had been strolling along with their backs to him when he first saw them; then, as he slackened his pace, they stopped at the river's edge and stood looking down at the flowing water, still laughing and talking so intently that he supposed they could not have seen him and that it was pure accident they had stopped, and anyway could even women have eyes in their backs? Still, they might have seen him; he must go on; it was ridiculous to feel this dread of doing so. He would only ex-change a greeting with them both, and then the King would come down the path and he would say all he had wanted to say to him; it would all be there in his head, just as urgent as when it had driven him on this frantic ride across country, the words he would say to the King throbbing and pulsing in his veins.

But now it was not words that throbbed there, words and thoughts too had gone. He saw Mary with her bare dark head bent like a flower towards the river, and the sunlit reflections from the water rippling up over her face, her lovely laughing face, shining in the river's light as well as its own, like something fluid and unsubstantial that might at any instant glide away into the water and flow into some rippling eddy and dis-appear.

He heard her say, 'Then you will go tell her now?' and Mag Kirke's clear high voice cry back, 'On the instant, trust me to deal with her!' and again that concerted peal of laughter that was full of secret feminine understanding. Mag swung round and came up the bank and there stopped dead, then turned back to her friend who still stood there, now a pensive wood nymph under the weeping willow, and called, 'Mary, who do you think is here?' – and Mary looked up, and came fluttering from the bank with chirps and cries of pleasure – 'The Prince himself! But you are far away conquering all the North. How is it you are here as well? Is it yourself or your familiar spirit?'

Mrs Kirke was protesting sadly that she must set about that tiresome business – 'fore God, she must run like a hare! She ran, and Rupert, looking after her, feeling a little light-headed from fatigue and hunger (for he had ridden all night and had not waited for any breakfast), wondered if they had really not seen him, so that he might have stepped away quietly after all.

It was too late now. He was here beside Mary, he could not be anywhere else, however much he wished it; but he did not wish it, that was a lie, he wished only to talk alone with Mary, if only he could let go of everything else – forget Digby, forget the King, forget Newcastle, forget the North – 'for I love you, and you know it and it is of no use to pretend the contrary', he heard his voice say in an unconsidered casual way – and then remembered that he had forgotten Richmond.

'No,' she said, and her tone was lighter than his – it might indeed have been their attendant sprites that walked here in this singing grove on this early clear spring morning and talked of the two bodies from which they were now apart – 'You say that because it has been jolted out of you by surprise, and already you are amazed at what you have said, but you do not love me truly, because you love so much else – the King, and your glory – all England is ringing with your praises, and off you must ride again on the instant to conquer more armies. You have no time to love me – and no room.'

'There is no room for Richmond's friend by your side. What am I doing then, walking here beside you, forgetting him?'

What was he doing? Was he walking, talking in his sleep?

Her voice seemed to be coming from a distance.

'No,' it said again – 'Must it always be "no" that I say to you? When you have given me no chance to say the one great "No" a woman ought to say!'

'You have said it. You said, "There is no time and no room."'

'For you. I was not speaking of myself.'

'There is Richmond.'

'It was not I who spoke of him. But you would put him between us always, even if there were not others between us.'

323

'Others?'

'You have never given your heart to a woman; you cannot now, it has never been your own to give. In ten years' time, perhaps twenty, it may be yours. But now you'd want from me what I can never give, nor any woman save one – and she's denied it!'

It was as though someone else than Mary was speaking to him, of things that he had known all his life but had never heard said before; not even in his thoughts.

And she, looking up into that proud face, knew that her hazard had been right – that only love for a woman that had remained unsatisfied from his birth could have given him the baffled, unconsciously reproachful look that sometimes made his face oddly childish in expression in spite of the sternness of its set purpose.

She had never seen it as now, fixed in deep lines of weariness and resolve; only the half of him was here. And yet this was the first morning, after all these long bitter months, that really felt like spring; the sun had a caressing warmth in it for all the cold wind; the celandines and wood anemones were all out, the birds shouting in the thin new green of the trees, and she was just twenty-one, and he twenty-four. Why could he never forget the war, let go, and snatch at his pleasures as all the others did?

'You are too ferocious a victor,' she said, 'perhaps you will have time for women when you fail.'

'*When I*—?' Absurdly, it had never occurred to him that he could fail. Others could fail him – yes, and had done so again and again. But he had never failed yet in his own part of the battle.

'And you never will,' she cried. 'I never meant that.'

But she had meant it, and that made it seem possible in a way that the ill will of his enemies had never done. She saw it, and saw them drifting apart as though the river that slid and whispered beside them now flowed between them. She stretched out her hand to him – 'You are going away,' she said. 'You are always going away. We have said no sense at all in these few minutes. Let us forget we ever spoke, that you ever saw me except in that moment when I was looking at the river.'

'I shall not forget that – ever.'

That at last was real, would be so always, until the dark closed his eyes for ever.

'Look,' she said, 'the King is coming.'

The King was walking towards them, fast as always, with the long determined strides of a short man.

Rupert stared at the slight advancing figure, attended by his courtiers. He felt as though he were trying to wake up. For a moment he could hardly think how it had happened that he was walking there with Mary.

The King was not at all astonished to see him there. He greeted his nephew with exclamations on the charm of Oxford in the spring, as if that were the obvious reason for his sudden visit. Mary curtseyed and went on her way. The Lords Digby and Wilmot dropped back in the narrow path as Rupert turned and walked back with his uncle, who was still rhapsodizing over the beauties of Oxford.

'The place has had its guts rotted by old learned men,' his nephew burst out in sudden irritation. It was an unfortunate beginning – he pushed his hand across his eyes, for whatever happened he must see clearly now, he must not let them swim and dazzle as they were doing. And he must remember the words that had been urging him forward all night.

'Sir,' he said, 'here in the South-West you have only to hold the centre safe with your garrisons while Maurice secures the West. Here there is but one enemy; in the North there are two, and they are daily nearer to joining forces. The loss of York would mean the loss of all the money coming in from the North, and it is money that will in the end win this war. The loss of York would be ultimately the loss of your crown. But if I am in time to relieve it and to beat those two armies before they join hands, then I shall have beaten the rebel armies of your two kingdoms, and the war is won.'

He could say no more. The grass was very soft underfoot, there were little wild white flowers growing in it – daisies, whose yellow centres had a dull surface like wool or cotton, while the celandines heaped in Mary's hat had been of a shiny gold like the polished metal itself. But he must not say that, or even his uncle, who liked to talk of flowers, might think him a bit mad.

'Nothing goes *in*,' thought Rupert, looking down at the exquisitely chiselled face of the little man beside him.

But something else had gone in. The King was ruminating over a piece of news that he hesitated to hand on to his nephew.

'Your brother —' he began.

'What of Maurice?' asked Rupert quickly.

'No, it is your elder brother,' said the King at last, in greater difficulties than usual from his stammer.

'Carl again!' Odd, how utterly he had forgotten him. 'He has been writing to the Parliament I suppose.'

'He has.'

'Sir, you need not hesitate to tell me. I know well enough what it is – more abuse of me.'

'No, it is not that. He is coming to live in London, as the guest of the Parliament. He will be lodged at Whitehall, with a grant of £12,000 a year.'

Rupert stared before him as he strode on, never realizing that his long legs had overshot the King's for the moment and left him behind. He swung round as he noticed it, and his uncle was startled by his face. He said, as Rupert fell into step beside him again, 'Indeed I think it will harm the Parliament more than anyone; it shows so plainly that they have an understanding with him, and they must realize this, for I hear they are doing their best to dissuade him from coming, but he does not care.'

'He'd never care for anything as long as he can take his ease in your palace, curse him!'

'It is not even as though he needed the money,' pursued Charles reflectively – 'the Parliament are paying him his pension. This is only as if it were to add another chicken to his dish.'

Rupert could not endure that accusation of his brother's meanness. He preferred to call him a traitor through and through, and did so.

'I cannot think that. He stayed with us so long as a boy and we were so fond of him – until we liked you best,' added his uncle ingenuously.

Rupert gave a short laugh. 'Timon wouldn't forgive either of us for that.'

There is power in a family nickname to recall intimacy if not affection. His less violent 'Twin' had once said to him, 'You wouldn't really want to kill old Timon.'

He was not at all sure. He had a flashing vision of himself riding into London at the head of his armies, surrounding Whitehall Palace, striding through its rooms until he came on Carl lounging in a comfortable chair, eating sweet cakes, of which he was very fond, and forcing him down on his knees to admit that he was a miserable cur and to promise never to

326

trouble them again. That was impossible. He would trouble them as long as he was alive. It would be better to kill him. It wouldn't look well – but – 'no one ever had a better cause for fratricide!' he broke out.

'Think of your mother!' exclaimed Charles, shocked. Rupert did – with a hardened face.

'This will do me most harm of all,' he said; and his voice dropped, for Digby, some yards behind them, had the ears of a cat. 'Your chief advisers hate me; they will do all they can to use this against me, that I have a brother in the enemy's camp – no, worse than that – sitting in your palace, showing openly how he hopes to step into your shoes. Will you let them work this against me?'

'Which of my advisers hate you?' asked the King's cold voice.

'By God, sir, you have only to turn your head to see them.'

'Nephew, you are mistaken. Digby has never hated you, but it is you who hate him. He has tried to make friends with you again and again, but you have shown him that you despise him; you flout his opinion on all matters —'

'On matters military, yes. He understands nothing about them. He has done what he can to ruin my work, and he'll do it altogether – if you let him.'

Once again he was looking anxiously down at his uncle, wondering which of his words would penetrate that masked face. All expression was hidden under its drooping eyelids, its sad shut mouth. In what dream world did he really hold his court? Not here, among the busy intrigues of Oxford. Did he see nothing ever, hear nothing?

*　　*　　*

He heard too much. He heard Rupert, and let him go with his promise that he should not meddle again with his plans in the North; and off rode Rupert, whistling as carelessly as the larks overhead, forgetting even that Carl was coming to London.

Next day the King heard Digby, wrote again to Rupert, abandoning his nephew's plan of campaign for him at Oxford. Rupert wrote back, and the King wrote yet again, thanking him with chill displeasure for his 'freedom' in expressing his opinion, but saying he was not of that opinion himself. But Rupert was too busy by now to heed opinions, as long as he did not have to obey orders.

He was rapidly marching north at last, defeating Parliamentary troops in skirmishes he did not think worth the mention ('but if Goring had done this you'd have had a handsome story', he told Trevor, who could see the sardonic grin with which he wrote it), storming Stockport and relieving the siege of Lathom House, taking Bolton, 'the Geneva of England', who testified to their Calvinist God by hanging an Irish prisoner over the walls in insult to the besiegers as they retreated from their first attack. It was a bad lesson in Calvin's doctrine of predestination, for Rupert had decided not to waste more time and men on the siege; but as he saw this crime, he leaped from his horse, called back his men and attacked again with such fury that they soon broke through and entered the town. This time he did not restrain his men from sacking it, for he swore that the enemy should learn the Irish were as subject to soldiers' laws as themselves.

Recruits poured in: Royalist Wigan was strewn with flowers to greet the conqueror; the little port of Liverpool, useful to receive troops from Ireland, but with its mud walls manned by a Parliamentary garrison, now fell to his sword; he snatched a moment to write a peremptory though thoughtful and humane letter to the Bishop of Chester, asking for church collections for the wounded soldiers; and there was a brief complimentary flourish when he sent all his captured standards to Lady Derby to adorn the house she had so long and nobly defended. The twenty-two Parliamentary banners that she had seen threatening her for so many weeks whenever she looked from her windows, now hung as ornaments in her hall.

The way was clear to York; the time was nearly mid-June, and Newcastle was writing that he could not hold out as much as a week more. It did not need Richmond's urging to tell Rupert that 'if York be lost it would prove the greatest blow which could come from those parts'.

But that was not the view of those nearest the King. To Digby, as to Rupert's other enemies, chiefly Percy and Wilmot, the greatest blow to come from those parts would be Rupert's success.

'The Parliament – or Rupert – what does it matter which of them wins, since either victor will reduce Your Majesty to a cipher.' So Digby said outright to the King on his morning walk in Christ Church gardens.

'Think, Your Majesty,' chimed in Percy on the other side, 'of that disgraceful scene in the farmhouse near Newbury before Your Majesty's own generals! Did he treat you then as his king?'

They told him it was common talk that the Prince aimed at the Crown for himself. It was what they had been hinting delicately for months; now desperation made them bold, for if Rupert returned in the blaze of glory that all his progress north had been, then it would be the end of their faction. If Rupert took the Crown or not, it would make small odds to them; – if he conquered England he would rule England, whether in the name of the King or his own. And the first thing he would do with his power would be to ruin them. He had sworn openly to remove them from the King, and he would then have the power to do so.

Now his elder brother was actually coming to live like an usurper in the King's own palace. It was an astonishingly lucky weapon for Rupert's enemies. Everywhere they were saying:

'He or his brother – it won't matter which of them calls himself King – Rupert will rule England with his army, whether for himself or Carl.'

And in echo of these crude suspicions, which the boldest would find it difficult to say outright as yet to the King, there were the sound opinions of wise moderate men like Chancellor Hyde – 'That young man is flying dead against all the instincts of the English people. You will never get England to endure a military tyranny.'

And the report of public opinion that reached Rupert was, 'The King grows daily more and more jealous of him and of his army.'

His uncle's version of it was another attempt to recall him rather than risk that army in a great battle.

The combined result on Rupert was a fit of such black rage that he swore to send his commission back to the King and take boat instantly for France.

'The tide is strong against him,' sighed Trevor, writing to his friend Ormonde and wishing to heaven the Irish Channel did not lie between them.

CHAPTER TWENTY-TWO

THE SIX days Newcastle thought he could hold out drifted into ten, and still Rupert did not march. He had not sent back his commission, he did not talk of leaving England, but then he no longer talked at all. The livid fury that had shaken him at first had passed, and left him in a cold rage like a trance that froze all the springs of action in him.

'He was tired out to start with, and now comes this shock,' said Lady Derby to her lord; for it was at Lathom House, with the draughty hall flapping with his twenty-two captured standards, that he stayed during this ten days' strange suspension.

But Lord Derby would not agree with her. 'No one's ever seen him tired yet. It's the joke of the army that he doesn't know what it is. No, it's temper that's the matter with him and I don't blame him, but what's the use?'

Trevor heard that Leslie's Scottish horse had already joined with General Cromwell's and were moving towards York, with all Lord Manchester's army guarded behind their cavalry screen.

Still Rupert did not move. And as with enemies, so with friends, however practical, sensible, coaxing, devoted – none of them did any good.

It was the thought of a man whom he had never known enough to call his friend that at last made him stretch his long arms, dragging them across his face, open his eyes on the blazing June sunshine as though he now noticed it for the first time, and walk into the house to find Trevor and tell him, 'I shall write to Montrose and ask him to come and help us to relieve York.'

Trevor gaped, felt an absurd impulse to burst into tears like a child at this relief of the horrible strain of the last ten days, swallowed hard, and said drily, 'Then we are to march?'

'Instantly.'

'That's as well, since I have just had a message that Goring is ready to meet us with 5,000 horse.'

'Then the King will try and recall them.'

'He has already written, doing so. What am I to say?'

'Nothing. Leave it.'

And he sat down to write to Montrose, who was still hovering about the Border, awaiting his chance to dash through the Scots

Covenant armies that were now as thick as the flies on this hot June day.

'He has only a midget army,' said Trevor. 'What can he do?'

'I don't know – yet. But I think it will be more than anyone else.'

He rode off, saying goodbye to his hosts as cheerfully as if he had never noticed that he had been in a black and silent rage all the time of his visit.

'But he is an extraordinary young man!' exclaimed the countess, helplessly lifting her plump capable hands. 'I sometimes think that he is not human at all – he has been changed at birth by the fairies for one of those northern giants.'

'He's not ugly enough for a troll,' objected her husband, laughing.

'But strange enough, you will admit. No, you will say he is a good fellow and leave it at that. Shut the doors for the love of heaven. I feel I am in a ship at sea with all these standards flapping round me. It was a charming thought of the Prince, but, dear God, what a dust they create!'

Her husband forbore to comment on the equally unpractical nature of her own parting present to her former playmate – a pair of beautiful Venetian mirrors, large for that time and in several pieces, as no way had yet been discovered of making looking-glass in a large sheet – 'but when there is peace here, we'll find out about it and make glass as fine as this and in one big piece' – so Rupert had said as he gazed in pleasure at the gleaming glass elaborately bordered with leaves and stags and little fantastic men chased all along the edge. It was certainly an inconvenient present to carry on forced marches, but they were carefully packed up and he promised he would do nothing so unlucky as to break them.

He now rushed his army across the Pennines, and joined Goring on the borders of Yorkshire.

Goring was very funny about 'my partner', Newcastle, whom he called 'Apollo's whirligig', all perfume and compliment, 'always toying with the Nine Muses or the Dean of York's daughters, and then braces himself to strike a blow for the monarchy, and writes to Prince Charles to remember his manners – "Pulling off your hat and making a leg pleases more than reward." Well, that's useful information, as our royalty are getting less and less chance to reward anyone. And then tells his pupil, "To women you cannot be too civil" – as if the young rascal needed to be told that by now! Newcastle's very unhappy at your coming,' he added inconsequently.

'Why, in God's name, when he's been urging it all this time?'

'Why, my Prince, because he's madly jealous of you! He could just stand your being a better soldier, though not easily – but that you should beat him at his own game and be an artist where he is only a critic and collector – what's the betting that he avoids the subject of pictures altogether and talks only of music?'

'He'll get no chance to talk of either – there won't be time.'

And Rupert asked what Goring had heard of Cromwell's cavalry up here in the North; from all he had heard, the man had been coming along twice as strong as anyone else on their side.

'Twice as strong as his commanding officers!' said Goring; 'he does what he likes with that sweet meek man, Manchester – but what he'd really like is to kick him out. The trouble is, Crawford does a bit what he likes with Manchester too.'

'Is that their Major-General of foot?'

'Yes, and he'll soon feel the weight of Cromwell's foot,' replied Goring with the hearty guffaw of a simple, good-natured man. 'They all hang Bibles on their belts now – they come in handy in bombing practice. Not a man among 'em but's called Zebedee or Zacharias or some such holy name – such an army of Hebrews as they've raised against us, you may learn the genealogy of Jesus from the names in Cromwell's regiment alone.'

They discussed the probable position of Cromwell's outposts.

Two days later they came in touch with them, and on the last day of June were only just over a dozen miles from York. The Parliament commanders drew off from their siege works and lay on Hessam Moor to bar Rupert's approach to York.

'Their Goliath himself is advancing, with men not to be numbered,' was an unfortunate bit of propaganda in one of their printed reports. They thought they had cut off his advance on the city, and expected him to attack them with his usual rashness. 'Grim with hunger,' as they growled, and with thirst too, for their commissariat had broken down, they were desperate and eager for battle.

In the light of a sultry copper sunset they saw Rupert's cavalry, squadron by squadron, deploying out from the forests and extending along its edge on a wide front. Behind them, so ran the rumour down the Parliament ranks, would surely be coming 'their inhuman cannibal foot'.

But Rupert did not attack that night, and in the morning they found that his cavalry had been acting only as a screen. His job was to relieve the city, and he determined to make sure of that first. Goring, who had reconnoitred all this country, knew of a ford across the river near Poppleton. Rupert swung his foot and artillery across under cover of the night, splashing through the shallow water, left his main body near Long Marston, and rode into York with two thousand horse.

He had most brilliantly outmanoeuvred them; and his highest tribute for this came from his disappointed enemies. 'Prince Rupert hath done a glorious piece of work; from nothing he had gathered, without money, a powerful army, and, in spite of all our three generals, had made us leave York.'

This generous praise from a Parliament soldier found its echo in the consternation of the 'three generals'; Sir Thomas Fairfax, Leslie, Lord Leven, and General Cromwell were in terror of having their retreat cut off, and fell back next day on Tadcaster.

Under the massive grey walls of York, Rupert met the Marquis of Newcastle at last. He led the Prince into his sumptuous library; a tall fair singularly beautiful man, stalking beside him in great but conscious dignity, like a king in a play. There he stood in that luxurious setting he had created for himself, of finely bound books and rare tapestries and musical instruments and pictures by foreign artists, stood bowing and sweeping his hat and flourishing compliments as formal and high-sounding as a blast of trumpets, but with not a single really cordial note of praise or thanks for the dexterity with which this young man had relieved the city from siege for him.

Sir John Hurry clanked after them down the long room, past the three windows, up to the big table where the Marquis was still rolling out his phrases – His Highness' deeds put the modern world to shame, no comparison with them could be found except —

Rupert interrupted hastily before they should be found. He wished to discuss the situation at once and tell the Marquis what he wanted him to do. The Marquis was equally anxious not to be told. He had just undergone the discomfort of a siege and that was bad enough, but at least his self-esteem had not suffered. He was not going to act as second-in-command to this terse hardbitten adventurer, a boy in years compared with himself, but with eyes furrowed like a veteran's from his sleepless night, who had not the smallest compunction in ordering anyone about, even the King.

Volubly, to prevent Rupert speaking, Newcastle told him that the best thing he could do now was to march back again to Worcester.

Rupert opened his eyes in no very pleasant manner. He had relieved the city for the Marquis and had not expected to get his marching orders from him like this. But Newcastle's voice rolled smoothly, suavely on, explaining that their combined forces were no match at present for the Parliament's, but that a very short time would do their work for them by disintegrating their enemies.

'True enough,' broke in Hurry, who had been nodding his head very wisely in agreement with the Marquis from time to time, 'their generals are all at loggerheads.'

Rupert was more impressed by Hurry's eagerness to back up his present superior officer than by his argument.

General Cromwell, he was saying in his strong Scots accent, was believed to have quarrelled already with the two Leslies – in any case he was known to hate the Scots as much as he did the Irish – 'though all he knows of Ireland is that he's invested money in land there.'

'What better reason for hatred than taking their land?' remarked Rupert. 'The dispossessed are always wrong.'

'A bad-tempered fellow,' said Newcastle. 'I cannot understand how he has risen as he has.'

'You can be a good soldier with a bad temper. I am one myself.'

Lord Newcastle flushed like a girl. This was the height of bad manners, to give so personal an application to his remarks, as though he had intended to imply reproof to his guest. But Rupert, who had never guessed at anything so subtle and had only thought of the question at issue, was pursuing the argument.

'You think then they may disagree as to their plans?'

'It is very likely. Their strength is nearly twice ours, yet they retired in such disorderly haste that they left a considerable amount of ammunition in their camp.'

'And about four thousand pairs of boots and shoes,' chimed in Hurry.

Rupert turned again to Newcastle.

'You secured them? You'll give us half?'

Again came that flush. What was the matter with the fellow?

'Oh, so the boots have already been grabbed by your Plunder-Quarter-Master-General?' said Rupert, reading the situation more quickly than the Marquis liked.

He replied with great dignity, 'Clavering and his reinforcements will soon be joining us from the North. I refuse no obedience to a grandson of King James' – it took Rupert a second to realize that this referred to himself – 'but if we wait till then —'

'Have you any news of Montrose?'

Newcastle stared at the abrupt question that had cut across his talk.

'Yes, the Earl of Montrose,' repeated Rupert at his pause.

'He has been created Marquis now,' corrected Newcastle in reproof. 'He came here in March for reinforcements, and I gave him what I could – two of my small cannon and a hundred troopers, but I fear their horses were poor enough. It is a mad scheme he is on, and I see no chance of his cutting through the Covenant armies into Scotland.'

Nor did Rupert see it, with two small cannon and a hundred badly mounted troopers.

Montrose should have got his message by now. Would he come? But he did not really doubt it – he knew he would come. And if Newcastle put his trust in Clavering's reinforcements, Rupert put his in the help of Montrose, almost single-handed as he was, but also of single heart and purpose.

This dilettante Marquis whose fingers itched to be at his harpsichord with the most single purpose in his life, but otherwise was so deeply concerned with his position in the eyes of the world – he could not serve one purpose; nor could a fellow like Hurry, who had once said openly that the markings of a good soldier were to spot the winning side in time to join it. He was a fine cavalry leader, but Rupert did not at all care to have him in the responsible position he would have to take among his horse.

At this moment the door opened behind him and —

'You will find an old comrade-in-arms here from the German wars,' Newcastle was saying with courtly geniality – 'Lord Eythin.'

'I never heard of him.'

'His title is new. But he knows you well, and has often spoken of your reckless gallantry at Vlotho.'

Rupert swung round in his chair, and saw a short stocky figure stumping slowly down the long room towards him, past the first window, and the second and the third, the spurred boots breaking up the three oblongs of late, red-glowing sunlight, until there was no longer any doubt of it; there before him was that same General King who through businesslike prudence had failed to support that charge of Rupert's at Vlotho which had landed him in prison for three years.

Of the two it should have been General King to be disconcerted at the meeting with the boy whom he had led as a tutor to war and deserted on the battlefield. But this squat stolid man approached and stared up into his face with a hard imperturbable assurance, neither aggressive nor defensive, but so certain of his own opinion as never even to be aware of any other.

The years since their last meeting seemed to fall away; the young Commander-in-Chief who had in two years of 'perpetual motion' built up the English horse into the best cavalry in Europe, felt himself once again on the threshold of manhood, with the cold shades of his prison closing in on him, and all round him that awful enforced stillness, that suspension of all his energies, when time had lain vast and empty as a desert – and he a prisoner in the midst of it.

General King, now advanced to Lord Eythin, congratulated him easily, calmly, on all he had learned and done in the way of soldiering since their last meeting, his little eyes blinking up at him under his white eyelashes. That manoeuvre of his just now, getting his troops across the river behind that screen of cavalry – it had prettily hoodwinked the enemy. To have relieved York without a man lost, it was a surprising *tour de force*. His sensible Scottish voice, clipping each word briskly into shape, went on to suggest what Newcastle and Hurry had already urged, that the enemy, cut off from the siege, would now certainly retire of themselves, 'if they don't wait to fly at each other's throats first, for they're near enough to it. You've put them into a devilish awkward position. Don't give them a chance to get out of it.'

The others buzzed assent; they had all got their opinions as pat as though they had rehearsed them beforehand.

Rupert's eyes were hot and dry with lack of sleep; he felt as stupid as an owl in daylight. He supposed these men were right, though he disliked the three of them and heartily distrusted two. Yet what they said sounded good sense; but it seemed ridiculous to have come all the way up here and never have a smack at the enemy. Well, if they were retreating in earnest, he could harry them with the cavalry on his own account. He looked up in agreement. 'Very well, then,' he began – and stopped as an officer came jingling into the room and up towards him with a letter in his hand.

CHAPTER TWENTY-THREE

ONCE AGAIN a letter from the King lay in his hand. He turned it over, reluctant to open it. What would it say this time? Would it recall him to Oxford again, or ask why he had not sent back Goring and his horse as before requested?

Questioning, hesitating, in a way that he could not have done before that sick pause at the sight of General King, he turned and twisted the paper before he even broke the seal, so that the other three watched him in amazement, thinking that he was really about to tear it through unread. 'Better if I did, perhaps,' Rupert was thinking. No letter from his uncle ever brought him luck.

But this was nonsense; he must open and read it, and so he did.

It was addressed to his 'loving nephew' as usual, and very long. The King was in desperate difficulties; he had not followed Rupert's plans for him, and now very graciously conceded: 'I believe that if you had been with me I had not been put to those straits I am in now. I confess the best had been to have followed your advice.'

Well, but he was not writing just to say that. (Get on with it – come to the point if you ever can!) Ah, here it was – apologies for such 'peremptory commands' – and here were the commands, stated, then qualified, almost contradicted, then repeated again and again with obstinate persistency.

'If York be lost I shall esteem my crown little less. But if York be relieved' – (so it is, then that's answered – no, wait till the end of the sentence) 'and you beat the rebels' army of both kingdoms which are before it, then, but otherwise not, I may possibly make a shift, upon the defensive, to spin out time until you come to assist me.'

The King must be in dire straits to write like this – 'you may

337

believe that nothing but an extreme necessity could make me write thus unto you; wherefore in this case in no ways doubt of your punctual compliance with.... Your loving and most faithful friend, Charles R.'

He must then, 'as he valued his honour and the King's cause', fight at once and 'beat the rebels' army of both kingdoms'. There was a familiar note in the phrase – whom had he heard use it? Presently it echoed back to him in his own voice, from the walk by the river that day this last spring when he had insisted to the King on the necessity of his marching north at once. Now his own words were being used against him, urging him to justify his hopes at once, whatever the conditions.

He pushed the letter into his doublet, turned to Newcastle with the first smile he had yet bestowed on that nobleman, and said, 'My lord, I hope we shall have a glorious day.'

'It is late evening!' replied the astonished Marquis.

'I speak of tomorrow. We will meet the enemy tomorrow morning. The bulk of my men are at Long Marston. Join me there with every man you can muster, and by daybreak.'

So he had begun to give his orders and without a word of explanation, treating Newcastle as though he were a mere subordinate, and in front of his own officers. The coldness of the Marquis' tone showed how deeply he was offended; he spoke of waiting, of manoeuvring, of anything but fighting. Rupert noticed neither the tone nor the words.

'Nothing venture, nothing have,' he replied abstractedly.

'Your Highness does not consider it worth the trouble even to answer my arguments!'

'Why, no, my Lord, it's never worth the trouble to argue when one has one's orders.'

'Of whose orders do you speak, sir? It is I who am accustomed to give them here.'

'Then you can't give 'em now. I have here,' he tapped his doublet, 'a positive and absolute command from the King to fight the enemy.'

'May we not see it?'

'You can take my word for it. Let's waste no more time.'

There was an outcry at that from the three of them – Hurry's the most sensible:

'The King does not understand the situation.'

But Newcastle began speaking at the same moment, his voice rolling on over Hurry's in deep indignant waves. 'I beg to remind Your Highness that I have His Majesty's commission to hold all the North for him, and that —'

'Let me remind Your Lordship that you'd not have held it much longer if I'd not come up here – at your repeated requests. God's blood, man, d'you think you can ignore the King's orders?'

'I have heard that Your Highness finds no difficulty in doing so when you wish.'

Rupert got up abruptly. 'I shall expect all your men at Long Marston tomorrow at daybreak.'

He strode out and galloped off with his troopers to Long Marston.

*   *   *

At dawn next day Rupert's cavalry scouts sent back word that they had got in touch with the rearguard of the Parliament horse under Manchester; they had had a brief skirmish with them and had gathered that the whole army was in full retreat. It was obvious that the Roundheads did not dream that Rupert would attack with such an inferior force as his had proved to be, and were falling back to hold the bridgeheads over the Ouse and prevent his marching south to the King.

At once Rupert's blood tingled with the desire to launch one of his furious charges on to their rearguard. What a chance to throw their orderly retreat into wild confusion and destroy their morale before the battle! If only he could be sure of extricating his men in time and getting them back to join forces with the garrison from York!

Why the devil wasn't that languid lackadaisical fellow up to time? He had told him to be here at daybreak. Did he lie in bed till seven? He fumed with impatience as he rode down the ranks, sending back messengers to York to hurry on the dilatory Marquis; there was no sign yet of the garrison turning up, and he had to check his impulse to gallop off in headlong attack on the enemy, though his own caution surprised him. A year, a month, perhaps even a day ago, he would have risked it.

But now a canny Scot and three years of cooling his heels in prison had slid forward out of the past and stood in his way, checking him with the reminder of what had come of his rashness; should he fail now by charging, unsupported, and getting cut off from the rest of the army, the consequences would be far worse than any personal disaster to himself. They would mean the loss of the best armies the King had got in the field, the loss of the North, and that, as he had himself been urging all these months, would mean the ultimate loss of the war to the King.

So he forced himself to wait for his belated allies, chafing, biting his lip till the blood ran; invented a hundred disastrous reasons for their absence, tried to keep himself cool while he worked out a plan of battle on paper and busied himself deploying his troops on the edge of the moor.

In an unwonted mood of anxiety and distrust, he tried to assure himself that the King's letter had made his actions inevitable. A man who was told to fight on his honour, had no choice but to fight. And it was what his instinct craved. 'Attack, always attack' – it was what he had always done and it had always succeeded as far as his part was concerned. A man did no good going against himself, and prudence was not his line.

'I am what I am,' he had said in his arrogance to Richmond. But a thin voice he had never heard before was whispering in his heart, asking what manner of man was that? A man whose fate it was to fight unsupported, from his cradle upwards?

Whatever it might be, his fate was here, let him go and seek it.

All this year too he had been longing to meet Cromwell, the only leader on the other side who had the wit to follow his own methods in cavalry and build up a body of horse comparable to his own. He was also the only one of their leaders who had never yet had a failure. Well, in this battle he must fail, or Rupert must. Today should decide between himself, the trained soldier of twenty-four, and the country gentleman and politician, turned soldier, of forty-five.

But he wished he had not quarrelled with his allies.

The men, anxious at the delay of their reinforcements and the reports that kept coming in of the enemy's enormous numbers, eased their horses by dismounting and loosening their girths, and kept up their own spirits by singing bawdy ballads about the Roundheads' wives, and rousing ones about their own Princes, who apparently fought shoulder to shoulder in their combats as in the heroic days of old. There was nothing heroic about the verse.

> 'Where, where are they, Prince Rupert cries,
> Gazing about with fiery eyes.
> Prince Maurice then to second his brother
> Fired his petronel, down fell another,
> 'Twere pity but news were sent to his mother.'

A more cheerful and ribald verse was introduced about Boy, whose white shaggy form was seen loping along as usual at his master's heels. Boy was now promoted to a subject for sermons. The Parliament ministers had taken to preaching against him.

Rupert was still 'gazing about' by the afternoon, but not for his enemies, who had turned back to meet him as his cavalry scouts had now reported – 'No doubt thanking their lucky stars for the chance to better their position,' growled the veteran grumblers. Dash and attack were all very well, but this was being a half and half business, dashing out to attack and then having to wait for one's allies.

It was not till about four o'clock that the main body of them came up with Newcastle and General King.

'Only about twelve hours later than I expected you,' Rupert told them sardonically.

There were all sorts of reasons for the delay. The troops had got out of hand, they had been demoralized by the siege and lack of provisions, even the famous Whitecoats, the best of the Yorkshire infantry and Newcastle's own men. They had got their name from their coats of undyed homespun wool, which had given them the further nickname of the Lambs, but they had apparently shown a far from lamb-like spirit this morning, having mutinied in the streets of York and refused to go to battle until they were given some of their arrears of pay, not one penny of which had they ever seen.

According to Newcastle, he and Lord Eythin had had to spend all the morning haranguing the troops and cheering them on with promises since pay there was none, and Eythin gave point to his former action at Vlotho by muttering: 'Hopeless game, hopeless – he who holds the cash box wins the war.'

Other reasons for the late arrival – that the Marquis had not finished plundering the deserted baggage wagons of the enemy and had made a good job of it by this morning – were not given officially, but whispered and hinted so that Rupert only got a vague idea of them, and feared to get a clearer, since for once he was afraid of himself; afraid of his rashness, of his temper, of anything that might further endanger the chances of this day.

He had made a very careful and deliberate disposition of his troops; putting Lord Byron in charge of the cavalry and artillery on his right wing, with Hurry in support, on ground that was excellent for defence, with strict injunctions to Byron not to move from it until he had his orders. Goring's cavalry he placed on the left wing, and Newcastle's infantry in the centre behind the front line all along a dyke, nearly dry, in the centre of the ground, that ran across the moor.

The day was thunderous and steaming with damp heat, the rolling moor before them rising dark against the sky. The enemy forces opposite had been slowly deploying into order of battle during the day; they were 27,000 strong and of these the largest part were the Scots Covenanters; the Royalist forces were barely 17,000. They were the largest armies to face each other in England since the Wars of the Roses, nearly two hundred years before. The cavalry had brought in one or two prisoners that afternoon, whom Rupert at once saw himself, in order to ask:

'Is Cromwell there? And will they fight?'

He was told 'yes' to both questions and sent the prisoners back to their own army with a message to Cromwell that 'they should have fighting enough'.

'If it please God, so shall he,' was Cromwell's answer to that; but Rupert could not hear it.

He turned back to General King (he could not remember his new title) who had been inspecting his line of battle, and in the strange new hesitancy with which last night's unexpected encounter had inspired him, he showed him the plan of battle he had drawn up, and asked him if he approved.

The old soldier took it, squinted at it horribly as he tried his long-sighted vision on it, then held it at arm's length from his nose.

'By God, sir,' he growled, 'it's very fine on paper, but there's no such thing in the field!'

'No such thing? These are the troops as I've drawn them up.'

'Then they've been altered. Go look at your right wing. Not but what I don't like it better as it is – it's the way we always fought in Sweden, and no commander can do better than Gustavus.'

Rupert swore deeply. The ghost of Gustavus Adolphus, that most troublesome ally, must have made mischief once again; no soldier who had served under him could believe that he was dead, or that his methods, though the best of his day, might in time be superseded.

He galloped off to the right wing, followed by King, and found that Hurry had broken up his cavalry lines into small squadrons, interspersed with groups of musketeers, to fire through the spaces at the enemy's cavalry. It was the Continental method, which Rupert had abandoned so as to give greater freedom and force to the charge. His horse had always been launched in close formation; they were grumbling loudly at this new arrangement, declaring that they would only get shot in the back by their own musketeers, and that they were so separated from each other that they 'could not find themselves in themselves'.

But Hurry declared it was the only way to meet the Scots lancers who would oppose them.

'I'm a Scot myself and I know them,' was his argument.

Rupert insisted that he must alter the dispositions; but the heavy precise voice of the old general came pounding behind him, 'No, sir, it is too late.'

A queer sensation came over Rupert in that instant, as though he had been listening to the talk of two people outside himself.

Could this tough elderly hard-bitten soldier be right, and had he himself lost all his practical sense of a battlefield?

If so, it could only be for a moment; he had lain dazed with his anger too long at Lathom House, and was still weary with it; so weary that for the first time in his life he felt he had not the energy to quarrel. For it would mean another quarrel with Newcastle and General King and Sir John Hurry, who were now all arguing at him to leave matters where they were till tomorrow – the men were tired out, they must have food and a night's rest – 'leave it,' they said, 'leave it, leave it'.

'They'll not do anything tonight. Leave it till tomorrow and then alter the line – attack at daybreak if you will. But nothing can happen tonight.'

'No, nothing can happen tonight.'

'It's getting darker every minute – there's a heavy storm coming up. Nothing can happen tonight.'

Their voices clacked against his brain; their silly faces thrust themselves under his; he felt he had never loathed his fellow-men so much – nor had less impulse to tell them so.

He would have supper, and that would make his head work clearly again. He gave the order for it, and for the men to feed, and sat down on the ground to eat it, while Newcastle went to sit in his coach and six (an odd equipage for a battlefield) to smoke a meditative pipe. The Marquis stepped delicately through the mud towards it, his fair head bent attentive to his feet, and every inch of his tall graceful figure expressive of his relief that for one night more at least he need not consider these tedious questions.

In his coach he sat private and reserved, inhaling the blessed fragrance of his tobacco, seeing in the wreaths of smoke that curled upwards against the darkening light of the window the notes of a charming fantasy he had lately played, written by that delightful old fellow, Jacobus Clemens non Papa.

Low thunder was growling from the storm clouds scurrying across the desolate scene. All the rye fields, near to harvest, were ruined by the tramp of the armies and lay trodden underfoot. It had begun to grow dusk very early. Rupert ordered prayers to be read to his men, greatly to the disgust of his enemies, who sent up a hasty counter-fire of psalms at the sound of Royalist hymns. 'Rupert, that bloody plunderer, would forsooth seem religious, just like a jingling Machiavellian.'

Gleams of stormy light of an unearthly brilliance were picking out here and there the great coloured banners that floated like sunset clouds among the thunderous darkness of the iron-clad troops massed together on the moor. These fugitive gleams wandered as in casual ironic scrutiny from the enemy to the regiments of Newcastle's Whitecoats, their rough woollen coats shining like flocks of sheep in the sudden floodlight; then lit up the dim hordes of Rupert's Bluecoats, the best Royalist foot regiment, into a stretch of blue; then vanished under a portentous cloud which came rolling up over the sky, sending up crash after crash of thunder.

Louder and fiercer rose the psalms across the moor in conjunction; 'Let God arise and let His enemies be scattered.' Their God was speaking to His hosts through the thunder – 'Heaven has resolved to second us!' the Parliament commanders shouted to their troops.

And in answer, the heavy rain suddenly sluiced down. Rupert sprang up – at the same instant there came a rattle of firing, the thud of horse on his right – the battle had been begun by the enemy as soon as they saw the Royalists did not expect it. Rupert knew that for the first time in his life he had missed his chance to take the initiative.

He swung himself into the saddle and rushed to his right wing. Raising himself in his stirrups he saw a heavy mass of horse come pounding down in a steady trot, splashing through the ditch, against Byron's men. The two lines locked and swayed, but the Roundhead horse were pouring through the gaps that Hurry had left in the Royalist cavalry, and trampling down the musketeers. As he galloped hell-for-leather round to them from the centre, he could hear the whole battle-line break into the roar of cannon and rattle of musketry. The rain beat against his face, men were shouting ahead of him, the stormy dusk seemed to be driving solid thunderclouds over the earth, the thunderclouds of Cromwell's Ironsides, slower in the charge than his, but weightier, as he saw when he joined his men and found them struggling against what seemed a steadily moving wall of horse and heavily armoured men.

In the confused and spattering wet dusk, he saw a swirl of horsemen hacking at each other, horses with empty saddles, shrilly neighing as they cantered wildly, swerving at the sudden glare and flashes of musket fire that frightened them from one place to another. Then among the groans and shouts and clash of swords against breast-plates, sounding like a devil's smithy on an enormous scale, he realized that his front line was being driven in on his second; the men were being slowly pushed back, whole troops of them turning round and digging spurs into their horses to gallop from the field. His own men were among them, the men of his regiment that he had led to victory after victory and never to a defeat. He yelled at them so that his voice rose high above the battle and the storm:

'God's blood, do you run? Follow me!'

They shouted to him that Hurry's regiment had broken and fled first of all, that Byron's was broken. He answered:

'Then we shall hold it – come on!'

He had done it, he swung them round.

Once again they drove against that wall. There was not space enough to get the impetus of a counter charge, they had no chance to carry out their shock tactics; but even so, hacking and thrusting, sawying this way and that, they broke sheer through Cromwell's first line and stayed his second.

Best of all, Cromwell himself was wounded and blinded, said men who had seen the Parliament leader swaying and groping like a drunken man with his face all grimed with gunpowder.

Rupert's horse drove on – Cromwell's fell back; in some places they stampeded, in another moment they would break into wild and hopeless rout.

But in that moment the new Scottish horse under David Leslie came to Cromwell's rescue. They crashed in on the Royalist flank, and Leslie, taking over the command of Cromwell's men while he was out of action, pulled them together from their retreat, and brought them again to the attack. Cromwell's wound was only the graze of a pistol bullet across his neck, and his blindness the temporary effect of a near shot flash. Dizzy as he was from it, he soon pulled himself together and took control again. He found grim fighting at close quarters, with nothing to say in the uncertain dusk which side was winning.

It was Leslie's Scots who finally said that. Thicker and thicker they came on, until their sheer weight of numbers broke what was left of Rupert's cavalry, pushed it back for nearly three miles and cut it clean off from the main army. Cromwell could leave Leslie's Scots to finish that work, while with the steady discipline he had ground into them, he re-formed and swung round the remainder of his regiments to retrieve the day for the rest of his side.

Things there were going badly for the Parliament armies, who had begun by advancing all along the line. Their infantry crossed the ditch and drove back the front line of the Royalist infantry. But in the centre of the Royalists' second line were the Yorkshire Whitecoats, hungry, unpaid, mutinous all this morning, who yet at odds of two to one drove back the enemy across the ditch and advanced to the attack, swearing to dye their white coats in the blood of their foes. As they advanced, Goring's left wing of cavalry, having driven Fairfax headlong off the field, and plundered the baggage wagons, returned, somewhat blown, to the infantry in the centre and helped the work of the Whitecoats so well that they drove old Leven also off the field, galloping northwards, shouting to the country people to ask the quickest way back to the Tweed.

Both these Parliament leaders thought their side had suffered complete rout, and well might they think so, for only a few Scottish regiments still held the position they had reached in their first advance.

Night was coming on, rain and hail still swept at times through the broken darkness; the black moor, reeking of blood and gunpowder, was a confused hell of screaming horses, groaning men and heavy masses struggling together and surging to and fro. Night should stop a battle, but this battle went on; and steady, inexorable as death itself, rolled on the slowly crushing weight of Cromwell's sixty troops of horse, reinforced now again by Leslie's.

They routed Goring's horse, they turned on the Whitecoats,

surrounding them with horse and foot, but could not make them surrender. With coats fast being dyed in their own blood, still they fought on with pike and musket, selling their lives as dearly as they could. Then Cromwell took the heavy guns he had captured from the Royalists and turned them on them. The men were mowed down by their own guns and trampled underfoot by the enemy's horse, who charged again and again until all that gallant company were blotted out.

The storm clouds split; the rising moon showed a few scattered groups still struggling here and there. Rupert, trying to rally the remnants of Royalist cavalry, found himself deserted; he put his horse at a high fence and leaped over it into a bean field, rode on and collected some of the broken cavalry squadrons, and held the narrow lanes towards York, keeping the Roundheads at bay with their fire.

Behind them they heard the bells of York Minster clanging out in peal after peal of joyous triumph, and saw the reflection of great bonfires leaping across the dark sky. All that they knew in the city was that Goring's horse had swept the Parliament's before him, that two of the Parliament's generals had fled headlong from the field.

'Another great Royalist victory,' people were yelling in the streets as they danced round the bonfires.

But Rupert, out in the wet darkness, collecting as many of his men together as he could in an orderly retreat to York, knew that the battle was lost.

CHAPTER TWENTY-FOUR

A THICK-SET middle-aged man with a bandage round his neck sat writing in his tent in the Parliament camp. His hand moved fast with big up-and-down strokes, the words dropped off his goose-quill pen almost as quick as if he were talking. They were fine words to write, words to taste and roll round your tongue – 'an absolute victory obtained by the Lord's blessing upon the godly party principally. We never charged but we routed the enemy. The left wing which I commanded, being our own horse (saving a few Scots in the rear), beat all the Prince's horse. God made them as stubble to our swords' – the grey goose quill was taking an even swifter flight – 'we charged their regiments of foot with our horse, routed all we charged.' Yes, he'd said that already – but no matter, it could not be said too often. It was no boast, no mere statement even; it was a proof that God, who alone gave success, was on their side.

The flap of his tent was lifted by his guard, and General David Leslie, a short sturdy Lowland Scot, stood stiffly before him. General Cromwell jerked back his head, winced from his sore neck, but managed to fix a genial and comradely look on his face.

'I see ye're writing,' observed his visitor with unnecessary deliberation; 'if it's an account of the battle, I trust ye're giving the praise for it where praise is due.'

'That is to the Lord, David Leslie. I have written that truly England and the Church of God has had a great favour from the Lord in this victory – aha, do I speak well, my little David, who marched out against their Goliath himself!'

'Little David' did not look as though he appreciated the humour of his name.

'I have come,' he said, 'from telling my men, who are inclined to the contrary opinion, that Europe has no better soldiers than your Ironsides. Are you doing as fairly by the Scots, who saved your horse in the nick of time, when you were all but routed?'

Cromwell's spread hand fell as by accident over his sentence – 'We never charged but we routed the enemy.'

'As fair as should be,' he said. 'The Scots have been well mentioned in dispatches.'

His wrist was over that careless parenthesis – 'a few Scots in the rear'. Perhaps it was rather a summary description of the 14,000 Scottish troops out of the Parliament's sum total of 27,000 – over half of the whole armies in fact – but then, so Cromwell qualified this unpalatable truth, the Scots horses were very inferior for cavalry work, no more than light moorland ponies. Still, he knew as well as Leslie that he had been all but beaten at the beginning. He certainly would have been routed but for the increasing persistency of Leslie's oncoming cavalry, and the promptness with which Leslie had taken over his command in the nick of time.

But that was at the beginning; it was his own resource and power of recovery that had won the battle at the end. And the end was all. Should he be dictated to as if he were a secretary by this precise little Presbyterian who was not even an Englishman?

'I take no pride to myself for the victory,' he said, 'except in that God has suffered me to be the executioner of His enemies.'

'You and your allies,' corrected Leslie.

'I did not mention all my allies,' replied Cromwell, grinning like a schoolboy at the cunning of his truth – 'it was kinder to leave out your cousin, Lord Leven, who was arrested by a village constable as he galloped back to the Tweed.'

'He's no cousin of mine; he's of base birth, a bastard of a Leslie of Balquhain. And as for his flight, your generals Manchester and Fairfax showed they could run.'

'Pooh! They're lords and so forth. What d'you expect of a lord? And who turned Manchester's infantry round from a retreat into a victory? *I* did – with the help of the Lord.'

'And of my Scots a second time,' pursued Leslie doggedly.

Cromwell made an exclamation not blasphemous but of plough-boy obscenity. 'What do you *want*, man?' he thundered.

It was the cue Leslie had been waiting for.

'We have come in to help your side win the war, but remember, upon a condition. You speak of the Church of God – that is, the Presbyterian Church of Scotland, which you have promised to make the one Church in England.'

Cromwell's keen eyes under their shaggy brows stared at him, heavy and brooding.

Suddenly he spoke – 'Were those boots recovered?'

'Boots?'

'Boots, man, boots! D'you not wear boots in your country? I forgot, the majority run bare-legged on the heather, don't they?'

'I'll not stand an insult to my country.'

'Insult? It was a joke; laughing and good fellowship make brothers before the Lord. Do Scots never see a joke?'

'I doubt any man seeing yours.'

'Now you're angry. Let it pass. I spoke of the four thousand pairs of boots that were left behind. Are they recovered?'

'Ask your Quartermaster-General. *I* spoke of religion.'

'A blessed thing to speak of, but why speak to me of it? You are having all you ask. The Assembly of Divines at Westminster are even now at work reconstructing the English Church on your Scots model.'

'Then there will be no more need for war. We can even now treat with the King, since we hold all the North; and if he is made to promise to uphold the one true Church of Presbyterianism, he can be set back at Whitehall.'

'You would not be such fools as to trust him?'

'We should see to it that we need not.'

'But we've not beaten all his armies.'

'Why should we? We have enough to bargain with.'

'Bargain! – when we might have victory!'

'For what purpose, General?'

Ah, that he could not say. A new England – tear up the old, and start clean. Shake off these irksome Scots and their rigorous Presbyterianism, which would start at once persecuting all the Baptists and Anabaptists and Independents – why, most of the soldiers he commanded belonged to these sects! 'I have a lovely company,' he had written as much as a year ago, and every month they improved under his training and multiplied an hundredfold. Were such men to be sacrificed to these Scots pedants? They complained that he had one whole company of atheists. But, to get good soldiers, he would willingly give toleration to all – as long as they were Dissenters. He would have no toleration for the Churches of England and Rome, and that ruled out about nine-tenths of the English people. They must learn to conform to nonconformity. But Charles was stubborn, he would not give up the Church of England. It was madness to put Charles back into Whitehall until he had undergone a change of heart – and how could one force that on a man? No signed treaties could ensure the relationship between man and man, any more than priests and set service-books could ensure it between man and God.

'And would ye prefer no legal contracts either, but to leave all to the inspiration of the moment?' inquired Leslie drily.

But Cromwell did not wait to argue with this arid Scot; his mind was rushing on ahead to the impasse that must come as soon as they began to treat with Charles. He could see no way out yet, but it would come, it would come; the Lord would provide His inspiration in His good time, and meanwhile there was the war to carry on. As he *could* carry it, all on his own shoulders, he knew that now, he alone out of the commanders on his side. He learned his job in these two years, and he had learned it chiefly from the young man he had just defeated. He knew that, nor did it dim his exultation, for surely it was the greatest triumph of all that he should be able to take his lesson from his brilliant young adversary, when he himself was growing elderly and had thought himself fixed for ever in his simple country pursuits.

But here he was building more and more regiments, and now he would have the whole army transformed on their model, and everyone should know it was something entirely new and different from Essex's lumbering machinery, for they would call it The New Model Army.

It was Waller's idea, not his, but he would take it and make it his, as he had taken the ideas of his enemy. There was no end to what he might do with this terrific energy and confidence now boiling up in his veins, a sign surely of God's spirit breathing into him for some great purpose.

To use himself to the fullest, to give out these powers he had never known till now that he possessed, that was what he must now do; and no king, no treaties, no calculating repressive allies should prevent him. 'You cannot plant an oak in a pot' – which of his friends had said that? Well, he was saying it now.

Words came rushing into his mouth, he felt an exhilaration blowing through him as though he were riding in the wind of his own thoughts – the Lord had caught him up and was bearing him along, putting the words from His Bible into his heart so thick he could not quote them fast enough.

David Leslie, with his head slightly cocked, watched him marching up and down. When at last the General had finished, he said slowly: 'Man, ye're in a great muddle. Has it ever struck ye to stop and consider *where* it is ye're going?'

Cromwell brought his fist down on the table with a crash. Now had the Lord delivered this dour, doubting, captious devil into his hand; for here was his answer ready, he had given it once before, he did not wait to think when.

'You never go so far,' he said, 'as when you *don't* know where you are going.'

'Oh, ye'll go far,' observed Leslie cannily, 'I've nae doot o' that.'

A slight chill fell on the General's exuberant spirits. He had had some such damping answer as that before, he now remembered; it echoed back to him, not in the shrewd pawky notes he despised, but in the voice of the man he had loved and admired above all others, a spirit finer and more delicate than his own, his friend and cousin, John Hampden, who had got his death-wound from Rupert's accursed cavalry on Chalgrove Field.

The flap was lifted again. A soldier stepped inside with a stiff shaggy carcass in his arms.

'I was ordered to bring you this, sir. It's Prince Rupert's dog. We found him on the battlefield, killed, among all the dead men and horses.'

The General stared. Suddenly he flung back his head and shouted with laughter, startling and rather shocking David Leslie. The poor beast, he had but followed his master into battle – what was there in that to give his ally such harsh, almost hysteric mirth?

Cromwell saw his expression and turned to him, wiping his eyes. 'You do not know,' he said, 'the reputation of this dog in England. It has had sermons preached against it – children shriek in bed for fear of it – grown men have fled from battle because they have seen it. It is held to be a minister of Satan. God has given us this clear sign. Now Rupert's familiar spirit, which helped bring him victory by striking terror into his enemies, is only a dead dog.'

CHAPTER TWENTY-FIVE

RUPERT HAD not remembered to order Boy to be tied up to the baggage wagons as usual, when he rushed headlong from his supper on the ground to his saddle. It was a moment in which matters of more desperate importance might well have been forgotten. Yet he could not believe that he had forgotten Boy. It was the final instance of that dead weight that had lain on his spirits and his mind this last fortnight – he had tried to shake it off in that rapid march across the Pennines, but it had kept coming back on him like a heavy dream.

Here it was again, like a drug or an enchantment, saying nothing to him but – 'Boy is dead,' although he knew that what he should be telling himself was that he and Newcastle had been utterly beaten, had lost all their guns, about 1,500 prisoners, many of great importance – and York, which they could not now hold, since there would be no other force to relieve it. Newcastle now had practically no army, and what was left of the Prince's was broken and scattered. The whole of the North was now lost to the King.

Worst of all for his uncle's cause, as he well knew, he had lost his own terrible reputation. No longer was he the Devil Prince, the Wizard Prince, whose charge no mortal man could stand against. He was the Prince who had only just escaped Cromwell's men by sticking spurs into his horse and leaping over a high fence into a bean field.

So he knew, but could not yet think, while that heavy genie that lay upon his mind muttered only through this accumulated agony of disaster and shame – 'Boy is dead.'

* * *

Said General King, 'What will you do?'

Said the Prince, 'I will rally my men.'

Said General King, 'Now you, what will you, Lord Newcastle, do?'

Said Lord Newcastle, 'I will go into Holland.'

Said the Prince, 'Recruit your forces, my lord, and I will stay and help you.'

Said Lord Newcastle, 'No, I will not stay to endure the laughter of the Court.'

And pathetically he begged Rupert to make the case for him there as good as might be.

Said the Prince, 'I promise to report that you behaved like an honest man, a gentleman and a loyal subject – but it will be easier if you prove it by staying.'

He did not state his own case, that it was unfair to him that he should be left to bear all the onus of failure, as well as the work of setting all the northern affairs in order before he started to march south. They knew that, both Newcastle and King who was also determined to run for it, and he was not going to remind them. He could even see that Newcastle, shrinking like a shorn lamb from the east wind, really could not stand up to it. He went, and so did General King, who asked also for Rupert's good opinion, but the Prince turned his back on him and walked away.

CHAPTER TWENTY-SIX

THE THUNDER had brought the hot weather. The little town of Richmond near York was like an etching of Dürer, Rupert's favourite master; thin spiral lines built up the huddle of small streets and smoking chimneys and peaked roofs like a cluster of witches' hats that climbed round and round the sharp conical hill, crowned so magnificently with its castle. Richmond Castle was so huge it could be seen nearly forty miles away; its mighty walls overhung the river that encircled it, blue and shining as a silk ribbon, three hundred feet below, flowing down from among the sultry folds of the green and purple hills that lay all round it. But the castle had never been used for any practical warlike purpose; this vast and ancient monument, a symbol, like an old suit of armour of the obsolete in warfare, immense and unimportant, overhung the town and the little inn in the Market Square where Rupert stayed for three days to collect his men.

It was just two days after the battle that he had a visitor. He was sitting in his tiny room upstairs where the old floor sloped unevenly down to the low window; it was midday, and the sun was blazing down into the square; and through the slit of window came the smell of dust and straw and sweat, the sounds of harness clanking and of hoofs ringing out against the cobblestones, and horses neighing and champing their bits in the heat, and the tired exasperated voices of men calling directions.

There was a different quality in their voices from any Rupert had ever heard before. Gaiety, hope, confidence, that note had sounded so continuously and increasingly ever since the summer day two years ago when he had come to England and taken command of his first little force of six hundred, that only now did he notice it, now that it had gone from their voices. He might win another battle, but they would never again feel certain he would win.

He should be down there with them, seeing to them, but he could not go. Their weary disillusioned faces were clear enough before him as he sat at the table watching the sunlight, through the greenish bottle glass of the window, ripple upwards over the ceiling.

He heard steps coming up the rickety stair, and the door open. It was only another messenger – but he looked up, and felt no surprise when he saw Montrose.

So he had come, as Rupert had known he would, ever since he had sent for him. But he had come two days late. He opened his mouth to tell him that, and found that all he had said was, 'Boy is dead.'

The man was staring at him, and he explained before he should think him mad. For answer, Montrose told him that he

354

had been far up at Alnwick, collecting provisions and smuggling them into Newcastle when he got the Prince's message, had then dashed south on the instant, only to find that Rupert had fought his battle without waiting for him.

'I was in a hurry,' said the Prince.

He heard how senseless it sounded. (Would he soon be known as the Mad Prince in sober earnest?) He had relieved York, he had joined forces with Newcastle; where was the hurry – where but in that piece of insensate paper, now folded inside his doublet?

They went on talking, Montrose in question, he in answer, but he did not think of what they were saying until he heard Montrose's voice commanding him, 'Show me the letter.' He would show it to no one, but this man, yes he must know. He pulled it out and unfolded it and saw the little black marks on the paper that had sent him to his downfall. And as he stared at them, not reading them, he thought how odd it was that words should have such power, and why had he allowed them to get the mastery over him? They were his uncle's orders, written by Digby and signed by the King; but his uncle's orders were very seldom his own, they were generally inspired by the last person to advise him. And as to his uncle's desperate position, which he could only faintly hope to hold until Rupert came to him, that too had only been his uncle's (or somebody else's) opinion of a fortnight ago, already contradicted – for report, travelling faster than any messenger, had just told of the King's successes down in the West.

Rupert had flung away the lives of his best men for this ambiguous, perhaps lying paper.

'He thought he dictated it,' he said – 'was it really Digby?'

And suddenly the sunshine in the room went black and it grew unbearably hot. Montrose poured brandy into a pewter mug and held it out to him, and he drank, remembering then that he had gone to the door and shouted to the man to bring it up for himself and his visitor. Montrose handed back the letter. All he said was – 'You would have smashed Cromwell's horse at the outset had it not been for Leslie's Scots. Their coming in for the Parliament has weighted the scales against us. We must provide a counter to them, and at once. Give me a thousand of your horse, and I will cut my way through the Lowlands and get Scotland for the King.'

'Will you take me with them?' said Rupert.

'And what is to happen to England? You are the one man that can save that for the King.'

'It is lost. The loss of the North, of the money coming from there, means the loss of all. The war may drag on another year or so, but that will make no odds.'

'Give me that year. We will see what I can do with it. But you must hold England.'

'If they let me. It was hard enough before. Now it may be impossible. They would not listen to me in success. Why should they in failure? Goring alone made a success of Marston Moor. It's he who'll lead the cavalry now.'

He sprang up, strode across the room, but bumped his head against the low beams and fell back into the rough wooden chair, rubbing it ruefully with one hand while the other long arm fell outwards across the table, pushing an ink-well and a quill pen, the two pewter mugs and the round black lop-sided brandy bottle this way and that on it, to show the depositions of his plan for his last battle. As he did so, he spoke of it in a low voice, sometimes almost muttering, for it was chiefly to himself that he was speaking as he tried to make out what had happened in the confusion of that stormy night.

'Leslie's Scots must have been here,' he said, 'they kept coming on and on upon our flank. I could never disengage my horse thick enough for a charge in the old manner. Hurry had interspersed the squadrons with companies of musketeers – it's the old Continental fashion, but I told him I'd not risk it, since my men did not know it. I only found what had happened when it was too late to change.'

'Hurry may have worked deliberately against you. I suspect him of being a double traitor. He deserted because he thought the King's the winning side. He'll soon desert back again.'

'Curse him! May he find himself on the losing side in the end.'

'Amen,' said Montrose; and an odd little silence hung attentive on the air.

Rupert pushed his hands up out from his face as though wings had brushed against it.

'It was the first time I could not use shock tactics,' he said, 'and the first time I met them from my enemy. That man, Cromwell, he's the finest soldier they've got. My men speak of his now as the Ironsides.'

'I'd heard it was you called them that.'

'Did I? I expect I was only thinking of their back and breast pieces.'

('How quick he is to deny his generosity,' thought the other. Only six years older than Rupert, Montrose felt himself of another generation.)

Rupert was still hot on the thought of Cromwell. 'He's grabbed my notions, and that shows his value. Take ideas from your enemy and work 'em up – there's nothing sounder. He took the initiative too, which I have always taken before. Was I dead asleep before that storm on the moor?'

'You may have been dead beat,' said Montrose, who was watching him closely; 'no man is at his best all the time. You will get the initiative again and recover your reputation.'

'By which time our enemies will have multiplied tenfold. All those who were waiting to see which side held the most chances of winning will now come in for the Parliament. It is always so in civil war. Reputation is a bigger weapon than big guns. Win, my lord, win always, and when you lose —'

'What then?'

'Oh, go overseas with Newcastle and General King – why not? It makes no odds, for the game will be up.'

Montrose did not answer him. His head was bent as he sat staring at the table, considering something deeply. 'I shall leave you my troops,' he said at last, 'I shall take only a bodyguard to Carlisle.'

'You'll need them after that on your way to Oxford.'

'No. I have thought of a new plan in this instant. You are the only man I shall tell it to, except the two who must share it. I shall leave my men, horses and baggage at Carlisle, they will go on to Oxford without me.'

'And you, where will you go?'

'To Scotland. We could not get through before because our force was not large enough. Now I shall try the other way and make it so small that we may slip through unseen.'

'How small?'

'Three. Two of my friends can pass as Covenanter troopers, I in disguise as their groom.'

Rupert felt so furious an envy that it tingled in his veins like new life. He was filled with longing to leave this country where words had conquered him, to ride by the side of this man who was setting forth on so desperate and lonely an adventure. If he were not discovered, taken prisoner or killed (there were thousands along the Border who could recognize him, and how impossible to disguise that bearing and those commanding eyes as those of a groom!), *if* he succeeded, he would have as his allies the half-savage Highlanders of the Western Isles and Ireland – and no slimy courtiers nor uncertain King.

He forgot that the King would have to be the ultimate factor in all their plans, however distant from him. He saw only himself and Montrose and his two friends, four men alone riding up into those hills in the North.

He said, 'You knew my fat friend at Oxford, Endymion Porter. He sang me a song of yours once, something about fate – what was it?'

Montrose sang one verse.

> *'He either fears his fate too much*
> *Or his deserts are small,*
> *That dares not put it to the touch,*
> *·To win or lose it all.'*

The keen-cut head, flung back, was outlined against the light as he sang, and his voice was gay and ringing.

' "To win or lose" ' – repeated Rupert.

'That's not our concern, once it's done,' he answered quickly.

And with the spell of those calm eyes upon him he could almost think he might one day believe it.

CHAPTER TWENTY-SEVEN

I T D I D not seem afterwards as though it had ever happened, that meeting in the little witchlike town of Richmond. Montrose went away the same afternoon, leaving the main part of his horse, as he said he would do, and Rupert, the only man to know the secret and incredible plans that had formed behind that cool, half-smiling face, wondered if he would ever hear of him again. Most likely he would be killed in some little encounter on the Border, too obscure for mention, and nobody would ever know what had happened to the new Marquis of Montrose.

Rupert himself, having collected what he could of the stragglers, left Richmond the next day and went on into the West. He stayed a night at Barningham Park and there left the pair of mirrors Charlotte, Countess of Derby, had given him. They were a nuisance on the march, it was polite to give a present to his hostess, and what did it matter that they had been a present to himself? It was a very slight straw to show the way of the wind, yet it did show an indifference that he could not have felt before to so old a friend.

But now nothing that he did or did not do could matter.

He went down to the Welsh marches to recruit more men, and it was difficult not to tell the recruits what damned fools they were to go on coming into this war, which was as good as lost. And that in spite of the fact that the King, Maurice, everyone but he, was winning victory after victory down in the South-West. Wilmot was disgraced by Digby, who told everybody it was by Rupert's doing, and Goring on his return was given his command. The exchange was about as useful as one pea for another in Rupert's opinion; though naturally he could not say so after Goring's successful charge at Marston Moor. He had been fighting drunk then or perhaps even, by a miracle, sober; in his next engagement he was dead drunk, and let his enemy get clean away while he sprawled across the table, shouting, 'Pox on old Pym,' forgetful that Pym had been dead six months.

In spite of such leaders there was certainly no evidence of the instant collapse Charles had threatened if his nephew did not at once return to his side. But there was all the misfortune Rupert had feared for the Queen when she had persisted in going to Exeter, for the town was at once besieged and nearly starved out. Her baby, a girl, named Henriette, had been born there in the middle of June, and less than a fortnight later Essex's army marched down upon the city. The Queen was so ill that her life had been despaired of. ('Mayerne, for love of me, go to my wife,' was the shortest and most poignant letter Charles had ever written, to his doctor and friend.) The Queen sent to Essex, asking for safe conduct for her and her infant to Bath, away from the fighting. A chivalrous enemy to men, 'the great cuckold' had no tenderness for a desperately sick woman and her new-born baby; his reply was that he intended to escort her to London, where she should stand her trial for high treason for 'having levied war in England'.

'He has a sense of fun, that elephant!' was her retort, before she stole out of the besieged city, disguised as a washerwoman, made her way to the coast, sleeping under the hedges, crossed the Channel in a gale, chased and fired on by Parliament ships, and at last found safety among the French peasants. The baby Henriette was left behind in Exeter with her nurse, the Countess of Morton, and was so small and delicate that she was not expected to live; but at least she had escaped Essex, for the King marched down and relieved the city and gave a splendid font to the Cathedral for his youngest daughter's christening.

So the Queen need never have fled – 'it was a pity,' said Charles in pathetic understatement of his lost and desolate sensations without her. She was away in France, where of course she had so much better be than here among such dangers, but everything grew more dubious every day, and who could tell for certain whether he would ever see her again?

For since Rupert could be defeated, anything might be possible. And unreasonable as it was, people blamed himself for it; Lord Culpeper had broken out in the most brutal way when he heard that that letter had been sent to Rupert – 'Before God!' he had sworn, 'you are undone, for upon this peremptory order he will fight, whatever comes of it.'

But what could he have done, since Digby had been so insistent? and Digby, as everybody admitted, even carping Ned Hyde, was a brilliantly clever man.

Rupert heard about Culpeper, knew about Digby, and cared now not at all. He heard that Sir John Hurry had changed his side again and joined the Parliament army, after providing them with intelligence of the Royalists' movements – a clear indication of what were now held to be the odds against the King. But Rupert, who had cursed Hurry, now only laughed.

As he laughed at Carl, now settled in Whitehall Palace, who had signed the Covenant against his uncle's 'Popish army raised for the subversion of the Protestant religion and the liberty of the subject'. His presence greatly embarrassed the Parliamentary leaders; they pointed out that the sooner the Elector left England the better it would be for his own interests. It was a clear confession of guilt on all their parts, for their alarm at his presence blew the gaff on the reason for it – but Carl, with Timon-like cynicism, gave not a jot for their disapproval. Whether he finally came in for his uncle's throne or not, he was very comfortable in his uncle's palace, and flatly refused to budge for the sake of the Parliamentary reputations. But at least he was made to pay for his perfidious position with a full share of boredom, for he was given a seat in the Westminster Assembly of Divines and had to listen to all their theological controversies, to his brothers' cruel satisfaction.

Rupert had gone back to Bristol, and there seemed to forget that he had an army. There were the Downs up beyond Clifton where he could ride; the soft air of the West fanned his face, the Welsh mountains were blue in the distance, and on the other side of the river, where Maurice had led down his troops towards the city they had stormed together a year ago, was the deep wooded gorge the people called Nightingale Valley, turning golden in the September sunshine. He needed rides to cool his head, for he spent most of his nights in the dingy and lurid little sailors' taverns and brothels down by the quay side where Cabot had set sail for America nearly two hundred years before.

He sat with swarthy seamen of different nations, who wore big gold rings in their ears and dirty scarlet caps on their heads, drank rum and smoked short white pipes and spat on the floor and held out handfuls of foreign coins to the girls that flounced among them. Rupert's ten modern languages were barely enough for all their talk. For the first time he let go of the iron control he had known to be essential to a soldier. He sent for women, got he did not care how; he drank with ruffians who thought it a joke to stab a stranger in the back for money, and sound sense to run away in fair fight; he smoked their strange Eastern drugs that bring a forgetfulness better than all sleep, another life lived in a dream, free of the fierce desire for action and endeavour and all the motives that had thrust on his eager life till now.

Now the pent-up years of his youth fell apart in an agonized relaxation. There was no purpose left to bind them together. Now that Goring had succeeded while he failed, what did it matter if he too sank himself stupid in drink and debauchery? He would take his pleasures where he found them, and little enough pleasure could his quick and fiery spirit find in them; but that was what he wanted – to dull his brain and all the nerves of pain and pleasure to an insensate pulp.

> *'A dead sleep it came over him*
> *And from his horse he fell.'*

Nor could his friends rouse him, anxiously as they tried. Arthur Trevor wrote to his friend Lord Ormonde that the Prince was so lost in his pleasures 'every man is disheartened that sees it', for he thought Ormonde might influence him. But

Ormonde could only do so in letters, and Rupert not only never answered letters now, he would not read them. At first he would fly into a passion if any were brought to him, but now he only laughed and coolly lit his pipe with them, unopened, and when Trevor expostulated, said it would have been well if he had always treated his letters so. Trevor began to fear for his sanity; the Prince saw it, and laughed at that too.

*　　*　　*

The rain fell in a grey smudge over the river. The foggy autumn dusk was shutting down on the town; his room looked mean and dreary; he still lay on the couch where he had flung himself in his clothes this morning to sleep off the night's debauch. He dozed, sated and unsatisfied; there was no savour in anything. His drugged mind craved a stronger stimulus; it brooded, darkened, finding pleasure in the mingling of savagery with lust. He heard his page come in behind him to bring the candles, but he would not stay, he would get up and go out and roam like a bat about the dark streets.

The boy had not brought the candles, the room was still dark. What was he waiting there for? He turned his head. A woman in a cloak was standing in the shadows by the door.

She pushed back her hood as he moved, and he saw that it was Mary Richmond. She came towards him, holding him with her eyes; hollow and black they were in her white face, like the valleys in the moon. She was saying:

'Rupert, I had to come. Do not be angry. I knew you were unhappy.'

'Who told you I was unhappy? I am learning to enjoy myself for the first time.'

'You don't look as though you are enjoying that,' she said softly, and now her eyes laughed at him in the old way for an instant, but they began to brim over with tears, and a gasping sob tore her voice across, and she was saying very fast and low – 'I feel it is all my fault for saying "when you fail" – do you remember, down by the river that May morning? – as though I had wished it on you, to bring you to me – but Heaven knows I never meant it so, Rupert, I would have done anything in the world to prevent it – as I would now to help if I could – but women can't help, they can do nothing, nothing – and that is why I came!' she added, with a sudden laugh spurting up through her tears.

He heard nothing that she said. He heard her voice go up and down, now sad, now gay; he heard her laugh; he saw her cry – crying for him. So she had come because she was sorry for him. He did not want her pity. He must have said so, for here she was coming close to him. She put her hands up against his breast, the scented warmth of her hair was close under his nostrils, she seemed to be flowing out towards him, into him; there was nothing in this dark room, in the whole world but her. She was here under his hands for him to do with as he willed. His head was reeling, yet still something within him kept a blind hold – 'wait,' it said, 'till you know what it is you do.' He tore himself away and dropped on to a chair, pressing his hands over his eyes.

She was speaking to him in a voice so light it only brushed his hearing. 'So you don't want my pity, Rupert? Is there nothing you want of me? They say you are wasting time, Rupert. Have you still none to waste on me? Is there any room for me now, Rupert?'

'There is no room for Richmond's friend by your side.' Was that still true?

He saw Richmond in a sudden cruel light, that light that shines so conveniently on those friends we hope to wrong. He saw him as a bit of a proser – so delicate-minded, so fussily concerned for his friend's good behaviour as well as for his affairs. That envious note in Richmond's voice – his words came beating in on his memory, though he had never thought of them since they had been uttered – 'When you are in love, you will give great happiness.'

But with that envious note he heard the grave tenderness also in his friend's voice, the intent affection that had never failed him, was not failing him now, in whatever depths he sank.

He rose slowly, staring down on her.

Why had she come? To take from him the last thing he had left, the honour between friends? He had failed in battle. Now she would make him fail his friend too.

She gazed up at him as he towered over her, and her eagerness turned to amazement and then terror.

Who was this stranger? In her excitement she had scarcely noticed the change in him; now she smelled the brandy on his breath, saw him unshaved, dishevelled, even dirty; saw his ravaged face, saw his eyes – those narrow, yellow slits between their dropped lids and the dark pouches beneath, the eyes of a soul in hell. She prayed that she might faint before she knew what he would do to her.

He bent towards her to snatch her up to him, to bring down his mouth on hers, not to kiss, but to tear and wound. 'If I touch her now, it is all over,' he thought.

His hands hovered out like birds of prey. Let her not speak now nor entreat, or his sense will leave him utterly and all will be gone; he will have destroyed everything – his honour, his friendship, perhaps her body, that stood so straight and fair, so near his ruinous hands.

She did not speak; she dared not; she could not even entreat him with her eyes, for she had closed them at the sight of his.

He saw her face as it would lie in death, a mask shut safe against the world and the flesh; he saw the lovely austerity of its bones, robbed of all its teasing charm, the eyelashes dark and quiet against the white cheeks, the lips unsmiling, unbreathing, shut fast in a terror they dared not show.

He stepped back, his hands fell to his side, he heard his voice telling her to go. He saw her go and did not call her back, he saw the door shut, and the room empty itself of her presence, holding only a faint clinging perfume. He looked down at his hands and saw that they were bleeding, he did not know how.

Book II

DEBATABLE LAND

PART II

CHAPTER ONE

GENERAL CROMWELL had reached full middle life without ever being of any particular consequence, or knowing exactly what he wanted to do. Now at last he knew where he stood, he stood for Parliament, he stood on his own feet, and he stood up, stamping them down into his stiff riding boots, thrusting his rather grimy shirt-sleeves into his buff leather coat with such violence that he heard a rent go somewhere in the linen, and thought with a wry tender smile how Elizabeth would scold him for that – yes, and for not having remembered to put on a clean shirt this morning either.

He would tease her when he next saw her, tell her how he had escaped from her bondage – that close sweet unbearably poignant affection of his godly home – stuffy, his worldly old uncle, Sir Oliver, had called it, complaining that the spacious days of the old Queen had narrowed to these little tight intolerant homesteads – 'Never thought to have 'em all round me in my own family though, all so loving and faithful and look after the children and bring 'em up proper and don't let the wives go out except to church – God, is *that* all a man can find to do nowadays?'

And although – or perhaps even because – he loved his children with such aching anxiety and his wife with desperate frightened dependence, mental as well as physical, Oliver's heart had held an insurgent echo of the old knight's careless impatience. His wife had gone about her house and garden, quiet, contained, fulfilled of all her powers for giving and being used, since her husband's need of her was as deep and helpless as that of her baby at her breast.

But now he had not that same need of her. Now he had time for nothing but the urgent needs outside him of the present moment, and that was why he was happy for the first time in his life. As he had been writing, so now he must ride, like the devil – but why did words like that trip up his mind when he fined his troopers twelve pence every time they swore? He would never swear aloud, but as always his thoughts betrayed him, even now when, praised be the Lord, he had no time to think!

So, as he strode out to horse after writing his glad shout of energy and triumph for the victory of Marston Moor, he never remembered the letters he had written years ago when he had been so wretched that he could only think of suicide, and all for that worst of reasons – nothing.

'I live in Meshac which they say signifies Prolonging; in Kedar, which signifies Blackness; yet the Lord forsaketh me not,' so he had written then; and even the last words had only been in frantic attempt to convince himself.

*   *   *

Oliver had respected his pious father, and despised his showy, extravagant and heartily Royalist old uncle, but it was the latter who had made the deepest impression on his childhood – chiefly because he had so much the larger house. The natural snob inherent in all children could not fail to observe that whereas Mr Robert Cromwell had a nice, neat, square, smallish house just off the High Street in the little country town of Hunting-don, his eldest brother, Sir Oliver Cromwell, had a vast and gorgeous Elizabethan Manor built by his father, 'the Golden Knight', within half a mile of the town.

Hinchingbrooke was of an almost royal splendour; in fact the royal arms themselves were carved on it, a huge lion and uni-corn and crown silhouetted against the sky, on top of the new bow-fronted walls that had been added when little Oliver was three years old.

The child came up from the modest gentility of his father's home in the High Street to a fairy palace of riotous fancy at Hinchingbrooke. There were pond gardens, where silver balls danced perpetually in the balance of the fountains, and stone nymphs paused shrinking as in palpable naked flesh before they dared to bathe; there were mazes of clipped yew where he could walk for hours and find no way out; chimney-pieces where fauns and cupids chased each other in wanton play; staircases built wide enough for a troop to march up without breaking ranks, in order to do justice to the old Queen's skirts when she had come to stay. The huge library was full of Italian novelettes and French romances and poetry and even stage plays, instead of the squat little brown volumes of theological controversy that ranged themselves so sturdily along the shelves of young Oliver's father.

It all reflected the splendid sprightly England that was now vanishing, so Sir Oliver lamented (Sir Oracle his neighbours called him) – and here instead was the earnest modern world, so sober, so self-restrained, so damnably dull, in their speech devoid of oaths and flourishes and their dress stripped of all jewels and bright colours – 'and my dismal brother Robert as bad as any of 'em. You see what it's done for him, all girls in the family – piety never breeds sons – barring that one young oaf. I do what I can for him, have him up here pretty often, but curse me if he's not more of a lout than a true Cromwell.'

For young Oliver was a clumsy little boy, whose nose was too big for his face, and head too big for his body, and trunk too big for his legs, and who altogether, said his six sisters, was too big for his boots. He knew he was uncouth and did not like it. But at least he was not as uncouth as some people. On one of his visits to Hinchingbrooke he saw a revolting old gentleman who flopped out his tongue at him as he spoke, so that Oliver felt quite sick, but his uncle made him go up close and be patted on the head, and was indeed so fulsomely respectful himself that Oliver at last had to believe what he had heard, that this unpleasing oddity who was gabbling away at him in so unintelligible an accent that he took it for a foreign tongue, was actually and most dismally, disappointingly, the King.

What the King was saying was that Oliver must go and play in the gardens with his younger son, Prince Charles, who was only a year younger than he; but that too Oliver could not believe, for he was so small and sickly and girlish-looking that it was an insult to ask him to play with such a baby. Oliver's legs might be rather short for his body, but they were splendidly sturdy, while Prince Charles' were so weak that he could not really run yet at all, 'though my n-n-n-nurse tells me I shall,' he said slowly, with a dreadful stammer, and an echo of that uncouth Scots accent that had so appalled Oliver in his father.

Off went that disgusting old man, hugging a gold cup from among the shower of presents Sir Oliver had given him and his suite, and gabbling, '*Now* I can believe I am King of England!'

If these were kings and princes, God help them, then young Oliver was glad he was not as they were!

And it did not improve his opinion of them that his sisters raved with excitement to hear he had seen the King and the little prince – 'oh, but they say he is the sweetest child, so grave and polite and pretty like a little wax doll!'

His sisters with their pert ways and prim names – *they* were not given hoydenish nicknames such as Bet or Mag or Doll or Peg, like so many modern minxes – spoiled him and teased him and worried him with their knowing little airs of the world, their reliance on the outward show of things. Through them he despised and secretly a little feared all women; there were so many things about them that were mysterious and forbidden; he must never see his sisters naked, nor think of any woman as naked, nor of his own body; he must not think of the maypole that his father had insisted on destroying on the green at Huntingdon in spite of the protests of all the people, including Will Dagge the Constable and Mr Trim, the parish priest.

Oliver's father scolded Mr Trim for his slavish obedience in reading the King's Book of Sports from the pulpit, telling the people they could dance round the maypole after service on Sunday; so that poor Mr Trim was in a great fix at having to combine slavish obedience to his squire and patron as well as to the King. But Mr Robert Cromwell was Member of Parliament for Huntingdon, bailiff of the borough, on the commission of the peace for the county, and landowner on a large and useful scale, for he grazed his neighbours' cattle and horses on his fields, and grew grain for malt to brew for sale.

So down came the maypole and was burnt, and then the villagers began to dance round the bonfire, for it was no good, folks must dance round something, Will Dagge told Mr Robert Cromwell, who came marching down the High Street to stop them, with little Oliver beside him, his round excited eyes staring at the flames leaping up from that monstrous heathen symbol of the phallus that the children of Baal had worshipped.

The village boys were leaping and laughing round it; they had been stopped from dancing hand in hand with the girls, and the occasion of all their future dancing now lay crumbling into dust and ashes; but their foresight did not stretch as far as next Sunday, they were watching a bonfire now and that was enough, they hurled sticks and branches on to the fire to make it the brighter and yelled with joy as the red flames licked out at them.

Oliver saw a stump of rotten wood near him that was alive

368

with wood-lice, and the insects, alarmed by the warmth, were running all over it; he took it and threw it on at his end of the fire and watched with fascinated interest their frantic stampede to the higher end where they dropped over one after the other and shrivelled as they fell into the burning ashes below.

His father was talking happily with Mr Trim of the last crying tyranny from Whitehall – the importation of cheap little Geneva Bibles had been prohibited, either because of the marginal notes, all strongly Calvinist in tone, or because they undercut the better-printed English goods – but in any case a monstrous oppression. Mr Trim countered this grievance with a complaint of having been stung by a bee on his nose, but he had at once plucked out the sting and laid on honey so that it had not swelled (in which he overestimated his cure, for Oliver had noted that his nose was like a strawberry) – 'thus Divine Providence reaches to the lowest things,' he declared, and seeing that his patron was not sufficiently impressed he added yet more fervently, 'Let not sin, O Lord, that dreadful sting, be able to poison me!'

It had been better for Oliver had Mr Trim stuck to Geneva Bibles. His father, bored and inattentive, was at leisure to perceive his son's preoccupation with the burning wood-lice; his father's hand fell on his shoulder; his father was shaking him, scolding him for his cruelty.

'They're worshippers of Baal,' Oliver protested. 'I threw them into their accursed temple to let them burn, they're the enemies of God.'

He was taken home and whipped, but all the same he had felt like a Hebrew prophet.

He found as he grew older what so many Englishmen had been finding in the new translations of the Bible; that it was the first book in the world to make a common bond between them, a book known to all men as no other book had been known before, making a new language of phrase and allusion to draw all men together. It was a weapon and a war-cry, it was a guide to God and a promise of salvation, it was a book of good stories, it was a thrill of excitement to both jaded and starved palates. Even Dick the ploughboy could understand and quote back as well as he, when young Master Oliver said the verses he liked to hear come roaring out of his mouth – 'Jehu the son of Nimshi; for he driveth furiously' —

'And Agag came unto him delicately' – (it called up a picture of a little boy with a face like a girl's doll, walking with precise careful steps down the steep grass slopes at Hinchingbrooke, where he himself had just run shouting). 'And Samuel hewed Agag in pieces before the Lord in Gilgal.'

The language went to his head like wine. Here were wild deeds, fantastic legends, the savagery of tribal war, denunciations of the wicked, stimulating his curiosity and desire at the same instant that he burned to smash down the sinners, cutting them off in the very act of their lusts. Unnatural sins of the flesh were common enough among the heavy earth-bound peasantry of his eastern counties, many of them little removed from animals. But there was an unholy excitement about the sinners of the Bible. There were dark terrors in it too, that had haunted him since he was little more than a baby. Was he one of the elect, that is, the chosen of God? Or was he condemned to burn in hell everlasting?

Sometimes God Himself parted the curtains of his bed to tell him which He had decided for him, but in his agony of fear Oliver always cried out, and so brought his father upon him, who whipped him for telling lies.

His mother comforted him by telling him that he was one of the elect, but she did not know the wickedness in his heart; for however hard he tried, he still thought of the things that he should not.

The older he grew, the deeper he buried his thoughts, trampled them down, down into the sun-warmed earth as he lay on his face in the woods round Huntingdon in the first soft days of spring. The white heads of wind-flowers tossing airily on their hair-thin stalks and the round surprised faces of primroses shone like stars all about him, rabbits darted out of their holes and scuttled away, birds sang on long tingling notes of piercing sweetness; all living nature was happy because it had no soul and could not think wickedness as he was doing.

He hurled himself into action, into furious rides and football and cudgel-play with his schoolfellows at the Grammar School at Huntingdon, then later during a year at Cambridge. The thoughts he had choked down surged up in his dreams, making their images hideously clear; there were symbols of wickedness, there were idolatries all round him – there was the Town Cross at Huntingdon which now he dared not look at, lest, as he told a friend, he should see there 'horrors beyond this world'.

Sometimes he gave up the struggle and plunged into dissipations with a furious determination to enjoy them that defeated its own end. 'Oh, I hated godliness!' he wrote, and so he might, but he could not love pleasure. His self-indulgence was always an attack, a struggle, tearing his mind in two.

He married as soon as he came of age, and brought his wife to live in his Huntingdon home with his father and mother and sisters. His family generally married well, and Oliver was no exception; his bride Elizabeth, a year older than himself, was the daughter of a rich London city knight – 'but it used to be Lord Mayors,' grumbled Uncle Oliver, who had married a Lord Mayor's daughter himself, and then a Viennese heiress, whose family had carried on a tiresome lawsuit ever since her death to reclaim the jewels she had left to them – but the jewels remained at Hinchingbrooke.

In Sir Oliver's opinion the family was going down. Land wasn't what it had been, you couldn't get a profit anywhere; he was riddled with debts; royal visits had made him a great figure in the country, but they had been a horrible expense and had led nowhere.

As for this Scots King (for all that he had given Sir Oliver the opportunity to say casually and incessantly, 'Yes, as King Jamie said to me when he was last here —') he was not playing his cards one quarter as well as the old Queen had done. ('Yes, as Queen Bess said to my father when she was last here — ')

It was a great mistake for a king to be an author, writing pamphlets on all subjects from tobacco to sorcery like those common scribblers in London who'd yark you up a pamphlet on any and every thing in a few hours – but the worst was when King James took to writing about his own trade of kingship, laying down all sorts of rules and definitions on the divine right of kings – which, complained Sir Oliver, 'makes conceited argumentative fellows like my precious brother Robert and his young cub of a son, Oliver, and all the rest of that Puritan host want to dispute it and make objections. The old Queen never defined anything, that was her cunning; she just took all she could without saying anything, and with as few Parliaments as possible.'

Like most Englishmen Sir Oliver was relieved for the country when King James died, having said too much and drunk too much and made a disgusting exhibition of the kingship he

371

would call divine, and left his sober, serious, well-mannered, good-looking son Charles on the throne. But his death removed Sir Oliver's last hopes of mending his fortunes through Court influence, and he announced at large that he would have to sell Hinchingbrooke. He had another rich estate at Ramsey; it was none the less infinitely pathetic to him that at sixty-five he should have to leave his stately park and woods, the scene of royal hunts, and the beautiful house by the river where he had been born only a year or two after it was built.

'We are of an age,' he said tenderly, 'and I shall not survive the parting,' – but he did survive it, until he fell into the fire at the age of ninety-three.

*   *   *

If Sir Oliver complained gently of the loss of Hinchingbrooke, it was nothing to the storm of protest it aroused down in his brother's household. Robert Cromwell had grown more and more to feel out of tune with his worldly brother, and scarcely ever visited Hinchingbrooke; his son Oliver was ill at ease there, defiantly conscious of his sisters' strictures on his clothes.

('But *why* not have them made while you are in London instead of always getting them from the local tailor?'

'It's affected to pretend to be poor when everyone knows you are not.')

But out of tune or ill at ease, disapproving, contemptuous even, the father and son might feel all these things among the splendours of Hinchingbrooke; yet they could not endure that they should pass out of the family. The Cromwells had always been men who knew how to get and how to hold what they got.

Thomas Cromwell had got the Church lands for the family nearly a century ago, when he destroyed the monasteries. Hinchingbrooke had been a nunnery since the ninth century, before it was pulled down to make way for the Cromwells' Tudor mansion; Sir Oliver's other great house at Ramsey had been a rich abbey, worth half the see of Westminster; even Robert Cromwell's humbler town-house had been an Augustinian friary since the thirteenth century. Thomas Cromwell had done well by his sister's family. She had married a Welsh brewer who had changed his name from Williams to Cromwell, without leave of Chancery, in order to advertise their connection with the man in power, and it was from them that the Cromwells were descended.

Thomas Cromwell's portrait by Holbein hung at Hinchingbrooke; the face barely human either in its grossness or its intelligence, the astute wicked little eyes looking out from fold after fold of flabby flesh – the face of a pig with a devil's brain. It did not hang in a prominent position, for Uncle Oliver was, absurdly, rather ashamed of the great minister who had made his master Henry VIII an absolute monarch, but had started life as a blacksmith's son at Putney.

Young Oliver scorned that shamefaced gentility. To him, Thomas Cromwell was a national hero.

'He's so ugly,' his silly little sisters had whined.

'He ruled all England, he gave us the Bible, he said "No" to the Pope, he chopped off the heads of the highest in the land – and all you can say is – "he's ugly"!'

'Why be so ill-tempered about it? You needn't think just because *you* are ugly that *you'll* rule all England and say "No" to the Pope and chop off the heads of the highest in the land.'

And Robina, the youngest, tossed her head and picked up her skirts and pranced away, humming a tune, as cool as cream. These smooth superior little people judged by vain shows; but that man, who had shown Henry VIII how to rule, had cared nothing for such toys as the outward pomp of state. It had been enough for him to govern England.

Thomas Cromwell's copy of Machiavelli's handbook on how to rule unhampered by scruple, written, unnecessarily one might imagine, for his master Caesar Borgia, was in the library at Hinchingbrooke. Thomas had known both Borgia and Machiavelli personally, and the book showed signs of his careful study, with tiny notes scored in the margin. Oliver had read it, a little shocked, but more impressed, for undoubtedly the core of this doctrine was that it showed how to *get things done* – and what else was the aim of any government?

If its teaching could be purified, combined with the Bible's, what a power for good would it not make in a truly godly man? Undoubtedly, if one saw one was right, if, as Thomas may have felt, 'Only *I* can save this country,' then one was justified in whatever means one used to achieve that necessary end.

So he said at dinner, the last time that they went up to Hinchingbrooke, and Sir Oliver, drumming his rather thick fingers on the edge of his gold plate, remarked, 'That's what the Jesuits say, isn't it?'

And his father said reprovingly that it was better to let things take their course than to do any action that was wrong in itself. Oliver could not make him see that there might be circumstances in which the worst wrong must be right – as when Thomas Cromwell had struck off the head of Sir Thomas More, the noblest and wisest head in England, seeing that for just that very reason, since it stood in the way of Protestantism, its removal was a stern necessity.

*   *   *

On the Church lands acquired by Thomas, the Cromwells had become the leading family in the county. But now with the passing of the great house at Hinchingbrooke, that proud position passed too, to the family of the Montagu's, who had always been their rivals. Worse still, the Montagu's were of 'the old blood', as the peasants with their persistent memories still called the families who had had power in the land for centuries before 'the new gentry', built up by Henry VIII out of the ruins of the old Church.

Uncle Oliver had not only belied his acquisitive and tenacious race; by selling Hinchingbrooke to a Montagu, he betrayed it, and to the very men at whom Thomas Cromwell had struck with such deadly power. Oliver resented this furiously; he had a strong family pride, though of a different order from that of his sisters who liked to think their mother was a cousin of the King's, because her name was Steward.

'She's one of the Leicestershire Stewards,' he told them, 'and nothing to do with a beggarly Scots family.'

'Why is it worse to be Scots than Welsh?'

'We're not Welsh – that's a lie. We've been settled in England for a hundred years.'

'We didn't *want* to be Welsh, or we wouldn't have changed our name from Williams. Cromwell sounds better.'

After four generations they might fairly look on it as theirs, but Oliver, with his hatred of shams – and shames – had been careful to sign his name as 'Williams (alias Cromwell)' in his marriage register.

It may have been partly his Welsh descent, making him as he knew more passionate and easily disturbed (his eyes always filling with tears, his temper always ready to burst out, his heart

374

full of unutterable, unappeasable longings) than the stolid fen-land neighbours whom he envied and tried in vain to emulate, that gave him so personal and religious a conviction that the English were not only the salt of the earth and the greatest nation on it (anyone knew that who had heard old men talk of the Armada) but that they were the people chosen by the Lord to do His work for him; and that wherever the Bible mentioned the Jews in this connection, God had meant one to understand 'Englishmen' – they not having then been invented.

This same free translation was applied to the prophets of Baal; by these, one should understand Popish priests or those of the English clergy that were so Popishly inclined as to wear surplices.

Later, the process converted the Amalekites, the heathen and the men of Belial, into all the Englishmen who stood for the King.

It was in effect the same as his pretence with the wood-lice, giving the capricious and irresponsible standards of a child's make-believe to human life and action. It was well on the way to madness, but that way madness did not lie for Oliver; for by the time he attained power, action had put his mind so firmly under his control that he could use this incipient madness just when and where he wished.

As yet he knew neither power nor control. Hinchingbrooke was sold; a Montague was lording it over him in his own county; he had been returned to Parliament for Huntingdon, and complained in the House that a Doctor Alabaster had preached black Popery at Paul's Cross, but had no other oppor-tunity of expressing his sense that everything was wrong with England – and then, to justify that sense, the session ended in a brawl, with all the members in tears, and King Charles refused to call another Parliament.

His wife was sure that something was wrong with himself, and made him see a fashionable London doctor for his depres-sion – prompted thereto by Dr Simcott at Huntingdon, who was sick of being summoned at midnight because Oliver thought he was dying, and of being stormed at when he told him he wasn't. 'Most splenetic' was his own opinion of his morbid patient; and Sir Theodore Mayerne (the King's own doctor) wrote 'melancholia' in his notebook against the name of Mr Oliver Cromwell, but could do nothing to cure it.

How could he, said Oliver, when it was the whole world that was wrong? The cause of the Lord was losing everywhere –

Protestant Germany crushed beneath the Catholic House of Austria, French Huguenots beneath Cardinal Richelieu, and here in England Papists were not fined and restricted nearly as much as they had been, only eight of their priests executed since the reign began, while at the head of the English Church was Laud, and the 'continual abounding nonsense' of the English Prayer-Book. 'Lean and dry', 'empty and unmoving', its liturgy could not satisfy a spirit that longed 'to soar upon the wings of zeal'.

He sold his house to get away from the spectacle of the Montagu's, and finally settled at Ely where he had succeeded to an uncle's fortune in land. He was getting more and more money. Elizabeth had more and more children. Their father liked the girls best, saucy monkeys and not afraid of him like the boys (they were in fact very like what his sisters had been, but that he did not see). But when his eldest boy died, his violent grief nearly drove him to suicide. His mother came and lived with them at Ely some time after his father had died. He could not do without her or Elizabeth or the children; if it had not been for them he would have lost his reason under the burden of his moods, now of a despairing sense of guilt, now of ecstatic certainty that he had found God's mercy.

His preoccupation was a common thing, though not the strength with which he felt it; many men in breaking away from all the guides and comforts and little warm assurances of a long-accepted religion, in deciding to stand alone before their God, were frightened and amazed, questioning themselves at every step, their thoughts all turned inward.

In such a mood, the peace and prosperity of England went for nothing. It was the salvation of each man's individual soul that mattered – and that might well be endangered by pushing back the Communion table to the East wall where it had stood in the days of the Romish priests (or the prophets of Baal).

Shows were shams in Oliver's eyes; to him it had been a true sense of religion that made men in the revolt against Rome hold up a dog in mockery when the priest elevated the Host, and corrupt the most sacred words of the Mass, 'Hoc est Corpus', into the modern contemptuous phrase for any jugglery, 'hocus-pocus'. His hatred of the Catholics was mixed up with his confused feeling about sex; the monks that his family had so rightly dispossessed were a lot of lazy vicious old men in petticoats, whose lives were as womanish as their dress, and who worshipped a woman.

But worst of all, they had put Rome above England.

It was Thomas Cromwell who had stopped that. If only he too could strike such a blow for England! He knew he had it in him to do it, if he knew where and at whom – apart from the Earl of Manchester, who as head of the detested Montagu family was his worst enemy.

He attacked him whenever he could, on land committees and in councils concerned with the fen drainage scheme, and so rudely that Mr Edward Hyde, sent down from London as chairman, had to rebuke him for 'shouting and brawling'. It certainly seemed a small objective on which to expend so much angry energy. But he had none of the ordinary aims of ambition, hated the idea of place-hunting, despised titles, refused a knighthood and had to pay £10 for doing so – the semi-compulsory sale of knighthoods being one of the King's desperate shifts to raise money. He was that unbribable and unbiddable creature, an English country gentleman, and there was nothing he wanted from other men.

His cousin, John Hampden, had resisted the King's demand for a tax to be paid towards the upkeep of the navy; he admitted that it might be reasonable to expect the nation to help pay for its navy, instead of leaving it all to the coastal towns. But the King ought to have called a Parliament first; only Parliament should now have the right to decide taxation.

Oliver, fond as he was of John, could not get sufficiently fired by a constitutional principle. That was John's way, not his – he wanted something more direct and practical for his energies, something nearer the earth.

He collected his rents, looked after his lands and the neighbours' horses and cattle that grazed on them, exercised his heavy body as he had to do continually – but however hard he rode to hounds or tramped with his gun over the open fields, it was seldom there was any joyful spring of life in it; life seemed to lie soggy and impenetrable within him like that unused marshland of the fens, while ever beneath his feet there lurked the quaking bog of his religious terrors, that bottomless pit waiting to swallow him up.

A deep reserve, inculcated by the iron discipline of his childhood, gave him little chance to express and so to some extent escape his wretchedness; he could only fling himself from it into the violent contrast of horseplay.

'What a great boy he is!'

'Oliver will never grow up!'

So said his kind friends when he threw cushions at their heads or chased them round the room to pommel them.

John Hampden knew that Oliver would have been healthier if he had grown up a bit more.

And to John, as they walked home with their guns one evening, Oliver confided his secret torments. Hampden was gently philosophic. Every age he said had its own sorrows. Theirs perhaps suffered from too much sense of religion; but the ancient Pagans had been as sad from the lack of it – their literature was haunted by the fear of death, the passing of youth and love, the terrible realization that all that belongs to the body must perish.

It was just like John to talk of the old Greeks and Romans as though they, or anyone in any age, could suffer as Oliver suffered. His eyes, which had been fixed upon his boots as he had talked, now raised themselves in despair upon the empty scene; the fields, unscarred by hedges, were as flat as the fens, the world seemed an endless plain under the globed sky. It had been raining all day but now the sun shone out as it set, and on the black banks of clouds in the east a rainbow towered up far above the great cathedral of Ely, and glimmered in a fantastic medley of colours in the rivulets that ran here and there among the reedy marsh. Oliver had not noticed it except as another storm sign, but Hampden now spoke of it, of the promise from God that it had once shown to a world that had seemed at an end.

Said Oliver, 'This world of ours is rotten and outworn – what promise can God hold out for it?'

'You know that I have purchased a grant of land in America,' said Hampden, in the quiet way he had when he was going to announce something startling. 'There on the other side of the globe is a New World and a New England. So they are calling it. Already they speak of their "capital", a little township of wooden huts that they have called Boston after the town in Lincolnshire.'

There was not a Puritan household that had not been discussing with rising excitement the extraordinarily rapid growth of this colony on the coast of the country with the heathen name of Massachusetts. Since John Robinson had landed there from the *Mayflower* with his small congregation of simple working-class people, thousands had sailed to join them, lured by no hope of gold and the fabulous riches of ancient empires that had urged the Spanish sailors to the south of the continent, but realizing that the true wealth of these barren shores could only be on the farther side of intense hardship and hard work. But there were compensations. There in poor cottages in the wilderness men would be free to worship God untrammelled by surplices and altar cloths, above all by bishops, who were abolished out there.

They were, of course, only free in one direction. Nobody might read the Book of Common Prayer, for it was prohibited; and a young minister who dared hold the doctrine of 'freedom of conscience' was turned out of the community and banished to Rhode Island. But all those who agreed with the ministers 'can now enjoy God and Jesus Christ, and is not that enough?' So they wrote home, and were answered with so mighty a wave of enthusiasm that it seemed as though most of the old England would soon be transplanted to the new. The tide flowed high as well as wide; three lords were now planning to emigrate, and the son of a secretary of state had already gone; it flowed especially from the eastern counties round the Cromwell and Hampden homes – and now it caught them too on the crest of its wave.

As Hampden told of his plan to sell his vast estates and settle on the strip of land he had bought on the Narragansett (of all barbarous names!) Oliver realized that this was what God had always held in readiness for him – America, God's last hope for the dying world.

He yearned for the effort, not for the result. All that his family had had to do for the last three generations was to settle down quietly and consolidate the gains that their founder had got for them. But all that he longed to do was to be himself a pioneer, to carve out his destiny, to build his house with his own hands, conquer the savage red-skinned hunters, tame them and teach them God's word or else exterminate them, stretch himself and breathe free of all these little cramping conventions and tyrannies here – Londoners who looked amused at his dress or winced if he spoke too loud – his sisters critical of him – his wife anxious for the effect he produced – even his cousin Hampden sometimes tactfully disapproving of his gross talk, in which he would deliberately use the coarsest country speech in order to relieve his mind of some of its pent-up matter.

Here had he no abiding city. He had already sold much of his land in order to have his property where he could quickly lay hold of it; now he would transfer it to America, and his family and even his old mother, who had enough guts for anything; and his wife would stand by him, as she had always done.

Now as the cousins planned to emigrate, there fell on them both the sense of an unutterable peace. On the other side of the world, in America, there they would find God.

*   *   *

Their emigration was prevented by a royal command, another hateful tyranny; another dull brooding pause in which he seemed to have nothing to do but wait for something to happen – and then it happened.

There was a riot in Edinburgh, a revolt against the bishops, in refusal to let the English Book of Common Prayer be read in the Scots Churches. An old washerwoman in St Giles' Cathedral flung a stool at the bishop's head.

Here was something practical and concrete with a vengeance. And here was the cause he had craved, with the weapons; not just passive resistance to a tax, but God's word and a sword. For the whole of Scotland was arming against the bishops – they were marching against England – and the King would have to call a Parliament to subscribe for an army to resist them.

Now was the moment that Hampden and his friends had been waiting for, for eleven years. The King had at last to put himself in their power, and not a penny would they subscribe against the Scots invasion until they had got their way.

And Oliver Cromwell, riding to Westminster as Member for Cambridge, was now heart and soul with his cousin, for the religious issue had been joined with the political.

The work of his blood had come full circle. That turgid welter of emotion, raw, hysterical, angry, that had been originally stirred up by Thomas Cromwell when he set up the Bible as a weapon against the Pope, was now all ready to hand for the politicians to use in their struggle against that very Crown that Thomas had exalted.

The army of Scots invaders, settled at Newcastle, gradually became the paid servants of the House of Commons ('No fear of dissolution while the lads at Newcastle are on guard!' it was gleefully said at Westminster).

With armed force as a Parliamentary weapon, civil war was bound to follow; but before that happened Strafford was executed, because he was suspected of being about to use armed force. War followed. Parliament was horrified to hear that Prince Rupert of the Rhine, whose family had been the hope and pride of the Protestant cause, had come back to England to fight for his uncle.

Oliver Cromwell went back to Cambridge to raise a troop of horse at his own expense, and came into his own. Here at last was what the Lord had made him for.

*　　　*　　　*

His war record was a steady advance.

He had begun by making a first-rate recruiting officer, bluff, hearty, full of God's words and dunghill expressions together, understanding the simple country fellows he had to deal with down to the ground, and they feeling they could understand him and know him honest since he talked like themselves as well as like a preacher.

At Edgehill in 1642 he was a captain in command of the 67th troop of Essex's horse, with three officers under him and sixty men; by the following January he was a colonel; by March he had five troops under him, and within a year of Edgehill, ten. God showed His approval by giving him continual success. Success was to him a direct sign from God; there was in him a deep uneasy craving that demanded this outward assurance that he was doing right; nor did it ever strike him as blasphemous to identify the spirit of God with that of worldly success.

But he had his work cut out to make it.

Edgehill was a bad business, and he learned his lesson from it. He might not be able ever to get his horse to charge with the incredible new speed and fury of Rupert's cavalry, but these very qualities had their defects; it had proved all but impossible for their leaders to recall them after the impetus of that first charge. If he could not attain that fiery gallop, he would get his men to charge at least at a good round trot, and above all to keep their ranks, and turn again when he wanted them to do so. By the following summer he had 'a lovely company'.

But by the following summer the King's armies were winning everywhere. Rupert had taken town after town, and London was clamouring for peace.

Now time, that heavy plodding thing which he had always had to kill as best he might, flew past Oliver on wings, and his one aim in life was to catch it up. He wrote from the North: 'It is no longer disputing but act instantly all you can. Raise all your bands, send them to Huntingdon, get up what volunteers you can, hasten your horses. Send these letters to Norfolk, Suffolk and Essex without delay. I beseech you spare not but be expeditious and industrious. Almost all our foot have quitted Stamford, there is nothing to interrupt an enemy but our horse, which is considerable!' (He had seen to that!) 'You must act lively. Do it without distraction. Neglect no means.'

Here were words he could use like weapons, not the cold logical arguments one had to make on committees before lawyers and politicians. The violence that had been a futile exhibition of rudeness with Hyde and Lord Manchester, was now as effective as if he were directing a charge. As indeed he was – a charge that resulted in the booty of fifty subsidies from the city of London, and an army of 10,000 men from the Eastern Counties, with Manchester at their head, and himself in charge of the horse and virtual second-in-command. It was bad to have the head of the Montagu's lording it over him again, but at least Manchester was a 'sweet meek man' and did whatever Oliver told him.

So did the Lord Lieutenant of the county, appointed by Parliament; Oliver, now created Governor of the Isle of Ely, allowed him no say at all in Ely or in Cambridge. He fortified Cambridge, as Oxford had been fortified for the King, and made the dignitaries of Ely Cathedral suffer for their precious tower that domineered over his fields.

By the January of 1644, the captain of horse was a Lieutenant-General; by February, a Member of the Committee of Both Kingdoms (England and Scotland) for prosecuting the war.

But Manchester must go.

Before he could manage that, Oliver must establish himself with some great spectacular victory; for he had no hold upon the will of the people; he knew as well as any man that if there were manhood suffrage in England, it would all along have brought back the King. Parliament did not represent the people; there was not a Royalist in it, and the majority of the country was Royalist. That naturally did not trouble Oliver. Nor did he care for democracy ('the creed of all bad men and all poor men', he called it, poor being as bad as bad). But he did wonder what good there was in this particular Parliament. It had seized bishops' lands and money, and Royalists', but with as much dishonesty as violence, for most of the money, instead of being used for the war, had gone into the private pockets of the Members of Parliament.

But worst of all his complaints was that which he wrote to a friend: 'It is a miserable thing to serve a Parliament.' It would be well indeed if Parliament too could be made to go, though his confidential opinion was that 'these men will never leave till the army pull them out by the ears.'

He and the army could not get to that yet. But they were getting nearer.

When he joined David Leslie and the Scottish horse to prevent Prince Rupert's conquest of the North, God gave him the crushing victory he needed at Marston Moor. Through sheer luck he got the initiative, which his dashing rival had seized on every other occasion except this, when he met with his greatest antagonist.

Why had Rupert not attacked at once with his cavalry? Something had clearly happened in the Royalists' camp which had caused their young leader to be out of fighting trim at the very moment of his supreme test. Whatever it was, it had been sent by God (for there was no such thing as luck to Oliver) to deliver him into the hands of his enemy.

Now he had conquered his chief foe, Oliver was strong enough to attack his friends.

He arraigned the growing peace party, which the people, and Parliament, and the Scots were all eagerly backing.

He arraigned his commanders, especially Manchester. He told him, 'we shall do no good till we have done away with lords, and you are plain Mr Montagu again'; he told him and Essex they were 'afraid to conquer'; but for himself, he 'would pistol his Sacred Majesty in battle as soon as any other man'. He made a passionate speech in Parliament, pointing out that many Members of Parliament 'had got great places and commands and the sword into their hands'; there was grave danger that between their political and military power 'they will perpetually continue themselves in grandeur'. So a Self-denying Ordinance was voted, that all Members of Parliament should lay down their arms.

All Oliver's enemies voted for it, since it was bound to get rid of him as well as others. He, too, was a Member of Parliament, who had got great places and command through the war, and might well 'perpetually continue himself in grandeur'.

They were short-sighted. In the spring of 1645, Manchester

went, Essex went (with a pension of £10,000 a year), and many others; and Sir Thomas Fairfax was made Commander-in-Chief. But Oliver's command was prolonged; and the post of Lieutenant-General in command of the horse was left open; nobody in the army wondered why.

Prince Rupert built up a fresh army, and petitions poured into Parliament to stem the 'mighty torrent of his successes'. Fairfax's Council of War suddenly discovered that there was no officer in command of all the cavalry, and pointed out this omission, recommending Oliver Cromwell to the vacant Lieutenant-Generalship on account of his talents and 'the constant presence and blessing of God that has accompanied him'.

A message was sent to Oliver at Ely, and nothing was said in it about the Self-denying Ordinance. He was ready for it. On the instant he was in the saddle and at the head of 600 men rode towards Fairfax, whose army was approaching the King's.

Fairfax's army was striking camp at Kislingbury and swinging into their line of march towards the village of Naseby, when they saw a cloud of dust and a large body of horsemen come galloping towards them. A mighty shout went up from all their ranks – 'Ironsides is come!'

CHAPTER TWO

I T S E E M E D at first that Cromwell had put Rupert out of action for good after Marston Moor. But that brutal self-indulgence at Bristol had not lasted more than a few weeks; his spirit burned with too fierce a flame to let itself be quenched. Drunkenness without gaiety, lust without love, inaction without ease, these had only deepened his depression.

It was Richmond who had succeeded in dragging him out of it; something of his deep unshaken confidence in his friends did finally convince him of the King's continued need of him – for Richmond said nothing to Rupert of the harm he was doing to himself, only of 'that great good' he could still do the King. He roused himself to join the King, only to find that Goring, unfortunately 'possessed of a great gaiety', had landed the Royalist army in another unnecessary and disastrous battle at Newbury. If Charles had waited only one day, Rupert would have been in time to prevent it. But he was in time to draw them off in a manœuvre of such perfect and intricate precision that not a man was lost on the retreat; and the admiring soldiers declared it to be as neat and pretty a movement as a country dance.

He was fast learning by his experience. In every direction he was showing a new, tempered judgement, cool as steel.

When he was made General-in-Chief instead of Ruthven, he was careful to ask that the Prince of Wales, not yet fifteen, should be made the nominal head over him.

When he flew into one of his rages in the Council Chamber (which now happened very seldom) he recovered mastery of himself far quicker than he used, and even brought himself to apologize.

When he drank deep, as he now did occasionally, he was as reserved in his cups as out of them, an icy watchfulness of himself and his companions keeping guard behind his smouldering eyes.

He even did his best to comply with his uncle's wishes and make at least outward friends with Digby; though it was as well Charles did not see his private opinion to 'Dear Will' in which he told Legge cynically in cypher – 'Rupert and Digby are now friends, but I doubt they trust one another alike.' And he added, 'Great factions are brewing against Rupert under a pretence of peace, *he being*, as they report, *the only cause of war in this kingdom.*'

This was bitterly ironic, for the chief sign of the new Rupert had been his earnest support of the Royalist efforts to make peace at Uxbridge, and he rode out the first to greet the Parliament Commissioners and bring them to the King.

But there was no hope of peace, for General Cromwell, ignoring his allies' attempts at it, was fast pushing on that huge new war machine of the New Model army, raised by conscription and enormous taxation from 'the bleeding, nay, almost dying, nation' of which he spoke in Parliament with so much pity. Twelve regiments of foot, eleven of horse, were raised from the national funds, with regular pay and supplies, and a uniform of scarlet coats, all sworn to impose Presbyterianism on England (for the Scots must be kept quiet).

This moment was also chosen to execute Archbishop Laud, who had been kept half-starved in the Tower for the last five years. Essex bravely protested against his murder, for there was no legal pretext for his death.

Coming in the very middle of the peace negotiations, these

things impressed Charles as a warning of profound and awful significance. 'They are only mocking me with this treaty,' he said, 'they do not want peace but the sword. They will not rest until they have my blood also.'

He saw this horror growing in the minds of his people, their leaders nursing it, encouraging it with outspoken brutality so as to make it familiar and no longer to be feared. Cromwell's assertion that he 'would pistol his Sacred Majesty in battle as soon as any other' had flown like wildfire through the country. There was no longer any meaning in the word 'sacred' as applied to Majesty.

Rupert had seen ever since Marston Moor, and for some months before, that there was only one enemy that counted, and that was Oliver Cromwell. Now the King realized it too, and sent away Prince Charles and with him his wisest counsellors, Richmond and Hyde, so that he and his heir should not be destroyed together. The struggle had ceased to be a fight for principles and prerogative; it was now a personal one between himself and Cromwell.

Shaken and bewildered as he was by these evidences of his enemies' implacable hate, Charles was cheered by their dissensions, for they were all at each other's throats.

That did not encourage Rupert; he saw that it was Cromwell's teeth that would get the hold on his allies' throats.

The chief hope of Rupert's friends was that the old fire was running in his veins, as well as the new caution – he had to keep an eye on every part of England at once – Prince Charles at Bristol – the King at Oxford, threatened by Cromwell's cavalry – the weakening Wales and Somerset – and, above all, the road to Scotland. A muster of troops at Stow-in-the-Wold in the May of '45 showed that they amounted to only 11,000 men; and these would have to be divided into reinforcements for all these scattered activities.

Goring's bloodshot eyes rolled heavily over their meagre forces. 'If we divide our men into all the quarters necessary, there'll be about enough apiece to cuckold a Cotswold village, and that can be a one-man's job – I've proved it.'

Rupert laid down his plans. Will Legge was to be sent back in charge of Oxford as Governor; Goring was to strengthen Bristol, take Taunton, keep Fairfax and Cromwell apart, and then join the King's army for a decisive combined blow at them: Rupert himself was to go north, to relieve Cheshire, win back Yorkshire, demolish Leslie's Scots, and double his army.

He did this last in a month. By early June he had increased the army to nearly twenty thousand men; he had subdued the Midlands, and taken Leicester in only two days, stoutly defended as it was, in one of the best pits of fighting in the war.

Once again the Parliament was showing panic at 'the admirable diligence and command of Prince Rupert', and the 'mighty torrent of his successes'.

And once again the road to the North lay open.

Rupert now had the best chance he had had yet to smash Leslie's Scots. Give them but one defeat, he argued, and in their present discontent with Cromwell (who said openly he 'would as soon turn his sword on them as on any in the King's army') they might easily back out of the war, or even come in for the King.

There was another widely different cause of hope from Scotland. Montrose had succeeded in miraculous fashion in slipping in disguise through the Covenanter armies on the Border last summer after his meeting with Rupert at Richmond. He had walked with only a single friend to find Alasdair Macdonald and his little force of Highlanders and 'Irishes', but they had accepted him at once as their leader, and within three days, with no horses or guns, and for many of them no weapons but the stones on the rough hillside, he had led them to the capture of the rich city of Perth. From then on he had won battle after battle; and his last despatch had been written from Inverlochy in the Highlands where he had just wiped out the fighting strength of the Clan Campbell, the chief support of the Covenant, and sent its leader, the Marquis of Argyll, flying from the scene of action. He assured Charles that 'I doubt not before the end of this summer I shall be able to come to Your Majesty's assistance with a brave army.'

The King longed to join Montrose, and Digby wrote many promises to him; but the first step to it, as Rupert pointed out, was to get Leslie's Covenanters out of the way. Never was there a better chance to do it. Montrose's victories had forced them to send some of their best infantry across the Border; it was the perfect opportunity to clear the North of England for Montrose's march south.

But the King, eager for the result, was dull as to the means.

And Digby did not agree with the northern plan. He had been appalled to see how fast Rupert had got back his old lead.

Now Digby recovered it.

There were recruits waiting for Rupert in Yorkshire, 3,000 Royalists marching to meet him at Leicester, the northern cavalry protesting against a return to the South, and all the soldiers appealing furiously to be allowed to finish the campaign they had begun so splendidly.

But Digby persuaded the King to turn south to relieve Oxford, which Fairfax was threatening to besiege, though without any heavy guns or entrenching tools. So the King turned south, only to hear that Fairfax had thrown up his half-hearted attempt at the siege of Oxford, and was marching north to meet them.

Rupert was justified, and the King's army turned north again, having wasted several precious days.

Rupert saw clearly the chief advantage that Cromwell had over him. It was a personal advantage. He could not brush aside his uncle, as Cromwell had brushed aside Manchester and Essex and all who stood in his way.

On his own side Cromwell was really the supreme power. But Rupert fought with one hand tied behind his back, tied and twisted this way and that by the King's shifting and bewildered mind.

Rupert had thought he could easily rule the affectionate uncle who so admired and leaned on him; now he had learned that the man who can be ruled by one is generally ruled by half a dozen.

CHAPTER THREE

THE KING'S army was making a leisurely march towards Leicester, over country as open and waving as the sea. Rupert and his Life Guards kept as usual the position nearest to the enemy; they had been in the van while marching towards him, and were now in the rear in retirement. They could hear no report of any enemy, but the country was hostile and Rupert was determined to take no chances. He left an outpost of his own horse at the village of Naseby in the centre of the plain, while he rode on to sleep at Market Harborough.

The troopers found themselves in comfortable quarters at Naseby; they sat down to supper at a long oak table and afterwards fell on a game of quoits in the inn, the onlookers drinking and cheering on the players, their belts, heavy with sword and pistols, thrown aside together with their steel back-and-breast bucklers, while the men took their slack and glorious ease. The evening was hot, the ale was cool; through the open door and windows of the little inn came the peaceful country sounds of slow heavy cart-horses trudging home and splashing down into the roadside pond, and geese hissing on the green. They hissed and cackled, disapproving of this loud intrusion into the accustomed quiet of Naseby, this undue number of strange horses neighing and clinking on their green, the shouts and songs that came reeling out from the inn into the still air of that blue June twilight.

A worse disturbance followed – the blare of a trumpet, calling to horse, and one of the vedettes galloped up at breakneck speed, shouting in sick torn-off shreds of sobbing breath, 'They're on us! To horse! To ho-orse!' The men came tumbling and jostling each other out of the inn, fumbling with their sword-belts, struggling into their breastplates, but too late. The thunder of galloping hoofs echoed through the village, and with triumphant shouts for 'God and the Parliament', Ireton's horsemen swept down on Rupert's and wiped them out before they had a chance to get together either weapons or horses. Most were killed, a few taken prisoner; only one man escaped, the man who had given the warning, and had ridden desperately on over the low hills to tell the King.

The King was in bed at the Hall House at Lubenham, but at once got up and rode to Market Harborough for an instant council of war.

Startled, unshaved, hastily dressed, the commanders came straggling in and stared sleepily at each other across the table where two candles threw an uncertain light, already paling in the first grey twilight of midsummer dawn. The King, rather oddly, was not perturbed, though he confided to Rupert that he had been dreaming of Strafford.

'Absit omen,' muttered his nephew as they sat down at the table, and brushed his hand across his mouth to hide the yawn that was rising irrepressibly in him in spite of his anxiety and sense of urgency, for he had been woken just as he had fallen into a heavy sleep after seeing to his troops until late at night, and could not at once shake off his feeling that this confused dream must soon resolve itself again in sleep.

The enemy was nearer then than they had thought. 'Gentlemen,' he said, 'why should we alter our plans? We were marching to Leicester – let us march, but with more speed. Three thousand troops have been sent for to meet us there; they are probably at Leicester by now. There are also reinforcements waiting for us at Newark and Melton. There is no point in risking a battle until we have collected all our strength. Goring's cavalry are to join us from the West – they might arrive at any moment.'

'So might Cromwell's,' said Digby, balancing a quill pen on his finger in his bored contempt of Rupert's arguments. But its wobbling and falling could not disturb the balance of Rupert's temper, the matter was too serious.

'Cromwell may be there already,' he replied.

'Then the country people would certainly have heard of it.'

'They need not have told us; they are not friendly to us here.'

The King now told them of a dispatch he had received overnight from a messenger that had caught up with him at Lubenham. Montrose had won a staggering victory at Auldearn, he had sent the whole Covenant army flying for fourteen miles, what was left of them.

'Where is Auldearn?' Rupert asked abruptly, leaning his elbow on the table and pushing his eyelids open so that he had a brief and narrow vision of the dark room and the raddled faces that swam behind the yellow flames of the candles, the flecks of light and colour here and there from a red sword-sash or a gleaming buckle out of the shadows, the large tired eyes of the King as they looked up from Montrose's dispatch, shining with new hope in his worn face, the fair pointed beard gleaming with white threads in the candlelight.

He answered his nephew that Auldearn was near the east coast of Scotland, farther north than Inverness.

'Then I do not see what it has to do with us here at this moment.'

But it had everything to do with them. The King in his happy confidence was determined on a battle, and Digby found the usual chivalrous reason that appealed to him. The King's gallant army would not like to retire before an army that was itself retiring from Oxford.

Rupert swore, but under his breath.

But even old Jacob, now Lord Astley, who was commanding the foot, was against him.

'We can take up a good position,' said the little man, shaking his white head, 'on that long hill we passed about two miles from here. I said at the time there could be no better defensive position for an army with that wide sweep of open country before us – good open ground that will give Your Highness' cavalry a chance.'

'The country looks open but the risings and hollows in the ground are deceptive.' But even as he spoke Rupert knew his plan would be set aside, for all the others had chimed in, echoing Astley; there could be no question, they said, of avoiding battle, it would not be practicable, the van of the Parliament armies was too close on their heels. Rupert pleaded for his holding a rearguard action to cover the retreat of the King and the main army, but the whole council was against it. Rupert's cavalry was the most valuable part of the army; it could not be risked as a unit – and a cracking yawn from Maurice seemed to tear up the last shreds of discussion. Rupert had to give in. Since there was to be a battle there was nothing to be done but move out his troops.

He staggered out into the sudden sunshine, blinking against the white freshness of early morning, like an owl among the small damnably sprightly larks that were shouting their heads off up there in the opal-coloured sky.

The men were almost as cheerful, whistling and singing as they got to horse, congratulating each other that they were going to get to grips with the enemy.

Rupert had sent out his scoutmaster to reconnoitre the moment he had heard of his outpost being scuppered – and here he was back again with the surprising intelligence that there was not an enemy in the neighbourhood. Rupert cursed him, and rode off himself with a handful of troopers and dragoons to reconnoitre.

He cantered back towards Naseby, and on some rising ground near the village of Clipston he saw a large force some way off on the side of a hill east of the village. It looked as though all Fairfax's army must be there, but if so the numbers were not as great as they had been told; moreover they were wheeling their front round to the West. They must have just got their scouts' reports of the nearness of the King's army and were now apparently retreating. In that case there was no point in rejoining the main army: he sent a message back to the King to tell what he had discovered and urged him to advance as fast as possible and attack the enemy while at the disadvantage of a full retreat.

He took up his position on some rising ground, and waited for Maurice to join him with the rest of their cavalry. Before they came up, a shepherd lad was brought to him who had news, he said, of Fairfax's army. They had struck their camp at Kislingbury yesterday and set off in pursuit of the King, and just as they had swung into their line of march, a large body of horsemen came galloping up to join them, and a great shout had gone down the ranks – 'Ironsides is come.'

Rupert questioned him himself – 'You are certain that is what they shouted?'

The lad was certain. He and his brother had been there with their sheep, watching the soldiers go off in their red coats. 'Ironsides was the word, "Ironsides is come."'

So his own especial rival and enemy was there after all. A throb of exultation rose in his throat, although he knew that the odds with this augmented force would now be heavily against their side. Once he had challenged Essex to single combat; but now he longed as never before to pit every ounce of strength in his body against his antagonist, with no others to confuse the issue, and prove once for all which was the better man of his hands. This was the man that mattered; kill or capture him, and the fate of England would be decided this day.

So Rupert knew as he sat his horse on the hillside and tried to guess what was the meaning of that flanking movement on the part of the enemy, for he was sure now that Cromwell with his extra strength of horse would not have counselled retreat. As he rode from one side of the low ridge to the other, the reason fell softly on his cheek, cool, refreshing, infuriating as he grasped its significance. It was a westerly breeze, from which they were sheltered on this side of the valley, but it must already be noticeable on the higher ground opposite, where the enemy had taken their stand. Their stand, as he now realized. For they were not retreating, they had shifted their front farther west only so as not to have the wind in their faces and the dust of their enemies' charge in their eyes.

He rode to meet Maurice as he came up with the cavalry, 'Ironsides is come,' he said, 'we will meet him together.'

He could see the whole army moving up on his left from behind him, with Astley's foot regiments in the centre in the old-fashioned solid formation of the Spanish infantry, musketeers on either side flanking the pikemen. These were veteran troops, sturdy and gallant as their 66-year-old little commander. Behind them marched Rupert's equally famous foot regiment of Bluecoats in reserve, with the Royal Life Guards round the King. Protecting the left wing, nearly a mile away, came the cloud of dust that meant the raw and untried Yorkshire cavalry under Sir Marmaduke Langdale.

The whole army amounted to 4,000 horse and 3,500 foot, for the most part experienced troops, as they had good need to be, for the enemy confronting them was 14,000 strong, with 7,000 foot and 6,500 horse. But this they did not yet know, for Fairfax's reserves were hidden behind a ridge. With red as the uniform of the New Model army, and so many of the King's forces wearing red, it was well to have some distinguishing mark between friend and foe, and so every man on the Royalist side wore a beanstalk in his hat.

'Let the watchword be "For God and Queen Mary",' said the King, knowing that was the name his subjects called her, and not even now knowing how little it would inspire the bulk of his followers.

'But let the Prince shout for the Whore of Babylon, for all they cared,' said Rupert's troopers to each other (and so he might as well, in most opinions) as long as it was his voice that was cheering them on.

Astley's centre opened the battle with a volley and then advanced down into the valley against the enemy that outnumbered them by two to one, 'in a very stately and gallant style' as that enemy declared, doing good work with their swords and the butt-ends of their muskets once they got to grips with them.

At the same moment Rupert gave the signal to charge on the right, and line after line of cavalry thundered down into the valley towards the opposite hill. But as they began to breast it the impetus was checked, a breathless pause fell on the cavalry, for the whole of the enemy army were now visible as they advanced over the crest of the hill. There was a check too among the enemy cavalry, and for an instant the two forces stared at each other – Rupert's men at an army far larger than they had expected, the Parliament men at Rupert. But seeing their check, he determined not to give them the advantage of a charge downhill but take them on the crest.

He swung his men on again uphill at the gallop, cheering and yelling, waving their swords, their cloaks streeling behind them in the soft west wind, gay with pride and desperation, the glimpse they had just had of the appalling odds against them being only an added spur. Dust rose from the cornlands in thick clouds, billowing up into the nostrils of the horses, who neighed and sneezed, whinnied and screamed with excitement, the smell of their sweat rising rank in the strong sunshine. Panting and snorting, as fiercely eager as the men who spurred them on, they struggled up on to the crest, plunged against the lines of the enemy, staggered at the shock, then drove on again, broke through their lines, pushed them back upon their own infantry in the centre and threw that too into confusion. The huge force of cavalry before them was crumpling and scattering, numbers were turning and flying headlong, and the pursuit swept after it.

'Is Cromwell there?' Rupert asked again and again. All this year he seemed to be asking this one question, the one thing that mattered. This swift and easy success was troubling him. There must be something wrong with it. It was not so that Cromwell fought at Marston Moor.

Then he heard that the Parliament commander had been wounded and taken prisoner. Cromwell his prisoner? His mouth was dry and choked with dust, the taste of his own blood was in his nostrils from the fury of his charge, but the exultation of that moment rose to his head like wine. It was only for a moment; he knew it could not be true, and it was not. Henry Ireton, the Parliament's new commissary-general, was the commander who had been taken, he caught a glimpse of him with his head bleeding and 'unpotted', having lost his helmet when he got his wound.

Then where was Cromwell? On the other wing of cavalry, leaving this new general to command the strongest position in the field, and show in so short a time how inadequate he was to do it? It did not seem likely, though the prisoners said it. A rumour was rushing down the field that Cromwell had fled back towards Naseby. Frantically Rupert now swept on at the head of his men, who were already making the baggage lines at Naseby their objective. As they rode up towards the ring of wagons the Parliamentary reserve cantered out to meet them, one troop advanced farther than the rest, and its leader shouted anxiously, 'How goes the day?'

Rupert, wearing a red cloak as usual, had been taken for Fairfax, also a very tall man, who happened to be wearing a scarlet cloak that day in uniform with the red coats of his army. No wonder the baggage guard were staggered to see their commander-in-chief, as they supposed, galloping back to the reserves so early in the day. They were still more startled when the tall leader called back, offering them quarter if they would surrender. Their answer was a volley, the answer to that a charge, in spite of all Rupert could do to hold back his men, for he was determined not to waste them in trying to capture the baggage wagons, which were heavily defended, until he knew how the rest of the battle was going, especially as it was now certain that Cromwell must have commanded the other wing of cavalry. He swung round all the men he could rally, but time was as precious as men, and he dared not wait until he could call off all of them.

Soon he was again on the crest of the hill from which he had driven Ireton's horse; he could see all over the valley below, and what he saw dried his throat more fiercely than the dust-choked heat of noon. A desperate struggle was going on down there which might break at any moment into a stampede and a holocaust. Langdale's cavalry were in full flight and halfway back to Clipston; the Parliament right wing of cavalry, having routed them, had evidently broken off pursuit and swung round to attack Astley's infantry in the rear. The Royalist foot were caught in a vice and, forming squares to receive this double attack from Fairfax and Cromwell, were fighting doggedly back to back.

Here and there groups of Royalist infantry had obviously surrendered; through the clouds of dust that obscured yet further that chaos below, Rupert could see what looked like whole regiments throwing down their arms and accepting quarter. But his own crack regiment of Bluecoats on the flank were being trampled down rather than surrender; while Astley's centre fought on indomitably. Whichever side could bring forward at this moment an overwhelming weight of cavalry and crash them down on that squirming struggling mass of men and horses below, would win the day.

There was no such weight of cavalry left on the Royalist side. Langdale's were scattered, and Rupert's exhausted and diminished to half their strength. But there were still the King's reserves of the Royal Horse Guards untouched. The one bare chance now of saving the field would be for the King to launch them down on the Ironsides' rear. This must be what he meant to do, for Rupert could see the Horse Guards moving forward on the hill opposite in steady formation. The one chance was being taken.

He saw that he must at all costs cut his way through Cromwell's Ironsides and reach the King before he changed his mind. He looked round him at his squadrons, all that he had rallied from the charge, and saw how few they were and how tired, shifting their seat in the saddle for greater ease, and mopping their faces. He raised himself up in his stirrups and shouted to them to follow him and make for the King, then spurred his horse into a gallop and came hurtling down once more into the valley, crashed against the Ironsides, was checked, and then began literally to carve his way through.

The sun glared down, the fresh earth was ground to powder, rising in volumes, the valley was a hell of screaming horses and groaning men, the smell of blood and gunpowder stank in his nostrils, the whole frantic field resolved itself into a nightmare wherein he kept seeing the King's pale inexpressive face hovering always just ahead of him, and himself hacking and hewing through a wall of human flesh to meet it. Bruised by the knocks he had got so that every bone in his body seemed broken and his sword arm hung helpless by his side, with his men gasping round him for lack of breath, urging on their sobbing horses, they won their way somehow up the opposite hill.

There they found confusion unutterable and the King nowhere. Men were turning their horses' heads and galloping from the field, despairing shouts rose above the clamour of their flight; whatever news they called, it was of some irremediable disaster, for its effect was as a spur in the side of their horses. At last Rupert heard it – 'the King has left the field' – 'the King has fled —'

It could only have happened a few minutes before he had fought his way to the crest. He might even now retrieve the King and this day from utter disaster. But as he dug his spurs into the Corsair's flanks, forcing him on to this supreme effort, he knew in his heart that it must be hopeless, he could never get this dismayed and broken force of men to rally.

About a quarter of a mile from the edge of the hill he saw the King being borne along in the centre of a group of horsemen, riding as men ride who are panic-stricken, yet he caught them up and drove the Corsair among them, shouting the command to halt. Some did not stay for that, some stayed only to try and force the King on with them. But Charles had pulled in his horse so sharply on seeing his nephew that it was rearing violently. Charles, steadying it with hand and voice, was looking across at Rupert. A babel of voices now added to the confusion; everyone was shouting different things; Rupert did not wait to hear them, he was collecting his men together, with what could be stayed of the demoralizing reserve and remnants of Langdale's, and once more advanced.

But by that time Fairfax and Cromwell between them had broken the last resistance of the Royalist foot. Astley's regiments and Rupert's Bluecoats had fought to the death, as the Whitecoats had done at Marston Moor. The Parliament army was free to re-form its infantry and sound a general advance, flanked on either side by the cavalry that had done such dreadful execution. The shaken Royalist horse saw them coming on at the same moment as they heard Rupert's call to charge as he rode down their ranks.

He was urging them as he had never done, had never had to do before, on the fine-drawn, unearthly note of desperation. They heard his voice ringing high and clear like a trumpet-call; they saw the victorious army that had annihilated their infantry and now was more than ten times the size of their battered remnant, marching in orderly formation against them. They turned, they broke and fled, and there was nothing for the King and his nephews to do but to fly too, on for fourteen miles to Leicester. There they pulled up, and Rupert at last heard what had happened.

Charles had led forward his reserves and rallied some of Langdale's; he had seen Rupert's horsemen struggling across the battle-ground towards him; he had himself headed the remains of Langdale's defeated and demoralized troops and shouted to them to make 'One charge more, gentlemen – one charge more and the day is ours.'

At that very instant someone had seized his bridle and crying, 'Will you go upon your death?' had wheeled the King's horse round, and the whole force of cavalry had turned and galloped off, sweeping the King with them. Rupert wondered that the King had not instantly cut down the traitor with his sword.

The King's main army was destroyed, all his big guns were taken, more than five thousand killed and taken prisoner and five hundred of his best officers among them.

As for the slaughter, that 'dismal carnage' lasted long after the battle; Cromwell's horse alone cut down and killed a thousand of the flying infantry before they tired. Then, refreshed with a prayer of thanksgiving to God and a psalm of victory, the Parliament army turned its attention on the captured women who had followed the King's army, and murdered between three and four hundred of them as being probably Irish and at any rate 'with cruel countenances'. The rest, being certainly their own countrywomen, many of them the wives of officers, were granted mercy in the shape of mutilation; the Parliament men slashed their faces and cut off their noses; their official report recorded it in print with pride as 'just rewards for such wicked queans', concluding the account with – 'thus now indeed did the Lord shew himself as Moses sweetly set him out, triumphing gloriously.'

With his New Model army, trained in the new strict discipline all this spring, making together with the Parliament's veteran troops an army twice the size of their opponents, and on ground that gave him full advantage, it should have been hard for such an experienced general as Cromwell to lose the battle. Yet the rest of his dispatch described the awe with which he watched his enemy 'marching in gallant order' towards his far superior position, 'and we a company of poor ignorant men at a loss how to order our battle ... I could not but smile out to God in praises in assurance of victory ... and God did it.'

CHAPTER FOUR

'... His Majesty hath now no way left to preserve his posterity, kingdom and nobility, but by a treaty. I believe it a more prudent way to retain something than to lose all. ... One comfort will be left; we shall all fall together. When this is, remember I have done my duty.

'Your faithful friend,
Rupert.'

He looked down at this last part of his letter to Richmond. He wrote 'Bristol' at the end of it, and then the date, 'July 28th, 1645.' It struck him that he might well have written it in 1644, nearly a year ago, when he had sat here in this sleepy western city and known in his heart that the King's cause would not recover the blow it had received at Marston Moor.

The King had lost more than his army, guns and officers; he had lost the baggage which contained his private correspondence to his wife, and this was now being printed in London and used as propaganda against him. It was the most powerful weapon of all, although the King himself, who best knew its contents, remained oddly unaware of it; certain that fair-minded people would find in them only the evidence of his constancy to his wife, to the laws and religion, and that 'bees will gather honey where the spider sucks poison'.

But three years of hostilities had wrought a great increase of poison in public opinion; and it was this more than any material losses that made Rupert feel it was essential the war should stop now, before it degenerated into the endless bloodshed, famine and bestiality that had been ruining his own native country ever since he had been born.

He had seen something of the hideous sack of Tirlemont as a boy; physically sickened as he had been by the work of blood-and lust-maddened soldiers, he was more appalled now by the Parliament's own report of the murder and maiming in cold blood of the women who had been 'kept under guard' after Naseby 'until order was given to dispose of them'. Any atrocity would be permissible to 'the profound enemies of God and of His Son', the phrase which was applied now in print to all who followed the King.

What Rupert saw was that the commanders against whom he had been fighting up till this last year had been men recognizably of his own kind – Essex, who had shown him the courtesy to send him back his falconer and hawks which he had captured – Waller, who had written to his enemy, Goring, after his men had been repeatedly beaten up by the Cavalier's raids, 'God's blessing on your heart, you are the jolliest neighbour I have ever met with!' But these were the men whom Cromwell had successfully plotted against, to make room for himself.

Every month that settled Cromwell more firmly in power showed the toughening and hardening of what had been so far a surprisingly gentlemanlike war. Now its ruling spirit, combining business-like efficiency with passionate religion and a shrewd instinct for self-deception, had no use for such amateur qualities as generosity towards ally or enemy. The Parliamentary reports that mentioned after Naseby that Rupert and his men fought 'with such gallantry as few ever saw the like', were not inspired by the Higher Command.

Richmond showed the King Rupert's letter urging a treaty. He was deeply offended. The matter was not to be judged 'as a mere soldier or statesman' but 'as a Christian'. Charles was certain that 'God will not suffer rebels and traitors to prosper, nor this cause to be overthrown'; three things he refused to abandon: his Church, his Crown, and above all his friends.

Digby wagged his great curled head over 'this popular and perilous design' of Rupert's for peace, which, so his most reliable spy had informed him, was 'but the medium to his *real aim*'. What that was did not need to be stated – everyone knew that Rupert's real aim was the Crown of England. 'Surely,' wrote the spy, 'there is no way left for His Majesty to recover, prosper and give life to his discouraged party but by expressing his high dislike and distrust of Prince Rupert.'

Digby was by now sole dictator of the King's will. He had been greatly strengthened by Naseby, as the civilian adviser always is after military defeat. He was in a position to be generous to Rupert, and he longed to be, for that he felt to be his true nature; though some accursed fate had always prevented him showing it to the Prince, and he did not know how to set about it now, for one might as well attempt to show oneself generous to a tiger. He tried to make friends through Will Legge in a letter of inordinate length; he spent hours composing it, determined that here at last his true self should shine out clear of the tangle of personal feelings and prejudices and misunderstandings that had ensnared himself and Rupert from the moment that they had set eyes on each other. Yet the writing of it proved so difficult even to his fluent pen that he longed at least to see Will and convince him of his feelings for the Prince – of at any rate the better half of them.

'I am very unhappy that I cannot speak with you, since the discourse that my heart is full of is too long for a letter, and of a nature not fit for it.'

He stated all the charges against Rupert after Naseby – but only to refute them. A little flattery of Will's own good sense should be enough to make him see where the Prince's had been at fault, so there was some tactful regret that Will had not been there. 'I make no doubt but you would have asked some material questions concerning a reserve, and the placing of the King's person first where it should not have been suddenly involved in the confusion. But really, dear Will, I do not write this as a reflection' (on Rupert) 'for indeed we were all carried on at that time with such a spirit and confidence of victory' – and so on and so forth, dealing praise and blame with an impartial and candid air that must surely convince Will of his sincerity; and ending on a brave hopeful note, half jocular, 'Well, let us look forward; give your Prince good advice as to caution and the value of counsel, and God will yet make him an instrument of much happiness to the King and kingdom, and that being so, I will adore him as much as you love him, though he should hate as much

'Your faithfullest friend and servant,
'GEORGE DIGBY.'

Colonel Legge's answer to this curiously feminine appeal came straight from the shoulder. He told Digby that the Prince's reluctance to his friendship was because of his belief 'that you both say and do things to his prejudice ... not in an open and direct line, but obscurely and obliquely; and this, under your Lordship's pardon, I find your letter ... very full of.' And lest even now the suave Digby should manage to elude his opinion, he added, 'and assure yourself you are not free from great blame towards Prince Rupert; and no man will give you this free language at a cheaper rate than myself, though many discourse of it.'

The effect on Digby was that of a physical blow. He sat stunned, the blood humming in his ears, his eyes glazed so that for an instant he could not read again the words that had done him this injury. All his efforts then had been in vain. Will Legge had taken every one of the points in his letter and turned them against him. It was war then between them. The Prince would never be friends with him; he had instead stolen his staunchest friend from him, and even as he bitterly told himself this, a sudden flash of laughter twisted his lips and sent those florid golden eyebrows curling upwards almost into his hair, as he realized that never had he appreciated 'Honest Will' so well as now when he knew he had lost him.

His spurt of cynicism almost revived him, but then his cleared eyes fell again on the brutal answer to the letter that had been so full of generous impulse, of the wish to be friends and fight by the side of this giant, instead of having to join with the little people who were too petty and clever to understand him.

A wave of self-pity welled up in him; his eyes, that had been cold and mocking this instant, were now brilliant with tears as he thought how those two great clumsy soldiers had seen nothing but ill in his letter, felt nothing for him but the contempt of the soldier for the civilian. Very well then. They should have what they saw.

The war throughout England receded, became remote and unreal, no more than a background to this agonizing, this stimulating, this intriguing, exasperating, internecine personal strife. He would hate Rupert to the death; he would ruin him, he swore it – and the word was taken up and carried to the Prince.

Digby was now assuring Jermyn in Paris that he had done everything he could to make up his quarrel with the Prince but in vain, and that in spite of it 'nothing shall provoke me to disserve Prince Rupert *whilst he is judged capable to serve the King.*'

It was an odd proviso; the person whose judgement would most influence the King as to his servants' capability was Digby himself; Rupert therefore would not have to wait long for Digby's 'disservice', and this he knew. He had heard rumours since last March of a plot to ruin him with the King. He wished he could spare but one day to go and clear it up, but he could not.

*   *   *

Montrose had just beaten all the combined armies of the Scots Covenanters at Kilsyth. He had sent the leaders flying into England and Ireland; and the victory over the thousands of routed infantry had been passionately commemorated by a breekless Highlander – 'Man, it was a grand day. At ilka stroke of my sword I slit an ell o' breeks.'

Montrose was now undisputed master of Scotland, and was marching to meet the King on the Border. Digby had been promising him cavalry since April; since the war in England had been so disastrous he had suddenly begun to encourage the King's yearning to join the great leader himself in Scotland. Digby had vehemently opposed the northern plan while Rupert was urging it; but now, at the last moment, he belatedly saw that it had points, or, as he expressed it in his emotional way, 'all this work of Montrose is above what can be attributed to mankind'. So he, and therefore the King, swung round to the North, marching first on Leslie's Scottish contingent who were besieging Hereford. But Leslie had heard the news of Kilsyth, thrown up the siege of Hereford, and was hurrying north to the relief of Argyll.

Charles reached Doncaster and was told that three thousand Yorkshiremen would join him the next day. But he did not wait for them. He heard that Leslie and his cavalry were at Rotherham. His own armies stood in the way of Leslie's path to Scotland; he had a good chance, as Leslie himself admitted later, to defeat him utterly. But Digby was shying like a frightened horse at the responsibility.

Once again Charles turned back. The Yorkshiremen, who had marched to their rendezvous with the King's troops, were left unsupported to be butchered by the enemy. And Leslie, finding the road to Scotland left open for him, went on with six thousand fresh cavalry to the Border, to where Montrose, unsuspecting, was waiting for the King.

* * *

Rupert rode out from Bristol to raise recruits in Wales and to try to win the wild 'Clubmen' of Dorset and Somerset to fight for the King instead of their own lone hand.

Their banner was a torn sheet, scrawled with their slogan:

> *'If you take our cattle*
> *We will give you battle.'*

They summoned their bands together with their swineherd horns, blown at night over the common lands that still covered most of the face of the English country – woods or heaths where men could graze their herds, free, until these armies had come to take toll of them. Now they demanded plunder in recompense, and did a good deal of damage in their sudden night raids with clubs and forks and burning torches, threatening to sack the towns.

The 'King's servants' to them meant Goring's utterly undisciplined troopers, who carried off their cattle, trampled their crops and raped their women. The steady power of money was turning the rebel forces into those of law and order and respectability. Ragged, starving, licentious Cavaliers were now as much a stock joke as canting, snuffling Roundheads.

Rupert had got to know the English peasants pretty well in this last year, a great deal better than did most of the English commanders, and he knew how profoundly indifferent the bulk of them were to the course of the war, as long as it avoided their own bit of land. Loyalty to them meant loyalty to their county, not their country. Poor Tom Phelps of Bristol had let himself be crushed to death in the last reign by the 'peine forte et dure' of the old statute because when tried for some small offence he insisted on saying his trial was by 'God and Somersetshire' instead of by 'God and his country'.

Let the war only be over and done with, they said, and they would not care who won – and what difference could it make anyway, for they were bound to put the King back on his throne in the long run, there was nobody else who was setting up to be King instead of him, and no one had ever heard of England without a King. This was not the stuff to make recruits. For the most part, all Rupert could do was to prevent their doing damage to his troops and to the nearest towns.

He rode out at night over the rolling Dorset hills that lay grey and misty and infinitely ancient under the moon. The primaeval figure of the naked giant and his club, carved out for hundreds of feet of the chalky soil on the hillside outside Cerne Abbas, relic of magic beliefs too old for anyone now to know what it had once meant, stood to him for a symbol of these Clubmen, gathering themselves together to defend their soil, naked of weapons and the arts of war, powerful simply because they were primaeval. To them England meant their own patch of ground, not to be sullied nor robbed by foreigners; and to them foreigners meant all those from other counties who did not speak and understand their rough dialect, so that Rupert with his quick ear and training in many languages was far less 'foreign' than a Londoner.

These deep valleys held memories dead elsewhere, as a curved shell holds the sound of the sea. The present Civil War would soon get confused with the Wars of the Roses; Queen Margaret had stayed at Cerne Castle two hundred years ago, or, so the villagers said, as much as forty year ago or more; and that was a thing they remembered far more clearly than that Queen Mary had fled last year to France. He saw again something of the unchanging English country scene that had been painted on the background of his first visit, delighting him with its vivid colours. He had thought it gone for ever, but it was still here, independent of politics and fashion. Plays might go out and prayers come in, but Dorset thought little about either.

With 'forty year or more' as the full gamut of antiquity, time here could not be measured, for the same things were done year after year as in the time of their fathers and their fathers before them; and though mad parsons in taller hats than heretofore might get up and tell them to break up the market cross and the maypole that had stood there since the oldest man's oldest relative could remember, still folk went on crossing themselves when a witch hare crossed their path, and children went on dancing in a ring though there was no pole in the middle. That the maypole was older than the cross, nobody knew nor cared – nor that when the children cried, 'We all fall down,' and flung themselves on the ground in the middle of their round game, they were performing an act of worship infinitely older than the sign of the cross.

But they could share the opinion of learned old lawyer Selden up in London who, though he stood for Parliament, observed that 'it never was a merry world since the fairies left dancing and the parson left conjuring'.

Time here could not be measured; so it slipped and merged. Queen Margaret of yesterday, Queen Mary of today, both fleeing from their rebellious subjects, reigned at only a short distance in their minds; it would take only a year or two more for that gigantic god of forgotten religion to stride forward out of the dark backward and abysm of time, and be taken for the patron saint of the Clubmen, set up by some of them on the hillside.

CHAPTER FIVE

THE COMBINED armies of Fairfax and Cromwell had marched to besiege Bristol.

The war for Rupert had narrowed to a single fortressed town, the besieging armies beyond its walls, the plague that was creeping on the bodies of rats through the houses of its sullenly hostile citizens. The burying bells of the twenty churches of Bristol and Bedminster were tolling night and day, striking a never-ceasing terror of the sickness into all hearts. The first order Rupert gave was to command their silence.

The plague had crept to Worcester also, and Maurice lay sick of it. Once again his life was despaired of by those about him; but Rupert did not despair – would not despair was this time nearer the mark. He dared not think of Maurice, nor of Carl. Brotherly love, brotherly hate, they bore an equal torture for his driven spirit.

It was a relief to see to the thousand and one details the siege demanded – to have the cattle swept in from the outlying country into the marsh near the city; to order beer to be brewed and stored; to collect supplies of grain and two thousand measures of corn from Wales to distribute among the poorer citizens – there were 12,500 of them in all, and if famine were added to plague, the Parliament armies would have little left for them to do.

The army was short of ammunition; he started a factory for it and kept it working in relays day and night. He longed to work out some of his experiments in it. He had thought out a method of making hail shot; and then there were these clumsy locks to firearms, these uncertain pistols that were always missing fire as he had found to his advantage again and again. He had toyed with the notion of a pistol made to fire shots in quick succession with a revolving barrel – but it was no use to think of that now, the war would not wait while he improved its weapons, the factory had to stick to its business of making bullets; and he had to try and make soldiers in a few days out of raw recruits from Wales.

He had none of the other reinforcements he had expected. His promise to the King to hold the city, made when he had counted on three times the number of his troops, began to look hollow.

Fairfax had reconnoitred the city and posted troops all round it; his generals had taken Bath, and settled a line of posts to the English Channel. Cromwell had driven Goring's troopers out of Taunton, his Ironsides chasing them down the long street at Langport, with flames arching over their heads from the burning houses on either side, and had joined forces with Fairfax. His new son-in-law Henry Ireton, who had found time to marry Bridget Cromwell since Naseby ('Their first child will be a cannon ball, their second a Bible,' said Goring), was stabling his horses in Bedminster Church.

The ring of their enemies narrowed closer and closer round the city in spite of all the sallies that Rupert's horse made to interrupt them. They dashed out of Prior's Hill fort down on to the besieging lines, a handful against an army, and in each case were driven back with the loss of their leader.

Fairfax shifted his quarters from the comfort of Stoke House to a poor farmhouse nearer the scene of action – 'the better the officer, the poorer the lodging,' said Rupert approvingly – 'and the tighter the siege,' growled his colonels.

Not a pailful of milk nor a basket of eggs could be got into the city now, and Fairfax, from the field behind his farmhouse, kept up a bombardment on Prior's Hill fort. It was plain he recognized this as the key to the city – once it were taken, Bristol must surrender. A battleship, the *Tenth Whelp*, commanded by Captain Boon, came flying up the Severn from before five Parliament ships that had entered Kingsroad. They were being surrounded by sea as well as land, and now the enemy were making a bridge across the Avon to join their two forces.

But their most formidable attacks were among the hearts of the citizens. Letters to the leading business men, signed and sealed by Fairfax and Cromwell, were discovered and brought in to Rupert, promising all the inhabitants of Bristol 'the enjoyment of their lives, liberties and estates, as freely as in former times ... notwithstanding any past acts of hostility,' if they would help to deliver up the city.

Rupert was continually in the great fort to keep guard against a surprise. The wall of the city would never stand any strong attack; but there was just a hope that they might beat off the first attempt so vigorously as to disguise its weakness from the enemy, and discourage them enough to draw off from the siege.

'It's our one chance,' said Rupert.

'A mighty thin one, sir,' his colonels told him, and small blame to them, for he himself had stormed this same city and taken it in three days, when it had been manned with a force more than twice as strong as that which now defended it, and with the bulk of the town in sympathy with it.

A messenger was brought in from Sir Thomas Fairfax with a personal letter to the Prince. It opened in 'as plain language as the business requires' (a direct way to Rupert's respect) with a summons to surrender the city to the Parliament, but continued as in a private letter to discuss the situation with him, as one well-wisher to England with another.

Never had the curious English quality of 'amateurishness' presented itself so attractively to Rupert. This country gentleman, his enemy, could write to him as to one who must really be aiming at the same end as himself.

'Sir, the Crown of England is and will be where it ought to be, we fight to maintain it there.' The King had been divided from his people by his division from Parliament; all that they fought for was to bring him back to that council and end these miserable dissensions, without further bloodshed and bitterness to make the gulf unbridgeable. 'Sir, if God makes this clear to you as He has to us, I doubt not but He will give you a heart to deliver this place.'

And so, with simple dignity, Fairfax begged the Prince in consideration of his royal birth and relation to the Crown of England, his honour and courage, to spare 'this so great, so famous and ancient city and so full of people' from the 'ruin and extremity of war', and reminded him that the Parliament and people of England had been the truest friends his own family had had in the world.

What Rupert most respected in the letter was its omissions. Fairfax had spoken of Rupert's obligations to the English Parliament and people; he did not mention those that the Prince owed to Fairfax's own family. Yet two of the Fairfaxes had fallen in that disastrous campaign at Vlotho, fighting for the Palatines; and Rupert had noticed their portraits at Denton, the Fairfax family seat, which had been on his line of march towards Marston Moor, and had seen to it that the place was spared from any injury out of gratitude – a gratitude that now included Sir Thomas Fairfax, who had not reminded him of this.

But his only answer to Fairfax was to ask leave to send a messenger to the King to know his pleasure.

Fairfax objected that this was a mere pretext to spin out time; he showed he would not be trifled with, and a week after he had sent that deeply felt and carefully reasoned appeal, he made a sudden night attack on the city, so that in the darkness the Royalists would not be able to turn their big guns on the storming parties.

It was a general assault. At two o'clock in the morning four guns blared out their signal, and the armies that stretched for seven miles round Bristol hurled themselves at the same instant against the city. Rupert was ready for them; his men drove them back with heavy losses on the south and south-east sides of the city; it looked as though his 'mighty thin chance' might yet be possible. There was little firing in the darkness; the thudding of the enemy's horse trotting up the old Roman causeway could be clearly heard, and all round the city, in an encircling storm, the crashing thunder of their battle-cry, 'David! David!'

'That's an appropriate shout for an army ten times our number!' snarled Mr Alderman Taylor, now a proud colonel since he had so distinguished himself at the storming of his city just two years ago.

Rupert smiled grimly.

'They're to have a better one, "The Lord of Hosts," when they've carried the outer line, so the prisoners say.'

'A truer one! Their hosts must be pouring in all over the marshlands and all the way up from Clifton Hill and Redland. Thank the Lord for the butchers of Redcliff! They've built their wall high and their ditch deep.'

'Listen there – where's that cry coming from?'

'St Philip's marsh, sir.'

'It's different, do you hear? It's a longer one.'

'It's "the Lord of Hosts"!' cried Taylor.

Men came running to say that the enemy were over the marsh, they were sweeping the line from the Avon to the Frome.

'May I go and see what they're doing at Stokes-Croft Gate, sir?' demanded Taylor.

'Stay here, man. Haven't you had your fill of fighting?'

But the big elderly merchant was hopping in unbearable excitement.

Messages came back; sconce, half-moon and redoubt had been carried by the enemy – now there was hot fighting round Lawford's Gate – then that too was captured with its twenty-two guns – and now their horse were galloping in by the Batch and the Bull-ring.

The defenders were pressed back, fighting every inch of the way until overwhelmed by the oncoming hordes and driven into the streets. They got no help there, and the storming party that pursued them got no hindrance from the townsfolk, who were many of them cheering them on. Now within the city, all through the ward of St Philip and Jacob, Back Avon Street to Wade Street, and right up to the castle walls came that yell of triumph, 'The Lord of Hosts! The Lord of Hosts!' Its message was spreading like wildfire – the enemy had carried the line, were in the city.

Then the news came back that Taylor had fallen while leading a charge of horse at Stokes-Croft Gate. 'So he went after all,' said Rupert, who had not noticed his departure in the press.

Well, he had cheated death more than once, at an age when many men are content merely to be old.

By that hairbreadth escape after the Bristol plot he had added two and a half years to his life, a friendship with Prince Rupert which gave him much proud and pleasant excitement, and a burning triumph when that Prince had seized Bristol from the hated Fiennes. And he had proved himself a gallant soldier. Now his brief respite was over; death had come upon him, not coldly and hideously in cruel execution or the stifling river mud, but, as he had prayed, in hot fight, defending his native city.

Still the forts held out, that on Prior's Hill for several hours after the line had been carried. But the gate at the foot of the hill was blown open with a petard, the way was cleared for Captain Ireton's horse to charge in, and more and more swept into the assault. The defenders fought on, refusing to surrender, until at last the few survivors ran for shelter into the rooms of the fort, but the attackers hunted them out like rats and finished them off, all but two, whose lives the officers ordered to be spared as testimony to their mercy.

As the autumn daylight began to break over the river mists, Fairfax and Cromwell rode up to the captured fort, and came out on top of it to see the good work.

'All this is none other than the work of God; he must be a very atheist that does not acknowledge it.'

As Cromwell spoke, the castle guns opened on them, and a shot hit the parapet within two feet of them, but without injuring either. That was so plainly God's work that it was unnecessary to comment on it; but lest they should tempt Providence too far, they went inside the fort. Certainly they had been well advised to make the attack in the middle of a thick night, for with those guns playing on them the loss would have been terrible.

'What can the young Plunderer Blunderer Cumberer Duke of Cumberland do now?' demanded Cromwell with his great laugh, 'the Earl of Holdernesse finds he holds less than he thought – aha, Henry, did you hear that one?' and he swung round as Captain Ireton came in; but his tone changed to one of sudden concern and tenderness as he exclaimed, 'What is the matter, man? Are you wounded?'

Captain Ireton's arm was tied up in a hastily improvised sling; very white and in obvious pain he admitted to a bullet in it. He had come to report that the town was on fire in at least three places; the whole city, being mainly built of wood, might be utterly destroyed if it went on.

'This is Rupert's accursed work!' cried Cromwell.

'And a hopeful sign,' said Fairfax.

The hot grey eyes of the Lieutenant-General rolled round in furious question on this superior officer, then flashed to his meaning.

'They hope to force us to high terms for themselves in surrender? Then they'll not gain them. Let them burn in their own flames now, as they shall burn hereafter!'

'It is scarcely worth the price of the second city in England, General; and a city in the main for the Parliament. All the countryside have been coming in to us.'

'Aye, since we're winning.'

But except in a moment's passion Cromwell was far too practical a soldier to care for the motives of his partisans. The results were what mattered.

*   *   *

Rupert was holding a council of war.

It was Lord Hawley, heavy-browed, insistent, who stated the case in short sentences, the grimmer for being so careful not to overstate it.

'The enemy are in the town. They've made lodgements within the curtain walls, they hold both line and fort, worst of all their infantry holds the ground between the castle and those of our forts that still hold out, so that we're cut off from each other. We can do nothing.'

Said Colonel Russell, scratching the stubble on his chin, for none had shaved this morning, and all their eyes were lined and blackened with lack of sleep and anxious strain, 'We were undermanned from the start. Fifteen hundred was all we could draw upon the line to defend a stretch of five miles.'

Said Lord Lumley, 'We can't hold the town with the town against us.'

They all drove in on that.

'My lord's in the right. The plague is rotting both our men and the town, they can't hold out against it – it's destroying body and spirit.'

'The town don't care a curse as long as Bristol trade and Bristol lives and property are safe.'

411

'Who's to blame 'em? It made me sick to see those houses burn.'

Their round of fire swung from the present scene to the outer world.

Said Sir Mathew Appleyard, 'We've had no word from Goring, though he's not far away. Not that it makes any odds, for there's not an army left in England that can relieve us. If there is, we've had no word from 'em; nothing from the forces round the King, nothing from the Prince of Wales.'

Said General Tillier, 'What odds what we hear? If the King were to draw together every man he has left and come to our relief, yet the enemy can spare twelve thousand men against him after blocking up the castle and the fort.'

Said Lieutenant-Colonel Osborne, 'What need of twelve thousand or even twelve hundred? They hold all the passes, they have barricaded all the ways. A very small force of theirs would prevent the advance of a great army. But the King does not intend any such advance. General Poyntz has assured us of that.'

Said Colonel Fox, on a sudden high note among all those heavy voices, disturbing as the first shriek of the gale wind that breaks the growl of the thunder, 'We are in a death-trap.'

Rustled, uneasy, the officers looked at each other's faces, to see their own despair reflected. In echo to that last shrill tone came Sir Walter Vavasour's correct official voice stating their ruin.

'The whole of England is shrinking to a death-trap. Every day there's another town surrendered. Any of our soldiers caught outside a town are slaughtered like beasts.'

Lord Hawley's hammer-tones drove the last nail into the coffin. 'The game is up. We must face it.'

Rupert faced it. The question was, as he well knew, could the King ever face it? No use to think of that. He himself was here now in Bristol on this tenth day of September 1645, with the enemy inside the city, and he would have to make up his mind within this half hour what he would do next. He looked round him on that ring of despondent and grimy faces that had kept up this steady battery of destructive criticism, but had offered no one active suggestion.

'There are three things we can do,' he said.

'Three? There's not one damned thing!' exclaimed Hawley explosively, but none of the others heeded him; they were

412

watching the drawn face of the young man who sat at the head of the table. It lightened for a moment; not with hope, but with the gay desperation of the gladiator who salutes his last adventure.

'The castle can be held a good while yet. We could leave just enough men to keep it, then lead out the cavalry and cut our way through Fairfax's army. What do you say to that?'

'Neither safe nor honourable to the infantry,' said Hawley, and this time the others answered with him, agreeing that it was an unfair division of their forces and chances.

'Very well,' said the Prince, 'the second choice is this – that I should take over the defence of the castle and fort myself.'

Once again there was a chorus of dissent. There was not enough water to supply the castle for more than a few days, and even that was foul. It was hopeless both within the castle and without, for it would mean abandoning all the main part of the garrison as well as the whole town to an enemy enraged by this continued resistance. Only a small portion of the cavalry could be held in the castle; the rest would be slaughtered. Rupert felt more strongly than anyone there that he could not leave his eight hundred horse, the last remnant now with him of that magnificent cavalry that he had created, to be butchered.

'We have then,' he said, 'the third and last alternative, to surrender on honourable terms.'

'There *is* no alternative to that,' they said.

So Rupert drew up the terms: that he and his officers and men should march out of the city with all the honours of war, and with a convoy provided for them, to any garrison of the King's that the Prince should choose within fifty miles of Bristol, and eight days allowed for their march there, with free quarters by the way; that all sick and wounded soldiers left behind should be protected until their recovery, and then be given safe conducts to go to His Majesty —

'Zounds, isn't it they who are the conquerors?' exclaimed Lord Lumley, amazed at such cool assumptions. Rupert paid no attention to the interruption, but continued to lay down his terms, safeguarding the citizens of Bristol and its suburbs from any plunder or violence.

'But they'll never grant such terms!' broke out Hawley.

'Then they shall watch the city go up in smoke,' replied Rupert.

'And us with it, sir?'

413

'No, by God, we'll sell our lives dearer than that. We'll ride out and meet 'em once more first!'

'Well might they call him Phaeton,' muttered Hawley to his neighbour, 'he'll never rest until he's burned the world!'

Aloud he said, 'Your Highness, consider, we are Englishmen and this is an English city, the second in the kingdom.'

'Gentlemen, I am considering it. And I am confident that the Generals Fairfax and Cromwell will also consider it – and grant our terms.'

CHAPTER SIX

'HAVE YOU polished that back-and-breast till you see every pock-mark on your ugly face in it?'

'Yessir.'

'Have you brushed those boots till they're as soft as a fawn's belly?'

'Yessir.'

'Is there no loose thread in the silver lace?'

'Nosir.'

'Nor a hair left on my chin?'

'Nosir.'

'Then I'll begin to dress.'

'As it might be for your wedding,' muttered the old soldier, thinking himself inaudible as he stooped to pick up the breastplate he had been so vigorously polishing; but Rupert's quick ear caught the words.

'You're wrong, Tom. I dress more carefully as a defeated foe than ever I would as a bridegroom.'

He put on his scarlet doublet, his collar and cuffs of silver lace, then his breastplate of bright steel, tied his scarlet sash laced with silver across it, then swung his famous scarlet cloak across his shoulders. There should be nothing shabby nor defeated-looking about him when he rode out this morning to give up Bristol to the victorious generals, Fairfax and Cromwell. The Corsair, still a magnificent beast, beautifully groomed by Tom Draycott, showed less sign of privation than did most of the lean and wretched-looking horses now in his cavalry. The 'Beggarman's Line' was graven deep into their thin flanks; their drooping necks and ragged coats showed the defeat of their long-dragged-out campaign as plainly as the haggard and despairing faces of their riders. They rode out for the most part before him, for he kept himself near the rear to safeguard their retreat. So he waited while the column of horse and foot and the few baggage wagons, not more than eight, filed out before him from the fort on to the wide green beyond the castle where the troops of their conquerors were drawn up to see them go.

As the Ironsides and the cavalry of the New Model army, sleek and well-fed and well-equipped, secure in the happy discipline that comes from regular pay and food, looked upon Rupert's Gay Riders, once so terrible, now so ragged and wretched, with such poor equipment and half-starved horses, a gust of derisive laughter blew up from them against the cavalry that they had superseded. It was at once suppressed by their commanders; damped down to a furtive sniggering, harder to bear than that hearty scorn had been.

Rupert had heard it as he came out of the fort, as lean as any of his broken-down troopers, but shining in scarlet and silver. He sat very straight and tall in the saddle, his fierce hawk's eyes gazing down under their heavy lids on to the little group of Parliament officers. They were waiting at the gates of the fort to escort him to General Fairfax. Colonel Hammond's regiment of foot were standing ready to receive the keys of the fort and march in.

Lieutenant-General Cromwell was at the head of the group of mounted officers, his helmet under his arm. Rupert swept off his plumed hat in a low bow; he lifted his head again; 'So you've won,' he said to himself, looking at the Lieutenant-General to see how he had done it, while his lips moved, making polite sounds that he himself did not hear, his brain was crowding so thick with the things that were not said.

Here at last he was seeing his rival.

He saw a troubled and determined face, thick nose, eyes passionate, swift, yet brooding, a bitterly repressed mouth. It was the face of a rugged neurotic, of enormous and unhappy power, the face of one who would always have to drug his soul with action to keep it from melancholia. Rupert's mind found no formula in words for what he saw, but he remembered the mighty and writhing figure of the father in the Laocoon – here, as in the statue, was a strong man, tortured and bound.

Words had to be formed with the top of his mind; his conquerors should not find him ungracious and sullen, a soldier who could not take his beating. As they came out upon the green, he complimented Cromwell on the splendid appearance of his Ironsides – 'for their sterner qualities I bore good witness at Naseby and Marston Moor. You have made the English cavalry the finest in Europe.'

His mind shot back to the five hundred untrained horse at Nottingham that had started his career as an English cavalry leader, and the splendid fighting body, nearly four thousand strong, they had become in six weeks' time when he led them to their first victory. ('Now if the fellow has the magnanimity of a louse, he'll admit we've made it that together, and that he got the hang of it from me.')

Then he remembered that Cromwell, who belittled his allies, was unlikely to praise his enemy, and smiled that he should have wished for it. Praise for praise, it was a cheap and easy exchange. His commerce with Cromwell went deeper than that. Here was a fine soldier, no genius nor originator in war, but a magnificent organizer, who had worked up his notions with his superior resources until he made a finished job of it. Those scarlet-coated soldiers on the green were the first English regular army; their work would be something far beyond what Rupert had begun and Cromwell carried on.

'We are both to be congratulated on our material,' he said, drawing rein to scan appraisingly the ranks of his enemies, as though he were a general come to review their troops, 'the English soldier is the best of any!'

A flash illumined the heavy face beside him. 'Your Highness does well to say so. God reveals Himself as His manner is, first to His Englishmen.' Remembering that the Prince was half a foreigner, the Lieutenant-General added hastily, '– at least that is what my friend Mr Milton says, but he is a poet —'

'And therefore lies? No, General, we are both of us sufficiently English to agree with him – ('And *that's* touched you up, Mr Williams from Wales.' He must go on quickly —)

'– But did you say Mr Milton, a poet? Did he not write a pretty masque some years ago – my lord Bridgewater's sons and daughter had been acting in it when I was here on my last visit, and spouted speeches a mile long whenever one spoke to them – it was called by some outlandish classic name, and I'm no scholar' – with a snap of his fingers he added, 'I have it – "Comus" – that was it!'

'A youthful folly, sir. He has long since given up the writing of verse.'

'A loss to England.'

'No, Your Highness, a gain. He writes political pamphlets and I am thinking of getting him some Government post as secretary.'

'Well, if the man prefers to be a politician, he's no poet, so it's no loss.' (No poet? The man who wrote

> 'Sabrina fair
> Listen where thou art sitting
> Under the glassy cool translucent wave'?)

Echoes were haunting him whichever way he turned, so that this present moment, and its huge ceremony of his conquerors' serried ranks staring upon him from every side, all seemed unreal. It could not be true, it could not be that this tough thick man with the tormented mouth now riding beside him had succeeded, while he had failed (but it is true, it is true, never think it that you will wake up).

Here was General Fairfax advancing to meet him. More bows, more sweeping of hats, more stately compliments, more easy and unforced than those of the Lieutenant-General, though sober, as became a Puritan officer. Sir Thomas Fairfax was carefully and beautifully dressed, the plain collar of exquisite sheer linen, worn over his breastplate, tied with little white cords, his fine hands as well kept as a Court lady's, his face smooth-shaven up to a thin curve of moustache and a mere point of beard, his manner gentle and sympathetically grave. He was nearly as tall as Rupert, who had been mistaken for him by Fairfax's own side at Naseby, where Fairfax had fought on gallantly after his helmet had been struck off, exposing that high bare head to the marksman.

There was more in common between them than their inches and a pair of scarlet cloaks. Without any obvious attempt at condolence he contrived to let Rupert know in his first few words how all England would realize the impossibility of his holding Bristol so insufficiently manned. He would make it his business that no derogatory pamphlet should be printed on the matter, in as far as he could control that uncontrollable and most unmilitary weapon – 'it is one of the new ways, like gunpowder, which spread so fast we cannot yet see what power they may attain'.

He was talking much, not to display himself, but to cover any sadness or embarrassment his defeated enemy might be feeling, and even as he talked his eyes sought Rupert's as if in apology, saying to him, 'You understand – these words are poor things, but we must juggle with them, lest our silence say too much.'

Here was an English gentleman; the other, the Lieutenant-General, was a medley, might even be a disaster, for all his infinitely greater force, so Rupert thought; but consoled himself that thank Heaven Fairfax and his like would always be at hand to exercise a restraining hand on him.

Fairfax and Cromwell asked him where he wished to go. He told them Oxford, and asked if he might borrow enough muskets for his infantry to protect themselves from the Club-men on their way, 'for as you must have noticed we are lament-ably short of arms. We will deliver them up to your convoy at parting.'

His trust that they would take his word for it made Fairfax feel in his turn that here was a man of his own kind; they looked at each other, liking each other. They might easily have fought together as Rupert had done with Fairfax's two uncles at Vlotho, instead of on opposite sides.

'I did not answer your letter,' said Rupert with something of his old abruptness, 'it was not the time. Some day I hope it may be.'

Fairfax was on his left, giving the Prince the right side out of courtesy, and riding between him and Cromwell. The two Generals were escorting him out of Bristol with their Colonels close behind; they rode up the sudden hill that shoots up above the green, and for two miles with him over Durdham Downs.

The polite ceremonial was broken into by crowds of people from the countryside, running to see the downfall of the Stranger Prince, the foreign wizard and robber who had brought all the misery of this war upon them. There he was riding tall and proud and stately as a conqueror on his splendid horse, and his conquerors bowing to him and paying him all the respect in the world – that was the way of the world, the great ones had it all their own way and the wicked never got their deserts.

'Give him no quarter! Give him no quarter!' they shrieked, trying to break through the ranks of the soldiers, but they were pushed back with pikes and swords; and the Prince rode on, with not a muscle of his face stirring, not even a glance in their direction.

The grey old city dropped away behind him, the river at low

tide between its slimy mud banks; beyond it the wooded valley clove a deep violet shadow among the surrounding forest. There the September sunshine shimmered in a soft haze, lighting up golden beeches and birch trees among the rusty green.

Once among woods like these he had wished that he might fall from his horse and break his neck so that he might leave his bones in England. With a passion far deeper than that boyish impulse of despair, he wished it now. England had greeted him then with cheers and praise, welcoming the fine upstanding young lad whose mother had been her pride. Now he was a hated foreigner, soon no doubt to be an outcast.

He did this and he said that, now to Fairfax, now to Cromwell, now turning in courtesy to include Colonel Butler or Colonel Harrison or Colonel Pride, who had been a drayman before he was a colonel and a foundling before he was a drayman, but the Prince did not know that, and made an unlucky compliment when he told him he had well earned his name in last night's attack on Prior's Hill. All that he did and said and saw, blue-shadowed woods, wide downs, the far hills of Wales, all seemed final and inevitable as if in farewell – as indeed it might well be, now that the most important city in the kingdom next to London was lost, and even the King would now see that the war was lost.

*   *   *

He said goodbye to them on Durdham Downs, yet they lingered as if in regret, asking questions as to the way he intended to take. It would lie across some of the Cotswold country, perhaps Chipping Campden – 'I know it,' broke in Rupert. 'I went there for the Cotswold games on Dover's Hill. But that's all past now, and Dover's dead,' he added quickly, remembering that they had been suppressed by the Puritans.

Now for the last time he looked at Cromwell, wondering what had come over the spirit of England, for this man was as English as Captain Dover had been, none the less for his mixed descent.

It was the alien strain of the rigid humourless Hebrew that he was helping to enforce on the mind of England; it would soon make all the land unrecognizable from that bright Whitsun scene on Cotswold, when thousands had disported themselves over the sunny plain as carelessly as mayflies over a stream, united by the Captain's simple passion for sport. A religious

419

passion it might well be called, since it had brought so many together in happy harmony that were now miserably divided against each other.

'When did Your Highness see them?' Fairfax was asking.

'It must have been the last time they were held, for it was in '37, when I was planning to go to Madagascar.'

'And I to America,' said Cromwell.

'We might both have done better to emigrate,' said Rupert.

Then, as he thanked them for their courtesy, he told Fairfax with an unexpected smile that lit his face with a sudden boyish charm, 'I have never received such satisfaction in such unhappiness; I hope it may some day be in my power to give the same to you.'

The last gallant compliment was paid, the last friendly farewell, the last sweeping bow performed; the horses' heads were turned, and the Prince rode on his way to Oxford, while his enemies turned back to Bristol, amazed to find how much they liked and respected the Bloody Robber, the Necromancer, the Mad Prince, Rupert the Devil. The Colonels Butler and Harrison were as eager in his praise and defence as if he were their dearest friend – they agreed that they had all been much mistaken about His Highness, it was an honour to have waited upon him – then, lest General Cromwell should think this a mere slavish regard for rank, 'Seriously, I am glad I had the happiness to see him.'

'– such satisfaction in such unhappiness —' the melancholy charm of the courtesy was still echoing in Fairfax's ears. It was the only time that that terse and forthright young man had ever shown a resemblance to his uncle, and Fairfax, not knowing its rarity, now commented on the likeness to Cromwell, who did not reply.

Rupert, as he rode towards Oxford, did not repay this last courtesy of Fairfax by thinking of the man who might have been his friend. His head was still too full of Fairfax's burly companion, of the turgid gloom, for all his air of the hearty soldier, that lurked in the depths of his swift and resolute eyes. Nothing could have been more unlike the exquisite yet strangely insensitive face of Charles, but the one had invoked the other; he saw his uncle standing once again as when he had first seen him, dazzled by his boyhood's eager vision of him in the centre of his gracious and splendid Court, devoted to the arts and a lovely way of living. An unreal calm had shone about it like the clear light before a storm. Even now it was not dispersed; the King saw all things in a false light, the enchanted calm of his bland optimism that was always brightest before the worst happened to him.

A piece of gossip about Cromwell's childhood (the kind that crops up round any growing greatness) had come into Rupert's mind; and now he saw, behind that circle of light, the shadow that lurked in Cromwell's eyes leaping to giant stature, parting the bed curtains of a small frightened boy who had woken shrieking from a nightmare.

Oliver and his strange visitor, Charles and the blood-soaked pall that darkened his cradle at Dunfermline – what foreshadowing doom was it that had haunted the infancy of both these men?

CHAPTER SEVEN

I T I S a mistake to see too clearly even those one knows best. No sooner had Rupert seen with the blinding clarity of a vision that nothing could ruffle King Charles' composure, than it was shattered, for the first time in his life, and by a storm against Rupert himself.

Charles loved him as he had loved no man since Buckingham. But Rupert himself had torn his love from him; Rupert, whom he trusted as his own soul, had betrayed him. He had given up the city he had sworn to defend, had made his own terms with the enemy, promised to plead their cause with their outraged sovereign, made such friends with them in fact that they were all busying themselves on his behalf, writing to the newsletters that 'no man can blame him', and 'On my word he could not have held it unless it had been better manned.' Such advocacy only proved his guilt.

'So do some eight thousand gold coins paid out by Parliament for the surrender of Bristol,' said Digby in a careless tone, twirling his moustaches to enhance the effect of nonchalance, for his fingers were trembling with eagerness now that this amazing stroke of luck had placed his triumph within his reach. In a few days he would have pieced together enough material, chiefly anonymous letters from spies, to impeach the Prince for high treason – 'and I'll have his head, or it shall cost me a fall!'

421

he had sworn, sobbing with excitement when he had heard the news of Bristol. He must show none of that to the King, he must go on being the cool man of the world – but he started as the King turned on him with an oath, in violence that left no time for his accustomed stammer, as he demanded where he had got hold of that God-damned lie.

'From his French Excellency, Monsieur de Sabran, now in London, who should know,' Digby told him. He was made to produce the letter, and had to pretend that he had not noticed the postscript that spoilt the story – 'perhaps it was his brother the Elector Palatine who received this sum'.

But why should it spoil the story? These brothers kept up a fine show of hostility, but they hung together no doubt in secret, playing – *and* paying – into each other's hands. So he suggested in his casual ironic fashion – but did not spoil the story with any postscript and following argument when he wrote the news out to the Queen. She hastened to inform all Paris that Rupert had sold Bristol to the enemy.

Charles could not quite believe it, though he wished he could. When love is turning to hate, it is better to hate thoroughly. His love for his nephew had been so deeply personal that he felt the dishonour as his own. 'Tell my son I had rather he were knocked on the head,' he wrote to the guardian of his son James, which made the astonished boy open his round eyes very wide until he heard the rest of the sentence – 'than that he should do so mean an action as the surrender of Bristol Castle.'

'So mean an action,' the word would give him no rest till he wrote it to his nephew also – and yet his letter showed a forbearance in anger such as Rupert could never have shown. What was the use of reproaches, what was there to be said or done, when he had been dealt this appalling, this irremediable blow by 'one that is so near me as you are both in blood and friendship? – I have so much to say that I shall say no more of it.'

Charles, like many stammerers, was an excellent letter-writer, but never did he write a better one than this.

Rupert, where Charles wrote with restraint and magnanimity, read black injustice and ingratitude. His uncle had deprived him of his command, dismissed him from his service, told him to 'seek his subsistence somewhere beyond seas', and sent him a passport for this purpose, signed by George Digby.

Yet there was not a port now in England where this could be

of use; Rupert could not leave the country without a pass from the Parliament, and he had not the King's leave to apply for that.

*　　*　　*

His mind went round and round, rattling the wires of its cage. He could not sleep; he dared not wake. Such a thing had never happened to him before; his huge young body had never got more than a fraction of the sleep it needed since he had come to England, so that whenever he got the chance, in whatever noise or discomfort, his sleep had been instantaneous, deep and dreamless.

Now it came slow and unwilling, and he woke from it with a start, staring straight at the thing that had lain waiting for him at the foot of his bed; in that first instant of return to conscious life he could see it so much more clearly than any other time. He did not know that such clearness never could be true, that nothing in human life, however shattering, can be seen with such sharp and final edges, such relentless and inevitable eyes.

This was, he decided, with that desperate four-o'clock-in-the-morning finality, the smashing of his career. He was publicly disgraced, a discredited soldier of fortune, banished under such a cloud that no one else would enlist his services, accused of treachery, of accepting huge bribes, when in actual fact he was hard put to it to buy food for his servants now his credit was destroyed. And all the money he had in the world did not amount to £50.

Yet that was not his first view of the monster that lay in wait for him. Before the last breath of sleep had left him, he knew that what he would see as he woke would be its eyes – sad eyes, eyes of a wounded stag, of a hurt child, eyes like his mother's; the eyes of his uncle whom he had loved and longed to protect, as he had never done with any man but Maurice – and who hated him.

This then was where the procession of the years in England had been leading him. Not to the victory that had seemed so certain with his uncle and aunt reinstated on the throne, smiling their affectionate gratitude; but in utter loss and ruin, and, worst of all, in hatred between friends.

*　　*　　*

All this last year Mary had avoided Rupert as much as he had her. There had been an annoying business with Dan O'Neill, whom Rupert had sent away for talking scandal about himself and the pretty Duchess. O'Neill, when questioned, had not denied the charge, but cursed volubly the man who had informed the Prince. He was transferred to service in Ireland under Ormonde, and nobody else was rash enough to neglect the warning. But it had increased Rupert's awkwardness with Richmond, and the friendship might have stiffened and cooled had the elder man allowed it. He had refused to do so; it had been his steady determination that had helped pull Rupert out of his despair at Bristol a year ago, and now, when things were looking infinitely blacker for him, Richmond showed him how deep and assured was their friendship. It was one of the strange compensations for misfortune that Rupert could walk with him again in Christ Church meadow and know that it made no odds to Richmond what Charles thought of him, for all his devotion to the King. But they did not talk of him; for some time they did not talk at all.

A cold October wind was blowing across the meadow. The cry 'All fellows to football!' had rung out, and they watched undergraduates from all colleges hurrying to join the game round the blown swine bladder, a confused rabble of indefinite number, with no positions allotted to any one of them.

Their life went on, they would grow up, Englishmen here in England, under what rule? That did not matter to them. The basis of their life was secure. England would still need her doctors, lawyers, teachers; and undergraduates would go to lectures here, whoever ruled in Westminster. The very security of the national life, continuing thus, while his father's lands lay waste in ruins, awakened a craving Rupert had never recognized before.

'England has beaten me,' he said, 'I've no place here. You English hate strangers, that is the root of it. I would have won the war with you, if you'd have let me. That plan of a concerted march on London, it was what Gustavus or Wallenstein would have thought of, and your true soldiers knew it – but there were so damned few of 'em. We'd have done it if we'd hung together. There was no strategy then on the other side. Now, what there is has been worked up by one man; and that is what makes the odds. He's neither king nor noble, but he's an Englishman, so he can hold 'em together – and I couldn't.'

'*He* an Englishman!' exclaimed Richmond with unwonted violence. 'Have you heard about Basing House?'

'That it's fallen to him? Yes, I've just heard it from Tom Draycott, my servant. Poor old Winchester, how grandly he held it all this time. A bad business, wasn't it? Did Cromwell's men get out of hand?'

'They acted under orders,' answered Richmond. 'Cromwell's own dispatches glory in it. He boasts that he was praying on his knees up on the hillside outside the house for the best part of the night before he offered it up as a burnt sacrifice, pleasing to the Lord.'

Rupert's face was sick with loathing. 'And then takes his fill of knocking priests and women on the head!'

'They stripped Inigo Jones naked and dragged him out in a blanket into the night – a man of seventy-five. And in a bitter frost.'

'Inigo Jones there? The best artist you've got! God, how you Englishmen appreciate your artists!'

'I tell you this is not English. This religious hysteria is a new thing. Men have grown like mad children through pretending to themselves that they and their enemies are the good and bad people in the Bible. They have got drunk on words.'

'So that's his vice. He doesn't drink, in spite of his bottle-nose, and he doesn't whore, but he holds prayer-meetings where they all sob together. That filthy flood of tears and texts —' Rupert broke off in disgust and exclaimed, 'The fellow's the best soldier in England, and he wallows in his emotions like a sow in its dung.'

He had a personal reason for bitterness. His own logic and sanity had never been recognized by either side; nobody could believe in the essential Puritan austerity of the young Cavalier, or in the frantic emotionalism of the elderly tight-lipped Puritan.

But Richmond believed in it. 'You are more English in bone and sinew and fibre than that bulldog-looking fellow who weeps like a woman and finds it effective. You know it. You are one of the things that will stay for good in this country – but that fellow, what he stands for can't last. The old good humour, the old good manners, the old respect for law and decency and kindness, they are the essential England, and however long we wait for them they will come back. Hyde was saying —'

Rupert did not want to hear what Hyde said. He broke out, 'It doesn't matter what a fellow is, but what other fellows think he is. Cromwell's a plain, honest, country gentleman to most of 'em, and that's his strength – a farmer, grazier, petty brewer, I couldn't quite make out which were the humble trades he was so proud not to be ashamed of. That's what they see. They forget his colleagues don't trust him, that he makes use of 'em and then ousts 'em. All they see is a nose like a cudgel with a good hearty wart on it – "Ah," they say, "you know where you are with a man like that!" But he doesn't know himself – and he's proud of it. He never knows what he'll do next. Oh, God, these men who can only do things when they "know not what they do!"'

'They were the men who crucified our Lord,' said Richmond in a low voice.

Silence fell on them, for both their minds had caught the glimpse of an unbearable vision.

*   *   *

They had walked back into Christ Church gardens as they talked. Other courtiers who were there stood aside in respectful sympathy with the disgraced Prince, sweeping off their hats and standing bare-headed in the cold wind. Two men were watching the little scene from the window of the porter's lodge. 'Do you want to see who is our new ruler?' asked the one, and pointed to the Prince.

'Fancy! There was Prince Rupert walking in the gardens, and the nobility and gentry standing there bare at a distance as if His Majesty were present!'

The other, having made this shocked observation, hurried back to write it to his friend Digby, who did not need to be told to 'fancy!'

He was busy with new plans every day, and dangling them before the King's eyes – now the Scots, now the French, now the Irish would be the saviours of his cause.

He had to keep Charles away from Rupert at all costs. The King had shown a most tiresome inclination to go to Worcester, but that would never do, for not only was it within easy reach of Oxford, but Maurice was Governor there, still desperately weak and ill after his attack of the plague, and raging in helpless indignation at the treatment of his brother. Worcester was no safe place.

Digby hurried Charles off to Newark, where it would be all but impossible for Rupert to get to him from the south-west, with the country between filled with the enemy's troops. The

King had sent his express commands to forbid Rupert to come to him, on pain of his severest displeasure. Digby put more confidence in the armies of Cromwell and Fairfax. Best of all would have been if the King had only consented to put his nephew under arrest, as Digby besought him to do.

'Now is the time to take the reins out of Phaeton's hands and permit him not a third time to burn the world.' The King had consented so far as to take them out of his hands, but not to bind them. And had power really gone from him with his official command? In misfortune and disgrace the Prince seemed to have more friends to stand by him than ever.

Richmond was staunch; he wrote on Rupert's behalf to the King as urgently as his deep respect for him could allow. More and more lords joined the 'Cumberlanders' as the Prince's party was nicknamed in compliment to his English title; the rich and astute Lord Portland was the latest. And even his enemies, even 'Constitutional Hyde', who had puffed and snorted his disgust at 'His Most Illustrious Arrogancy' all through the war, had expressed himself scandalized by Will Legge's arrest, and was of opinion it would harm Digby's cause far more than Rupert's.

For Will had been deprived of the Governorship of Oxford and imprisoned in his own house. Digby was preparing articles of high treason against him also. It was a mistake to go so far, for nothing could be urged against Colonel Legge but the crime of being Rupert's friend.

Rupert had told the King that he was surprised at having been condemned unheard, and asked for leave to lay his case before him. That leave was refused.

Rupert fumed to Legge – 'He can't do this. I've been deprived of command. I insist on a court-martial.'

'Well, you won't get it,' said Will, 'not with the King at Newark.'

'Then I shall go to Newark.'

'With Cromwell's armies sprawled across the country? What force can you take off from here?'

'None, since I have no command.'

'You know well enough they'll volunteer. But they can't spare many.'

'They can spare eighty.'

'Exorbitant fellow! Why not say ten – or none? They'd be as much use in face of the enemy's armies.'

'We'd cut a way through somehow.'

But he was not thinking of that. He was striding up and down, biting his nails, pulling at his hair, scratching his head in that inelegant fashion that had been the despair of his mother.

'Who's "we"?' asked Will, 'I'm a prisoner. Richmond can't leave Oxford.'

'I know. I asked him. He wants to, but he won't. He's against my going, in the face of the King's command. But I'm going. And I shall tell Maurice. If he's well enough to sit a horse he'll come with me.'

'And the King's commands —?'

'Can go hang,' said the Prince.

He told Maurice to meet him at Banbury, though he did not tell him his plan. There would be time enough for that when they met.

He arrived in the evening and found Maurice already in bed, his inordinate length of limb stretched under a counterpane too short to reach his feet, his grey-shadowed face filled with his eyes. They turned listlessly as the door opened, stared, and with one movement the whole long lifeless form jerked up on his elbow.

'The Devil!' he exclaimed, 'the old Devil himself!'

Rupert flung himself down on the bed. 'What have you been up to, getting ill again?'

'What have you been up to, getting —' Maurice could not finish 'in disgrace', it went too deep. He could only plunge straight into what lay always now at the back of both their minds.

'Here is the King's letter to me,' he said, turning and thrusting between the leaves of a book on the table beside him. 'He calls it a "great error", so he can't really believe those damnable lies about it – though he says it's given him "more grief than any misfortune since this damnable rebellion".'

'What does he write to you for?'

'To say that whatever you've done, it won't stagger the good opinion he's always had of me – as if I want that – or his employment. He says he'll continue to find employment for me, but I've told him I'll have none apart from you.'

'He's a fool to abuse me to you.'

'He doesn't abuse you, that's the worst of it; he says he'll never forget your former services, "whensoever it shall please God to enable me to look upon my friends like a King".'

'He'd best look upon his friends like a sensible man first, and see which are his friends.'

Rupert tossed the letter aside as he spoke, as if it were not worth his glance. 'What is the book?' he said, taking it up as he spoke.

'Your man, John Wilkins – I remembered your telling me of his rocket to the moon.'

'Not my man – Carl's. They both sit snug in London.' He threw down the book as contemptuously as he had the letter. 'Carl's put his best spoke in our chariot wheel,' he said, 'taking all this money from Parliament just now. Digby's been saying that I was in correspondence with him there, and that that proves the money was really for me. Eight thousand yellow boys! Pity it isn't true. Tom Draycott told me yesterday I must get a new sword-belt. I told him he'd have to find the seven and sixpence for it first.'

'But you've never written to Carl?'

'Not one letter, for – how many years? Is this good?' He was turning over the pages of the book.

'It was published the year before the war,' said Maurice, as if in extenuation. He picked it up in his turn and read out the title – ' "Mercury, or the Swift and Secret Messenger, showing how a man may with Privacy and Speed communicate his thoughts to a Friend at any Distance." '

'We need that, don't we?' said his brother, and fell silent; then broke out with the sudden fury of pity and resentment that his brother's illnesses always roused in him – 'Are you never going to get well? How long have you been lying in bed? Weeks now, and here you are flopping back into it as soon as you get here.'

Maurice grinned in feeble insult at him.

'There was nothing particular to get up for.'

Rupert gave him a quick glance from under his half-shut eyelids. He was seeing how this blow to himself had knocked the heart out of Maurice so that he had lost all impulse towards recovery. Once again, but this time with far more urgent sense of responsibility, there came that warning, 'I must not let Maurice die.' To drag him now from convalescence on this the most dangerous ride of the whole war, might well seem the way to kill him. But Rupert did not think so. He leaned forward and grinned down at that sallow hollow-eyed mask under the tousled hair.

'You'll get up at dawn tomorrow, you old ruffian, and come with me to Newark, and see if it doesn't put life into you to see me put a bullet into Digby.'

CHAPTER EIGHT

THEY STARTED off with just over a hundred men in all. They came through Northampton and went on past Burghley, a house that had belonged to the Duke of Buckingham but was now a Parliamentary garrison.

They found some of the garrison posted across the wide straggling road to cut off their line of march. These the Princes scattered, but behind them the main body came up unexpectedly under the Governor himself, the dark shapes of men rising suddenly over the hill-top against the sunlight.

Rupert found himself looking down the wrong end of a pistol held cocked at him by a hand that had shot out at arm's length. He recognized a man who had fought in his own troop, ratted to the winning side and been rewarded with the Governorship of Burghley. The instant that they stared at each other stretched into eternity while the man pulled the trigger, firing point-blank into Rupert's face. Perhaps the hand shook, for there was no report. Rupert was still erect, untouched. The renegade had missed fire, he flung away his useless weapon with a shriek for quarter. With a grim smile at the impudence of such a hope, Rupert shot him dead.

The Roundheads saw their leader fall from his saddle, killed by that unnaturally tall, dark man, whom an instant since he had had at his mercy. Once again the Wizard Prince had proved himself beyond the power of any mortal-made weapon. They dragged at their horses' bridles, swung their necks round, and fled helter-skelter back into Burghley.

Maurice's lips were grey as he whispered, 'I thought you a dead man. Within a few yards – and he fired point-blank at you!'

'Blank it was. These pistols are clumsy fellows. I've got a scheme for improving them some time.'

430

'Glad you haven't done it yet, then.' At the moment Maurice was thankful for inefficient firearms.

The enemy were well warned now of their movements, though indeed they had guessed as soon as Rupert left Oxford that he would go to Newark. Fifteen hundred cavalry were dispatched to intercept him at different places along his line of march; but by night marches and his old bewildering swiftness of movement he managed to slip through them, until they had all but reached Belvoir Castle in Leicestershire. There they should be safe, for Belvoir was garrisoned with Royalist troops and less than a day's march from Newark. Rupert had stayed some weeks at Belvoir on his last visit, had hunted all over the wide fields round Melton Mowbray, and knew every lane about there. He had good need of his knowledge, for since fifteen hundred had not been enough to catch him, three hundred horse had been sent to guard a bridge that was on his way to Belvoir.

The Prince with his hundred odd came coolly on over the fields as if to charge the troops so solidly planted in front of the bridge, then suddenly turned his horse and led his men away at the gallop, as though he had only just recognized the odds against him. As he had intended, the enemy gave chase, whereupon he swung his troop round and charged them, trying to get between them and the bridge. Twice the manoeuvre failed, and he could see that more horsemen were coming up on the right. In another moment their little force would be completely surrounded.

Rupert called out to his men, 'We have beaten them twice – we must beat them once more, and then over the bridge and away!'

Spurring their blown and panting horses, they charged once again; furiously thrusting and cutting, they forced their way up to and over the bridge. But more and more reinforcements were riding up behind and Rupert saw they must split forces. Sending on most of his men by the main way to Belvoir Castle with his baggage and papers, he and Maurice with some twenty men slipped down a side lane which he remembered as a short-cut to Belvoir from his visit nine years ago.

'I used to stroll down here with a gun, shooting rabbits,' he told Maurice as they jogged easily along, feeling they had shaken off their pursuers. The hedges which had then only lately been planted were now tangled masses of brown and golden leaves, scarlet berries and over all a mist of grey old-man's beard; it was an absurd haphazard little lane, winding and curling itself into loops, gay and fantastic as a girl's ribbon.

Maurice felt a pang of envy that he had not been with Rupert then. What sport they would have had here together, had it been he and not Carl to share that visit with him; to stay in these pleasant country houses, to hunt over these wide, un-bounded fields, and go shooting down these English lanes. He began to say something of this, jerking out a word or two as they urged on their tired horses out of the lane into open ground. As usual, what Maurice said, and did not say, was enough to let Rupert know what he was thinking.

'We're getting sport enough here now,' he answered. 'What better rabbits than the Roundheads at the bridge?' He pulled in his horse for an instant to listen. 'Damme, they're after us again.'

He had heard hoofs thudding in the soft mud, pounding along the steep slope in the lane behind them. Soon men's heads could be seen bobbing along above the hedge, and it looked as if there were more than forty of them. When they came within earshot their leader bellowed, 'Will you have quarter?'

Rupert laughed back at him.

He had turned some of his men to block the lane – in that narrow space the difference of numbers made little odds – and with the remainder he leaped the hedge plumb into the middle of the struggling mass. This sudden flank attack finished the Roundheads; they broke desperately over the farther hedge and galloped away pell-mell across country.

Maurice struck a man down from his saddle just as he was swinging round to escape with the rest. He caught his mount and handed it over to Rupert, whose horse was spent. Now they rode on peacefully to Belvoir with nothing more to break the calm of the golden evening.

It was the home of the Earl of Rutland, who had joined the Parliament side when war broke out and had lost his house to the other side. Sir Gervase Lucas, the commander of the Royal-ist garrison, now entertained the Prince in the castle where he had danced and sung and acted in absurd impromptu plays with his fellow guests when he had stayed here as a boy. Those charades had been an echo to him of the impromptu acting and merry-making at home, when Louey had worn his out-grown clothes and he had flung a cloak over his head and doubled

432

himself up as an old woman. It was odd to come back to such reminders here at Belvoir, when he was to see his uncle tomorrow to account for the last loss of this lost war, and soon leave England perhaps for ever.

'All life is but a wand'ring to find home.'

He had heard that often in his mother's voice, from one of her English playbooks no doubt, which she loved to have sent out to her as soon as they were printed.

They spoke of her, he and Maurice, as they walked under the tall elms whose branches were already thinning from the autumn gales, the brown leaves drifting down all round them in the damp evening air, while the rooks cawed their immemorial council, conducting their laws and arguments with a decorum Westminster never knew.

A strange peace fell on them both, fell like dew, cooling and softening all the harsh outlines of this present moment, their furious dash across England, hewing their way through their enemies, and tomorrow their interview with the incensed King – and with Rupert's chief enemy.

Yet at this moment none of these things seemed very near; they did not discuss the escapes they had had on this ride, nor what they would say or do tomorrow; they wondered what was happening at home, and compared what news they had had in the past few months. 'Wilful Ned' had been proving his nickname in Paris where he and Philip, his 'Twin', as Maurice was Rupert's, had been leading a very gay life. He had just proved his gallantry too in a very plucky duel; but his mother and his aunt Queen Henrietta thought he could employ it better in England, fighting for his uncle, where he would be out of mischief.

So rushed had Rupert been when asked about the matter, that he wrote saying he would ask the King for his consent, and then remembered he had already done so! But it made no odds, for Lord Jermyn had just written from Paris that Ned had eloped the week before Rupert's messenger arrived, ' "with a very beautiful young lady" he says, and "very rich; six or seven thousand pounds a year sterling is the least that can fall to her, maybe more." '

'*Our* heiress was worth more than that,' said Maurice complacently, 'but it is something to have one in the family. What is the trouble?'

For of course there was trouble. Nothing the Palatines did

could ever fail to make trouble. Ned's private marriage without asking consent had deeply offended the Queen Regent of France, Anne of Austria, and Ned had been ordered to retire for a time to Holland, where, however, as Jermyn cynically assured his brother, 'there will come no further disadvantage to him than a little separation from his wife'. She was the Princess Anne de Gonzugue, daughter of the Duc de Nevers, as showy and dramatic as she was beautiful; the Queen of Bohemia was far from approving of a daughter-in-law who had already had such startling adventures and moreover was a Papist – and worse was to follow, for it turned out that since his marriage Ned had become a Papist too. That made his peace with Anne of Austria and his Aunt Henrietta, but furiously alienated his mother.

Family quarrels were raging to and fro; as for Carl, still snug at Whitehall, he was in a terrible twitter, writing to the Parliament that his misguided brother could not really 'be persuaded of those fopperies to which he pretends', and sending his commands to Philip to abjure his bad company in Paris, a town, according to him, populated with 'only atheists and hypocrites'.

In the morning a messenger rode up to the castle with a letter from the King, forbidding Rupert to come to Newark on pain of his extreme displeasure, and telling him 'you are no fit company for me'. Rupert tossed the letter over to Maurice without a word. His face was set again in the hard lines that had grown there this last year; it looked much older than it had done last evening under the elms. He would say nothing about his uncle. He ate an early breakfast in silence and then they set off for Newark. On the way he mentioned Digby briefly and in some trivial connection, but Maurice, looking at his brother's eyes, found himself considering the chances of Digby being alive this time tomorrow.

They rode through rain that beat against their faces, rustling and roaring through the forest trees, then sheeting over the naked plain. They were still about two miles from Newark when they saw a large company of horse come riding towards them. There was a momentary alarm, but then they saw Sir Richard Willis, the Governor of Newark, at the head of them. He had come to escort the Prince into the town that lay like a smear of smoke in the distant hollow, with the jagged shape of the castle thrusting up above the plain. With him were all those who wished to show that they took Rupert's part against Digby. It was a great muster, and the honour they did him greater than that they had shown the King when he had entered Newark two days ago, for then they had only met him at the gates.

An ignoble pleasure lit Rupert's eyes as they scanned that troop of gentlemen, there only to do his pleasure. But it blazed into fury when he heard that Digby had not stayed to see him. He dared not meet the Prince, Sir Richard told him, but had dashed off with nearly two thousand horse, the chief strength now left to the King, 'to help Montrose'.

They had had news that Montrose's army had been surprised and practically annihilated at Philiphaugh only two days after Rupert had marched out of Bristol. The King's old secretary Sir Robert Spottiswoode, whom he had sent to Montrose after his victory at Kilsyth, had been taken prisoner, and was now under sentence of death; the chief evidence against him being a letter he had written to Digby a day or two before the battle, urging him to 'fulfil that which you lately promised'.

Now, when it was too late to be of any use, Digby was fulfilling that promise. So he had given out with a heroic true-to-the-death air, while everyone at Newark was saying that he had galloped off in such a hurry with the bulk of the cavalry to avoid meeting Rupert.

Rupert had been thinking far more of his coming meeting with Digby than with the King. The King by now was someone who might or might not be made to understand what had happened – if he did, good – and if he did not, then there was nothing more Rupert could do. But Digby was his 'dearest foe' with whom he had been going to settle for once and all.

And now Digby had escaped him.

They rode into Newark against the rain, but in spite of it people were all thronging the narrow streets and massed in the great market square, to cheer themselves hoarse for the disgraced Prince.

'It's like a royal progress,' they said to each other.

They knew that he had been blamed for everything that had gone wrong since the beginning of the war, they knew that the usual adjectives to apply to him were 'rash' or 'reckless' and the formula for his part in a battle was 'a fine charge but went too far as usual – young fool can never wait for the others to come up'. But now that he was publicly attacked and had been told to leave the country, men had begun to look round and ask which of the other commanders would take his place, and who else had ever had a tenth part of his victories. He had rescued them from the grim hunger of their siege eighteen months ago, with a daring and cleverness that had been the town talk ever since; a good joke for their stomachs it had been when he told them to 'beat the old drum,' meaning old Meldrum, and beat him soundly he did.

In the courtyard of the castle Sir Richard Willis said goodbye for the moment.

'If things do not go as you hope,' he said, 'come to my house for the night.'

They thanked him while their horses stamped and shuddered under the rain, and the old grey towers of the castle loomed up above them into the dirty sky.

Rupert waited for no preliminaries; he dismounted in the castle courtyard and, followed by Maurice and two or three of his friends, he marched straight into the King's presence without asking for permission. The King was sitting at his table; his secretary at the other end of it, busily writing, while the King, with a pen in his hand, was reading a letter he was just about to sign. He looked up, startled. Rupert could not find his voice; in the sudden dimness of the room after the steel-cold light outside, he saw his uncle's pale face, ending in the shadowy point of his beard, as though it were swimming in space, isolated. It was only for an instant – then he saw the dark shoulders, the long hand resting on the table with the quill pen in its fingers – that flutteringly balanced weapon that had clashed with and conquered Rupert's sword.

He said in a loud voice, 'I have come to render an account of the loss of Bristol.'

The King's lips moved in his beard, he tried to speak, but the words stuck in his throat as if they would strangle him. Anger and the helplessness of wounded affection completed what his continued fatigue had begun. For the last few weeks he had been hurried from one place to the other without any pause for rest, often without any dinner and glad if he could get supper at the end of the day. He had marched over the mountains that separate England from Wales, sometimes from six in the morning till midnight. His desperate flittings were getting to look more and more like a continuous flight. Once his utter fatigue compelled him to stop and snatch a few hours' sleep, but he was woken up and hurried on again. Hurry always bewildered him; he needed calm to compose his mind and speech.

Now when he was suddenly confronted with the man he had been most dreading, most longing to see, all the things he had been saying to him in the restless watches of the night when he was too weary to sleep, surged up in his mind. How often then he had reproached and appealed to his nephew!

But now the young man stood before him, towering dark against the doorway, angry, impenitent, and nothing Charles could say would make any difference. And he could say nothing; no single word would come. If he tried to wrestle with his stammer he would only make himself ridiculous. Silence, as so often, was his only refuge. He abandoned the effort, and without any sign to his nephews, walked through a doorway into another room.

The brothers followed him. He was sitting down to supper, attended by two of his gentlemen. Rupert came up and stood on his right hand, Maurice on the other. A page was lighting candles that hung on the wall within glass cases to prevent their flickering in the draught. The glass was of a thick greenish quality and the light came faintly through it as if under water, the candle flames balancing themselves in their glass tanks like goldfish standing on their heads, thought Rupert in that crazy impulse to draw what he was seeing, which always seized him in moments of suspense and emotion.

He would not speak again till the King did. The King would not speak. But presently the food and wine began to have their effect. Charles, feeling less chilled and weak from emptiness, found the two overbearing shadows of his nephews on either side of him too oppressive to be borne any longer in silence. He turned to Maurice and asked how he was after his serious illness. His concern for Maurice, though warm and kindly, came only from the top of his mind and gave him no trouble to put into words.

Maurice replied curtly enough that he was well, but when Rupert scowled at him over the top of their uncle's head he pushed out another short sentence or two. Charles relapsed into silence. It was the most uncomfortable meal he had ever had.

Rupert watched the listless movements of his uncle's hands with his knife and fork, the lines that exhaustion and disappointment had graven deep on his face. Pity intensified his anger; his uncle had enough to put up with, God knows – must he add to it by making enemies of his truest friends? But he

437

wished he had not marched in on him so rudely, and pushed after him to where he sat at supper. Now he was there, he was as helpless as Charles himself from his own presence, for nothing would induce him to turn tail and acknowledge his defeat by marching out again.

As Charles rose from the table, Rupert made another attempt to speak.

'Sir,' he began, 'I ask only —'

He could ask nothing, for the King, too slow or too angry to notice the softening of his nephew's voice, turned his back on him without a word and went to his bedroom – his only refuge. Rupert turned to Maurice, who turned away from him, sick with shame that the King had spoken to him and not to his brother. Without a word they left the castle for the house of Sir Richard Willis, who showed no surprise at seeing them back.

The Governor's house gave them a warm welcome after the chill hostility of the castle. They sat after supper in a room with a fire that blazed up a wide chimney where the raindrops fell spluttering down into the flames. The fire-dogs ended in tall iron stands, where they could place their mugs of mulled wine to keep warm. They sat close to it, resting their wet boots on the ends of the burning logs, which hissed softly under the impact. In this sudden ease, with the friendly bustle and clamour of the market square outside the windows, they heard how Digby had been working the case against Rupert all this summer.

'He has sworn to have Your Highness' head, through proving that you intend the Crown for yourself.'

'That old charge!' Rupert gave a short, bitter laugh. Morosely kicking at the great heap of golden wood ash under the fire-dogs, he seemed to pay little attention; it was Maurice who suddenly flared into angry defiance.

'Let them take care not to say it so often as to make it true!'

Rupert looked at him, startled and not too well pleased. Maurice was flushed; his head, weak after his illness and the exhausting adventures of his ride, was obviously swimming with the warm wine. Unlike his usual self, he was suddenly determined to talk. 'We have stood enough,' he said; 'we came here to fight for our uncle and they say it's for ourselves. Let them look to themselves who say it. Do they *want* Rupert to make himself King that they say it so often?'

'Let them say.' Rupert's gruff contempt had the effect of silencing his brother. He saw that Rupert was annoyed with him, but he did not care. When they went to bed he broke out again. 'Why shouldn't you be King? They've made everything else impossible now. The King's lost all his following, he's lost his country, his army —'

'Oh God damn you!' said Rupert.

They slept in one bed, a very wide one and the longest in the house, in a room like a small church, with rafters arching upwards to a point. His body taut and rigid, Rupert lay stretched out at full length; while Maurice tossed and turned feverishly, now all doubled up, now suddenly sprawling, and muttered in his sleep.

Rupert heard him say, 'He ought to be King, he ought to be King.' He said it over and over again in a cross grumbling voice, and then more urgently, then in a loud shrill tone. Rupert could bear it no longer; he leaned over and gripped his shoulder and shook it to wake him, and Maurice's fist shot out and caught him a furious blow on his cheek, while he shouted out, 'Knock up his pistol! Knock up his pistol!'

'Wake up, you fool. You've nearly cracked my jaw.'

Maurice was clutching at his brother's arm. 'That fellow at Burghley – I thought he was shooting you.'

His voice sounded much weaker now he was awake.

'Well, here I am as large as life.'

'Larger.'

A fire had been lit in the room; its smouldering light sent a shadow of Rupert's head and shoulders halfway across the rafters. He was sitting up, looking down on his brother's dim outline in the bed. 'Why do you go on saying it?'

'Saying what?'

'That I ought to be King.'

'I've never said it. Others do.'

'Who?'

'They all say it, Roundheads and Royalists alike. They say it was your skill and direction that managed everything when things were going well, and that now they're not —'

'Well?'

'Well, now it's because your enemies have undermined you with the King. If you could have dealt with them direct you'd have got 'em out of the way long ago, and the war over.'

Rupert flung himself out of bed, the stone floor striking like ice upon his feet, and leaned right down to look out of the window, which was nearly on a level with the floor. The church steeple opposite pointed sharp into the sky, clear-washed now of clouds. Behind it was the castle, which he could not see.

A waning moon hung over the wide and silent square that had been so full of people, all clamouring their loyal welcome to him, as ardent as when he had ridden at the head of his conquering army into this town that he had saved. 'Our Prince!' 'Our Prince!' they had shouted then and today, proud to claim him as their own – as Oxford had done again and again – as London had done, long years ago.

He did not speak for some time. At last he said: 'That's true. But I can't be King. You know it. Don't ever say it.'

'I don't. Ever.'

Maurice's tired voice was weighed down by his complete conviction. Rupert found himself wondering for an instant whose was that strong high voice that had proclaimed in the night that he ought to be King.

CHAPTER NINE

RUPERT AT last got his court-martial, as he had insisted. It was composed very fairly of both his friends and his enemies, and the result was a complete acquittal of any suspicion of treachery or corruption. But it took a long time to convince the King of this sufficiently to declare his innocence. His verdict still questioned Rupert's discretion, still spoke of the relief of Bristol as a working probability, when there had been no force in the field that could have relieved it – even Rupert's enemies at the court-martial could say no more than that the expected relief 'was a very plausible design on paper'.

On paper – that was the King's favourite field of action. He acquitted Rupert from 'any the least want of courage or fidelity to us' but added the corollary 'withal we believe that he might have kept the castle and fort a longer time'. So of course he might. That had never been the question – but the question as to whether it had been worth while to do so when the town was taken.

These little damning thrusts at him, quite beside the point, and without Digby there to prompt them, gave Rupert a contempt of his uncle such as he would never have dreamed possible before. Charles had been forced by public opinion and the decision of the court-martial to absolve him of all the major counts against him, yet could not resist these feeble, feminine digs. Rupert regretted that he had ever come to Newark to win only this perfunctory reconciliation, and that on the outside only, for the King was as cold and distant to him as ever, and never spoke to him when he could avoid it.

They were shut up in the little town in the hollow of that wide plain, with the year closing in on them, and all round them the war narrowing down to a few last forlorn hopes. They heard that Digby never reached Montrose. His army was scattered and destroyed on the Border; Digby himself fled in a fishing-smack to the Isle of Man, and thence to Ireland.

No one knew what the King felt about this last crushing blow. He drew the farther into himself under a crustacean shell of obstinate calm. It had no calming effect on his followers, who saw in it a fanatical resolution that would hold to his purpose, or even one part of his purpose, quite regardless of any practical means or results. Whatever plans were brewing in his head, he confided them to no one whom Rupert knew.

The cleavage between the Prince's friends and the King's now seemed complete, when the King found a way to make the division deeper yet, so deep as to threaten a secondary war. He removed Sir Richard Willis from his post as Governor of Newark, and appointed a close friend of Digby's in his place, for no reason but that Willis had shown himself a friend of Rupert.

These friends were dangerous, now that they were being pushed into isolation, for they were all soldiers, taking their stand against the influence of the civilian Digby.

The Princes and Willis and about eighteen of the chief military officers went to the castle together to demand justice for the Governor. It was Sunday; the King had returned from church and was just sitting down to dinner when this formidable body of men marched into his presence, headed by Rupert, who came straight up to the King with a dark and furious face. Charles rose from his chair and told the servants to take away the food. With slow precise steps as though picking his way through the mud, he walked over to the deep window-seat, and there stood looking out on the crazy up-and-down roofs of the little town, seeing nothing.

Rupert strode over to him, and Willis, and Willis' friend,

Lord Gerard. The small figure in the window turned and faced the three big men. He was at a disadvantage standing, but every one of his comparatively few inches was that of a king. Sir Richard Willis began to ask in respectful tones for what reason he had been publicly dishonoured. Rupert could not wait for the King to answer. He burst out, 'By God! This is done in malice to me, because Sir Richard has always been my faithful friend.'

The King's eyes, fixed on Willis, never wavered towards Rupert as he spoke. His silence hung on the threatening air. Gerard began to speak, lodging a correct and formal protest, but nobody really listened; they were still listening to what Rupert had just said, and for what he would say next. It came soon enough, crashing through Gerard's polite sentences with the missile that he had longed to fling at his uncle for months past now – no, for years – ever since the war began and Rupert had found his plans for it checked and thwarted in every direction. He placed his foot on the window-seat and leaned forward over his knee to stare down into his uncle's face in the casual attitude of an equal, but with a fierce intensity in his gaze as he said, 'The cause of all this is Digby.'

This was what he had come to Newark to say, cutting his way with a few horse through the armies of his enemies. The King should know it at last.

The King said in a small, frozen voice, 'So I am but a child, and Digby can do what he will with me!' He did not stammer, his indignation had given him the mastery of his voice. But that thin contempt pushed Rupert too far.

'By God, that is true!' he cried, and his loud young voice in its turmoil of grief and rage made that other sound very old, even in Charles' own ears. 'Digby can do what he will. I fought against odds at Marston Moor – not your will, but his, dictated your letter telling me to do that. Digby made you drop our joint attack on London. Digby's promised help to Montrose this year past – not one man or horse did he send him. Montrose has had a year of such victories as never general has known – but what good has it done you? Digby waits till Montrose's army is routed, his friends sentenced to death, his soldiers butchered in droves on the Lowland hillsides, and *then*, when it's all too late, keeps his promise to go and meet him on the Border – and why? Only because he daren't stay and face me. So he goes and loses the best that's left of your cavalry, scatters them over the hills and leaves them to die, while he runs away to Ireland. That's how he *helps* Montrose.'

That chill toneless voice of the King cut in again; 'You slander him worse than ever he did you. He has been burning to march north for months. He worships Montrose, as he would have worshipped you if you had let him.'

'I tell you, he's betrayed Montrose as surely as he's betrayed me. If he had kept even one of his promises to him, if he'd not undermined all my power, then Montrose and I between us would have won this war before Cromwell's new armies had grown strong. But it's lost, lost, lost – and you won't see it, you won't see what has lost it – to the end of your days you'll go on thinking it's because I gave up Bristol.'

The word Bristol fell like a stone, stunning the King, who had begun to speak again, determined to silence this insolence. But once 'Bristol' was said, of what use to say any more? Bristol had finished him, had finished something for ever between him and his nephew. For this raging intolerable young man who towered over him and stormed at him and stirred up all his followers against him, breaking in on his privacy and filling it with such gusts of passionate hostility as his worst enemies would not show, was yet his nephew, whom he had loved and who had loved him, but who had given up Bristol.

He looked now for the first time at Rupert, with eyes that seemed to have been hollowed out of his white face, so huge and dark and empty they showed, drained of all anger now, but also of all hope or belief.

'Oh, nephew —' he sighed out, then turned away.

The room was silent. Rupert stood staring at his uncle, wondering what had happened. They had been so much to each other; he had wanted to protect and fight for his uncle more than ever he had wanted anything for himself – even that island on the other side of the world. Yet now they could never meet; they were irreconcilable, as far apart as though all the seas in the world rolled between them. Anger had dropped from him also; a misery of bewilderment and loss filled his mind. Why had it all happened? Desperately anxious to believe his words, he said, 'Digby is the man that has caused all this distraction between us.'

He had better have left it, remembering his own dislike of words. Even as he spoke, he knew that in one sense Digby was not worth dragging in again. If he or Charles had been different,

Digby could never have mattered. The quarrel was between Charles and himself. All that his last appeal had done (for appeal it was, far more than accusation) was to split that moment of memory and longing that had fallen on them both; to separate them once again, now more widely than ever. The King turned sharply back to his nephew, determined to end the matter.

'They are all rogues and rascals that say so,' he said loudly; 'those who seek to dishonour my best subjects are in effect traitors.'

His words were heard clearly all over the large room. There was an uneasy stir among the group they had left standing by the door. The three who were with the King drew themselves up stiffly and looked at each other. They would not stay to be called rogues and rascals, even traitors. Gerard and Willis bowed and left the room, the others followed them. Rupert remained where he was for a minute or two. He seemed about to speak, but he did not, and nor did Charles. He looked at the King, but the King did not look at him. He turned on his heel and marched out after the others, without bowing or showing any respect.

He rode back to Sir Richard's house. Everything there was confusion; the market square clanged with angry voices; more and more men kept coming in to hear how things had gone and to repeat the news to each other with growing embellishments. The King had called the Prince a traitor, the Prince had laid his hand on his sword, the Prince had drawn his sword, all the company had pressed in upon the King's presence with drawn swords.

Rupert paid no attention to the wild and various reports. Baffled and dazed by his rage, he found he could think of nothing but his longing to pursue Digby to Ireland, tear the heart out of his living body and present it to his uncle who would say, 'Yes, I now see you are right. It is entirely black, and you are completely justified.'

This ridiculous image had presented itself with the clarity and conviction of a dream, and persisted in haunting his thoughts however sensible he strove to make them, as he sat with Maurice and Gerard and Willis. They had shut out all their eager new partisans, and were concocting a letter to the King. The first letter he had ever written to King Charles had also been in conjunction with three others, when as children he

444

and Carl and Maurice and Ned had all written their appeal for help to the magnificent uncle they had never seen.

Now the fourfold appeal was either for a general court-martial in which their case could be tried fairly, or for passes to go overseas. They pointed out that their commissions had been taken away 'without any cause or reason expressed, whereby our honours are blemished to the world, our fortunes ruined, and we rendered incapable of command from any foreign prince'; they explained that 'we do in all humility present these reasons unto your sacred Majesty rather in writing than personally, lest we should hazard a second misrepresentation'.

'In other words,' growled Rupert across the table, 'I lost my temper.'

'If you were to say so, it would help considerably,' said Gerard.

But Rupert would not say it.

The letter contained no apology, and was sent to the King that evening. He replied by their messenger that he would not submit his actions to the judgement of a court-martial. He sent the passes instead, thereby dismissing his best officers from his service. Willis and Gerard were astounded; but Rupert had all along, in spite of his furious struggles, felt uncomfortably certain that the King would not yield an inch until they had reached this deadlock. That did not suggest to him that he on his side might yield a little.

He and Maurice and Gerard went to the King's bedchamber next morning for a private leave-taking, and Gerard, hoping to give Rupert a lead, murmured regrets for the 'folly' shown in yesterday's interview. But Rupert would not apologize.

He heard the King warning them that it would bring but little credit to them if they should now nourish any secret design to turn into his adversaries, either through fear or hope – 'hope', he repeated in a dead, anguished tone, his eyes fixed on Rupert.

Did he think then that Rupert hoped to snatch at the Crown? Then he had known nothing of him, nothing, ever since he had come over to fight for him, thought Rupert, raising his heavy eyelids at last to stare at the man who had never known him.

Very stiffly he said he hoped for nothing but that His Majesty should acknowledge his innocence.

'I do acknowledge it,' said the King.

Yes, when it had been dragged out of him by a court-martial he had striven to prevent. Rupert, having got what he asked, saw how futile it was to ask for anything. He went out with the other two, and they got on their horses and rode away, through the great stone arch where King John had been carried in on his litter to die. Rupert would not let himself look back at the castle or at the window of the room where he had left his uncle. If he had, he would have seen that Charles, forgetting his pride at last, as Rupert could not do, was standing at the window in full view of whomsoever happened to look up, and that the tears were running down his face.

CHAPTER TEN

THEY RODE out of Newark for Belvoir Castle with an amazing following of about four hundred officers. One thing had grown increasingly clear, that practically every officer of importance left on the King's side was now determined to show himself on Rupert's. Rupert had had no idea of this widespread popularity. One and all were prepared to follow him on whatever project he cared to lead them, whether in England or abroad, and with them the bulk of the army, what was left of it.

Their indignation was far louder than his own. Gerard wrote furiously to his friends, 'This is an excellent reward for Rupert and Maurice!' But all that Rupert casually told Will, who was still a prisoner at Oxford, was that he hoped he had heard from others what reasons he had to quit the King's service – if not, Rupert could not wait to furnish them, he had something more pleasant for his pen – 'I forgot to tell you that Lord Digby was beaten back again to Shipton. Alas, poor man!'

Digby's papers had all been taken by the Parliament; a quantity of them were in cipher, but these after weeks of careful de-coding turned out to be all his love-letters, a surprising testimony to his discretion. It was too much to expect him to carry it into his public affairs; all the important papers were preserved in straightforward English for anyone to read. This engaging topsyturvydom had one helpful result for Rupert, for among the papers was a copy of the King's answer to him, showing how strongly Rupert had urged him to treat for peace with Parliament.

This impressed the Parliament. Their surprise, indignation even, at his treatment by the King was almost equal to that of his friends. 'It is remarkable that Prince Rupert and all the Protestant leaders should be deposed for Popish Digby.' They readily offered him and Maurice a safe-conduct out of the kingdom, but on one condition – that they should never again bear arms for the King against the Parliament.

'And how can we do that if we are going overseas?' demanded Maurice '– it's nothing but a formula, and we need not mind complying with it.'

But Rupert would not comply. He could not give up hope of fighting for his uncle ever again. And this was in spite of the fact that he told himself that he hated his uncle, that cold, obtuse and ungrateful man who had looked at him with his mother's eyes, seeing nothing of all he had done and tried to do.

There was nothing to be done now but fight their way back again across country to Woodstock. Their numbers were far larger this time and they had no particular adventures, though they beat the Roundheads once again as they drew near Woodstock. The deadness of an early winter now lay on the land: black frost, dark sky, and thin tormented trees. There was nothing to hope or fear at the end of their journey. They had reached the end and turned back and that was all.

Some of his friends wanted to go farther. Gerard and Willis told Rupert how they heard on all sides the complaint and aspiration —

'If the Prince were King, he would have won the war.'

'Once he had a free hand, he might do so even now.'

The question haunted his mind, heavy and drugged with anger – would he after all declare himself the King's 'adversary', even as Charles had openly feared?

Maurice was silently longing for it; some of his friends were indignantly urging him to do it; but Richmond he knew was not even thinking of it, and would find it inconceivable that Rupert should do so; and all the time at the back of his mind was an image of Will puffing at his pipe and saying with comfortable certainty, 'You won't do it.'

He would not go on to Oxford, for the King was going back there. He remained at Woodstock. Once again, as on that ten days' pause before Marston Moor, but now far worse, his black mood had become a physical condition. Maurice was still wretchedly delicate after his illness, but it was Rupert who looked the more ill of the two. Prison was on him again, shutting him off from all he had ever cared for. He rode with hawks or hounds in Woodstock forest, and it meant nothing to him that often he had hunted here with his uncle. He got letter after letter from Will, from Richmond, from all his truest friends, even from anonymous well-wishers, all entreating him to try and make his peace with the King;

'You shall not have the heart to leave us all in our saddest times ... surely you should not abandon your uncle in the disastrous condition these evil storms have placed him in?'

'It is your uncle you should submit to, and a King, and not in the condition he merits.'

'You should write to your uncle – you ought to do it – he is a King, your uncle, and in effect a parent to you.'

That was Will's, that last, insisting on the plain facts again and again.

But all their appeals were no more than black spidery marks upon the paper. He had lost his chief battle for a letter. Never should letters have power to sway him again.

*　　*　　*

Will had only just been freed from his imprisonment; King Charles had seen to that as soon as he arrived in Oxford, though he did not restore him to his Governorship. The unfairness of his treatment made no difference to Colonel Legge. He was working every day with the King to get him reconciled with his 'most dear Prince'; he told Rupert how Charles had admitted what great happiness it would give him to have his nephew with him again, if only Rupert would satisfy the King's honour by admitting his fault, which was no more than he would ask from his own son – 'if Prince Charles had done as you did, he would never see him again without the same he desires from you'.

'What do I care if he never sees his son Charles again? He probably never will, since he can come to terms with nobody, either friend or foe.'

Only one sentence had come alive to him out of all those meaningless words, and that was where Will had told him that he must thank the Duchess of Richmond for getting this letter to him, 'for she furnished a present to procure this messenger – I being not so happy as to have any money myself.'

So she was interesting herself in this affair too, 'for his good', like all the rest. How mighty good everybody had become! She hadn't been good when she had come to him at Bristol. But like a fool he had been good himself then – why? He could barely remember! Richmond had been his friend, that was it, and he had still thought friendship mattered. But King Charles had been his friend – that showed how little it mattered.

He should not have begun to think of her again; it was like opening a door where all had been securely fastened. Now he kept seeing her again as he had done at first, and then forgotten – at her wedding in the dim candlelit chapel which the murdered Laud had so enjoyed restoring to its former beauty. A child's face, surmounting a little stiff brilliant figure like an image,

'When she came in like starlight, hid with jewels.'

(Who had said that? His mother? Or a gross wheezing groaning old man under a mountain of pink counterpane?)

She had come in on the King's arm, and he had handed her over to his tall cousin Richmond as though she were a sacred treasure.

Now she had brought Charles in after her through that opening door. He saw Charles walking through the galleries at Hampton Court, showing him his pictures – Charles asking him casually if he would like an island of his own – Charles turning towards him with that slow sad smile that lit his face so seldom, when his nephew had burst out that he wished he could break his neck in this last hunt of theirs together, since then at least he would leave his bones in England.

Now he would go away and leave nothing of him in England; no victory, no kindly memories – he might just as well have never come and fought – better, for then Charles would still think kindly of him.

It was not a door opening in his mind, but an open wound.

He would not be made to feel again. He would see nothing but what was here in front of him.

Then one day there was Will in front of him, as large as life, larger since his imprisonment.

'Not enough exercise, I've been putting on weight,' he said, with the grin that seemed as broad as his massive shoulders. He discussed the news. Goring had just bolted to France with all the money he could grab. Prince Charles and his followers had been pushed farther and farther west and south until at last he had reached the Scilly Isles. His father did not feel he would be safe even there, and was making plans for him to join his mother in France. Will did not add what plans the King was making for himself; before he had intended to do so, Rupert found himself asking what they were.

'Oh, Ireland or Scotland,' said Will casually, as though he were speaking of a proposed holiday.

'What the devil do you mean? Montrose has no army now.'

'Montrose? No, not Montrose. I believe he intends to ask Montrose to join with Leslie of Leven.'

'Montrose join with Leslie? And I with Cromwell, I suppose? Is he stark staring mad?'

'Well, if that's not feasible,' continued Will imperturbably, 'he may have to ask him to lay down his arms and leave the country as you're doing.'

'God alone knows what I'm doing!'

'You lay too much upon Him,' interposed Will solemnly.

'Confound you, man, this is not a joking matter. I've been told to go ever since Bristol – do you think I want to stay, disgraced, deprived of command?'

'What do you want to do, my Prince?' asked his friend with sudden real gravity.

Rupert said slowly, 'This country, it's not mine, I've been shown that clearly enough. For all that, I still feel it matters more to me than any other. It matters what happens to it. It was a lovely country — '

'It's a pity,' said Will, 'that Hyde is not here now. You've no reason to like him, I know, but for all that, he stands for the old things in England that will come back when all this is over.'

'*When* will all this be over? How will it be over?'

'God alone knows,' echoed Will, serious enough now as he puffed at his long white pipe. Rupert suddenly sprang forward and knocked it out of his mouth.

'God damn you!' he cried, 'will nothing ever put you off your taste for tobacco?'

'I trust not.' Will was looking ruefully at the broken pieces of clay on the floor.

'I must finish this fooling.'

'I'm glad, if you refer to the breaking of pipes.'

'I must see the King.'

'The King is quite as anxious to see the Prince.'

'Then go and tell him I'll apologize in whatever terms he likes

– say anything, say I sold Bristol if he wishes – whatever he chooses that will get the business over so that we can talk.'

'Wouldn't it be best to write your message?'

Rupert made a wry face. What could he write?

'I must see you —'

'This is folly. Let us leave it.'

No, they would none of them do. The King must have his way in those few things where it was still possible. After much tearing of paper and some ribald suggestions from Will which curiously lightened the burden of his quill (it was odd to find himself laughing so freely again without any sardonic bitterness, but easily, foolishly like a schoolboy), he wrote, 'I humbly acknowledge that great error which I find Your Majesty justly sensible of —'

'Which error? D'you think you've so few to your account?'

'Then he can choose.'

'Why not make it particular? You don't want him to think you mean Bristol.'

Rupert did not. He hastily added that the error had taken place at Newark.

His apology was not sufficient. Charles wrote to explain this, Rupert wrote again, Charles wrote to tell Rupert what he ought to write, and Will brought the final letter with a very rueful face, for this last ungenerous gesture of the King's had struck him as the greatest incentive to open rebellion the Prince had yet received.

He stood looking down at the bowed shoulders, the drawn forbidding brows of the young man who sat at the table, staring at the letter in which the helpless King had dictated terms to him. The Prince had only to lift a finger to raise the strongest part of the King's followers against him. That did not strike the King as of importance equal to the question of the exact terms in which Rupert should 'confess his fault'. One might discover a certain nobility in such imperviousness to self-interest, but Will felt that the Prince was the last person likely to recognize it at this moment.

Nor did it give him any surprise to see Rupert at last straighten his shoulders, draw back in his chair, hold the letter at arm's length over the table as though he wished it no nearer him than necessary, and deliberately tear it into small shreds.

'And what will he do now?' wondered Will, watching these dangerous movements of 'his dearest Prince' as he might those of some wild beast that has been rudely awakened from its sleep. He saw the long hands drop the scraps of paper, wipe themselves free of their touch, then drum a steady contemptuous tattoo upon the table. At last he spoke, and now he did amaze Will, for the words were the last he expected to hear.

'Give me a piece of paper.'

So he was going to write once more after all.

But when he handed him the paper, Rupert did not write. He pushed it from him till his hand hovered over the bottom of the sheet, then scrawled his name across it. Then he folded it, handed it to Will and rose, stretching his arms above his head.

'What am I to do with this?' demanded Will.

'Take it to the King.'

'There's nothing on it!'

'There's my name. He can fill in the rest.'

It was a gesture of surrender more arrogant than any defiance. Rupert would put his name to anything the King wished him to say, since he despaired of the argument. So Will saw it, but Charles, who had not seen his nephew make it, was so deeply moved by Rupert's humility that as he looked at the blank sheet and the bold untidy signature, the tears started to his eyes. Will told Rupert of that, and thereby caused the young man some discomfort. 'Well, anyway, the ground is clear now for us to meet,' he said ungraciously.

And he went at last to Oxford.

He rode through the familiar grey streets in a December mist that struck chill to his bones. He noticed as he dismounted how his breath hung on the air and his horse was outlined with a thin exhalation of steam.

He stayed a moment to pat the sweating, shivering beast; he did not know what he should say to his uncle. He went into the room in Christ Church where he and the King and Montrose had discussed the plan for the conquest of Scotland.

The King was rising and coming forward to met him, was reaching up to embrace him. 'My dear nephew,' said Charles, and Rupert no longer wondered why he had come. He did not say anything, and it was his uncle who spoke again – 'We shall have one more Christmas together. You remember – it was just before Christmas when you first came, ten years ago.'

Rupert spoke with more difficulty than his stammering uncle. 'Not one more – many,' he said, and wished he had not said it, for he did not think Charles believed it, nor he himself.

THERE WAS one more battle, fought up in the Cotswolds in the cold and gusty spring that followed that last Christmas at Oxford. It proved an easy victory for the Roundheads, for few of their enemies had their heart in it. Of what use to win a battle when the war was so plainly lost? Their leader, old Astley, knew that as well as any. 'Well,' he said to the Ironsides who had taken him prisoner, 'you have done your work and may go and play – unless you fall out among yourselves.'

Even the King saw that it was the last battle. But he told Rupert there was still hope for him in Scotland.

'Then I am with you,' said Rupert, 'we'll fight our way up north once more – though what to do when we get there —'

He stopped, suddenly remembering that he had never been restored to military command and that he was speaking as though he were. So natural was it to assume that he would share the King's adventures that this had not occurred to him. But it was not that that was making his uncle hesitate to accept his offer. The oddest reason came out.

'You cannot go with me, Rupert. Your height would betray us both.'

'Betray – By God, sir, do you mean to go in disguise?'

The King intended to disguise himself as a servant and, accompanied with only two attendants, to ride up to the Scots army at Newcastle and give himself into their hands. The Scots might well be induced to accept him as their leader against the Parliament, for they were by now deeply disgusted with the allies, who had refused flatly to keep their promise to the Presbyterian Church.

'But do *you* intend to establish the Presbyterian Church in England?' asked the nephew; to which the uncle replied very quietly and without any trace of his hesitancy.

'I will die sooner than betray the Church of England.'

'Well then – what can you offer the Scots?'

'The matter may not proceed as far as that.'

He was a little ruffled that Rupert with his usual uncompromising directness should have gone so straight to the root of the matter. He had to collect his reasons; the Scots would understand him better than the illogical, muddle-headed English – though they had not done so when he visited them. He said, 'They are my people and a gallant people. I was born there and am one of them. If I throw myself on their honour and chivalry they will not betray me.'

'Of whom are you thinking?' asked Rupert, who saw plainly that his uncle's head was full of the image of Montrose, whereas he himself was remembering all he had heard of Argyll. Charles was determined to do what was on the face of it the chivalrous and noble thing. To fight on was hopeless, to treat was impossible; very well then, he would put himself unreservedly into the hands of his enemies and let them say what was to be done. Whatever the issue, he would then have saved his country from further torment, and future ages would see that his motives had been selfless and disinterested. 'If I cannot live a King,' he said, 'at least I will die a gentleman.'

Did he think people would always stand so – and so – wherever his precise and deliberate thoughts had placed them? A sudden rage possessed Rupert at the sight of that confidence. His Scottish enemies – posterity – Charles could believe in anything as long as it was far enough away.

'Whoever succeeds in this struggle,' the young man burst out, 'will be called a great man and the saviour of this country. Englishmen don't care to distinguish qualities, they only value success. They are generous to their enemies if their enemies beat them, but they've never forgiven Ireland for the crime of being conquered by them, and they never will.'

'You have no opinion of this country,' said his uncle sadly.

'Because I know it will have no opinion of me – nor of you. They have defeated us.'

It was a statement made quietly, but so bitterly that even Charles was startled. It struck him that Rupert might have endured rather more than was usual at his age. He began to say that he had never valued Rupert's services the less because they had not always been successful. But his voice, that unwilling servant of his emotions, faltered timidly over his words, where he longed to rush into warm and impulsive speech.

Rupert's mind was hurrying on, seeing his uncle make this chivalrous gesture as the 'veray parfait gentle knight' that Rupert had first thought him; knowing that he intended it in all good faith, but knowing also that, though perfectly brave in despair, he would not be able to resist the agonizing temptations of hope; that he would try to juggle with minds far shrewder than his own, would walk into traps, be 'so sharp that he'd cut himself' as his old nurse used to say; and, worst of all, fritter away all that noble impulse in degrading subterfuges, excusable enough in a poor trapped prisoner, but not in the hero-victim that he suspected his uncle was holding as his model.

To hear him speak now no one would think he had no other hope nor motive than self-sacrifice; but he had talked otherwise when in cheerful mood of the possibility of playing off the rigid Presbyterians against the multitudinous Independent sects of Cromwell's army. Rupert made a desperate attempt to drag his uncle from his heights down into those sordid depths where the matter was only too likely to end.

'You may think you can outwit Cromwell,' he said in his violent way, crashing through Charles' tentative expressions of affection and gratitude and showing too plainly that he had not even been listening to them. 'You'll never do it. He'll read you like a book, he'll twist you and lay traps for you and you will most obligingly walk into them. *You* outwit him!'

He became uncomfortably aware of Charles' thoughtful regard. Even to himself he sounded surprisingly unlike a nephew talking to his uncle, let alone a king. He heard his own angry and despairing voice as though it were the voice of another man, and knew he would not have talked like this to his uncle before their quarrel. It was not in him to retract, it was too late to change; he could only hammer on relentlessly, 'You've never learned to deceive yourself one quarter as cunningly as he does, and that's more than half the battle. The man who can write those dispatches doesn't tell lies, he doesn't need to. His lies are all truth – to himself.'

He had transferred his violence to Cromwell to cover his attack on the King; but it was a transparent move and Charles eyed it coldly.

'What has Cromwell to do with the matter?' he asked. 'It is not to him I go, but the Scots.'

Rupert swooped upon that. 'Sir, you may go to whom you like, but it will be Cromwell you will have to deal with at the end. His army will back him whatever he does, and there's no army in Scotland now that can meet it. He's bound to get the last word.'

'As you have got now,' said the King with his faint smile.

Last word to first, Rupert realized they would make no difference. Yet he went on trying to dissuade him, passionately, doggedly, hopelessly.

'This is my fault,' he said, 'because I have made you lose faith in me. If you had gone on believing in me you would listen to me now.'

But he had to learn that 'no man may deliver his brother'.

Sullenness succeeded to his passion. At least he would take care not to be blamed for this scheme, as he had been for so many others. He would have it on record that he had nothing to do with it.

Charles was perfectly reasonable on this point; he wrote 'your opinion is, I should not undertake it', but asked him to 'assist me as heartily in it as if you fully concurred with me in opinion'. He added that his resolution was not because he was ignorant of the danger, 'in that differing little or nothing from you'. Indeed, his appreciation of the danger seemed to give him a curious ecstasy such as Rupert experienced in the height and fury of battle, but could not understand in this deliberate march into the enemies' power. He was too young and strong to realize that to anyone as desperately tired as Charles and dazed with his misfortunes, it was something to be welcomed.

Here was the thing that Charles instinctively knew he could do perfectly, and that was to accept his fate, whatever it might be, with the dignity of a true king.

*   *   *

On the light spring night within a week of May Day when Rupert at last saw Charles in his humble disguise ride with his two companions over Magdalen Bridge away from Oxford towards his self-appointed destiny, he remembered with aching vision that it was just ten years since that May Day when the Queen had come running into Whitehall Palace calling to the King, come running with a streak of sunlight dancing after her through the open door, and had stuck a branch of may-blossom into his hat.

There had been some sort of scurry – that infernal woman Lucy Carlisle snatching the white branches from the Queen's arms and crying that it was unlucky to bring them into the house, for so in old days the victim had been chosen to be crowned with garlands as King of Summer for a day, and sacrificed at the end of it.

What a thing to remember for ten years, and poor jolly red-nosed Suckling twirling on his toes at his malicious couplet, and Lucy scolding and the Queen laughing and throwing away all the white blossom – because 'she would not make the King a victim!'

The figure on horseback behind the two taller riders was growing smaller and smaller, a mere black dot behind two larger dots in the grey glimmer of the surrounding night. He would not watch till it was out of sight; it was mawkish, womanly, so he told himself as he turned away, lest he should recognize the fear that had whispered to him it was unlucky.

In that instant he knew, though soon he did not believe it, that he would not see Charles again.

CHAPTER TWELVE

IT SEEMED impossible that the three fugitives should manage to thread their way through their enemies; the Parliament armies had got wind of the King's flight, for they at once published a warning that anyone found sheltering or helping him in any way would be instantly executed. But at last those waiting in Oxford heard how he had reached Newcastle, how the Scots generals had hurried to meet him, not with any respectful courtesy and welcome such as Charles had been fondly imagining, but with a shrewd determination to exact their own terms before they even offered breakfast to the exhausted wanderer.

Rupert was given a good guess at the nature of those terms from a private message that succeeded in getting through to him. It told him that Charles had asked Montrose to lay down his arms and leave the country. The best way for his best friends to serve him was to leave him, so he told them.

So all hostilities were over. Oxford capitulated. The Princes were given remarkably good terms. They were not this time asked to give any promise of future neutrality to the Parliament, but were given free passes for themselves and all their household, down even to their laundry-maid, to leave the country from whatever port they pleased any time in the next six months.

Such sudden magnanimity was a trifle bewildering. 'What can they want of us?' asked Rupert, scratching his head. The only condition was that they were not to go within a certain distance of London. Well, that was easy. They had no wish to go near London. But no sooner did they agree on that than an urgent message came to them from Carl, entreating them to meet him at Oatlands, within the forbidden radius.

The war that had ravaged Germany for nearly thirty years was gradually ending, peace terms were being discussed at Munster and Osnaburgh, and it was there mooted that the Elector Palatine should be restored to his dominions. For this he must have the consent of all his brothers, and he had written to the Parliament telling them this and asking their leave 'to confer with my brothers Rupert and Maurice before their departure out of this kingdom, about this, and other domestic affairs'.

So here was the fruit that had been dangled in front of their struggling hands all their lives; it would fall into the family's hands again at last; and Rupert looked across the table at Maurice, and Maurice at Rupert, and both knew that it had ceased to be of any importance to them. Let Carl go home to the Palatinate. Small odds would it make to them, for they would never go – nor, so they shrewdly suspected, would it much help their mother or the rest of the family. Carl would get what he could out of it for himself, and that was all.

Rupert's first impulse was to refuse to meet his brother. But Maurice, less vindictive, and realizing what a storm this would create with their mother on their return to her, urged him to relent. It would be said that they had tried passively to prevent Carl's recovery of his land. Rupert did not care for the accusation, which savoured too much of Carl's own quiet methods. Finally all possible excuse for their avoiding the meeting was removed by their enemies; for Fairfax, official Commander-in-Chief for the Parliament, gave them full permission to go to Oatlands to meet their brother.

'There's nothing they won't do to oblige us!' said Maurice, and Rupert again felt the puzzled suspicion that there must be something behind all this compliance, and what could it be?

They rode to Oatlands, they rode up a two-mile drive of beech trees, straight as a die, planted in King Harry's days when people had begun to take long peaceful views for their property, to build their houses without battlements for defence and to plant trees that would be tall when they were dead. Under a century of waving green they rode, then out into the courtyard.

It was a dark June day, the clouds heavy, the lights silver and cold, the trees a violent green against them and the blown clouds of the last fruit blossoms of the late spring scurrying like snow before the wind. On top of the courtyard walls poppies and daisies were dancing, small torn banners of white and scarlet. A figure in black, young and tall, had come out on the steps of the great house to meet them, but it was not Carl.

'Who the devil is that?' asked Maurice; and Rupert, though he knew there was something familiar in the form, could not at once answer. But as he rode up and saw the leonine head and rosy cheerful face above the broad shoulders that had grown more robust than he remembered, he recognized his brother's chaplain, John Wilkins, whom he had last seen here in England ten years ago. They had been good friends then, he had liked and admired Wilkins almost more than anyone he had then got to know in England, but that was all changed now, Wilkins had turned his coat.

'So you are a Parliament man now,' Rupert said as he dismounted.

'No, Your Highness, I am as before, a Court chaplain,' he replied with a glance of subdued merriment which showed Rupert he knew all that he was thinking. But he gave no pause for embarrassment as they went into the house, his voice rippled on in the light balanced tones Rupert remembered so well, giving the Prince Elector's apologies for not being there to greet his brothers, but at that moment there had come an important message from Westphalia that had had to be dealt with on the instant, he would be with them immediately, and in the meantime would they not take refreshment after their ride – had they dined?

They had dined; Rupert had seen to that, not relishing the thought of convivialities with Carl. And as usual he refused wine.

' "Toujours soldat," ' murmured Wilkins consideringly. 'That being Your Highness' reputation throughout Europe I expected to find you no more of a wine drinker than in your boyhood, and have provided other liquor.'

He motioned to the servant to take away the tray of bottles and glasses.

'It's not the construction the English generally put on it then,' said Rupert. 'Here, to be "toujours soldat" is construed as always drunk. But what other liquor is there? You're not going to offer us milk in the name of God.'

For the life of him he could not help talking in this easy, half chaffing, half argumentative tone with Wilkins. It was exactly as though their last discussion had been interrupted only yesterday and they were now just about to pick up the threads again. There he was throwing back that massive head to pounce on his theoretical hare as eagerly as when his youth and ardour had made him look like a chubby schoolboy in canonicals.

'I have long suspected,' he was saying, 'that our European civilization was raw, immature, and inferior in many respects to those we are only beginning to discover. The practice of tea-drinking confirms my suspicion.'

The footman had re-entered the room, bearing this time a polished silver tray that gleamed as clearly as a pool of water from the reflected colours of three or four tiny porcelain bowls. Behind them a teapot of carved white jade bulged serenely like a cloud, and from it as Wilkins poured the tea came a faint burnt fragrance, more delicate than incense. Rupert had met with tea on his last visit; it had been the latest extravagance of the Court ladies and he had condemned it as insipid as hot water. In the irritation and suspense of this moment he drank it only to have something to do, but found the hot scented golden-brown liquid tasted both refreshing and soothing. He began to be amused at its effect on his companions. Maurice found it difficult to hold the hot thin porcelain without a handle, and was plainly contemptuous of the effeminate novelty, while Wilkins was drinking in bland and reverent satisfaction as if he would drink in the whole ancient culture of China with its tea.

He was speaking now of those strange nests of Cochinchina made by birds upon rocks 'of a certain viscous froth of the sea – and these nests when they are grown dry and hard are said to become transparent. The Chinese dissolve them in water and they then serve as an excellent seasoning to their meats. A traveller told me they are also a great restorative to nature, and much used by the lecherous Chinese.'

'I see no signs of superior civilization in eating birds' nests and drinking thin hot water-brew,' said Maurice haughtily.

Wilkins replied happily – 'Let us agree to differ. We can raise contrary imaginations upon any and every subject without any danger of a civil war.'

'Who are "we"?' asked Rupert.

'Your Highness' self, myself, and all who wish to clear away the thick deceits of spiritual frenzies by a candid and dispassionate inquiry into nature.'

'Thick deceits – spiritual frenzies' – the words had given Rupert an instant's vision of General Cromwell's hot brooding eyes. Wilkins was to have married Cromwell's sister – was that why the General's big head had thrust into his fancy? But he could not trouble to ask if Wilkins had married her or not, other questions mattered most – 'who are we?' still echoed in his mind.

'You know nothing of me,' he said.

'I know that you should have been Prince of Madagascar.'

Spoken in that deep triumphant voice the name was like the crash of surf on a far distant shore; it echoed down the caves of his memory that had lain empty of it all these years, it awoke again the longing and regret of his boyhood. Wilkins was calmly reminding him of all the observations he was to have made concerning the satellites of Jupiter, the nature of rivers that turn wood to stone, the healing properties of the rhinoceros' horn, and above all the customs, language and religion of the inhabitants, to be preserved intact for the purposes of comparative philosophy.

'You would not convert them?' gasped Maurice.

Wilkins plainly did not care to consider this question too closely. He reminded the young Prince, who was staring in amazement at this unusual parson, of the endless wars and disputes now waged in God's name. Was Prince Rupert to expose to the savages the hatreds that rend the body of Christ? 'I am certain,' he continued, flinging back his head with proud confidence in human destiny, 'that religion ought not to be the subject of dispute, it should not stand at the need of any devices of reason. The belief in God, the fate of man, are not to be confined by words.'

'You are a very clever fellow,' Maurice said, 'but I don't know why we are sitting here listening to you. Where is the Elector?'

'He is coming as soon as he can,' replied Wilkins.

'Soon enough – too soon,' muttered Rupert, staring down into his minute fragile cup which the chaplain had just refilled. The sun had come out between the storm clouds with that sudden and contrasted brilliance that makes the most homely scene look portentous; it was shining full through the open window on to the tea in the cup, and in this light instrument lay the cause of that goblin of reflected light that was dancing more madly than any will-o'-the-wisp upon the shadowed plaster ceiling, spinning itself into the circles and curves of a geometrical design, into clusters of butterflies, and now, as he held the cup very still in his hand, concentrating into a close-locked pair of Japanese wrestlers, crouching, leaping, rolling over and over each other.

The room where they sat was small; the walls were darkened by old-fashioned tapestries and solemn smoke-blackened portraits; the heavy carved furniture had remained stationary in it since King Henry's time. Wilkins' talk seemed to mock the solemn stuffy little store-house of the past with the wild possibilities of the future. He spoke of the parts of the human anatomy which Nature has not yet perfected; of injections into the blood and their possible effect on medicine; of the wonders and curiosities observable in deep mines. Rupert could now remember when all these questions had seemed of more importance than any other human activity.

Maurice made an effort against his brother's growing acquiescence.

'To hear you talk,' he said, 'no one would think that this country has been at war for the last four years.'

'And the world,' replied Mr Wilkins, 'has been at war for nearly six thousand years, against powerful and barbarous foes which have not yet been fully subdued – the foes of ignorance and false opinions. That is a war we are all bound in honour to wage until the end of time.'

'How do you propose to muster your army?' asked Rupert.

'Some few generals are enrolled, Your Highness.'

'It's an odd way of beginning, but you take long views. The raw recruits may not begin to come in for a few hundred years I suppose. And what's your plan of campaign?'

'To meet and discuss if possible at each other's houses at least once a week. We make experiments, compare discoveries, observe the motions of the stars, and each week we arrange some special subject to investigate. One week we examine spiders in amber – another, the methods of making that ruby glass, said to be a lost art, found only in old churches and cathedrals.'

'You'll not find much of it,' growled Maurice. 'Wasn't it a thousand windows and pictures, "all very superstitious", that the Roundheads ordered to be smashed in Clare village alone? It may be fun to smash glass, but why can't they leave the pictures?'

'I know that,' said Wilkins. 'It is precisely such love of senseless destruction that our society hopes to counteract.'

Rupert asked inconsequently, 'Does my brother attend your meetings?'

'His Highness,' replied Wilkins ambiguously, 'was, you may remember, never very good at mathematics.'

'Are mathematics essential to the meetings?'

'They are of great assistance. Last week a clever young mathematician, one Christopher Wren, showed us a globe he had made of the moon with its hills and cavities all moulded in solid work. Only politics and religion are never discussed, and no man is allowed to ask the opinions of his neighbour. So for a few hours each week, we of the Invisible College, as some of us like to call our little society, can forget the miseries of this present time, and plan towards a happier one.'

Rupert wondered when, and not if, that happier time would come, and whether he would be here to share it in England. What explorations could be made from this land with men of this spirit! Along the African coasts or to Guinea where the savages tipped their arrows with poison and devoured their prisoners? or to find the North-West passage among the floating ice rocks that were huge as mountains, blue as sapphire and as transparent? Surf breaking on a far distant shore – the Prince of Madagascar had gone on his travels again as he stared at the light reflected from his tea-cup.

A spiderweb traced in water, it fluttered, faded, vanished. The fugitive gleam had fled from the sky, the sun had gone in.

Rupert rose in respect to the head of the house as his brother Carl came into the room, and at once forgot that the past six thousand years and future ages had, through a brief enchantment, seemed more important than this present moment at the end of a four years' war.

Carl looked a man many years older than the youth that he remembered, many more than the actual number that had passed since their meeting; all the features were elongated, pulled down, while the upward twist to his moustaches and peaked eyebrows seemed to be making a self-conscious attempt to contradict this bitter and disillusioned look by an uneasy swagger. He was dapper as ever, dressed as though he had just come in from riding (rather oddly for one who had been closely occupied with messengers from Westphalia), in long boots of soft leather, brushed to a peach-like bloom, and carrying his hat and gloves.

His hat he tossed into a corner with a superb gesture, slightly marred by the anxious glance he sent after it to see if he had hurt the feather. His gloves he kept to flick and smack against his hand.

Rupert had not seen him since the beginning of the battle of Vlotho when he had been taken prisoner. Now that he saw again that superior mocking air, that cold glance and twist of eyebrow, he found that the words that were rushing hot into his throat were – 'why the devil did you and King never back me up at Vlotho?' He choked them back, of course – and made an effort to match his mood to Carl's exaggerated air of Olympic calm.

The latter was certainly overdoing it, and that showed his discomfort; he looked inquiringly at Wilkins, while Wilkins, refusing to meet his eye, looked with disapproval at his own boots. Rupert had a sudden suspicion of collusion. Had Carl come in too soon? Had all Wilkins' eager, rambling talk been merely preparatory to some suggestion Carl had wanted him to make, and had the blundering ass with his usual quiet tactlessness come in before he had made it? But Wilkins was preparing respectfully to leave them.

'Wait,' Rupert said sternly, 'I have something to ask you.'

For the life of him he could not yet think what it would be; but in the pause that followed he found himself asking nothing after all of the immediate moment, but rather that Wilkins should define his position.

'Where do you stand in all this?' he said. 'You cannot stand aloof these days, you must be for either King or Parliament – or is it only for the winning side?'

'For the winning side,' answered Wilkins, with not even a look to modify his statement. An astonished oath broke from Maurice, but Rupert checked him.

'You once told me,' he said, 'that you gave up your country parsonage because you could promote your interests better by attaching yourself to persons of influence. I know enough of you now to know what your interests are – they are not self-interest.'

'No – but they run parallel,' interpolated Carl with a twirl of his moustache. It was counter to his own design to belittle his chaplain, but he had to assert himself somehow; he had been ignored as soon as he had entered.

'Wilkins should have taught you enough mathematics to know that parallel lines never meet,' replied Rupert. At once turning back to the chaplain he went on as though the other did

464

not exist – 'But you can't stand aside in all this. You must think one side good, the other evil.'

'I think the chief evil is in their being sides. My aim is to lead men away from narrow notions of belonging to parties, from their superstitious conceits that they alone know God's intentions, and from the fierceness of opinion that leads to. You have met John Selden, a very wise man – he once said to me, "Opinion is that wherein I go about to show why all the world should think as I think." I have no opinion of opinions. I hate differing with men, for by differing comes division, and division is death, the death of society. Back we go to the savage, each for his own. The history of humanity is of the growing power of unity. That will continue, in spite of all this struggle is doing to rend it, and life will go on towards a brighter light of reason, of moderation and kindliness than seems possible today.'

'But you – you yourself?'

'I, sir? I was a watchmaker's son. But I am of more use as a scholar, in touch with other scholars, than as either a watchmaker or a country parson. And, for that end, I consider it right and reasonable to submit myself to the powers in being, be they who they may, or established how they may.'

'You would not lift a finger to defend your King?'

'You have realized yourself, sir, that it is useless.'

'*Now* I have.'

'I placed the "now" rather earlier than Your Highness has done, that is all.'

'Of all cold-blooded, atheistical parsons —' began Maurice.

'Hush,' said his eldest brother softly, 'we must not interrupt Rupert.'

The sneer brought Rupert wheeling round on his brother.

'What have you to do with all this? You would not care a rap for what he has been saying.'

'I don't know what he has been saying, only what he has not, since he has obviously neglected to come to the point.'

'I lost myself in other matters,' said Wilkins. His voice was mild, even apologetic, but he continued in the same respectful and friendly tone, 'Your Highness' annoyance, though very natural, will not help your point with Prince Rupert. I had best remove the cause of it.'

He bowed low to all three brothers, and Rupert held out his hand. 'Curse me if I understand what you're at,' he said, 'but I'd give a deal to share in it.'

'I will defend what I can,' said Wilkins, looking him straight in the face, 'and those are the persons and places of learning which the ignorant and superstitious commanders will certainly try to destroy. For the sake —' he was speaking more and more slowly, his mild clear wide-open eyes fixed on the sad hooded eyes above him, '— not merely of England, but of all mankind, I ask Your Highness not to leave the rule of this country to a mob of raw soldiers who mistake themselves for saints.'

He went out of the room, which now seemed stuffy, small, and incapable of change. There would always be these heavy chairs and table in it, these wooden portraits of ruffs and staring eyes, this long, complaining face that he had not seen for seven years and that now seemed to have been always with him. Carl was beginning to put on his jaunty air, Carl was clearing his throat, 'Well, now that we are alone together —' began Carl.

And Carl came to the point, which Wilkins had overlooked among the satellites of Jupiter and the wonders and curiosities observable in deep mines.

CHAPTER THIRTEEN

'I SENT FOR you,' said Carl, raising his eyes to Rupert's and as hastily transferring them to Maurice's, 'on business even more to your advantage than mine.'

His curious tactlessness with men could not have shown itself more characteristically. Rupert had been sufficiently puzzled and interested to determine to bury the hatchet, but now that detestable word 'advantage', on top of the cool assumption of authority in 'I sent for you', made all his pent-up fury with his brother surge up again to the surface.

'What advantage can you offer me?' he asked haughtily. 'Is it a share in that eight thousand you received so opportunely from Parliament at the moment when I had to surrender Bristol? A great advantage that was to me, as was all your stay here, almost as much advantage as to our uncle.'

'You are absurd if you blame me for that. All it amounted to was that our uncle was spared the expense of my pension since Parliament paid it instead.'

'You are very reasonable,' said Rupert through his teeth, his upper lip curled back like an angry wolf's. 'Is it from living so intimately with the London shopkeepers that you've learned to think like a tradesman?'

It seemed inevitable, the quarrel was on them just as in the old days, and as then with Rupert the aggressor, putting himself more and more hopelessly in the wrong. But this time Carl was determined to keep the peace.

'It would be just as well,' he replied almost good-humouredly, 'if a family like ours could contrive to have one tradesman in it. We can't all go for knights-errant – our mother said none of us should, but you've all gone against that.'

'So you think that justifies hanging on here—' Rupert choked the rage back in his throat. What was the use of going on like this as though they were still in the schoolroom? He would never know what Carl's scheme was if he told him all that he thought of him – he had even learned enough from his quarrels with Charles, with Digby, and a hundred others, to know that he could never make Carl see himself as he saw him. But some insidious trick of family feeling always betrayed him – he did not recognize that what he really wanted was to make his mother see Carl as he saw him.

'Will you govern by Parliament in the Palatinate?' Maurice asked unexpectedly of Carl, who as surprisingly answered him. 'I intend there shall be government in the Palatinate, not a succession of compromises. That may suit this country, it wouldn't suit any other.'

'You speak very oddly for a champion of Parliament,' said Rupert.

'I play the national game while I am in the country – but I can see it is a game, which they can't.' His considering, doubtful eyes flickered from one to the other. 'This is all private, every word that I've said and am going to say.'

They nodded at the unnecessary warning. This was a family conclave. Of course it would be private. For all that, Carl seemed to find it difficult to come to the main point. He smiled a little as if to try the effect on his brothers, but quickly abandoned the attempt on finding it to be unsuccessful. Rupert jogged him on.

'You want our consent to whatever may be settled in your interests at the Treaty of Munster,' he said; 'well, it's given. What else?'

'What are the "other domestic affairs that concern us"?' asked Maurice.

Carl caught at this question quite eagerly. It was plainly not the chief one in his mind. ' "The other domestic —" – oh, well, things are not being very satisfactory at home.'

'They never are,' remarked Rupert. 'Has anyone boxed Louey's ears again, or anybody else turned Catholic?'

Carl gave him a wry grin. 'No, thank God. Ned's done me harm enough. Now they've got Philip away from Paris at last.'

'Where is he?'

'At home again with Mother, and I've begged her to get rid of his rascally Papist tutor and tell him she'll put a mother's curse on him if he ever changes his religion. It would be fatal if anything were to happen now, just as the peace negotiations have started. He talks of taking service with the Venetians, but he's very young for that. Perhaps one of you might undertake it instead?'

He looked at Maurice, who looked at Rupert, who replied haughtily, 'Wherever we go when we leave here, it will be on our uncle's business.'

Carl bolted back to the refuge of domestic affairs.

'I have had some rather disturbing reports,' he said; 'they can, I am certain, be only the result of ill-natured gossip —'

'Well, spit it out, man.'

In proof of the egoism of man, Rupert could only think of the reports spread by Queen Henrietta that he had sold Bristol to the enemy.

'Have you heard of the Marquis d'Epinay?'

They had not.

'He's a French refugee, has a great reputation with women – well, he's added to it, that's all.'

Never had Carl's indirect methods been so irritating. Maurice questioned once again, Rupert swore, and at last Carl said, 'Well, there seems to have been some flirtation with Louey as usual. She is always giving trouble – cares nothing for our reputation. But that's not the worst by a long shot. He seems to have wormed himself into Mother's confidence – and now there's scandal about her too. They say he boasts of both his conquests – mater pulchrior, puella pulchrissima —'

His Latin tag died uncompleted, Rupert's face had flushed dark red, his hand had gone to his sword.

'And he's alive? Is there nobody at The Hague to stand by her?'

'She doesn't want to be stood by,' said Carl crossly; 'you

don't understand, that's the whole difficulty – she's infatuated with the fellow.'

'That's a lie.'

'I hope so. It isn't one I want to believe any more than you. I'm sure I don't know what ought to be done. It isn't as though anything like this had ever happened before. Men have always lost their heads over Mother, and she's never cared a rush – till now.'

Rupert had turned away long before Carl had finished speaking. A hot sick wave of fury and disgust engulfed him. He had always taken it for granted that his mother was adored and invulnerable; it had never occurred to him that she might be desired as well as adored; and it naturally never dawned on him that he was madly jealous. All he knew was that there was no truth, faith nor honour anywhere; he did not think of asking with whom it was that his mother had not kept faith.

Carl began to say that with Louey it might be more excusable, though very trying, if she chose to make herself the talk of Europe, but that with their mother now just fifty —

Rupert swung round from the window out of which he had been staring and seeing nothing.

'We'll leave this,' he said. 'Tell us what you want of us.'

'Nothing for myself, except indirectly. It concerns our family, it concerns this country.' He watched Rupert to see if he had yet caught his attention, but there was no sign that Rupert was even listening. 'By this country,' went on Carl argumentatively to gain time, 'I mean something more than Parliament or the Court. You can't know it in the same way because you've always been with the King, but I've been away from Court —' ('My God, you have!' muttered Rupert, his attention caught at last, though in a flash of angry contempt, but Carl ignored that. The self-restraint on both sides made the ground feel like the edge of a volcano.) – 'I've lived and talked with Londoners for years,' Carl continued with something now of his old imperturbability, 'and I know what the country has always wanted – all over the country. It's nothing to do with the war, it goes back a dozen years before that started, it goes right back for that matter to the King's wedding. They all hated to have a French Papist for a Queen, they hated it still more when she refused to be crowned by the Church of England – refused even to walk in the Coronation procession. That finished her —'

'At fifteen!' exclaimed Maurice in a spasm of unwonted

sentiment at the thought of their plucky, maddening little aunt. Rupert was wondering dully why they were bothering about her, why he had ever bothered about her – all her French airs and graces, her little coaxing ways that had suddenly turned to clawing scratches – they had never really mattered.

What had mattered was the woman with the brooding eyes and the glorious bursts of laughter who had ridden and hunted better than any man, who had never been fair to him, who whenever she looked at him talked about Carl, who was now 'infatuated', so Carl said coolly, with some little French rat who boasted of his conquest of her. He tore his mind from the images that were now rushing into it, filling it with obscene horror; he forced himself to listen to what Carl was saying.

'At fifteen? Why not? They condemned her son and heir as soon as he was born – they wouldn't ring bells or offer thanksgiving in some of the churches – and everywhere they were saying, "What do we want with a French Papist's brat for our Prince of Wales? When our own English Elizabeth has given so many fine sons to the Protestant cause?" '

He paused to look impressively at his brothers, whose faces had shut down like masks. He could not guess what they were thinking; he went on piling up his evidence. 'It reached even into Whitehall – when I was with the King there before the war began, someone had scratched on the window that England wanted the Queen of Bohemia's sons for heirs instead of Prince Charles. He had the pane removed before the Queen saw it, but everyone knew of it – I saw it myself.'

'I'll bet you did,' said Rupert in a low growl, 'and a deal of comfort you must have been to our uncle!'

'I never referred to it with him,' said Carl indignantly, and stared at the rude laughter this provoked.

'You've got less and less like an Englishman since you've lived with 'em,' said Rupert.

Carl's patience was little short of heroic; but as a matter of fact he was for the most part enjoying himself. For all his brothers' antagonism they were now listening to him as he had never got them to listen before. He knew that he was putting his case well and fairly, without any exaggeration.

'You can laugh at me like boors if you will,' he said, 'I am only telling you the facts as impersonally as Wilkins would have done if he had been describing a condition of nature. The English people have wanted one of us for their King before even we

470

were born. They have always adored our mother – "She's an Englishwoman through and through," they say – "Our second Queen Elizabeth, that's what she should have been!"'

('That's what she should have been, and she's given some sneaking French rat the chance to call her his whore! – Be still you fool and listen, or you'll go mad.')

But Rupert's words were silent. It was Carl who was talking. 'They wanted her for Queen, they wanted her brother Harry for King. They feel they've been cheated of the two they wanted; but sooner or later it will come, they say. Those here who take long views can see it coming,' he added portentously.

There was no doubt that Carl was telling what he had heard, and heard often.

'So it's true,' said Rupert, in that soft voice of his that was the most dangerous, a voice that sounded positively happy, for here was a sound and legitimate object for the anger that was tearing him inside, 'it's true – that you have been waiting here in hopes of the English Crown.'

In the instant's pause that followed, while the blueish flush went up from Carl's cheekbones round the edges of his nervous eyes, it seemed that anything might happen.

But Carl only said, 'I don't deny I've thought of it for myself, it would have been inhuman if I hadn't. God knows I've had it rammed into me enough. Two years ago the French Ambassador was talking openly of the Parliament's plan to put me on the throne. But now things are changed. I'll put it as cynically as you like; I've got this firm offer of the Palatinate, and if I linger on here I might lose the substance for the shadow. But that's no reason why it shouldn't still be kept in the family. With two reigning princes in it, think of the power we could be in Europe!'

'You suggest that I should make a bid for my uncle's throne?' asked Rupert.

'I do, and I suggest that you should not be such a hypocrite as to deny that you've never thought of it for yourself. If I've had it put to me in private, you've had it shouted from the housetops, stated in cold print again and again.'

'As an accusation, which has done me more harm than anything else, and that's why their cursed pamphlets went on saying it.'

'Their tune has changed a deal towards you this last year. You might even manage the whole business quite peaceably.

Ever since it became known that you were advising the King to make peace, there's been a strong feeling for you – much stronger than there's ever been for me,' he added, glancing from one to the other to see how this generous concession was taken. Like all that he had offered, it was not taken with any graciousness, but Maurice nodded in unexpected confirmation.

'I know,' he said to Rupert; 'the Roundhead prisoners have told me so – they all wish they had you to deal with instead of our uncle.'

Rupert began to walk up and down the little room. Another gleam of sunshine had made the trees outside a glaucous green, like glass against the dark clouds. He stopped to stare at them out of the window and then walked on again.

What did it matter now what anyone did since there was neither decency nor honour anywhere in the world?

Carl drove it home. He was sitting on the edge of the table now, casual and easy in manner, swinging a leg while he flapped his riding-glove against it, his air at last that of the old Timon, the boy who had so soon become a man of the world but had not quite lost the piquant charm of that precocious cynicism.

'I'll tell you what they say now, here in London. They say of you, "we know where we are with him. He fought well and he gave us some bloody hard knocks, and now he's fought as hard on the side of peace." But of the King they say, "We shall never know where we are with him." '

'That's true,' said Maurice, who was staring under his thick fair eyebrows at Rupert, urging him with all his will to consent. 'He's ruined every battle and every campaign you fought here, and now he blames you for them all. You've broken yourself for him – but what's he ever done for you first and last that you should consider him any more?'

Rupert met his angry pleading eyes as he walked past him. He wanted to say that you didn't fight for a man in order that he should do something for you – but what was the use of saying that sort of thing now? Old Timon would only jeer, and he was probably right, for it did make a difference how a man treated you – Marston Moor had made a difference (that maddening contradicting equivocating letter that had yet been so damnably insistent – he still had it on him), and Bristol had made a difference – by God, yes! Bristol had made all the difference.

Maurice, watching his brother's darkening face, pushed home one more thrust, and said, 'Let him go.'

'He's gone,' said Carl, 'gone into the Scots camp, to the enemies of both his side and the Parliament's. He's finished.'

Rupert stopped in his walk and stood looking down on his brother. All their animosity was for the moment forgotten. They were friends of the same family who had shared as many anxieties, fears and hopes in the past as they had quarrels.

'What do you think they'll do with him?' he asked.

'Sell him to England most likely, and *then* England will be in a pretty fix! But they'll never dare let him have any real power again, that's certain.'

'*Sell* him?'

'Well, the Scots have never yet got a penny of their army's pay that the Parliament promised them.'

'What do you say in London about him?'

'Some talk of making him abdicate in favour of one of his sons – the baby one, Harry of Gloucester, if any, for they won't have Charles or James; they were brought up by their mother. Her reputation as a devoted mother has only gone against her – and them. The Puritans know what the Jesuits say – "Give me a child's first seven years and you can have the rest," and so that's what they say of the first two – "She's had 'em the first seven years and they'll both die as Papists, mark my words." '

Carl's imitation of the Cockney accent was rather funny, but Rupert did not smile. He was still standing motionless, biting his thumb, chewing the nail, sullen and ferocious, as when he had been a schoolboy. Carl thought he was in doubt, and cleared up Harry's position quickly.

'He'd be nothing but a puppet for the Parliament and army of course. That's what the bad ones among them want, as a cloak for power for themselves.'

Rupert gave no sign of having heard him. The words, 'sell him' were still echoing in his mind.

If the world were nothing but a dirty market-place, must he be one of the hucksters?

'I won't,' he said.

'You won't what?'

'You know well enough, and I won't do it.'

'Oh, so you won't, won't you?' It was a ridiculous echo of their childhood, growling the same brief words over and over again at each other, but none of the three young men heard that – they heard only the angry rift widening between them, splitting them apart where just now they had spoken in unity.

473

'So you'll be noble and self-sacrificing,' Carl was saying. 'Well, you'll sacrifice a good deal more than your own private ambition – and you needn't tell me you haven't longed to be King of England ever since you were a boy here, for you know you have. And it's England you're sacrificing. If you won't rule this country, it won't be Uncle Charles who will.'

'Who then?' asked Maurice, and Rupert held his breath, knowing the answer himself and dreading to hear another acknowledge it.

'General Cromwell,' said Carl. 'Parliament don't count now. Nothing counts but the army, and he rules the army. Fairfax may be Commander-in-Chief, but it's what Cromwell says that goes. He'll not want to rule in his own name – it was his notion to put up a child by way of pretence – but he'd rather do that than have Charles rule. I don't think he'd be out for power for himself once the war's over – but he'd want things done the way he wants them, and he's said good things of you. What's the use of leaving the country to be distracted by more civil wars and revolutions before we take what *must* come to us – or our children – sooner or later?'

The reasonable voice slipped on, lightly flicking his words into the air on that faintly disdainful note that used to flick at his younger brother's raw temper with a lash like a whip. But now at last it was Rupert who could take the whip-hand, and not for anything, not to be King of England, could he forego that pleasure. He would show that 'mother's darling' what he really was – fit darling for such a mother, a mother who could squander herself at fifty on a little womanizing rat.

'So you hang on here, waiting to snatch what pickings you can out of the King's defeat! Did I call you a tradesman just now? I was wrong. I've seen how the Cockney tradesmen can fight, and they are grand fellows. There's no word for you but jackal. Even Uncle Charles saw it – wrote it to you – "Merely to get another chicken in your dish" – that's what he said to you!'

'Then he lied!' roared Carl, suddenly at breaking point.

'He lied, did he? He did you an injustice when he told you "it would have been a design more worthy of his nephew if you'd openly tried to take the Crown from his head"? He'd have had more respect for you then, and so would I.'

'Very well then, he hates me. I know that. His letter showed it plain enough; it had things in it that would have moved a saint to anger. I don't know of anyone but our Saviour who'd have ruined himself for those that hate him.'

'What's our Saviour to do with it?'

'You can snarl yourself hoarse. But I have done what I could here to smooth things over for him, and he's never been just to me – never – since you first came to England and spoilt everything. We were good friends then, till you came swaggering in with your precious plans of Madagascar. It's easy for you to play the knight-errant, you're only a younger son with no responsibilities. Nobody ever sees how difficult my position is.'

'Why couldn't you fight then? That's easy. No, I forgot – it's easier to drive off with General King and the cash box.'

'Or surrender Bristol?'

Rupert hurled himself forward. 'You sneaking French rat!' he roared, and nobody, not even himself, noticed how odd it was he should call his brother a Frenchman, for his fist was clenched, drawn back to swing into Carl's face. Maurice flung himself on to him, pinioning his arm. Over his head Rupert saw Carl's white anxious grin that was trying to look contemptuous.

The red mist cleared before his eyes; they could not fight with fists at this age, nor could they have a duel between brothers. He was even a little shocked to find that his hands had been itching not so much to strike as to lock themselves round Carl's pale throat, pale from living much indoors, and shake the life out of him as a dog shakes a rat to death.

That was over. He drew back, roughly pushing Maurice's hand off his arm.

'I lost my temper,' he said, unnecessarily, except that it was by way of apology.

'You've taken your last chance with me to behave like a madman,' said Carl, his voice as cool as ever and a good deal more scornful, but with a nervous twitch flicking his under eyelid furiously up and down – 'If you had been visiting me in the Palatinate you would have been placed under arrest.'

Rupert said slowly, 'As long as I live, I'll never set foot in my father's country while you rule there.'

He turned his back on Carl and walked out of the room. Maurice walked after him. They summoned their servants, got on their horses, and rode away.

Rupert felt his bridle hand still shaking with rage. He tried to think that he had done the right thing and that he was glad of it, but he knew that his chief reason for doing so at that moment had been his hatred for Carl and for anything that Carl could suggest.

As he rode through this smiling summer land that had been offered to him and that he had rejected, silly whining words crept into his angry mood – 'after all I've done', they whined, 'after all I've done', for he was thinking now of his uncle Charles who had hurt him as Carl never could, had wrecked all his plans for him and then done his best to blast his reputation and spoil his career, worst of all, had given Carl the chance to taunt him with Bristol – and this after all that Rupert had done for him.

And this just cause for complaint he nursed as he had never done before, because, for the first time, it was bearable to think of – it was better to think of it than of something else that lay red and raw and unbearable at the back of his mind and of his eyes.

CHAPTER FOURTEEN

THAT SAME night, when the clouds that had been blowing past all day had piled themselves up into a heavy and still sky, with low thunder threatening from time to time along its borders, Mary Richmond slipped a dark cloak round her shoulders, pulled it over her head and half across her face, and went out of the house by a little garden door, down by the tall yew hedge, across the herb garden and into the pleached alley where the dark sky made a round of faint light at each end of the tunnel of black trees. And there, though it was just what she was expecting, she gave a little choked cry when something as black and tall as the trees stepped out from among them and came towards her.

In desperate hurry she began to speak, tumbling her sentences over each other and finishing none of them. 'How did you come here all alone, and where – It is the most mad, foolhardy – And your note to me, how did you —'

She knew they would not be answered, were not heard even; she knew before he bent towards her that this would happen; the next instant she was caught up into blackness and knew nothing, for all thought, all feeling, except that of blind pain and terror, was being battered out of her by his kisses. Her feeble struggles were quickly crushed, she had no breath to cry, soon she lay so limp and dead in his arms that her terror now invaded Rupert; he began to wonder what he had done to her in the fury of his desire and mad discovery that she was in his arms at last.

He carried her out from under the blackness of the trees and stared down at her face, a grey glimmer against his dark sleeve, and all the black hair rippling back from it, running like water over his arm and across his breast. He pushed his free hand over her hair, and took it up and twisted it round his fingers and tugged at it, not knowing what he was doing in his agony of fear and doubt, and cried to her to speak to him and tell him he had not hurt her. A voice as faint as the flutter of a moth's wing came out of the darkness.

'Not hurt me?' it sighed; 'do you take me for a suit of armour?'

He all but dropped her in his amazement. Who could crush or hold this woman? Kill her, and she would laugh at you as she died. His senses had come back to him under that flick of mockery; he peered down into her face, hoping those deep shadows were not bruises. 'What can I do for you?' he asked humbly.

'Take me into the shelter at the end of this path. It is beginning to rain.'

He had never noticed that. Now as he straightened himself again, tossing back the hair that had fallen forward over his shoulders, he felt the raindrops running down the back of his neck under his collar.

He carried her into the little summer-house at the end of the path, scarcely more than an alcove in the wall, with a stone seat in its embrasure and a mass of white clematis that came tumbling down over the wall and fringed its roof. Its star-shaped flowers shone dimly between them and the dark rain which seeped and slithered down now all round their narrow shelter. She slipped out of his arms as he set her on the seat, and he did not dare touch her again after his late roughness; he sat beside her and could not see her face. Only he knew she was there beside him, warm and living in the darkness, and the scent of that night-black hair, that he had just now coiled and twisted round his fingers, stole into his nostrils, and he knew that soon he would no longer be able to bear it that she was beside him.

He stared out into the darkness and the rain falling, and heard the little sucking sighing noises as it sank into the ground and pattered on the leaves and dripped off them into the earth. He said, 'Leave Richmond and come with me, and I will make you Queen of England.'

She was leaning back against the wall in her exhaustion and had closed her smarting eyelids; but now she opened them painfully and stared out too at those slanting dark lines that made the night, and saw against them his face as it leaned forward, carved in black silhouette; the great arrogant nose and chin, and the mouth pulled tightly in between them, shut down in restraint.

She knew then that what she had just heard had not been said on the impulse of his passion; it was what he had come here to say; and it seemed to her as though the world itself must have turned over in its sleep and set everybody changing places. It was not Rupert of the Rhine that was saying this, it was not what he could ever have said; it was what her father would have said, but not through stern-shut lips on that note of tragic doom – he would have said it with a laugh and a flourish, delighted to think of a new way to prove himself irresistible, to plunge his country into another war, yes, even to betray his two best friends, since it was all for the love of a lady.

'But *you* can't do that?' she said, 'your King and uncle, your friend, you could never betray them. Your honour —'

'That damnable word!' he said, 'it's a trick, a game they teach to fools, so that knaves shall win. Well, I'm free of it now.'

'You are the soul of it!'

'There's no soul in honour or in anything. I've been its unwilling victim all these years, and now I see what it's worth.'

'Rupert! This is not you —'

'This is I – I – I. Don't think of the fool whose precious honour held him back from you all this time – that's over – the honour's gone, trampled in the mud. I've been turned off in disgrace as a traitor to my uncle – so why not to my friend too? What does one dishonour more or less matter now?'

She saw then that here was no Buckingham but the same Rupert, furious with pain such as her father would never have known how to feel. The hurt that he had done her so that every inch of her was throbbing, but in a deep triumphant exultation as well as discomfort, was nothing to the hurt that had been done to him. Pity and indignation for him stirred her to life; she forgot everything but that he must not feel like this.

'You are wrong,' she cried, 'there's never been dishonour in your heart. You have kept faith with your friends – think when they all wanted you to take arms against the King at Newark, and you would not – think when I came to you at Bristol.'

'No, I'll not think of that, nor of Newark – nor of this very afternoon.'

'What happened this afternoon?'

'Nothing; I'll not speak of that. Yes, though, I'll tell you of one thing this afternoon. I forgot that. I was offered the Crown of England and refused it. Never mind how. It was all very quiet and unofficial, but there's good backing for it. If you come with me, I will take it. Will you come?'

He turned in the darkness so that she no longer saw that black outline of his face, only of his great shoulders towering over her. She shrank back, but he did no more than take her two hands where they lay limp and pale on her cloak, and he held them in his very gently, and said her name under his breath, the name she had not borne since she had been a very little girl in a scarlet and silver apron who had been told that she was to marry the King's nephew and might one day be Queen of England.

'Mary Villiers,' he whispered, 'Mary Villiers,' and drew her towards him until his lips found her face and then her mouth, and sank on it as though they would never leave it again.

Then she longed to go with him to the ends of the earth.

But would she go? She had been sheltered so tenderly since her childhood that she had scarcely had opportunity to notice it. But what life would she lead with this man? Would she ever feel safe with him? She remembered Bristol and shuddered.

And though her senses were swooning under his touch, that had been so brutal and was now so gentle, her cool, subtle and lively brain woke to consciousness; and she knew that he could never make her Queen of England without hating her and himself with the hatred that leads to madness. Nor could she let him take her now, lightly, as if she were only Mary Villiers, for she was not that, and had never been since he had known her; she was Mary Richmond, and she had learned her lesson once for all at Bristol when she had seen what that meant to him, and what he would become if he betrayed it.

479

Very carefully, so as not to startle nor anger this uncontrollable creature, she withdrew her lips from his and said softly, 'When I lie in your arms, you will remember your friend, and you will hate me as I saw you hate me in Bristol.'

'By God,' he cried, 'it is you who hate me because of Bristol and rightly, for I was a fool. Can you never forget it?'

'Never, dear Rupert.'

Her voice was more tender than he had ever heard it. He stared baffled into the blackness, wishing he could see if those long slanting eyes were laughing at him. She was speaking again now, but as strangely. 'I will never forget what I saw you to be. You all call me frivolous, but nothing will make me forget that.'

'But it's over,' he said, 'the game is up. Who cares what happens now? We have reached the edge of the world. Who's to care how or with whom we go over the edge?' ('With a French rat even? Who cares? Nobody cares. We've all got our own fish to fry.')

Kissing her again, mockingly, insolently now, as she had never imagined he could kiss, his hands taking his toll of her with the cool mastery of a man practised with women, his wild rambling thoughts ran on out into his speech – 'a pretty kettle of fish – a very pretty little fish – have you no warm blood in you after all, my little fish?'

She surrendered trembling to his strength; all the pleasure-loving sensual nature inherited from her father revelled in his caresses, and the more for their new insolent command of her making her only a plaything in his cruel and tender hands.

She whispered, 'How you have changed – what woman has been teaching you?'

'My mother!' he said, and broke into terrible laughter.

For an instant's frozen horror she thought he had gone mad in earnest – then she remembered gossip she had heard lately from The Hague; remembered too what she herself had once said of him and his mother. She pulled herself from him and he let her go; he did not want to hold her now that she had made him say that. Now she would probe and pry and pretend to comfort; he had wanted her as a woman – but he was damned if he would let that give her the right to interfere.

But she said no word of his mother.

Silence filled the alcove. Only the rain sighed and swished all round them, and one big clematis star hung down from the roof like a pale transparent face looking in on them from the night

The hush that was on them was carrying them down the years, farther and farther away from the snatching, eager, desperate moment that had locked them together just now. So that when Mary spoke her voice seemed to come from a great distance, after a long time.

'Whoever reaches the edge of the world,' she said, 'the world goes on, life begins again.'

She choked back the sob in her throat and laughed breathlessly and a little wildly – 'and for us too life will begin again – but not with each other while I am Richmond's wife. Neither he nor you could bear that, especially you. I may be a Butterfly but I won't be broken on the wheel of your hate – yes, hate, and it's no use to deny it. You are a great gentleman, I see that, and I dare say my dear disgraceful Dad, whom I always thought one, was only a great mountebank!'

'Mary, Mary, are you laughing? You are not crying, are you?'

All the cruelty of his bitterness was tamed. He had thrown himself into her power by flinging out into the night, like a stone at an unseen enemy, the name of his mother whom he had never meant to speak of. But Mary had not used her advantage, she was not even thinking of it.

'You are more of a great gentleman than I,' he said with a new shy admiration, 'but what are you crying for?'

'A few tears are for myself and one or two for you. And now I am going back before they find I'm gone.'

He put his hands on her shoulders, then let his grasp slide to her elbows, holding her there, but at arm's length.

'I will not hold you against your will,' he said; it was a question, his last.

'You'll know some day,' she said, 'that that is what I would not do with you.'

For a moment he still held her, and the fates of more than themselves hung in the balance. He had not listened to her words. Had she resisted or even stiffened in his grasp, they would have been no more than straws against him. But in the deep stillness of her flesh he read their meaning. His hands fell. She moved from him and he let her go. She melted into the wet darkness. He sat on, staring at the face of the white clematis.

H E R E J O I N E D Maurice next morning, one of those splendid mornings of high summer that blazingly contradict the fact that it has been pouring all night. But Maurice's face was a thundercloud in itself.

'These bloody treacherous English,' he burst out on seeing his brother. 'They don't know what it is to keep their word.'

'Do other nations?' asked Rupert wearily, for nothing irritated him more than when Maurice ran down the English on the tacit assumption that he was more of a foreigner than Rupert.

'Perhaps not, but they don't invent pompous proverbs like "An Englishman's word is as good as his bond". In this case it *was* his bond – we had direct written permission from the Commander-in-Chief of all their armies to go and visit Carl, and now they've gone back on it – look what they're doing' – he was flourishing a paper so furiously at Rupert that he could not keep it still enough for Rupert to read – 'they say we've broken our terms – they're seizing the pretext to push us out of England straight away. It was a trap, that's what it was – there they were ready to jump the moment we left Carl. These letters must have been prepared overnight – and now here we are being told to go within a week!'

Rupert took the paper out of his brother's hand and stood reading, frowning, furiously pulling at a long lock of hair that had fallen forward over his shoulder. It certainly was very strange. Here had the Parliamentary army been behaving like the most courteous of hosts; they had pressed them to stay in the country for a full six months, only making a very natural proviso that they should not go too near London; and then modified even that, when there came that question of visiting their brother, and granted them full leave to do so. And now, ignoring the permission they had given, they were protesting that the Princes had broken their terms and must instantly leave the country.

Maurice went on fuming – 'We'll raise hell over this – we'll expose them – we'll get Carl to ask a question in Parliament —'

'*How* will you get Carl to do that?' asked Rupert. 'No, they couldn't be acting like this for no reason. They knew what they were doing when they sent us to Carl, they knew what Carl was doing. And now we've refused his suggestion, they're bundling us out of the country as fast as possible, before we give anything away. They needn't have worried. Not a soul will ever know what was said then.'

'You think Parliament was really behind it?'

'I can only guess. It looks like it from this. Or perhaps Fairfax wanted it, and when Cromwell came to hear of it he wouldn't have it. But whoever was behind it,' he added, looking sternly at the wistful hopes that were even now raising themselves again in Maurice's eyes, 'that's finished. And we've finished with England. So we may as well go in six days as six months – and better.'

Since last night he was in a fever to be off. What was the use of staying in this country, since he could not woo Mary? 'I had her here in my hands,' he found himself thinking whenever he looked down on them, 'and I let her go!'

He could not take Mary, and he could not take his uncle's throne. Mary had been right, and he would be grateful to her for it all the days of his life – but Maurice knew nothing about that, and he should not know. For three years his pent-up longing for Mary had been repressed so sternly that of late he would not admit it even to himself; but now it walked free and acknowledged in his breast, a living thing, glorious and terrible, tearing him in two, yet making him see the world as if he had never looked on it before. That force of passion was now rushing through him on a tide of immense bitterness as he realized what the power was that would henceforth master England.

But he could not do anything more – and the King would not. The King was confident again, almost happy, busying himself in correspondence with Henderson, the head of the Scottish Church, writing about bishops, that he was willing to learn Henderson's views on them and see if there were any doctrine which he himself had not understood.

Maurice was speaking of this now, asking in his direct fashion, 'Will he really let the Church of England be turned Presbyterian, do you think?'

'If he did, he'd get back his throne. But he won't.'

'Then why does he act as if he might?'

'He must do something. He's their prisoner, he's sent away all his friends – what else can he do?'

'Doesn't he see how dangerous it is if he's only playing with them?'

'The King sees nothing. He spins webs in his brain and he thinks he can catch his enemies in them, but it is he who will be caught, and in his heart he knows it; he spins webs only to "spin out time", as he is always saying, and every twist and turn gives him a fresh false hope.'

'Then Carl's right. You ought to take over.'

'Damn your eyes and Carl too!' snapped Rupert.

The well-trained Maurice always kept a wary eye out for the Devil's spurts of temper. Today something seemed to have made him peculiarly irritable; he wondered where he had ridden off to last night by himself, but knew better than to ask as he watched Rupert's savage and anxious eyes.

Rupert went on almost apologetically, 'It's not our concern any more. Let England go. The sword and the Bible, those will be her rulers now. And you can guess what texts they'll choose!'

The tyranny of texts, that would be the cruellest.

Only science and art seemed clean and pure, free of the intoxication of words. Would Wilkins still be able to do anything for England?

And himself? He could see nothing yet. There was d'Epinay. After that, there was fighting to be had in France; many of the Cavaliers were taking service there – he might do that to 'spin out time' until he saw what could yet be done abroad for King Charles. It had not needed Charles' favourite phrase to bring that haunted face into his mind again.

'I'll manage something,' he said, nodding as if in reassurance to his absent uncle, to Maurice's puzzled annoyance; he saw that his brother had forgotten his existence, and did not know what he was at.

'I shan't go on to France,' he said, when Rupert sketched his plan. 'I've had enough fighting for the present. I'll stay at home for a bit and walk behind my mamma when she pays visits, and be the good boy Carl always was.'

The rather sheepish flippancy of his tone was to allay the anxiety that leaped into Rupert's eyes at such unnatural slackness. It was no good blinking it; Maurice had been tired out ever since the last bad illness, and he had had two of them in England besides wounds. Suddenly Rupert, in faint echo from last night, remembered Mag Kirke and asked Maurice if he had seen her again.

'No,' was the answer. 'What's the use? She's sure to have got more interested in somebody else by now.'

That settled it. Maurice must be really bad. 'You stay at home,' said Rupert (it seemed odd to be calling The Hague that), 'and when you're ready I will come for you.'

So they went home.

Book III

SOMEWHERE BEYOND SEAS

CHAPTER ONE

E N G L A N D W A S slipping away over the edge of the summer
sea – a dotted white line wherever the chalk cliffs caught the
sun. She was shrinking, fading; now she was invisible; now she
was 'somewhere beyond seas'. The seas flowed all round her,
enclosing her, shutting her away from him, every minute more
remote; she was no longer a green land all round him, blossom-
ing into gardens and orchards, clustering into woods, throwing
up hives of little sleepy angry towns under grey or brown roofs,
which he and his soldiers would have to march into to disturb.
She was an island now; she was a memory; soon he and
Maurice would be saying, 'When we were in England' – and at
thought of that he could have broken down and wept as easily
as ever did General Cromwell.

They came to the important Dutch town, as neat as a new
pin, that used to be so familiar and now seemed so strange; they
went down avenues of pleasant trees, past shops and bright
gardens, and still smelled the tang of the sea, and heard the
harsh Dutch guttural voices and the clatter of sabots on cobbles.
Everything was clear, sharper, more metallic in this light northern air. England was far away now, a dim misty place where it
always rained during a battle or a forced march and sometimes
thundered and lightened. Rupert wondered what his family had
heard about Marston Moor, that murky bewildering battle
fought during a thunderstorm.

His mother had never dared write since her letters had been
intercepted by the Parliament and caused such an outcry. It was
ironic that only his enemies should have witnessed the warmest
sympathy and admiration she had ever expressed for him. He
would never hear it now, he told himself grimly, as he thought
of his intention to kill d'Epinay. He would meet and challenge
him instantly, which would leave the choice of weapons to his
opponent, an experienced duellist as he had since heard; but
Rupert as a crack swordsman and shot left precious little chance
to the man he meant to kill in a duel. That would finish him

with his mother for ever most likely. It seemed a pity when he had been fighting for her brother and her early home, and she had written those letters.

They went up the steps of the pleasant modern red-brick house they knew so well and into the hall; and a single servant they did not know came forward belatedly and gaped at them and exclaimed that they had had no notion – he would go and inform Her Majesty on the instant.

'No, wait,' said Rupert.

The evident alarm of the fellow, the confusion of the house where no one was about to take charge or even see who might walk in, all made him suspicious; but he would not ask questions of a strange servant, he would see for himself. 'Do your duty at the door,' he told the man, and strode on with Maurice down the scrubbed passages paved with neat marble squares that smelled so fresh and cool after the dark stuffy corridors lined with old wood that they had known in England. They went through one little room after another, past plain pale-coloured walls and big many-paned windows that let in the late evening sunlight in a smooth checkwork pattern on the shining floor. Nobody was in any of them; all were empty and bright, and the house was quite silent except for the steady clank of their boots on the stone.

Rupert ducked his head under an arched doorway without any door that led into the corridor again, went a little way down it and opened the door into the room which used to be the schoolroom, where he and Louey used to draw and Eliza read and Etta sew; and as he put up his hand to the latch he remembered that that was what they had all been doing that winter's day four and a half years ago, just before that last bad quarrel he had had with his mother, when he had ridden off to take ship for England and fight for his uncle. He had cursed her and ridden off to his ship, and had torn up the letter she sent after him, without reading it, and before the eyes of her messenger, and so sailed away. He had returned from England almost at once for several months, but it did not seem now as though that interval had ever taken place, or, if it had, as though he and his mother had ever spoken during it. They had remained aloof from each other by tacit consent in a sort of armed neutrality, while between them King Charles' little Queen buzzed to and fro, making plans, making mischief, making enemies and dazzled adoring young friends.

No, he had never really spoken with his mother since that quarrel when he had cursed her; and this he now realized for the first time as he lifted his hand to the latch. Very softly, as though the memory were acting as a spell which might bring back time to that moment and start from there all over again, he raised it and opened the door, and stood there without moving, looking into the room.

For an instant it seemed as though time had obeyed him. There was the room, in a mess as always with Louey's painting things littered in every corner, and Eliza's books neatly stacked along the wide bookshelves, and Etta's big workbox with the picture of Adam and Eve on its lid in padded embroidery.

And there, as motionless as all these things, were Louey and Eliza and Etta – yes, and the child Sophie – all quite still and silent, with their eyes staring at the door, and alarm in them that changed to incredulous amazement and then relief.

Eliza was the first to speak. 'Rupert! Maurice! Oh, thank God, it is only you!'

Louey was the first to move. She flung herself into Rupert's arms, sobbing, 'The Devil himself! Speak of the Devil! Now we know you are really he!'

Maurice had gone over to his favourite, Etta, and was kissing her; Sophie was exclaiming, 'How quickly you have come! You must have flown!'

'You're still the Wizard, you see, even here,' Maurice flung back over his shoulder to Rupert. 'Why should we have flown? It was a good wind as it happened, but our boat was slow.'

'Ah, then you cannot have heard the news,' said Eliza.

'We have heard some news,' said Rupert as he came forward, looking round on his sisters. It struck him that none of them had been doing anything when he and Maurice had come into the room; not reading nor writing nor drawing; even the industrious Etta held no piece of sewing.

'Have you been holding a council of war?' he asked.

'War is exactly right,' said Louey.

'Who is the enemy?'

'Our mother,' said Sophie brightly.

He turned on the child, a pert black-eyed fledgling, already showing beauty in spite of her sharp movements and arms like brown twigs. 'That is not the way to speak of your mother, or to your brother,' he said, his acute artist's eye making a note of her

488

attractive immature angles even as he rebuked her. 'You'd best go now.'

She dropped him a mocking curtsey but remained, holding Eliza's hand.

'His High Illustrious Arrogancy has forgotten how old I am by now,' she said. 'Tell him, Bess, that I'm nearly sixteen, and know quite as much of all this as any of you – except, I dare say, Louey!'

Rupert decided that it was a pity Sophie had not been born a boy; but he did not wait to attend to her, for Etta was saying, 'We thought you were the armed guard come back with poor Philip.'

'What has Philip done?' asked Maurice.

'Killed d'Epinay,' said Louey quietly, looking Rupert straight in the eyes. He found the look inscrutable; was it in denial or defiance of the report that d'Epinay had been her lover?

So Philip, the youngest of the men in the family, not yet eighteen, had done his job for him.

'When did they fight?' he demanded.

'It wasn't a duel,' said Eliza, 'that is why we are afraid of the armed guard.'

'He didn't murder him?'

'Not that either, but it was very irregular. D'Epinay had insulted Philip the evening before – d'Epinay was walking with his friends and Philip was alone – insulted both him personally and our mother – and Philip attacked them then and sent them flying.'

'Single-handed – and he routed them!'

Eliza paid no heed to Rupert's exclamation. 'The next morning he was riding across the Place d'Armes and saw d'Epinay, and he leaped from his horse and rushed on him then and there.'

'Was d'Epinay armed?' asked Maurice.

'Yes, he had his drawn sword in his hand, and wounded Philip in the side as he came for him. It was Philip who was unarmed – except for his hunting-knife. He killed d'Epinay with that.'

'Were there no people about?'

'Several. But it all happened so quickly, there was no time to interfere.'

'And then he got on his horse again and galloped straight for the Spanish frontier,' Sophie put in eagerly.

What a boy this would have been to have had beside them in the English fighting!

'It all happened only four – no, five days ago!' sighed Etta.

Eliza, shuddering, had sunk on to a chair, putting her hands over her eyes.

Rupert still could not look at anyone but Louey, and still she met his gaze, and still he did not know what her eyes were saying to him.

He was feeling an odd mixture of regret that he had not killed d'Epinay himself, and relief that he had not at once to make his mother his enemy again. It was plain enough now why Sophie had said she was the enemy.

'She is angry,' he said musing, in statement rather than question.

Sophie gave a laugh like the yap of a puppy.

Etta with grave childish awe said, 'She has cursed poor Philip. She says she will never look upon his face again.'

Eliza tried to speak but was shaking from head to foot, twisting her hands together in vain effort to control her body; 'it is four years since I have seen her,' thought Rupert, in surprise that it was not more. To his younger sisters, especially Louey, those years had brought more beauty, and to Louey they had brought something more – an elusive quality that he did not yet know for fascination. But Eliza, his senior, though by only one year, seemed to have ceased to be a girl without ever becoming a woman. The severely classic beauty of her profile was severe now in another sense; there was something too sharp about the chiselled lines of her nose and lips; the emotion that was shaking her, the first time he had ever seen emotion in her, was somehow painful to him. She was speaking now, but in broken words utterly unlike her old considered preciseness.

'She is mad —' she was saying – 'she has made our lives impossible to us. It is not merely Philip – she hates us all – all. She makes all thought, all reason, all decent civilized life impossible.'

Louey gave a little inarticulate exclamation. 'Oh, ma Grecque!' she cried but could go no further; she had flung an arm round her sister, but that was shaken off. 'She doesn't really hate us,' Louey said to Rupert, 'but she is so unhappy.'

'Unhappy? Hasn't she made all of us unhappy? Because we none of us could bear d'Epinay and the shame he brought on us,

490

none but *you* —' it was plain enough now why she was glaring at Louey.

'She's never cared for us anyway,' Sophie's shrill chirp chimed in against the deeper note of her eldest sister's tragedy. 'She always liked her pets better than us – we've come second in favour to her monkeys and a long way after her dogs.'

'Oh, you're a tiresome brat,' sighed Louey, but Eliza held the child's hand, an evident sympathy linking the sad scholarly mind of the eldest sister with the precocious intelligence of the youngest. To this budding shrew Eliza could be tender, as Rupert had never seen her with Etta the Cherub whom they all adored; yet not to any practical purpose, for she was even now proposing to desert her favourite.

'I can stand it no longer,' she was saying in clipped, breathless sentences – 'I am going to leave home. I shall go and live with my aunt at Brandenburg. It is all arranged. I shall go at the end of this week.'

'But not now Rupert and Maurice have come home!' cried Etta.

'What difference does that make?' asked Eliza.

A smile, the first since the brothers had entered, hovered between Rupert and Louey.

'You shall give my love to my Sweet William and his wife,' she said flippantly. 'How odd it is that our dear Aunt of Brandenburg has never extended her invitation to me!'

'You think of nothing but your lovers, your broken engagements and intrigues,' her sister burst out as she rose from her chair. 'Thank Heaven I shall get some peace from them there!'

She went out of the room, borne onward on the wind of her passionate impersonality, once again looking the part of the tall Greek goddess. She swept Sophie with her, though she seemed unaware that she was still holding her hand, and the child herself looked back wistfully at the scene, so much more lively and dramatic, that she was leaving for the honour of being singled out by her sister.

Etta burst into tears as they went. 'You have come back, and we should be so happy,' she sobbed; and then on a long sigh of sheer weariness, 'These quarrels – they are so tiring.'

Never had she looked so like a pink and white flower, but more white than pink. Maurice put his arm round her. 'Come and see if they've brought the trunks from the ships yet,' he said. 'I have got something pretty for you from England.'

491

So they too went out of the room, and Rupert remained where he was, leaning his hand on the table and looking across it at Louey.

She had grown a little taller still, as he had noticed when she had flung her arms round him, for he had not had to stoop his head so far to kiss her; but she had lost all that gawky air of the overgrown girl; her limbs belonged to her, lovely and flowing from her; even that shock of tangled, light-brown hair floating out like a nimbus round her head, shining with red and gold sparks in the light from the window behind it, was now only an added grace, making her look like an untidy angel. Untidy she still was certainly; her clothes seemed to have been flung on anyhow; there was a smear of paint on her skirt and a rent in her sleeve.

She put her hand down on his, and then lifted his up and looked at it; first the lean brown back of it, showing the veins and sinews and long strong fingers, and then turned it over and felt the hard palm and the lines deeply graven by continual holding of his bridle.

'It's been a long time since I've seen this,' she said. 'And it has been fighting for England and King Charles ever since. And you have won and you have lost, and then you come back here, and all that's said of England is that Maurice has brought something pretty from it for Etta! You come back and find us all at it just as you did when you left – "cackle, cackle, cackle!" – do you remember? And then you said, "No, but I am sick of the sound of your voices," and strode out of the room. And now you're back again and four years hasn't made any difference; you find us all just the same, except that the place is rotten with over-ripe virginity.'

'I am not sure of that,' said Rupert, looking intently down at her face.

'You may not be sure. But I'm damned if because you are my brother and three years older than I, that you shall have any right to make sure.'

'So you swear too. There is something rather like a man about you, but not on that account, for plenty of women swear but they look at you sideways as they do it.'

'Dear Devil, you are an angel!'

'What was d'Epinay like?' he asked abruptly.

She shot a quick glance to see if he were fishing for more than the direct answer, but there was no sign of that.

'An amusing, agreeable fellow. A rake, but not insensitive. He really adored Mother.'

'And you.'

'No. He was amused by me, that is all. I wasn't playing very fair with him myself, for I did try to draw him off from her – she is so much older and more helpless.'

'Helpless! *She!*'

It seemed the worst of insults.

'You will never know her,' said Louey. 'No man could. They look at her and are dazzled. But be kind to her for all that.'

And with these astounding words echoing in his ears, Rupert went to his mother.

CHAPTER TWO

H E W A S more astonished when he saw her. He had expected animosity or worse still, indifference. She was pacing up and down her room; and when he entered she swung round and stared with strained haggard eyes that slowly filled with wonder, and then – yes, he had never seen it in her eyes before when she had looked at him, but it was surely joy. She interrupted his formal greeting, would not let him kneel to ask her blessing, but threw herself into his arms and sobbed out that thank God he was here, her favourite son. (Yes, she was calling him that, and seemed to think that she had always done so!)

'You have heard?' she said. 'My own son has killed the man I loved – and the rest of my children applaud him. They have broken my heart.' It was so sad a cry, yet so unaware, it might have been a cry without words, the cry of a curlew on a lonely shore.

Now he must break their strange truce, but he must say it.

'As I applaud him. If he had not done so, I would have killed d'Epinay.'

Would she now call him Nero, as she had done in that last terrible quarrel? But he had forgotten, she did not remember things like that, as he did, though as he did only with her. It was not in anger, but in sad, even envious statement that she spoke to him.

'You have a hard heart. You are young and can afford it – but

493

be careful. It is the hard hearts that get broken. I have found that. As for Philip, he has no heart at all. He is a monster. To rush on him with a hunting-knife as though he were slaughtering a wild beast!'

She covered her eyes with her hands, twisting her head this way and that to escape the images that thronged there. He knew the horror of such images that lurk within the eyelids. Let her see reason, truth itself, anything rather than such horrors.

He took her by the wrists and drew her hands from her eyes, so that she was forced to look up into his own.

'Mother, he heard you insulted. It was his love of you, his pride in you drove him mad.'

'D'Epinay would never have insulted me. He worshipped me. You think of him as a heartless gallant, a Don Juan – that is Louey's doing because she flirted with him, and no man takes her seriously, because she does not take them so. But with me it was different. He was grateful, humble even – you none of you know —'

His hands had tightened on her wrists unknowingly, until he saw the pain in her face and the pride that would not let her cry out.

He let go abruptly and walked to the window and then back again, and said, 'You will want to hear of the King.'

'Yes, yes – my poor little brother. Sit here beside me and tell me all.'

Hastily, nervously (could this be herself?) she began to ask about King Charles – why had he gone off like that to the Scottish camp? A hare-brained notion it had sounded – what did Rupert think of it, and what on earth was going to happen? What doom lay on the world that revolution should have struck even so happy a country as England? The whole thing seemed so purposeless – the Puritans did not want a republic – nor had they thought of setting up any pretender to the throne.

Rupert felt his face grow hot at that; his mother, staring at him, said, 'Did they ever really want Carl as much as he hoped? I know they thought so in Europe – but in England?'

'They wanted *you*. They always have. They still do.'

'Ah, yes, I could have managed that. It is strange that God should enjoy thrusting square pegs into round holes; my brother Harry always said Baby Charles should be Archbishop when he was King, and that would have suited them both perfectly – and I have always understood the English, and they me – but

494

what a mess I have made of every other country, and every other relationship! In no one thing have I succeeded.'

He had expected her to speak of his own failures; had wondered what she had heard about Bristol, and whether she realized that he had built up an English cavalry better than anything on the Continent and had set the standard for the New Model cavalry.

'I went and fought for my uncle,' he said, 'and it was all for nothing. He's given himself into the power of his enemies, and God knows what will be the end. I don't know what went wrong through it all, but I know now that if I could have kept my temper we might have won.'

She looked at him as he sat beside her, his lean cheek resting on his hand; she saw in his face the rugged beauty that comes from having known both power and remorse.

'I am prouder of you,' she said, 'than I have ever been of any of my sons. And so I wrote to you when those rascals stole my letters – but I was not then as proud as now.'

So she had written that, and he might have seen the words on paper years ago and known how she had changed towards him. She was prouder of him now than of Carl? – so amazed was he that he heard himself asking the words aloud.

'Carl? *Carl!*' Apparently she had never been proud of Carl! 'Do you know what he has done since he heard of his good fortune, that I have striven for all his life? Told me he can do nothing to help me, of course – that is not surprising, for I know how burdened the country will be for many years after that terrible war, though I do not see that it need add so very much to its expenses for me to go and stay with him there – I have simple tastes now, God knows, and no wish to live as a Queen Dowager.' Her sigh showed how deep was her belief in her economy – but it was caught up by a sharp intake of breath, the beginning of a laugh or a sob, as she said, 'No, but it is his generosity that has confounded me. He has sent me a case of wine – and it is all sour!'

'He can't have known it! He'd know how everyone would laugh at him!'

'Ah, that's his subtlety. He'd guess people would say that, and traded on it. It has taken me a long time to know him, but now I do.'

They were the words he had longed to hear all his life. At last she knew what Carl was like, and had turned to himself instead.

Yet there was no exultation in his heart; he even tried to defend his brother for her sake, not Carl's, since he could not bear her to suffer the bitterness of such disillusionment. 'It has been hard on old Timon, you know. He does care about the family, he is always worrying about it; but he thinks us all so mad and foolish that he has to be doubly careful to make up for it.'

'Mad and foolish! So you all are. My daughters want to leave home, my sons are murderers – accursed — '

'Mother, you must forgive Philip. He is your youngest son, he is not yet eighteen. Carl is concerned for him taking service so young with the Venetians – do you feel no concern that he should do so with your curse upon him? You must have pity.'

'For his youth?' She would not look at him. 'Should I pity what I envy? You are too young to know how blessed he is – and you. You talk of failures, regrets. You are twenty-six, and here it is high summer with nearly half a year more before you'll be even twenty-seven. What does it matter what happens to you, as long as you are young? The flying moment when we can know happiness, that is all that matters. That is what Philip murdered as remorselessly as he would stab a boar with his hunting-knife. He murdered my moment.'

Her long fingers, hard and lissom from continual riding, were pulling at her rings, twisting and tugging each other.

'We make plans for kingdoms,' she said; 'we talk nobly – all is nothing. Only love matters – and I have lived to be fifty and had many glorious men in love with me, before I discovered it.'

Her bewildered eyes opened on him, the eyes of a tragic child suddenly waking to find that she is fifty.

And he had seen her as a caged creature, beating against the bars, as he had done those three years in prison. She should have been a leader and a great queen, a second Elizabeth, with none of the caution and economy of the first, but with an equal or greater ability to charm the whole nation to her, as indeed she had done even at a distance.

He could not see also that she was a daughter of the pagan Renaissance, framed to take her place among such glittering princesses as Marguerite de Valois, Beatrice d'Este, or her own grandmother, Mary Queen of Scots, and of France, the France of Ronsard and of Rabelais; but that she had been forced by the times into the arduous and ill-fitting rôle of the unlucky heroine of the Protestant Reformation.

496

But what he saw had been enough to awake him, for at last he had seen herself. She was no longer the mother who had never understood or judged him fairly, had baffled and enraged him, denied him the affection he had craved from infancy, so that he had unconsciously shunned giving his heart to any other woman, since no other could appease that craving. She was a woman whose generous powers had been baulked and driven in on herself, rending herself and those nearest herself.

And for herself he could love her, not merely for what love she could give or had not given him. He was free of that. At last she had given it, but he had ceased at last to crave it. Mary had set him free. He loved Mary now; he was a man standing on his own feet; he no longer needed to ask of his mother, but to give.

He stood up, squaring his shoulders with a shake like a dog's, and their broad outline rose dark against the window, blocking out the light. She had made him think of Mary Richmond, which he had not meant to do.

It made no difference that he might live for many years, enjoy other women, perhaps even fall in love again. Not all his life to come could ever bring back the moment when he had held her in his arms in the darkness of the summer night with the rain falling round them.

His mother saw that he had followed his own thoughts, and wished that she could enter them.

CHAPTER THREE

THE TWO English princes, Charles Prince of Wales and James Duke of York, now living with their mother in France, were staying at The Hague on a visit to their eldest sister Mary and her husband the Prince of Orange. The hospitable young married couple gave a grand reunion dinner to all the younger generation of Stuart and Palatine first cousins, and a large and merry company they made; though when they came to drink the old toast to absent friends there were almost as many of the two families absent as present.

Eliza had insisted on leaving for her aunt's home at Brandenburg, not to be deterred even by so delightful a prospect as this family dinner. Ned was back in Paris with his rich and lively

French wife. Poor Philip was writing to Rupert in some dis-illusionment about the Venetians, whom he had discovered were 'unworthy pantaloons'. And Carl was not improving Philip's case with his mother by his rather pompous attempts to win her pardon. His own affairs were marching very slowly, and it looked as if after all he would not get to the Palatinate for some time yet.

Of their Stuart cousins, the ten-year-old Princess Elizabeth and her little brother Harry were still in England, but the baby of the family, Henriette, whom Prince Charles called Minette, 'because she is just like a kitten, so small and dainty', had just been brought over to her mother in France by her governess, who had escaped with her in disguise from the Roundhead armies.

'They wore rags and slept under hedges,' said Charles with amusement. 'We are all living in one of the romances now, but somehow it does not feel like it!'

He had grown into a fine boy of sixteen. 'They think I shall be nearly as tall as you,' he told Rupert proudly, and it was plain that he still kept his childish hero worship of his big cousin. He had many messages for him from the French Court, all very flattering. The Duke of Orléans and the Cardinal Mazarin, the virtual ruler of France, had written at once to offer him command as a Field-Marshal of the French army 'upon whatever conditions of preferment or advantage he could desire'.

It was very pleasant to read eager entreaties for his service, still pleasanter when young Charles, with a roll of his black eye which showed a precocious understanding of men, added to them, 'Goring applied for a commission, but they would not have him at any price; so what does he do but promptly hop over and join the Spanish army to fight against France. You may pay off old scores on opposite sides of the field yet.'

Rupert smiled down at the lad. 'Have they refused Digby too?' he asked.

'Not yet. But you could kill him off in a duel now you're both out of England. The French are mad to have you, Cousin Rupert. They say you and Montrose are the greatest generals today. Will you join them?'

'It depends on the King. They would have to let me leave the moment he needed me elsewhere.'

'They'll accept any conditions – they say so.'

'They don't seem to believe I sold Bristol then,' said Rupert, watching the boy flush to his ears.

'My mother doesn't say that now,' said Charles quickly. 'She's bristling with compliments and welcome for whenever you shall come to Paris – and so is my aunt, Queen Anne. She takes her tune from Mazarin; he's probably her lover – but perhaps I'd better not say that.'

'You have said it.'

'No, no, Cousin, it's not true, I'll swear. You are too apt to think ill of people, you are indeed, I have heard men say so.' And he put his arm round his sister and hostess, Mary, as she went by, and told her, 'I am warning our cousin not to speak scandal.'

'He'd best never speak of you then,' she replied laughing and slapping his cheek, as she danced on past them to arrange who should sit where at the table. Charles was following her, but remembered something and turned back, fumbling in his pockets.

'My father has written to you – he wrote to Mam too, and told her to behave decently to you, though he didn't put it like that, but that's what he meant – she showed me the letter, and there was one for you inside her package.'

He brought a screwed-up roll of paper out of his pocket; Rupert unrolled it and saw the words – 'his passions may sometimes make him mistake, yet I am confident of his honest constancy and courage, having at the last behaved himself very well.'

'You have brought away the wrong letter,' he said with a short laugh, hastily handing it back.

'God's flesh, so I have! Mam will be wild to find hers gone! Look, they are bringing in the first course – what a lot of dishes! Moll is treating us royally. I am to sit between your sisters. Louise looks charming, but I think, don't you, that Sophie is at an awkward age.'

'It's the same as your own.'

'That makes it the more awkward.'

And having backed out of that difficult moment of the letter quickly and smoothly, Charles took his place at the table between his she-cousins. His brother-in-law, Prince William of Orange, was on the other side of Sophie and had Maurice on his other hand, for there was no order or precedence; Maurice was also next his sister Etta, and then came young James, the

Duke of York, not yet fourteen and the youngest of the party, next his sister Mary, whose favourite he was.

She presided at the end of the table, a girl of fifteen with shining eyes, proud to feel that she was a married woman and able to entertain them all at dinner.

She told James that when she had a baby he should be its godfather, and then he would feel older than all the rest of them here instead of the youngest.

'No, don't,' he expostulated gravely, 'I might drop it on the way to church.'

He was a very pretty fair boy, quite unlike his brother Charles. He at once began to talk earnestly about the French army, and to beg his sister to persuade their mother that he was old enough to join it.

'There's no fighting now in England, and I must do something besides lessons. Cousin Rupert once said I had the makings of a good soldier. I know he'd back me up.'

'I'll ask him,' said Mary, and turned to Rupert, who was between her and his sister Louise; but James, instantly bashful at the notion of his career being the subject of discussion, begged her not to. 'There are plenty of other important things to talk about,' he said; and told her how his little French cousin, King Louis XIV, had given him a splendid bay horse so that he could go hunting with him in the woods round Paris.

But Mary, to tease him, though she too stood in some awe of this famous fierce soldier who was so much older and taller and more stately than any of them there, leaned towards Rupert and said, 'If you take command in the French army, Cousin, will you make James your lieutenant?'

'Yes,' he replied, 'when he writes me a letter in ten languages to ask for it.'

There was an outcry.

'Well,' said Rupert, 'that was the condition my Dutch uncle put on me when I was a deal younger than James.'

'Listen to your brother talking to mine like a Dutch uncle!' whispered Charles to Sophie.

She took him up sharply, and there was a battle of crude young wits like the friendly snapping of puppies.

Rupert was telling Louise of Montrose, and of that day after Marston Moor when they had met in a Yorkshire inn, and Montrose had left him to embark single-handed on that year of amazing victories that was now being talked of on the Continent as 'Annus Mirabilis'.

She said meditatively, 'I believe he is the only man with whom I could ever really fall in love.'

'Small good to you then. He loves his wife.'

'Has he told you so?'

'No.'

'Then how did you know?'

'He has never been in love with anyone else.'

'There might be various explanations of that.'

'They would not apply to him.'

'No, I see that.'

'As it happens,' continued Rupert casually, 'I believe I heard last winter that his wife had died.'

'Ah, now indeed you've killed my hopes. There's no rival so cruel as the dead.'

He looked at her laughing, glancing face and asked, 'Do you always say sad things in joke?'

It struck him as he spoke that most of them had some reason to be sad; yet there they were, thank Heaven, enjoying their dinner and their family jokes, the ordinary course of life rolling on through quarrels and love affairs and debts and money troubles and the happiness of getting together and eating and drinking in familiar company – all this going on just the same, the women hungry for love and angry with the men who would prevent it, Eliza leaving home, Louey growing more beautiful, his mother less – all as though these were the most important things in the world, and the last four years of civil war in England a mere interlude, providing employment for Rupert and Maurice, who must now instantly take service with France lest they should find themselves 'idle' again.

So he saw it with bitter-tasting amusement through his mother's eyes; while with his own he watched a strangely cheerful little figure in the dress of a servant ride out of Oxford over Magdalen Bridge, on a glimmering night late last April, riding as on a high adventure, never quite knowing what, but only that as it was new it must be good – a figure that now sat with the same curious serenity in his enemies' camp, writing long, learned, beautifully polite letters to Mr Henderson, Moderator of the Scottish Kirk, in argument on the subject of bishops. What hopes did it give the captive king to write those letters? Was he writing now this very evening?

'I wish I were a man,' Louey was saying, 'and then I should get you to talk about the war, but I don't know what to ask.'

The directness of the attack pleased him. He did not know what to tell any more than she knew what to ask; but he began somehow about the cavalry charges, for that seemed the simplest, and soon found himself remembering the dazzling intoxication of that cold fine autumn day at Edgehill when all the different colours of the regimental banners had glittered over the frosty plain, and he had tasted the blood in his nostrils from the furious speed of his charge as his cavalry swept down upon the enemy and drove it before them for miles.

He saw again the thunderous sky that had hung over Marston Moor where everything had gone wrong as in some heavy, drugged dream, and he could give no reason for it but to say stupidly that the devil had helped his servants.

And then he remembered that desperate dust-choked struggle at Naseby when he had again driven the enemy's cavalry off the field, and thought he was driving Cromwell's, and that Cromwell had been taken prisoner, and then found it was only Ireton – and had come back from his victory to find it turned to dust and ashes, all the rest of the battle lost, and with it the war.

'There was no point in going on after that,' he said.

She knew he was thinking of Bristol, and presently he broke out, 'One day I shall write the history of the war, and then they will see —'

'Don't do that. It's the mark of a defeated general. They all write the history of their war, and think "then they will see", but they don't. Chancellor Hyde is going to write a History of the Great Rebellion to show how right he was.'

'He'll give me a bad character then.'

'He'll do worse, he'll leave you out. Nothing makes people see anything but what they want. The rest of your life will make people see what you are.'

'I have no notion what I'm going to do with the rest of my life. I have no more reason to suppose I shall win then than before.'

'You have won in almost every battle you fought. I have heard that again and again, that you always won your part of it, but were never properly supported. Oh, why did they never really give you the supreme command?'

'Because I was a stranger. A foreigner. Because I got angry

and told them all what I thought of them. Because my aunt came back and made trouble. Because of Digby.'

He stopped at that, brooding, then said, 'He and I have had to fight like women till now, that is why it has been so deadly. Women can only fight with words.' He was thinking of the hatred that had leaped out like a flame from Eliza for his mother. 'The natural action of hate is blows, but you women never take action. I've felt all the time with Digby as though I were fighting a woman. He beat me with those weapons. But now I shall take my own ground and my own weapons.'

'To what end?' asked Louey.

He gave that short laugh that had frightened her before now. 'Because the war's at an end, do you think I will not take my satisfaction?'

She wished she had not begun to dispute this dangerous subject. He was looking straight before him, and the line of his mouth and jaw was forbidding. If she crossed him, would he go off into one of his old black rages and not speak to her again? It would be a pity, just as they had begun to be friends. But they could not be friends if she did not dare say what she thought with him. So she said boldly, 'It's over. He can't do you any more harm now. You've nothing to fear from him.'

He did not like the word 'fear', but he knew it to be true. And the moment he saw his hate was born of fear, he did not care to remember it. He had been conquered by Digby's wordy weapons, but to use his own 'in fair fight' would be no more fair than if he were to shoot him in the back. As a crack shot and swordsman the certainty of victory took away its zest.

But for all that, 'I shall fight him,' he said, 'but I may not kill him.'

Musicians had come in, and sang some English madrigals and then swung into a rollicking drinking song of 'old Suckling's' which Prince Charles had asked for.

> 'Come and let the State stay
> And drink away — '

The young company joined lustily in the chorus. Soon they were all singing song after song themselves in turn; their host, Prince William, sang a Dutch drinking song, and Maurice a Swedish marching song, and the Princess Mary a French canzonette, and her two brothers a French ballad in question and answer form which they had learned in Jersey, and Etta a

German cradle song, and Louey an Italian love song, and Rupert, 'as you have all left out England', a sea shanty he had heard the sailors sing in Bristol city, which made them all laugh and vote it very low.

The music and the ring of gay faces round the table transformed it into a magic island secure from the strife and anxiety of the outside world. The window curtains behind them were of Persian silk; on the walls the Dutch paintings of still life showed this nation's industrious passion for beautiful objects. Material civilization in all that made for comfort and the beauty of homely things was striding ahead in Holland faster than anywhere else. It was a pleasant friendly welcoming country, the country Rupert had been brought up in since he was old enough to remember any; yet it had never seemed to him like home, and still less did it now.

England was the only place on earth that he could think of as home, even as his mother had always thought of it – and did so now, he believed, for all that she was too distraught to realize yet what was happening to her land and to the brother she had not seen since he was twelve years old. Through the songs round him he could hear her voice singing as she rode ahead of him in the hunt, while he as a small boy furiously spurred his pony after her —

> *'One foot up and one foot down,*
> *That's the way to London town.'*

Well, he might jog that way again yet. England in her icily altered behaviour now seemed more remote and alien than the cold moon. But one day he might yet find her the old merry England again, and come back to leave his bones there.

Would Mary Richmond be there when he returned? No use to think of that. He had sworn not to think of her. From this time on he would keep his vow, and not be cheated again by the tune of a madrigal and the glimmer of wine in a glass, the polished surface of porcelain, the unconscious gaze of white wide-open flowers shining over this bright table to remind him of the star of white clematis that had glimmered so faintly in the dark and the rain. These had all cheated him into thinking of her, who was so like some rare bird that she had nearly been shot for one, so like a butterfly that she had been called it all her life. He would not remember that again.

She was called Mary Richmond, and that was all he would

remember. That was over, as the war in England was over. No woman could permanently share his life as it would be now, the life of a Prince of no country, a penniless wanderer. He would not whine and long for what he could not have; he would not think of it again.

But though he determined not to think of her, she was helping him to think of all things with a keener and enfranchised vision. He was free of the old obsessions; the four years of maddening neither-one-nor-t'other war in England were over; Digby no longer mattered a straw; his aunt could do him so little harm that Mazarin could write from her side to offer him the highest command. And from his own turbulent and distracting family he was also free. They could no longer hurt him as they used to do. Carl was no longer in his way; but no longer was that way limited to his mother's heart.

Freedom, power, exultation even – for no reason that he was conscious of, they had caught him up on a high wind that blew from the future and not from the past, though it was the tune of the shanty from Bristol city that had begun to whistle it to him.

> 'Bristol city is my home;
> In Bristol city I met my doom.'

Across his future there fell the shadow of a great ship, her sails spreading like wings against the sky.

They were pulling young Charles on to his feet, telling him he must make a speech. He stood, flushed and smiling, and at his every movement the candlelight rippled like sunny water over his satin coat. Precocious as he was in his wits and his pleasures, he was still a boy; disillusionment and distrust had not yet touched him; he was hopeful, sure of himself, and perhaps a little drunk. He told them what good fellows they all were, and especially his sister's cook; how delightful it was to meet everyone here and find so many pretty cousins to welcome him – too many, that was the difficulty – they all knew what trouble Paris had got into among three goddesses! He looked forward to entertaining them all in England when he went home – and that would be his toast next to his father's health, the day when they should all go home to England.

'And here's to my father!'

Glasses were raised, glowing like rubies against the light, clinked together, ringed hands stretching eagerly across the table towards each other. Mary blew a kiss to her brother. Etta was all but crying.

'King Charles, God bless him!'

'King Charles, and may he soon enjoy his own again!'

'Here's to England!'

'Here's to the day we go home!'

Louey took Rupert's hand in hers. Each knew what the other was thinking – of the old childish days when they used to play that they were going home – home to the Palatinate first of all – then, after Buckingham's visit and Henry's betrothal, home to England. The memory struck chill into the future. Were their young cousins, still almost children, to be kept out of their own as long as they themselves had been?

And who was to support them? Their mother had had the English throne behind her; but now that that too had fallen, who would feed and clothe the English royal family? Rupert's keen common sense went straight as usual to the core of the problem, while Charles, though his speech was finished, was still talking, gaily, confidently, of all that he would help his father to do when they were at home again.

He would bring back French cooks and French plays and French actresses too – it was ridiculous that women should not act as well as men; it was all the fault of the Roundheads, who hated women because women hated them; but he would change all that, he would turn out the Roundheads, put up the may-poles again, bring back dancing and the theatres and games and horse races and ride in them himself and sup with the jockeys.

'What does anything matter as long as you are young?' echoed in Rupert's ears. His mother was right; it was better to be Charles as he was now than some gouty old prince who had always sat secure on his throne. Wherever he was, this lad would always find himself at home in the world.

And he himself? His young cousin's dreams for the future made small appeal to him. His fancy was following that vision of a great ship out on to a wider sea than the crossing to England.

England was not only an island. She had her kingdom of the sea. Mutiny against the Parliament had begun to break out here and there in the navy. Given a little more time (an interval which he might as well spend in fighting in France if his uncle approved), and he should soon be able to fight for King Charles away from him – the only way it could be done, he had discovered.

He thought of the essential things that must translate his vision into fact. He had learned a good deal about shipbuilding in the days when he had haunted the London dockyards, and something of navigation; it would not take the inside of a week for him to be able to con his flagship himself.

He had done business with Dutch traders and could drive a hard bargain; he had learned much from old Taylor and had listened to the Bristol merchants and sea-captains comparing the prices of raw hides and indigo, sugar and elephants' teeth, with the close attention that an artist gives to the subject of the picture he might one day paint. He and Maurice had always got on with the common soldiers, he had made friends with farmers and peasants in England – it would all help.

'What are you thinking of?' asked Louey, who had seen his deep gaze travel beyond their company and this moment.

'I am thinking that sea-bread costs a penny a pound, and cheese and butter between fourpence and fivepence, and that dried peas are sixty-three shillings a bushel.'

'Why?'

'Because civil war sends up prices.'

'No, but why think of that?'

'For the price of a seaman's rations per day.'

'Do you mean to be a seaman?'

'I do. When the Royal cause is all at sea, I might reclaim it there.'

'Devil you do! And will you be Admiral of the British fleet?'

'They wanted to make me one at sixteen. Well, I may be one yet; and when I am, two things I will have – iron discipline and good pay. Twenty-four shillings a month with food and clothing would give a comfortable margin.'

'So you'll be a sailor as well as a soldier! Oh, poor Mother! Do you remember Madagascar?'

'Often.'

'How mad she was against it! No sons of hers should go for knight-errants!'

'I can't help it.'

'I know that. How will you do this?'

'I don't know. There'll be no money for it. We'll be the Beggars of the Sea. But we'll raise it somehow.'

And again his eyes looked beyond her and she saw that he had

507

forgotten her. His dream was still severely practical. The King's enemies at sea should be made to include the ships of all nations that did not support him, and as no other nations had supported him, so much the better – they would fly at every flag that could furnish them with a prize; and their booty should buy food and clothes and lodging for the royal family now in exile, and for the host of ruined Cavaliers that were daily escaping to France and Holland, often with no more of their possessions than the clothes they stood up in.

The Pirate Prince was what the Roundheads would call him then, and much he cared! He would be no more – and perhaps no less – a pirate than the sea-dogs of Elizabeth's day who had sailed round the world in search of booty and plundered the Spanish galleons of their gold and emeralds. But it was not the glitter of these spoils that shone in his eyes.

Maurice should be his second-in-command on the sea as he had been on land; he should stay at home as he had wished until Rupert was ready for him, but not a moment longer! He and Maurice on the high seas – on a rover's ship – on the other side of the world! God had taken that prayer of his, made long ago at Linz, very literally. He had cut out victory, women, money – but he and Maurice would go on together.

Together they would discover new islands, explore the Caribbean seas and the coasts of Africa and Guinea, learn the tribal customs, the strange religions, the medical and magic lore of the savages of the West Indies and the Azores.

The vision widened. Seas beyond seas were opened. He saw himself talking again with Wilkins, in no neat withdrawing-room, but in some scientific laboratory, exploring together the fruits of his explorations. Experiment, research, in art as well as in science and discovery (he was remembering that plan of a new method in etching which some day he would make time to perfect) – these worlds, free of strife yet full of endeavour and excitement, were also waiting to welcome him; in them too he would make himself at home.

But that further peaceful shore could not be reached yet. A fiercer adventure would come first. He would be living hard again, testing every sinew and nerve and muscle to the limit of its endurance. Sleep would be dangerous again, and drink; to take his ease might prove more quickly fatal than in war. He would leave this cosy, stuffy little civilization of warm, well-lighted rooms and large soft beds and dainty cooking, for a world where their wooden walls would depend on the mercy of the wind; where the weather, instead of a subject for polite conversation, would be the integral part of their lives; where the storm clouds and the hollow waves would be his enemy instead of a golden-curled liar, and the Pole star and the swift rains would be his friends.

That wider wilder world lay even now beyond this snug circle of candlelight and music and soft voices; outside this room lay the night and the restless waters dark under the stars; and that would be his home.

MARGARET IRWIN

Margaret Irwin's novels of the Sixteenth and Seventeenth Centuries have been popular for over three decades. She blends exciting adventure, romance and penetrating character-study with scrupulous historical accuracy.

YOUNG BESS 35p
With the death of Henry VIII, the young Elizabeth stands second in succession to the throne. She must use any weapon to fight a succession of ruthless enemies to defend her right to the throne.

ELIZABETH, CAPTIVE PRINCESS 35p
Imprisoned in the Tower, consoled only by Robin Dudley, Elizabeth found herself a pawn in a ruthless game of politics where the wrong move meant death . . .

ELIZABETH AND THE PRINCE OF SPAIN 35p
Unwilling bridegroom to Mary Tudor, Philip of Spain found himself more and more fascinated by the warmth and vitality of her younger sister.

THE PROUD SERVANT 35p
The story of James Graham, Marquis of Montrose, the soldier-poet who fought so magnificently and so fruitlessly for his King, Charles I.

THE BRIDE 30p
The story of the romance between the Marquis of Montrose and the enchanting, wayward Princess Louise, sister of Rupert of the Rhine.

ROYAL FLUSH 35p
The story of Minette, sister of Charles II of England and wife of Philip, Duke of Orleans, who was the brother of Louis XIV of France.

THE GAY GALLIARD 35p
The ever controversial story of Mary, Queen of Scots and of Bothwell, her lover.

JEAN PLAIDY

'One of England's foremost historical novelists' – *Birmingham Mail*

The story of Henry of Navarre
EVERGREEN GALLANT   30p

The story of Jane Shore
THE GOLDSMITH'S WIFE   30p

The persecution of witches and puritans in the 16th and 17th centuries
DAUGHTER OF SATAN   30p

The story of Mary Stuart
ROYAL ROAD TO FOTHERINGAY   30p
THE CAPTIVE QUEEN OF SCOTS   35p

The infamous Borgia family
MADONNA OF THE SEVEN HILLS   30p
LIGHT OF LUCREZIA   30p

Life and loves of Charles II
THE WANDERING PRINCE   30p
A HEALTH UNTO HIS MAJESTY   30p
HERE LIES OUR SOVEREIGN LORD   30p

Catherine de Medici
MADAME SERPENT   30p
THE ITALIAN WOMAN   30p
QUEEN JEZEBEL   30p

Robert Carr and the Countess of Essex
THE MURDER IN THE TOWER   30p

The Tudor Novels
THE SPANISH BRIDEGROOM   30p
GAY LORD ROBERT   30p
THE THISTLE AND THE ROSE   30p
MURDER MOST ROYAL   35p
ST. THOMAS'S EVE   30p
THE SIXTH WIFE   30p

REGENCY ROMANCES
BY GEORGETTE HEYER

VENETIA 30p
'Enchanting ... Georgette Heyer has so steeped herself in the Regency period that atmosphere and situation seem to flow effortlessly from her pen.' – THE SCOTSMAN.

FARO'S DAUGHTER 25p
BEAUVALLET 25p
THE CORINTHIAN 25p
APRIL LADY 30p
BLACK SHEEP 30p
SYLVESTER 30p
COUSIN KATE 30p
BATH TANGLE 30p
FREDERICA 30p
ARABELLA 30p
SPRIG MUSLIN 30p
THE MASQUERADERS 30p
THE TALISMAN RING 30p
THE CONVENIENT MARRIAGE 30p
THE TOLL-GATE 30p
THE QUIET GENTLEMAN 30p
THE BLACK MOTH 30p
DEVIL'S CUB 30p
ROYAL ESCAPE 30p